Philip Boast is the author of *London's Child*, *The Millionaire* and *Watersmeet* (also published by Headline). He is a full time writer who lives in Devon with his wife Rosalind and two children, Harry and Zoe.

Also by Philip Boast

**London's Child
The Millionaire
Watersmeet**

Pride

Philip Boast

HEADLINE

First published in 1991
by Random Century Group

First published in paperback in 1992
by HEADLINE BOOK PUBLISHING PLC

10 9 8 7 6 5 4 3 2 1

ISBN 0 7472 3629 1

Printed and bound in Great Britain by
HarperCollins Manufacturing, Glasgow

HEADLINE BOOK PUBLISHING PLC
Headline House
79 Great Titchfield Street
London W1P 7FN

For my son
Harry

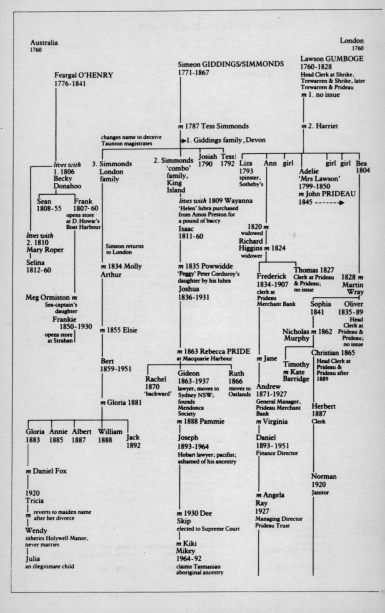

Australia
1760

London
1760

Feargal O'HENRY
1776-1841

Simeon GIDDINGS/SIMMONDS
1771-1867

Lawson GUMBOGE
1760-1828
Head Clerk at Shrike,
Trewarren & Shrike, later
Trewarren & Prideau
m 1. no issue

m 1787 Tess Simmonds

m 2. Harriet

changes name to deceive
Taunton magistrates

→ 1. Giddings family, Devon

lives with
1. 1806
Becky
Donahoo

3. Simmonds
London
family

2. Simmonds
'combo'
family,
King
Island

Josiah
1790

Tess
1792

Liza
1793
spinster,
Sotheby's

Ann

girl

girl girl Bea
1804

Adelie
'Mrs Lawson'
1799-1850
m John PRIDEAU
1845 - - - - - →

Sean
1808-55

Frank
1807-60
opens store
at D. Howie's
Boat Harbour

lives with 1809 Wayanna
'Helen' lubra purchased
from Amos Preston for
a pound of baccy

Isaac
1811-60

lives with
2. 1810
Mary Roper

Selina
1812-60

Simeon returns
to London

1820 m
widowed
Richard
Higgins m 1824
widower

Meg Ormiston m
Sea-captain's
daughter

m 1834 Molly
Arthur

m 1835 Powwidde
'Peggy' Peter Corduroy's
daughter by his lubra

Frederick
1834-1907
clerk at
Prideau
Merchant Bank

Thomas 1827
Clerk at Prideau
& Prideau;
no issue

1828 m
Martin
Wray

Frankie
1850-1930
opens store
at Strahan

Joshua
1836-1931

Sophia
1841

Oliver
1835-89
Head
Clerk at
Prideau &
Prideau;
no issue

m 1855 Elsie

Nicholas m 1862
Murphy

Bert
1859-1951

m 1863 Rebecca PRIDE
at Macquarie Harbour

Christian 1865
Head Clerk at
Prideau &
Prideau after
1889

Rachel
1870
'backward'

Gideon
1863-1937
lawyer, moves to
Sydney NSW;
founds
Mendonca
Society
m 1888 Pammie

Ruth
1866
moves to
Oatlands

m Jane

Timothy
m Kate
Barridge

m Gloria 1881

Andrew
1871-1927
General Manager,
Prideau Merchant
Bank
m Virginia

Herbert
1887
Clerk

Gloria
1883

Annie
1885

Albert
1887

William
1888

Jack
1892

Joseph
1893-1964
Hobart lawyer; pacifist;
ashamed of his ancestry

Daniel
1893-1951
Finance Director

m Daniel Fox

1920
Tricia
m reverts to maiden name
after her divorce

Norman
1920
Janitor

Wendy
inherits Holywell Manor,
never marries

m 1930 Dee
Skip
elected to Supreme Court

m Angela
Ray
1927
Managing Director
Prideau Trust

Julia
an illegitimate child

m Kiki
Mikey
1964-92
claims Tasmanian
aboriginal ancestry

PRIDE FAMILY TREE 1760-1992

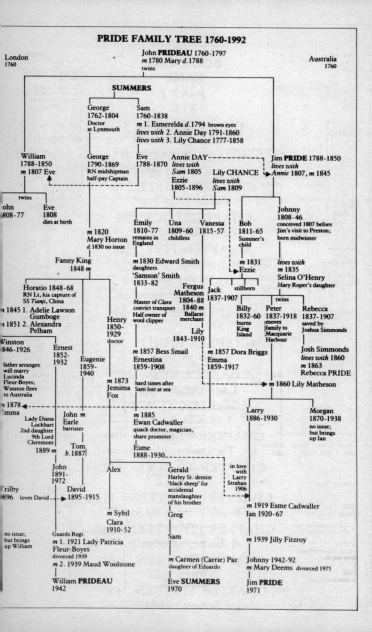

Contents

BOOK ONE

EZZIE

My conscience hath a thousand several tongues,
And every tongue brings in a several tale,
And every tale condemns me for a villain.
Perjury, perjury in the highest degree,
Murder, stern murder, in the dir'st degree –
All several sins, all us'd in each degree,
Throng to the bar, crying all, 'Guilty! Guilty!'
I shall despair. There is no creature loves me,
And if I die, no soul will pity me:
Nay, wherefore should they, since that I myself
Find in my heart no pity to myself?

Richard III
William Shakespeare

Part I

Eve

1

1788

The woman he loved

They said John Prideau loved fishing more than he loved his sons.

But a husband must be excluded from the birth of his longed-for first child, and he had never seen Mary look healthier, or stronger.

'Woman's work,' she teased him, touching his cheek. She had wide, trusting eyes, whose gaze held him. They were in the tall front room of Prideau's House, deep in the Watersmeet valley.

He said simply to his wife: 'You are my heart.'

She laughed and kissed him, then groaned. 'Go to your fishing, sir, and trust in me.'

'I shall wait outside the door.' He jumped to his feet.

'Go!' she said in her agony, and he could not bear her cries. Fetching his rod and line, his broad green hat and his boots, John Prideau walked to the river whose rush drowned all other sounds, because he loved her.

A beautiful place for a birth: Mary's confinement in the sunny parlour, every window a vista of treetops rising up the valley walls, was attended by her widowed cousin Rose, a sharp-faced, capable woman with a pure twist to her pale lips. 'Give me your hand,' Mary gasped. Rose concealed a kind heart behind her pinched looks, but she had been much put upon by the years.

'My!' she fussed, 'don't squeeze my hand so, my bones will crack.'

'Is it over yet?' cried Mary.

'My sweet dear,' smiled childless Rose Shrike, 'it has hardly begun.'

But Mary seemed so quickly distressed, the sheets growing appalling with her blood, that Rose knew something was wrong and was frightened she would be blamed. The doctor was a dangerous freethinker and she did not want to be beholden to him. Only when Mary's grip weakened did Rose send the manservant to Lynton, the village on the hill, for Doctor Summers. But the doctor, younger brother of Mr Prideau's wealthy London business partner Samuel Summers, could not be expected before evening.

Then when Mary was nearly exhausted the baby was at last born.

He was a perfect boy.

Rose held him up into the last of the sunlight streaming through the room so that Mary could see her son: this was William. Mary was too weak to hold her child, but she touched his tiny fingers, then Rose laid the baby's face close to Mary's cheek on the pillow, and let her stroke him.

But still the placenta did not appear, and Rose's tugging broke the cord.

The cruel contractions began again. Mary fell silent and unresponsive, even when the most sensitive part of her flesh was twisted by pincers; and the blood beading her bitten lips now bled so dark it seemed blue.

Rose knelt in prayer.

Mary was hardly breathing; her breathing stopped.

Dr George Summers, dust-covered, his hair wild, arrived: Rose Shrike kept vigil by the dead woman. In two strides he examined the body. He drew his knife, and with gigantic hands plucked a second baby from the cooling womb.

'Leave *him*,' Rose Shrike instructed, her hands clamped white on her Bible.

Blue and wrinkled, it seemed impossible the child should live; but the doctor sat cradling, squeezing the tiny body, gently blowing in the baby's mouth. Suddenly the little frame heaved, and gasped for life.

'But look what it did!' Rose cried.

This was James.

2

1804

John Prideau's legacy

'It was my Christian duty to look after those boys, even though every penny was out of my own purse,' sighed Aunt Rose in her loneliness, knowing how empty her life would be without William. *'Their father never left them anything. He had lost everything.'*

Rose, standing blindly at the window of her cottage on Mars Hill, cast her mind's eye back sixteen years, to Watersmeet Valley and John Prideau's figure coming home through the twilight with a fish, a twelve-pound salmon to go in a glass case for the death of his loved wife and the birth of his two sons.

In the nine years of life remaining to him, John Prideau never loved again, neither any woman, nor his sons.

Rose had cared for them since his death. The cataract had not completely obscured her left eye, and by opening her window on the noisy dawn air, the shadows she saw on the busy Lynmouth waterfront became real and full of life as their voices echoed up – and she heard William's voice calling to someone, 'Have you seen my brother?'

William searching for James; of course. William was a saint.

Today they would leave Devon for the first and probably last time.

But where was James?

'Have you seen my brother?'

8

His sons had been shadows to John Prideau; but they adored him. By ignoring his boys, their father dominated their lives, and the more that in his grief he rejected them, the more they loved him. As the rest of his life went wrong for him John Prideau's's brooding moods, his flashing temper and worse his legacy of the days and weeks he simply ignored them, his *absences*, were their fault. But William earnestly wanted to be faultless. William believed in crime, he knew that there are *good* boys and *bad* boys, and he was determined to be good. But . . . there was James.

The children had lived in their own world at Prideau's House, James always full of fun and the spontaneous silliness that so infuriated William, who as the elder was expected to keep him out of trouble. His twin's wild ideas and boundless enthusiasms sent William almost frantic: James imagined a boat out of an old barrel, he got from a book how to fly a kite with a key hung from the string to absorb lightning-strikes, and once he disappeared for days living carefree in a house in the trees. But his father didn't whip him, he whipped William for letting it happen. It was William's duty to look after his feckless younger brother, to save him from harm; never mind that it was usually William who fell from the tree, William who tore his jacket, and William who was always caught. Miraculously unharmed and untouched, James hardly noticed the responsibilities that gnawed William. In church the Reverend Gough spoke of Original Sin, the certainty that all men are born guilty. When William confided that the vicar's gimlet eyes seemed to bore into him personally, James laughed, and called the Reverend 'Old Guffy'.

He could afford to be carefree. He had William to look after him, the elder brother by less than an hour, but that was everything.

John Prideau had died when the twins were nine.

Prideau's House had been instantly seized by a frenzy of creditors, and it became clear that he had ended his life an empty shell, cheated of his capital in remote speculations, paper companies and bubbles on the Royal Exchange, always wilder and more desperate as his fortunes declined. Or perhaps he had not cared and this was the conclusion he desired: certainly he remained friends with the partner whose mistakes had planted him in Queer Street, Mr Summers of the City, whose resources were so much greater to survive misfortunes. The two men, local boys, had known each other since childhood, and though Sam no longer maintained a country house close to his doctor brother in Lynton, having made his fortune on the streets of gold, he and John Prideau remained bound by the understanding of common experience: Sam was a widower too. When he saw the Prideau estate coffers were empty, he had agreed even to forgo the money owing to him from outstanding commissions. He had been John Prideau's one real friend – strange, Sam Summers's gift for retaining the friendship of the man he ruined, while his brother the doctor remained unforgiven for a death no man could have prevented.

So the twins went to Aunt Rose. And over the next seven years she did her best for the two frightened, lonely boys, and came to love them like the children she never had.

Now, in her cottage this chilly late summer's morning in 1804, she had closed the door behind them for the last time, and she wished she could weep. She regretted penning the appeal to her long-dead husband's brother Elijah Shrike in London so persuasively; the almost indecipherable letter that at last returned from The Temple did indeed hold out the hope of two places as clerks for young gentlemen of assiduity, application and demeanour. No subject so gross as remuneration or accommodation was mentioned – The

Honourable Society of the Middle Temple, one of His Majesty's Inns of Court! Sixteen years old, the boys were London-bound, a vast distance, to a different world, and she would probably never see them again.

William's voice echoed up to her plaintively: *'Please sir, have you seen my brother?'*

William would look after James and make sure he fulfilled his duties, but who would look after William?

Below, the 'Cabriolet Service' to Bath made ready in the churned mud outside the Rising Sun tavern. Simeon Giddings, the coachman, lurched down the tavern steps on his skinny leg of English oak, beer-froth clinging to his mouth, already drunk: all the Giddings were either mad as May-butter or dull as dogs, but Simeon was clever as well as being a man of surpassing criminality. In the glowing dawn by the steps William waited, blowing on his hands and looking around anxiously.

Still no sign of James: William kept an eye on Simeon Giddings's cart in the centre of the muddy patch, shifting from one foot to the other, trying not to choke on the oak-smoke blowing from the curing-houses. The opened herrings hung in bright orange ranks, like rows of early morning suns glimmering through the smoke.

Two women arrived down the hill on donkeys pulled by lead-reins, and as the servant doubled back to help them dismount, William noticed how pretty one of them was. The women were ushered into the tavern.

But where was James? On Lynmouth foreshore seagulls fought over the piles of guts unbucketed by the fishwives. The tallow chandler lit the fire beneath his maggot-boiler, and the wives who took in washing to their ramshackle houses along the river – the old curing sheds from when the industry enjoyed its peak in the last century – were beating the winter out of grimy red petticoats in the foaming stream: plenty of work for the seamstresses there as the rotten stitching gave way. A calloused hand fell on his shoulder and William jumped. He said the first thing that came to his head.

'Please sir, have you seen my brother?'

Simeon Giddings eyed him speculatively. The young shaver was shabby genteel: his britches were patched and that coat had seen better days. There was no money to be had from him, so he clapped the boy's shoulder reassuringly.

'That lad James? He's in the tavern, drinking beer.' He liked the Prideau boys because the family had sunk so far. Anyway he wouldn't cross the old widow: Captain Shrike had apprenticed him to the owling and prisage trade – smuggling – long ago. They were bound by ties of blood, the Captain dying in the same clash with the armed Revenue cutter that lost young Simeon, screaming drunk on a butcher's block six days later, the foul-smelling ruins of his leg. Everyone was related, smuggling had been traditional in the West for a thousand years, and the number of men and women living in the twin villages of Lynton and Lynmouth had hardly changed in that time. Their great-great grandfathers smuggled wool to Florentine merchant vessels, and most of the world's tin and copper was free-traded at night from pilchard boats. Now, in wartime, with Europe united and Great Britain isolated, gentlemen's yachts, fishing boats, brigs and schooners, even galleys rowed with banks of oars, ran the Royal Navy blockade for French brandy. The dozing donkeys hitched to the Rising Sun's rail weren't there only to carry imports of Welsh coal and limestone up for Exmoor farmers: last night, Giddings knew – for he had organised it – their panniers were loaded with the half-ankers of brandy now concealed in cellars from Woody Bay to Brendon, and the mast-top showing on the horizon was Daniel Coppinger's schooner *Black Prince*, standing well out from the four Revenue officers stationed at Ilfracombe. Giddings was lost in his reverie.

'Please sir, if you have seen my brother James – '

'I told you!' Giddings shouted, startled. 'Last I saw, he was in the Rising Sun drinking beer and carving a fourpenny plate of beef for his breakfast!' He added cruelly, knowing how poor the boys were, 'And a half-penny tip for the waiter.'

It rang all too true. William looked at him miserably.

Giddings leaned on William Prideau's shoulder and they watched the drab luggers, propped on sheerlegs as the tide dropped out of the shallow river, unloading the early catch of herring at the gravel quay. 'It's a hard old world,' the older man sighed, scratching the cleft of his buttocks. There was no profit in tea since the tax was cut. The thought made him bad-tempered. Irritated with the boy, suddenly Giddings pushed him away, and everyone roared with laughter when William slipped and fell in the mud.

Giddings stumped away, shouting orders.

William scrambled up.

James leaned in the tavern doorway, still chewing, laughing at William spattered with mud. Then he went down and Giddings, watching them, thought it was like looking at a man talking to his reflection. But the longer he peered, the more distortions in the mirror were revealed. James was taller, standing at ease without any of William's tension. And his smile was wider. James stood, in fact, like a young man who had enjoyed a fine breakfast very much, and expected an equally fine lunch.

'I'm falling in love!'

William scrubbed the mud from his face and hid his anger. 'Where's my share of the beef?'

'Oh, I forgot to save you any, but I got you some apples. . . .'

Men were pushing and pressing all around them

13

now, ale breath and sweat. Giddings was in his element. He loved people, and *his* reputation kept him safe from them: he took out his prized pocket-watch which no footpad or highwayman, knowing Giddings, would dare touch – a magnificent gold watch such as a French nobleman might own, and indeed had, a man saved from the guillotine only for a watery grave in mid-Channel. To impress passengers with the sophistication of modern travel Giddings made a great show of setting the hands twenty minutes ahead, to Bristol time. Giddings's son Josiah, a nervous dirty-faced boy who worshipped his father, hung on his every word, and held the horses' curb-chains hoping his work would be noticed. The hefters were still swinging boxes onto the cart, heaping them into a swaying pile crisscrossed with ropes, and behind the driver a canvas cover had been erected, the famous 'cabriolet', with a padded seat beneath and some privacy for three or four passengers of gentility to sit across: the war had been good for business. 'Hurry-scurry there!' Giddings roared from beside the lead horse, which twitched and stamped, excitement at the impending departure sharp in the air. 'Porlock! Minehead! Bath! The ends of the earth!' Giddings called, laughing to the figures now coming down the tavern steps.

'That's her!' James said. He pointed at the girl with a broad-brimmed hat, trimmed with royal blue. 'She looked at me.' Her dark travelling cape swung slightly open, revealing a royal blue dress trimmed with antique lace. She steadied the older woman beside her but still the broad brim hid her face.

'Who is she?' William asked.

'She called the other one her aunt,' James said distractedly. 'The aunt had asked the landlord for a private room to wait in.'

'I heard of that scheming woman, she was the doctor's wife,' William said in his flat undescriptive way.

14

Ten weeks ago free-thinking Doctor George Summers of Lynton had been struck down in his prime, complaining of pains to the chest in the evening, found dead in his chair next morning. This natural justice caused much self-congratulation in certain sections of the community and Gough's sermon was 'Physician Heal Thyself'.

'No wonder she's leaving, they must have been awful to her,' James said, but he was looking at the figure of the girl. She was wonderfully tall. Perhaps he would glimpse her leg as she was helped into the carriage. There was something very unromantic about his feelings.

'She's not the doctor's daughter,' William said dismissively, 'he only had a son, and he's a midshipman in the Navy.'

'Look at her,' James said.

'You're making a fool of yourself.'

'Look at her fingers, how slim they are.'

'I saw her first,' William said suddenly. 'They were led down from Lynton on donkeys, with two more donkeys to carry their baggage.'

But James had already gone forward and swept off his hat in front of the girl. He held out his hand to help her across the muddy gap between step and cart. Her fingers trembled. She was no goddess. He looked frankly into her face.

She took his breath away, and the words he had been going to say were lost from his mouth. James simply stared; he had never seen a face so full of expression.

She stepped into the shadow under the cabriolet hood with not a word of thanks. He had never even heard her voice. Her aunt arranged the blankets over their laps and now he could not see her at all – except a sudden flash of her eyes glancing at him.

15

Giddings cracked the whip and the horses shied. 'All coming who's coming!' he roared.

William said: 'Wasn't she beautiful?'

'I touched her.'

'I saw her first,' William said again.

Then with Giddings shouting, 'All right! all *right*!' they had to scramble for a place on the baggage, and hung onto the ropes.

Although they had to get down almost at once to walk the long, steep ascent of Countisbury Hill, the break had been made: they had departed. Through the red dust kicked up by the straining horses, William looked back for the last time at the tiny village laid out below them like a map. Already they were almost too far away to make out Aunt Rose's house.

'I wish father could see us,' William said to himself.

James had no eyes for the past. He walked near the front of the vehicle, although in some danger from Giddings's lashing whip, because from that position he could glance into the shadows, wondering what her name was.

At the Blue Ball Inn at the summit two of the horses were taken off. James took advantage of the pause to lean across the wheel and offer a couple of apples to the ladies under the hood.

'How kind,' the aunt said, taking them both, a look both wise and amused in her eye, handing one to her niece. James tilted his hat-brim and could have skipped for joy, but instead had to run for his place on top as the coach departed. William pulled him up. James hardly looked at him.

'I know who she is, I asked the publican,' said William at last. 'She's Eve Summers, the daughter of Sam Summers, the doctor's elder brother. He lives in London and for some reason, after her mother's death, she had to live down here with the doctor's family. But now George Summers is dead and she is returning. . . .'

16

The horses were changed after the steep descent into Porlock, and again at Minehead. Here Miss Summers and her aunt transferred to the faster stage-coach, but the driver told James that as long as Giddings's cart drove through the night and arrived in Bath before dawn next day, all its passengers could be on the same Mail to London tomorrow.

Giddings's journey across the flatlands seemed interminable. Finally the horses' hooves clopped wearily onto the cobblestones of Bath. Giddings threw down the baggage in the stableyard and went towards the inn. 'Goodbye, Mr Giddings!' William called, and James saw that his brother was already overcome with homesickness. Tomorrow Giddings would be returning to the little village of their childhood.

Giddings merely glanced back. 'Won't see you again,' he said churlishly, then swung and thumped up the steps.

As well as being homesick, James knew that William was worried about money. Poor Aunt Rose had found ten pounds to give each of them, after Giddings's fare, but tickets on the Mail coach cost nearly four pounds ten shillings, though that included breakfast, dinner and tea on the way. Rather than waste money at the inn, therefore, William found a wall to sit on, eating apples and bread while they waited for the Mail to emerge. James talked all the time, trying to cheer him up. Her hair was dark, and full of curls, her eyes were blue, bright blue, her complexion not pale like the fashion, but dark, almost sultry. . . . something different about her. William said little. He had seen her first.

'You don't know the first thing about her,' he said.

When the London Mail bowled out into the dawn light, Miss Summers and her aunt, well-rested, were inside. The guard carried a blunderbuss: four well-fed horses strained at polished leather harness. The boys rode on the coach-box, and the journey from Bath to

London was accomplished in just seventeen hours on the new toll-maintained Turnpike Trust road.

And so quite suddenly, they breasted the last hill and saw London spread out before them: vast and smooth, four miles long and two miles wide, its rooftops already dusk-shadowed, pierced only by church spires gleaming in the last light of day, like glorious spears pointing the way to God.

The Mail tore proudly through the narrow streets and was reined to a stop outside the wooden front of the White Bear in Piccadilly. Guests enjoying an evening smoke gazed from the third floor balcony at the frantic activity below, barefooted urchins clinging to the stamping horses, dogs yapping.

They had arrived in London.

'James?' William shouted. James was already on his way.

He pushed through the crowd. At last he saw her. Porters had loaded their two portmanteaux onto a hackney. Why had Mr Sam Summers not sent his own coach for his daughter? The older woman was inside the carriage and must already have told the driver his destination, for he flicked his whip impatiently when the girl did not get in. But she stood with her hand on the door, looking back into the crowd. For a moment her steady gaze met James's eyes.

He heard her aunt call, 'Get inside, Eve. It's only London.'

The vehicle rattled away. James ran after it for a few paces then stopped, helpless. In the rush of gigs and chaises jostling along Piccadilly he saw half a dozen lumbering hackneys. This was a city of a million people. All he knew was her name, Eve. And that he was in love. And that somehow he would find her again.

3

1805

The watching brief

But the weeks passed and he didn't find her. London, a jostling swarm of life hurrying forward, had swallowed Eve Summers as though she never existed. Yet James would not forget her, and finally William put a stop to this dreaming.

'I don't want to hear any more about her,' he said sternly.

It was for James's own good, yet James looked at him miserably.

'You always used to be so happy,' William said, locking away the ledger of accounts for Mr Gumboge's signature first thing on Monday morning. 'You were the happy one of the two of us.'

In the basement office of Shrike, Trewarren and Shrike at Nos 2 & 3, Brick Court, the last wintry daylight had faded from the row of barred tunnel-windows along the top of the front wall: even the homeward tap of shoes and old men's canes had long ceased across the courtyard above as the chambers emptied and silence settled over the Middle Temple. Once they heard the watchman's boots clumping along the cloister, and his mournful call, 'All quiet, and a clear and frosty night.'

'Why are you so miserable?' William demanded, pocketing the key and shuffling back to his bench-desk.

His voice echoed between the bare walls. Below the windows, situated to snatch the best of any light, stood

Mr Gumboge the Head Clerk's desk and empty chair, on an intimidating raised platform. Once twenty shivering clerks in meagre surtouts, bringing their own coals to feed the single tiny fire, had toiled here beneath Gumboge's sweltering eye, but nowadays only half a dozen remained, the partnership having fallen on hard times since Mr Shrike's illness. Seven thousand Wills were stored in the medieval subcellars, dating back to slim volumes from before the Reformation, passed down generations of legal firms to occupy this site to make a trove second in numbers only to the huge new Wills Depository beneath the riverside terrace of Somerset House, a few furlongs upstream. But until the uncertainty about whether Mr Shrike would return was resolved, Mr Trewarren took no action except to cut wages, and kept a watching brief.

The other clerks, including James's friend Honeyman, had finished their work at eight, bowing to Mr Gumboge, shuffling out stiff-jointed after carefully snuffing the candles: only two remained alight. William would lock up, Gumboge trusted William. James had appropriated the Head Clerk's chair and leaned back with his feet on the desk. Work bored him.

'You know why,' he said at last.

'You should find some other girl,' William told him smugly, not looking up from the document he was copying, dipping his goose-quill lightly into the porcelain well at the end of every line, as though each working day were not fourteen hours long; and then there was the work he was doing for his Articles exams. 'You'll forget this infatuation in no time.'

James stretched. 'William, I don't think you know what I feel.'

'Don't I? We're the same,' William said. 'By the bye, your shoes need re-soling.'

James flicked ink at him and William hunched over – protecting not himself but his fastidious script.

'She's too good for you,' William went on. 'There's no fool so great as a fool who *thinks* he's in love.' He put down his pen and leaned back with a yawn.

'That's true,' James said obediently, but he didn't believe it. She was of the same social class as he, they were separated only by his straitened circumstances, and he remembered the life-light in Eve Summers's eyes. He couldn't explain his feelings to William who was so determined not to understand. James thought it might really be possible to die of love. By now he lived not in the perpetual hope of his first weeks in London but in perpetual disappointment that dragged his spirits down and made him such a burden for poor William; William had been wonderful, doing much of James's work. But he had obviously decided that his support was encouraging James's depression, the pursuit of his lost cause.

William was right, as always.

The streets of London were not paved with gold.

At first, not realising how many people he had to choose from, James had simply kept his eyes open, thinking he was bound to see her. Later, James had checked the City street directory at the General Post Office in Lombard Street but it only covered the main thoroughfares, and he found no address for Samuel Summers – more than a hundred and thirty thousand people lived in the City, and the lists were not alphabetical but by street. If Summers had his residence outside the square mile, or the two women were lodging elsewhere for some reason, they could be anywhere. He found no mention of anyone called Summers in Webster's *Royal Red Book*, and a last-chance visit to Debrett's bookshop to consult the *Peerage*, in the faint hope that the financier had been ennobled, turned up nothing.

James stared at his brother's face. He was asleep. What a terrible life it was, and how terrible to be in love. Unlike William, James didn't enjoy work; he hated it. Without Eve, it was not worth living.

But William didn't understand. Although William was exhausted by his studies, he was ambitious and needed the approval of the employers who exploited him, Mr dry-as-a-stick Trewarren who fawned on the few remaining wealthy clients in the dusty labyrinth of his chambers upstairs, and Gumboge the Head Clerk. James called them Wet & Dry. Old Trewarren was dry and dusty, Gumboge fat and sleek as a frog: in his fifties, with lank white hair affected in curls, his flesh gleamed. His belly filled his britches like a baby elephant straining to be born. He had a high laugh and a gross temper, and he was ambitious too.

William completed the tasks Mr Gumboge set him as though they were interesting and important; Gumboge soon realised this enthusiasm for hard work was a stick to beat the other clerks with, and called him 'my Sweet William'. Twice William was dunned in the yard by other clerks, led by Honeyman, Gumboge watching through the window-glass with a smile on his moon face, the half-gnawed beefbone in his hand forgotten. Both times only James's speedy arrival saved William from a bad bruising.

James covered William's sleeping figure with his coat. They needed one another. It was still them against everyone else, but he wished William would understand about Eve. He sat staring into his brother's sleeping face. Slumber had smoothed the careworn lines, but it was definitely an older face than his own. At the first interview with Mr Trewarren, still holding out the letter of invitation sent by Mr Shrike, William had surprised James by himself raising the subject of tracing Miss Summers.

'I'm a Devon man myself,' Trewarren nodded agreeably, glancing at the scrawled letter, 'I like to look favourably on Devon boys making their way in the world.' Something snuffled under his desk but Trewarren appeared not to notice.

'Thank you, sir,' William said smoothly. 'If you were to consider favouring us. . . . Mr Samuel Summers, once of Devon, is an old friend of our family who may furnish us with lodgings more cheaply than we could otherwise afford. . . .'

The name did not have the expected effect. 'Never heard of a Summers.' Trewarren took a large pinch of Number 37 snuff and sneezed. It seemed extraordinary that so skinny a frame could have contained so large a sneeze. Mr Trewarren pulled at his lapels. 'Cheaply, you say.' He sighed and shook his head over the letter. 'Shrike is in Bedlam,' he said with sudden brutality.

James laughed nervously before William could cut him off. Mr Trewarren's high, domed forehead creased into a dusty frown. The scuffling noise beneath the desk was repeated. A small dog perhaps?

Resourcefully William returned to his earlier point. 'You see, as to Mr Summers – unfortunately we are not aware of his present address –'

But Trewarren waved the letter, lost in his own thoughts. 'A brilliant man, but you see from his handwriting how Mr Shrike declined. We did everything we could, Mr Gumboge and I. But he never liked poor Gumboge, who really should have been made a partner years ago having joined us on that understanding. He has been most unfairly kept down.' Trewarren could not entirely eradicate his own distaste from his voice, and Gumboge was still not a partner, although his services were obviously too valuable to be dispensed with. Trewarren said earnestly: 'Of course the Bethlem Hospital for the Insane is very humane, and spectators are now admitted by ticket only.' There was a dry, genial edge of hardness behind his papery smile. 'And we mustn't find ourselves too downhearted, must we? I saw his old suits for sale in Monmouth Street, that's the place to go. And just behind the hospital for wonderful old books.' James was looking at him horror-struck. 'Thames Street for cheeses,' Mr Trewarren said. 'Oh, how I envy you being young.' He sat back, carefully placing his feet.

Obviously he had not heard of Mr Summers.

'Yes, young and inexperienced,' Trewarren said abruptly. 'I am aware of the effects of the current war, however I can only treat you as Juniors, at four shillings per week. You will start on Monday.' He had smiled that smile they already knew too well, and from the door they had looked back to see the source of the snuffling and scuffling beneath the desk: the hedgehog that, they discovered later, he used for catching beetles.

Now James stared down at his brother's sleeping face, almost his own.

Sometimes he felt Eve was so close to him that her knock would come on the door. But it did not come. He put his head on the desk and closed his eyes for a moment. Suddenly, it seemed, the candles were blackened stumps and the fire was cold, but the room had filled with light: three brilliant oblongs of glare stretched across the scrubbed floorboards, and a fourth along the side wall, flooding from the tunnel windows. All over London church bells were ringing out. James jumped up and tousled William's hair. 'Come on! I'll buy you breakfast!'

'I've got to finish these papers,' William said contentedly.

James dragged him outside by force. The sunlight struck into their eyes, the fresh air hurt their lungs, as they walked up Middle Temple Street through the Gate House into the Strand. Opposite them rose Newgate Prison, rebuilt since the riots and replacing Tyburn as the place of execution, its massive walls already black with soot and grime. Of more interest was the man hawking farthing dips in a sidestreet. They walked munching the bread fried in pork fat, wiping their fingers on the painted shop-boards along the Strand's narrowing highway, admiring their reflections in the bowfronted windows darkened for the Sabbath, then running towards the rising smoky warren of Charing Cross and the Bermudas where they had their lodgings among the cranked roofs and jutting attics, and there had never been such a good day to be alive. William put his hand flat against James's chest, stopping him.

'How can you be miserable?' he demanded.

The very next day, Monday afternoon, James was handed a roll of documents tied up in red ribbon and instructed by Mr Gumboge, who thought he was doing him no favour, to deliver them to the hand of Mr Cathcart, clerk to the Marquess of Breadalbane at Breadalbane House in Park Lane. James had to ask the way in Piccadilly and was directed to a dirty track running north from Hyde Park Corner to Tyburn. Though unfashionable despite one or two houses of consequence, Park Lane led up the east side of Hyde Park. Mr Cathcart took the legal papers and James was free almost at once. He stood for a moment beneath the tollgate's enormous tree-shaped arrangement of seven great light-globes, hoping with the other fashion-watchers to see someone famous pass the Park gates, and saw Eve Summers being driven past in a one-horse gig by a whiskered man in a tall hat, black jacket and white hose.

He passed so close, James could make out the flea-bites speckling his wrists.

James gazed at Eve Summers and saw his attention returned in her startled glance. Such fine clothes she wore: a bonnet trimmed with green, green cashmere cape, her hands concealed in the largest fur muff he had ever seen, and the surprise he saw in her blue eyes made him smile, because he knew she recognised him.

Everyone but he and she was in the shade: the young blood in the military uniform courting her, glittering epaulettes erect as golden hairbrushes across his shoulders, a hussar's busby atop his head, seemed hardly more than a shadow on the red leather beside her. And though she was so obviously of private means, as the gig continued round the curve, sand spraying from the wheels, he saw her pale face turn back to him for a moment above the folded-down hood.

James's legs unfroze and he ran into the Park, the gig far ahead of him as he sprinted along the tree-lined ride towards the gate at the northern extremity of the Park. Fortunately the driver was delayed at the Tyburn turnpike before turning along Oxford Street, a thousand white balloons of horse-breath. James ran with the flagstones pounding through the soles of his shoes, knocking aside shoppers, weaving between the bollards that kept traffic off the pavement, then tripped over a terrier that pounced after him yapping, and took to the road, dodging along the central line of parked carriages where there were fewer people. His coat-tails flapped behind him, clipping his heels.

He almost came too close to the gig and could walk for a while, stumbling because of his worn right shoe, holding his ribs and gasping for breath. These were fine, clean shops. He leaned his steaming face against a butcher's cold window, the sides of beef inside bleeding over the spotless cloths, then pulled off both his shoes and, stuffing them in his pockets, went on stockinged feet.

The gig turned left up the Tottenham Court Road, the driver snapping the whip to set the horse high-trotting past the gloomy orifices of the St Giles rookery so that his smart passengers should not be distressed by the sordid conglomeration, the terrible world that lived beyond. James ran with the woollen hose fraying long threads under his feet, keeping to the mat of compressed straw and dung that softened the roadway. A boy walking a pig on a leash banged smack into a head-high rail for staring at him, and the pig scampered away squealing for joy.

The fine gates of Bedford Square were closed as always; James groaned when the gig passed the gate-keepers by and continued towards the open country of Paddington. The great houses fell behind and women and children worked amongst the brickfields and dust heaps, sorting bones from the ash, rags from old leather, holding broken bottles to their chests like prizes. The gig turned right along the New Cut and pulled up in front of number twenty-nine of a large, curiously-shaped building, three storeys high, sur-rounded by pleasant gardens showing snowdrops, primroses, a few early daffodils. James had heard of this, The Polygon, a revolutionary new style of build-ing. He stopped by the Brill Tavern, staring.

He had discovered where she lived.

The young hussar jumped down from the gig, leaving the driver scratching his wrists, and walked Eve Summers hopefully up the steps on his ostentatiously pre-sented arm. The door was opened by a maid in a white cap and the officer took off his busby but he was obviously not invited in. Eve went inside – and the door closed. He returned down the steps and the gig drove away.

Number 29, The Polygon. James knew what William would advise and of course William would be right: think it out, sensible approach, calling card, borrow money for clothes, get the aunt on your side first. James couldn't wait. He rubbed the uppers of his ruined shoes clean on his coat, brushed his coat with his hands, lifted his hat and ran his fingers back through his hair. Then he expended a penny on daffodils from a Chapel Street flower-seller; they would be his card. He ran up the steps and beat on the door. It was answered by the white-capped maid, who sniffed her red nose and said, 'What yer want?'

James held out the flowers.

A voice called from another room along the hall: 'Ask the gentleman inside at once, Nellie.'

'It isn't that Captain Perceval,' Nellie called over her shoulder.

The widow of Doctor Summers appeared in the hall-way looking at first disappointed, then flustered. Her grey hair had misled him: she was a handsome woman of only forty-five years. She might be as independently-minded a woman as her dead husband: her eyes gleam-ed with a pleasant glint of humour.

'The boy with the apples,' she said.

James held out the flowers. 'Mrs Summers, I for-mally ask your permission to call on your niece.'

She inclined her head. 'Are you always so hasty, young man?' But he hardly heard her, his eyes fixed on the figure who had appeared behind the older woman.

'Eve,' James said, going down on one knee.

Mrs Summers looked at them both. 'Now, Eve, our circumstances – '

'Perkin Perceval,' Eve said with fortitude, 'is a pomp-ous prig.'

'Oh, dear!' remonstrated the older woman, now wringing her hands, then turned back to James. Her fingernails were trimmed very short and businesslike. 'Don't move! Stand back! Nellie, take those silly flowers.'

But James instead held them out to Eve, who leaned down and took hold of them, and he inhaled her scent of lavender. Her mouth was too wide and supple for the ideal of feminine beauty, though lightly dusted with red pomatom, and her eyes much too full of amuse-ment, yet seeming earnest too. They stared curiously at each other, their hands almost touching on the daffodil

28

stalks. Then she backed away, but did not take her eyes off him.

James stood and turned to the older woman respectfully. 'I am James Prideau, younger son of Mr John Prideau, of Watersmeet in Devon.'

'Shall I shut the door, ma'am?' Nellie asked patiently.

'For goodness' sake continue with your duties!' snapped Mrs Summers. 'Yes, I knew John Prideau. Now you are here you had better come in, my boy.'

Eve slipped into the front room and the older woman stumped after her, whispering, 'He hasn't got two brass farthings,' but Eve just laughed. James followed them into a parlour much more sparsely furnished than he had imagined. Mrs Summers had needlework, a slide-mounted sampler that could be adjusted to keep the fire's heat from reddening her face. Two good chairs, a reasonable rug, a table by the window, a square piano: that was all.

But the room was vigorous with books, in glass-fronted cases or lying open, Harvey's treatise in Latin on the circulation of the blood with a notebook translating it into English, a bound volume of Johann Hasse's opera *Sesostrate* in music and words, works by the French freethinkers and Addison; but also the latest copy of the *Tatler* scattered amongst such fashion monthlies as the *Lady's Magazine* and *The Fashions of London and Paris*.

Eve stood in the corner. Mrs Summers said: 'Yes, I knew of John Prideau's younger son.' She left a long pause. 'And your brother?'

'William is well.' James hid his impatience.

Eve watched James, seated with the flowers clasped in her lap. There was no nonsense about putting them in water, she held them close against her. Her eyes filled James's vision while he struggled in conversation with her aunt. Aunt Sarah was unstoppable. She rang

29

for cups of tea to lubricate her flow, and he realised she liked him, and that he need say nothing.

'Poor Sam Summers,' chattered Aunt Sarah, 'the death of his wife Esmerelda desolated him, it was what joined him to John Prideau: their mutual understanding of a widower's grief. Mary Prideau, Esmerelda Summers. Eve's mother was a great beauty – as you can see,' she gushed. 'Her death was a tragedy and Sam never recovered. She was the daughter of the Spanish Ambassador you know, a nobleman. Sam was very proud. But of course Sam is related to Lord Somers of Evesham – they were Lord Chancellors you know. This village is called Somers Town, which is how Sam obtained this accommodation for us after my husband. . . . It was quite impossible for us to stay in Devon.'

James murmured, 'Eve. . . . Miss Summers could not continue to live in her father's house after her mother's death?'

'Sam lives in the City,' Aunt Sarah said hurriedly, pouring the Twining's aromatic tea into tiny cups, reserving the cracked one for herself. 'It's better this way. He was never the same since Esmerelda passed on. I do not think he would even recognise Eve.'

'All my life,' Eve said, 'he has been absent.'

James felt himself transformed by emotion; his eyes filled with inexplicable tears. *Absence.*

'It's unforgivable,' he said in a rough voice. 'I searched, but I never found your father. I'm glad I never found a man who could treat you in such a way.'

'James,' she asked gently, and now it seemed there were only the two of them in the room, 'who were you really searching for?'

'I searched for you.'

'No,' Eve said, 'I found you.'

4

The waiting game

'I wanted you to meet her,' James said anxiously. 'Aunt Sarah said bring William.' William knew why; she wanted to know more about James. 'What did you think of her?' James begged.

'Who – the Aunt?' William said, 'I liked *her*.' And that was true, but James only laughed. 'You know who I mean!' he said, his eyes shining. The twins were walking home through St Giles, near the tavern called the Good Woman, the sign portraying her without a head.

'Didn't you love The Polygon?' James enthused, 'isn't it perfect?'

'It's too far from town,' came William's voice at last.

'That's the only way they could afford to live in London.' It being Sunday evening idle crowds lounged about the street corners. 'Say you like Eve. Tell me I'm the luckiest man.'

'What do you want to hear?' William told the truth. 'She's very pretty! She's beautiful.' But what could she see in James, so without money or the determination to acquire status? 'I don't trust her. She's too ambitious for you.'

'Ambitious! Look at me,' James scoffed, showing his threadbare cuffs. 'They're not rich and you couldn't blame her for wanting a good marriage. But yet it's me she loves. And I love her, William.'

'That white muslin dress was hardly ladylike.' William changed tack, pushed through the crowd down St Martin's Lane. 'The way she walks, knowing you're looking at her. . . .' He stopped by a hot-apple barrow, and the grimy girl held one out hopefully from the upturned saucepan used as a griddle. It was starting to rain.

'Don't you think Aunt Sarah is a wonder?' James said excitedly, building castles in the drizzling air as they walked on. 'She's read all those books. Did you see the rug that Eve chose? Wasn't the room comfortable?'

'You're making a fool of yourself,' William said, putting up his collar. They passed the church of St Martin-in-the-Fields, almost obscured by the tenements around it, and entered the tilted, slumped tangle of collapsing buildings where they kept their room. It cost them three shillings a week, a big lump out of their combined income of eight shillings, but it was let as furnished: it had a bed big enough for two, and James had re-stuffed it with hay which William was sure he had stolen. Almost all the money Aunt Rose had scrimped for them was now gone and William fretted after every farthing. The memory of James in Lynmouth blithely eating the fourpenny plate of beef, with a ha'penny tip for the waiter, made him cringe with anger and worry for the present. James's extravagance, his lack of responsibility and seriousness, his cleverness, the way he relied on Lady Luck to turn up, tormented William. He would lie sleepless in the middle of the night, while James contentedly snored beside him, dreaming of Eve.

William bunched his fists in his pocket. They just couldn't make do on eight shillings a week; they could not. James was still dreaming of her now, as they climbed the narrow steps from the dripping alley.

'When I left her house the first time,' James whispered amongst the creaking boards, 'I stood on the street corner, watching. The piano began playing, so faintly at first through the glass, then I heard her voice.

Soft at first, then growing. Unfolding. I have never heard so fine a voice.'

William knew it would end in disaster.

They came upstairs. The garret window was glazed with paper that hung limply as the rain intensified. James threw himself down on the bed, his hands behind his head, and William lay beside him, then smiled.

'Yes, James,' he murmured under the rattling downpour, 'she's perfect. Now all you've got to do is earn a living, make a fortune, deserve her.' But it was wasted; James wasn't listening.

Life was being so good for them. London was a fine place to be young and full of hope. William was keeping James up to the mark in his job, covering for him with Mr Gumboge where necessary, even finishing paperwork James was too lazy to bother with. Nothing had ever threatened them while they were together, and William's silver tongue kept James out of trouble. . . .

But as the weeks passed and spring had its way with the trees in the squares and parks, James's absences from the office began seriously to irritate Mr Gumboge. The clerks scribbled busily among the tiered desks, with one place conspicuously empty, illuminated by a single hot shaft of sunbeam from the tunnel window.

'My dear William,' came rumbling from Gumboge in his oiled, reverberant tone: 'where is Master James this time?'

And for the first time William said, 'I'm sorry, sir, I do not know. I am not my brother's keeper.'

Gumboge's features bulged into creases of mirth and he wiped under his ears with the dank grey kerchief. 'A fine and wise sentiment. You do not claim he is sick as usual?'

He was with Eve. William looked down loyally.

'Your attitude does you credit,' advised Gumboge complacently. One of the clerks, Honeyman, made a small farting noise between his lips.

'I do not know at all where he is, sir,' William said, and Gumboge smiled broadly, showing lower teeth like distant yellow sails on a red sea. He descended from his platform and came close to William.

'Mr Trewarren is taking an interest in your career,' he confided.

'Thank you, Mr Gumboge.'

Gumboge winked one wet, hooded eye.

In fact when the summons arrived from Mr Trewarren, shortly after morning prayers, by chance James was working beside William, having been in every day that week hoping to make up with speed what he had lost in time, though succeeding only in blotching his work with an unsharpened quill. William gathered his papers neatly and followed in the wake of Mr Gumboge's wheezing progress upstairs. James hastened after, looking like a worried schoolboy, whispering, 'What's it for?'

William shrugged.

'William, I find myself most satisfied with your conduct,' Trewarren said at once, not getting up from the shelter of his desk in the airless chamber. 'Mr Gumboge has spoken well of you.'

Gumboge nodded modestly, stuck where he had been waved into the corner.

'Thank you, sir,' William said. 'It is an honour to work for Shrike, Trewarren and Shrike.'

'Yes, well,' said Trewarren, flustered, 'poor Mr Shrike.'

'Has he died?' asked James.

'Last Saturday,' rumbled Gumboge, his hand rested reverently on his chest.

'There is so much to consider. . . .' said Trewarren, opening a desk drawer pointlessly and closing it. 'I will make no changes for the present. Decisions in haste are often repented in leisure.'

'Quite so,' William said.

34

'However Mr Gumboge has recommended to me that you, William, should be promoted to the position of full Junior Clerk on a wage of eight shillings a week. I think I may see ahead to a time when you are a Clerk – eleven shillings a week, my boy.'

'And perhaps raised even further,' Gumboge hinted smoothly.

'What about me?' James said.

'Your work has been unsatisfactory,' Trewarren said frostily. 'You will stay where you are.'

James said: 'But I can't get married on four shillings a week!' He sounded so upset and overwrought that both older men laughed.

'Then your work must follow your brother's example,' said Trewarren. He slammed his desk drawer, and the interview was over.

William grabbed James on the stairs. At first James laughed, but then he looked startled as William pushed him back against the dusty law-books. A spiral of dust trailed down the stairwell.

'What did you mean about getting married?' William hissed, his face distorted.

'It is my intention to ask Eve Summers for her hand in marriage,' said James levelly, and smiled for William's approval and good wishes.

William stared at him. He was shaking. James realised he had come within a whisker of getting them both thrown out on the street. Yet he still smiled.

'My best wishes,' William said. 'I wish you every happiness.'

That night William stayed late, as usual, to work on the ledger of accounts. He was alone in the office; only a single candle by his head. Ages passed before he made the first mark, then his hand moved with increasing confidence, his hands turning back through the months, not re-dipping from the inkpot until the tip scratched at the paper. He was using an unsharpened quill.

When he was finished he locked up and, carrying a heavy bag, walked calmly along the river bank towards the first glow of midsummer's dawn. The deserted terrace of the Inner Temple Gardens was still gloomy: the Piranesi arches of the nearest river-crossing rose out of the vaporous mist like a pale dream of Portland stone. He crossed the concealed mouth of the Fleet River and walked out to the centre span of the William Pitt bridge, beyond the sandbanks that clustered this reach of the Thames, and leaned casually against the parapet having carefully ascertained he was over deep water; when he yawned and turned towards home, it was with empty hands.

'James!' Eve welcomed him, her face lighting up with pleasure in the mellow afternoon sunlight across The Polygon, then her expression faltered.

'It's me,' William said. 'William.'

'Close the door, Nellie,' called Aunt Sarah.

Eve looked at William with concern. He was hollow-eyed, but it was the change in his manner, so unlike his usual cold self-control, that had made her mistake him for James. For the first time she felt William would be honest with her.

'What is it?' she asked anxiously, 'what's the matter?'

'Something terrible. . . .' he said, standing in the hallway with his tall hat still on, his hands hanging at his sides, the very picture of a man dazed by a shock greater than he could utter. 'Something terrible has happened to James.'

He stepped forward, just in case, but Eve did not do what women were supposed to do: she did not scream or faint, though he had smelling-salts in his pocket. 'Is he killed?' she asked calmly. 'No, you would have said that at once.'

'It might be better if he were,' William whispered. 'The constable arrested James this morning. He has been taken to prison. Newgate. My brother has been thrown into Newgate Gaol.'

'I must go to him,' said Eve.

He stepped in front of her. 'Even I was not allowed to talk to him, Miss Summers. This is the worst day of my life.' He covered his face with his hands.

'Come in, William,' Aunt Sarah said kindly, bringing him into the parlour by the elbow. 'Sit down. Be calm.'

William sat with his back to the light. He took off his hat and held it on his knees.

'It was I who was the cause of his discovery!'

'You must not blame yourself,' Aunt Sarah said.

'Let him speak.' Eve crouched in front of William, her face earnest with self-restraint. 'Never mind her, speak to *me*.'

William said, 'Mr Gumboge signs each page of the accounts ledger up to date, first thing every morning. The ledger is prepared for his inspection by me, or my dear brother, or Mr Honeyman – anyone, in fact. It was I who discovered the discrepancy.'

'Discrepancy?'

'Forgery,' admitted William. 'False accounts added, money paid out, totals altered.'

'James would never – ' Eve said.

'It never crossed my mind that it was he,' William said, turning his face slightly to the light, and they saw he blamed himself. 'I thought it was Mr Gumboge, the Head Clerk – all the changes were over his signature, you see.' William looked down. 'I went to Mr Trewarren. Sir, I told him, I have come to see you over Mr Gumboge's head on a very serious matter, forgery. When confronted Mr Gumboge proclaimed his innocence, of course, anyone would.'

'James is innocent,' Eve said.

'Then it was noticed that the changes had been made

37

with James's quill. Comparisons were made; it was unmistakable. And the style of hand was his.'

'But surely James protested his innocence?' asked Aunt Sarah.

'Of course,' repeated William, 'anyone would.'

'If James said it,' said Eve calmly, 'it must be true.'

William nodded. 'Yes. There is still hope. The judge must believe him.'

'It will not come to a trial as though James were a common criminal?' protested Aunt Sarah, horrified.

'The amount in question is several hundred pounds.'

Both women gasped. 'My dear,' Aunt Sarah said, 'This changes everything.'

For the first time Eve put her hands to her head. 'No, he did it for me.'

William said: 'You are aware of his feelings for you. . . . did he mention. . . . marriage?' Eve's lips trembled, holding back desperately, then she melted into tears. William looked to Aunt Sarah for permission then touched his hand comfortingly to the girl's shoulder.

'That's why he did it,' William said, 'for love.'

'There must be a way of paying the money back,' Aunt Sarah fretted. 'Oh, my sweet darling, don't weep so.' But Eve had lost heart.

'Several hundred pounds?' William spoke quietly over the top of her head. 'Not while James claims he doesn't have it, didn't steal it. Maybe he spent it some-how – gambling for a marriage stake. . . . Lord knows there are enough gambling dens.'

'Not James,' Eve said, looking up with a trembling mouth.

William shrugged helplessly. 'The constable searched our room. Miss Summers, there was nothing there. The money could be hidden anywhere.'

Eve said quietly, pulling away, 'You believe James is guilty.'

'How he thought he would get away with it I do not know,' William admitted. 'Gambling is the only reason I can believe: he thought he could win enough to, if you will pardon the expression, Miss Summers, win you, and replace the amount before anyone noticed. But he lost – two hundred and forty pounds in gold sovereigns!' Gold was doubly precious since the French invasion scare in Wales – the Bank of England was only issuing money in paper notes. 'And now he has lost you too.' Eve shook her head in denial but William continued remorselessly. 'Please recognise the gravity of his situation. Most of the stolen money was held only temporarily on behalf of clients, as is standard practice, awaiting transfer to Coutts's Bank on the Strand. It is a disaster for our firm. Mr Gumboge is plainly guilty of a dereliction of duty and may well be dismissed – he has a wife in poor health and seven daughters who depend on him. His situation is desperate.'

'I only care about James,' said Eve. 'He is all I think about.'

'Of course,' said William smoothly. 'I merely wished to explain no one can help James, only myself. Gumboge and Honeyman are both tainted; only I am in good standing, because it was I who made the discovery.'

'Two hundred and forty pounds,' sighed Aunt Sarah. 'It is a small fortune. And in real money, not paper! I would never have thought such wickedness of James.'

William shook head sadly: 'And there will be the legal costs to consider.'

'But surely Mr Trewarren would – ' Eve stopped.

'Please understand,' William explained gently, 'how vindictive his feelings are towards James. He is accustomed to ease, an old man contemplating retirement with the respect of his peers, facing the loss of his entire life's work. He will pursue James with the implacable rigour of the law.'

Eve rose slowly to her feet. 'What may happen to him?'

'Don't worry your head about that,' William said.

'Tell me all. Leave nothing out.'

He did not spare her. 'Since the sum in question was more than ten pounds, the death penalty is mandatory.' Eve stared at him as though she could not bring her mind to bear what he was saying. He jumped up and held her elbows. 'However, I assure you there are so many mitigating circumstances,' he said rapidly. 'First offence, and he is of previous good character. . . . Perhaps a short prison sentence – '

'Are the prisons as evil as they say?'

'No,' William said.

'But you must prove him innocent!' She looked up into William's face. 'You must.'

'Rest assured,' William said, 'I shall leave no stone unturned.'

Still comforted by William's arms, Eve turned to Aunt Sarah. 'Can we not pay it back and persuade Mr Trewarren to dismiss his action?'

'Dear,' responded the older woman softly, 'if I had such a huge sum, it would be yours.' She explained to William, 'There is only the small pension from my husband's residue, invested in the City.'

William said, 'I have no money, and legal fees are ruinous. It seems most sensible to leave James to his fate, and live in hope. We must pray for him.'

Ever drew a breath. 'No. We will turn to my father.'

'I thought you were estranged from him,' said William.

'I will do anything for James.' Her eyes gazed steadily into his, and he came to a decision.

'It would be best if I saw him by myself,' William suggested. 'Alone, a man can speak honestly and forthrightly to another man, especially on the subject of money.'

She still acted so wonderfully calm. He wondered what it would take to break through that shell of hers.

He bowed to her, then picked up his hat and went into the hall followed by Aunt Sarah, leaving Eve standing in the centre of the room, the light from the window slanting across her slim form. 'No creature in the world can be more unhappy,' she called after him, 'or any circumstances seem darker than mine.'

William bowed again, and thought: *How little you know.*

Aunt Sarah closed the door. Now she thought herself in private they overheard Eve weeping. 'I fear her heart will break,' Aunt Sarah whispered, 'we are so alone.'

'I am on your side,' William promised earnestly. 'Trust me.'

'You will find Mr Samuel Summers in the Rotunda of the Stock Exchange,' Aunt Sarah informed him, 'or some deeper sink of iniquity nearby.'

5

'A gentleman of leisure'

'A gentleman of leisure? Never! As you see, I am a very busy man,' claimed the ridiculous Sam Summers impatiently when he at last turned up, ostentatiously consulting his fob watch, on the pavement outside the chophouse.

'I understand,' William said, raising his hat to this amusing, quick little robin of a man who had come bouncing smartly towards him along the pavement.

'I've no time for chatter,' claimed the garrulous Sam. 'What do you have to say that takes me from my work?'

'What is your work?' William asked.

'Everything that lives and breathes!' said Sam extravagantly.

'And what is that?'

'Money.'

William, never in the City before, was impressed by what he saw. From the Middle Temple it was only twenty minutes' easy stroll along the fashionable end of the Strand to the bookshops lining Fleet Street, climbing past the fine drapers' shops of Ludgate Hill, and coming to the summit at St Paul's Cathedral, aswirl with birds returning with scraps for their young from the Billingsgate or Smithfield markets. Here William had stopped to take a tuppenny glass of strong peppermint water from the stall, sipping the pepper-minter's illicit sky-blue gin while he got his thoughts in order, enjoying the hot sun and the view ahead of him, the City of London's grand new buildings glaring above the skyline. The Bank of England was almost completed, standing opposite the Mansion House with the Lord Mayor's Nest on top, the bulk of the Royal Exchange just visible beyond.

Fortified, using these buildings as a guide, William had found his way to Change Alley under the shadow of the Bank, navigating the last few yards by the volume of uproar. In the Rotunda a red-coated beadle whirred an earsplitting watchman's ratchet in a vain appeal for order over a mob of stock-jobbers and money-dealers who jostled him aside. William felt the excitement of money. He stared, rapt: the brokers were all of a disreputable description, wearing limp tricorne hats and greasy coats with the gilt rubbing off the buttons, but the thrill in the stinking air was palpable. This hot odour of breath and sweat was the smell of money, and here was what it bought: William looked around him at the vast buildings. Respectability.

But first he must find Sam Summers.

One man coming out tearing up a dirty piece of paper in disgust had told him to look at John's Coffee House in Cornhill. Lounging there in the doorway, an Italian merchant in parrot-bright finery recognised the name at once. 'Sam, he is like me, a lover of the opera, he sing. You sing?' He brushed the side of his nose with his fingers.

'No,' William said.

Signor Versucchi glanced around the crowded interior and shrugged. 'You try find him. Won't do you no good, if he owe you money.'

'If you see him,' William said, 'tell him a friend wishes to buy him a good square meal, there.' He pointed at the chophouse up the road.

The Italian had waved him away with a polite flourish and did not move while William remained within sight; but when William, after waiting a few seconds, looked back round the corner, the doorway was empty.

William stood in front of the chophouse, waiting.

The Italian must have given William, the outsider, a good report, for when Sam Summers at last strode busily down the pavement, his wine-red coat, complete with gold braid, still carried the pawnbroker's creases.

'Money is a subject close to my heart also,' William now said. 'Perhaps it would be best if we ate.'

He tipped the waiter to force a way for them through the crowd of diners, the gentlemen leaning back after their meal with their ankles crossed on the tables, smoking long pipes. The waiter, slapping at its grease spots with the cloth over his shoulder, showed them a table by the window, and when they sat the world beyond them was warped and fragmented by the cheap panes.

William called for ale. 'We have an interest in common.'

'Interest?' Sam said quickly, thinking William was talking about money – as, indeed, in a way he was, for money alone could save James, and thus was the last thing William wanted. He had come to Sam Summers not to get money but specifically *not* to get it. Already he was reassured: Sam Summers, for all his puffery, was obviously one of those speculators ekeing a living on the margins of City gossip, and when the soup was brought the hands of his watch still pointed to the time of his arrival. William was in control.

He watched how Sam, with quick movements and eyes fixed hungrily on the bowl, although attempting to feign indifference, tucked his napkin eagerly into his collar. William, amused to see weakness so clearly revealed and so briefly resisted, called for another loaf for his guest. He hardly touched his own bowl; he had eaten a jam pastry while he waited. Sam slurped busily, all his concentration on his food. He wiped the last piece of bread round the bowl, then saw William looking at him and put it down ashamed.

'I work in the futures market,' Sam said, running his hand tiredly through his curly, greying hair. Twenty pounds lighter, Summers would be a handsome man whose aura of energy might bestow a stature greater than his inches. But Sam had squandered his dead wife Esmerelda's fortune and been estranged from Eve long ago, and his spirit had shrunk. Still he puffed himself out: 'I am a speculator of capital wherever a penny may be turned,' he claimed chirpily, though obviously starving for the meat course. 'A penny turned is a penny earned. A young man with money to invest could not come to a better man than I.' He surveyed William with cat-bright eyes.

William put his cards on the table. 'My name is William Prideau. I am the elder son of your old friend John Prideau.'

Sam was instantly wary, quick as the flipping of a coin. Then he said sadly: 'Was it so long ago?'

'You ruined my father.'

'Your father ruined himself. He lost heart,' Sam said impatiently, 'lost heart when his wife died. Ah,' he greeted the arrival of the mutton chop, and poured on sauce liberally. 'You're very young,' he said. 'Let me guess. And very ambitious, aren't you?'

William said nothing.

'What do you really want of me?' Sam said bleakly.

'Eve asked me to come and see you.'

Sam munched with the appetite of a starving man. 'Is she well?'

'She's very beautiful. She has fallen in love with my brother.'

'And you think this is a bad thing.'

William spoke warily. 'My brother has stolen some money.'

'Yes?'

'Yes.'

'I see.' Sam hardly glanced at him, still busily eating. 'And my dear daughter has asked you to appeal to me for funds.'

William shrugged.

'Which is the last thing you wish, naturally.'

William said nothing.

'You're in love with her,' Sam said.

For a moment William lost his nerve. 'No, I'm not.'

Sam gnawed the bone. 'I fancy a bottle of port,' he said.

William ordered it.

'To go with my cheese,' Sam said. William called the waiter back.

Sam looked searchingly into William's eyes.

'I know something of human weakness, Master Prideau.'

'Doubtless because you move in such circles!'

'I know my own soul. I despise myself, if that reassures you.'

William drank a glass of port and smiled. 'My conscience is clear.'

'If that's so, you'll go far,' Sam said, wholly in command. 'You have nothing to fear from me.'

'I don't know what you mean,' William protested.

'You *are* in love with Eve. Why are you here?'

'I am not in love.'

'You will do anything for her, and that is love. *Anything*, am I not right?' Sam washed down a wedge of cheese with port and gestured for William to recharge his glass. 'Don't worry, there is no danger of reconciliation between my daughter and me. You may have her all for yourself, my self-contained young man. Yes; she deserves you.' He helped himself to a piece of cheese from William's plate.

William said, 'Why does she hate you?'

'I treated her cruelly as a child, I could not help myself. Naturally I blamed her for living while my wife was dead. Later I saw how her mother was still alive in Eve and I would have done anything for my dear daughter, but it was too late and she would not stand

46

on the pedestal I put her on.' He ignored the worthless fob watch dangling on its plated chain and pulled a small locket, perhaps the last memento of genuine value he owned, from under his collar on a finely-woven chain of gold. Leaning forward so that it reached, he let William examine it.

William flicked the hasp and glanced at the young and pretty woman, painted on a coin-sized circle of china, who smiled with eyes as brown as her hair beneath the glaze.

'Esmerelda, whom I loved,' Samuel Summers said, one half his face illuminated by the window. 'Do you not think her blood lives on?'

'I see a resemblance,' admitted William, thankful he discerned no trace of Sam Summers in Eve, except in her blue eyes.

'There is only room for love once in a life,' Sam murmured. He leaned back and belched. 'There's nothing new in sibling rivalry. Did you deliberately plan to erase your brother as a competitor, or was it an accident?'

'How dare you make such a suggestion! How can you fall so low. . . .'

'Because, like you, I am flesh and blood.'

William hesitated. Challenged by this man to find the truth, he said at last: 'James brought it on himself.'

'Ah, yes,' Sam said softly. 'That, I understand.'

William paid the waiter, and Sam held out his palm too.

6

A sinner beyond redemption

Sam jumped the gutter and stood observing the young man's retreat: William Prideau, so ambitious and so immune to guilt that he could look Sam Summers in the face. What crime had William committed? Sam did not care to know, he was weary of vice. He stepped into the shadows that clung to the south side of the street, and William walked self-righteously from sight among the riders and carriages passing along the grandeur of the thoroughfare.

Behind this grandeur, Sam knew, so close to the tall back walls that its rotten wood and mouldering plaster almost touched the pale Portland stone, the darkest rookery in London dropped down to the river. Here a man could lose anything, if he was not already lost.

Sam leaned back against a filthy brick wall, holding the notes crumpled in his hand, his eyes gleaming beneath the brim of his tall hat. His belly was full for the first time in weeks, his head spun slowly from the combined effects of ale and port, and he knew what he had to do. Already he had forgotten William. The alley led down, and he had the very woman in mind, he could smell the river already.

Her name was not Esmerelda. Annie or some such. Annie Day. And she was younger, she said fourteen. But ignore her matted hair, the bright blueness of her eyes – he always made her close her eyes – and forget that it was the ingrained filth that made her skin Spanish-dark, and she looked like Esmerelda. He had even trained her to parrot a few Spanish words as though she loved him.

Sam turned left and right and left again along dank alleys that showed no sky, empty but for the clusters of pale children too young to work the streets, left looking after the babies. The slimy walls crowded Sam's shoulders as he hurried down. But here he felt peculiarly safe; people worth robbing did not enter these strange communities. A gentleman was in more danger on the faraway steps of Covent Garden Theatre.

Sam ducked through a doorway and descended into a tiny room, the bar of a public house breathtaking with a fug of urine and vomit; Pitt's tax on gin meant these people got piss-giddy on beer. A bunch of women, their money gone, glowered at him from the counter. Girls in the money lay with their bonneted heads askew on each other's bellies, knees apart, grinning up helplessly as he stepped over them. In the corner a baby tried to play with a kitten, then coughed itself purple. Someone was humming aimlessly in a low, pretty voice: sitting on a table with her ankles showing, her wrists on her knees, leaning back against the wall, was Annie.

'Want a threepenny bit?' she said hopefully, then saw who it was. 'Why Sam! I don't do it with no one but you, honest, until my man comes home.' She smiled prettily in her red dress, jumping down. '*Con ti amo?*'

She'd forgotten how to say it properly, and for a moment, trembling with desire, he loathed her almost as much as he loathed himself.

Annie held back her long brown hair with one hand, her elbows pressed tight against her sides to deepen her cleavage and please him. She looked straight into his eyes.

'I'm flush!' he begged her, old enough to be her father.

He was all right; Annie let him lead her out, the

other girls sniggering because she was taller than he was.

But as they walked towards the river he suddenly said: 'You don't go with other men, do you, my dear?'

She felt pity for him because he had never hurt her. 'Not until my Dick Dodds gets home again,' she repeated, loping beside him.

He showed her the pound note in his hand. 'Promise me you won't, and you can have this.' Annie's eyes widened and she hung onto him affectionately, promising him anything while he bobbed fatly along beside her as fast as he could.

The loophole of light at the end of the alley held an arch of London Bridge, slowly traversed by a triangular sail.

She hitched her dress and he followed her up long flights of steps to her lodging-room among the rooftops, then looked down on the bridge and river foreshore through her bare draughty window. He spoke without looking round. 'Esmerelda, do you love him?'

'Dick Dodds, he's my sneaksman,' Annie smiled proudly, 'I never know when he's coming back when he's gone off. He works alone, houses in the country mostly, in the summer when the grand folks is in town. No clink can hold Dick Dodds, though Ilchester kept him for six months. If he came here now he'd have your liver out. What did you call me?'

'I forget,' he said sadly, running his hand back through his greying hair.

'It's a lovely name, that,' she said tenderly.

'Does he love you?'

'Dickie Doddie? He has me, don't he? He's not peculiar, Sam, like you are, he's not just a dreamer.'

'You're beautiful,' he said.

He hung a blanket over the window so that the room was dim. Her dress now seemed the colour of claret, fine as a lady's; her hair almost black falling over her shoulders, her complexion sultry. He left the pound note on the sill. She knew what he wanted, and closed her eyes. He put his arms round her, and held her gently. She wondered what pictures ran through his memory.

'Call it me again,' she whispered. 'Esmerelda.'

He murmured that name, his face in her hair, groaning aloud in his despair. Annie slipped out one hand and got the note between her fingers. 'My true love,' he demanded of her, pulling in his stomach like a young man.

'*Con ti mio*,' she whispered.

'No, say it properly: *amor mio*, my own true love, my sweet love.'

'*Amor mio*,' she murmured obligingly. Letting her dress ride up her long thighs, wearing nothing beneath, she let him possess her for the few gasping moments it took, no time at all. His spirit wasted, he flopped facedown on the bed, ashamed, and she stole his locket.

He was such a funny little man with his pot belly and skinny white buttocks, she almost liked him.

For the first time she offered: 'Do you want me to lie down beside you for a while? You can hold me if you like.'

'You?' he said, offended. 'I wouldn't expect a whore to understand.'

'You made me one,' she said.

'What have you done to me?' he said with earnestness. He touched her hair longingly, then looked at his hand with disgust: it was crawling with lice. 'You're a sinner,' he said, turning away, 'a sinner beyond redemption.'

'No,' she said, 'I think that's *you*.'

Ignoring her, he searched for his britches. 'I shan't see you again,' he said.

He pulled on his clothes, not looking at her. When he was young he must really have loved that Esmer-

51

elda, like in one of the penny love stories hawked around the publics perhaps, and for a few moments she felt quite sorry for him; then she forgot him, and looked forward to getting drunk.

One morning, riding down Bow Street, Eve Summers saw her father come striding from the alley beside the Covent Garden Theatre, where attendants at the stage door reserved places for the following nights. She sat back in the carriage at once, turning away, and he did not notice her.

Then she looked back, her face disturbed.

So, as always, he could raise a pound or two when he had to, but not for her. She saw a handbill advertising, fittingly, *The Beggar's Opera*.

'Is anything wrong, ma'am?' Nellie asked.

Eve stared after her father until he disappeared.

She thought she had learned to hide her feelings long ago, since he first confused her with his love, and even now her feelings about him were complex.

Ironically, Eve had been almost pleased when William came back to The Polygon after his visit to the City, and informed her that 'her father had no money and cared not to see her.' No horrid pity showed on his calm features, he uttered no soulful commiserations. She was grateful for such lack of emotion to reinforce her self-control. She had always withdrawn from the ambiguous area her father occupied in her emotions. And indeed she had hardly thought of him. Her real childhood started at her uncle's house in Devon, everything she felt deeply from before that time pretended forgotten.

And then something extraordinary had happened to her: there in the parlour Eve wept, and William held her. He looked like James Prideau, felt like James, smelt like James.

She looked at him uncertainly, gathering her composure.

'I'm sorry,' William said stiffly, and she took her lead from him.

'It's not your fault. It was unforgivable of me.' She felt a tear on her cheek and wiped it away, now truly ashamed.

His eyes shifted past her. 'I feel terrible that I can't do more for James. I've given him what little money I can afford – '

'But why does he need money in prison?'

'Don't bother your head with such concerns. He is content, you know James, always lands on his feet. Frankly I wish he took his situation more seriously – as seriously as I do. I'm sure he misses you really. You must save all your strength for his appearance in Court. Eve,' William said kindly, 'I implore you not to attend such a ghastly place.'

'I love him. I've written to him but I am sure he does not receive my letters.'

'You must not torment yourself.'

'But I love him.'

He bowed. 'It is several months away at least. The mills of justice grind slow, and Mr Trewarren is drawing up a damning case.' He stopped, as if unwilling to give her more bad news. 'I feel worse because Mr Trewarren has promoted me to a salary of some twenty-two shillings a week while Mr Gumboge is suspended. It makes me feel like a traitor. Of course I give it all to James – except my bare living,' he added.

How much thinner he looked – almost gaunt. 'You must eat with us!' she said at once. 'You will!' She could be as impulsive as James. 'I won't take no for an answer!'

This time he bowed deeply. 'My brother does not deserve you.'

During breakfast the next morning she told Aunt

Sarah: 'I am going to Oxford Street to buy some Brussels lace. Nellie will accompany me.'

Nellie, glad of the chance to dress up as lady's maid, was easily sworn to secrecy. Eve sent her into a premises to buy a bob's worth of lace and hurry back, then ordered the driver to take them to the Strand; perhaps she would look in Mr Cadell's bookshop. In fact Eve had quite another purpose in mind. She was determined to look at Newgate Prison, where James was.

Seeing her father disturbed her.

'What's the matter, ma'am?' Nellie asked indiscreetly.

'No one,' Eve said. She had meant to say *nothing*.

Turning left into the Strand, the old horse clopped a few yards eastward along the widening road through increasing crowds of jolly people until the carriage could hardly move forward. Eve saw the melancholy black walls of Newgate, deliberately designed to intimidate and overawe with the ponderous majesty of their justice.

'Why are all these people here?' she asked calmly.

'Look, to see them sinners hanging,' Nellie pointed.

Two men, their hands tied into a position of prayer, hung like sacks from a crossbar over the roadway. They rotated slowly above the milling heads of the crowd, the grandstands no longer used. The third dangling body was that of a woman in a bonnet which half hid her ghastly face. The breeze ruffled her skirts as she swung.

'The crowd thought it was going to be Haggerty and Holloway,' Nellie sounded quite miffed to have missed it. 'Everyone's sure they're innocent, so a lot of people'll come to see how they hang.'

'Turn home!' Eve ordered the driver. Even as she said it she did not think she could ever forgive herself. She had thought there was no one in the world unhappier than she. Now she realised how lucky she was.

*

Throughout the summer, waiting for the case to inch its way to trial, William tried desperately to keep Eve's spirits up with his thoughtful good company, talking of this and that, anything but James and his awful predicament. The Keeper of Newgate Prison was a monster who demanded fees for everything – fees to arrive and fees to depart, three shillings and sixpence for rent of bed and foul bedding, fees for the turnkey, fees for food and fees not to be held in chains, and fees for the chains to be struck off once they were on. It was almost impossible to save much for a defence despite William's increased earnings from Mr Gumboge's vacated position as Head Clerk. That brute Honeyman, who considered the place should have gone to him, finally had been dismissed for his continual insolence to William. 'I pleaded for Mr Honeyman to be given a good reference, that he may find another employer,' William said, 'but Mr Trewarren would not hear of it. So you see, Eve, my influence with him is really very small.' He sighed. 'If only I could do more for James, but he's his own worst enemy. He still claims he is innocent, and such protestations do him nothing but harm, since of course everyone makes them.'

'But he is innocent,' Eve said.

'I wish to believe so,' William admitted, and her lips trembled.

'Then you do not – '

'I no longer know what I believe,' William said.

He had moved into better rooms just east of Covent Garden, on the excuse of being nearer James, with a high ceiling and a good fireplace as winter closed in. A maid, Deb, came in daily to empty his chamber-pot into the cellar and brush the rugs, sand the floorboards and turn the bed once a week, occasionally to cook for him, and after one such meal of good English beef it was to her he lost his virginity, she letting him take her with a self-interested casualness that entranced him.

Later he bought a commode so he could relieve his bowels without getting up from his desk.

He felt no pity for what he had done to James, who would have done it to himself sooner or later – William was still convinced James had stolen that hay for the bed. Already on the slippery slope, James would have fallen anyway. Besides, William had seen Eve first. It was in her own interest to see that William was a far better catch, but she persisted in loving James despite his faults, and failed to see that William was the one who could look after her. Very well, her obstinacy sealed her lover's fate. Without hope for James, when he was gone she *must* love William. So her suffering, and James's, was their own fault not William's, and Eve's happiness up to her to see the obvious, that William was the one she must trust. The only one.

But still Eve talked of James.

Deb had been around long enough so William dismissed her.

7

The river's child

A girl could get drunk for a penny and blind drunk for
twopence, but it was awful wildfire, and every summer's day seemed to start with Annie waking with her
head split and the front of her dress soaked with
alcoholic vomit, no sign of food there, nor any memory
of yesterday. Sometimes she was in the Flat Head
public, but later, as the mornings grew cold and the
days and nights lost their meaning, she was often lying
in an alley, and finally she found herself coming to
consciousness not recognising at first where she was.

She was lying on the muddy foreshore of the river at
low tide, the crumbling spans of London Bridge arching
away from her in the dawn. Old ragged women and
children searched like magpies among the pebble-
dashed slime for any poor flotsam and jetsam, stepping
over Annie where necessary. Sometimes the mudlarks
found Roman coins amongst the sewage, and occasionally they pulled up some poor suicide with clothes and
shoes, and gold to be cut from her swollen fingers, or
broken from her teeth.

Annie sat up and vomited.

Even after all this desperate remedy, her belly still
bulged.

She sat with her head between her knees.

Boats crisscrossed the flat, bright water. Around her
it lapped jagged and brown with breaking wavelets as
the tide rose, and the pebbles began to slither against
her thighs. Footsteps splashing past her towards the

steps stopped, then a foot enormously cloaked in rags kicked her in the ribs.

'Wouldn't stay there,' Old Slane said, her clothes stiff with dried faeces. 'Back to Dick Dodds's fine room with you, Annie.'

Annie shook her head, but then the woman took her hand and dragged her to the steps with surprising strength.

'You don't weigh nothing,' muttered Old Slane, 'and you was so tall and all. I knew your mother. She were all right herself but she never found the right man.' She sat on the step beside Annie and emitted a bone-weary groan. 'Tragedy it is, you being pretty and all,' she said, looking at Annie lower down, winking. 'And not his. They say Dick Dodds is still in Taunton gaol.'

'It won't hold him.'

'He'll cut your face off if he sees you like that,' Old Slane said.

'Not if I get him in bed first.'

Old Slane slapped her raggedy hands on her knees and gave a cackling laugh, then pushed herself up on Annie's shoulder. 'That looks like a December baby to me. Call me when you're ready.' She looked back, a grin splitting her filthy face. 'Or come round before.'

But Annie wouldn't go to the old woman's cellar. Her baby had survived the gin; now she felt quite curious about the little fighter she nourished inside her. And as it swelled and kept her in Dick's room unable to work – but she had saved back some of Sam's money – make-working on a shawl while staring bored from the window, Annie often recognised Old Slane's distinctive crow-shape, her rags stiff as armour with dried mud, plodding among those others pecking at the mud-banks, driven from the shipyards and the precious copper nails by men with cudgels. Old Slane came to fascinate her: *I knew your mother. She was all right herself but she never found the right man.* Annie arrived at the extraordinary determination to keep her baby. She found herself thinking about her own mother and it seemed unbearably sad that she held no memory at all of her. Was she tall? Annie was. Was she like Annie? Had she felt these same feelings Annie felt?

Winter came, but the baby came before winter, much too sudden, with unstoppable pains that gathered themselves like waves on the sea, great waves unfolding and flowing down her body. Old Slane came stumping up the stairs and looked around her with appreciation. 'Blimey, Dick Dodds set you up in fine style, don't it echo nice.' She sat herself down comfortably, smelling overwhelmingly of the river. 'You just carry on.'

Annie screamed as her baby was born, in pain and finally joy, on the bed where she had been conceived with indifference.

'All that fuss about such a little one,' Old Slane said, holding the pink, squalling thing up. 'What you want me to do with it?'

'Her,' Annie murmured, holding out her arms.

'Not a good idea,' said Old Slane, hanging back.

Annie caught at the old woman with all her strength. 'All right!' Old Slane said, 'let go, *let go*.' She handed the baby back. 'Well,' she said, watching Annie cuddle her too-tiny daughter, 'I could do with a slug of gin, and I reckon you could too.'

But Annie wasn't listening, so Old Slane drank straight from the bottle's mouth. 'What you going to call her?' she demanded with a sigh.

Annie glanced up. 'Esmerelda.'

'Never heard a name like that.' Old Slane tilted back the bottle, then smiled benignly. 'Ezzie. I like it though.' But Annie didn't hear her. All her thoughts were concentrated on her baby, all her emotions involved in Esmerelda's every wince and wrinkle. It was love.

*

From the courtroom dock James simply stared at the woman he loved, as though nothing else had existence in his mind but she, not the shabby candlelit room that held him or the row of chatting clerks, the periwigged counsel, or Judge Mainwaring leaning forward to hear, his nose a hook of old leather curved over his toothless mouth: only Eve.

She stood alone. William had cleared a space for her against the railings. The motley crowd who attended such events pressed forward, hungry journalists hoping to puff up a petty crime to a sensational broadsheet, fat sentimental women crying into handkerchiefs. Below, beadles were shouldering men in chains forward, leading others away. The tipstaff was very jolly, tilting a bottle of port to his lips behind his lapel.

'I begged you not to come,' William murmured to Eve. 'You could have saved yourself this pain.'

Now she knew why those women stuck their noses in their perfumed kerchiefs: on account of the gaol stench from the poor prisoners shambling forward, shackled with irons so that they could not wave to their friends and supporters who whistled and hooted in greeting at their entrance. Waving annoyed the judge, but not the noise, since he was almost deaf.

Someone shouted, 'How d'ye plead?'

James said with dignity: 'Not guilty. I plead *Ponit se super patriam*. I put myself at the mercy of the jury.'

The judge cupped his hand to his ear and the usher obligingly shook his head in the negative. '*Po se*, m'lud.' Mr Trewarren passed across a sheaf of papers and the arguing began.

'What goods does he have?' demanded the judge.

'The trouble is,' William murmured to Eve, 'James *looks* guilty. You've got to have the right face to get off, and after eight months in Newgate, nobody has the right face.' He was right, Eve admitted to herself. James *did* look different: he was emaciated, despite all the food

William brought him, all the care of him William took. James looked like a man who *should* be in prison: made brutish by that brutal place. The refinement had disappeared from his features. He looked ten years older, his skin pastry-white from that sunless interior, aged with lines of congealed dirt. James looked guilty. But his adamant eyes did not move from Eve's face.

'What? What?' the judge was cupping his hand to his ear. 'Guilty?'

Looking harassed, the foreman of the jury nervously repeated the word.

'Death by hanging,' said the man beside them, snatching his silk kerchief from his cuff and waving it in front of his nose, 'Damme, the stink of them.'

William interposed himself quietly. 'Eve. . . .'

'He cannot die,' she said.

'Trewarren is a vengeful man,' William said.

But Judge Mainwaring said: 'What? What? Transportation, fourteen years.'

William looked thunderstruck. 'It's the same as death,' he said quietly, 'they don't come back.'

Eve burst into tears, and William kept his hands by his sides, clearly embarrassed by her public show.

'James Prideau,' yawned the Clerk, holding out a warrant to the tipstaff, 'Gaol Delivery, to be contracted under the care of the Transport Office to the hulk *Captivity* at Portsmouth, as soon as may be convenient.'

Two beadles flanked James, one to each elbow to stop him falling, as he was taken down. Eve held out her hands but his were chained.

The Clerk instructed his juniors: 'Append the name Prideau to the List of Offenders ordered to be transported beyond the seas, in order that this List might be annexed to an order by His Majesty in Council, appointing the East Coast of New South Wales the place to which they should be transported. . . .'

'It's over,' William said.

'James thinks I believe in his guilt,' whispered Eve.
'Oh, I'm sure not.'
'What must he feel, William?'
William tried visibly to imagine it.
'He must feel,' he said, 'that justice has been done.'

Shivering, leaning forward to look from the carriage window at the snowy streets leading her down to the Strand, Eve felt guilty about her determination to come here alone, without even Nellie to chaperone her, in case she seemed disloyal to William. William had been wonderful. . . . but it was James she had to see.

The wheels turned in eerie silence on the packed snow, even the horse's hoofs muffled, as though the vehicle was pulled by a magic force. The carriage passed through the feathery silence in front of Edward Cross's menagerie; in the shadows of the arcade lay ranks of chained animals, a monkey dressed as Napoleon Bonaparte shivering on a pole: the year was 1805, and although the Grand Army's attempt to mount a lightning-strike attack on London had failed, the nation was in mourning for Nelson's murder at Trafalgar.

All Eve could think of was James. Thank God no bodies were hanging in the roadway this time, the street-market was busy and bright, and Newgate prison, which had presented such a fearsome aspect before, seemed lower than she remembered, softened by a stained, sooty mantle of snow.

She knocked on the door, thinking only of James, and when it was opened she stepped innocently into the prototype of hell. The turnkey greeted her with a smile and after she had paid him, led her through throngs of drunken men and women sprawled along the stones of the wards, past the filthy sea-coal fires claimed by the strongest. The bowing turnkey prayed her to ignore the babble of voices, curses, appeals. 'These people say any lie. The sluts get with child to plead their bellies.' Eve saw inmates practising their trade: a cobbler repairing shoes, women sewing as though they would die tomorrow. Eve held a handkerchief soaked in vinegar, that the turnkey had sold her, to her nose while he kept encouraging her to peer into cells on the way. Did she wish to pay a little extra to look into the Condemned Hold, where the men and women lay chained on stone beds until it was time to have their necks stretched? Eve shuddered, so he showed her anyway, for the pleasure of her horror.

'Poor creatures!' she said.

He was outraged. 'Why,' he told her angrily, pointing, 'those two killed a ewe sheep what was not theirs, and would have eaten it too. There's Johnson that broke into a house and stole some curtains, and those there are Dowder and Needs, what stole five pounds from a gentleman. Where would it end, ma'am, if they did not die?' When it seemed Eve could barely comprehend his words he dragged her to a sleeping woman. 'This here, Mary Jennings, attempted to suffocate her child in a cesspool, but she's been commuted to twenty years' transportation, taking her brat too. Justice is too merciful. There's none but the guiltiest of the guilty here, ma'am, the poorest of the poor. You thank your God for your fine birth and your fine clothes or you'd find yourself in here too, I dare say!'

The turnkey picked up his lamp that he had dropped in his righteous passion. Then he held out his hand for more money.

He led her to an ironbound door, at least four inches thick, as though constructed to contain a rhinoceros.

The light fell across James's face as the door opened. He looked up at her, then he made no further movement.

'James,' she said.

Two dark lines trickled down his face.

63

'James,' said the turnkey, leaning in the doorway, 'how I does love you, James. Oh Jim, how I does!'

She held out her gloved hands to James and he gripped them, staring up. Then he pulled off her gloves and kissed her hands, her fingers, holding them to his lips, her knuckles against his eyes.

'You must be mad to come here,' he murmured.

'Jim, Jim! I loves you!' said the turnkey in a high voice, clasping his hands over his heart.

James lunged at the man but the chains snapped taut, throwing him back. The shiny skin of his wrists and ankles was rubbed raw, veined with blood. 'Don't,' she whispered, kneeling, 'don't.'

Was he the same James she had known?

'I still love you,' she whispered, touching his sore flesh.

Screams along the hall; the turnkey cursed and left them.

'William's been marvellous,' said James rapidly, his eyes still fixed on the open door as though he were not chained and could run through it to freedom, 'almost all his eight shillings a week is spent on me.'

'He gets a little more than that now.' She tugged his shoulders. 'James, please don't accept your fate! You've done nothing wrong.'

He turned his haunted face up to her, his skin cold and pale as a dead man's. 'I'm so out of touch, I don't know whether I'm innocent or guilty. You don't know this place. Without William I'd die. He brings me food, he dotes on me like a mother. He's launching an appeal for the Royal Mercy. Trewarren wanted death but William begged him not to and that was why Trewarren didn't push for it.' She could hardly understand his gabble: 'Hush, hush,' she whispered. James said: 'I love you and I'm never going to see you again.'

Back in the streets of London at last, Dick Dodds

smiled as he thought of Annie, her warm welcome. She knew how to welcome a man. If she'd looked at anyone else he'd kill her, after he'd done her. He thought of her a lot.

He was the ruins of a handsome man, the sort girls like to throw their arms round in the dark, and he knew how to look after them. He'd grown heavy, but he was still enormously strong, and feared no man. He prowled eastwards along the Strand at his best time, the dead of night, stepping into a doorway when any watchman's lamp glowed on the snow.

Taunton prison had held him despite all his cunning, all for a bit of sawney bacon, though they talked it up to being worth half a guinea. Still, his brutality made it a comfortable enough life for him over the other prisoners. The Western Circuit Assizes, Sir Alexander Thomson presiding, chose to be soft even though it was a second offence – it cost two shillings and sixpence a week to keep a man in gaol, a little over a shilling in a hulk, and two pounds to hang him and get rid of him forever, but because in Portsmouth a great transport fleet was assembling, Dick Dodds was lucky. He would be transported overseas for the term of his natural life.

The transport contractor's chains that could hold Dick Dodds hadn't yet been forged. He knew something would turn up; meanwhile it was time he saw Annie again.

'Thank you, sir!' he said, pulling his forelock.

The next case was a man called Simeon Simmonds, down for handling stolen goods, a very serious matter, though apparently his first offence. But Dick Dodds knew an old lag when he saw one, and this man Simmonds – if his name was really Simmonds – had a smile even Dick respected. Simmonds too was sentenced to transportation. Back in the icy cells, Dick observed him carefully. Simmonds limped, yet tried to conceal it. He was a ferocious-looking bastard. In the evening his son

Josiah visited him and as Dick watched them embrace, he saw a flash of steel pass between them. He clamped his hand over theirs: two tiny spring saws, small enough to be concealed in the lining of a collar. 'Two of us,' he said. 'Or none of us. Depend on it, hearty.'

Working with bloody fingers they got their chains cut half through during the night, and there were three other men chained with them in the freezing van. As the cart jolted onward they finished the job off, then cut a hole in the bottom of the van, hurrying as it got dark: they had to get the job done before the overnight check at Yate's Lockup.

'If they catch us escaping,' Dick said, 'it's the drop.'

Simmonds dropped down first and the two men ran, but the pale snow showed them up, and Simmonds hobbled in the soft drifts like a man with a wooden leg. The guard tripped Simmonds into a ditch but Dick Dodds, who was loyal, flung his chains round the guard's neck and pulled tight, pulling the man's boots clean out of the snow, strangling him. By now the pistol-waving driver was blundering towards them and Simmonds knew he stood no chance of escape. As Dick Dodds ran off into the night, he crawled back to the vehicle as though he'd never got out in the first place.

A few days later, in Bedminster, Dick Dodds was proud to see a handbill nailed up offering twenty guineas on his head. He had reached the pinnacle of his profession. He was wanted for murder.

Winter was a bad time to be on the run; he generally avoided it. But Annie's room would be good and warm, and so would she; he was almost home.

As soon as she heard his footsteps on the stairs, Annie sat up blinking the sleep out of her eyes, pulling her hair from her face. She knew at once Dick Dodds was back. She was wearing a shift partly because it was cold and partly because her breasts were so heavy with milk. Quickly she pulled it over her head and dropped the folds to hide her baby's crib, where Esmerelda lay swaddled in a shawl, then ran naked to the door.

'Dick!' she greeted him in the doorway, arms wide.

'Get me a bottle,' he said, then reached for her instead, and there they stood in the doorway, him guzzling at her breast, his great paws searching her body. Thank God she'd hidden the locket in the baby's shawl. He reached for his belt, her milk running down his chin, then stopped, putting his hand to his mouth and looking at it with disgust.

'What's this?'

'Come to bed,' she begged him, hugging her arms around him, 'I'll bring your bottle to bed and we – '

He pushed her aside and searched the room. 'Don't,' she said.

He plucked the baby from the crib and held her up by the ankles.

'Don't,' Annie murmured, 'Dick, don't.'

He stared at her with flat eyes as Annie reached out, letting her fingertips almost touch her baby, then swung her away.

'Whose?'

'No one's, honest.'

Esmerelda began to cry. Annie covered her breasts with her hands.

'Whose man are you?' He caressed his thumb to her Adam's apple.

'Yours, Dick.' All Annie's inner being screamed with terror.

'I should break your back,' he said, and she closed her eyes.

Instead, she heard the door open and his footsteps thump downstairs. Annie stared uncomprehending. Now she could hear her baby's cries in the street below. With numb fingers, still not understanding, she pulled her shift over her head then ran down the stairs in her bare feet. The street was outlined by starlight, she heard faint cries and saw Dick Dodds's shadow walk onto London Bridge. The arches rose against the sky-line. Annie ran like the wind towards his shadow lean-ing over the parapet.

It was done before she reached him. Dick Dodds flung her baby sheer off the bridge.

Gripping Annie by the throat, strangling her shrieks, he dragged her home along the street. No doors were opened or windows thrown wide. Annie screamed and screamed but her mouth could make no sound. His footsteps thumped up the stairs, his ankles rising and falling below her. She had never felt such pure hatred. She got her foot behind his, and pushed with all her strength.

With flailing arms, his heels racketting down the steps, Dick Dodds fell backwards. He grabbed at the air with his great strength and landed on his forehead, lay piled against the bottom step with his head bent down his back. Annie sat on the top step, she couldn't move. It was one of those days.

She didn't like his staring eyes.

She wandered. When she was hungry, she ate. When she was arrested, still clothed only in her shift, she slept like a dead woman.

It was Old Slane who found the river's child. Left by the falling tide, the bundle lay on the mudbank in the eddy below London Bridge. A baby here was a not uncommon occurrence, and the raggedy old woman approached it without getting her hopes up, because they were usually dead and no use to anyone except for their clothes, sometimes a nice bit of lace, but the poor draggle of shawl that clung to this one didn't augur well. Then the baby gave a low cry, and Old Slane gave a little hop of pleasure as she splashed

68

across the mud. A live baby was a different proposition. It could be sold.

Wriggling her filthy fingers out of her half-gloves, unwittingly dropping mud over the glint of gold trapped in the folds of the shawl, old Betty Slane peered at the baby's exhausted face, the bruised left arm. No mistaking those Annie-blue eyes: Betty Slane recognised the baby she'd brought into the world six weeks ago.

'What you doing here, Ezzie?' She looked back at the bridge towering above them. Babies were amazingly resilient, and Ezzie must have landed in the slick of shallow water over the soft mud, but she didn't like the look of that arm. 'Your ma didn't drop you over here, did she?' She couldn't think so: Annie had been a fool for her little girl.

Betty wrapped her in rags and took her back to Annie's. She barely glanced at the body at the foot of the stairs, but backed straight out and disappeared into an alleyway, knowing trouble when she saw it. Dick Dodds's clothes had already been snatched from his body; even his garters, his shoes were gone. His balls hung down between his hairy thighs. The white soles of his feet almost touched the back of his head, and the look on his face was terrifying.

'Looks like Dick had a bit of a fall,' she told the baby. 'I don't think you'll see your ma again.' In this, she was almost right.

Old Slane crossed herself and hurried on. It was difficult to imagine a buyer for a baby with a broken wing. But she would think of something.

8

1806

The ferryman

The grandly-titled Clerk of the Calendar of Prisoners Awaiting Transportation aboard the hulk *Captivity*, a harassed little man called Chas Dowling who was dying of consumption and was desperately worried for the fate of his children, made a small mistake in his tally of prisoners copied from the Home Office list. He left the last two letters off a prisoner's name. There were so many names. It was never noticed, and by the time Dowling was dead and his children in the Workhouse, James Prideau no longer existed.

None of the prisoners had ever known him as James; in flash talk he was Jim, even his own sense of identity now leaking from him in the hopeless, vicious world of the *Captivity*'s tween-decks. James Prideau had always been too clever and too quick with his bright outgoing smile, never serious enough about anything. Until he met Eve, and fell in love. Such men were marked.

There were only twenty-seven guards aboard the *Captivity*, one of them a woman, for there was no escape. To swim was to drown, entered DD for discharged dead, or Dragged Down, and the old lags said many men slept in their heavy chains on the sea bed where the ships swung at anchor above.

At work he was a number. Ferried to the Arsenal in chains – God help them if the rowboat overturned – the convict gang toiled all the daylight hours, then were marched back still in fourteen-pound irons to the

Captivity, whose mastless bulk wallowed in the brisk, windswept waters of the harbour.

Even to himself he possessed little sense of his own worth. He did what he was told. The system had succeeded.

But he remembered Eve.

The man lay head-to-toe with three hundred others, the healthy and profane, the sick and dying, the lost and never to be saved, in the cramped gallery of the hulk. He believed in love; he believed in William. No man could have done more than William to save him, or more to care for Eve since Aunt Sarah had fallen unwell with her lungs; William had been a saint. But all his appeals had been turned down by the authorities. The last hope was his petition to King George III for the Royal Prerogative of Mercy.

The prisoner lived in hope for that pardon, and the days passed as heavy as lead, each the same. But slowly, off Spithead, masts appeared, and the great transport fleet for Botany Bay began to assemble.

Time was running out.

On 19 December 1805 Lord Hawkesbury had written to Bradley, the Commissioner of Convicts, enclosing the list of convicts in the hulks, desiring that one hundred and fifty of those male and female prisoners free from infectious distemper should be removed on board the transports *Fortune, Paragon* and *Alexander* in order to their being sent to New South Wales.

On 6 January 1806 a guard detachment arrived on the *Captivity* and for the rest of the month the prisoners, in driving snow, began to be embarked aboard the *Paragon* and other ships. Among them were thirteen prisoners sentenced to be transported at the Sessions of Gaol Delivery for Somerset. Some convicts were permitted to take their wives with them as an indulgence, to save the burden of beggars on the parish.

There would be thirty guards, several of them accompanied by their wives and children.

Aboard the longboat ferrying prisoners across the churning green sea, the cowering men huddled down into a chained misery against the boards, only one man upright in the bow. Snow matting his hair and beard, he stared at the ship whose form became solid ahead of him out of the blizzard: making out the name blazoned in flaking gilding across her square stern below the windows. One of the others called through chattering teeth: 'What do she be, Jim?'

'We're for the *Paragon*.'

'Sit down, Pridey, or you'll have us all in the drink!'

The cox'n lashed out with a knotted rope's end. A marine clutched his musket nervously as the longboat wobbled, and the oarsmen cursed.

The prisoner stared, ignoring all complaints. He didn't believe he would have to go.

In Lynmouth they would have considered the tarry old *Paragon* a big vessel. To cross the world she was tiny, a three-master with poop and quarter decks, of only six hundred tons or so, and a hundred and twenty feet long, but she was almost forty across the beam – a tubby, sea-capable old matron, at least.

The snow lifted for a moment and James saw the flush-decked *Alexander* swinging to anchor a couple of cables' lengths to starboard, only half the *Paragon*'s tonnage. The last ship in the Weather Division was the *Lady Sinclair*, and even as he watched the pendant of a ship of war broke out from her masthead. His Excellency Captain William Bligh of His Majesty's Navy had embarked already.

Fifteen years had passed since the mutiny on the *Bounty*. Bligh, now Captain General of the little fleet, was going out to take up his appointment as Governor in Chief of New South Wales.

The prisoners climbed the scantlings onto the deck

of the *Paragon*. The miserable shivering crowd, tame as rabbits, treated as dangerous wild animals, guarded by armed marines, were herded below into the swilling dark of the gallery.

And no pardon came.

Almost at midnight the prisoner, his blue eyes downcast, bribed the guard with a penny for a quill, a further penny for a thimble of ink, and the last of his money for a lamp and a corner to write his letter in. Bent almost double under the low beams, he crouched near the bulkhead and began to write. The horn lantern swung by his face as the ship rolled. Tomorrow the fleet sailed for Botany Bay.

My dearest Eve, he wrote,
Tomorrow I shall die, if tomorrow comes without you. The new world is the prisoner of the old, and I cannot live without my freedom, without hope, without the woman I love.
Eve, I love you.

He looked up, hearing a noise, but it was only creaking wood, lapping water.

The women wearing the canary yellow dresses of shame were taking turns to press their eyes to the knothole, ogling the chained men sleeping in rows beyond the bulkhead. The lags looked better asleep, their faces softened by slumber. 'I like the one with the loaded britches,' Becky whispered, her strong hands knobbly and stained like potatoes. 'He looked at me earlier, he noticed me and a gleam came into his eye.'

'He looked at me first,' Mary hissed, the willowy girl with a madonna's smooth features and wide eyes. 'He smiled at me, with sauce on it.'

Becky turned with her hair over her face. Mary pinched her and Becky kicked out skilfully, bruising Mary's ankle where it would show.

Annie had pressed her eye to the knothole. Almost close enough to touch, a man with long hair had come to write a letter, the lamp swinging by his face casting a light as dim as an old painting. His was a strange, strong face, she thought, a face made for smiling. But the lines were harsh, the eyes hard.

Becky had pulled Mary's hair and left her sobbing. Now she elbowed Annie aside. 'Well, who's the pretty gentleman?'

Annie, who was considered mad, kept her mouth shut. She'd heard someone call him Jim, but she didn't see why she should share this information. Becky wasn't interested in him anyway. She was all for the one asleep with his hands over his bulge, since finding out Mary wanted him.

'Feargal O'Henry's only an Irish, anyway,' Mary sneered, her tears forgotten in her hatred for her competitor.

'What's wrong with Irish?' said Becky dangerously. 'You know what I am, and proud of it too.' One of the other girls groaned and complained she was trying to sleep. Becky Donahoo went and stood over Catherine Sidmouth with her fists bunched on her hips, defying a sleepy chorus of complaint. The marine on deck beat on the hatch-grating with his musket. Becky cursed them all roundly, they were all being sent Bay Side and she was as good as any of them. Finally she threw herself down and crossed her arms, jumping up if Mary made a move towards the knothole. So Annie, half out of her mind for the death of her baby, having been sentenced to seven years transportation for stealing a mutton pie and being a disorderly woman, was free to sit quietly alone, staring through the knothole. It was already tomorrow.

Across the choppy water of Spithead, a boat was landing another load of coffins on the mudbank called Rats'

Castle. Other vessels crisscrossed the channel in the stiff breeze. The prisoners, shivering at the clean cut of the wind, wincing against the bright sky, clanked obediently round the poop deck of the *Paragon*: their irons would not be struck off until the fleet had weighed anchor and lost sight of land. The women kept apart up on the foc'sle jeered and strutted for the men below, who responded with crude gestures and oaths of undying affection. The cheeks of one young officer were the colour of his scarlet tunic. Before prayers that morning two soldiers, Edmund Germany and Levi Chance, their crime substantiated by an officer, had been tied to a metal triangle and flogged by the bo'sun for filthiness, twenty-four lashes for one, twelve for the other, and the blood that had run down their legs was grossly magnified by the salt water sluiced over them, a thin red gruel that dripped through the planks into the gallery below, a warning. Only then had prayers been held, the sun rising behind the captain like a halo.

The wind blowing his long hair, one man ignored the service. His eyes searched every boat that came near, parents and lovers brought out by fishermen as a profitable trade, their appeals drifting like little screams across the surging waters. Finally, as signal flags unfurled from the *Lady Sinclair*'s yardarm, and the tars began to heave round the clanking anchor-capstan, and still others swarmed up the ratlines along the yards to set sail, he turned away like a man who has lost his last hope.

The old prisoner ahead of him on the chain limped, tugging on him as they traipsed round the deck.

The *Paragon* began to drift forward, the sails snapping as they caught at the wind, then billowing. One of the longboats that had set off too late from shore, rigged with a small gaff sail, still slowly caught them up. In the smooth water to the lee of the *Paragon* she lost the wind to the great bulk of the ship and began to fall back. Then an eddy drew her close, and Eve Summers, seated, looked up straight into his eyes.

She cupped her hands at her mouth. 'I'm sorry. . . .'

'Eve!' he shouted, fumbling with both his chained hands for the letter in his pocket. The circle continued to move, the man ahead tugging at him.

William, sitting below with his hands on his knees, shook his head. He had lost his appeal for Royal Mercy. He looked from the shabby creature in chains and ruined clothes above them, to Eve.

Eve had stood up and opened her arms to the struggling figure. She wore her fine clothes, cream wool, a long cape, she looked lovely, like a woman in the last moment before she throws herself over the side, giving up everything for the heat of the moment. William stood up beside her and held her.

'Eve,' Jim shouted, and then stopped as he gazed at the scene below him, at Eve holding up her arms to him, knowing the look in her eyes was true because he felt it himself. But there was William beside her, hugging her, turning to look up with a smile, a self-satisfied warmth, a kind of peace on his face. And in that moment, in the exuberance of victory, in his happiness, it was James Prideau's face he wore.

William loved her.

High above, the light went from Jim's eyes as he understood how stupid he had been not to see William's love for Eve. Conflicting emotions began to chase themselves across his dull features. The letter went fluttering into the sea. Ignoring the frantic prisoners pulling at him, Jim dragged them forward as though to plunge over the railing into her arms.

A marine levelled his musket, but the prisoner with the limp and a Devon voice knocked the barrel aside, then calmly picked up a belaying pin and cracked it smartly across Jim Pride's head so that he fell unconscious.

76

'Poor fellow,' William comforted Eve, watching the ship wear round in a storm of clattering canvas then steady towards the open sea, 'I fear he was not quite in his right mind towards the end.' He did not pat her, he held her tight now, and she turned her face into his shoulder.

In the carriage returning to London William sat opposite Eve, facing her, but apart. He observed her with the eyes of a man dying of thirst, gazing at a delicious mirage. He made no move to hold her again, keeping his face very serious, very William. He watched the pulse beating in the pale curve of her throat and desired to caress her.

'I should never have allowed you to go to Portsmouth,' he chided her gently. 'I should have spared you.'

'I did not want to be spared. It's my fault.'

He spread his hands obligingly: if that's what you prefer. He was keeping her shut inside herself, and in this she cooperated as always. The days when Eve Summers, prodded by Aunt Sarah, took life lightly were long gone, and such petty distractions as Captain Perceval were inconceivable.

She looked at William, and he saw James Prideau in her eyes.

'You look so like him,' she admitted, 'sometimes I think you are him.'

'Not at all.'

'Are you like him, William?' The scenery passed beyond the window.

'Do I look guilty?' he smiled.

She was on the brink of tears. 'You are very cruel.' Her lip trembled.

'It's cruel world, Miss Summers.'

She glanced at him with hatred. 'Of course you are right,' she sighed: 'You always are.'

77

'And right about this,' he said.

When she looked at him questioningly, William leaned forward, took her hand, and kissed her skin.

Back in London, he plunged into a different sort of work. He purchased a fine beaver hat from Mr Lock, a good, solid, respectable coat from Whitehead's, and silk hose that set off the shape of his legs. Ushers bowed to him from shop doorways. He went with his own sort to the proper theatres and opera houses of Covent Garden. He learned to take snuff and sneeze through one nostril, visited Aunt Sarah's bedside and brought her small gifts, sugary confections in the shape of flowers, making sure he was never absent from Eve's thoughts, never less than polite to her and sometimes a little more. He was wearing her down. All this was work to William. He had always known what he wanted.

'I want to be the son you never had,' he told Mr Trewarren. 'Sir,' he confessed, 'you are the father I have always missed.'

The old man's hands quivered to hear such a revealing honesty so calmly delivered, his eyes watering with affection at the implied compliment. 'Well! I have always tried to treat you fairly, William, and to reward you after the unhappy events that are now in the past. . . .'

'Quite so. I look forward to it.'

'Your work as Head Clerk has been exemplary.'

'I intend the fortunes of Shrike, Trewarren and Shrike to flourish,' William said coldly. 'I respectfully wish you a happy and peaceful retirement, undisturbed by worries about. . . .' he glossed smoothly over the word *money*, 'anything my brother may have done. You cannot handle the burden of work alone, sir. Forgive me for speaking to you so forthrightly, it is my personal respect for you, Mr Trewarren, that makes me do it.'

'Naturally, my boy.'

'I do not ask you to take me into partnership, I merely give you the opportunity to let me earn it.'

Trewarren felt all this was going much too fast. He knew he was being manipulated, but the sensation was flattering. He could not see how the situation could be to his disadvantage; the business was derelict anyway, and a young man could always be reined in – especially one without qualifications.

'I want to serve an apprenticeship,' William said meekly. 'I beg this of you. I could have no more knowledgeable master than you.'

'You certainly know how to present a persuasive case.'

William eyed the anteroom at the head of the stairs, the position of power, that would be his office.

'Yes!' Trewarren decided, trusting William, 'yes, by God. Put some life back in the old firm.' His poor, withered old face lit up. 'Come on, William, it's nearly three, let's take our dinner at the Cheshire Cheese.'

'I have a client already waiting for you,' William said.

'No, no, not now.'

'I think you will find him most interesting,' murmured William. 'His name is Signor Emilio Versucchi, an Italian merchant unfamiliar with English law, who requires clarification on some aspects of company liability. . . .' He scratched the side of his nose.

'Ah, I see,' sighed Trewarren, 'very well. You will sit there, and take notes.'

'Thank you, sir,' said William deferentially.

At the end of the day William walked across to the Surrey side of the river, finding his way to the Gumboge residence in a street of cheap, neat little houses in Southwark. He rapped on the door with the head of his stick. A small, dumpy woman answered his summons, and looked frightened as soon as she saw him.

'No good!' she said. 'We haven't got it.'

79

'I'm not the rent collector,' William said tersely, 'I've come to see Mr Gumboge.'

'I'll see if he's at home,' she said pathetically.

Impatiently, William followed her down the hall. In shirtsleeves, Lawson Gumboge was playing with his family at his kitchen table. They were all girls, and so many that there seemed to William, as he ducked under the washing, not to be one square inch left unoccupied. The baby was in a basket carried on the hip of the eldest, a strong-looking lass who stared at William defiantly.

The gigantic Gumboge had lost stones in weight. Diminished and defenceless, he pushed the girls for his wife to take away, and she retreated into a corner with them while he pulled on his coat like a man acquiring his dignity. It hung in loose folds from his anxious frame.

'Now then, what can I do for you, Master Prideau?'

William pulled up a chair and sat, his hands propped on his stick. 'You strike me as a man, Mr Gumboge, who – when it comes down to it – knows what's what.'

'I pride myself on it, sir.' Gumboge was plainly unsure, but his slanted yellowish eyes had lost none of their cunning, watery light. 'What do you have in mind, Mr Prideau, sir?'

'Your carelessness with the ledger signatures cost you dear, Mr Gumboge.'

'I've learned my lesson, sir,' Gumboge fawned, plainly loathing himself.

'I wish you to return as Head Clerk,' William said. 'I think I can persuade Mr Trewarren that your oversight was a temporary lapse.'

Gumboge swallowed. 'You can depend on me, sir.'

'You are a wise man, Mr Gumboge.' And a dangerous one. William wanted such a man working for him, not against him. Gumboge had never rated James Prideau, believing him too lazy to be bothered even to

80

steal. Perhaps Gumboge believed Honeyman was the thief; perhaps not.

Accompanying him to the door, Gumboge said, 'It occurs to me, Mr Prideau, that your brother's stupidity was the best thing that ever happened to you.'

'Yes; that is the greatest tragedy.' William doffed his hat to Mrs Gumboge and said goodbye until tomorrow.

'I'll be there,' Gumboge called from his doorway. 'You can count on me.'

Harriet put her arms round her husband, who watched William walk tightly down the street, not swinging his stick but rather chasing a steady questing angle like a blind man or diviner, until the twilight hid him.

'You've got your job back, husband,' whispered Harriet.

'He's got my loyalty,' Gumboge murmured. Then he said, 'He wants to be loved, and to show he cares, and be cared for.'

'You look after him, now.'

Gumboge turned back into his house, to his daughters, embracing them with a laugh. But he looked over his shoulder one last time.

'That man's heart is an empty place.'

81

9

Crossing the river

'Bunch your fists,' Simeon Giddings whispered, 'it makes your wrists thicker. Jim, are you listening, boy? Then the ropes won't feel so tight.'

Like the slave ships that still plied from Africa to the Americas, Bligh's fleet already trailed its human stench downwind. As the *Paragon*'s sails caught the wind and behind them the long grey line of England slipped like a coffin beneath the sea, finally dropping from sight, the irons had been humanely struck off the prisoners. Instead of sleeping on the bare boards, hammocks were strung like giant grey sausages, filling every available nook and crouching-space of the tween-decks, all slowly swinging in time to the roll of the ship, filled with men groaning in their seasick misery. And after the night, the dawn.

'Jim Pride, twelve lashes, for disturbance.'

The convicts assembling in the waist of the ship wore coarse grey shirts like wrapping, and canvas trousers. Their bare feet slapped softly on the deck planks as they were called to witness punishment in the wan dawn. A cockerel crowed: the stock animals the ship carried, sheep, hens, goats, a hutch of rabbits, half a dozen cows and the chained bull, Gorgon, stared out indifferently. The muscles stood out along Jim Pride's arms and down his back as the shirt was stripped from him.

'String him up!'

Staring down from the foc'sle at the figure wrenched forward below her, Annie wondered how she had ever thought him a gentleman. Beneath his matted hair, his face showed no expression as his arms were lashed to the upper corners of the triangle, above his head, his ankles bound tightly together to the lower corner. The eight-tailed cat, each leather tail whipped with thread, hung from the bo'sun's hand, whispering on the deck as the ship rolled.

'We'll start as we'll carry on, bo'sun,' called the first mate. 'I'll see his fingers white.'

As the bonds were heaved tighter, dragging back the tendons so that the whitened fingers splayed helplessly, Annie stared in fascination. Every man wanted to be an iron man, but she reckoned he'd crack by the fifth.

The bo'sun was a man of great experience, twisting half round on one foot to add flourish to the lash. The women were interested, never having seen a flogging before. The punishment for a woman was much worse, they thought. Her hair was shaved.

The heavy tails thudded, not slapped, into the man's back, making an echoing, resonant sound like a paving stone being dropped into place. But Becky Donahoo said, 'I'll lay odds on, he won't crack.'

'He's a sandstone,' Mary wagered, 'he'll crumble before seven, my rum says so.'

Becky said, 'Done.' They stared eagerly, their pretty curls falling down their backs, as the quartermaster kept count in a tolling voice. The sheep, chickens, rabbits were silent in their pens and hutches, but one cow seemed to low mournfully in time to the lashes like a groaning man. Catherine Sidmouth pretended to ignore one of the marines who winked at her. On the fifth stroke first blood showed across Jim Pride's back. By the ninth a fine spray of blood accompanied each flourish, and the deck showed a crescent of red beads.

Annie watched that unmoved face. He was totally unbroken.

'Twelve,' said the bo'sun after the domino, the last lash. 'Take him down and bucket him.'

As the icy salt water was rubbed into his back, Jim Pride showed no awareness of pain. The bo'sun swore he'd get double next time. And the ships ploughed on, *Lady Sinclair* leading to windward.

'It hurt bad?' Simeon Giddings said softly, below decks. 'I remember you as you was, boy. I prefer that.'

Jim looked at him indifferently, and not for the first time Giddings wondered if this man, who as a lad had set off for London with such high hopes, recalled him. He watched Jim shrug on his rough canvas shirt over the tangled flesh of his back. Giddings, one-time proprietor of the Cabriolet Service, understood men who were indifferent to the fate of others, but a man who could be indifferent to himself chilled him to the marrow.

'It hurt,' Jim Pride said.

'The streets of London are paved with gold,' said Giddings, trying to get in close, 'and so are the gutters, eh, boy?'

Jim looked at him with eyes like holes in his head.

'We've all got secrets,' Giddings whined. The timbers creaked and he put his mouth close to Jim's ear in the semi-darkness. 'I am your friend.'

'I'll never trust a man who calls himself my friend.'

Simeon Giddings scratched his head, laughing, appalled.

Jim Pride said: 'What do you want?'

'Well now, there's one or two things I'd rather were kept secret.'

'That's why you hit me so hard,' Jim said. 'You didn't mind if you broke my head.'

'Oh sir, it wasn't quite that way at all!' protested Giddings winningly. 'One little belaying pin to save you from the bottom of the sea? Best headache you ever had. I'm a kind man.'

Jim Pride said bleakly, 'I want the bottom of the sea.'

Giddings stopped, then nodded. 'I'll put it man to man. I was caught in Somerset for a lesser crime, so I told the constable a false name or I would have got my neck stretched for a greater. So Simeon Simmonds I am,' he said anxiously. 'You're the only one who knows.'

'What else, Simmonds?'

'And they don't know about this.' Simeon tapped his leg, which made a wooden sound beneath his trousers. 'They think I'm able-bodied, or I'd have been kept in clink in England polishing the king's iron with my eyebrows, and I'd die there never seeing the sun. Die there, sir. I'd rather take my chances.'

'Your secrets are safe with me,' said Jim Pride indifferently, going.

'Just like that? Want some baccy? Or rum. I'm in with the cook, I can get you extra food. You must want something. . . .' he called along the gallery, but the other man did not turn or look back.

Simeon Simmonds sat down in confusion. Jim Pride worried him: it seemed impossible to get a hold over him. The man had a dead heart. Then Simeon snapped his fingers. The Surgeon Superintendent, a drinking companion of the cook, was looking for a reliable man as an assistant. . . .

Then Simeon thought of his own boy, hundreds of miles away. Who would look after him? And what of his daughter? He covered his ears with his hands, and the ships rolled on.

For weeks there was no sign of the black-painted masts of the French, but more deadly enemies began to arrive. Already the water was green, the salt pork adipose with decay. The first case of typhus, called spotted fever, had shown up on schedule, a fortnight after leaving port, with the warmer weather off Tenerife. In the custom of transports the women took up with the marines and crew, hoping for favours, a better life. One or two, like Catherine Sidmouth, would only tilt her hips at an officer. Becky Donahoo, by her cunning choice of watches, kept two marines and a bashful little midshipman juggled on the trot, each bringing her extra rations. She slipped them to the winking O'Henry who sold them amongst the male convicts, and it was for the bull-hung Irishman she reserved her truly lustful embraces. Annie's marine bothered her at every opportunity, treating her with contempt because she was mad, passive beneath his kiss and his cruel squeezing of her breasts under her yellow dress of shame. Because she didn't care what he did, he despised her. Mobley was a man of very considerable strength and far more intelligence than he could express, which made him dangerous company. Annie was the lowest of the low, with only the sick and dying below her, so he treated her rough and told her she liked it, and she believed him.

He surprised her, catching her alone and sending her thumping wearily against the bulkhead, her hands dangling. But as her face caught a harsh angle of sunlight, he let out an oath. Annie's grimy skin was peppered with dull red spots. He backed away from her as though to distance himself from the contagion. Holding his breath, he dashed up the steps almost weeping with fear.

By the time the surgeon was roused from his stupor, Annie's spots were bleeding pin-points, more were flowering on her body and legs, and she was running a fever. Keeping his hands safe in his frock-coat, the surgeon turned to his assistant. 'She'll have to be carried down. Find someone.'

'I'll do it.'

Jim Pride did work no other man would do. The gangways emptied of people ahead of him as he carried his limp burden down to the hospital, in the lowest part of the ship, a room kept as airless as possible to contain the infection. The heat was stifling and bilge-water sloshed beneath the boards. He laid her in a cot and waited for the surgeon to return, staring at her by the light of an oil lamp. Then, as she groaned in her feverish lassitude, he found a cloth and wiped the dirt from her face. He stared at her pale features for a long time. Her name was Miss Ann Day.

The lieutenant surgeon bled her, prescribed ammonium acetate and camphor to be taken every four hours, and left as hastily as possible.

'Drink this,' Jim Pride said, holding a glass of wine to her lips. Her eyes flickered open and he helped her take a second sip, then put his hand comfortingly on her forehead as she lay back exhausted.

Within the week the hospital was full, the sick sprawling in the gangways. In such heat as now oppressed the vessel the suffering was terrible to see. But the weeks Annie spent in the sick bay on the point of death, she hardly remembered except for their fear and misery. And she was transformed by her experience of desperate illness, of almost dying, into a different woman.

Annie had recovered from more than typhus. In the sick bay she had come to terms with her baby's loss. There was life on the other side: under the tropical sun she found her old cheerful, sociable self, her grief buried in a secret compartment. Marked by infection, she was isolated by the other women as though still a source of it. To be sent to Coventry was the worst punishment she could imagine. Worse, it meant she had no man to protect her or obtain better rations, and soon her situation became the worst of all the women. Even Mobley shunned her as though she had the clap.

The fleet ploughed on, crossing the line into the southern hemisphere with the pitch bubbling in the deck seams. The captains of the vessels communicated by flags, hailing, or longboat. They were afraid that the Cape of Africa might not be in British possession, afraid of running out of water and wood for the fire, afraid of the scurvy that now swept through prisoners and crew loosening teeth from gums, and afraid of mutiny. On another level, the captains resented William Bligh's overbearing manner. With less than two weeks' water remaining, the captains of the *Paragon* and *Alexander* gained permission to abandon their efforts to reach the Cape and change course downwind for Rio. The first the *Paragon*'s convicts knew of this was by the changing position of the sun and the sudden loneliness of their ship on the vast ocean, with only the tiny *Alexander* for company. But as soon as land was sighted, those convicts not already fettered were placed in irons and kept below deck, seeing nothing of Rio harbour, and were pleased when the ships sailed again.

Whatever their Botany Bay destination was like, it could not be worse than the ship. The rumours said life in New South Wales was good and many of the convicts, especially those accompanied by their wives, considered themselves lucky to go. As the ships wallowed in the steady westerlies across the south Atlantic towards Cape Town, disease broke out again. Desperate for company, Annie was driven to return to the sick bay, where alone she would find people to talk to her. It was a ghastly place. Jim Pride sat slumped in a corner, his knees drawn up, asleep. She looked at him tenderly, thinking he was exhausted by his duties, then saw the empty pannikin clamped possessively in his hands against his chest, and the spittle hanging from his lips. When she knelt and lifted his eyelid, the eyeball stared whitely at her, totally blank. He was blind drunk, and on impure Rio rum too.

She moved between the cots, then someone asked her for something, another pleaded for water, so she rolled up her sleeves and started to help since no one else but her and Pride had the guts. Many of these patients, nourished by Argentine beef broth and denied the fiery Rio *aguardiente*, would recover. But she quickly learned that Jim was useless. He woke and drank his hangover down, then vacantly attempted to help, wandering among the cots until a roll of the ship tumbled him over, and there he lay. He was drinking himself to death. Sighing, Annie bent over him. His pallid skin was filthy.

'Haven't you got no friends?' she said contemptuously.

He vomited on her foot and she gave him a good hard kick. 'I hope it hurts,' she said, then relented. 'Let's get you washed,' she said, and pulled his nose.

He did have a friend. 'Welcome, m'dear,' boomed a voice. Simeon Simmonds came thumping down from the gallery most days, a welcome sight in his baggy trousers and painted straw hat, bringing with him some small delicacy for Jim, a piece of duff wrapped in his handkerchief, or cook's precious slush of melted salt pork fat. In the stern-seas the ship had acquired a heavy, twisting roll, and Annie screamed when a brass-bound chest broke free, skidding across the deck and crushing Simeon's lower leg against the door combing. He showed no sign of pain but cursed, giving a great pull, and his leg came off. 'Now the three of us know,' he said, eyeing her, then took two hops towards her like a vast shaggy bird, holding his splintered wooden shin in one hand.

'Don't you touch me,' she warned.

'Leave her alone,' Jim croaked from the deck.

'Thought you wasn't with us,' Simeon said genially, taking one more hop. 'I thought you was three sheets to the wind.'

'Leave her alone, Simeon.'

'You aren't in a position to insist, my shaking boy,'

Simeon remarked. Annie laughed from nerves because the leg still had his shoe stuck on it. 'You're frightened, aren't you?' she said. 'You live in fear.'

He stared at her.

'All right,' Simeon admitted grudgingly, 'the three of us.'

'How will you repair your leg?' Annie said.

'I'm friends with the carpenter, so I can get hold of another length of wood.'

But Simeon, Annie soon learned, had no friends, only Jim Pride – and that friendship was not returned. But Simeon did have a very wide circle of acquaintances, and from Mr Murdoon the Second Officer down to the poorest waisters there was no one aboard ship he did not know how to use. It was he who had obtained the rum Jim craved, and his position as cook's assistant gave him considerable influence bartering scrapings for tobacco, spirits, favours. Only the captain strolling the weather side of the quarterdeck was safe from him – though even the leftovers from his table found their way through Simeon Simmonds's hands sooner or later. He did it not for personal advantage but, he said, for fun. He was frightened of not living as he had always lived, of losing himself.

The ships rolled and twisted in the mighty ocean. Africa was a dusty speck of land: the Cape was in British possession but it was dangerous to anchor in Table Bay so they joined the rest of the fleet in False Bay to the east, already preparing to depart having arrived early in June. As suddenly as he had started, Jim ceased drinking. He ignored Annie, helping her listlessly in the sick bay, or standing passively by the hammock nettings in the waist staring out, nothing in the way he stood giving her the slightest clue to the thoughts inside his head.

The anchor-capstans clanked, the patched sails unfurled to catch the Roaring Forties of the southern ocean, and within an hour the speck of Africa was gone. Soon the sick bay began to fill up again as the fresh food ran out. Jim was indifferent to her help but Annie made herself grit her teeth, sometimes staring at his back while he worked among the dying, or covertly observing him in Mr Murdoon's group on deck, wondering how to unlock him.

Second Officer Orin Murdoon was young and intelligent, of a pleasantly sunny disposition, but careless, which made him variable, and so he was widely unpopular with the sailors under his command who liked a tough, consistent officer who told them where they stood. When his brow was knotted with some problem of trigonometry, working out the ship's position, he was a tiger to approach. At other times he was too friendly, unwilling to treat men with the brutality that earned their respect. He held mathematics classes even amongst the convicts, who could hardly count; and at night, on the heaving deck among marching seas like mountains of black glass, he taught the stars. It was the end of June, which he called midwinter.

'But June's midsummer,' said Simeon comfortably, chewing his quid of baccy.

'Everything's opposite in the southern hemisphere. I've been down here before and it's the most magnificent sky in the world.' Murdoon pointed wildly in the blazing dark. 'That arch like a glittering serpent – the Milky Way. Those Magellanic clouds on the horizon to the south really are clouds – vast clouds of stars. . . .'

Simeon spat a stream of juice in disgust at such enthusiasm.

'D'you see the Southern Cross there, Jim?' Murdoon pointed, turning up his eager face.

'I see it,' Jim murmured. A huge slow wave gently lifted the ship as though the mastheads might scratch the sky.

91

'No, that's the False Cross, but it's an easy mistake to make. Look in the Milky Way. . . . just to the right of the dark patch.'

'One thing I know that sharp idiot don't know,' Simeon said when the lieutenant had gone, 'is that the warnings of clouds don't change. You see those ones like feathers? See the halo round Venus? Going to storm.'

But the ship pressed on through the dark. In these latitudes the winds and the seas encircled the world from Cape Horn to Van Diemen's Land, with nothing to stop them.

10

A swim in the forest

At first the wind was from the north, carrying a strange dust that coated the sails like rust, as though a vast red desert sailed along with them below the northern horizon. The criminal continent of New South Wales was a gritty taste in their mouths, and their eyes watered from its sting. But they never saw it, and never would. There were thousands of miles yet to go to Botany Bay, and they stared silently at the glowing horizon, an island folk contemplating the scale of such a mighty land.

Then the wind backed and blew clean, growing in power so that the topsails were brought down, and the ships sailed among seas like vast mounds of jewels, opal and shimmering sapphire, and by afternoon the sky was a featureless pale glare. The gale began to moan in the rigging and when Jim came up after dark it was raining torrents and spare sails had been strung up to catch the fresh water. He could taste the salt on his lips and knew the tops were breaking off the waves and blowing in the wind. The girl in the yellow dress was sitting on the foc'sle, her long dark hair bannering like part of the night. He went below. Months in the hot sun of the Antipodean winter, still 1806, had sprung the decks and the deckheads poured glittering streams in the dim reflection of the horn lamps. He lay in a corner of the sick bay listening to the water thumping in the bilges below. When he woke spurts of it were splashing up between the gratings with the gyration of the ship, and the deckheads poured salt water. The

Paragon groaned and creaked from the pummelling she was taking. The hatches had been battened down, and dawn did not come that day.

In stinking seasick darkness, lying in terrified rows, they listened to the seas roaring across the deck above them. The ship pitched slowly, picked up by giant waves then slowly tilted, accelerating. The fall was as slow, ending in a shuddering crash in the trough of the waves, and they could hear the storm-canvas flapping limply, cut off from the gale that roared overhead by the mountainous, watery slopes lifting all around them. And then the ship rose again. In the sick bay Annie Day turned, her blue eyes enormous with fear.

'Are we going to die?'

'Yes, of course, one day,' Jim told her.

'I had a daughter.' She wept. 'A lovely little girl.' She stared at him, but she couldn't get past his expressionless gaze. 'Hold me, don't mock me,' she shivered, 'I don't want to die.' Something crashed above and the motion of the ship changed, becoming jerky and unrestrained, and someone screamed, not a woman. 'We've lost a mast,' Jim said calmly, disengaging himself. 'I must report to the surgeon.'

Left alone, she stared at the bilgewater pouring to and fro across the drowned gratings, the wildly swinging lantern, the sick men and women gagging and clutching at her for succour. She knocked their hands aside and ran after Jim along the tilting gangway, skidding to her knees, seeing him stop to pick up one of the ship's cats from the water and drape the poor limp creature considerately over the back of a bolted-down chair. She watched him climb the ladder, then followed him.

Jim was astonished to see that it was night still, or again, the deck a dimly-seen chaos of spars and rigging interspersed with floods of spume. A canvas dodger had been strung behind the helmsmen who battled with the wheel so that they should not witness the tallowy seas curling up behind them. With each breaking wave the ship surfed forward in a brief glow of illumination from the white cascades of foam surrounding her. Orin Murdoon recognised him and pressed his mouth close, shouting over the roar of the storm, 'Couldn't shoot the sun today – dead reckoning puts us a hundred miles either way. The fleet's scattered. We must be close to the entrance to the Bass Strait, between the mainland and Van Diemen's Land; it'll funnel the storm as it's some of the roughest water in the world. . . .'

Gaps showed briefly in the flying storm-cloud, the stars winking out almost as soon as they appeared. They saw the first officer shouting to the captain on the quarterdeck: the Southern Cross.

'It's too early,' Murdoon muttered, but they ignored him. 'That was the False Cross – the Southern Cross hasn't risen yet! We're fifty miles further south than they think.'

Jim shrugged. 'It's a big ocean.'

But Murdoon set off across the waist of the ship to warn them, the yeasty floods of spray knocking him over, tangling him in broken rigging. Annie saw Jim make no attempt to help the struggling officer, but Murdoon got free by himself and clawed his way onto the quarterdeck where he reported to the captain, the two of them hanging together in their sodden blue uniforms, but the captain merely shook his head, he was in control. A sailor was washed overboard, gone without a scream. Spars fell with great clouting bangs onto the deck, followed by looping coils of rope. The body of the seaman was washed back aboard from the sea, left hanging in the ratlines like a ghastly omen, then again disappeared. The captain looked calm. Murdoon talked to him urgently again, and again he shook his head.

95

Someone shouted: 'Breakers ahead!' Annie looked but saw nothing, and still the captain was shaking his head. Murdoon threw down his hat and came forward. 'He says it's Cape Otway on the mainland,' he shouted. 'We're changing course two points southward to clear the headland and obtain some sea-room.' He frowned as among the cordage on deck something like the tentacle of a gigantic sea-squid appeared, washed in by the sea, wriggling and flopping, and one of the seamen crossed himself superstitiously. 'It's only bull kelp,' Murdoon said.

'What does it mean?'

'Shallow water.' A seaman was told off to take a sounding from the bows, but even as he swung the lead, again they saw breakers ahead. The sea rose up in pinnacles around them, kicked up by the sea bed close below. The helmsmen spun the wheel hard to starboard but the breakers seemed endless, a white swathe of broken water with humps of low land to their left. Further off they saw a dimmer line of breakers stretch across the horizon. 'It's impossible,' murmured Murdoon, as calm as though he were working on a problem of triangulation. 'It can't be. It's neither Otway nor Van Diemen's Land.'

Annie ran forward. 'You've got to let everyone up on deck!'

'There'd be mutiny.'

'All the women and children! And the prisoners under guard must have their fetters struck off. . . .'

Murdoon shuddered. 'Better a quick death. Wherever we are, we must be a thousand sea-miles from Botany Bay, and this coast is infested with aboriginal tribes. . . .' He looked away from her. 'Much better a quick death, madam.'

Nevertheless, he jumped down into the waist and gave the order, then tripped among the strands of kelp flopping across the deck, each as thick as a man's leg at the roots, torn away by the storm. The ship struck before any of them had expected it, at first as gently as a caress so that they thought they were saved, then with an interminable grinding as they were flung off their feet, the ropes they clung to burning through their hands, the wooden railings and decks battering at them. Suddenly the decks seemed full of people pouring up from below in the last extremities of terror, and a musket went off as though the marine captain feared the mutiny had started. The ship lifted and crashed and they heard the awful sound of the ladders breaking down below, trapping the survivors on each deck. The seas washing over the ship were solid with kelp fronds, and men skidded comically in their slithery embrace. The mainmast toppled, crushing a screaming tangle beneath its yards, then swept them over the side. Jim stood with his hands calmly laid on the foc's'le railing, watching.

The howling had begun. The captain was still on the quarterdeck saying he was in command, and the sea started pouring in below among the trapped people. Their piteous screaming echoed through the gratings. With the ladders gone survivors stood on one another's shoulders to get out, then reached back to help, but only as the ship was distorted did many at last force their way out through the splintering timbers, pale shadows to be swept away or to fall onto the streaming razorbacked rocks on which the vessel was impaled. Still Jim watched, like a man looking down into a bucket of rats, struggling and fighting for life as the water rose. Many gave up hope and let themselves go down. Others fought for their last breath, drowning in the morass of kelp. The darkness was full of shouting and confusion.

Jim turned and saw her still there, her eyes fixed on him. 'What are you waiting for?'

'You,' Annie said, stripping off her yellow dress of shame.

'You're wasting your time,' he said sadly.

'No, I'm not, she said fiercely, gripping his hand. 'I want to live,' she groaned, her red petticoats fluttering ridiculously, 'and I can't swim. Can you?'

He seemed to remember. 'Yes, I can,' he said. 'I used to swim from Lynmouth beach. There was kelp there. Not so big as this.'

'It's not worth dying before you have to, is it?' she urged him. With a scream of halliards through the blocks a spar dropped from the mizzen and fell across the captain and Murdoon arguing on the quarterdeck. Neither figure moved again, crushed beneath the heavy baulk of elm. 'Jim,' said Annie insistently.

'You're very beautiful, Ann,' he said in a voice quite without desire.

'Then let's swim for it,' she begged, and he let her tug him across to the other side, where the sea foamed clear of kelp. 'I trust you,' she said, and jumped.

He looked over the side where she had disappeared. She didn't come up.

Then he plunged after her, coming up beside her dark form drowning in the foam, and a wave lifted them clear together. She clung to him, wrapping her arms and legs around his warm frame in the cold water. 'Swim,' she hissed, and he swam obediently, letting the buoyant seawater do the work.

The current sweeping them towards the mainland was strong. He realised that the ship had grounded on the reefy tail of a tiny offshore island. They drifted in the silence, hearing only the occasional crash from the shipwreck, the dark waves of the channel jostling them like friendly dogs.

Below them, the forest of kelp reaching up from the sea floor touched their feet, then twined their legs with its slimy embrace, and Annie screamed. They were

close enough to the shore to see the clotted surf breaking ahead of them, and suddenly the water round them
was slimy with fronds, and drowned bodies. A wave
curled up behind them, submerging them in slithering
vegetation that washed them forward almost to the
sandy beach, then sucked them back. The second wave
dropped them ashore but the retreating water almost
dragged them out again. The beach was swept by
waves: they climbed the cliff to a ledge. Jim slipped,
clinging on by his fingers to the rock, the pale surf
surging below him. He stared up calmly, slipping down
from her inch by inch.

Annie, kneeling at the brink, held out her hand to
him. Would he take it? Her gaze was steady. She forced
him to choose rather than meekly acquiesce in his life
or death. If he was to live it would only be by exerting
every effort. Their fingertips quivered two inches apart,
then his hand clamped over hers, and for a moment
she saw the most terrifying expression cross his face.
In the glow of dawn, she saw for the first time coloured
light in his eyes, the love and betrayal there.

'Jim,' she whined, 'you're hurting me. . . .'

'I don't love you, Annie,' he said.

He almost dragged her over the edge as he pulled
himself up. Annie wept, not letting him see. Shaking
off cold and exhaustion, carrying her, he fought his
way to the clifftop. He stood with her beside him, and
they turned to face the sea. Annie had saved him, *but
he would always love Eve.*

The sun rose behind them. It was the first morning.

11

The unpromised land

Jim and Annie stood on the yellow rocks. Whatever the name of the great bay that stretched out to one side of them was, it wasn't Botany Bay. The smooth curve of sand was mounded with kelp and human debris. Inland, they saw no sign of settlement among the grassy hummocks of the dunes rising into the level dawn sunlight like great, green breasts. No threads of welcoming hearth-smoke rose from the thick woods of oak or elm that cloaked the flat hinterland behind them to the glaring, undulating horizon of treetops.

They were alone.

She clung to him atop a low granite cliff stained with orange and yellow lichen, the jumbled spines and pillows of rock below them softened by the sea into strange comfortable shapes exactly like sofas and elbow-chairs, a chaotic furniture depository carved from solid stone by giants. Neither of them were tempted to sit: they stared along the fans of sunlight streaming past them at a scene of terrible desolation.

There could be no sight sadder or more pathetic than a shipwreck. The chilly wind blowing in their faces from the wrinkled blue ocean was veering from the southwest back to west. There were two islets a mile or so offshore, both low scrub, with sandy beaches. The *Paragon* lay on the rocks that trailed into the channel from the southern islet. Broadside on, white fountains lifted over her and they realised that the waves were still pounding her without mercy: listening hard, they heard the hollow booming of the sea into her, and by narrowing their eyes discerned the shattered woodwork and twisted decks, the bodies rolling in the scuppers.

They saw survivors who had struggled ashore across the rocks onto the islet lying outstretched. Only one man, who had deserted the wreck later than the others, was standing up, even at this distance unmistakable in his white shirt with his beard and enormous belly: it was Simeon, standing on his wooden leg, balanced on a splintered length of spar, his other leg tucked up fastidiously.

Annie pointed. 'What's that?' At the north end of the islet Gorgon the bull, still trailing the chain from the ring in his nose, trotted angrily through the bush tossing his horns this way and that, apparently aimlessly, then charged from view.

'I want that bull,' Jim said with a flat determination Annie had not heard before. 'The survivors out there will claim it, but I don't reckon they've got any fresh water. . . .'

Closer to the mainland shore, the sea was a beautiful green, with sandy shallows of brilliant turquoise. 'I don't think that no human footprint has ever been here, ever before,' Annie said suddenly, and Jim looked at her closely for the first time. 'It's like heaven,' she said, relishing his attention.

'Or hell,' he said, walking to the very edge, then turned. 'Why are you following me?'

'Someone's got to look after you.'

He said swiftly and brutally, 'I don't need you.'

She was crushed. 'Suit yourself!' she said, and flounced away like a lady until she realised she was wearing only her scarlet petticoat. She glanced back, but he wasn't looking at her. She picked up a rock, sulking, and threw it at another rock. Instead of the clattering sound she expected there was a deep hollow thud. The large black rock she had aimed at rippled, then

101

quivered, then rose up seven feet above her and gaped a tusked mouth.

'Why aren't the survivors on the islet moving about?' Jim muttered.

'Jim. . . .' Annie, backing away, found her voice.

'There's only Simeon and he's just standing there.'

'*Jim!*' Annie backed into him, clutching him. They stared at the strange creature, which emitted a high bellowing roar from beneath its long blubbery nose. It seemed shocked about being rudely woken rather than aggressive. 'It's an elephant,' Annie said in wonderment. They watched it heave itself slowly away from them, still complaining loudly. Then it turned and galumphed down to the sea, and the great ungainly mass dived in, becoming suddenly graceful, porpoised once, and was gone. 'No, an elephant of the sea,' Jim said. Now they knew how to look they saw other shadows slipping through the clear water, the sea elephants returning after the storm. Smaller shapes darted among them: seals, seals racing by the thousand, clouds of seals shimmering through the shallow seas.

The small, sharply curving bay they overlooked held only tiny deserted beaches between spines of yellow rock. Oystercatchers swooped and poked their beaks earnestly for tidbits in the tons of kelp thrown up. But the large sandy bay arcing away to their right, swarming with seals, a sea-eagle soaring above the dunes, showed a few survivors now staggering to their feet, turning their faces to the sun. Amid the heaps of flotsam and kelp many more lay with their heads in the surf, moving only when the waves moved them.

Jim climbed down to the little bay and Annie, staying where she was, watched him splash out to a body in a dark brown frock-coat rolling in the slime, and drag it ashore. He had chosen well: it was the purser and Jim helped himself to the fine cotton shirt before tying on the black silk neckerchief and shrugging the waisted

102

coat onto his lean figure. The felt hat jammed on the purser's head had lost its shape but Jim punched it out and slapped it rakishly on his own head. He turned with his hands on his hips and grinned up at her with his mocking blue eyes bright beneath the brim: Annie with the sky glowing through her petticoats. She crossed her elbows over her breasts.

'Can't you find something for me?' she wailed. 'I don't want to wear dead people's clothes though.'

'Only dead people here,' he called levelly, pushing the purser's brace of pistols through his belt. He found the body of one of the soldier's wives, holding a baby's clothes in her hand with no baby in them, and stripped off her dress and shoes. When he climbed back to Annie he found her staring out to sea.

'Wasn't the ship sideways on earlier?' she asked.

'Yes, it was.' But now the bow was pointing at them, and they saw Simeon hop clumsily across the rocks and hang onto a rope as the ship swung free, propelled by the veering wind from the reef which had held her. He pulled himself up arm over arm and disappeared over the taffrail. Low in the water, the *Paragon* rolled horribly, and in mid-channel the seas started washing over her waist-deck as she filled, yet that stabilising weight made her roll less. It seemed the current would take her ashore somewhere on the broad length of Seal Bay, a distance she could not last. 'Come on, ship,' Annie urged her, but Jim watched silently. Then he said: 'Come on, you old bitch.' They stood together shouting, 'Come on you old bitch, come on!'

The wind kept veering, pushing her towards them. Simeon stood at the helm, now proudly spinning the wheel, as thoroughly in command of her as was the captain whose crushed blue-jacketed body sprawled beneath the spar. He heard Jim and Annie's cries and waved, then knelt beside the second trapped officer. The ship rotated in the tide, lifting and falling in the waves gathering towards the shore. 'I think Murdoon's alive,' Jim said, tapping his pistols. 'I won't let him take me to Botany Bay.'

The *Paragon* grated over a shoal of rocks offshore, rolled as if she would turn turtle, then drifted silently on her shadow over the brilliant sandy shallows.

'Put your dress on,' said Jim.

'Oh, a lot you care!' Annie said. He paid her no further attention and she pulled the dead woman's dress on with a scowl of distaste, then hopped after him pulling on the shoes.

The *Paragon* was finished. She had settled in the shallows fifty yards from the tiny beach, her bowsprit overhanging one of the yellow spines of rock. The wind blew her dank stink over them, and they could hear the miserable lowing of the cows trapped in their pens. A cockerel crowed from the broken stump of the main-mast. They scrambled out along the rocks and Jim swung himself up through the chains, made his way aft along the sloping deck past the smashed boats. Simeon hobbled to meet him. Close to, Jim hardly recognised his friend. Simeon's hair was white, and so was his beard. His eyes seemed to have aged ten years in the one night.

'Jim, thank God,' Simeon said, embracing him. 'I thought I was dead.' Jim could feel this tough man still trembling.

'Sit down,' he said calmly, and now that he had permission Simeon almost fell. 'Tell me what happened.'

Simeon drew a breath. 'See, about fifty of us got across the rocks onto the island.' He shivered at the memory. 'Fifty, sixty of us maybe. We were in good shape. Couldn't see for the dark, but we got gathered on the beach. Further back there was grass and some people lay down and started. . . . excuse me, ma'am.'

'That's all right,' Annie said.

'Started,' Simeon winked at Jim, 'what people start doing when they're glad to be alive. Jim knows what I mean.'

'No, he doesn't know,' Annie said. '*We* didn't.'

Jim ignored her.

Simeon said, 'So the first time someone screamed out, we didn't pay no mind, you understand. Then they all started hollering and people were blundering, panicking, in the dark, you could hear them running and falling down, them sandhills are mighty steep. No trees, nothing, just the sandhills and low thorny bushes. I had a stick to lean on but I couldn't run, and soon it was quiet, deadly quiet. And then I heard slithering all around me. I stood there on my best leg. . . . through the stump I could feel things going past brushing against the wood. I thought it was the sea monster but at first light I saw the ground moving around me. The place is alive with snakes. I saw one girl nipped by something not much longer than her hand. . . .'

'Only you survived?' Jim slapped his hands on his knees. 'Then the bull's ours!'

'You're in a charming mood this morning,' Annie said.

'I ain't going back there!' said Simeon, trembling.

'You don't have to,' Jim told him.

'Gorgon's safe enough where he is,' Annie pointed out. 'He's lasted one night, and he looked lively enough to me. After all, he's got a thick furry coat, and he's wearing leather beneath it, ain't he?'

'Can't take the risk of losing him, this ship's never going to sail again,' Jim said. 'All we've got is what we've got. The cows are useless without the bull.' He slid across the deck and with a belaying pin started knocking the hasps off the pens that imprisoned the animals. They broke free with rolling eyes into the sunlight, scrambling, then the leader saw the grass growing on the dunes, and took the plunge into the turquoise interval of water. Meanwhile Annie had gone aft on the quarterdeck, then they heard her anxious call.

'Jim – quick, it's Mr Murdoon.'

Jim merely stood looking down at the unconscious officer, making no effort to help her lift the spar from his chest; the captain's body had shielded him from the worst impact but dark threads of blood dribbled from Murdoon's lips and ears.

'I won't go to Botany Bay,' Jim repeated.

'His chest is crushed,' Annie whispered, 'he's no threat to you.'

'He's an officer.'

'Jim's right,' Simeon warned her in a low voice. 'The only good officer's a dead one. Look away, lass.'

'You'll have to knock me on the head first!' Annie threatened.

Simeon looked at Jim.

'Leave her.' Jim shrugged. 'We've got more important things to do.'

Annie sat weakly on the wet planks. She was shaking and she didn't dare ask the men to help her lift the spar. She cast round for a lever to help her. 'We can't live aboard the ship,' Jim was telling Simeon, 'as she'll break up with the next storm. Throw everything in barrels over the side and drift it in; we'll drag it above the tidemark later. Rig a line to the rocks to swing across the implements we'll need, like axes, muskets, hammers. . . .'

'You reckon we're going to be here a while?' Simeon asked him.

'We're going to be here forever.'

Jim picked up a batten and went to Annie, inserted the end under the spar and lifted, holding nothing back: the tendons stood out in his neck, the muscles in his face like cords.

'Then, my friend, you just remember we're free men,' said Simeon, dragging out Orin Murdoon by the legs.

'Yes,' Jim said. But Annie saw his eyes, prisoner's eyes. Jim would never be free. He would make this his place, but his heart was somewhere else. She stared after him as he leapt away, down on the rocks, and cursed herself. Then Murdoon groaned, and she tended him irritably.

Jim crossed the tiny crescent of beach and climbed the grassy slope skirting the low cliff. From this vantage point the whole of the great sandy curve to the north was spread out below him. The dark form of the swamped cutter was almost lost among the kelp rapidly blackening in the sun. He ran down and pushed through the people wandering aimlessly around, shaken and disorganised. Some of them he recognised, George Tatham, Amos Preston, old Bob, some not. Women had survived the cold water better than the men. Catherine Sidmouth clung onto him sadly, drunk on rum – barrels of cargo were bumping in the wavelets, probably the captain had hoped to turn a tidy profit at Botany Bay. A barrel of flour had already been opened by mistake and thrown down, wasted. Becky Donahoo was hanging on O'Henry's arm, both of them tattered and bruised, but Becky wore a smile like a cat that had been at the cream. 'It's an outrageous happening,' O'Henry complained, helping himself to the bellamine of rum nestled in the crook of his other arm. 'They sent us to Botany Bay and it was their responsibility to get us there, surely.'

'Mind out for the snakes,' Jim said.

'But isn't that right, Jim?' They followed him in a group. He found the beached cutter no longer full, the water having escaped through the strakes stove-in along the keel. He pulled the sail from the locker and rolled the boat over, tying the canvas over the exposed hull from the stern cleats to the bow. 'All I know,' he told them, 'is that ships are lost in these waters and never found. If we're somewhere on the southern coast of the mainland, it's uncolonised, and if this is the west coast of Van Diemen's Land, it's unexplored.' Jim surveyed his handiwork; most of the hull below the waterline was covered with canvas. He was counting on water pressure to seal it tight over the holes. It looked rickety and very dangerous.

'You're not thinking of going any place in that little coracle, now?' O'Henry flexed his enormous muscles, but he had little inclination to use them except for show.

'You can row if you like.'

'Oh, I don't like to take orders any more, my boy.'

'We've got to have that bull, Feargal, or everything else is a waste of time.'

'I'll stay and look after the women,' O'Henry said. 'I'll do the work I know best.' Becky Donahoo laughed and hugged him. Mary Roper stood in the background watching them tottering together like a chaste madonna, but Jim did not mistake the sly passion in those wide eyes. They would soon all be drunk as Catherine Sidmouth. 'I'm going out to fetch that bull,' Jim said patiently, 'and I need a petticoat to do it.'

O'Henry roared with laughter and the women followed his example. Jim did not laugh. 'You won't tie up the great Gorgon with a petticoat,' O'Henry chuckled.

'You can have mine,' Catherine taunted, turning like an actress and daring Jim, then squealed when he bent down, grasped the hem, and pulled the red flannel garment from under her dress with a rotten ripping sound. 'Start thinking about surviving,' he told them angrily, facing the group, bunching up the material in his fists and tossing it into the boat. 'Start thinking.'

He pushed the boat through the wavelets and jumped aboard. 'Did the man say, start *drinking*?'

O'Henry's genial call followed him. Jim tugged at the oars, keeping the little craft in the calm leeward waters of the islet. In mid-channel he stopped to bail out, then beached the cutter on the clean sand. It was silent as a graveyard.

He called, but there was no reply.

The sandhills were pocked with snake-burrows but only big birds moved, feasting in the hot sun. He climbed carefully up the scrabbled sand. The birds rose into the air. A man lay locked in death in fornication with his back to the sun, the woman staring up with her pecked eyesockets at the blazing orb, like a portrait of sin.

From this new angle Jim surveyed the channel that separated him from the mainland. Seal Bay ran north to a distant headland, he saw nothing more of the coast beyond. To the south, on such a brilliant day, he saw at least fifteen miles of coastline revealed, jagged headlands running out from tall grassy dunes, dense bush starting a mile or so inland. He stiffened, narrowing his eyes. From here, almost directly in line with the wreck of the *Paragon*, he saw a stand of taller trees like cypresses towering above the alien skyline of the bush, probably several miles in from the coast. He took a bearing, since he would not be able to see them from the bay shore.

Then he looked again at the couple in the sand. The sun beat down out of the northern sky. He had lost everything that meant anything to him and gained a strange, empty kingdom.

He heard a bellow and turned. Gorgon, his horns smeared with slime, his eyes bloodshot with rage, trotted into view. The ring through his nose flashed as he advanced, the broken chain dangling between his legs. Jim retreated, sliding down the sandhill between the mouths of the burrows, and Gorgon charged. Jim hared

109

along the beach towards the boat with Gorgon gaining on him, then dashed into the sea. Gorgon stopped.

'Won't you taste the water, my good sir?' Jim called.

Gorgon hated the sea. Jim waved his hat, taunting him.

The bull paced up and down the sand, afraid of getting his feet wet. Jim splashed along to the boat and clambered in, rowed a few yards offshore and shipped the oars. Gorgon stormed along the margin of the sea, but still he wouldn't take the plunge. Jim held up the red petticoat, and Gorgon stopped, then pawed the wavelets. Jim mocked him, flapping the material provocatively over the side. Gorgon lowered his head and charged, out of his depth before he knew it. He bleated with terror at the current sweeping him away, struggled to get back, then fixed his gaze on the infuriating red square, and it became his whole world. Gorgon swam for his life, roaring and gurgling, with Jim rowing just ahead of the flared nostrils and rolling eyes. 'Good old Gorgon. Fine old man. What a fine gentleman you are.' Jim had to bail out twice in mid-channel, and the sun was at its highest before he got back near the wreck of the *Paragon*. He threw the red petticoat onto the sand and Gorgon waded ashore, losing all interest in the garment when he saw his cows grazing on the dune-grass, and chased after them on wobbly legs.

Jim beached the boat on the sand.

Leaving most of the others dead-drunk where they lay, O'Henry had walked along to find more rum. The two men stared at one another, then O'Henry gave a nod of respect. But he wouldn't help unload the ship, just flapped his hand amiably when he had found the bottle he was looking for, and wandered off with it to rejoin the party along the beach. Jim swung aboard and found Annie in the captain's quarters. She had laid Murdoon in the truckle bed.

'Your face looks like you stuck it in a frying pan,' she told Jim unsympathetically. 'You look stupid.'

'Even though it's winter the sun's rays here seem quite direct.' Propping himself against the slope of the deck he reloaded his pistols with dry powder from the captain's supply and stuck them back under his coat.

'That was a stupid thing to do with that bull.' She still wouldn't look at him. 'Don't expect any compliments from me.'

'I won't.'

'I'll leave that to Catherine Sidmouth,' Annie said.

'Will Murdoon live?' The second officer's face was feverish in the close heat of the cabin, and his shallow breaths whistled.

'What do you care!' Annie scoffed. 'His ribs are broken, I think they're caved in. He might, he might not. Why didn't you tell me about that Sidmouth woman?'

'Shut your jealous mouth.'

'I hate all men. I always fancy the wrong ones.' He cut her off impatiently, but Annie said, 'No, it's true, awful ones. I love you.'

He sighed and rummaged through the map drawer.

'I've decided,' Annie said brightly. 'It's something I've decided.'

'What?'

'Listen,' she said, and put her hand over his. 'Stop all that. Listen, Jim, stop thinking like the man you are, listen to me. You think it's going to be so simple and sensible. Unload the ship, share it out, hoping a company of dragoons aren't camped over the hill – and maybe they aren't. You see, we're the enemy, Jim. We are going to start fighting among ourselves. Look at that load along the beach. All they want is to get drunk.'

'Let them.'

'And then they'll fight among themselves. And then they'll fight us.'

'I don't think men are quite that brutal.'

'Oh,' Annie said, 'I think they are. That's why I decided I love you.'

'To protect you from them.'

'Yes. Only the ones with strong partners will survive. There's another reason. Pardon me for sounding like a stupid woman.'

'You don't sound stupid.'

'You are the love of my life, Jim. There's something about you. I knew it the first moment I saw you.' She sighed: 'The very first moment.'

'But you mean nothing to me.'

Annie said, 'Tell me about her.'

He shook his head.

She said: 'Never?'

There were too many maps for him to examine. He rolled them up to look at later.

The weather here in the path of the Roaring Forties never felt as though it would be calm, but for a few days of grace the wind was no more than a strong breeze driving the bright waves ashore. They called the place Quarantine Bay to stop the party-goers helping themselves to the rum or the growing accumulation of stores. The stores were floated to the beach or swung across on endless ropes, Simeon's patent system, helped by the ship's carpenter, a leathery old man called Dawes, quite without hair or teeth or ambition, but still vigorous when told what to do. Simeon worked with a will, an energetic figure stumping along the deck on his latest leg of good English ship's timber. The proprietor of the Cabriolet Service was a good organiser who persuaded the seamen who had gravitated back to the ship to work harder than they ever had in their lives, even though they were obeying the laws of convicts, until the lure of the party along the beach became too strong for them and they drifted away to join in the celebrations, vain creatures picking up bright articles of clothing to adorn themselves, scarlet kerseymere waist-coats and shoes with big silver buckles, licks of grease to glisten their braided pigtails. Half the night a distant fife piped *Drops of Brandy* and *Nancy Dawson* around the bonfire.

In the cove, the stores piled under sail-tents strung between the rocks grew quickly. They took everything they could get at, not knowing what would be of value. They had to re-rig the broken ladders that had trapped so many below to be drowned. Now in the heat the stranded bodies were swelling and the reek was cloying in its sweetness, unendurable; they had to spend a day swinging the pathetic things out, stripping them, and burying them in a mass grave. Jim said a quick service, only able to remember a few words from the Reverend Gough. Standing with bared heads, they thanked God for the wind: the stink of the kelp rotting around them, buzzing with flies, was almost worse than the smell in the ship.

But that same wind was rocking the *Paragon*, soften-ing and smoothing her outline as she worked herself into the gritty sand, literally wearing herself away. Soon the poop and foc'sle were two islands separated by sea. 'The rest will come ashore when she breaks up,' Simeon said.

Orin Murdoon was moved to a sail-tent ashore as it was now too dangerous to leave him aboard. The young officer had regained consciousness but was in great pain, and feverish. Annie listened to his babble. 'He's definitely been to Van Diemen's Land, I think,' she told Jim. 'His father was captain aboard HMS *Guard-ian*, a Navy ship carrying convicts, and after she struck an iceberg ten days out from Africa officers, seamen and convicts drunk on rum mutinied, thinking she was

113

going to sink, and one of his own drunken officers knocked Captain Murdoon over the side, drowning him. Poor Orin.' She brushed away the flies from the sick's man's face. 'He keeps saying Ocean, I think he means a ship, and somewhere called Port Phillip.'

'Port Phillip,' Orin Murdoon repeated clearly. 'The storeship *Ocean*.'

Jim leaned close. 'Is Port Phillip near here?'

'Collins said no good for a penal settlement, no water. No water. . . . father, father I'm drowning.'

'*Where are we?*'

Annie protested, 'Leave him alone!'

They listened to Orin ramble feverishly about Sullivan's Bay and the Derwent, then he murmured: 'Hunter's Island, Hobart Town, carrying the fine ladies ashore.' He groaned in his agony.

'That's the settlement on Van Diemen's Land,' Jim said. 'I saw it on the map and I've heard of it.' Annie went out and fetched a bucket from one of the freshwater springs in the rocks, laid a damp cloth on Orin's forehead.

His eyes flickered open.

'Ah,' Orin told Jim, 'so the convicts are kings now. Mutineers.'

'We don't accept your authority.'

'I am not in a position to enforce it.' Orin's hands fluttered weakly over his chest and his face contorted. 'Laudanum,' he begged. Annie gave him a sip of rum.

Jim said, 'Is this Van Diemen's Land?'

'We could be anywhere facing west.'

'There's a stand of trees visible only from the sea, that look like cypresses.'

'Cypresses? No, those are pines.'

'They don't look like pines,' Jim insisted.

'Don't tire him,' Annie said.

'They're Huon pines,' Orin murmured, and smiled. 'Fabulous trees, magical trees. The finest shipbuilding

114

timber in the world. Among savages its oil is precious, said to counter putrefaction, and heavier than water, yet the timber floats, and it never rots. And old. I saw a tree felled for a bridge, I counted the rings. More than two thousand years old. . . .'

'That's older than Christ,' Jim said.

'He's dreaming,' Annie said gently, 'there's no such tree.'

'Magical,' Orin murmured, closing his eyes, 'magical trees. . . .' He slept.

Simeon could not write, so Jim was making the inventory of the stores with slate and chalk, sitting at the captain's desk incongruously placed on the sand, but he could no longer settle to the work. He had found the ship's manifest. A roll of needles was more important to them than a barrel of salt pork, and many of the most useful stores had been loaded unofficially, put aboard by the captain for sale on the Botany Bay quayside: farming implements, household goods, bolts of cloth, everything settlers needed enough to pay for. Yet he kept thinking of the stand of Huon pines. Simeon plumped down beside him with a sigh and closed his eyes.

'Got five more cows ashore, one of 'em sick, and six sheep with a couple of rams. Chickens, a couple of goats. Don't know where they are.'

'They won't go far. You've done well.'

'The rabbits drowned. I love rabbit pie better than anything. Them dunes would have made fine warrens.'

'I hope all the marines drowned. The seamen are no problem, and the fourth officer has drunk himself into a stupor along the beach, but the bos'un is a tough nut and too used to giving orders for my liking. A couple of marines with muskets might feel they had to do their duty.'

'Duty? What's that?'

'We're still convicts. Rounding us up and putting us in chains.'

'I've hidden all the muskets I've found.'

'Well done.'

'It's a pleasure to watch your back, squire,' Simeon said, then stumped off to curse a sailor who had dropped a barrel and burst the hoops.

It was evening before Jim could get away. He climbed to the grassy summit of the highest dune. The orange sun set behind him, the dunes trailed long spikes of shadow away from him and a bird he did not recognise gave an angry, grating call. The treetops were a rolling purple plain. Above them the distant stand of Huon pines stood their shaggy heads against a sky already glimmering with stars. He heard a soft footstep behind him.

'Are you planning an expedition to Murdoon's magic trees?' Annie asked, keeping her hands at her sides.

'Not an expedition, Annie. Only me. I can be there and back in a day.'

'Only you. Of course. What if you meet savages?'

'I haven't seen any.'

'There's quartz chippings been flaked out of the rocks above the beach. Someone did it. They make spears and things, don't they?'

'That might have been years ago. Besides, I have my pistols.'

'Suppose you don't come back?' She didn't mention that she thought she had seen Mobley, the marine who had been the bane of her life, come walking down from the north and join O'Henry's party on the beach. 'Suppose you're killed? What happens to me?'

He shrugged.

'What . . . *who* exactly do you hope to find out there, Jim?'

He didn't answer her for a long time and she thought he had forgotten her, as usual.

'No, not myself, Annie.'

'A place? It's a bloody wilderness!'

'A place worth fighting for,' he said finally.

'Home. That's called *home*,' she appealed to him.

'No,' he said vehemently, 'this is never home. But a place worth fighting for, Annie. A home made out of the wilderness. That's a thought.'

12

The stand

The sun was rising in his face when Jim walked up past the cows grazing in the fine melilot clover, leaving Gorgon regarding him suspiciously, and set off across the rolling hills of the unexplored land.

One day he would know this wilderness as well as the back of his hand, but for now everything was nameless. He would have to learn how to look at this land. Brown badgers as big as barrels bumbled around him amiably, and he saw something striding across the distance like a gigantic shaggy chicken wearing stilts. Some creatures he knew: the tall triangular bounding animals that came close enough to sniff him, must be kangaroos. Wallabies grazed the hills in thousands, so many, and so unafraid, that he could have knocked them over with his stick. As he came out of the pussytail grass down to the trees, he found a stream meandering towards Seal Bay with watercress growing in its bed. He saw snails in the clumps of rushes and grimaced: the sheep would get liverfluke.

Swans and duck floated placidly on the rippling waters, a tall heron hunted from the bank. He crouched on the dark soil as a pinky-coloured kestrel flashed overhead into the grass for mice or lizards. To the north he saw brown falcons, and swamp harriers revealed the line of the stream towards the stand of pines inland. Scattering some stupid birds like big blue hens on bright red legs in front of him, oversized coots perhaps, he splashed along the watercourse.

He stopped with an exclamation of disgust. His legs

were crawling with leeches, and he had to drag them off between his fingers. When he slapped his face his hands came away spattered with blood from the mosquitoes.

Taking the cutlass from his belt he slashed a path through the boobyalla scrub away from the water and entered a tangled bushland of tea-tree, then dense clusters of celery-top pines, myrtle and sassafras, growing so tight he often had to turn and slide his shoulders between them. So, finally, he came to the trees he had mistaken for oaks or elms. In fact they were great blue and white gums standing in a fine mulch of their own leaves, long shucks of bark hanging like skin from their trunks, the space below them cathedral quiet, broken only by rowdy outbursts from birds in the high branches. Pressing through the bracken and ferns, he doubted there had ever been a fire here, and imagined how bounteous this soil would be with a good coating of ash.

And then he saw the valley open up ahead of him.

Its tumbled walls were a granite-quartz outcrop, the end of the clover-covered dunes rolling away to the north. He stood on a grassy platform overlooking the dell. He swore that for ever this would be Pride's Valley.

The stream meandered along the valley floor, forming shallow lagoons. It was by these that the stand of ancient Huon pines grew, captivating his attention, the tallest rising from a low mound to well over a hundred feet above the walls of the little valley which had sheltered it.

Jim knew this place, vacant of men except for himself, was *his* place.

'Mine,' he said, planting his seaboots in the grass. Then he shouted it out and for the first time, he thought, the valley echoed to the challenge of a human cry. 'Mine!'

Here he would build his house.

To have a house he must have a woman.

He saw Eve's face in the shape of the clouds, the river's mirror, the treetops. He squeezed his eyes shut, and he was alone.

He went and pressed his hands reverently against the thick scaly bark of a Huon, staring up at the overhanging branches, feeling the immense age of the tree radiate through his palms. He dug down with a stick through the mat of recent dead vegetation, peat and sandy loam, then suddenly the stick broke. He pulled out the tip: it was coated with dense black soil, and he guessed that these trees were the last remnant of a vast forest left over from perhaps more favourable weather conditions long ago.

He slapped the soil from his hands, and began to climb.

From the topmost swaying branch he saw sea all around him. They had been shipwrecked on an island. He saw no other land.

The island was shaped like a primitive flint to be held in a man's fist. About forty miles long – stretching almost to the horizon in the south – by fifteen miles broad, his domain was drowned beneath dark primeval forest, fringed by dunes and forbidding sawtooth headlands.

He stayed there, staring out from the angle of a branch, until the sun sank towards the west. He thought about Annie, but to desire her was to forsake Eve, and that love was more precious to him than anything.

The forest would be a bad place to spend the night; he did not know what dangers it contained, either slithering on their bellies or walking on their feet like men, but once he heard an eerie cry, and saw something like a dog with an enormous mouth, fanged as the devil's,

120

slinking through the bush. The mile struggling through the dense understoreys of growth took him more than three hours, and the sun had set by the time he reached the dunes behind Quarantine Bay. There was no moon; he made a small fire of deadwood, and slept exhausted.

He woke shivering. His fire had burned out a crescent of grass almost to the stream while he slept. He stamped out any remaining embers and walked, stiffly at first, navigating by the constellation Annie called the Saucepan. As the first rays of sun lit the sky behind him with orange, Jim stared down at the beach from the top of a dune.

During his absence everything had gone wrong. The party-goers had invaded the sail-tents of Quarantine Bay, probably in search of rum. The stores were scattered over the sand and drunken people staggered in search of booty. No life showed from Orin Murdoon's tent.

Simeon had been knocked to the ground and bound up with rope. At first Jim thought he had suffered some horrible injury, then saw that his false leg had been torn off, further immobilising him. Many of the revellers lay on the sand exhausted but Becky was still dancing while O'Henry clapped. A man in a marine corporal's uniform, white breeches and crooked pipeclayed sash, chased a woman who was thrown from man to man. The woman was Annie.

They forced her to her knees. She bit one of the men in the crotch and ran into the dunes, chased by the corporal in his uniform. She recognised Jim's silhouette, his distinctive waisted coat and floppy-brimmed hat tilted back against the dawn skyline. She dodged desperately uphill towards him. She didn't call out.

Jim could hear the breath whining in her throat, could sense her thudding heart, her terror. Something had changed in Annie and the masculinity that would once have led her to tolerate the brutal Corporal Mobley, even to fancy him, was now the cause of her fear.

His hands in his pockets, Jim watched her frantic attempts to escape.

She scrambled towards him, climbing out of the dark, the sand sliding away under her fingers as she tore at the grass. Mobley loped up the footholds she had made. She looked up at Jim, holding out her hand. The sand gave way under her feet, she slid down. Mobley opened his arms and claimed her.

'Mine,' he said. 'Mine, or I'll have you flogged in chains, convict.'

'We're free,' Jim said, very gentle. 'This is our land.' He walked downslope slowly, his boots making no sound in the soft, sliding sand. 'Let her be.'

'She's mine.' The marine backed away dragging her.

'She's neither property, or animal, nor a child. Her name is Annie and she's a free woman.'

'Don't he talk fancy?' Mobley called to the others on the beach.

Jim said, 'This is an island. There's no help for you here, Mobley. No orders for you to follow. Let Annie choose.'

She looked at him pathetically. If she chose Jim she knew Mobley, who was much stronger, would beat him to a pulp.

'I'll go with Mobley,' she said.

Mobley laughed.

'I'll fight you for her,' Jim said softly, his fingers hooked in the belt beneath his jacket.

Mobley roared with laughter. 'Ho, yes, a fight between gentlemen!' He tossed Annie to the bo'sun, also a man used to giving orders. Jim hardly glanced at him – such a man would also accept taking them. Becky and the enormously powerful O'Henry came to watch. Jim knew O'Henry would go with the victor.

'Queensberry Rules?' Jim said, making his stand.

Mobley spat. He pulled off his sash and circled eagerly, bunching his fists, his naked toes digging for a hold in the wet sand. Jim watched him without taking off his hat. Mobley sparred forward.

In a smooth motion Jim opened his jacket, pulled the pistol from his belt and blew half Mobley's head away. The marine's body stood upright in a bloody turmoil, then fell without a sound.

'He wasn't a gentleman,' Jim told them.

13

1807

The cold heart of the south

Annie could smile now, looking out over their valley from her own doorway, remembering those early days before the real struggle began. She had walked away from the crowd with Jim Pride and as soon as they were out of sight she would have let him do anything he wanted to, and she wanted him to.

But Jim didn't attempt to seduce her. Instead, he made her work, stacking and tallying the stores.

Annie faithfully worked her fingers to the bone for him. Her muscles grew taut, her hands seamed hard from the endless lifting, scalds from the billy pot marked her forearms, and she tied her long hair back as the sun browned her face like a peasant woman's. But he treated her as a companion, he didn't take her as a woman. She looked at no other man, but Jim hardly noticed her. She told herself he appreciated her, but he never looked at her with love in his eyes. It was a hard life for her on the beach, together and apart.

Sometimes, waking alone in the sail-tent where she tended Orin Murdoon, lying in the dark with only the sick man's gasping for company, she cringed beneath the tarpaulin covering her, remembering, not knowing whether to laugh or cry in her fear and desire: perhaps Mobley would have been the better bet after all. Jim was cruel, not in what he did, but in what he did not do. Nothing was worse than coldness.

Annie learned humility. She always made herself

cheerful for him. She talked to him with a straight-forward practical look in her eye. She knew he couldn't last her out. He wasn't nearly as tough as her, and she knew she had only to stick with him long enough. Annie knew what was best for them. Even if she had not loved him, romance was common sense. A woman couldn't live without a man in this land.

It was a hard land, this island.

By smokey lamplight they held up the maps for Orin Murdoon to study from his sickbed. He lay back, nodding.

'This is King Island,' he told them. 'No doubt about it. The sentinel at the entrance to the Bass Strait, about half way between New South Wales and Van Diemen's Land.'

'King Island,' Jim said thoughtfully, 'never heard of it.'

'There's the map – you can recognise the curve of the two bays. The island was first named about half a dozen years ago by the *Harbinger* when she all but ran on a reef. Flinders did a brief survey a year or two later, this is his Arrowsmith map. A team of French naturalists aboard the *Géographe* tried to claim the island for Napoleon, but the crapauds were seen off by an English lieutenant without a shot being fired. That's the last time anyone came here.'

'Why?'

'No all-weather harbour, and a bad reputation for shipwrecks: it's deserted, of no value – except as a prison, perhaps.'

'This land isn't our prison,' Jim insisted, 'it's our opportunity.'

Orin Murdoon said sadly, 'The Government will catch you one day. They always do.'

'Not if we're dead,' Jim said bluntly. 'As far as Governor Bligh is concerned the *Paragon* was lost at sea with all hands, and that's the end of the story. Bligh experienced that storm personally. How many ships are lost in these waters?'

'More than we know,' Murdoon admitted. 'Have you never wondered how the melilot clover got here? Mattress-stuffing washed ashore from some unknown wreck, I'd swear.' He sat up painfully and reached for the strong pine crutches Dawes the carpenter had made him. 'I fear this is not Robinson Crusoe's island. The climate is rigorous and, should any sealers call, the captains are known for their ruthlessness.'

'They will have to learn to value us,' Jim said. The two men went out to walk on the beach, leaving Annie to stare at the map. South of King Island, the large heart-shaped island of Van Diemen's Land hung like an exquisite green pendant down chains of islands from the angry red face of Australia.

She rolled it up, packed it away and crept out to follow them; even men's conversation was better than nothing.

Jim and Orin Murdoon walked along the beach above the tideline of kelp thrown up by the constant winds. The moonlight flashed off the glittering bay waters and gleamed along the steady line of the two New Year islands. The *Paragon* had first struck off the tail of Christmas Island. The only safe approach to the bay was the least obvious one, the narrow channel of water running between the two islands to the deep anchorage in their lee, called Franklin Roads after the midshipman aboard Flinders's ship *Investigator* who discovered it.

'Feargal O'Henry came to me today,' Orin said, as much Jim Pride's friend as any man could be. 'As senior ranking officer I'm technically captain, with the power to hold marriages. Becky Donahoo's got him. They want to squat a few miles south, the Pass river I guess, near George Tatham's. He was a farmer before. . . . before.' None of them used the word *convict*

126

now. 'Amos Preston's found better land on the east coast, but we can't spare the stock this year. We can't afford to scatter.'

'We can't afford to do anything else,' Jim said. 'Each squatter needs land to support himself. Neighbours can help one another, but we've got to make our own way, we're too vulnerable close together. Besides, you don't think O'Henry would ever do what he was told, do you? And none of the seamen listen to me, they've got the sea in their blood, not the land.'

They looked as something moved on the hills, one of the Herefords in calf.

'Gorgon's mine,' Jim said. 'That's all I ask.'

'That makes you king of the castle,' Orin said.

'That's right.'

'You're really determined to make a success of it, aren't you.'

But Jim repeated in a low voice, 'We're dead men.'

Annie, eavesdropping, knew what he meant. Any day, perhaps tomorrow, a ship might anchor in Franklin Roads, send a boatload of marines ashore, and take back their pathetic group in irons. But it was not his callousness in shooting down Mobley that had shocked her, it was the depth of sadness she had sensed in him as he pulled the trigger. He had known exactly what he was doing: if he was taken now, he would swing. The tears came to Annie's eyes. Everything joined them except love.

'Are you crying?' whispered Mary Roper out of the dark. 'I'm so sorry, Annie, I didn't think you ever did. I'm so lonely. Stay with me here.' She sat quickly behind a rock, looking up appealingly with the moon in her large slanted eyes.

'I'm not crying,' Annie said, but she sat.

'George Tatham is taking me south,' Mary said. 'He's a good man, but it's Feargal O'Henry I love.'

'There's no sport in this game,' Annie agreed. 'Don't that seaweed stink.'

'George says we'll use it to fertilise the fields we've cleared by fire once the ash has lost its goodness,' said Mary in her meek little voice.

'You're not strong enough to carry much,' Annie said.

'You'd be surprised the burden I can bear,' said Mary softly. 'I've got to be near Feargal even though it's a torture to be. Just to see him.'

Annie said, 'You stick with sensible George.'

'Yes, he's much older, and he's kind.' Mary threw a little handful of sand. 'I want a child, my own child. Why are you crying, Annie?'

Jim's murder of Mobley had put a blight on the beach party. Over the next few days, shivering in the wintry rains that lashed the exposed coastline, the sheepish revellers had returned one by one to the sheltered nest of sail-tents, daring to make no complaint when Simeon put them to work. As the breaking seas completed the final ruin of the *Paragon* they laboured to drag every last piece of debris safely above the watermark. On calm days Jim even had those who could swim diving for the shipwright's copper nails that littered the sandy seabed. When they tallied the final inventory, they thanked God. Ten tons of Government salt pork helped them little, since fresh meat was to be had for the trouble of knocking a tame wallaby, or the bouncing red pademelons that clustered curiously around, on the head with a stick, and the divers often came up struggling with succulent crayfish as long as their waists to their chins, holding them at arms' length to avoid the clacking pincers. But the goods the captain had intended for wharf sale in Botany Bay were invaluable. Surgical instruments, shovel-blades, tomahawk-heads, adzes, hoes, one single plough, needles, hooks, pails, saws and hammers, all the things colonists needed to make other things. There were barrels of flour for bread to last them to the end of the year, and seed ready for planting now, all consigned in casks of twelve-pound canisters marked for the general traders and seedsmen Riley & Jones. The lid of each tin canister was pasted down with paper and packed in matted hair, and here their choice was bafflingly wide: not only wheat and barley, but names they had never heard of, lucerne, chicory, burnet, bumas, marram, orientalis, sainfoin, meadow fescue.

'They's grasses,' old Peter Corduroy said, sniffing them between his gnarled fingers. 'They's good grasses for cows later. Here's white clover, and this here's a smooth-stalk meadow grass, they spread themselves by running root as well as a little seed.' It was the first time anyone had seen him smile. 'We're all right, me jackeroos! We'll grow beef here to be the envy of Old England.'

But this wasn't Old England. There was no intimacy in this disconnected land of dense bush and trickling creeks, blazing sun and sheeting rain. There were no homely glades, dales, spinneys or thickets in these woods. Their mates drifted away, Mr and Mrs O'Henry shaking Jim's hand, straitlaced George Tatham standing like a father by Mary Roper, who winked at Annie. They had chosen the calmest day for weeks, and Jim and Annie stood apart watching the cutter loaded to the gunwhales with stores row southward hugging the coast, seals playing round it, until the little vessel was gone from sight. That evening a thin column of smoke rose above the bush, and they knew the voyagers had arrived safely.

'Now there's no boat,' Jim told Orin Murdoon, 'it's impossible for you to sail for help.'

'At last my conscience is clear,' the Englishman drawled ironically.

Jim spat over a rock. The bored sailors larrikined roughly on the beach, and he frowned. They wouldn't go inland, and it had been his constant fear that they would seize the cutter, escape, and take the tip to the authorities for a reward.

Orin Murdoon was dying, Annie thought. His nose ran with a constant cold, and his cough was worse, otherwise Jim would not have brought him with them when they went inland. Annie liked Orin, he had pleasant eyes and his mind was lively, but this wasn't a gentleman's land, and she resisted the dangerous temptation to get Jim jealous. She bided her time.

Without horses or bullocks what they could carry from the shore was strictly limited, but Jim did it somehow, poling stores up the Yellow Rock river, more taciturn than ever, or roping together a travois like a Devon trackamuck and dragging it overland. Under the high summer sun the dense bush made this back-breaking labour almost impossible, but he wouldn't let her help him. It wasn't woman's work. She had stayed back at the tent near Simeon's slab-hut in the dunes with Orin Murdoon, him standing in his sun-faded blue jacket with the once-white lapels and white duck trousers, leaning on his stick enthusiastically pointing out the different varieties of butterfly, or the tiny white wombats, but Annie looked anxiously across the tree-tops for any sign of Jim. When they saw smoke rise and fan out away from them in the gentle wind, they knew he had decided to clear his path with fire.

None of them ever forgot how quickly the wind fanned that fire. Within minutes a pall of smoke obscured the bush, red flames licking up within it like tongues coming through the earth, and they heard the crash of trees. Thank God the fire couldn't jump the marshes and it petered out along the line of the Yellow Rock river. The Huons stood out safe from their swamp, an island of green in the black swathe. When

Jim returned, ash in his hair and his face blackened, he held out his hand for his billy without a word. A lesson had been learned.

It would have been sufficient for him to have built a slab-hut like everyone else, with a door for the wind to blow through and no windows. But Jim wouldn't do things that way once he'd got to the valley. No stringy-bark settler, he did nothing easy now. He rested his hands on the bark of one of the great pines, staring up, and that was where she found him.

'Jim?' she said.

He looked round, startled. He showed her a level grassy space sheltered by the granite outcrop, and she knew this was where her house would be.

'I'm going to have a vegetable patch down the side,' she said, and he nodded his permission. 'No, it's my place too,' she insisted.

'It's mine.'

'It's ours, or I'll walk out on you right now, Jim.'

'You're free.'

'Jim?' she said, 'look at me.'

He looked her in the eye.

'Jim,' Annie said, 'I'm sorry I'm not her.'

'You'll need a fence to keep the animals out,' he said.

'Not even memories last for ever,' she murmured.

Then he showed her the outline of a fallen tree almost buried in the damp earth, a Huon centuries old covered with lichen and moss.

'It hasn't rotted,' he said. 'It lasts for ever.'

This was the fragrant yellow wood which framed her doorway, hacked out of the earth as fresh as though it still grew. In return for the loan of Gorgon, Dawes the carpenter had carved, tenoned and morticed the wood immaculately, so her home was the strangest that had ever been, fashioned of the earth and the sea: double front doors taken from the captain's cabin of the *Paragon* and fitted so exactly that not the slightest draught sneaked through, with brass doorknobs that she burnished with a fine paste of rockdust. The roof was copper sheathing. Decking clad the walls, with two enormous stern-gallery windows one on each side of the door, one of them still carrying the ship's name on a gilt scroll beneath it. The feature she loved most was the ship's figurehead Jim had mounted over the door, beneath the eaves of the verandah: the Paragon of Virtue, her golden tresses flying. The light in her left eye was severe and disapproving, but Annie decided the old girl wasn't so virtuous as she pretended: that right eye held a saucy gleam.

The hut had two rooms, a day room where the men bedded down at night, and a small place for Annie alone. She made it pretty with a few rugs salvaged from the cargo and hung a brass lamp from the roof.

Once it was finished she hardly saw Jim except for meals. It was natural for her and Orin Murdoon to grow closer. The invalid was good company and entertaining, keeping her spirits up. Jim was away for days at a time, dragging stores upriver, arriving home too exhausted to talk. He surrounded the house with a cockatoo fence of split branches bound to uprights to keep the badgers – Orin called them wombats – and hopping pademelons out, but no fence could keep the kangaroos from breaking into the paddock cleared by the fire. Jim had seeded the ash with lucerne and within a few days of rain the most extraordinary sight greeted their eyes: the black had turned green with a mist of growing grass. A few days after that, the wild animals moved in to enjoy the tender shoots, and the returning cows, who had found quiet places to calve in the dunes, went hungry with their young. At first the unfairness of it nearly drove Annie frantic, she ran around waving her arms and shooing the tolerant marsupials, who bounded obligingly away from her then settled in a new place. Strips of white cloth fluttering from sticks in the wind had no effect on them and Orin, sitting on the verandah, passed his time making English scarecrows which also had no effect. Jim returned from a visit up north to Peter Corduroy, who had showed him how to make snares. But still the kangaroos ate, and everyone else got hungrier. Annie sensed Jim tense up with rage. He had lost weight, his arms like whipcord, but his face was gaunt, the gentleness leached out of it. He no longer shared Orin's joking, bantering manner: like a stranger he came home to bolt his food, and sleep.

And Annie tried hard with the food. Only one stove had been saved from the *Paragon* – by lottery it had gone with O'Henry, but Annie had a fine selection of pots and pans for her woodfire smoking and reeking in its makeshift iron hearth at the back of the hut, and the finest cutlery and Staffordshire plates she had ever dreamed of. Kangaroo tail soup was her wonderful invention but Jim bolted it and went out. Until the young generation of bulls were old enough to be castrated for use as bullocks, the plough was no good to them, and Jim hoed the east paddock by moonlight, while in the west paddock the wildlife ate the seed from this year's ripening crops. Annie sat on the top step of the verandah and cried. Orin stood behind her. She got up and threw her arms round him.

'It isn't working,' she wept, 'the only man I never took pity on, worth loving for himself. He doesn't care about me, and he's right. I'm a worthless woman.'

'You're lovely,' Orin said in a low voice. 'I desire you.'

'I know. That's always been my trouble with men, they're too easy. Except Jim. Isn't it perfect?' She stared up at him, crying.

'Perhaps he conceals his passions.'

'I want a new life, I want everything different. I'm

a battler.' Her hands hung by her sides. 'Is Jim doing this to us deliberately?'

'So you do love him.' Orin stared at her, then pulled away bitterly. 'I see how much you love him.'

'He doesn't,' she said.

But Jim, she knew, wasn't trying to drive her into Orin's arms. Jim was being faithful to the girl in his mind. Annie couldn't persuade him that the past was far away and long gone. Sometimes he climbed the tallest tree and stayed there for hours, staring out. He didn't see Seal Bay or the New Year Islands – he was looking, she knew, beyond the horizon. He was looking home.

Annie knew that Orin loved her and once she would have loved the fun of having him, the life. Orin Murdoon's good breeding meant nothing here, she was as good as he was. In England Annie could only ever have been his whore; here she could be, if Jim went bad, his woman. But Orin still thought himself a gentleman; an uninvolved man. That was not good enough here. Jim had no breeding, he was no dreamer, all that was past in this place. He was fighting for his life, and for Annie's life.

Each day was a little worse. They might starve.

Jim never smiled. Everything he did was serious. She took him seriously, as faithful to her love as he was to his. He never touched her but she supported him like a wife, feeding him, asking nothing in return, taking out his lunch to him in the paddock he was clearing and handing it to him in the shade of the great gum trees. He leaned on a fallen trunk and ate without a word of thanks. When long after dark Jim came back exhausted, walking as wearily as though he carried another man on his shoulders, she had a hot dinner ready and slid the bowl between his elbows, sometimes even pushing the spoon into his fingers, he was so tired,

134

and they sat on boxes round the table shovelling back the food in silence. Except Orin Murdoon, sitting on the long side of the table between them, who made conversation. Here was autumn in May, and the crops grew tall but thin, and the kangaroos knocked them down. Jim staggered to his mattress and dropped. Annie washed up, then pulled off Jim's boots and covered him with a blanket. 'G'night,' she muttered to Orin, closing herself in her own little cubby-hole of a room where the strength went out of her legs and she dropped down as exhausted as Jim.

Orin sat unmoving at the table, quietly sucking his cold pipe – his lungs could not take smoke. Rain pittered softly on the roof. He hated this place, this island of ceaseless wind and rain and blazing sun, seeing these people disconnect themselves from the civilised world. Because of his weakness, unable to escape, he lived among people who willingly sacrificed their spark, their elegance of manner merely to survive – Annie had never been elegant, of course, but she could have learned. She was still so beautiful that she made his heart ache; to see her gobbling her food with a slave's blank face infuriated him.

Yet they were his friends, his mates. The bonds that had bound them to Simeon aboard ship had been widened to include him. They could have left him on the beach, but instead they looked after him although they could barely support themselves. At first his knowledge of the antipodes had made him useful to them, but now they knew more than he, and he had nothing more to offer.

He could have escaped. The bo'sun and a delegation of seamen had made him an extraordinarily tempting offer. It would be possible to steal the cutter from the squatters at Pass River and fit it out for a passage to the mainland, any good seaman could do that, but they needed Murdoon to steer their course. There was only one settlement on the whole wild north coast of Van Diemen's Land – the military camp that Murdoon had last heard of at Outer Cove, on the Tamar estuary. Torn, he kept this information to himself, because revealing it meant betraying Jim and Annie and all the others to the authorities. And yet it was his duty. And he wanted to escape from this ghastly place more than anything.

'Will you not lead us, sir?' They had met at the edge of the dunes and the bo'sun, at the head of the delegation, watched him steadily. Simeon sat nearby with his large knife in full view, whittling a stick.

'I fear I cannot help you,' said Murdoon stiffly. The four seamen shifted their feet impatiently. But for Simeon's presence he would have feared an attempt at kidnap.

'At least tell us what's the name of this place we're on, sir?'

Murdoon hesitated, then continued with his own mutiny. He would not give his friends away, even though they were condemned convicts. 'It is the island of Never Never.'

The bo'sun tugged his forelock respectfully. 'And what course do we steer, sir?'

'Southwest,' Murdoon said, sending them to their deaths.

So Murdoon had gone against everything he believed in for the sake of his friends. He would never fit in this land, and when he heard that the cutter was stolen, he was tempted to join them and steer them to the southwest through the hail and snow until the icebergs claimed them in the cold heart of the south. He didn't have the courage. He stood on a dune-top with his distorted body hanging from his crutches, watching the little craft dwindle between the marching rainstorms, steering bravely to the southwest, until the sea was empty.

'Good riddance,' Simeon said, 'though it's a pity there's still some of their friends left on the beach, and doubtless they'll make trouble when the rum's gone. Come on, chum, I'll take you home.'

But it wasn't home. Orin stood on the verandah staring out at the dark, the rain blowing in over him. Soon he was shivering and as his fever rose, he thought he saw icebergs cruising like mighty ships through the dark. They were only clouds; but he never knew.

'He must have been mad,' Annie said, 'standing out in the rain like that.'

'I'll have to take a morning to dig the hole,' Jim said, wearing his usual frown, and when Annie turned on him angrily he looked amazed.

'You're an effing failure, Jim Pride – you aren't half the man he was. You aren't worth anything, you're useless to everyone, especially me.' Her tongue ran away with her. 'Oh, it isn't worth living like this! You're driving me mad, I'm not going to let you lock me up, Jim, like you are. That might suit you but it isn't good enough for me!' Tears were running from her eyes so that she couldn't see, she bumped into him then ran to her room, slamming her door so that the hut shook.

He stood there listening to her crying.

Then he fetched the shovel and went down to the tallest Huon growing from the soft soil of the knoll above the lagoon, and began to dig.

The day was beautiful. He stopped, and looked around him: the trees standing in their waving shadows, enormous white clouds sailing above the blue-ish treetops across the brilliant sky, the lagoon so blue in reflection it almost ached. There was no sound but the sigh of the wind, the rustling of the rushes, the cry of a bird. Jim sat dangling his legs in the hole, watching everything around him. A smile broke over his face.

He finished digging in the hard, compacted layer of

fertile soil from the ancient forest, then piled up some cut tea-tree nearby for a bonfire. Going up to the house he found Annie had bound up the gape of Orin's mouth with a strip of cloth and cleaned up his uniform somehow, even put a gleam on the brass buttons. Jim took off his battered hat and watched her. Annie ignored him.

'He was all right,' Jim acknowledged.

Standing, she still ignored him. Jim picked up the body and crutches and carried them down to the knoll.

Annie said: 'Say something nice.'

'I don't believe in words,' Jim murmured. He put the crutches on the fire and lit it from his tinderbox, and they watched the pale flames consume the wood. 'That's all that needs to be said.' He shovelled back the earth until the two of them stood alone.

'We won't work this afternoon,' he said. 'I've got something more important in mind.'

Annie looked worried, then realised his tone of voice.

'You,' Jim said. 'Us.' He reached out and took her hand in his. 'I need you. I know that now. I do need you, Annie.' They walked back to their little house in the shelter of its rocky outcrop. He didn't say any more, just sat on the step, as though it ended there. She wouldn't leave him.

'I love you, Jim.' She knelt beside him, breathing quietly.

'Annie,' he said, 'give me time.'

'No, Jim,' she said, 'you've had enough time.' She waited.

'Don't ever,' he told her earnestly, 'don't ever go in your bedroom again and make me hear you crying.'

She said simply: 'Don't ever make me go in there alone again.' He must kiss her now: she kept her gaze steady.

He kissed her bluntly and she responded, putting her elbows on his shoulders, curling her hands round the back of his head, twining her fingers in his hair so that he could not escape her. He put his arms round her, then held her tight. Rising to their feet they backed up the steps, and he thought he was leading her. He didn't say her name. He carried her inside and she longed to get him undone, her hands pressed to the heat of his belly, but she knew he wanted her to be passive so she hung from his arms with her eyes closed. It was dark in her room; the brass casing of the oil lamp glinted a little. 'Close your eyes,' Jim said, and she realised he was nervous: he had never been with a woman before. His hands were rough and she helped his clumsy efforts in ways he could not sense, but he knew what he wanted and when he found her he pushed at once, so that in her surprise she cried out like a virgin. It was enough.

'Oh my love,' he whispered, 'oh my heart, my sweet love.' He stroked her eyelids, caressed her hair, her smiling lips. Annie kept her eyes closed as his passion convulsed him, and pretended the same. She knew it wasn't really her he was speaking to, but that wasn't what mattered. They had a future now.

14

1808

A business opportunity

Last year, soon after Annie had taken Jim to her bed, Bass Strait sealers had landed at Sea Elephant Bay on the east coast of the island. The twenty miles to Amos Preston's place was a hard three-day journey through tangled tallow-wood scrub and gigantic stands of blue gum, blackwood, ash, cottonbark and celery-top; but by chance Jim was taking over two hardy Durham cows, both pregnant, the east-coasters' share of the first generation of King Island cattle. The land was cut by creeks where enormous manferns grew as tall as palm trees, and high in a gum he saw the great nest of a sea-eagle. The arching caverns of the treetops echoed with the laughing Joe-Witty call of the butcher bird and fantails and blue wrens fluttered around him.

Fortunately, both Amos and Sam Rafferty used fire-sticks liberally, and Jim made better time through the swathes of cleared land. He noticed last year's burn already overgrown with tea-tree, hazel and bracken-fern, choking the melilot. Black cockatoos showing the yellow flashes under their wings flew over in mobs, which meant rain. And the rain came.

Rafferty was demoralised; the rain poured through his roof and the wind blew through his walls. His woman, Jane, ten years older than he, cut him with her tongue and called him useless. 'I wish Amos would take her, but I'm stuck. He's found himself a lubra.'

'A what?'

'An aborigine woman. He found her living on kelp.'

This was the first Jim had heard of savages alive on King Island. The settlers had seen no footprints in the sand or trace of campfires other than their own. Feargal O'Henry, on an exploration to the south of the island, had found a skeleton in a cave, but there was no telling if it had been there fifteen years or fifteen thousand.

'Amos says she picks up English phenomenal quick and foul. The sealers left her.'

'Sealers? Here?' Jim demanded. 'By the God Almighty, why didn't you tell me before?'

Rafferty shrugged. 'Amos stays well back from the beach when Cowper's here. That Cowper would sell you for your hide.'

'Let's see what he's up to,' Jim said.

'No fear!' said Rafferty. 'Leave the cattle here with me, or we'll lose them. You'll find Amos hiding down at the creek above the beach.'

In his previous life Amos had been a gardener and the grass-thatched dwelling he called his cottage was almost hidden by mimosa. He grew cabbages and pumpkins, carrots and silver beet in his vegetable garden, potatoes with the choking bracken fern patiently plucked out, even a row of tiny peach trees, and there was a passionfruit vine over the door. He called his lubra Helen as though that made her European, respectable. She was a tall, spindly creature. Jim said: 'What is your name?'

She turned to him with large, lustrous brown eyes. 'Wayanna,' she said softly.

'But that's a lovely name.'

She looked at him sadly. 'It means seal.'

'Have the sealers really come back?'

'Answer him, Helen,' instructed Amos self-importantly, and smiled proudly when she spoke.

'Those men are savages,' she said.

'Now, now,' Amos warned her. 'And enough of you rolling your *r*'s like a Scotch woman.'

'They kill their children by us at birth, because they stop us lubras working.' Her eyes filled with tears.

'I told the wicked girl,' Amos strutted, 'no white man would do such a thing.'

'Show me these men,' Jim said.

Wayanna slipped like a will o' the wisp through the bush ahead of them, Amos crashing and puffing behind. When they stopped for a rest Amos explained: 'It's the oil of the sea elephants they're after – each sea elephant can be rendered in try-pots to yield half a tun of oil, and that's worth twenty pounds in London. Wonderful for lamps, burns without smell or smoke. The skin makes leather for harness. A couple of good seal skins, no holes, fetch a pound. A gang kills about six hundred sea elephants in a month, maybe four or five thousand seal – it's a fortune, man! An endless supply. Some of the skins are shipped to China to keep prices up.'

'Fewer seal,' whispered Wayanna.

'Nonsense!' said Amos. 'I wish there were, then we'd get some peace from their noise.'

They wriggled through the bush until they came out on a cliff edge above the beach. The rain had ceased but everything was shades of grey: the smooth sea, the sky, the rocks and even the sand. Sea Elephant Bay was well named: the creatures drowsed and lolled in their lazy, yawning thousands – thousands of tuns of living oil. The seals seemed very small among them. 'A dozen sealskins buys a gallon of rum,' said Amos wistfully. He pointed out the headland he called Cowper's Point, a rough settlement of A-frame badger-box huts with grey smoke eddying between them, and they heard the distant barking of dogs. 'Kangaroo dogs,' Amos nodded, 'they'll attack a man as soon as a kangaroo.'

'And you can't trade with these brutes of sealers at all?'

'Rough men kill one another,' Wayanna said, showing no sign of distress.

'She's a savage, she has no emotions,' Amos explained. 'She feels no misery, and no happiness.'

They watched the sealers' lubras crawl silently through the seal herd, clubbing the heads with such expert smoothness that the others, although watching curiously, remained unalarmed. For the gigantic sea elephants the lubras used their traditional technique, encircling a number to keep them from the sea, then jabbing at the mouths, locked open in submission, with lighted sticks so that the lips swelled up and suffocated the great beasts. The females wept floods of tears as they died, and Jim thought it was the most distressing sight he had ever witnessed. He looked away and saw Wayanna watching him intently.

Amos said, 'Jim, we're not official-like serving out our sentences here, are we?'

'Officially we don't start serving our time until the day we're mustered on the quay at Botany Bay.'

'So we're for sale,' Amos said miserably. 'Those sealing brutes would sell their own mothers. I was hoping to barter a few things with them. I need a grindstone and. . . .'

'If you let them catch you,' Jim said, 'I'll do for you myself.'

'Remember what you saw here today,' Amos said. 'It's a disaster.'

That was true: they could not trade with these sealers, men who lacked every scruple for money, who had good reason to give them away. Seals would not be the only prey to be wiped out: they would be as happy to hunt humans for profit. But it was not a total loss. Jim returned to his house with a gift for Annie, a cutting

143

of Amos's passionfruit vine to plant by the back door. She greeted him with a kiss.

'What's that for?' he said.

And so the year turned. Jim was creating a world, *his* world. Annie wanted to populate it with a family, to give it meaning. Annie had not been in his plan, but he was part of hers. She didn't give up her battle to win him, to keep him constantly in her heart, any more than he gave up his battle against the soil. She didn't care whose face he saw in the dark, as long as he was kind to Annie. If he saw something in the shape of her nose, the curls of her hair, flashes of someone else in the way Annie looked up or smiled, she was happy, because it was Annie who would have his child.

But she was frightened, badly frightened, that Jim would lose his battle. Despite his toil they seemed condemned to eke out Robinson Crusoe lives on the grim margin of subsistence farming, not daring to reveal themselves. Grass didn't regenerate so swiftly after a second fire, and wooden fences weren't much good at keeping the kangaroos out – they needed wire, needed money to buy it. Yet they dare not reveal themselves to the sealers.

Their great stroke of good fortune had been in their cattle – these Herefords were hardy, perhaps the first Herefords in the southern hemisphere, not prone to disease or cold like the Bengali stock. Even so, their condition was not now as good in the second year as in the first. And they had found Bess, their finest cow, lying dead with her mouth full of poisonous tare, her calf lowing piteously beside her. In these calves all their hopes resided, and Annie would have fed the little fellow from her own swelling breasts if she could, but a new mother adopted him in a day or two and soon he was trotting around with her other calf as cheerfully as a twin.

A summer storm kept them off the land for almost

a week, and then Jim saw the ragged smoke of Simeon's warning fire in the dunes.

It was too late to start out that evening, but Jim was on his way before dawn. The sealers' vessels had stood off the land overnight, but now they were passing confidently down the deep channel between the New Year islands.

'Trouble,' Simeon said, scratching sand out of his beard. The two men lay on the summit of a dune peering through the bent stalks of marram grass, the wind hissing between them throwing occasional flurries of sand into their faces. Simeon looked round, the wind now thundering in his ear, fluttering the red kerchief tied around his head. Jim, cleanshaven, had grown a moustache and his twinkling eyes, at first glance, lent him a raffish air with his hat and stylish long-tailed coat. You would have thought he was a man at peace with himself, but peace was not where Jim derived his strength: behind those eyes was a man constantly at war. His gentleness in Annie's company was a source of wonder to Simeon. But Annie was a mile inland, and now Jim stared out at the scene before them with eyes as hard as stones.

The two ships, a small schooner and a larger brig of about two hundred tons, had been sighted on the horizon by Simeon last evening, and he had lit the fire to warn Jim at once. Sealers were coming to Seal Bay.

'The brig's armed with at least half a dozen twelve-pound cannon,' Simeon commented. 'I wonder why?'

'Perhaps in fear of other sealers,' Jim said. 'Look at those slim lines. They're foreign. Americans build graceful ships like that, don't they?'

They watched the two ships turn into the wind in the sheltered lee of the islands. 'The captain knows these waters all right,' Simeon said bleakly. 'Yankee traders.' The storm had left the long curve of Seal Bay piled high with kelp, and the stench of this mingled with the stink of seal in their nostrils; at times the whole shoreline swarmed with movement, in and out of the sea, the seals so tame as to almost encircle the two ships anchoring in Franklin Roads.

'What do you think, Simeon?' Jim asked.

'Both vessels show storm damage – I can make out smashed boats, lost spars, and the bigger vessel was handling wrong, trouble with the rudder maybe. And you're right, that curve on the bow is pure Massachusetts.'

'Americans. They're a long way from home,' Jim said thoughtfully. 'They look laden, but I guess they don't get a welcome from the British sealers.'

There was no hope that their presence would not be noticed: the seventeen sailors living in miserable huts were prancing on the foreshore waving their arms to attract the sealers' attention, if the smoke of their fish-curing fires had not already done so. A boat was lowered from the larger vessel.

'Come on,' Jim said, 'the current will sweep them north.' The sailors shouting and waving in Quarantine Bay were lost to view as he slid down the dune and waited on the shore of Seal Bay where the Yellow Rock river meandered into the waves, his thumbs hooked in his belt pushing back his stylish coat to reveal his pistols. Simeon stood to one side of him and slightly behind, a blunderbuss clasped across his chest. The rowboat gave up its struggle to achieve the sailors and allowed itself to be swept around the bluff. Rather than land through the pounding surf the cox'n navigated expertly into the calm waters of the river, grounding the stem in the sand between Jim's feet.

'Welcome,' Jim said, holding out his hand to the grizzled old ruffian who jumped down. They shook hands. Simeon could hear the bones cracking.

'My name is Amasa Delano, sir. I have the honour

146

to command the *Perseverance*, sir, more years than I like to remember out of Boston, Massachusetts.' Indeed an American: the smallest sigh of relief escaped Simeon's lips. 'This is my brother Samuel Delano, captain of the schooner *Pilgrim*. Our last call was Kangaroo Island.' He spat. 'Used to be kangaroo, used to be seal, but no more. We're loaded with more preserving salt from the saltpan there than we found skins for. Looks good here.'

Jim said: 'I am Jim Pride, and this is my island.'

The American shrugged. 'Has the island been leased to you, sir? I had not heard of it.'

'I hold it by force of arms,' Jim said. 'And force of friendship.'

Delano exhaled, examining the blank faces of the dunes and doubtless wondering what enemies they hid. 'Friendship is by far the better way.'

'The businesslike way,' Jim said.

'These are my business,' Delano said, nodding at the seals.

'Difficulties lie in the way of an American in these waters,' Jim said. 'I know how deeply the British sealers resent you – don't they?'

'Some,' admitted Delano. 'Dick Cowper, Murrell and others have taken it into their heads that we have no right to procure seals in these straits, and a long time they've spent trying to drive us out of them.'

'So you Americans – and there must be other captains in these waters? – all have difficulty in obtaining fresh supplies, stores, replacements. . . . for spars lost to storm damage, for example. . . . or a rudder.' They looked at one another mischievously, in complete understanding of each other. 'Walk with me alone together, sir.' Jim put his arm around the Bostonian's shoulders and they strolled by the river. 'I think we friends should do business together, not be competitors. The seals are yours, you know your trade.'

'We don't use lubras; my men are expert with lances, quick and clean.'

Jim said: 'How many kangaroo skins buy me a horse? – or a grindstone?'

'Keep talking,' Delano said.

Jim took him to the top of a dune and pointed across the treetops to the shaggy-headed pines. 'The finest shipbuilding timber in the world.'

'I never heard they were to be found so far north.' Delano shook his head in wonder. 'Yes, I need a new rudder, and new gudgeons too, and the *Pilgrim*'s started half her timbers through the nail-heads. We could careen her. . . .'

'Let's make a deal,' Jim said. 'I have a river to float logs down, I can offer you the services of a skilled carpenter. I can get you sweet spring water, not this brackish stuff. I'll sell you smoked abalone, trumpeter, live crays, fresh fruit against scurvy. Everything you need. In time I may even be able to supply you with fresh beef.' Simeon watched them talking, and heard Jim go on: 'And there are a few things I need in return. . . .' After much haggling the two men clasped hands, and Simeon carefully relaxed his thumb from the cocked hammer of the blunderbuss.

15

1808–1810

Winter's child

On this foundation Jim built his new world. From now on, Annie knew, pushing her knuckles into the small of her back with a sigh, life would be hard but not impossible. Forbidden to build boats more than fourteen feet long in the straits, the Americans had good reason to keep their island haven secret, and Dawes the carpenter was kept busy. As the seals deserted the beaches, he built light double-ended sealing craft for two or three men, still showing the marks of the tomahawk that chopped the tree. And Amasa Delano, returning with a full cargo to Boston via New Zealand, with his crew of sixty between the two ships reduced by mutiny, disease and natural wastage to a number hardly sufficient to man the rigging, was doubtless surprised on clearing King Island to find seventeen stowaways bound and gagged under the *Perseverance*'s foc'sle, good seamen all, though with sand between their toes and smelling strongly of smoked fish.

Annie gave birth to her baby on a still and perfect midwinter day, her cries echoing down the valley denuded of trees where the men worked with their saws. They looked up then calmly continued with their own labour. Mary Roper had come up from Pass River partly to be with Annie during her time, partly because her delicate features were bruised black and blue. She was defiant. Annie had demanded, outraged: 'Did George Tatham do that?'

149

'George doesn't care enough about me to lay a finger on me,' Mary said bitterly. 'It was Becky Donahoo caught me.' There were older bruises on her body too.

'You're not still going on and on for Feargal O'Henry,' Annie said. 'He's Becky's. You are a fool. Get that Irishman out of your mind.'

'I can't help myself, Annie. Everything I do I think of him. George is a kind man but Feargal is a man. I don't understand myself, I just love him.'

'You be careful of Becky,' Annie warned her.

'She doesn't love him, she just uses him.'

'Perhaps he likes to be used.'

'Sure and he does! I don't say he's perfect, Annie. Just that I love him.' She smiled, as though that explained everything.

'You're obsessed,' Annie said. Her baby boy was born the next day while the men worked. When Jim came in the women were still trying to get the baby to take Annie's milk, but the lad refused the nipple away every time. Jim surveyed the scene. 'That didn't take you long,' he told Annie with a nod of approval. 'It's as though you've done it before.' When Annie didn't reply he held out his hands for his son. 'Come on Johnny, take your milk!' The baby's mouth closed round the tip of his little finger and sucked fruitlessly. 'That's better,' Jim said, 'he's going to be strong.' He listened as the saws stopped and they heard the creak of sundering timber. 'Got to go,' he said, relinquishing the baby into Mary's arms, leaving the two women struggling to get the lad on Annie's breast.

That quiet evening of the day his firstborn son arrived in the world Jim climbed the last Huon to the topmost branches. The soles of his bare feet and hands had smoothed the wood almost to a polish up there. The captain of the American ship *Charles*, arriving under jury rig after being dismasted, had offered him

150

a fortune beyond measure for this tree; free passage to Boston, and from thence home. Home.

Home to England, and to Eve.

Jim stared at the red antipodean sun dipping towards the horizon, the dark purple bar of the southern ocean shimmering beneath it with red highlights. The same sun was rising over the rooftops of London on the other side of the world, midsummer's day. Here was midwinter: he tried to remember Eve and could not – she looked like Annie, and yet not. . . . He remembered the transforming sparkle in Eve's eyes, all felt in his heart, not in his brain: no picture now accompanied his aching loss. Eve believed James Prideau dead, and he was.

She had married. He was certain of it, feeling the knowledge as surely as he felt her in his heart. Whose arms held her? The arms of William Prideau. An outcast in an outcast land, Jim could never go home. He might meet the man he might have been.

'Please, God,' he whispered, 'let her be happy.'

On his third return to King Island the captain of the *Charles* said that in less than half a dozen years of sealing in the Bass Strait more than a hundred thousand skins had been sent through Sydney Heads, more to China and Massachusetts. The industry was doomed through extinction. Seal Bay was now white sand and black kelp, and a few penguins. Carrying his son, Jim walked the dunes in the silence.

'You see that grass, Johnny? Pussytail. There are never frosts at Yellow Rock, the grass grows all year round, which is why the other farmers winter some of their cattle here.' The boy stared incuriously. 'There are wild cats living here,' Jim said. 'I think they come from shipwrecks, don't you? This is the worst coast in the world for shipwrecks, that's why the captains steer clear unless they have to.' He knew Johnny was too

151

young to understand what he was saying but it was important to say it. 'I remember when all this was covered with seal, Johnny. . . .' He climbed a dune and put the toddler down, pointing across the flatlands of reedy flats on the north-east of the island, illuminated with tiny patches of brilliantly green lucerne by Peter Corduroy's shack. The cattle grazing the dunes were looking even scrawnier this year. 'If we keep them inland,' Jim said, 'they get milk fever. But if we keep them near the shore, they get coasty and die. I think if we move them regularly they'll get better.'

Johnny pointed excitedly: a band of smoke hung above the dense treetops about three miles south. O'Henry was burning into the Bungaree flatlands. Grass had to be burned off in January or February every year once the cattle had fattened. Even so it grew poorly, and by the third year had to be fertilised. O'Henry's great discovery had been the Bungaree lime sand, a far better fertiliser than kelp, but there was the backbreaking difficulty of transporting it, so Jim bartered a bullock team in return for a share of lime. Now O'Henry's broad shoulders and almost equally broad white smile, waving his sassafras whip in greeting from his laden bullock cart, were a familiar sight at Yellow Rock. Simeon went into business with O'Henry, but it was a far cry from the days of the Cabriolet Service; the forests had to be burned off and the tea-tree scrub rolled flat with tree trunks to make a track, but then the bracken fern sprang through fifteen feet high, and fallen logs a hundred feet long and ten feet in diameter were always blocking the way – and the traders' bullocks were recalcitrant creatures always tipping the cart or the bullocky into a bog-hole, taking more than a week to get across the island from Bungaree to Preston. . . . Jim realised that Johnny wasn't listening to him: he was watching the kangaroos.

'Catch bad roo,' Johnny said, knowing his father's

feelings about the destructive animals always breaking into the paddocks. They were valuable for their skins, and Jim checked out the snares. They weren't made of wire, which slipped. White hemp rope was best, brown hemp not quite so good. Johnny was very interested in the snare – anything mechanical fascinated him. Then he tripped and rolled to the bottom of the slope. 'You're naturally clumsy,' Jim sighed tolerantly, and as soon as he said it realised it was true. For the first time, in this merciless world, an old school-saying passed across his mind: Queen Elizabeth of England wishing her commanders well in their enterprises abroad with the words *Be brave, be wise, be fortunate*. Of these the attribute of good fortune was the most important, and some men had it, and some didn't.

Of course it was wrong to seriously accuse a twenty-seven-month old child of anything, least of all clumsiness. At that age nothing was set, nothing could be beyond change. Nevertheless, Jim could not afford tolerance.

They went back to where their American horse waited, grazing. Jim swung into the broad American saddle with its tall pommel, and rode holding his little boy in front of him, not at all preserving him from the bumps, to learn the feel of the horse's motion.

'Sit up straight!' he said.

Johnny was Annie's boy. Such a thought was desperately unfair, but nevertheless, riding home with the little stranger in front of him, that was the thought Jim could not escape.

Annie's eyes softened as they rode up. She was happier than she had ever even dreamed of being. Her life as a London whore belonged to another person, and indeed she now disapproved of the men who, like her old friend Simeon, took up with one of the lubras left by the sealers. The skinny girl had matted hair and no sense of property, she was a little thief. In Annie's view the aboriginal word *lubra* covered a multitude of sins. 'You don't love her,' she told Simeon, 'she's just a concubine.'

'Anything's better than being alone,' Simeon said. He'd brought Wayanna from Amos Preston for a pound of tobacco. Annie had come over rather righteous since becoming a mother, but he was amused rather than angry at her sticking her nose in his business. Annie of course wanted to marry Jim but he never would. She hardly thought of it. She believed in love, which was why she disapproved of him and not of Mary Roper, old George Tatham's woman, who had now proudly produced a daughter of her own, Selina, weighing eleven pounds at birth, the longest baby Annie had ever seen. Selina would be a tall girl, she already had her father's wide smile and sunny, casual nature. She was O'Henry's of course. Becky Donahoo had exhausted her threats and Mary had got what she wanted. Becky, busy with two sons of her own each of them as much of a handful as their father, decided to compromise. If Mary promised never to encourage Feargal again that was the end of the matter. Mary, with her obsession now concentrated at least for the moment on Feargal's daughter, agreed.

Annie held the horse's bridle while Jim dismounted.

'He's too young to ride like that,' she said.

Jim glanced at her.

'He is,' she said gently. 'Why are you so hard on Johnny?'

'Don't love him too much, Annie. You'll make him soft.'

Annie knew that was true, but she got her revenge in bed that night. In the moment of exhaustion, moulded and exploited by her expert caresses, his spirit transferred to her and his body defeated, was when Jim was most vulnerable. She stroked his face fondly.

154

'I've got a secret,' she whispered.

'Oh no,' he murmured, sitting upright. 'Not another one! Annie?'

'A summer baby.' She kissed his rib. 'Maybe a girl this time.'

16

1811–1822

Summer's child

But he was a boy. Bob was born in the summer of 1811 in the midst of a gale lashing the island, so that Annie always remembered the contrast between the calm weather of Johnny's arrival with the sound of the wind roaring over the top of the outcrop, shaking the roof, setting the tall Huon down by the now unsheltered lagoon swaying regally from side to side – she could see its slow progress forward and back again through the window. He was a more difficult birth; she yelled and swore he was stuck, but as she grew tired all Annie's attention concentrated on the rhythm of the swaying tree. By the time the tree stopped she would have her baby, she told herself over and over. As the storm eased, with a roar Annie brought her baby into the world. He gazed up calmly at her and smiled, though Mary said it was just wind. But Annie held him close to her and never forgot her child had been born with a smile.

For this reason, although she never showed her feelings, unaware of her small displays of tenderness towards him, Bob was a touch special to her in a way Johnny was not. This wasn't Johnny's fault, though of course he thought it was.

Being older, Johnny was soon helping his father about the place, doing the endless fencing, setting snares and learning to salt skins for sale to the American whaling captains who still occasionally called. By the time he was seven years old Johnny was as lean as a hard-worked boy of ten, obedient and never happier than when his father straightened his back with a groan and winced up at the midday sun flickering through the roof of leaves, wiped the sweat from his brow, then smiled and sat down against a toppled tree for a smoke. 'Get the billy on, Johnny,' he'd say, and Johnny would light the fire and settle down against the tree with exactly the same groan as his father. That made Jim laugh, and Johnny laughed too. He never felt so at ease with his mother who ordered him about like a child and made him do girl's work. Bob was happy to do it, Johnny sulked: but Bob was only a baby of course.

Johnny loved the burning better than anything, watching the line of relatively cool flames sweeping away from them across the grassland, but setting off the dried matting of felled tea-tree scrub was another matter altogether. His father would sniff the wind carefully and decide it was safe, then they rode out with firesticks, dropping them as they went along. Those broad bands of hot fire rippling into the night made a fine sight. By dawn the fire would have burned out to the shore leaving a broad trail of ash, hundreds of acres of new land to be seeded and flourish overnight with the first rain.

Even so the thousands of square miles of virgin forest dwarfed any indication of human habitation, and no sign at all showed from the sea except the smoke of an occasional campfire.

Annie could neither read nor write so as the years passed Jim taught the boys. Johnny hated these classes even after Annie joined in. His father seemed to turn into another person and the work was almost impossible. What made it worse was that Bob could pick it up effortlessly, becoming garrulous in his fascinated delight in words. Johnny knew the important things: he knew how to tie a snare knot, how to fell a tall tree

157

from a springboard, how to steam cajaput oil from tea-tree leaves, he knew how to salt a seal's tongue, and he loved the excitement of the kill. He was a practical boy and he didn't pick up learning easily like Bob, and often when Jim shut them in the skillion at the back of the house to get on with the bookwork he had set them, Johnny cribbed from his facile little brother, menacing him so that Bob was too frightened to tell. Annie saw it one November day and told, and Jim beat both boys, Johnny for doing it and Bob for not standing up to him.

The family ate enormous meals. That night it was kangaroo steak casserole with the last of the winter's carrots and fried soda dumplings, since they had no yeast, and the boys ate standing up.

'You were too hard on Bob,' Annie had told Jim earlier.

'There's more to life than learning.'

'But he took it harder!' Annie said, and Jim looked angry.

'We won't talk about this any more,' he ordered her.

But as the boys were wiping the last of the gravy off their plates with the soft insides of the dumplings, Jim said with a kindly gleam in his eye: 'Well, boys, what would you like to do most for a treat?'

'I want to see the birds,' Bob said at once.

He didn't mean the cormorants, or the pardalote with its forty spots to count, the eastern spinebills, or the pheasant escaped from the *Paragon* that had now multiplied to thousands. Bob knew that on the twenty-fifth of November without fail the flocks of muttonbirds, having bred ashore in September and October, would return to King Island to lay. So Jim took the boys, Bob riding on his shoulders, into the dunes at the north end of Seal Bay, and they hid on the headland at Cape Farewell. Each bird would return to exactly the same spot as last year in the rookery around them.

The sea-horizon seemed to move upwards, then streams of birds flew out of the sunset, their numbers obscuring the sun and making it dark, skimming the sea with wingtips touching as Bob gazed, enthralled. He could not have passed his dinner-plate between the birds and the water. Johnny watched, then practised knots in a piece of old string. The evening filled with an orchestral thrumming and yowling as the birds, tens of millions of them, swirled towards the New Year islands in clouds, then many more arrived like a crescendo into the burrows around the boys and not until night fell was it silent.

'Not bad!' Bob told his mother when she asked him, 'not bad at all.'

'Your clothes smell bad,' Annie said, holding out her hand in demand.

'Aw, ma,' Bob said, but gave them up, and hopped shivering from one foot to the other while she dunked them in the copper and Johnny sniggered. 'You too,' Annie said, then pointed the tongs at Jim, 'and you.' She wouldn't let the boys run around naked but made them wear nightshirts and show their hands were clean before she put them snugly to bed behind a curtain.

Their mother was a proud woman and the hut she called Paragon House, though now rather rickety from the unrelenting weather and the rough attentions of her boys, was full of homely details: the rugs Annie had hung round the walls to keep out the draughts she'd by now persuaded herself were for decoration, and what remained of the Staffordshire dinner set was much too valuable to be used, kept on show in a crate turned on its side to look like a sideboard, and they ate off rusty iron plates. Jim had offered to turn her new ones out of celery-top pine, which took a good polish, but she wouldn't give up her old plates because they came from the ship, and not many people had them any more. Most of the islanders made do with wooden platters, but Annie's enamelled iron plates were from Home and their rarity conferred class; the Staffordshire enshrined, in her view, the Pride family as the island's aristocracy. Since George Tatham died Mary Roper let her tall daughter Selina run wild and unwashed as a savage, as uncivilised and uneducated as Simeon's lubra Wayenna. But Annie would never let her children go out dirty. Even though no one would see them, *she* would know.

Annie forgot she had ever been a city girl, for the wilderness had many compensations – King's Island's natural beauty even when it was cruellest could not fail to touch her; the discipline the surf-bounded island enforced on their lives, the sense of fulfilment from their natural existence that she gained and the primitive satisfactions with Jim after a day of exhausting toil. At last she was getting her way with him, Annie told herself; getting him to love her for herself. And when one night his lips whispered another name, *Eve*, in his sleep, Annie pretended nothing had happened.

Strangely, no more children came along. Two, she told herself with a sigh, were quite enough. At first after Johnny was born Annie had told herself life would be easier when, oh, when he'd learned to crawl, to walk, or control his bowels, but then he was into everything and she worried about snakes, and each stage seemed to make more trouble, and then Bob came along and she had to go through the same stages again with him, plus stop fights.

But now she realised sadly how fast they were growing up, before she had known enough of them as children.

Johnny was an adolescent, Bob was the emotional one; Annie knew he loved his home, and her, deeply. Her son was her best friend, but there were vast gaps in his knowledge she could never fill: it would have been entirely impossible for him to have imagined

London, the life and power of the place, and she never spoke of it.

In the end there was so much she never spoke of; nearly everything; in a timeless land only the present could be lived in.

'What's the matter, mum?' Bob asked kindly, touching her elbow.

'Nothing,' Annie wept, 'nothing and everything.' Bob stood tall and gangly, watching her with bright eyes. She wished he wasn't so gentle; it wouldn't do. 'Go on!' she said, 'go away, get on with your mutton-birding with those savages.'

'They aren't called muttonbirds,' Bob said angrily. 'They don't even taste of mutton, and the aborigines call them yowlers.' *Yollas* in fact, he knew, but his mother hated savages for their submissiveness of manner, their flagrant nudity and willingness to make love in public, and he didn't want to infuriate her unnecessarily. He knew she was just trying to protect him from sex, but of course he and Johnny already knew it all. From the trees they'd watched Simeon and Wayenna sitting by their campfire with her legs around him, as naturally as two people having a conversation. 'Cor,' Johnny had whispered, 'look at them go.' But Bob, by the flickering firelight, had seen only the tenderness in Wayanna's dark eyes.

'*Yollas*,' Annie sneered.

Bob said furiously: 'The aborigines call them that because of the sound their wings make in the wind, and their calls.' He stormed out angrily and Annie called after him. 'Bob. . . .'

He swung up onto horseback, then his face softened and he took the swag she offered. 'There's sassafras bark in it for tea,' she said, 'and there's biscuit, and a big piece of cheese. Leave some for Johnny.' She didn't try to kiss him. Bob nodded and touched the brim of his hat just like his father did.

161

He rode north scattering the herd of Paragon cattle in front of him, proud that it was these cows, not Annie's Staffordshire dinner set, that made Jim Pride a man of consequence – not wealthy, there was no money on the island – but a man to be treated by other islanders with respect, because he could choose who got the services of the prime bull, the best calves, other such favours. Jim used this power; it was what survival was about, and because of it they probably lived better than anyone.

He paused at the thatched dome of Simeon's gardown hut, decorated with the feathers of cockatoos and currawongs, but he had already set off north with his lubra Wayanna. Avoiding the impenetrable bush Bob rode his horse Right – so called because he was blind in the left eye and always pulled in the direction he could see – across the Yellow Rock River, sending up sheets of spray just for the joy of it, then cantered along the broad featureless beach to Cape Farewell.

It was the end of March and the yolla chicks were almost ready to fly: this year of 1821, as at the start of every other winter, the adult birds that survived the harvesting would keep to their precise schedule and fly away in mid-April, the chicks following a fortnight later. When Bob arrived at the camp he found only the children left amongst the huts. The thirty or so adult birders, the cliff-hanging lubras by far the most skilful among them, and most prepared to risk plunging their hands armpit-deep into burrows where a snake and agonising death might lie in wait instead of a helpless bird, were already hard at work. They'd catch at least a hundred and fifty thousand, probably more. Women were returning already with loaded spits of forty or fifty birds, dumping them for the children to start work on. Johnny had got himself out with the adults. Bob helped squeeze the gurry from the stomachs of the dead birds into barrels, ready to skim the valuable oil off the top come evening. After scalding in boiling coppers, the feathers except from the wings were easily removed, and after gutting the whole birds were boiled in try-pots to remove the thick layer of fat, then laid up in racks for smoking and salting. Now that the seals and the sea elephants were gone, when the next ship called bound for Boston the thousand gallons of oil, several tons of feathers and hundreds of pounds of fat would go to grease the wheels of American industry.

But few ships called nowadays.

One of the girls slipped on the grease and Bob reached out to save her. Knocking into a boiling copper, he gave a cry of pain: he had scalded his hand. He bandaged it and tried to carry on but when Jim came back he told Bob to go home, he was no good like that. 'The birds will come back next year,' he said, tousling his boy's hair, knowing how disappointed he was. 'They always do.'

Bob had to walk home; the horse would be needed to pull the laden sand-sledges to the storage huts at Yellow Rock. He thought of the Boston captains as he walked, imagining their ships anchoring in the bay, their voyages like tenuous threads binding the world. As if each ship trailed a long reel of string. He must have been feverish by now because he imagined the world hanging in outer space like a ball of string growing larger and more intricate, the ships winding round and round.

Annie took one look at him and put him straight to bed.

When he woke, she was not there and he was thirsty. He realised it was early in the morning and she must be milking. He drank from the pitcher and wandered outside. The light of dawn was soft yet intense. He found himself down by the Huon, staring up, his good hand resting against the bark. His other hand didn't

163

hurt so much once he'd started climbing. At the top he stared out into the vast silence, the empty ocean.

He came down and as soon as his feet touched the ground Annie grabbed his shoulder. 'Don't ever tell your father you've been up there, and don't you ever go up there again.'

Bob didn't know how to explain what he had felt.

'Mum,' he said, 'is it a holy place like a church?'

Bob had never seen a church. 'It's a place where an exile remembers his old life,' Annie said. Then her tongue added before she could stop it: 'And love.' It was true: Jim did still love Eve and he was thirty-three years old and could pass for forty, and he would love her until he died, and then it would be Eve he chose to be with him in heaven, not Annie.

Bob watched her then hugged her, allowing himself to be vulnerable, to show love, in a way few boys his age on the island would.

'Oh, my child,' Annie said softly, 'you are growing up so quickly.'

17

1822

A house divided

Growing light eroded the darkness from the features of
James Prideau. Eve lay watching the first faint outline
of her husband's forehead appear and brighten, gleaming in reflection of the tall bedroom window. The maid
had omitted to draw the curtains last night and the top
panes already held the cloudless sky, pale and boiling,
glaring above the smoking rooftops of London. Another
blazing hot day.

Eve lay with his hand on her thigh, floating between
sleep and waking. The man she truly loved slept on
the sea bed, lost with the *Paragon* a lifetime ago. The
real James Prideau lay with pearls growing in his
mouth, his bones fabulous with rainbow coral in shaf-
ted caverns of golden sunlight: living for ever in her
heart. She cradled him.

Then winced against full daylight, awake.

The sun slanting through the smoke dug deep
shadows across the lines of William Prideau's face. Her
heart softened: how human he was, in sleep revealing
how much he genuinely needed her; a weakness he
would never admit in his waking hours. After the opera
last night he had come to her bed without so much as
a knock on the door or a murmured endearment. A
husband could not keep telling his wife *I love you;* treating her like a lovesick suitor. The cheap theatre of
such displays was improper for their class; mindless

gratification was for the common people, not for the middle class such as they, the backbone of England.

William loved her. She had everything to be happy for.

For her, at her command, anything: all she had to do was say it. He lived through her, her interests became his. He knew she loved opera so last night he had taken her to Covent Garden for the Drury Lane opening of Bishop's opera *No Man is an Hero to His Wife* adapted from the Restoration play, Madame Vestris playing the Wife, in modern dress of course, her wonderful voice soaring above the babble of the audience that filled the stacked layers of the auditorium. The prices were stunning – three and sixpence even for the pit. In the break in the singing Donaldson, the Bow Street runner, waved his gilt-crowned baton and made his cry: 'Take care of your pockets, gentlemen!' and everyone patted their valuables to check they were still there. 'Just tells the pickpockets where to work,' grumbled William. When Eve applauded the encore, William nodded at the singers prancing on the bare stage; then, as the red velvet curtain came swinging down, he opined: 'Well done, well done.'

'She is magnificent!' Eve said radiantly.

'Magnificent,' William said, pushing a way to the steps past the coffee room, then looked back noticing the sudden stillness in her profile. 'What is it?' he asked, but could not follow her gaze through the crowd, the eddying oilsmoke from the lighting. The building must discharge more than three thousand people, and the entranceways were solid with the rush from the pit-lobbies. But he followed Eve's gaze to someone near them on the grand staircase and thought he glimpsed a white head bobbing out of sight between the shoulders of the throng. Frowning, he stood on tiptoe peering through the fug. 'Who was it?'

'Don't make a scene,' Eve said, taking his arm. 'No one. Let's go home!'

William kept up appearances even in bed. He wore a linen nightshirt and bedsocks she had bought to make him laugh, but he faithfully wore them. And during the daytime he called her Mrs Prideau, or my dear, or my good woman in case the servants overheard more familiar talk and lost respect for the gulf of manners, accent, money and position that now sundered them from their superiors. The threat of Napoleon Bonaparte no longer bound the nation with common purpose and the fraying social fabric – the country was going to the dogs – was held together by only the class system and a million such men as William Prideau, that tenth of the population with their noses above the property line, who would properly dismiss a girl for forgetting to pull the curtains. Standards were there to be maintained. Standards: these new men made them their own. William would give a penny to a starving sailor, providing the man was neatly turned out and tugged his forelock respectfully. But behind this cold, righteous shell he loved Eve more than life itself, and was watching her in bed secretly through his almost-closed eyelids. She could see his eyes glinting.

Whatever happens in childhood lasts forever. Eve didn't want to be loved, she wanted to feel love. William had not the faintest idea what she felt; he desired her appearance, her feminine gloss: her clothes, her face, her hair or eyes, not aware of the real woman. She couldn't tell him what *she* really felt, explain her bitterness when he was most loving, her retreat when he was most passionate, making her the guilty one. Because she *was* guilty, remembering the distorted face – almost William's face – of her lover above the ship's railing, his splayed arms, the fluttering sheet of paper, and the ship sailing away never to be seen again. The boatman had hooked James's letter from the water and she remembered holding it in her hands, the illegible shreds leaking between her fingers, and how in her grief she had thrown herself into William's arms.

Her heart was dry as dust. She felt sorry for William.

His hand stroked her thigh, pretending to be asleep. She swung her legs quickly over the side of the bed. He sat up too. 'You woke me,' he grumbled. 'Who left those curtains open? You are too casual with your girl, my dear.'

'Oh, what does it matter!' she cried.

Seven months and fifteen years ago he had come as a young man to The Polygon to show her the report in the *Times* newspaper. *Lost with all hands:* William had always been there when bad news was around, reliable and dependable.

'Eve, my brother is dead.' This time he simply held out his arms and let her run to him.

But then something in him had broken and as she held him while he cried, his head to her bosom, she realised the simple truth. William wasn't crying for his brother. She and James had been so obsessed with their own selfish love she had missed the truth: William had loved her all the time.

'You cannot!' she had told him, offended. 'It is *wrong*—'

'I love you.' He looked into her eyes. 'I love you, what can be wrong with that?' She stared at him doubtfully. 'Have you ever caught me in a lie?' he whispered. 'I'd do *anything* for you. Eve, marry me.'

She gasped: 'No!'

'I see.' He had learned a lawyer's tongue and knew how to use words as weapons. 'You prefer to remain in love with the memory of a criminal!'

'Yes! No – I don't know!' She glanced upstairs, fearful that their raised voices would disturb Aunt Sarah in her sickbed.

'In that case,' William said, 'I accept your verdict,'

168

and stormed out. She followed him into the street and called his name.

'I can do nothing more to help you,' William smiled, 'if you will not let me.'

When Aunt Sarah died, the creditors moved in, and Eve married William Prideau.

That had been a boiling summer's morning too, the interior of St Andrew Undershaft striking blessedly cool as they filed off Leadenhall Street followed by William's City friends, inevitably led by Versucchi father and son. Eve stood numbly while the voices whispered around her. The sun glared through the various faces of kings and queens of Britain in the east window, blinding her, the shrill piping of the Harris organ deafened her. She was married alone. The tears trickled down her face.

As they came out into the sudden heat, she saw her father. She stopped. No rumour escaped Sam Summers and he stood in the roadway like a puffed-up, ragamuffin little robin in scarecrow clothes, his shadow beside him, a smile on his lips and loss in his eyes. William interposed himself fiercely. 'Go away!'

'Eve?' Sam Summers said.

'She doesn't want to see you!' William said.

Sam walked away with all the dignity he could muster and she watched him until he was gone. Then William laughed, and the fiddler struck up a merry tune. Yes, William was right, she had not wanted to be reconciled with her father. . . . and yet her feelings were confused and so she clung to William. William has always been right in those days.

William's business prospered, and she fell pregnant. The increasing burden of company law handled by Trewarren & Prideau kept him from their comfortable house in once-fashionable Mayfair. They were not rich in those early days but they were certainly no longer poor since William had secured the partnership, and she was attended by a doctor in her confinement. William was working late at the Middle Temple; he was sent for. The doctor took Eve's pulse but did not even lift her skirts to examine her, smiling calmly and drinking porter while she groaned and writhed. The wretched dull-faced woman who was attending wouldn't touch the blood that soaked the sheets, then when Eve was almost exhausted the baby was at last born, a perfect boy: this was John, the name William desired, his father's name.

Still the placenta did not appear, and the contractions began again. 'She's got another one in there!' the dull-faced woman said in an outraged voice, but it was very quick this time. 'Have I another little son?' Eve gasped, 'is he another little boy like his twin brother?' There was a silence.

She heard Doctor Commyns speak in a low voice, his lips almost touching her ear. 'What religion have you?'

Eve murmured automatically, thinking of being married to William: 'Why, Church of England of course. Why do you want to know?'

She heard him telling the woman, 'Better fetch the Church of England pastor.'

'What's wrong?' she begged.

'Nothing's wrong,' said the doctor, sounding just like William.

'Let me see!'

'Prepare yourself.' He laid the little girl against Eve's face. She was very tiny, hardly larger than Eve's hand. 'Oh, she's beautiful,' Eve said.

The doctor looked away.

'I'll call her Eve, my name, then she'll live, won't she? Oh isn't she lovely?'

'Calm yourself, madam. There is nothing you can do.'

'She won't die,' Eve said. 'Help me sit up.'

'There's no point in distressing yourself.'

'Help me up!' But he didn't move. Groaning, Eve pushed herself up in the pillows. She looked down at the little naked body cradled in her gigantic arms: a tiny animal blue as a bruise but fighting valiantly for life, eyes wide, the effort to breathe rocking it like passion. And then it stopped.

'That's all,' the doctor said, buttoning his coat.

'She's alive,' Eve said. 'She's alive.'

William arrived taking his hat off behind the Anglican clergyman, then pushed past the mumbling cleric.

'Thank God!' he said, laying his hand on the squalling, healthy boy in the nurse's arms, 'I have a son!'

Those were words that echoed down the years and Eve remembered them as though they had just been spoken: the moment that revealed her husband as a stranger. *Yes, but look what died.* She would never understand him.

Eve threw herself into caring for her baby. But he was William's son, and a nanny was engaged. John was sent away to school and Eve was happy because it was all for the best. 'You'll soften him,' William said: she remembered him saying that, and she was sure he was right. Everything they did was in their boy's best interest. He was a fine boy.

And Eve thought she was happy.

'What have I done?' William said. They sat on opposite sides of the bed. 'You employ these moods against me too extensively.' His voice was calm and she knew he was very angry.

She said tenderly: 'I remember you last night.'

He patted the hand she laid on his shoulder, and rang for the servant.

They were growing old. No, that was not the word. She was unhappier than she could ever have imagined.

171

'Dear,' she said, shattering William's calm, 'last night I saw my father at the opera.'

Poetic types, who never rose early enough to go out in them, wrote of the beauty of London's smokeless dawn. Idiots, William grumbled to himself. He blamed Wordsworth, who saw nature everywhere. London always smoked. The hot dawn was acrid of the smell of fumes, and William walked his smooth walk, following his stick. He was bothered.

William Prideau believed in human progress. He no longer spoke with a Devon accent, dialects were for servants, he had mastered clean, educated Oxford vowels. William believed his son would live in a better world, that tomorrow was as important as today. Work was rewarded, solid respectability a hard-won prize. The reappearance of Sam Summers, feckless and extravagant, bothered him more than he could say.

The blood of the woman he loved flowed in his son's veins. But that meant the blood of Sam Summers flowed there too, a latent infection that might bloom into a disease. William was stiff with the boy for his own good, and John took to it well – so far as anyone could tell of a lad of fourteen, but William understood him well enough. William was closer to John than anyone, though he only saw him a few weeks of the year. *A man of substance* – that would be a fine epitaph for the boy to live up to. 'The day you join Trewarren & Prideau,' William had promised, 'that very day, the name of the enterprise shall be changed to Prideau & Prideau.'

But John did not say thank you as he had expected: he was as self-controlled as William himself. John said: 'Who was Mr Trewarren, Papa?' and William respected him all the more for cutting to the point of the matter.

'An old man who died,' William said.

Remembering this talk, he swung his silver-topped cane pleasurably – it was his sole luxury – as he walked to work in the morning sunlight, already sticky-hot, through Covent Garden market. He wore good, plain clothes and an expressionless face. His feelings had soured again: *Last night she saw her father at the opera.* He had been so sure that Sam Summers was all in her past. Damn him! The eyes of that man had always seemed so wise to secrets – so knowing that they made William feel guilty. Where did that scarecrow get the money for a box at the opera? Half a guinea if a penny! Summers was an evil man; William was convinced of it.

The smell of vegetables rotting in the heat wafted across the piazza, mingling with the delicious odour of roasting beans from the shanty coffee-houses, and the rear colonnade of the Covent Garden Theatre, at present in Chancery to the great benefit of lawyers, threw back the shouts of the swarming vegetable-hawkers. Porters weaved daintily between the booths, carrying swaying towers of baskets, ten or twelve at a time, piled on their ugly heads. William snorted: he disliked this chaotic scene intensely – he nearly tripped over an urchin gazing in wonder at a pineapple, doubtlessly planning its theft – there was talk of a new Act of Parliament to regulate the market into a large single building, and of erecting a new police court. Crime in London was a scandal, it was hardly safe to walk the streets. A girl of about six tottered alongside him under a tray of watercress and he increased the length of his stride until he left her behind in the wretchedness of Bow Street. A dozen offers were called to him from front parlours for a shave or a plate of fine red herring, while whores, only the ugliest working so early, yawned in the doorways and complained to him about the heat.

Passing the confusion of drays wedged as usual across the narrow passageway of Temple Bar, William's footsteps echoed beneath the gate house as he entered the peace of Middle Temple Lane, the nest of lawyers. He touched the brim of his brushed-beaverskin hat with his stick, acknowledging everyone he knew by sight with varying degrees of warm servility or cool aloofness, depending on whether they were above him or below. Then he entered the doorway of 2 Brick Court, and his demeanour changed: here his power was absolute.

The clerks scribbled busily, not daring to look up from their desks. There were more downstairs, rows of scratching quills and bent heads: the sight of money being made. The Head Clerk, Mr Verty, bowed – once they had all stood up and bowed, interrupting work, wasting time, spilling ink – but now only Verty, a man William would once have regarded as a god, respectfully made himself available for instructions.

'Good morning, Mr Prideau.' William glanced at him severely: Verty had brown hair arranged in curls across his forehead and William suspected him of French blood. He was efficient but excitable.

'Good day.' Verty was a small man and William surveyed the busy scene over the top of his head. This was an *office*, a factory whose product was words – and, increasingly, numbers. Quietly, as a natural development after a chance meeting with a Captain Lansdowne of the 1st Foot Guards, and a crafty piece of work by Mr Gumboge over a disputed will, the law firm of Trewarren & Prideau now handled regimental business as Regimental Agents, negotiating contracts, holding money, authorising payments. The 1st Foot was a prestigious regiment and others had followed. These days the law business was confined to the basement, and all the ground floor was given over to regimental and banking accounts. It was profitable, but officers were always in debt, and financing their increasing numbers as the business expanded meant it was not all jam today; it was always jam tomorrow. Every penny of profit invested in expansion. Invested in the future. In his son.

'That man looks half asleep!'

'Higgins, sir. His baby girl–'

'Can the man not speak for himself, Mr Verty?'

'She wouldn't sleep,' Higgins said, standing. 'She cried all night and I was worried, sir.'

'She cried and you worried. Is that all?' William's tone rose. 'I *lost* my daughter, Higgins.'

'I'm sorry, sir. My lapse won't happen again, sir.' With the peacetime economic situation it was very hard for them to find work.

'I should watch your work very carefully today, Higgins.' William gave Mr Verty a cold look on his way to the stairs, blaming him too. It never paid to be happy with anyone.

'His wife died,' a young clerk called Wray dared protest.

'Oh!' William said, 'that excuses *everything*,' and Wray went quite pale. William went upstairs feeling angry. Wray was Gumboge's pet.

'Mr Gumboge!' he called. 'You'll oblige me!'

A shadow rose from the desk silhouetted against the bright windowpanes. Gumboge, vast and astounding with the odour of sweat, had half-drawn the curtains against the heat. The gap showed a bleached view of the Pitt bridge, now renamed Blackfriars, the open sewer of the Thames running through its central spans glowing false blue in reflection of the sky.

'Yes, Mr Prideau?'

'It's dark in here,' William said, forcing himself to be calm. The essential Gumboge knew his work far too well to be given orders; William made comments, Gumboge offered suggestions. He was worth his mighty weight in gold, was paid almost as much as William, and had somehow acquired a dwelling north of the

175

river more commodious than William's. But Gumboge would never be a partner: obviously he was still fiddling the books – William had by now persuaded himself that he always had. Gumboge was cunning but soft, lazily devoted to his grown-up family, their marriages and grandchildren; he had a life outside the firm. William worked so hard his life was hardly his own, his virility locked to his business.

Gumboge had been eating an apple out of his handkerchief to preserve the documents he was reading from stains. Now he took the apple in his long, flexible fingers and placed it on the desk, then folded his handkerchief neatly in his top pocket. While William fidgeted impatiently he pulled the curtains in one smooth sweep.

'I wish discreet enquiries to be made concerning the whereabouts of a certain Samuel Summers,' William said in a rush.

Gumboge turned, revealing his gross features, pocked after a bout of smallpox, to the illumination. 'Summers? This would be Mrs Prideau's father, sir?'

William faltered, unaware that Gumboge had known. He must be more reserved in future. Gumboge loved gossip.

'He was well known in the City before his retirement,' William said importantly.

'Hard times are the fault of no man, sir,' said Gumboge obsequiously.

William flushed. 'I saw him at the opera last night.'

Gumboge followed William through to his spartan room, a classical painting above the fireplace but otherwise cold, stripped-back and manly: dark wood and simple furniture, and not much of it. Gumboge, with his fondness for Persian carpet and Italian ornaments, was less at ease here.

'Go on,' William said.

'Yesterday I was speaking to the elder Mr Versucchi,

who wishes to raise more capital incidentally, and apparently Mr Summers has reappeared in the City, much changed. He asked after his daughter, sir.'

'He has no right!' William's face was pale.

'He mentioned the possibility of seeing Mrs Prideau.' William's mind worked busily: Summers would be sixty years old, perhaps a little more. Men who lived to sixty lived often until eighty, and of course he would demand money. There was no end to the lies he could tell.

Worse, suppose there was a reconciliation between Eve and the old man – then William would lose his sole hold over his wife's affections, obliged to share the woman he loved, and would do anything for, with a man he despised. 'Mrs Prideau would refuse to see him,' William said, but her emotions couldn't be trusted – she was an impetuous woman, she might do the wrong thing. He loved her but he couldn't trust her.

'Where might I find Mr Summers, should I have a mind?'

'Oh, but you have appointments, Mr Prideau.'

'I will deal with all such matters first, naturally.'

Gumboge coughed apologetically. 'I fear, sir, Mr Summers has been seen hawking his wares on the corner of Cornhill and Mansion House Street – a very central location between the Royal Exchange and the Bank of England.'

'Wares?' William was baffled. 'You mean securities?'

Gumboge coughed again. 'Ginger beer, sir.'

All day the thunderheads piled higher in the shimmering sky, and the atmosphere grew closer. A woman fainted in the office waiting room and had to be revived with a glass of porter from the public house. The stench of the river, motionless and appalling at low tide, permeated every niche and interstice. William betrayed no sign of discomfort, drawing strength from the weak-

177

ness of others. But the thought of Sam Summers selling ginger beer in front of the Bank of England nagged at him secretly until by afternoon he could bear it no longer.

He took up his hat and cane, and walked along the diffuse glare of Fleet Street to the City. Thunder rumbled; rain would be a relief. A crowd stood by the steps of the Bank of England. At the centre of it, maestro of a showy cart made up as a ginger-beer fountain, stood Sam Summers dressed in a cheerful gold-braided hat, gold-braided coat, pattering his wares.

'Cool ginger beer, tuppence, thruppence, according to the quality! Soda powders!' Indeed he had a fine baritone, rolling his *r*'s as sonorously as Incledon the ballad-singer, melodious and powerful.

Ginger beer!

William hung back until the mob had eased, then purchased a glass.

'Thank you sir, that's thruppence.' When William kept his fist closed on the coins, Sam Summers looked up with his eyes bright gleams under his silly hat.

William got in first. 'Hallo, Sam.'

'My dear William.' They smiled with mutual dislike. Then Sam took the coins into his hand, sticky with evaporated sugar from the drink. 'Tuppence or thruppence, William,' he confided, 'it's exactly the same. What a game! Only the price is different.' Somebody complaining about the heat bought a fourpenny soda, given the glass to hold while Sam the showman mixed in the acid and alkali powders with a flourish, urging the man that it was most refreshing to drink while effervescing. The man drank, and sneezed. 'Excellent!' he said.

'You've sunk this low,' William said.

'The ginger beer sells better,' Sam laughed. He was happy and William was suspicious. 'My dear Lily makes it up the day before, and very well it's done us this hot weather. A pound of ginger to three gallons of water, a little lemon acid, cloves, yeast, a pound of raw sugar, and there you are. Pure profit. *And* it's half froth.'

William touched the cart with his cane. 'This is how you make your sole living?'

'And a very good living it is! Oh, my boy, I grew so weary of low lodging-houses. I'm a miserable failure and I know it. But look at me.' He swept off his excessive hat: his hair was white but his eyes had lost their pain. 'Do I look unhappy? The support of a good woman. My dear widowed landlady – her late lamented husband was a soldier who gave his life for his country – my dear Mrs Lily Chance of Candlewick Ward! Nowadays it's a proper street of terraced dwellings, and I have a front room and I can almost see down to the river. I owe it all to her.'

'This is pleasant enough – I had not tasted ginger beer before.' William sounded like a nob with his Oxford accent.

'Oh, don't bother with your disapproval,' Sam chuckled.

'You were at the opera last night,' William said.

'You see,' Sam said, looking at the lowering sky, the emptying streets, and starting to pack up his wares, 'I've tried my hand at everything. Getting back into the Exchange. . . . I've starved. I sold peppermint water and lost my shirt, I've blacked boots. I tried selling fried fish pieces but my fellow lodger complained – and fifty pieces take a quart of pale rape oil, and a Billingsgate plaice is a penny, so where's the profit in that? I stank of fish like a fish, and everyone twitted me with using lamp oil, and then a gentleman knocked me over and I lost my stock, but I didn't give up. Now I've finally hit it, I've been doing well. Ginger beer – my salvation! I've made thirty shillings a day clear profit during this drought – nine pounds a week. Now isn't that an irony?'

'You upset my wife,' William said.

'I couldn't resist going, William. I took Lily to the opera for the first time in her life, and the last time in mine. And not to the pit either: our own box, like swells. Seeing Eve was God's gift to me – for a moment we were close enough to touch.' He took up the handles of his cart and pushed it downhill in the direction of the Monument, the urn of brassy flames atop the two-hundred-foot stone column very bright against the massing rainclouds. 'That's the end of the fine weather,' Sam said as they walked. 'I'll sell no more ginger beer. I'm tired, William. I'm tired of you people and I'm not fighting for you any more. I'm a free object. I was locked up in the Marshalsea prison nearly four years for debt and I thought I would die. Lily got me out, God bless her, I've been her lodger. . . . oh, a long time now. Now I've had my stroke of luck. I've saved thirty-five pounds, and I need thirty-five more.' He returned the hired cart to the supplier's yard and walked, wiping the sugar from his hands in the first drops of rain starting to fall.

'Thirty-five pounds. Inevitably you ask for money.' William turned up his collar.

'I'm emigrating to New South Wales.'

William stared at him. They stood in the road with the dust and dried horse-dung turning to dark spatters around them.

'You won't see me again,' Sam said, lifting his lined face up to the rain. The roadway seemed to slide downhill to the silvery river through the haze of rain, the street now brighter than the sky. 'Tomorrow is a better day. I'm going to end my days in honest labour, William, breathing fresh air. I've got ten good years in me, and the Government will help.' He grabbed William's

180

elbow paternally and led him splashing to a sheltered porch.

'You are mad,' William said. Sam, standing on the dubbined step, just grinned. 'They don't want old men like you,' William said.

'This house has done us well,' Sam told him, opening the door and beckoning William inside. 'Of course, it's nothing to compare with a dwelling backing onto the garden of Chesterfield House.'

Obviously he knew where William lived. 'How long have you been spying on me?'

'You? I don't care about *you*,' Sam almost spat. 'When you're at business, many's the time I've waited in Chesterfield Street and seen Eve at the window, where the light is best, and watched her reading. Sometimes just a glimpse of her. I deserve what *she* thinks, her hatred. Once I saw her reading for an hour, her hair on her shoulders, and a dozen times I almost knocked on the door.'

'For forgiveness?'

Sam sighed: this ruthless, righteous young man understood nothing of sin, his life was a clean white page. His brother had taken the entire load and left him pure. Sam did not have the words to comprehend such a man as William, or make him understand.

'To wish her farewell,' Sam said finally. 'Come and meet Lily. We're on the first floor.' His eyes twinkled. 'I'm part of a new family. Do you not know the word?'

William watched the plump white-haired figure bounding upstairs into the shadows. Then he dropped his hat over his cane and followed.

The door opened on chaos, children jumping up from the back window where they had been watching the rain and bounding into Sam's arms, three girls of different sizes, him swinging them round with their skirts and scuffed black boots flying. Then the littlest girl flew off and knocked into William.

181

'There's a man!' she said, taking William's hat from his cane and putting it on her head, where it promptly plonked down over her shoulders.

'We were watching the rain,' explained a tall girl. She was old enough to be losing her girlish stalkiness, and her cheeks burned with shy spots of colour. She curtseyed rather casually. 'My name is Emily, sir.'

Her sister, almost the same age of adolescence, had measuring eyes and cheeks that burned for, William was certain, quite another reason. She had a passionate nature. With such heat, such sensuality, one look at her and he *knew* she would end up on the streets. 'My name is Una, sir. May I take your stick?' From her mere glance, the way she turned away, he gained the most extraordinary sense of her hunger and unhappiness.

'I'm Vanessa and I'm seven,' piped up the little one under the hat.

William took back his beaver before it was spoiled. 'Vanessa, very unusual name,' he said.

'Jonathan Swift made it up,' Sam said. 'Mrs Chance is very literary.'

They were obviously Sam's children. They had, except Una, who was even more like him in other ways, the same twinkling gaze. William's heart tugged: Eve as a child must have looked a little like these girls.

'May I introduce my, ah, cousin,' Sam said. He had called her his landlady earlier. 'Mr Prideau, Mrs Chance.'

The woman who came gushingly from the corner was younger than Sam – considerably younger, in her middle forties perhaps. 'Take a chair, do!' There was something elegantly beautiful about her, in a foreign way. She wore lustrous brown hair in curls to her shoulders, and her eyebrows had a pleasingly aristocratic curve in a rather dark complexion. She was dreadfully nervous, touching her hair in ringlets as though it was bound to be out of place, and William could see how much she needed Sam. 'Charmed, Mr Prideau,' she said. 'Lovely. The mess – forgive us! We were not in expectation of an anticipation. Mr Summers never warns me.' She turned to practical matters, ineffectually trying to locate a chair for their guest.

'I can't stay,' William said.

'Wait!' Sam gripped his elbow. 'You see, they aren't girls,' he said, surprisingly. 'They are our passports to a better tomorrow.'

In the woman's company William turned formal. 'Pray elucidate, Mr Summers.'

The coldness worked, putting a distance between them, and into it Sam made his pitch. 'The colony in New South Wales *needs* two imports – it gets labour for free, convict labour that is – but it *needs* capital, and it *needs* the female gender; there is an overwhelming preponderance of the male sex. In time my girls–' in his passion he had admitted the awful truth of his fatherhood, and William frowned, '–my beautiful girls, Mr Prideau, will find good land-owning husbands, gentlemen far better than any they would attract here. When I was young I could do anything; now we have no friends left. Mr Prideau, seventy pounds sterling would make me a rich man in *Terra Australis*, and set us up in a land where I can be free – a land where I can have servants, and not breathe smoke or be dunned every time I put my nose in the street. I don't want my daughters to marry pale-faced hollow-chested London hog-grubbers, and raise children who die of cholera in this stinking, shameful metropolis.'

William waited. He could see no reason why he should help out a man who made a virtue of irresponsibility.

Sam swallowed. 'I beg you, Mr Prideau, sir.'

William reminded himself the man was still dangerous, and worth getting rid of. The thought of this animal, sunk so low as not to marry the woman who was mother of his children, being Eve's father, revolted him. William lived a good life, and he was more proud of his wife and loved her more than he would ever put into words, but Sam Summers might be waiting outside the bright windows of his family home – one day he might knock on their door. William knew he was being exploited.

'I'll loan you thirty-five pounds,' he said bitterly. 'I expect it back, mind!'

They hardly heard him in their rejoicing. Mrs Chance kissed him, leaving the taste of pomatom on his mouth, and Sam Summers, at the ridiculous age of sixty-two, attempted to lift all his four women at once.

'The banker's draft will be with you tomorrow,' William said angrily. 'Good day!' He slapped his hat on his head and went downstairs, almost running by the time he reached the bottom. His breath was short and he leaned in the doorway, his heart fluttering in his chest.

The little girl, Vanessa, came down behind him. 'Are you feeling poorly?' she piped. *Not that anyone would care if I did*, William thought. When he shook his head she asked, 'Uncle says, how about a glass of ginger beer?'

'Leave me alone!' William said, and went out into the rain to get rid of her.

'Thank you for letting me wear your hat,' she called after him, then stomped away upstairs and left him alone in the empty street as he had asked.

William limped the few yards down to the Old Swan steps at London Bridge. He hoped to hire a sculler but had to pay double for oars, though it was a tilt-boat with a tarpaulin against the rain. The boatman swore with every stroke all the way to the Temple steps despite the rising tide to help him, and took his eight-pence with a bad grace. But William felt better as he crossed the shallow stretch of Middle Temple gardens and re-entered the world he knew.

His mental picture of the young girls so happy in Summers's poor little room nagged at him with its familiarity. He had never been there in his life! But as soon as he saw Lawson Gumboge he realised his memory had played a trick.

Many years ago he had visited Gumboge's house for some reason or another – a house, too, full of girls. The youngest, only a baby at that time, had recently married Wray, one of the junior clerks downstairs. The oldest worked for Mr Sotheby the literary auctioneer in nearby Wellington Street, a determined spinster. The rest of them were scattered over London like buckshot, probably bleeding Gumboge white with dowries. One, Adelie, had gone onto the stage as Miss Lawson and must require support. Yet Gumboge looked grinningly prosperous, like a man who thoroughly enjoyed his life, and now William eyed him with distrust.

'Did you find him, sir?' Gumboge asked.

'No,' William said, 'there was no one there!'

Not today, not tomorrow, but one day, Gumboge must go.

'I've been a fool.' William almost never talked about business at home, and his voice was so low that Eve could hardly hear him. William had drawn the curtains himself, cutting out the sound of the rain. The bed creaked as he got in on the other side, then there was silence.

Eve said: 'Everyone's a fool some of the time.'

'I love you,' his voice came, confessing. 'You really do know that, don't you?'

'What happened to you today?' she murmured.

'I saw that I have no friends, only people who use me.' From him, such humility was an admission of weakness, and she felt no sympathy – she lay without moving, staring into the dark. His hand fumbled for hers, found her wrist instead, and she kept her fist closed. 'I can't trust anyone but you,' he confided to her in his nocturnal anguish. 'I felt it today. The cold breath of mortality. My life is dust without you, Eve.'

'What have I done?'

'I love you!' he said sadly, 'I can't help myself.' As though he hated himself for loving her – still trying to live up to the memory of his dead brother.

'Don't take yourself so seriously.'

He was silent for a long time, thinking of his son, his hope for the future, the blood of Sam Summers flowing there too. The sooner William got young John solidly into the business, the better. Until then the important thing was to keep him away from his mother. For the present there was board school, and then there would be Oxford University. And then there would be Prideau & Prideau.

He sat up. 'What is to become of us, Eve?' Still the thought of Sam Summers nagged him. 'Put him out of your mind,' he advised her earnestly.

Eve said something he never forgot. 'Who do you mean?'

The scales fell from William's eyes.

He was alone.

Part II

Ezzie

18

1830

The empty tree

Australia. At last the name of their country appeared officially on maps. They had a name and a place. And the sun beat down, and the wind blew.

Each year the muttonbirds, the *yollas*, returned. Each bird lived for thirty years and they did not breed until their lives were a quarter done. Every twenty-fifth of November without fail Bob watched from the dunes, wearing his greasy 'bluey' coat bartered from an American whaler, as the birds flew out of the sunset until their numbers filled his eyesight, then left them in peace to lay their eggs.

Bob loved King Island – as he grew up through adolescence he came to love the place for itself in a way no one else did. Jim Pride respected the island in his fatherly way, and he loved the trees and fenced boundaries of his own small valley, his wired and ditched redoubt, but he was unsentimental about the rest of it: the animals, poisonous or voracious, that threatened his family or his crops, the backbreaking work of felling the forest. . . . and he was no longer a young man. But Jim had spirit, by God he had spirit, and both his sons were devoted to him. Thin as a fence-rail since his heart attack, his features sinewy beneath long greying hair swept back to his shoulders, in his forties Jim could still outwork Johnny who was half his age, chopping one of the mighty blue gums from a springboard a dozen feet above the ground or hacking a path through the dense storeys of brush with a machete until Johnny beside him was almost crying with exhaustion.

It was Johnny, not Bob, who was the lonely one.

Johnny comforted himself: *I'm the eldest son – I'm the one who will inherit all this work he's doing. In a way he's working for me – he's doing it all for me!* And at this satisfying thought Johnny's sulk would melt into a smile. One thing he became very expert at was pretending to work as hard as his father. But, twenty-two now, Johnny was mooning, in love. As soon as he could escape from his chores he would be off meeting Selina at their rendezvous in the woods. And there were always Bob's absences to blame for work that was not done. 'That boy's a dreamer,' Johnny would say, 'not a stockman.'

But Bob always kept his promises: he made up the work he had missed, though often alone, where the results were noticed too late. Bob was happy in his own company: the waiting silence of the bush that filled with sound and activity around a motionless watcher, until he was surrounded with life where there had seemed to be nothing before. Butterflies would settle on the brim of Bob's hat. Then he would begin his work.

Jim understood this. He knew Bob climbed the Huon and stared out to sea, as he did. But his heart filled with sadness when he looked at the boy: Jim knew he had a hard choice coming.

There was always a billy steaming for Johnny at Simeon's gardown set amidst grazing cattle in the rolling, grass-covered dunes. Johnny liked the old man, now in his sixties, almost bald with his fringe of white beard and high voice telling his weird and wonderful, and increasingly wistful, tales of Home. 'I could go back,' he told Johnny, rapping his wooden leg. 'I'll live to a hundred, less work for the heart, see.'

Heart. He stopped as Jim's heart attack of nine years ago came back to haunt both their minds, both thinking: *What would we do without Jim?* It happened during the yolla season: Bob had hurt his hand, been sent home on his old half-blind pony Right, and suddenly Jim fell down among the burrows. At first they thought it was a snake bite, but it was his heart. He claimed he was all right, but he was trembling and his hands were icy cold: the cold breath of mortality had blown over him. Simeon had stood no nonsense: he must rest, and they sent him home on a trusty nag with strict instructions to Annie to keep him in bed for a week. As soon as Jim arrived back at the house, he knew Bob had been up the tree, but he said nothing, just nodded quietly and let Annie take him inside.

'Dad would've exploded right enough if it'd been me went up there,' Johnny asserted through the haze of Simeon's tobacco-smoke. The gardown, despite the cheerful peacock colours of its feathered exterior, was grimly unventilated to keep the wind out. Simeon had gone native, Johnny knew, allowing himself to live – however much he denied it – like a savage. Wayanna, his lubra of Van Diemen's Land aboriginal stock, probably very similar in looks to the tribe who died out on King Island in ancient times leaving only their bones and a few flakes of quartz to show any sign of their existence on God's earth, sat cross-legged by the reeking hearth playing with their son. From time to time Simeon reached across and pulled him away from her, pretending to bring him up as a white even though he was only a half-caste, calling him Isaac. 'Listen to us talk, boy,' he told the six-year-old importantly, then sneezed. The boy folded himself like a insect into an impossible cross-legged pose, watching intently, and Simeon kept sneezing and cursing him for Johnny's benefit, telling him to sit properly. The boy could stand on one leg like a bird, which had infuriated Simeon with its alienness until once Jim had pointed out it was exactly the characteristic that had saved Simeon from the snakes on Christmas Island, and that imitation was the sincerest form of flattery.

So while Isaac listened and Johnny sat smoking his tree-bark tobacco, Simeon jawed about a distant land called Home, where you could buy vegetables in shops, and there were wars, and taxes, and smuggling. Johnny turned the talk back to King Island.

'I remember when Seal Bay was full of seals,' Simeon rambled wistfully. 'I remember half a dozen American schooners anchored in Franklin Roads. It's all changed, Johnny. It's going bad.'

That was true. They all remembered last year, at the end of the yolla season, the huts at Yellow Rock full of oil, and not one single ship had come to anchor. Bob camped there keeping watch for any passing vessel, the oil gradually going rancid while the horizon remained blank.

They had to pour it away. There was no trade, but their needs were no less.

They were losing their battle against King Island. Jim would never admit that, but they were. Johnny could remember going to almost any rock pool and heaving out a cray as long as his arm, but now only the less accessible locations were really good, and the abalone were gone completely from the shallow waters. On land, O'Henry's Bungaree lime sand sweetened the soil for a year, then it again decayed, and they were growing barely enough wheat to keep themselves in bread. The coastal dunes, which looked such fine grass, lacked some vital ingredient and cattle kept on them too long simply died. And now they could not trade beef to the whalers, the herds were too big for the paddocks to support. Burning virgin land was the only way to extend their property, and it was backbreaking work felling the underbrush to dry it enough to take the flame.

It was evening by the time Johnny left the gardown, and as he walked home through the paddocks he wondered, almost panicky: *What would we do without my father?*

One day, no longer such a pleasurable thought, the responsibility for all this would be his.

Johnny could hear the chink of pickaxes and shovels still going down by the river although it was almost dark. His father and Bob looked like pale ghosts labouring at the dam they were building – in summer the Yellow Rock River often dried out except for clumps of marsh between the shallow lagoons, and Jim's heartrendingly laborious improvement scheme was the water-dam. Johnny knew what to do. '*Burn it,*' he whispered, then instead of joining them sneaked quietly to bed.

Wayanna had suffered colds before, but this time it settled on her thin chest. On the third day she was too weak to bring Simeon his breakfast. She lived through the day with the arms of her son Isaac wrapped round her, and died in the night when the fire had gone out. She said only one word to him: it sounded like *Droemerdeene*.

Isaac sat beside her, and waited.

And then instead of the arrival of the ancestral being, his father came stumbling over and pushed him away. Simeon stared down at the body.

'Dead, by God!' he said.

He had her laid out in a wooden box by dawn and sent Isaac to get Pride – he didn't trust the boy alone with his mother's body, not knowing what blasphemy he might get up to: Simeon had held the woman in affection and she had loved him in her way, and she deserved a Christian burial. Johnny and Bob dug the grave, wetting the sides to shore up the sandy soil, and Jim said a few words. The wind blew over them and Isaac stood on one leg, watching from a distance. Jim called to him and held out his hand but Isaac shook his head. O'Henry and Mary Roper had come up from Bungaree with supplies in the bullock cart, which his sons by Becky Donahoo, Frank, and Sean the short one, were unloading. They acknowledged Selina, tall and careless, as their sister but with her high forehead and wide, bewitching eyes she was plainly Mary's, born long before Becky had died a defeated woman, and perhaps a cause of that strong woman's early death. Feargal O'Henry had held a cheerful wake when Becky went, but he missed the tyrant who kept him on a leash.

Mary was sweet and very pretty; and she had passed her sensuality on to her daughter.

Selina, standing beside Johnny at the graveside, was tall and well-formed, with mischievous Irish-blue eyes. While his father's voice droned on Johnny slipped his hand through the pleats at the back of her dress and fondled her bottom. Jim looked round, aware of movement, then continued reading the service. At the back of the crowd Selina made no attempt to remove Johnny's hand, which slowly kneaded her left buttock with caresses that made her breathing quicken, and her nipples show points in the front of her dress.

Jim closed the book and left the mourners by the graveside. He crossed to Isaac and spoke a few words they could not hear. Selina moaned, then covered it with a cough. Jim came back leading Isaac by the hand, and they crouched together by the grave. 'Go on,' Jim said. Isaac took a handful of sand and scattered it into the hole. Turning, he nodded to Jim and walked away.

'Shall I talk to him?' Bob said.

'Leave him be.' Jim shook his head. 'Since we've got

Feargal and Mary here, and they know the island pretty well, I think we should have a talk. Let's get together at Paragon House.'

'Count me out,' said Simeon bitterly. But Jim argued him into coming.

The men sat at the table, the women at the stove. Bob had to let a mob of stock down to the lagoon; he left them churning the mud happily then sat alone in the corner where he could keep an eye on them through the old glazed stern-window. Nobody had noticed Johnny and Selina weren't there.

'We've got to talk this out,' Jim said, putting down his sassafras tea with an expression of distaste. 'What it comes down to is we aren't making a go of it alone and we've got to face the outside world sooner or later.'

Annie said: 'We're still convicts, aren't we? I don't want to go to prison at my age, thank you. I'm happy here, Jim.' She had gone quite pale.

'Nor me,' Mary Roper said. 'I mean, what would they do as soon as we stepped on the waterfront?'

'Arrest us,' Jim said, 'but there may be a loophole.' He read out from a yellowing paper that one of the captains had left him: ' "Article Seven of the Act regulating the transport of convicts to New South Wales: all the Time during which any Offender, being removed under the Provisions aforesaid, *shall continue confined* – " ' he paused significantly before finishing – ' "shall be reckoned in Discharge, or Part Discharge, or satisfaction of the Term of his Transportation, so far as such Time shall extend." ' He put the paper down. 'If the authorities regarded our time on this island as time in prison, then we'd be free.'

Annie covered his hand. It would be impossible for Jim ever to admit that his island was his prison.

'But why should they oblige us?' Bob asked. 'And they'd have to ask permission from London, wouldn't they? It'd take months. Years.'

195

Jim said: 'Convicts have clearly defined rights under the law. We aren't slaves. You can be born a slave, Bob, but you are a free man: you can't be born a prisoner.'

'Except of your own sinful nature,' Simeon said. He puffed a cloud of the tree-bark tobacco he smoked. 'I've had enough, boys. I'm tired and I want to go home. There's nothing to keep me here if I'm a free man.'

'But this is my home,' Bob said, 'of my own free will.'

Jim said: 'I'm coming to that.'

Bob, glancing out of the window, saw Johnny and Selina creeping along by the lagoon, slipping out of sight among the trees, and hid a grin.

'I've got a proposal to make,' Jim said. 'We have one or two cards to play. Our beef, for example. The markets are crying out for fine quality beef. If we play it right, we've got something of value to bargain with.' He looked at Bob.

'It's me, isn't it,' Bob said. 'You're sending me.'

'You've got the job,' Jim said. 'I wish I had a choice, but I don't.'

Bob said: 'Send Johnny.'

'Johnny is a fool.'

Bob closed his eyes. He wasn't crying; he just sat there alone in the corner. This is my home.

'I wouldn't do it to you, Bob,' Jim said doggedly, 'if I didn't have to.'

Selina pulled Johnny's mouth against her own, leaning back against the tree, feeling bits of bark trickling inside her dress as their heads moved. Johnny muttered endearments: 'You're so soft.' She pressed her breasts into his hands, complaining when he used her too roughly, then laughing, egging him on. 'Isn't the sunlight beautiful through the leaves?' she said, helping

196

him undo an extra button so deftly that he didn't notice, sighing her pleasure.

'I'm going to have you right now,' he grunted, and did – right there against the tree.

It was nearly dark when Jim came prowling down across the moss to the Huon pine, his footsteps making no sound. There was no one there; he began to climb and the tree tops fell away beneath him. He could have reached up into the windless stillness and touched the arching campfires of the Milky Way above him. With a faint, seesaw whistling sound two black swans soared overhead, shadows against the stars, then turned below him, bellying the slipstream from their wings as they slid across the sheen of the lagoon. The ripples died away in the complex pattern thrown back by the earth dam built by himself and Bob.

'It's not a prison,' he whispered aloud.

But it was; and that was a stain that might never be wiped clean.

Slowly Jim started down. It was possible that he was sacrificing his second, favourite son. And the look on Bob's face! In being sent away from the island Bob believed he had been disinherited. Jim could not bring himself to admit to Bob he loved *him* most – he could hardly admit it even to himself. But it was Bob who held Jim's trust.

With all his heart Jim believed that Bob would come back. That was what Jim told himself. He knew sons didn't really come back.

He was getting old. He didn't climb the tree again for a long time: something had gone out of him.

19

1831

The new chum

Bob wore his faithful bluey jacket and cord trousers
against the cold, seaboots against the wet – the day
was as miserable as a shag on a rock. He stood at the
whaler's taffrail looking back: he had never seen his
home from the sea before. First the orange rocks of
the King Island's seashore disappeared then even his
mother's white handkerchief, energetically waved, was
finally lost to his sight, though he was sure she was
waving still.

Bill Delano, the captain and youngest of the three
Massachusetts brothers, a grizzled seadog with his
beard varnished by dried tobacco-spit, stumped along
the deck cursing the crew, sobering up now after Jim's
farewell grog party, but still tender. His new mainsail
yardarm, the reason for his visit to King Island after a
cyclone, was of spanking smart celery-top pine, looking
very yellow and fresh against the weathered timbers.
Bob found the smell of the vessel below decks appalling,
every item slick and dank with whale grease – he was
a Murrumbidgee seaman, an unskilled deckhand working his passage to George Town, and he was determined to pull his weight.

Having beaten clear of the island the captain set
course to the south-east. Bob's first sight of Van Diem-
en's Land was three green hummocks sticking out of
the sea, then the endless sandbanks off Cape Grim, the
lines of bursting foam sheltering the vessel from the

rolling Southern Ocean, so that the coast they sailed along seemed more like the shore of a harbour than the open sea. Bob stared, rapt, as extraordinary mountains, humped, or flat-topped as tables or spiky as though pulled up by great fingers out of the earth, rose unexplored inland of the sandy beaches and stretched down the cloud-wreathed horizon southward. It was a wonderful sight, and it stuck in his mind.

Lower ranges of hills rolling down from the tiers hid the entrance to the Tamar River. Outer Cove had been renamed George Town, a once-thriving place with a grid of straight streets still showing, but now derelict except for the waterfront area, the bleached skeletons of Bengali cattle still showing on the beach. The captain hove to, and by good luck the first decked boat he hailed, setting sail upriver, agreed to take Bob.

Taking advantage of the wind, the little supply-sloop tacked upstream between the wooded shores of the Tamar River towards the town of Launceston forty-five miles upstream. In places the trees had been burnt by natives: 'They've all gone away now,' the captain's wife Alicia told him, a jolly soul about fifty years old with a face almost as weatherbeaten as her husband's. 'When we first came here I remember their fires along the shore. Those devils pretended to run away at first, then killed a lot of people. Some of the children are being brought up as whites, but the elders cannot be trusted, and have been taken to a place where they will be happy – better than they deserve, too. The Black Drive. They have Mr Robinson to thank for that, a man with too soft a heart for his good or theirs.'

'How can that be?'

She said directly, 'You must be a new chum,' and when Bob finished his luncheon she wanted him to pay her in money. He fumbled with the unfamiliar coins – part-payment for the new spar – so she took them kindly from his hand and with a smile charged him

199

double for his meal. Only when he said goodbye to Launceston waterfront, where the two rivers joined, did she take pity on him.

'This is a hard place,' she told him, 'a good place.'

Bob swung his swag of a few personal items, rolled in a blue blanket, over his shoulder and surveyed the town. He had come to civilisation.

He saw houses made of brick, half a dozen or more with pretty gardens, and long crowded streets petering out in the bush lined with wooden houses, shops, warehouses, more or less ramshackle but often two storeys high. He stood on the busy dock gaping at the bustling scene around him: George Town's decline had been Launceston's good fortune, and the failure of the drought-stricken harvest on the New South Wales mainland a couple of years ago had established a busy export trade in wheat, goods and timber. He had never imagined so many people, or such wealth: men with tall hats, women wearing clothes that looked fresh put on that day, carts rumbling along deep ruts in the mud. Above the smoking rooftops, on the outskirts of the town at the corner of Elizabeth Street, a single tower rose: St John's Church, by far the largest building he had ever seen. The lime render around the clock was still fresh, brilliantly white. He wandered over Prince's Square where more bricks were being fired in a kiln. Launceston was growing fast.

A man who had been watching him, perhaps following him, sucking a stalk of grass plucked from the roadway, came over and looked him in the eye.

'You're a new chum, I gather.'

'Listen, chum,' Bob said, 'I'm as Australian as you are.'

The man said coldly: 'I'm British. I am surprised you couldn't tell.' Then he smiled and tilted back his hat, stuck out his hand. 'I'm Gibbons.'

Bob said: 'Bob Pride.'

'Pride! And very *proud* I am to introduce you to our fair town.' Gibbons winked, still shaking his hand warmly, looking him straight in the face and not at all noticing Bob's roll of swag, or the way Bob's pockets rattled with cash as they shook. 'Fair Launceston. Don't worry, nearly everybody is a new chum here, the numbers have doubled in the three years I've had the pleasure. Why, a new public house arises every week! Thirty pubs to choose from. You look like a man who can hold his liquor.'

'Yes, but I need somewhere to stay first.'

'Ah, the very place.' Gibbons guided him into a doorway. 'Brandy, a full nor'wester,' he called into the gloom, then as the bottle was put down on the counter, the landlord's other grubby palm held out as threateningly as a fist, Gibbons turned to Bob with a slightly contemptuous look in his eye. 'I say, you aren't a dry hash, are you?' Seeing Bob's confusion he explained, sighing: 'A man who drinks alone and won't buy his shout.'

'Maybe I am pretty new,' Bob admitted. 'Is this my shout?' He'd never tasted brandy before and it was fine. .

'Breathe deep,' Gibbons advised, pouring more glasses. 'That's rozner stuff, sets a man up, what?' They were talking man to man and Bob nodded seriously.

'Try this,' Gibbons said, 'it's called White Lady.'

'What is it?'

'Methylated spirits and ammonia. The mosquitoes won't bite you tonight.'

'I feel great,' Bob said. 'I could bite the mozzies right back!' He laughed uproariously.

'Still going?' Gibbons said wearily. 'Come on, lamb down. Try this.'

'This is good,' Bob said seriously.

'It's called *Bidgee*,' Gibbons said, not bothering to catch Bob as he went down. 'It's made of methylated spirits with a tablespoon of boot-polish, and just a dash of tobacco to give it flavour. . . .'

Bob woke with a terrible hangover. He felt very bad. He was not where he had any memory of being: a sloping area of rough grass near a cheap board proclaiming that this was The People's Park. He stared up through the swaying leaves of the small pear tree above him and the midday sun lanced into his eyes. He was sure he was dying. He could hear the angels singing.

He pulled his knees up and rolled very slowly to his feet, holding onto the pear sapling for support. He looked round for his swag but it was gone; he patted his pockets, but they were empty.

He'd let his father down – let everyone he loved down. Tears would have flowed from his eyes but he was so dehydrated his body seemed to have no more water to give.

Yet still he heard the heavenly voices.

Holding his head, he staggered along the fence of Government House and crossed between the proud Free Settler yeomen riding their fine Cleveland horses along the slimy entrails of Tamar Street. Because of the depth of mud their smart ladies travelled in gigs or sedans carried by convicts.

Bob followed the voices along Cameron Street. The end of the street, beyond the military barracks, held a view of Cataract Hill and a steep gorge; the cottages dotted along the verges were surrounded by pretty patches of garden trailing honeysuckle or wisteria over the door, and dogs barked over the paling-fences at him.

It was Sunday, and in this area those citizens who were not drunk or working – he could distinctly hear the clicking of a treadmill in the punishment yard of the gaol factory – were worshipping. He followed a few people walking on foot to a single-roomed cottage, a schoolroom, near the Customs House. Bob had found the Wesleyan Chapel.

With a groan of relief he dropped to his knees at the horse trough by the gate and drank from his cupped hands, unaware that he was being observed by a ruddy-faced, grey-haired figure on the steps. The door was about to be closed, but the man stayed it and put his hand firmly on Bob's shoulder. 'You drink like a soldier of the Lord, friend,' he said in a deep, resonant voice, a voice used to public speaking. 'I shall call you Gideon, whose soldiers drank from their cupped hands, neither lapping like dogs nor kneeling like slaves: thus were they saved, and the Midianites delivered into the hands of Gideon, and their princes slain. Judges, chapter seven.'

His big shoes were scuffed and worn, the black clothes old but neatly brushed. Bob stood awkwardly. 'I followed the voices,' he tried to explain.

'Yes!' the missionary trumpeted, gripping both Bob's shoulders in his reddened muscular hands, 'the wicked-ness of the people of Launceston exceeds all description! Turn .from drink, my boy. You heard the voices of Hope and Faith uplifted!'

'Hope and Faith? And Charity?'

'There is no Charity,' said the missionary, 'and Beauty is in the eye of the beholder.' He held Bob tight. 'Yes,' he said quietly, 'we shall see. I am Brother Fisher. Come in, follow me,' he held a finger to his lips, 'say nothing. Do as I say, my friend who drinks from his cupped hands, and come in.'

It was a wooden building, ordinary and dark. The floor creaked between the narrow walls in the silence; the singing had stopped. Two girls, heads down, their long smooth skirts seeming very pale in the gloom, waited to hand out texts and copies of the *Arminian* magazine from the pile stacked in their right arms.

Obviously they had hoped for a greater attendance than they had achieved. Bob smiled at the one on the left and held out his hand for a sheet.

He couldn't see her eyes.

She bobbed shyly, and he realised he was supposed to take it himself. She wore a locket at her throat and her empty left hand remained folded beneath the curve of her breasts. The other girl held out a text boldly, intervening, but Bob kept his eyes on she who stood in front of him.

She looked up at Bob, slanted snake eyes, but blue eyes, ravishing him, her hair in brown curls around a sultry complexion, and he fell in love.

Slowly she lifted her withered left arm, closed her fingers on the top sheet, and handed it to him.

He couldn't take his eyes off her.

'Hope,' her father said fondly. 'Hope and Faith, take your places now.'

Bob thrust past a couple of worshippers and got in first, just to be near her. *Hope*. The key was given on a tuning-fork and the God-botherers' singing began. He peered at the dissimilar profiles of the two girls, not the text of the hymn. He was in a daze, craning forward to see her so that the people beside him shuffled in irritation – those slanted eyes, and that demure smile. Just to look at her was a sin. Now he understood the minister's cryptic *There is no Charity* – he had no third daughter. Hope sang beautifully: it was definitely her voice he had heard, the other girl's singing was a hoarse counterpoint. Hope sang with all her heart, the little wooden cross on the shabby end wall the focus of all her emotions, her eyes upraised through the roof, her mouth open on fine white teeth. How different she looked from her sister, though they shared the same dress and manner.

Silence. Bob remembered to sit.

What Fisher lacked in attendance, he made up for with the muscular exuberance of his preaching, and by the time he was well-launched the room was full to overflowing, with more outside. 'This is the final day of the Quarter, the last time I shall talk to you here in Launceston. What advice do I have to pass on to my successor, Brother Leach? The duty of a clergyman in Launceston is most arduous, placed as it were in the very gorge of sin!' He eyed his daughters fondly, their pure pale dresses shining in the brilliant slants of sunlight from the little windows, their heads bowed. A shrunken woman with most severe features, a pinched impatient mouth, sat beside them and must be their mother. Bob thought Hope flashed him a look from the corners of her eyes; like an angel.

Her father's voice boomed and rolled, and Bob tried to pay attention.

'Australia is the receptacle for the worst characters in the world,' Fisher thundered, 'and a clergyman is compelled to grapple at the very gates of hell if he would rescue a soul from its headlong ruin.' He sounded as though he thoroughly enjoyed grappling. 'But the pride, self importance and officiousness of some of our leading men, with the notable exception,' he added, 'of Lieutenant-Governor Arthur, occasions such grief and trouble that a missionary feels himself almost without protection. . . .' There was an awkward moment for Bob when the collection was made – Brother John Leach had been appointed by the District Committee in Hobart Town at a salary of £50 a year, and a subscription started for a new chapel to be built in Launceston. Bob had to fumble in his sock for one of his small store of promissory notes left by the American whaler in payment for the spar, forty dollars payable at five shillings each. He felt Fisher's eyes on him. And when the meeting ended Fisher and his wife, with the girls in tow, walked straight past him. Hope did not even glance at him, his tongue was tied, and he lost his opportunity.

Bob sat alone. The bench creaked as Fisher, returning, sat beside him. 'You interest me, my cupped-hand friend,' Fisher said. 'I cannot see through you. You talk in the native style, yet you seem innocent of our wicked ways. At the same time,' he glanced at Bob's feet, 'you are a man of consequence. And your manner is one of consequence – almost, I might say, of passion. I like a man who knows what he wants. Tell me your story, sir.'

Bob came to a decision. He took Fisher into his confidence, and told him all he knew.

'My dear boy, the Lord works in marvellous ways,' sighed Fisher at the end. 'I see our path clearly. I can help you, to my advantage as well as yours.' He put his arm round Bob's shoulder and they went outside where Mrs Fisher and the girls were waiting. 'This is Mr Pride,' Fisher said. 'He is on a journey, and he will travel with us to Hobart Town tomorrow.'

Mrs Fisher looked at Bob. She said only one word to her husband: 'Samuel.'

Fisher pulled out all the stops. 'It is the will of the Lord,' he said.

She gave Bob an ugly look. The daughters didn't look at him at all.

'Come,' she told them, and ushered them away. Samuel Fisher watched them anxiously out of sight.

'I guess I've offended her,' Bob said.

'My wife is an unhappy woman.' Fisher glanced at him. 'The one thing that would have made her happy, the Lord has not blessed me with the power to give her.'

'What is that, sir?'

'Children.'

206

20
Hope

At about eight next morning Bob came out of Dicky
White's Hotel having exchanged all his dollars with
the owner for much less than ten pounds and spent
fivepence of it on a plate of mutton for breakfast, to
find Cox's mail cart waiting for him in the mud. From
Launceston to Hobart Town was a hundred and
twenty-four miles by coach road. The Fishers were
cramped on the wooden bench-seat although they were
the only occupants, their portmanteau strapped on the
back, and he got a very cold stare from Hope's stepmother, Mrs Fisher. The girls wore white bonnets. The
one called Faith looked at him and smiled, but Hope
kept her head down. 'Quickly, Mr Pride,' their father
called, 'Mrs Fisher is a woman of punctuality.'

'But I do not be,' Cox the driver said, not to be put
down by any woman, spitting an arc of tobacco juice
over the wheel, grinning at the clock of St John's
already showing ten past. 'That be five pounds, Mr
Pride.' Bob paid it over, grumbling. 'I'm saving up for
a proper stagecoach,' Cox said.

'You will sit up beside Mr Cox,' Mrs Fisher told
Bob. The lady wasn't a romantic like her husband, she
wasn't having Bob Pride anywhere near her precious
girls. She told Cox: 'My husband is a personal friend
of Lieutenant-Governor Arthur' – Cox yawned – 'and
we have been invited to the Ball at His Excellency's
Residence on Wednesday eve. We shall arrive at the
Ship Inn in Hobart Town promptly at three of the clock

on Wednesday afternoon, as set out in your published schedule, is that clear?'

'Yes, ma'am,' Cox conceded, holding out his hand for Bob to scramble up on the high seat beside him. 'Clear as mud, ma'am. Wednesday, you say?'

The great advantage of the cart over a sailing vessel was that it could run to a schedule, but Cox had only the vaguest idea of what his schedule was, and could neither read nor write. This was a poor attribute for a mailman and the Executive Council threatened to revoke his licence but no one else wanted the work. Bob knew all about this by the time they reached the town limits.

The cart stopped at the top of the first hill and they looked back at the magnificent view of Launceston, Cataract Gorge lit by the rising sun, and four large vessels unloading in the Tamar to show the prosperity of the place. 'You wait until you clap eyes on Hobart Town,' Cox promised, '*that's* a town, three, four times the size – and you should see the government buildings!' He flicked Launceston off his fingers. 'Mind you, I'm a Hobart Town man myself. . . .'

The rolling agricultural countryside of the Midlands road opened up around them. 'Looks just like the south of England, dried out,' Cox prompted, but Bob was a rarity, a native-born Australian, and what England looked like didn't interest him. 'It do have a friendly look,' Cox explained. 'It looks cared for. And rich! Look at that soil! Why, don't it make you want to crumble it in your hands? Lambs in a month or two.' Bob closed his eyes and pretended to sleep. With the jolting of the cart he could peep at Hope's shoulder behind his right hip, an occasional glimpse of her face.

Near Gibson's Inn at Snake Banks they passed convict road-grading gangs, the men working in rows across the road, connected by chains. Fourth-class convicts then; third-class men would have worked unencumbered, while men of the fifth class would have been ironed down. 'Excellent road this,' Cox said, nudging Bob, who pretended to drift back into sleep. 'They're going to metal it soon.'

Hope was a lovely girl, and flawed – it was Hope's flaws that brought her to life for Bob and fascinated him, her broken wing, the withered arm she tucked strengthlessly against her front. Yet despite her demure smile and obediently bowed head, she could look up at him with a sudden flash in her narrowed eyes, almost a glitter, that touched Bob like ice, and he noticed she was the only one – certainly not her father – with the strength of personality to stand up to her strident stepmother: they *would* stop for lunch even if it made them late to arrive at their first night's stop, Somercotes, Hope insisted in her quiet way, and it was Hope who insisted on laying out a blanket on the edge of a grassy vista to eat the hard-boiled eggs, bread and crumbly cheese they had brought with them. Hope had boiled two extra eggs, one for Mr Cox who stayed back at the cart, and one for Bob. He sat down beside her but Faith slipped between them, looking him in the eye.

'Who would have believed,' said Samuel with a sigh at the lovely view, 'that this is one of the strongholds of the devil.'

Hope kept her head down.

They did not arrive at Somercotes, owned by Captain Horton, the cousin of a Wesleyan missionary, until it was dark. The house was a stone fortress with windows iron-barred against bushrangers, and the courtyard surrounded by spikes. In a barn massively constructed of whole treetrunks Samuel Fisher, keen as mustard, held a service for a small congregation of local people, farmers who put their feet on the seats – Bob saw them from outside through candlelit chinks in the wood. Hope sang, but then her voice broke off. A door slammed and he heard footsteps running lightly across the stableyard. He caught a glimpse of her against the lights of the military station at Ross, down in the river-valley, then he cut behind the stables and came out in front of her, and she ran into his arms.

Neither of them moved.

'No,' she said. Her right hand twisted at the lapel of his coat. She was as tense as a colt straining at a rope.

'What's happened?' he whispered.

'Our feelings are obvious,' she said.

All he could see of her was her pale dress, her blurred hand against her face, and he knew she was angry with her tears. They listened to one another's breathing, saying not a word to break the spell, breathing together.

'Everybody knows,' she murmured.

'Do you care?'

'Do you not have eyes?' Her voice came sadly: 'I am an imperfect woman.'

'No! Don't talk like that.'

'Don't give me *orders*,' she flared, 'like everyone else.'

He whispered: 'Never. You are beautiful to me.'

She lifted her withered left arm with her right. 'Tonight I could not sing.' He could not tell which upset her more, her arm or voice, or whether it was that all her emotion was concentrated on him.

Bob kissed her.

'I wanted to,' he said.

They heard Samuel Fisher calling. They stood with their fingertips touching, as though this moment between them could extend for ever.

'Hope?' called a voice from the stableyard, facing the wrong way, echoing.

'Your father's worried,' Bob said.

She said nothing.

'I don't want you to go,' Bob whispered. 'Hope – '

She kissed his lips, staring at him defiantly.

'He isn't my father!' Now she had begun, her confession rushed breathlessly out of her. 'He is not my father – she isn't my mother – Faith is not my sister. We are orphans.' Tears gleamed in her eyes, sure she had lost him now. 'And my name is not Hope!'

She ran and he chased after her, caught her by her thin elbow. 'But what *is* your name?'

She said: 'Ezzie.'

21

Carving the turkey

Ezzie. It was a pretty name. Was it short for Esmerelda?
She didn't know. Who gave it to her? She knew nothing.
Hope and *Faith* were her foster-mother's vanities, but
Samuel Fisher had confessed the truth about her adop-
tion when she came of age about five years ago. *My
wife, your stepmother, pretty, merry creature Eleanor once was
– but she could not conceive. . . . you were the hope of our
prayers. An old woman held you up at a Prayer Meeting in
London, a bundle wrapped in rags: a baby with a broken wing.
She wanted a guinea. We took you in our arms, and when we
looked up, the old woman was gone.*

Bob and Ezzie whispered their secrets together in
the warm dark evening at Somercotes like conspirators,
her stepfather's calls floating over them in the night
air. *Hope.* . . . His lost girl. Bob held Ezzie in his arms
and the calls faded in the distance.

'I knew you the moment I saw you,' Bob murmured,
'I loved you Ezzie.'

'They never knew when my birthday was,' her breath
whispered on his throat, 'I was the river's child: Ezzie.
My foster-mother said it was a common name. Samuel
was a cabinet-maker come down from Lincolnshire and
knew himself called to the Lord – he loved me *because*
of my broken wing. But Eleanor wanted to own me, as
she owned Faith.'

'This was London? What a ghastly place!' he said
impetuously. 'My own father and mother came from
London.'

'What crime did they commit?'

He wanted Ezzie to admire him. 'I don't know.'

'I must always have known I was not their daughter.' Ezzie sighed. 'When Samuel told me the truth, in a storm on the voyage out to Australia when we thought we would die, it made sense at once. . . . I felt so alone.' She shuddered, then clutched him. 'Hold me, quickly. Don't be afraid, I'm not china.' They stood close, his arms round her, her stepfather's cries echoing between the distant buildings.

'You must go back,' Bob said at last.

'We must be strangers again,' she said impishly, and this time the flash in her narrowed eyes contained amusement. He wished he understood her. 'This will be our secret.'

'This?'

Her lips brushed his for the briefest moment. 'This.'

She had kissed *him!* – she was shocking, and irresistible. Her voice, her touch, the flash of her eyes, echoed in his imagination all night.

And she was right: the next day they played strangers again. But Samuel Fisher knew, because he took every opportunity to speak with Bob, getting to know him thoroughly, and by the time the cart rolled down into Hobart Town on Wednesday the Wesleyan minister seemed not displeased by the turn events had taken. Faith sulked; she knew. Only Eleanor Fisher, secure in her domination of her purchased family, was left ignorant: Ezzie played Hope, and the old woman snapped out her orders as usual, not realising her foster-daughter had slipped away.

'Exactly on schedule,' she said with self-congratulation as the cart stopped in Hobart Town and the church clock chimed three times.

Samuel Fisher took Bob quietly aside. 'Remember, eight o'clock at the Governor's Residence. You will need a better frock coat than that, sir.' He took something wrapped in a parcel from behind his back.

*

Bob walked along Macquarie Street. In the blue expanse of the Derwent Estuary beyond the shingled rooftops falling away below him, a whale spouted white spray against the green woodlands of the far hills. Soldiers drilled in scarlet uniforms and bright regimental cockades. The window-drapes of Thomas Birch's yellow freestone mansion were royal purple, imported by the great merchant from the mills of England, and the sun gleamed off cannon mounted on the battlemented roof. Most dwellings, made of orange handmade brick, and single-storey except in the very centre of town, were dwarfed by the broad thoroughfares where tax-carts ran swaying, full of shop goods and building materials. Labourers shambled under heavy hods from the brick piles to the shops and houses springing up everywhere. Bob stared at these ignored figures in coarse yellow and grey; *convicts*. Nobody else saw them. What awful crimes had they committed? And yet they had been sent to this wonderful place, this land of opportunity, to make it theirs. He stared uncomprehending at their passive faces, slack movements. They craved anything denied to them – tobacco, drink, women – everything except freedom. Divided and ruled by a rigorous system of espionage, they knew only the certainty of punishment.

Along the street a convict-constable was checking papers, and Bob turned aside.

He blew on his hands and saw his breath. The scaffolded copper-green spire of St David's was pastel with frost on the shadow-side, winter ending with a cold snap. Snow-capped Mount Wellington towered flat-topped above the town nestling in the foothills, and the great vertical rock-face called the Organ Pipes was ribbed with white.

At one shop by a creek lined with watermills chuting white foam into the bay Bob purchased a secondhand pair of shoes with good-looking shiny buckles, and in

the front room of another shop a fine cotton shirt was
freshly ironed for him. Coming out he paused to look
at the causeway built out to Hunter's Island, a street
of white warehouses three storeys high, the commercial
centre dominated by Wesleyans and Quakers. Hundreds of little boats clustered like flies around the
wooden wharves, such a swarm of activity everywhere
that it was difficult to believe this was a town of only
ten or twelve thousand people, three-quarters of them
men, and desperately insecure.

Bob took a room at a skilling, a lean-to of sawn
eucalyptus planks behind the wooden façade of a
housefront. Mrs Deems's was close to the water's edge
by the Wapping jetties and she was full of rum and
kangaroo. 'Welcome aboard,' she greeted him with a
polite flourish of her arms, anxious to seem respectable.
'Just arrived, have we? Free settler, I can see that, sir.
You'll be wanting run goods, of course. . . .'

'What are they?'

'I have the honour to be the official marriage agent
for the Immigration Society,' she curtseyed, 'free
females only. Run goods, sir – only the finest goods.'

'Not today, Mrs Deems.'

'A maidenhead – being a commodity never entered,
sir,' she said, very ladylike.

'Thank you, Mrs Deems.' He closed the room's door
on her and leaned back against it, then undid the
package Samuel Fisher had given him and held up
a bottle-green frock coat. Tonight he must be a real
gentleman, and he had only what his father told him
to go by. But Ezzie would be there.

Lieutenant-Governor Arthur communicated with the
common people, whose lives his bureaucracy regulated
in the finest detail, by means of edicts and regulations
nailed to the doors of pubs. The hurricane lamps above
these doors were Hobart Town's only street lighting,

215

so the wharf area glittered cheerfully and Bob found his way without difficulty. But then he was in the dark of more sober areas, following the dimly lit windows of the homes above the shops, until he found the big lantern illuminating the gaol stocks of St George's Square, surrounded by fine public buildings. He stood beneath the gaol wall: Australia's second town was first and foremost a prison, the whole island of Van Diemen's Land was. Arthur regarded free settlers merely as visitors, bystanders to the island's main business, which was incarceration.

Bob had come too far, and turned back.

'There you are at last!' Fisher met Bob outside the Residence, wrung his hand, and swept him up the steps. 'He's with me,' he told the soldiers on guard. The house was not at all grand, and the male guests looked like clerks: it was only Eleanor's snobbery that had elevated George Arthur's regular Wednesday gathering of virtuous citizens in his drawing room to the status of a ball. 'A ball? The house is too small, and the Governor is too mean,' murmured Samuel, not letting go of Bob's elbow as they nodded and bowed to various matrons. He beckoned to a lanky, sardonic-looking man who escaped gratefully from an enormous lady lecturing him in a corner. 'Alphabet, I want you to meet someone who will fascinate you. A noble savage.'

Bob bowed; he was getting the hang of it. 'This is Alphabet Boyes,' Samuel introduced them, 'we call him Alphabet because he shows off with too many initials before his name.'

'My mother's fault,' yawned Boyes, but his eyes were bright and sizing. 'She couldn't decide whether she preferred G or T, or perhaps W or B or –'

'He's very clever,' Samuel said, 'and you may depend on him, the only man who can make sense of the finances of this extraordinary island.'

216

'But they don't make sense,' Boyes said languidly. 'How d'ye do.'

Bob said: 'What *is* that awful smell?'

Boyes sniffed as though he had just noticed it. 'Like the ripescent steam from a tallow-chandler's copper? That wicked aroma, my dear sir, is the off beef the Lieutenant-Governor hopes we shall eat tonight. I should have the turkey.'

'I shall, sir.' Bob looked around the dusty drawing room, airless from the roaring fire, then pointed at the watercolours hanging along the wall.

'I like the pictures.' At the entrance he'd seen one close enough to read the foreign-looking title. 'Spanish, I'll wager.' In the books that reached King Island gentlemen said *wager* and *oath*. He was the only Australian here; for the moment he must deal with them on their terms.

Samuel was laughing, and Boyes coughed modestly. 'You are obviously a person of taste and discrimination, my friend.'

The crowd jostled them in the cramped space. 'There must be at least twenty people!' Bob exclaimed.

'Everyone knows everyone here,' Boyes said. 'This is a class-ridden society, we know only our own layer – allow me to educate you.' Boyes swept a glass of wine from the tray offered by a bulky servant. 'These people are all Hobartons – now that's something you must learn, the socially exquisite classes affect to call our little town *Hobarton*. They are boringly respectable and excruciatingly virtuous, in public, and, I greatly fear, in private too. Relax, young man. You look like an outsider.'

Bob relaxed.

Boyes said, 'The tragedy of the aboriginal race is that to our eyes they have no nobility. They are stringy folk – worst of all, frightened of us. Can't make Treaty with them. We can't respect them.'

'Is that nobility?' Bob said, nodding at the man who was the centre of attention.

'Very much so! The only man in this room who is important,' Boyes said. 'Our lieutenant-governor with his personal supply of Madeira.' He gestured his glass of cheap Cape wine at the lacklustre figure sitting like a tailor on a music stool with the fashionable ladies. 'His Honour may consent to notice you. Beware of him, his is a dog who pleases his masters, mind his wagging tail does not knock you. He is an Evangelical, and he regards democracy as insubordination, even if it is purchased at ten pounds a vote.'

'He knows the heart of every man is desperately wicked,' Samuel said. 'The way to *his* heart is chess, as Alphabet well knows.'

'Whist was your treat, Samuel, was it not,' joked Boyes.

'Before I found the Lord,' said Samuel, offended.

'Ah, you're a canny Lincolnshire man, you play your cards close to your chest. . . .'

Bob let their talk wash over him, closely observing the man on the stool: his flicking blue eyes, long ear-lobes, light brown hair greying at the temples, the small smile he wore for the ladies. He obviously did not share the colonial Hobartons' high opinion of themselves. He merely encouraged them because they were useful.

'His Honour is all-powerful,' Boyes warned. 'He has a mind like a machine, and being a colonel – it cost him thousands of pounds to get so far – he holds the military command here. The Colonial Office in London respect him and he's a personal friend of Lord Bathurst, so there is nothing Arthur cannot do. He's a skilful administrator and his powers of patronage are vast, greater than any English monarch's, sufficient to elevate any friend or break any enemy. He never delegates *anything*, the Colony is run all in his own personal handwriting: police instructions, appointments, the

218

smallest regulations, the ratification of death sentences. They say he owns land here worth sixty thousand pounds.' Boyes tossed off his glass. 'And the man looks like a tailor.'

'Hope – my dear.' Samuel greeted his daughter coming from another room with Mrs Arthur, an insipid woman with Eleanor Fisher fawning on her, and Faith trailing two army officers holding in their stomachs to pay her court. But Bob could not take his gaze off Ezzie who lit up the room to his eyes. No one else was interested in her, quick to spot the painfully thin arm in the long white glove. These men knew that everything is genetic, passed down in the blood: nobility, Original Sin, a withered arm, criminality.

'The punishment of crimes and the reformation of criminals are the grand objects.' Arthur, with his thin, precise voice and small smile was shocking the Hobartons by referring to the reason for the existence of Hobart Town. 'It costs twenty-eight pounds a year to keep a man in an English penitentiary, but less than half that amount in Van Diemen's Land – and the man can be made to work. Against that must be set, in this humanitarian policy, the eighteen pounds required for his transport out. But what an opportunity! Punishment alone, ladies, is insufficient to prevent crime. But banishment to this island creates a vacuum in the human soul that can be filled with religious instruction before the season is lost.'

'My own thought exactly,' Samuel Fisher murmured.

Arthur overheard him. 'My dear Samuel, at last you return to us! Now, such men as these Wesleyan missionaries,' he confided to the ladies, 'I send them to the penitentiaries at Port Arthur, Maria Island, or Point Puer – that's for the incorrigible children – in fact the Wesleyan Missionary Society penetrates even the remote fastness of Macquarie Harbour, and we find

219

these honest workers far better qualified for the office than liberal gentlemen with university educations.'

'It is a grim office, sir,' said Samuel Fisher.

'Believe me, dear ladies, the moral desert of Macquarie Harbour is more reformatory to the criminal soul than any amount of flogging. And all the more humane because impartial.'

Samuel Fisher said: 'Sir, convicts on their deathbed are often indifferent to sin, believing, at such places as Macquarie Harbour, that they have suffered so much in this world that it could never be the design of the Almighty to punish them at all in the next. I have received letters from Brother Schofield that would make your heart – '

'We shall talk of this later,' George Arthur chopped him off, turning away. He clapped his hands, the doors were thrown open and they went into the supper room, seating themselves along the dirty linen. 'Mr Boyes!' Everyone avoided the beef. 'You will carve the turkey. I shall have white meat.'

Bob found himself separated from Ezzie, but only two seats from Arthur, who made a point of putting Samuel Fisher opposite himself. While Boyes struggled with the knife to satisfy everyone who wanted particular cuts, Arthur ate little. Someone asked him a question and Bob heard him reply, 'Money is the only essential qualification for agricultural settlers. We need them! We give them ten per cent off for prompt payment – up to ten thousand acres – and I assure you no purchase price is ever rejected.' Bob listened, hardly aware of the food he was eating. Now he understood the way business was done in Van Diemen's Land: it was done on the nod of George Arthur. When a settler he approved of needed a few more labourers from the Convict Department, George Arthur would nod and it would happen. When another man wanted extra land

220

Lieutenant-Governor Arthur would nod, or not, and so the turkey was carved.

'Our police system is so excellent because so many are guilty,' Arthur was saying, 'and the strong must be saved from the weak.' He waved his knife at Samuel Fisher. 'Samuel, while St David's is being repaired, we find the Court House less than suitable for divine service. I and my suite shall be pleased to attend the Wesleyan Chapel this Sunday – if you can promise us a not too argumentative oration.' From Samuel's face Bob realised that this recognition by the churchgoing gentry was important.

Samuel pulled a subscription book from his pocket. 'I have opened a subscription for a new chapel to be built in Launceston.' He waved the book, undaunted by the sour looks he was getting. 'Building can start when the subscription reaches five hundred pounds,' he said loudly.

There was silence, then Arthur smiled, and everyone else smiled too. 'Very well, Samuel,' Arthur said, 'you may put me down for ten pounds!' He looked from face to face, and the guests reached into their pockets. Ten o'clock struck and the women left the men to their port, Mrs Fisher and the girls returning to their lodging. Arthur lifted his finger and Samuel leaned across the table. Bob heard Arthur murmur: 'I am aware of the loan request for eight hundred pounds your Hobart Town chapel trustees have submitted to the Executive Council. Perhaps we should discuss this in another room – there is another matter I wish to mention.'

'Myself also,' Samuel said, 'with your permission,' nodding to Bob to follow them. The three men took their port into a small study and Arthur sat in a rumpled red armchair near the fire where he had worked all day. He got down to business. 'I detest these ceremonies, but it does keep the people in line. On the mainland the settlers grew so above themselves as actu-

221

ally to imprison Governor Bligh when he got between them and their profits! These cliques are deadly; they must be used.' He leaned towards Samuel, but his eyes flicked constantly between him and Bob, wondering about the young man standing in the shadows of the firelight. Samuel, soldier of the Lord, took advantage of the colonel's momentary distraction.

'Your Honour, I pray the Executive Council will see fit to lend our cause this money – at five per cent.'

'That is the Executive Council's business.' Arthur changed the subject. 'I am not satisfied with your Schofield, the chaplain at Macquarie Harbour, an appointment for which I am responsible.'

Samuel tried to keep him talking of money. 'Your Honour's help seven years ago with the building of the Hobart Town chapel was of momentous importance for us, and we have not forgotten our gratitude. But now more money is required. The chapel was very poorly constructed and the front wall is five inches out of true. . . .'

'The Executive Council will turn you down,' Arthur said clearly. 'Let us talk about the vacancy at Macquarie Harbour since William Schofield, though desperately needed, refuses to remain at that place any longer. I offered it to Esh Lovell. He refused. I have even applied to London for a preacher, but. . . .'

Samuel looked uneasy. The nature of the deal being proposed was becoming clear to him.

Bob said, 'What's so bad about Macquarie Harbour?'

'It's a prison – '

'A penitentiary,' Arthur interrupted. 'A place of penitence.'

'At the end of the earth,' Samuel said. 'A wilderness beyond Hell's Gates. Literally.'

Arthur smiled his small smile with his small mouth. 'Sarah Island is a fastness so remote that a man cannot escape, cannot know hope, can only repent sin. What punishment is more impartial or humane than a wilderness?'

'I understand,' Bob said.

'Now, Samuel. I have issued instructions that a small but comfortable cottage with a garden is to be built for you at Macquarie Harbour, on Sarah Island, and chairs and a table shall be provided for you and your family along with beds and all articles of household use, buckets, a candle ration, and so forth. Passage for you and your family will be paid, and an additional salary of a hundred pounds a year.'

If Samuel agreed to go, Bob had lost Ezzie. 'You cannot take her to such a terrible place!'

Samuel said: 'Be silent.' He turned back to Arthur with hunched shoulders, outmanoeuvred. 'Please complete what you have to say.'

Bob was aghast. 'But – '

Arthur tied up the deal. 'I am prepared to approve the eight hundred pound loan before the Executive Council meets, on my personal authority.' He waited. 'The poor penitents need your services desperately, Samuel. You have no choice. As soon as Brother Schofield returns, you will take ship for the Macquarie Harbour penal settlement as chaplain.'

'If I agree – ' Samuel was not quite finished. 'I have one small favour to ask.'

'Really, Samuel, I think you have drawn quite enough on my favour for one night!' But Arthur was flushed with victory. 'Very well. If it is only very small.'

'Simply this. I pray you listen to Mr Pride. He is an honest man, and freeborn. And what he has to say will not, I believe, be to your disadvantage. I hope you will permit me to say, Your Honour, that the boiled beef tonight was disgusting.'

For a moment Arthur's face did not move. Then

the impossible happened. Lieutenant-Governor George Arthur laughed.

'Thank you, Samuel,' said Bob. They clasped hands on the steps, then pulled up their collars against the chill night air. 'Thank you from the bottom of my heart.'

'I am doing the Lord's work. It is my hope to one day baptise you into our circle of friends.'

'Did you see his face!' Bob said as he walked the missionary to his lodging near the chapel in Melville Street. Someone brushed against them in the dark with an apology, and Bob lashed out with a curse, keeping his hand tight on the folded document in his pocket.

'You learn our ways quickly,' Samuel said.

'I have a good teacher.'

'I knew Arthur would find your proposition irresistible,' Samuel said. He ran his hand over the raised letters of a shopfront to locate himself in the dark. 'His Honour laughed because he has been cornered, checkmated, in his battle with the Van Diemen's Land Company and he saw how your proposal gave him a way out. Live cattle off the Cape or India ships are mostly of the Bengali breed accustomed to tropical climes, and they sicken and die here, or are stolen before they reproduce. Arthur feuds with the Van Diemen's Land Company because their vast Emu Bay estates in the northwest were given by London, not sanctioned by him, and in return the VDLC are as difficult as they can be with the supply of livestock to Arthur's friends, in order to strengthen their hand against him. And they have Durhams – '

'So when I said I could deliver Durham stock, no wonder he was pleased.'

'Keep your hand on that order,' Samuel advised. 'Arthur's signature is good anywhere. You'll see what I mean.'

He stopped at the door beneath the lighted windows of his lodging. 'My wife is waiting up for me,' said Samuel uncomfortably. The clouds sweeping over Mount Wellington tore across the moon, sending shafts of cold light racing down the slopes above the town. 'This news that we must go to Macquarie Harbour will test her. She has come to appreciate the pleasures of civilised society.'

Bob said: 'You won't really take your foster-daughters to such a place?'

'It is my duty to lead, and theirs to follow.' Samuel hesitated, then wrung Bob's hand. 'Good night!'

Bob walked away with his thumbs hooked in his belt, the moonlight sweeping over the rooflines below him to the Prussian blue of the Derwent. The door closed softly behind him and flying footsteps caught him up.

'Is it true?' her voice whispered.

He said: 'Lieutenant-Governor Arthur will issue conditional pardons to my parents the day the first consignment of cattle from King Island are swung ashore on the Hobart Town wharf.'

22

Hope redeemed

Ezzie had been able to bear it no longer. She had watched her stepfather and Bob talking in the street, then Samuel Fisher's footsteps came softly up the stairs; Eleanor took his news about Macquarie Harbour with her eyes lidless with fury, and then her face shrank into its familiar embittered grooves that her enjoyment of the party had softened, and she began to curse her husband for his weakness, for putting his Church before his family. The girls left the room. For a moment the two orphans stood at the head of the stairs while their stepmother wept and bewailed her fate through the thin lath walls as though she wanted the whole street to hear her. Then Faith's eyes filled with tears and she rushed into the little bedroom she shared with Ezzie – but Ezzie rushed downstairs.

She chased after Bob's figure in the moonlight and clung to him. '*Is it true?*'

He smiled with surprise and pleasure. 'Lieutenant-Governor Arthur will issue conditional pardons. . . .' she listened sadly to him prattle joyfully of his parents, not of *them*. She pulled away, and he understood. If he had not she would never have forgiven him.

'Surely Macquarie Harbour cannot be such a dreadful place,' he said. She would not look at him. 'Your father will not take up his appointment for a month at least.' Still she would not look, wearing him down, forcing him to think of her feelings, not his own.

'I shall never see you again,' she said.

'Ezzie.'

'Only you call me by my real name,' she murmured.

'Your stepfather is a good man, Ezzie.'

'He is one of God's sheep,' she blurted viciously, 'and you, you'll marry a Hobarton lady and be a sheep too.' She let him see she meant every word. Then she turned on her heel and ran.

He followed her. She had nowhere to go and the taverns were emptying: the silent town echoed to slamming doors and the oaths of stumbling figures. Ezzie looked over her shoulder then disappeared into a courtyard set back from the road. Bob tilted back his felt hat and ran. He found her up the steps at the chapel door, a blue key gleaming in her right hand, and she thrust it into the lock.

He said: 'You are more important to me than anything.' But she disappeared inside. He plunged after her.

The chapel was blue glow, black shadow: the narrow aisle illuminated by small, high windows along one wall pouring moonbeams. The characteristic eucalyptus smell of Hobart Town was replaced by a fresh scent: the rows of pews were of cedarwood imported from Sydney. She ran past the benches at the back and paused, hearing his running footsteps, then barked her knees slipping into one of the pews.

He sat beside her, banging his knees with a crash. Her mother-of-pearl hairpin gleamed in the moonlight.

'Why should I love them?' Ezzie murmured. 'They do their good works to redeem their *own* souls.'

'That is blasphemy, Ezzie.' It was chilling, and exciting: how far she was prepared to go, how much she cared about him.

'What about *us*?' she demanded, looking down, her elbows on her parted knees. Bob said nothing.

She whispered: 'Love forgives all, redeems all, is all. Do you understand?'

He pulled her hairpin and her hair fell around them as he kissed her.

*

Ezzie crept upstairs. The house was silent. She opened her bedroom door and slipped inside. The curtains were a dim square of moonlight, the bed's pale rectangle almost filled the room. Faith's hair was a dark circle on the pillow. She watched Ezzie undress.

'Did he kiss you?'

'Faith!' Ezzie said demurely. She had done more than kiss.

'What's wrong with kissing?' Faith grumbled. 'I've been going mad, I thought you'd never get back. Don't let them make me go to Macquarie Harbour.'

Ezzie slipped her nightshift over her head and combed out her hair, then got into bed. 'Don't trust him,' Faith begged. 'With that crippled arm you'll never find a man worth having.'

'You didn't warm my side of the bed,' Ezzie complained, but not with her usual vigour. She was remembering Bob's touch.

'Don't pretend it's love,' Faith said.

'But it is.' Ezzie floated.

'You don't want to go to Macquarie Harbour.'

'Only because it would separate me from Bob.'

Faith wept tears of envy.

Bob was strolling back to his room at Mrs Deems's skilling on Wapping Flats with his hands stuck in his pockets and a smile on his face. It was long past midnight and he enjoyed the fierce emotions coursing in his blood. He had been in Van Diemen's Land less than a week: been fooled and robbed, attended divine service and fallen in love head over heels, made new friends, negotiated man-to-man with the Lieutenant-Governor for the pardons to absolve his parents of crime, sold an initial hundred head of cattle to the beef-starved Colony, lost his virginity and proposed marriage to Ezzie Fisher. He had started as he meant to go on.

23

Beneath the tree

'Not this morning, Mrs Deems,' Bob remarked cheerfully on his way out. Mrs Deems lay in wait for him morning and night. As soon as she heard him getting out of bed her footsteps rattled across the rotten boards of the front room and fell silent by his split eucalyptus door, which she would happen to be passing as he came out.

'Oh sir, you surprised me!' she feigned. 'There's a new ship coming in, sir, only the very best ladies of the finest taste.' She followed him into the street. 'You *must* want a wife. It's respectable.'

'Not this morning, Mrs Deems,' Bob repeated.

'I don't want to be disappointed in you. There is a lot of competition you know,' she called after him.

It was September, and in the spring foliage of the imported poplars, oaks and elms of St George's Square, wattle birds quarrelled boisterously for nest space by the gaol's white walls and plovers stalked in aggressive circles on the convict-scythed grass. Only those human figures toiling in yellow and grey were so common that they receded unnoticed into the background: part of the scenery. Bob whistled cheerfully as he walked, hardly able to restrain his excitement. Seeing his son striding up Elizabeth Street, skipping the puddles, swinging a newly-purchased cane, Jim Pride would have recognised the man he had buried long ago inside himself, a young man in love. Heredity had asserted its power, but as always there was a price, and Bob would never call King Island home again.

Honey-eaters nested busily on the corner of Melville Street. He found Ezzie alone in the chapel and they kissed with open mouths.

'I want to be completely alone with you today,' he said. Samuel Fisher's departure for Macquarie Harbour could not be much longer delayed.

Ezzie pretended to arrange a few flowers as Faith came in to the chapel, Lieutenant Proctor in tow. Her catch was a very tall and dashing officer on leave from the Indian Army, with an irresistible moustache, and everyone had been amazed that Faith had caught him. 'G'day,' he drawled, 'foine day for a trawl, says I.' They would hire a dory and sail across the estuary to Kangaroo Point. Bob had first met him one evening at the Macquarie Hotel and they'd done some walking and drinking together, which was how, through Bob, Niall Proctor had been introduced to Faith.

When Bob had asked Samuel Fisher, one evening in front of the lodging room fire, for his foster daughter's hand in marriage, Samuel showed not the least surprise: Bob had played his cards shrewdly and would be baptised. Samuel would have counselled delay in calmer times but Macquarie Harbour and Sarah Island hung over them all. And though he had little faith in human love, it would be wonderful if it were true. What had made up his mind finally was the certainty of Eleanor's opposition. 'I knew this day would come,' Samuel assented by the firelight. 'I know. . . . *love*. Yes, my young friends, you have my blessing.'

'You do *not*,' Eleanor said, and by now even Bob recognised that lidless look of her eyes. 'Samuel!'

'It would be best if you left us, Bob,' Samuel said. Bob took Ezzie's hand, not backing down.

'She stays,' Eleanor ordered, her round face and red round cheeks making her look like a doll, innocent yet embittered, in her black dress.

'I go with Bob,' Ezzie said.

The little woman actually grabbed her, so great was her misery. There ensued a ridiculous but very serious tug-of-war that embarrassed them all, while Faith watched with mockery on her superior features. Ezzie, head down, dry-eyed, wouldn't let herself be taken. Finally Eleanor relinquished her and appealed to Samuel.

He shook his head. 'Not this time,' he said.

Eleanor's face collapsed. He would do anything for anyone, those ruined lines said, except his wife. He was no good.

'Go now,' whispered Samuel to Bob, and he led Ezzie outside. Faith followed, spoiling their embrace.

'A whirlwind romance!' she whispered excitedly, staring at their faces with her eyes glowing, and laid her own plans.

Bob was busy most weekdays, and Sunday was taken up in chapel, so the four of them usually met there on Saturday, when Ezzie was arranging the small bundle of flowers that sweetened the bare interior without risking accusations of ornamentation from the devout. Now they walked to the wharf where Bob had hired a dory, passing the Female Factory still smoke-blackened above the windows where the desperate women had tried to set fire to it with themselves inside. On their way Bob nodded to many men on foot or horseback, or lounging in doorways, who were already his friends. In such a class-ridden society, where everyone knew their place, it was essential to be *placed*: even the lowest scum were complacent because they had the convicts beneath them and this contentment made for the town's peaceful atmosphere and safe streets: many pickpockets but little violence.

Bob played the rules of Hobart Town cleverly. Born free, he was respected by the Lieutenant-Governor, so the Hobartons were bound to respect him: they placed him. With a government contract for the supply of stock in his pocket, he was credit-worthy with the merchant classes, all directors of each others' companies, and so he was placed with men like John Dunn the storekeeper and Gamaliel Butler, the banker; and he was devoutly Wesleyan, a Church whose fast-growing moral leadership, vigorously expounded, made it far more influential in the island than the Catholics or even the Church of England. And he was shortly to marry the minister's stepdaughter.

From the dory's midship thwart Ezzie watched his hand swinging on the tiller between the ships and hulks in the harbour, and dabbled her fingers in the sparkling water. It was no wonder she loved him: the raffish light in his eyes beneath his sun-streaked hair, the range of tones in the way he looked at her, his energy, made it impossible to imagine not loving him.

What she hardly dared believe was that he loved a cripple. There was no strength in her arm, there never would be. He could have married a beautiful woman. This was the fear she hid.

He watched her: she was wearing fluttering white muslin beneath a waterproof cape, and the sun had brought roses to her cheeks. He hardly dared believe she was so beautiful.

Ashore, they collected deadwood from the forest, lit a fire on the beach and sprawled around it. Faith went for a walk, with a glance over her shoulder, and Niall, ever the gentleman, accompanied her. Ezzie sat against Bob. He cupped his hands over her breasts, the back of her head against his shoulder, his mouth whispering in her ear, and on the deserted beach they watched the occasional sail tack across the brilliant blue, and the flat-bottomed scows rowed back full of stone for the new wharf, towed by convicts in rowing boats. The Bruny Island channel shone like a green paint stroke beneath the misty mountain shapes of the distance. Ezzie sighed and Bob led her into the trees, found her a fallen sheoak trunk covered with moss and clematis, and in the green silence among the tiny bright flowers where she lay back with her eyes open, he loved her, and she loved him, giving a small cry as usual.

'Ssh,' he said.

'They'll just think it's a little bird,' she murmured. They walked along the sand, she sensually in her bare feet. 'Take off your shoes,' Ezzie said and he walked as though he expected the sand to bite him, his britches turned up, holding his shoes dangling from two fingers. They heard giggling from the trees and Ezzie covered Bob's lips with her finger. 'We aren't alone.'

'Is she letting him?' Bob said.

'Yes.'

They walked on, holding one another closer than ever.

'Does she love him?'

'She hates Macquarie Harbour,' Ezzie said, then ran, and he caught her up.

Bob squeezed her hand. Having her was opposite to what Johnny told him love was like: afterwards Bob wanted her more not less. Ezzie sauntered, then kicked the fine sand like spray, looked at him with a smile, the sun pulling blonde highlights along her hair, her arm forgotten – with him. She was always new, never what he expected.

Where a stream ran into the bay they crouched, thinking they saw a platypus, and watched penguins play in the surf.

'I don't hide anything from you,' she murmured, 'you alone.'

'I love you, Ezzie.' That was all between them, simple as the sunlight, and she held him close.

Turning back at last, they found Faith in her blue dress and Niall in his uniform sitting upright on opposite sides of the fire as though they had never left it, brewing tea. Niall surveyed the horizon with cat's eyes and Faith looked heated and victorious. 'Where have you been?' she said sternly. Ezzie laughed aloud at such effrontery, and Faith blushed.

A missionary on his way to do God's work at Port Jackson on the coast of New South Wales called in at King Island to hand over Bob's letter. Annie watched on tenterhooks as Jim scanned the page: the promise of conditional pardon, the recognition that was emotionally so important to her, meant *nothing* to him, so deeply had he never forgiven himself; to him it was important only for trade and that was the only, businesslike, satisfaction his face showed. 'Are we free?' she asked.

'You are.'

'*Us*,' she said.

He read on. 'Bob is to be married,' he said, and Annie gave a scream of excitement. 'Her name is Hope. We really have lost him,' Jim said.

'When will it be?' Annie hugged him and while she danced he stood like a pillar.

'Here,' he said. 'When the first stock is shipped out. Then they return to Hobart Town with the cargo. Oh, Annie, I've lost my boy.'

Isaac, the half-aborigine lad, came in and slipped silent as a shadow into the corner. Simeon his father came thumping up the steps and knocked on the door. They showed him Bob's letter. 'You're no longer a criminal,' Annie said.

Simeon cuffed the lad. 'Learn to knock on doors, boy.'

'Sit by the fire,' Annie told Isaac kindly, then turned to Jim. 'Does this mean I can have a proper stove?'

Simeon sat tiredly by the fire. 'Now I can go home.' He rubbed his brown face wearily, his fringe of white hair and beard.

'They don't want you back,' Jim said. 'The pardon only works if you stay in Van Diemen's Land.'

'I'll go anyway. Once a crim, always a crim – my name wasn't always Simmonds, remember. I've nothing to stay for, I'll take the first ship. Don't you want to go back, Jim?'

'No,' Jim said. 'I've got nothing to go back for.'

Annie looked thoughtfully at Jim: he had never referred to his life long ago, and whatever memories returned to him in his silent moods, standing in the vee of branches high in the tree, he did not bring back to earth with him. But if he thought of revenge, she feared it, because anything he did must destroy her first.

'Oh Jim,' she said, 'don't be sad.'

'Got to get to work!' he said. 'There's a jetty to build.' Isaac slipped out to help him: he liked Jim. Alone, Simeon looked at Annie.

'Won't he ever forgive himself?' he asked.

'He can't take his revenge,' she said, 'because of me.' So she must mean something to him after all.

Bob raised a loan with Gam Butler of the Commercial Bank to charter the *Emma Kemp*, a staunch cutter of thirty-seven tons, to bring the first cargo of live cattle from King Island – Captain Steen would call in on the return leg of his regular Port Jackson supply run. Frank Lipscombe would fatten them at Sandy Bay if heavy weather had thinned them down, and John Dunn purchased rights to the wholesale contract.

'You strike a hard bargain, Mr Pride,' he said as they shook hands over the deal. They wouldn't have trusted him if he hadn't: shrewd merchants didn't like dealing with fools. Bob grinned to himself. The real shrewdness of the deal was that it spread plenty of profit around to everybody in on it. They were hooked, and though he would play fair with them, he would make sure they were played to the last penny.

'I am going to King Island to oversee the loading personally,' Bob had promised as he put on his hat. This was only half the truth, but that was best in business. He was really going to get married.

The schooner *Currency Lass* was taking Samuel Fisher to Macquarie Harbour via King Island – they would all sail with him that far, even Faith, who stood tearfully at the ship's rail staring at the sliding shore of Kangaroo Point. She had been so sure that Niall Proctor would marry her after all she had given him, but he had simply gone. Ezzie held her hand: Faith, ashamed, must go to Macquarie Harbour, and live without love.

As Mount Wellington dwindled until only its wreath of cloud showed above the horizon, and the little schooner turned northwards for King Island, guilty tears ran freely down Faith's cheeks, or perhaps it was just the salt spray.

'I am a sinner,' she whispered during the dark night to Ezzie in their cabin, the groaning of timbers so loud her voice was almost lost beneath them. 'I acknowledge it. I repent and accept the justice of my punishment.'

'You're just feeling seasick,' Ezzie said, and the ship sailed on.

King Island weather was never safe. The *Currency Lass* hove to for only six hours in Franklin Roads – at ninety tons she was too big to come alongside the simple blue gum jetty jutting into the channel of the Yellow Rock River. The wedding party were rowed ashore and Jim Pride, who believed in no god, shook the hand of the man who would marry his son to this girl with the sunstreaked hair.

'Welcome to King Island.' Jim's voice was rough with emotion. He punched Bob then hugged him.

'I'll stay until the *Emma Kemp* arrives from Port Jackson.'

236

Jim knelt on the jetty to reach down into the boat. 'And you're Hope.'

'Ezzie,' Ezzie said eagerly, ignoring her foster mother's *tsk*. She was starting her new life.

Jim told Bob: 'She's lovely.'

'Too right,' Bob said, observing the look in his father's eyes.

'If I was twenty-five years younger,' Jim said, 'I'd fight Bob for you!' He took her right arm and lifted her smoothly beside him.

'Well!' said Mrs Fisher, putting out her hand to be helped.

'Where's Ma?' Bob said.

'Now, Bob, Annie turned her ankle carrying the milk in, I keep telling her not to, it's bruised to hell – sorry, Samuel.'

'A fine of one Ticket,' Samuel Fisher smiled, inhaling the bracing air. 'Come Eleanor, Faith, we must walk.' He sounded pleased. 'There are no such conveniences as carriages on King Island!'

'Yes,' Jim said. As they walked he told Ezzie, 'Don't mind Annie, she's always been closest to Bob. There was everything to get ready at Paragon House, she's laid out a spread.'

'Paragon House?' Eleanor Fisher said over her shoulder, holding her fluttering black parasol so as to keep the sun from her face. But when she saw the little patchwork of a house in the valley, she looked disappointed.

'We call it our home,' Jim said, 'though it looks funny enough to town eyes, I daresay.' He didn't sound amused.

'I had expected something larger.' And Eleanor had not expected a ship's figurehead above the door. She threw Samuel a look, her warnings vindicated: *Told you so*.

'Bob and Ezzie will be living in Hobart Town

237

anyway,' Jim said shortly, and realised that he had become quite attached to his cottage, neatly garlanded with wisteria and passionfruit vine, woodsmoke whipping cheerfully from the chimney. Annie had planted welcoming rows of flowers beside the path; the paling fence had been given a lick of precious white paint and the lovingly tended vegetable gardens were as precise as a military display.

'It's wonderful!' Ezzie exclaimed, and Jim tried not to appear pleased.

'It's nothing.' But it was quite something, of course. 'This is just a working ranch.'

Not to Bob. His home had already changed. The outhouse had new planks added out back and it was all smarter than he remembered. It was part of the past now. He stopped, and Ezzie squeezed his hand.

Suddenly Faith said in a sad voice, 'We've never known a home.'

Ezzie said: 'I hope I never grow up.' She walked alone towards the house.

Inside, Annie listened to the blur of their voices through the wooden walls. She wanted Bob to be happy, but the *Emma Kemp* would be here in only a day or two; she didn't see why they had to rush back to Hobart Town so quickly, unless Hope had put him up to it. She forced a smile on her lips and hobbled outside.

Ezzie said: 'Pleased to meet you, Mrs Pride.' The vivid grass dappled her white dress with a pale, greenish glow. Her eyes were very blue and the sun lit her hair.

Annie just stood there by the table laden with good things, her curly brown hair streaked with grey, her work-hardened hands hanging. Suddenly her eyes filled with tears. 'No, girl, I'm not Mrs Pride. Jim never would. We never married, it isn't to be. *You* are Mrs Pride.' She knew from the younger girl's straight-

238

forward gaze they made love. She wasn't the young lady she appeared; or it was true love. Annie said: 'I hope you'll make my Bob happy.'

'I'm sure we will be.'

'I've knitted some woollens, proper merino, for you to take back for him, what with those Hobart Town frosts.'

Bob came over. 'I see you've already met Ezzie.'

'New suit,' Annie grunted, then held her boy tight. 'Now, does she look after you?'

'You can see she does,' Bob said. 'Be happy for us.'

Samuel Fisher called, 'Well, shall we get down to business?'

The party walked towards the lagoon where Simeon, Isaac, the O'Henry's who had been drinking, Johnny and Selina were waiting beneath the tree. Annie was the same height as Ezzie and they walked in step. 'I suppose Ezzie is a common name nowadays,' Annie said.

Bob turned in irritation. 'Ma, stop trying to put her down, will you?'

'Bob's nervous!' Johnny murmured, jabbing Selina in the ribs with his elbow.

She didn't give him one back as usual. 'Don't, Johnny.'

'Ho!' he said, 'you and your bellyaches, you used to be a sport.'

She looked at the black swans cruising the blue waters. She had something to tell Johnny and she supposed she ought. 'Johnny. . . .'

'Well, what is it?'

'I've got a little one in there.'

'So what?' he shrugged.

'It's yours.'

'I'd bloody kill you if it wasn't!'

'You're pleased about it then?'

'Long as it doesn't slow you down,' he said and

239

she sighed, relieved. 'Here come the church mice,' he scoffed.

Bob and Ezzie were married beneath the tree, their voices quiet in the calm air down here, though the wind roared in the upper branches. They thought Annie was crying because mothers did. In reality she was remembering her poor dead daughter from all those years ago, remembering when she herself was young.

When the ceremony was over Samuel Fisher seized the opportunity for a little preaching to this wilderness that had never heard the word of God raised in its domain. His face came to life, his eyes lit up, he lifted up his arms to encompass them all. Feargal O'Henry shook his head, a staunch lapsed Catholic. Selina noticed his boys by Becky Donahoo, Frank and Sean, still avoided her mother, Mary Roper. Selina was far from stupid, though she had been held back by hardly being brought up, but now she was older she saw her mother really loved O'Henry, even though work had bent his back and drink had taken much of his strength: her mother was happy with him because of his faults, not in spite of them. She supposed she felt the same about Johnny. She loved him more than he knew, and felt the pride of carrying on the line, feeling the new life stirring within her. Feargal, followed obediently by Sean and Frank, sat in the bullock cart rather than listen to the Protestant devil. Annie, Selina saw, didn't like it either: her expression was lemon-sucking sour, and her eyes were fixed on Ezzie, the flash of gold at her throat. Jealous old biddy. When the sermon ran out of steam and they were walking uphill to eat, Selina hung back with Annie. 'Your face is as long as your foot,' Selina said. Annie, trembling, ignored her.

The others sat round the table and tucked in. King Islanders did not know the meaning of the word temperance: the hooch was blindingly strong. Elbows were stuck out, jaws chomped. Jim kept glancing at Annie. 'Cheer up, old girl.'

'No,' Annie whispered, 'it can't have happened.'

Bob and Ezzie were laughing together. 'Look at the way she laughs,' Jim said fondly, 'don't spoil their day. Come on, Annie, this isn't like you.'

'Isn't it?' Annie said, not looking at him. Jim shrugged. The mouthful of food Annie had taken swelled up in her throat. She pressed her hand to her mouth and had to go inside.

Jim looked over his shoulder then got up and came in. Annie closed her eyes. 'Go away,' she said.

'Don't you feel up to it, old girl?' he asked kindly.

'Where did she get that deformed arm?'

He lost his geniality and frowned. 'It doesn't worry Bob.'

'I'm sorry, Jim.' She forced herself to smile. 'Go back and enjoy yourself.' She picked up a knife and pretended to cut the bread.

'Are you sure you're all right?' he asked from the doorway, and she smiled brightly until the instant he turned away.

Annie hated Ezzie. She couldn't stand the sight of her. For the first time in her life, Annie understood justice. The real concept of sin – really nobody here felt they were convicts for real crimes – struck home to her. The dead came back to life. The coincidence of the name was too great. And that locket. She was sure Ezzie was her baby.

Ezzie was the girl Dick Dodds threw in the river, the ghost of Annie's old life come back to haunt her with its taint, its stain.

She didn't really hate Ezzie, Annie hated herself. Guilt.

24

October 1831 – 1833 December
Two islands

Bob was still furious with his mother for spoiling their day yesterday but he got no joy from Johnny. 'Ah, you know what the old girl's like,' Johnny said carelessly from the saddle as they rode, and loosened his hatbrim with his thumb.

'Maybe I don't,' Bob said.

'Let's load this bloody mob and have a drink,' Johnny said. 'What does it matter, any right?' He pulled on the reins, a fine horseman, and stormed past Selina, strong and dark with matted hair that she kept sweeping back from her face as she talked to Ezzie by the fence rail. Ezzie looked very slight beside her: a slim lonely figure. Bob had set his horse galloping after Johnny's and the milling cattle, the first load to be taken to the jetty at Yellow Rock. It all looked dangerous to her and she realised how little she knew her new husband.

'Don't worry,' Selina said, 'they know what they're doing.'

'Do they?'

'Johnny's showing off,' Selina grinned. 'Look at that – not a thought in his head, the dear man.' Horses, men and cattle swirled together in a dust of fine sand. The sail of the *Emma Kemp* had been sighted tacking beyond New Year Island but the easterly that took the Fishers' *Currency Lass* safely away last evening, bound for Macquarie Harbour, now kept the cutter out. An easterly was a rare wind on King Island, and a bad one; it went against the order of things in the Roaring Forties.

Selina laughed and scratched her ribs. 'Look at Johnny go. He'll inherit all this, you know. The first-born, and that's important to him. I don't know what he'd do otherwise. I wish we had a proper bed. Him living with his parents makes me feel like an outcast.' Ezzie looked with new respect at the dark-lashed, strong-boned girl who carried the smell of the earth engrained in her skin. 'I like you,' Selina said. 'Johnny's not what he appears, he's so frightened of failing. They all are, aren't they.'

'No,' Ezzie shook her head in certainty. 'Not Bob. I'm sure it's never occurred to him.'

'I can tell it from the way Johnny makes love, quick in, quick out, afraid of giving himself away. He's so straight and simple.'

'Are you carrying Johnny's child?'

'That's only part of it. We'll have a home of our own. . . .' Selina narrowed her eyes for a moment. Ezzie held her hand and they watched the two men circling the cloud of dust. Uncharacteristic though it was, this was the image of King Island Ezzie carried ever after in her mind: the figures of men and dust and cattle under the glaring light, the easterly wind blowing over the treetops and dunes.

In the afternoon the *Emma Kemp* tied up at the jetty and anchored King Island to the world. The cattle were driven aboard into deck-stalls and secured by cleats. Jim said goodbye to Bob and Ezzie. 'She'll come round,' he said, nodding at Annie watching from the bank of sand, 'it's just one of those woman things.'

Bob kept glancing back, hurt Annie wouldn't come down to say goodbye. The little vessel could wait no longer: the sail was hoisted before the wind changed. Bob and Ezzie stood in the stern. Ezzie waved. Jim clambered back to Annie. They stood watching the cutter follow the dark channel through the turquoise shallows and cross the bar.

Jim said to Annie's ear: 'Why did you give the impression that you are a heartless and loveless old woman, when the opposite is true?'

The first thing Faith did on arriving at Macquarie Harbour, before even disembarking from the ship, was to write home: *home* was Ezzie, Faith knew no other.

They had a fine voyage. Faith was happy for Ezzie and very interested to see King Island, and she was sure Bob would make a fine husband. She prayed for them and loved them. The voyage was fascinating! Light winds, and the Southern Ocean calm but full of curves, vast mirrors of blue glare half a mile from peak to trough sliding slowly beneath the frail vessel. The sawtoothed, almost uninhabited western coast of Van Diemen's Land crept by for days, then the captain pointed out the two sentinels, Mount Heemskirk and Mount Zeehan, and turned for the shore. It revealed itself as a line of surf, unbroken, thrilling, stretching along the sandy beach to their left until the blowing salt obscured it. They stared excited at the rolling backs of the breaking waves: on their right a promontory pointed straight at them with the sea that seemed so calm bursting against its cliffs like explosions. Between the beach and the cliffs were Hell's Gates. The sea became unsteady, pushing them on, drawing them back. Faith gasped, staring over the ship's side with round eyes as beneath them crawled the sea bottom, a field of beaten gold, the shimmering sand thrown down by the mighty currents swirling around Cape Sorell. Ahead of them in the mouth of the harbour broke a strange amber surf. They had been seen: the red flag was flying to indicate that the narrow entrance was navigable, and the arms of the semaphore on Entrance

Island moved, summoning the pilot who would be their guide through Hell's Gates. The captain ordered the women below so they should not see the sight. They sat in the dark praying, listening in an ecstasy of terror as the ship shuddered and banged. They sensed the sandbanks sliding only feet beneath them, and heard the sails' flapping and sounds of rattling cordage come clapping back off rocks or islets. The channel must be barely wider than the ship was long. Then all sound ceased: they had entered sheltered water, and praised God.

The captain permitted them on deck. Macquarie Harbour stretched away like wrinkled metal between misty headlands as far as the eye could see, one of the great harbours of the world, surrounded by a wilderness. The captain assured them several hours later, 'Only people are here who deserve to be,' as Sarah Island appeared in silhouette against the mouth of the Gordon River.

There was no time for Faith to write more in her letter to Ezzie.

The *Currency Lass*, having unloaded its stores at Sarah Island and shipped a cargo of Huon pine for Hobart Town, departed carrying this letter with her. Almost immediately, even before the ship had shrunk from sight, Faith started another letter. She lived through her letters. The government schooner took away a pathetic pile of them when it called, every six months. A girl could write a lot of letters in six months.

In Hobart Town the colossal ironstone extension of the Stone Wharf into deep water at Hunter's Island meant Bob's fat cattle could be safely unloaded straight onto the dockside. One or two, panicked by blasting-powder explosions and the clang of jackhammers, broke loose and swam for it, pursued along the quagmire of reclaimed shore towards Battery Point by men waving

245

neckerchiefs, shovels and jumping-bars. But Lieutenant-Governor Arthur was a man of his word, and by evening the conditional pardons and the lease granting 275,000 acres of King Island to Jim Pride for £20 per annum were delivered to Bob by private messenger.

So Arthur had won his victory over the Van Diemen's Land Company and Bob had legally vindicated his parents. He would have been less pleased if he had seen his father's face when the captain of the *Emma Kemp* handed him the sealed envelope a couple of months later, when the second batch of cattle had been loaded at Yellow Rock.

'Hell!' Jim said, then bit his lip rather than go on: a name from the past. Annie took the document and struggled to read it, her lips forming each letter before she uttered the word, then gave up. 'What's that one?'

'Whereas,' Jim said.

' "Whereas James Prideau, alias Jim Pride, who arrived in this Island under a Sentence of Transportation, hath by his good conduct and behaviour during his residence in this Island appeared to me the said Lieutenant-Governor to be a fit object for the extension to him of a Conditional Remission of his Sentence. . . ." ' Why do they write it so you can't understand it?' Annie asked.

Jim stared at the sky. 'James Prideau is forgiven of his crime,' he sneered. *He* had forgiven nothing.

'Who is he, this James Prideau?' she said, and he looked at her sharply.

'Annie – ' He stopped. By the gangway Johnny, a broad smile on his dusty face and a lasso hanging from his hand, was looking at him. Johnny the firstborn, Bob the favourite. 'It's all too late,' Jim said. 'What a mess we've made of our lives.'

At the gangway it was his twin brother, a rough, rawboned, sunbrowned William Prideau he thought he now saw, just from a flash in his son's eyes. 'Have you done that work on the south fence?' Jim shouted angrily. Startled, Johnny rode away jabbing his spurs into the flanks of his horse. There was no such thing as redemption. Jim watched until he was gone, his face dark with fury to witness such treatment.

Annie continued: ' "Now therefore in consideration I the Lieutenant-Governor aforesaid remit all the residue or remainder of the term of Transportation, upon this express condition: that the said James Prideau also known as Jim Pride shall continue to reside within the said Island of King Island." '

To her surprise Jim began to laugh. 'Don't you see? It doesn't mention you, Annie.' He hugged her, laughing. 'Because you aren't formally my wife – you're a bureaucratic oversight – you're still technically a felon!'

Annie looked down at the piece of paper. The mistake had amused him, but she took it seriously. 'I'm glad,' she said at last. 'I don't want to be forgiven. Or to forgive. Do you, Jim?'

He didn't reply. He took the paper. A quarter of a century had passed since he killed the marine on the beach for her and nothing had changed: Jim Pride was as close and as far away from her as ever. Annie despaired. Still she did not have his heart. He glanced at her and she thought he would tear the paper up, let the wind take it, but then he folded it and put it in his pocket. But he did not put his arms round her.

They stood on the shore together, staring out at the straight horizon of the sea that bounded their prison.

Ezzie took no part whatsoever in religious work now; Bob was her life.

In Hobart Town they first set up house in the Melville Street lodging near the chapel. Ezzie adored fun in bed and showed Bob she treasured him more than words could say. She soon got the old place homely and different from how her step-parents had it, rearranging the chairs and adding tasselled cushions and a sumptuous embroidered bedspread. Bob wondered where she got her love for these little luxuries – certainly not from her upbringing, where plainness was a virtue. Nor was she afraid of running up accounts. She delighted in buying a fancy Honiton lace lambrequin for the mantelshelf from John Dunn's store, a bookshelf of gold-tooled first editions from Tegg's, and a few warm, dark red, patterned rugs as the changeable Hobart Town weather turned back towards winter again. Her fireplace burned Macquarie Harbour coal for the sense of connection it gave her to Faith; mined by the convicts, it smoked more than enough, and she always put on a few sheoak logs to show a cheerful flame when Bob returned home.

Bob attended chapel at first simply because he thought the contacts he made there would forward his career – the one thing nobody could afford in Hobart Town was to be an outsider. But gradually he came to believe in what he heard there and genuinely to respect the people he joined in worship; as he became more prosperous he did a little lay preaching himself. Ezzie worked to fill the gap taken by King Island and the withholding of his mother's love, unfailingly cheerful and faithfully supportive. They had both grown up, a respectable and well-regarded couple with a widening circle of acquaintances, and soon Bob had acquired the row of small cottages further down the street, with a rateable value of £55 a year. In almost every way they were happy as could be. A year passed, and Ezzie did not conceive.

They were regular guests at the Governor's dinner parties each Wednesday night, suffocatingly formal and patronising on the surface, a web of Hobarton intrigue beneath. In winter Ezzie carried a little Chinese fan to stir the bitter New Town coal dust from her face, in summer she stood near the open window with its cooling draught and view over the thick copse of gum trees to the sparkling cove below. Black smoke trailed across it: the first steam engine had arrived in the Colony, paid for in apples and consignments of Huon pine for the Clyde shipwrights. In the room behind her the other women disapproved of her obvious, naive happiness and easy manner: the matrons found her too approachable. Mrs MacDowell had been cut dead for admitting she lived with her husband and knew him before marrying him – just *admitting* it. Ezzie did not believe in her own perfection, she did not twitter about the unreliability of servants, and she did not live in New Town. At least her clothes were fashionable, and she knew how to be genteel. But was she whole-heartedly one of them? They liked her, but there was that narrowed laughter in her eyes, and they did not trust her.

Ezzie made smiling conversation with the plump, white-breasted matrons. Bob had to do business with their husbands.

She was a wonderful actress; she'd lived a lie all her life, demure and faithful, the Wesleyan daughter. She looked round the solid, stolid faces of the men Bob was talking to – what a bunch. It was an open secret that the Treasury had been robbed of more than a thousand pounds in gold bullion about five years ago – not a robbery by convicts, but an appropriation by some of these respectable men who had done so very well out of the boom. It was whispered that the money had been used to finance the Commercial Bank of Van Diemen's Land – John Dunn had personally found from somewhere the funds to purchase half the share-holding. Bob's cynical friend Alphabet Boyes, with his close links to the Colonial Treasurer, had taken him aside and repressing mirth, told him the same thing had happened again – thousands of pounds missing, embezzled. The Lieutenant-Governor's problem, Boyes chuckled, in this land of convicts, emancipists, adventurers and the dregs of the British military and bureaucratic establishment, and very few Australians, was whom to trust. Bob realised he was being given a message.

'Go on,' he said.

Boyes twirled his glass and looked Bob frankly in the eye. 'The Great Arthur has let it be known that he expects the money to be returned. It will be, of course. But henceforth – this is the order straight from London – Treasury funds will be deposited in a private bank. But whose? John Dunn and Gam Butler are directors of the Commercial Bank, the Bank of Van Diemen's Land and half a dozen others, and Arthur is determined they won't have returned to them as deposits money they embezzled in the first place.'

'He needs an Australian bank,' Bob said.

Boyes said: 'I've always wanted to be a shareholder. . . . George Walker, the draper, has banking experience. And Frank Lipscombe's honest – he's up for Alderman, did you know?' He looked Bob in the eye.

'I have a venture in mind,' Bob said.

So the Paragon-Pride Bank of Australia was born. Ezzie liked to think she conceived on the very same evening, he whispering his secret while she stroked his thigh with her right hand: they both knew their big business opportunity had come and she always liked to celebrate Bob's successes in bed, binding their two lives and bodies into one. So perhaps it was true. They moved to the florid-fronted two-storey house at the end of the little row of cottages Bob owned, which had more space for a child. But Ezzie's baby miscarried after only a few months, whereas with the funds attracted by Treasury deposits, Paragon-Pride went from strength to strength. While she was recuperating in bed two letters arrived for her on the same day. Ezzie chose the writing she did not recognise: the long-awaited news had at last arrived from King Island that Selina had given birth to her boy, and called him Billy. It was so easy for her. 'He looks just like his father,' Selina wrote fondly in her big untidy hand, 'everyone says so.'

The other letter was from Faith.

'My dearest sister in God,' Faith wrote. 'What a wonderful place Sarah Island is! I see our Father's hand at work in this place. The island is small, low and bare. All the trees have been cut down, a windbreak has been erected instead. Our cottage has a view of the jetty and, several miles across the water, we can just make out the line of Farm Cove, Mount Sorell rising gloriously behind it. On a clear day, the broken peak of Frenchman's Cap, more than one mile high, may even be seen! The forests are impenetrable and unin-habited, there is no escape except to certain death, it is a wild and pure place. There are several hundred penitents undergoing reform here. Hard labour turns useless characters into good workers – and they are worked vigorously, mostly at felling the trees up the Gordon River, floated down in rafts, dangerous work but improving, and they are fed little more than monks. Bricks are made, boats built, furniture made for the profit of the government, and crops grown on Philip Island and at Farm Cove so that the officers may enjoy fresh vegetables and avoid the scurvy that plagues the penitents. Since the aborigines have been removed from the lower cells, the men have grown violent, and many have been confined to Grummet Rock, windswept and constantly wet. The rainfall here on the west coast is measured in fathoms! Mr Fisher says these men are all incorrigibly wicked. . . . Samuel is weary, and God's light seems to have been withdrawn from him. He makes every effort to save them, but they relapse. He has *lost Hope* – forgive my wicked pun! He spends much

251

of his time trying to persuade the commandant that the graveyard casualties, those fortunates who have achieved peace, should be dignified by markers of stone, not initialled planks stuck in the earth by the Dead House or on Halliday's Island. We do miss you, and wish you were here with us. Eleanor and I have taken over some of his ministry but we can only work among the officers as Major Baylee, the commandant, says we must be protected from the men. How quickly one comes to hate the condemned – they are so dull, and let the irons chafe their legs almost to the bone although they are supplied with leather gaiters. However, there are ways around every rule. One of the men made me a good pair of kangaroo-leather shoes, soft and they have lasted very well. There is not very far to walk on such a small island! Mostly we walk in the house, which has two rooms. If Mr Fisher dies, we will have to leave. . . .'

Ezzie confronted Bob. 'I feel awful about her. She sounds half crazy.'

'I don't think she would agree. She's just unhappy.'

'She's driving *me* half crazy with these letters. Can't you do something for her? Drop a hint to someone who matters?'

'Leave it,' Bob advised.

'You could speak to Arthur. Just a word from you. That's the way you do things here, isn't it?'

'Do you think Faith would thank me?' he said gently.

'No,' Ezzie said. 'Do it for me.'

So he did, and when he tapped Boyes, one of the few men he could mention the existence of convicts to, the administrator gave a mocking laugh. 'Don't you know? Arthur took on a couple of servants Fisher was supposed to have reformed, brought to God and all that, and they broke fifteen pounds' worth of cut glasses.' The two men amiably walked to work in the warm January breeze, then paused before parting on the broad corner of Elizabeth Street. 'Quietly, now,' Boyes confided, 'Macquarie Harbour is to be closed down, it's got out of control. The horror will revert to unbesmirched antipodean never-never land and Port Arthur will be extended. Discipline will be total and humane, convicts will have their heads in bags and never be allowed to see each other, only the chaplain. A true reformatory. It'll take until the end of the year, but Arthur will probably give the Port Arthur chaplaincy to Fisher.'

Bob told Ezzie in bed. 'I don't expect Arthur would let him leave Macquarie Harbour early.'

'You don't seriously think Samuel would agree to leave before his work was done,' she said.

When Ezzie was expecting again Bob took her out in the carriage and showed her, through the falling leaves of the oak trees that grew so tall and strong here, one of the good Italian-style houses on Elboden Square. 'That's our new house,' he said, and kissed her, and she fainted with her face as pale as death.

Bob shouted to the driver, 'Take us to Doctor Agnew's house – quickly!'

'No. . . .' Annie said. Another stillborn child: it was a kind of murder going on and on like this. And that had been in April 1833: now it was June and it could have happened again by now. Being half in touch like this was worse than not hearing anything at all. Annie walked along the line of the Yellow Rock River, the winter mud squelching over her shoes and the cold rain trickling over her stony features – she did not notice her discomfort, she hardly saw where she was headed. The sins of the grandmother visited on her grandchildren could not be fair, but the Biblical justice of the punishment convinced her of her own guilt. Like Jim, she bottled herself up inside, helplessly forcing them still further apart because she loved him and couldn't bear to tell him how she had failed him. She still wanted him to love her; to be worth loving.

'Jim means more than anything to you,' Selina said.

'Of course he does!' snapped Annie impatiently. 'And Bob,' she added. Selina looked down when Johnny was not mentioned.

Johnny had built their shingle hut near where Simeon's old gardown used to be, on the Yellow Rock River near the shelter of the dunes. The grass outside hissed as loudly as though it was inside, and the wind blew between the slatted walls, flapping the blankets hung over them and blowing the smoke of the fire about. 'Can't Johnny be bothered to do anything properly?' Annie demanded furiously.

'He's *your* son,' Selina said. 'Calm down, why don't you?' Only Selina could speak to Annie so casually.

'Your baby's crying,' Annie said, and Selina watched, amused, as the older woman plucked Billy out of the incongruously solid, smartly blue-painted crib. Annie's gift had been imported from a mass manufactory in High Wycombe, England: they had money to spend now. Selina would have been just as happy wrapping Billy up in a packing crate.

'He's no longer a baby,' she said, 'he's a little boy. Johnny's had him on horseback. He's going to train Billy to whistle like he does to make the horse come over.'

'Billy can't even crawl yet,' Annie said. 'They grow up too quickly nowadays.'

'What was Becky Donahoo really like?' Selina asked, and Annie looked at her in surprise. Of course; Selina would have seen her father's first woman only from a distance, and been too young to understand.

'She was a battler. . . .' Annie said, but that described all of them. 'I didn't know her. What was she like? She was just Becky.' She sighed: 'Who knows? It's past now.'

254

'Why did you come here?' Selina asked.

Anna cuddled the baby. Billy stirred, then settled back on her shoulder, his thumb in his mouth. The most important secrets must be secrets for ever.

Faith stood at the graveside at the north end of Sarah Island, in the Cemetery of the Free, with the wind cutting through her black clothes like a knife. Some things could not be put down in words – perhaps nearly everything could not. She would never be able to write what she now felt in a letter to Ezzie: the wind blowing through her, the bands of rain scouring the harbour white and grey and wrinkling her skin, the mighty wilderness. She looked around her. Eleanor was weeping: the soldiers seemed relieved by the demonstration of human emotion, and clustered around the warmth of it in this awful place, Major Baylee holding up the sobbing woman, his hair blown ragged, leading her gently to the shelter of the windbreak. Faith stood alone and knew there was no God – none that she would recognise. The surf broke into white feathers on the island rocks. Samuel Fisher was dead.

The wind made her eyes trickle. A mile westward Cape Sorell, the long jagged headland that kept Macquarie Harbour from the sea, was riven with a thousand streams from the interminable rains: they glinted their silvery veins across the wild button-grass heathlands created over millennia by the aborigines' firesticks. The tribes, Mimegin and Lowreene, were completely saved now, gone. She twitched as a piece of brick clinked behind her: Sarah Island shook almost imperceptibly to the vast, primitive heartbeat of the waves breaking on the seaward cliffs of Cape Sorell. The shock was transmitted through the hard rocks that comprised the Cape and the floor of Macquarie Harbour, with Sarah Island its isolated peak.

She had never known how much she needed Samuel Fisher until he was gone.

His name was carved in full with convict skill on a headboard of Huon pine, the rainforest tree that grew everywhere here. Not stone, the penitentiary was winding down, few remained to do the labour; and not in the convicts' burial ground on Halliday Isle, the water was too rough, the haste of departure too great. The golden wood probably would last longer than stone in this climate, Faith thought. She could not write this in a letter. The funeral party wound its way back Indian-file and bedraggled to the buildings, many of which were already dismantled. He had died because he had lost heart, and he had been all heart. Faith could not write that down either.

'We shall return to England,' Eleanor said. She loved him now he was dead. 'We shall carry his memory Home with us.'

By chance the government brig *Prince Leopold* of eighty-one tons, the old *Rosetta*, one of the first ships to be built in New South Wales, lay at the jetty loading treenails and logs. Her masts and spars were massive, of heavy blue gum, and she had a reputation for rolling. Bearing in mind the ladies' circumstances, Captain Harris agreed to take them at once. The wind was dying away to a steady breeze; the *Prince Leopold* cast off at first light, keeling across the flat tea-coloured water incandescent with a faithful reproduction of the dawn. As the sun rose over the bare shoulders of Mount Sorell, cloaking the rainforest of the lower slopes with steam, the decks and rose-tinted sails of the ship steamed too. It was a scene of extraordinary beauty, but Captain Harris swore an oath for more wind.

By mid-morning, as the harbour narrowed towards the entrance, the white arms of the semaphore on Entrance Island still hung down unattended and the pilot's boat did not appear. 'Lucas is drunk, by God!'

swore Captain Harris. But the flag remained raised to indicate the narrow entrance was navigable. The peaty current, swollen after the rains, swept them out past the island, and as the headland of Port Sorell fell away the wind blew down a gully, shivering the sails. The masthead lookout reported a strong wind up there, but on deck it was calm. The captain frowned.

Behind the island, Hell's Gates appeared, the breaking waves higher than the ship's masts from Ocean Beach to Cape Sorell, seething foam and swirling whirlpools. Captain Harris tried to turn back; the vessel rotated helplessly with clapping sails in the flood. Eleanor went below and Faith wondered if her prayers would save them. Faith stood with her hands calmly on the rail. The approach of a great blue wave sucked the ship forward in a gathering roar of spray and sand.

The wave broke white, the ship turned turtle; falling timbers crushed them against the sea bed.

Ezzie seemed to take Faith's death very lightly: there was a hard edge to Bob's lively, lovely wife, an unsentimentality that cut. He, the businessman with his energy and enthusiasm, was the romantic. He thought: *Suppose I had married Faith?* It would have been Ezzie who went to Macquarie Harbour. Lieutenant-Governor Arthur had let Bob know personally that the *Prince Leopold* was six weeks overdue – Arthur had used the ship to entertain guests at the civil service regattas at Geilston Bay and grown deeply attached to the little vessel, the tears in his eyes belying his cold-hearted reputation, a deeply emotional man revealed in private, even if it was over only a ship. He had wrung Bob's hand in silent distress.

Deeply upset by the bad news about Faith he carried, Bob returned home to Elboden Place. Graves opened the door, bowed, and took his hat and coat to brush. Bob crossed the broad sunlit parlour and lifted Ezzie in his arms, held her tight. 'You are all the world to me,' he whispered.

'I know,' she said to his chest. 'And I know that Faith is dead. She never wanted to go to that place, Bob, and then she never wanted to return.' She put back her head and looked at him steadily.

'Don't you care?'

'All I care about is life!' Ezzie said impetuously. 'I have some news of my own.'

'Oh my God,' he said, pleased and frightened.

'This time,' she promised, very determined, 'this time will be all right. Doctor Agnew says I must be quiet. Perhaps even stay in bed for the last couple of months.' She made a face. 'But I will be *all right*, Bob.'

'You make me so happy.' He tried to get Faith out of his mind.

'I've got a terrible confession.' Ezzie mimicked the drawling English accents of the Hobarton women, their overblown speaking. 'You'll be *devastated*!' She laughed when he looked genuinely worried. 'Bob, I only go swimming! The exercise is good for the baby – '

'Swimming? Where?' He was shocked. 'What about *you*? Were you seen?'

'Of course not. There are any number of deserted beaches. Graves – ' the stocky convict butler assigned to them, with a face like a flatiron and the inevitable forename of Lazarus. 'He drives me to Sandy Bay, or we take Allender's little ferry to Kangaroo Point. He stands guard while we swim, staring like a statue into the forest, a white towel hung over his arm.'

Bob's mind raced. There was his baby to consider – this silly swimming must stop. If Ezzie were seen the social consequences would be incalculable.

'I forbid it,' he said.

'But I enjoy it! I love the water, Bob.'

'Think of the child.' He waggled his finger. 'No more swimming!'

She pouted, but saw he was serious.

Again he thought: Poor Faith! and imagined her dead, her belly swollen with seawater and the eels nibbling her wide eyes.

25

May 1835 – 1845 August

The death of illusion

The convict barque *Neva*, a hundred and twenty-five days from Cork bound for Port Jackson, struck the north tip of King Island on the thirteenth day of the month at five in the morning. Her cargo was one hundred and fifty female convicts and fifty-five children, not including babies born during the voyage, and nine free women. It was a windy moonlit night, her rudder was ripped off, and despite Captain Peck's brilliant box-sailed seamanship she wedged on the reef with seas breaking over her, and her decks collapsed within four hours. Twenty-seven survivors reached shore. Five wandered into the bush and were never found, seven died on the beach of cold and rum poisoning. The captain and six seamen survived; all the children were killed.

Jim Pride, his long iron-grey hair blowing in the wind and a tough grimace on his face, buried ninety-five soft, wrinkled bodies in a mass grave on the beach. Annie toiled beside him with features of stone. To her each child wore Ezzie's face: each of Ezzie's dead children, Annie's punishment. The shovels clinked on pebbles and the men cursed as they worked. Jim remembered the wreck of the *Paragon* nearly thirty years ago: the same scene haunting him. When Johnny arrived, his horse picking its way fastidiously between the bundles staining the sand, Jim turned on him.

'Get off that bloody horse,' he roared, 'and take your bloody hat off.'

'What have I done?' Johnny demanded.

'It's what you haven't done,' Jim swore. He snatched Johnny's hat off in his horny hands and pushed it against Johnny's chest. None of them had ever seen Jim so raw with anger.

'I'm sorry, all right?' Johnny shouted.

'Dig, you lazy bastard,' Jim said, turning away, but the word hung behind him in the air.

Selina was waiting when Johnny got home. His blue jacket smelled of death and he had lost his hat. She watched him cross the yard and put his head in the water butt. 'Run off and play,' Selina told Billy, but the three-year-old watched his father sloshing water over his shoulders then tried to fit his arms inside the arms of the discarded bluey he picked up from the hard-packed earth.

'Bad, was it,' Selina murmured.

'Nah,' Johnny shrugged, 'nothing to it.' He stood looking at Billy.

She sighed: 'What is it now, Johnny?'

His face showed almost no expression. They went inside, she held out her arms and hugged him, the water on his chest wetting her shift and making her shiver. Through the gaps in the door Selina could see Billy wrestling with the jacket outside and she wanted Johnny to take her to the pile of boards covered by a straw palliasse that passed for a bed. She stroked him, reassuring him. He twisted away from her, leaving her looking at her hands, a strong ordinary girl. Johnny, who could ride like the wind, knock in fenceposts all day and drink with his Bungaree mates Frank and Sean all night, couldn't live up to her between the sheets. It wasn't his problem, *she* was his problem, the situation was her fault: she was too demanding, like an animal in heat. What had been raunchy, illicit and wonderful between them lost its appeal for him now they were settled, and he worried about her being as promiscuous with other men as she had been with him. When she said how much she loved him in bed he called her dirty, or a hungry hunter, or crude, yet asserted to his mates he gave her a good time.

'They're getting in our way,' he stormed, 'they're keeping us out.' This was the familiar refrain against his parents. Johnny was always greedy for what he asserted was denied him, his rightful place at Paragon House, more space, a better horse. He refused to visit Hobart Town because Bob would show him up: making Van Diemen's Land Bob's own so that King Island could be totally *his*. Johnny had the cattle and one day as the older brother the lease to King Island would be his. Johnny had persuaded himself he held the whip hand, that Bob needed him more than he needed Bob. Selina wondered if Johnny really understood about the Paragon-Pride Bank, the profits that purchased the ornate cast-iron stove Annie had coveted for years, and a hundred helpful items around the place. Selina's proudest possession was the dark red patterned rug Ezzie sent her, that Johnny put his muddy boots on.

'Bob and Ezzie have been good to us,' Selina said. They had not been back to the island since Annie's unwelcome. If the stove had been a peace offering it made no difference at all. Annie was only forty-three, but after a hard life she was old, and she deliberately let herself look older. She was embittered from choice. Selina liked Jim and knew Annie wasn't present in the restless look she saw in his eyes. Jim had been very kind to Annie, and very cruel too.

Johnny insisted, 'My father's too weak with Bob, just follows his advice, the Great God Bob.' The word *favourite* trembled on his lips. 'I never get my chance to have a say! Those bloody merinos tear out the grass down to the roots, but *Bob says* we got to have wool. . . .'

'We get good prices.' The island had exported five bales of wool to London, and mimosa bark too, for £25 a ton.

'I don't want shearers here.' Johnny had a cattle-man's hatred of sheep. 'It's our island, and God knows what those Barcoo spews steal. And what about the convict gangs? We want the bush felled and tracks made, and we need the dams to water the stock, I know all that – don't say it – '

Selina didn't interrupt the familiar tirade. Everything would become her fault if she put herself in his way.

'There's no need for so many Derwent Ducks,' Johnny protested to himself. 'It won't be our island any more. What happens when they get their tickets-of-leave? They'll squat. There's ten or twelve at least'll stay. Who'll keep them off our women?' So this was what he talked about working with Sean, or the rough lads up by Egg Lagoon, or the witless Sidmouth snaggers; Selina felt as if she was hardly here. Johnny almost never came inside during the day, and at night he snored. Selina's only full friends were women; as for the man in her life, most of him was a stranger to her. Johnny was proud of her because she was a good looker, and his mates knew she was the property of his cock.

'Johnny,' she said, 'look at me.' He stopped.

If she said *hold me* he'd run away like a shot. She had to stand apart from him to bring him close. Suddenly he hugged her.

'Selina, he called me a lazy bastard.'

'Oh, Johnny.'

'He's right. My name's nothing, isn't it? I don't have a name.'

She held him tight.

He said: 'I was thinking about Billy.' She glanced anxiously through the door, wondering what the little boy was getting up to. 'I want him to have a name.

There's a missionary from the little *Tartar* that was wrecked down south near David Howie's Boat Harbour a while ago. He could splice us.'

Selina stared at him, astonished at what Johnny was almost saying.

'Marry me, all right?' he said to the floor. 'Yeah, we'll do that. Give Billy a name.' He went out nodding, the matter settled, and she heard his horse galloping away.

'Yes,' Selina called. She held up her trembling hand and smiled. Billy waddled past with his father's jacket trailing in the dust behind him. 'Come here, Billy Pride,' Selina said fondly, doing up the brass buttons and plonking his father's spare hat over her son's head.

And so Johnny and Selina were married in a ceremony on the sand at Howie's Boat Harbour.

In a moment of weakness the tears poured down Annie's face at the wedding she herself would never have, but still Jim didn't acknowledge the pain he gave her. Bob and Ezzie weren't invited of course – Annie and her son Johnny were united on that. And obviously they were right – a contagion clung to that marriage – Johnny sensed that Ezzie's dead children represented some fault with the parents. Johnny had long ago taken one of his instant dislikes to Ezzie, finding her far too feminine and intimidating, too full of life for him: and appreciated a kind of justice in that too-vivacious body producing death – or else he would have to be envious of Bob. And so he drew closer to his mother, and further from his father.

For her most recent pregnancy, forbidden to swim and submitting to Dr Agnew's strict regime, Ezzie lay in bed for six months and three weeks. She was not allowed to see the sun or exert herself in any way, prescribed a strict diet without meat or fruit. She was forbidden to worry. For the last month a nurse was

264

with her every hour of the day. The baby was born dead.

Ezzie wrote to Annie every month, and when she read those words, Annie was glad. The situation she had come to terms with was confirmed – almost justified.

When Ezzie was almost recovered Bob begged her: 'Come to chapel with me this Sunday.' It was almost Christmas.

Ezzie refused. She would not think of it. They both knew what his words concealed, the acceptance of defeat.

'Please,' he said.

'I love *you*,' she said, pale as death from her sunless obedience.

He drew a breath. 'If we are to be childless, so be it.'

She gripped his hand with surprising strength. 'I'm going to go swimming,' she said, and raised both her eyebrows in a straight, determined line. 'I'm going to eat beef and apples and apricots and anything I want, I'm going to live like a human being and I'm going to give you a son.'

'But why?' He held out his hands desperately. 'I love you and I can't hurt you any more.'

'If you give up,' she said quietly, 'that hurts me most.'

In the final months of 1836, as spring flowered and pink blossom filled the square brick-walled gardens along the rank of fine houses, the sky plumed with feathery mares' tails in promise of hot days to come, Ezzie fell pregnant for the last time.

Annie crumpled that letter when she read it; it was almost evil, the blind hope that girl lived in, as though she could assert her personality above fate, bend the way of the world to her own personal will. And she was more than thirty years old! Worse, Jim read her

265

letters with interest, even affection, while Annie watched behind a mask of indifference.

'Why do you like her so much?' she asked casually.

'I don't know,' Jim yawned. 'Ezzie's got something, I suppose.' He smoothed the letter out again and read it at arm's length. His eyes weren't as good as once they were.

Annie wanted to shake his hurtful complacency. 'Selina told me something yesterday. Her too.'

'I'm surprised,' he said calmly, 'considering the amount of time Johnny spends drinking with his mates.'

'My son works bloody hard,' Annie flared.

'Our son,' he said mildly, glancing over the page.

'What do you care, we don't matter to you, do we. Your family are lost to you, just shadows. You don't care, you're obsessed with yourself.'

'We don't talk of this,' he said stiffly. 'We agreed.'

'The past exists,' Annie said.

'I'm going to check the south paddock,' he said, opening the door.

Before he could leave her alone she called: 'Jim, is there any history of twins in your family?'

He stopped. 'Twins?' he said.

'Selina is carrying twins. She can feel it. Did you have any brothers who were twins?'

'No,' Jim said.

'Did you?'

'No!'

'Jim,' she protested.

'Who knows where we come from,' he said. 'I made me what I am.'

'Jim,' she asked quietly, 'are *you* a twin?'

He looked back at her, his hand on the door. 'The past is dead and buried,' he said, then slammed it closed behind him.

'Is it?' murmured Annie to the half-darkness,

imagining Ezzie lying in bed swelling with child, and closed her eyes.

Ezzie was not in bed. Ezzie was swimming like a dab-chick in the blue waters of the Derwent estuary. Laza-rus Graves, holding the reins gently in his great hairy hands, had driven her carriage down the Sandy Bay track past the scrubland of Dunkley Point to Nutgrove Beach. The giant decorticating gums of the forest, and the orchards that interspersed it, hid her from view of the smallholdings, the convict station and Frank Lipscombe's house as she splashed through the shal-lows and dived forward into the sudden deep water. Her long blonde-streaked hair, unbound, swirled along her back like a sensual caress. If only Bob were here.

It wasn't his fault; he was so worried about her. He thought he knew what was good for her, but *she* knew better. This time, floating on her back, her body immersed in the cool embrace, the blissful January sun scorching her face, she was confident that all would be well because she was enjoying herself. 'Don't worry,' she told Bob in bed, touching his lips, but he wouldn't make love because he was worried about hurting the baby. He loved her so much that all his old exuberance was gone, consumed in concern for her. The sun had browned her fashionably pale skin – he worried about its effect on her. And didn't she know that a shark had recently been caught in the Derwent, twenty-five feet long and fifteen feet in girth? She touched him with her breasts, lightly brushing his nipples with her own, her nails pricking his thighs. 'The sharks don't eat women,' she murmured, 'the water isn't hot enough.' He groaned and she knew she was irresistible. She cuddled him with a lump in her throat because she was so happy.

'Do you pray for us?' she asked.

'You,' he admitted. 'Do you mind?'

She laughed and shook her head. 'It's nice,' she said. 'It's wonderful.'

But she saw little of him during the daytime. The 'Antipodean Princes' – the *Colonial Times*'s catchphrase for the cream of the Hobarton set, the 20,000-acre gentry – were doing well, indeed too well. The importation of capital from foreign banks at high interest rates, and the vast increase of the pauper and prisoner population, increased the gap between rich and poor. The price of wheat collapsed as cheap American grain was sold in Hobart Town, bankrupting many farmers. Though bank interest rates climbed well above ten per cent, the number of defaults broke many local bankers who had overextended themselves in the boom years of the 1820s. Free settlers from Britain were no longer men of £500 capital but 'perishing millions', pauper emigrants with no money of their own, the worst class that could be introduced into the Colony. As Lieutenant-Governor Arthur's period in office came to an end and his influence waned, he was prisoner of the Antipodean Princes he had himself appointed to the Legislative Council. As the bankers loaded with wheat debts crumbled, Bob took over their good loans to sheep and dairy farmers, and prospered. His work seemed so important to him; he was so afraid that his child must again die. He expanded his interests into shipbuilding ventures along Battery Point, including Daniel Callaghan's yard which a few years ago built the first paddlesteamer on the Derwent, ventures that because of the cost of boilers required more capital than sail did. These smoky eager vessels churning profitably to schedule along the Derwent were now a common sight, warm and friendly puffers trailing foam in all the sheltered waters of the tortuous coast.

Only a few miles inland, to the west and north, rose the jagged hinterland of the island, wild and unexplored. Amazing marvels rewarded dangerous journeys: circular Lake Pedder amidst a whirlpool of mountains in the heartland, bordered by an extraordinary shining white beach, had been discovered eighteen months ago and dignified with the name of the Chief Justice. It was Pedder, with Bob on the other side, who helped Colonel Sir George Arthur, rewarded with a knighthood for his irreproachable administration, down from Government House to the quay to board the ship that would take him home to retirement, a sad and very rich man. Arthur wept every step of the way. An ex-Governor had few friends.

In January the new Lieutenant-Governor arrived, Sir John Franklin the explorer. 'King Island?' he laughed, dismounting from his bay horse when Bob told him his birthplace, 'why, I know the place!' The shy midshipman on Flinders' *Investigator* who at the turn of the century had given his name to Franklin Roads, the anchorage in the lee of the New Year Islands, had returned as ruler of all he surveyed. He touched his hat to Ezzie coming through the garden gate, and she curtseyed with a grunt. He admired her tanned face, liking a woman who liked the fresh air as he did. Only his military secretary, Captain Wood, accompanied him. Ezzie came over faint so they took tea indoors.

Bob and Ezzie came to genuinely like Franklin, an easy man to underrate because not good at public speaking, bluff and ponderous with glowing eyes. His only weaknesses were his hatred of Americans – because of the rebellion against Her Majesty by United States citizens in Upper Canada – and his wife Lady Jane, twitching with intelligence and determined to civilise these rough natives, by which she meant not aborigines but Hobartons. She got her way with her husband; she would get her way with them.

With Arthur gone, Bob was free to cut a deal with Arthur's old enemies, the Van Diemen's Land Company. Ezzie had recovered from her fainting spells and he had never seen her look healthier or happier. The water was by now too cool for swimming, so Bob felt few qualms about his business journey to see the Chief Agent of the Van Diemen's Land Company, Edward Curr, at Circular Head. 'I won't go if you don't want me to,' he told Ezzie.

'I am perfectly all right,' she told him, exasperated. 'You won't be gone for an eternity, I can live without you for three or four days, you know!'

'I wouldn't go if it wasn't so important,' he said.

She gave him a great bussing kiss.

Cox's stagecoach left the Sun Inn for Launceston at eight on Monday morning, and after a smooth journey on the new metalled roads across the fertile farmlands, arrived at Dicky White's Hotel at three on Wednesday afternoon. Windblown and weary, Bob reserved a horse from the livery stable, and rode west along the northern coast of Van Diemen's Land at first light. After stopping at Emu Bay, the evening sun glittered off the sea in the direction of King Island, below the horizon, as he arrived at Highfield House to be greeted by Edward Curr.

The Van Diemen's Land Company, the VDLC, was supported by the highest levels of the British Government and the City of London as a steady, and cheap, source of wool in times of European political turmoil. Huge tracts of the deserted and unexplored northwest of Van Diemen's Land were granted to the company directors in London. High hopes had been held out, and still were, but the venture had not yet been very successful. But its London friends were so powerful that the Company was actually paid for taking on convict labour, though everyone else had to pay, and Curr bragged he was claiming a rental rebate of more than fifteen thousand pounds this year. Bob was interested in men who could run things to their own advantage so well: now that Arthur was gone and Macquarie Harbour closed down, there was nothing to stop the Company – suitably financed – spreading southward into the mysterious, verdant west coast wilderness, opening up new territories. He had never seen such fine stock – heavy horses, deer, Berkshire pigs, merino sheep, more than a thousand head of Kyloe and Hereford cattle. The Company lacked for only one thing: grassland as good as King Island.

'We can help one another,' Bob said as Curr showed him the estate.

'One more push and we're there,' Curr said, clenching his hand into a fist. 'We're by far the largest company in the Colony, and we can be the most profitable; people must always eat, and they must always wear clothes.' Bob looked round at the sound of a distant gunshot, but Curr showed no reaction. 'There are small bands of aborigine guerillas in the area; the Government makes no effort to capture them. We've boobytrapped our shepherds' huts with spring-loaded guns aimed below the waist, and mantraps. We should stick some aborigine heads on the roofs.'

'I thought all natives had been removed to a place of safety.'

'Wybalenna, on Flinders Island,' spat Curr, 'bringing God and civilisation to the poor devils. I kept one myself you know, brought it up as one of my own family, but it didn't work. Like dressing up a monkey in proper clothes. Whined itself to death. They aren't like us.'

He took off his hat at a small stone funeral monument beneath a weeping willow. Two years ago, Curr explained, his daughter Juliana had been playing in a dog-cart when the animal rushed off to join other dogs in a fight, dragging the screaming youngster behind.

Beyond its white-painted paling fence Highfield House was lovely, the last rays of the sun fingering the warm stone. Juliana had struck her head against the fencing and died in her father's arms. Bob felt his lips go white with dread and an almost irresistible premonition to return to Hobart Town, to Ezzie's side. 'My other daughters are coming from England soon,' Curr said, looking at Bob with concern. 'We are converting the roof into attics for them. . . . Are you not well, sir?'

'I must return to my wife at once,' Bob said.

He could not follow the track that passed for a road in the dark; he allowed himself to be pressed into staying for supper, then set off with a local guide supplied by Curr as soon as the moon rose after midnight. Pale sheep grazed the blue pastures beneath the tiers of silver mountains. The horse was a fine Cleveland and went like the wind across the rolling terrain. Bob's initial panic had settled to a dull throb of worry. Nevertheless, he compressed two days' leisurely ride into a frantic dash of a single night and one day.

Exhausted and covered with dust, he ran to Elboden Place and beat on the door. Graves opened it calmly.

From upstairs, Bob heard the strong voice of a baby squalling.

'I had my babies here,' Annie told Selina, looking out from the window of Paragon House. The tip of the Huon pine growing from its bed of moss by the lagoon in the valley floor scratched the windy sky.

'All of them?' Selina murmured, almost asleep in the corner bed. Her labour had lasted a day and a night.

'Both of them,' Annie said, turning. She touched the two bundles Selina cuddled to her breasts. 'Twins,' she said. 'You aren't going to have much time to yourself.'

'Aren't they amazing?' Selina said wonderingly. 'I wish Johnny was here.'

Annie parted the swaddling with her fingertips.

'Peter and Rebecca,' she said. 'Welcome to your life on King Island.'

'Peter and Rebecca Pride,' Selina said fiercely. 'Bring Billy in so that he can see his new brother and sister.'

'Johnny took him out riding,' Annie said. 'You know what Johnny's like. You keep a grip on your children, girl, while they're still yours.'

'Peter and Rebecca Pride,' repeated Selina, clamping her babies to her breasts.

'He's just like you,' Ezzie murmured.

'Is that a compliment?' Bob looked down into the red, scrunched-up face of his son. 'Come on Jack, give us a smile.'

'He was born with a smile,' the nursemaid said, then added, 'it just means wind. Now, Mr Pride, you must let your wife rest.'

'I don't want to rest,' Ezzie said. 'I want to get up and run and fly.' But her eyes closed. The nursemaid ushered Bob from the room, but Ezzie said: 'It was my swimming. I was right, wasn't I? Happiness goes to the happy. Admit I was right.'

'You were right,' he said, 'as usual.'

'Leave her in peace now!' the nursemaid said severely. Ezzie opened one eye and took back her baby. 'Welcome, Jack Pride,' she murmured as she fell asleep, 'welcome to your home in Hobart Town, Earth, the Universe. . . .'

She knew she would never have another child and, after Bob, Jack would be her life.

Dan Callaghan's steamers dared only coastal waters. Usually it was one of the solid sailing vessels from Petchey's yard on the Esplanade, another of the Paragon-Pride Bank's customers, which made the twice yearly voyage to King Island to deliver stores and pick up fat cattle and wool for delivery to the VDLC at

Emu Bay, where Bob was now – because of the Bank's involvement as well as that of the Paragon Kings Livestock Company – a director with a non-executive seat on the VDLC Main Board. He had formed a close letter relationship with Burnie, the senior director in London, and knew his suggestions carried weight.

On King Island, the channel to the Yellow Rock jetty silted up until not even the blunt, valiant cutter *Royal William* of only 42 tons could negotiate the entrance safely. The jetty fell into disrepair and the vessel loaded down south at David Howie's Boat Harbour instead. Originally a trader against old Feargal O'Henry, Howie could not compete when Feargal's hardworking son Frank moved south from Bungaree and opened a part-time store, made out of blackwood shingles, by the harbour. Sir John Franklin appointed Howie constable of the straits because of the numbers of lawless sealers and escaped convicts who found their way there and made their living from the wrecks, which as shipping increased, ran onto the ghastly shore. Even the seasoned skipper of the *Royal William* found the razorback rocks lining the entrance to the harbour, involving a sharp twist to starboard, daunting.

The rapid improvement of stock on King Island, with the influx of fresh blood from the VDLC stud, only partly offset the decline in the quality of grassland. The settlers had to run to stand still: using fire to open new fertile lands and allowing the old cleared lands to revert to scrub. The Yellow Rock loam was still rich, as were the black beds of the old drained lagoons up north around the Corduroy place, where dark-eyed Isaac Simmonds was chief hand, having taken up with Corduroy's daughter by his lubra. Everyone called this shy, thin girl Peggy, but that was not the name Isaac whispered as they sat making love beneath the stars: he called her by her euphonious aboriginal name 'Powwidde', robin redbreast. Their son Joshua, a year

274

old, gurgled beside them in a crib of woven grass. From somewhere in the unknown time before his grandparents the little boy had acquired his pair of striking blue eyes, and his pale, lustrous skin. Corduroy, increasingly senile and difficult, was fatally bitten by a tiger snake and without him to give orders about the place, Isaac let the land slip back into itself; staring into the starlight in Powwidde's eyes he had achieved all he needed in the world.

One wintry day Jim Pride came and saw them shivering miserably in their badger-box hut. They watched him approaching, striding across the reverting landscape, the wind blowing his long silver hair. He'd not yet seen sixty summers, Isaac knew, but his fierce eyes were webbed with lines from years of toil under the harsh sun. Isaac stood respectfully. Joshua was toddling and talking by now and Jim scooped him up effortlessly. Joshua squealed with delight. He curled himself up like a monkey and gripped Jim's hands. 'He must be the same age as my own grandchildren, Peter and Rebecca?' Jim said. He did not mention Jack, whom he had not met. Beyond the borders of King Island was beyond the borders of Jim's mind: he had not climbed the tree for years.

Isaac made a deferential gesture. Actually Joshua was almost a year older than the twins, but it did not seem important. 'Yes, Mr Pride,' he said. Jim nodded politely to Powwidde, who giggled. Jim pulled his coat closer around him and crouched. He told Isaac: 'You can't go on living like this.'

Isaac was ashamed without knowing why.

'Listen,' Jim said kindly, 'you don't remember what it was like here at first. You can't let things go like this – fences down, everything wild. Land is there to be improved.'

'Yes,' Isaac said politely.

Jim tried to explain. 'The poisonous tares you are

allowing to grow are seeding on my land. Your stock is mingling with mine. It has got to stop.'

'Why are you speaking to me in stilted English?' Isaac asked.

Jim was blunt. 'You've got Johnny's dander up. You know what he's like when he's been drinking with Sean. I don't want trouble.'

'You just want your way,' Powwidde said.

'I just want good neighbours,' Jim said. 'We need land this good. How else will you support Josh here, except by making it pay?'

That got through to her. She looked anxiously at Isaac, who stood twisting his big toe into the earth floor of the hut, caught between two worlds.

'All right!' he said. 'But I'm not ashamed. We don't live no worse than Johnny.'

Jim said: 'Don't say one word against Johnny.'

In the 1840s Jim, who had slowed down because of his heart, was increasingly leaving to Johnny the day-to-day running of the farm. Johnny had a chip on his shoulder. He resented the merinos bought by Bob at his father's command, he hated and feared the gangs of convict labour whose assignment was arranged through Bob's influence with the authorities, building the first proper track from Yellow Rock to David Howie's Boat Harbour, which in the summer reduced the journey by bullock cart from weeks to days. But at least Johnny dominated his household, or thought he did. Selina did not complain when he took Billy stock-riding with him, the ten-year-old a natural in the saddle of his galloping pony, or when Johnny went out without a word after tea and spent the evening drinking with Sean. His horse brought him home. But Selina wouldn't go out to him and Billy put his father to bed. Soon he would be old enough to go drinking with his father.

And yet his father kept Billy at a distance too. Like

father like son, Billy did not really know him. It was not love; it was worship.

Selina loved Billy, and hoped she could keep him. But the twins were her victory. It was they she hugged to her ample bosom and they put their arms round her without restraint. What little bundles of energy they were – Annie's prediction had come true – they were never still, and she was sure they were brilliant. Billy's childish jealousy was natural: 'When can we send them to market?' was one of his first questions on seeing them, and Selina had laughed, but now as they grew into active youngsters Billy, excluded and superior only in age and seriousness, retreated and stuck to his father.

Selina kept the twins to herself. She learned how to seal the leaks in the roof and do simple woodwork herself, so that she did not have to badger Johnny into doing it, and the twins helped her: Peter had a natural eye for a line, even at six years old, and ways of doing things came naturally to him. It was different from intelligence – he was not as *intelligent* as Rebecca – he must be artistic, she decided. Where Peter was warm and instinctive, Rebecca thought things through. Selina waddled across the yard, washing piled in her arms and sassafras clothes-pegs stuck in her mouth, dust pluming from her big brown feet jammed in their wooden clogs, at least fifty pounds overweight with contentment.

Johnny cantered his horse, Billy galloping his pony Shorty beside him, along the neat painted fence-rails of Isaac's squat. Johnny looked over his son's head with a sneer at the abo half-castes working their paddocks as earnestly as white folk. They even looked like whites, but he remembered their mothers. Billy didn't understand his father's sneer, but he imitated it. When he met little Joshua alone, four years younger than he, Billy pushed him around. But once when Billy cornered him, Josh turned out to be strong too, and lashed out blackening Billy's eye.

Billy was too ashamed to admit what had happened, his father might not take him drinking, but he took to leaving a few gates open around the place, and Johnny went berserk, blaming his neighbours. He rode over to sort them out and Billy nearly died of choking from amusement. It didn't come to blows; Johnny wasn't drunk. Still the gates got left open.

But Johnny took no further action. Gradually Billy understood it was grandad holding his father back, stopping him behaving like a man. Billy had listened and knew his mother and Johnny didn't make the love business that Sean and his boys bragged about: lay there silent and apart. Because he didn't love her Johnny almost feared Selina, hardly coming home now and treating her as she deserved when he did. On Johnny's behalf Billy hated his mother as much as Johnny hated Jim Pride. But Johnny accepted his father's authority, just as Billy accepted his mother's. So the open gates were Jim Pride's fault. This was Billy's signal. The old man was getting soft, it was time for his own father to take over.

Intoxicated by the rightness of what he was doing, Billy went out again one night and left a few gates swinging behind him, when a figure rose up in the darkness. It was Johnny, drunk, and Billy hardly knew what hit him.

He never again saw properly out of his left eye. This injury was Billy's fault: he understood he had done a terrible thing. He wanted to please his father who punished him even more. Because of the mistake about the eye, which never ceased hurting, he understood his father was just a human being, with error built into him, and loved him. They were on equal terms. Johnny took Billy drinking now, and Billy drank himself stupid to be happy.

This was the state they were in, around the table in Sean's hut at Bungaree, when a ticket-of-leave man burst in with news that there had been a good wreck south of David Howie's Boat Harbour. Jim Pride was already waiting outside on horseback, and he looked at the men staggering out of the hut into the rain with contempt. He wouldn't wait for them but spurred on alone. The gale made the treetops roar. Johnny found Jim with David Howie on the beach a few miles south of the harbour, trying to get a line to the vessel almost lost in the furious surf. The waves were throwing up kelp-drowned bodies in piles and still Jim kept trying, but the desperate crowd of emigrants clinging to the foc'sle were swept away one by one as the light faded. By dawn few remained. The line parted time after time; Jim risked his life like a desperate man, but each time the surf flung him back. Shattered by the waves, the ship collapsed into pieces, the foc'sle unstitching into the sea. Of the four hundred and twenty-three souls aboard, including seventy-three children, only nine reached the beach alive.

The wind died away to a flat calm. The sand was strewn with wreckage for two miles. Johnny picked up a gold fob-watch. 'Let's get to it,' he said. Someone else found a brass telescope marked *Cataraqui*.

A ticket-of-leave man made off with a puncheon of rum to bury for later. Jim knocked him over.

'But everyone does it,' Johnny said.

'No,' Jim said.

'You did it once,' Johnny screamed, '*you did it!*'

That night Jim couldn't sleep. His memory had been provoked, the sights and smells of the beach and the work he had done today merging into recollections forty years old. He woke sweating. The bodies must be buried: he helped like an automaton. Later he rode home alone. Too weary to descend from the saddle, he sat there bent forward over the pommel.

Annie watched him from the doorway, then came down the path and touched his knee. 'Come in for a cup of tea,' she said, and reached up her arms to take his weight.

26

1845–1850

Jim Pride's legacy

Jim climbed the tree. It seemed taller and himself
smaller, his joints clicked, and his body grew more
heavy and clumsy as he climbed. He clung to the top
with trembling legs and arms, angry, feeling the years
of his mortality. He was no longer young.

He didn't lie to himself. By colonial standards he
was a wealthy man, a success, but he had never valued
that.

Eve Summers. He could not even faintly imagine her
face. The reality of her was totally lost to him.

Jim Pride stared out at the empty sea.

The sun set almost due west. A few handspans to
the northwest Venus twinkled among the wings of light,
burning brighter as darkness rose.

'You old fool, what do you do up there?' Annie said
fondly, taking his hand as he fumbled for the last step
down. 'Ah, my poor man. Your hands are so cold. I
don't know.'

'Eve,' he said.

'I'm not Eve,' Annie said anxiously.

Jim hugged her with sudden force.

'You're a lovely woman.'

'If only you knew. . . .' Annie bit her tongue. Then
she said flatly: 'Do you still love her?'

'Yes. The Eve I never knew, the happiness we lost.'

'After all these years, you're still angry.'

He said gently: 'Didn't you know?'

He did not come to her bed that night. Alone, Annie lay staring at the angle of candlelight stretched across the roofbeams, listening to the scratch of his pen, the clink of the nib dipped in the porcelain inkwell, Bob's gift. It was almost dawn before he came to bed.

Annie said in a rush, 'Maybe she's dead by now.'

Jim touched his heart. He would know if Eve died.

'I'm so happy and so unhappy,' Annie said. 'I wish I was her.'

'You are a wonderful woman,' Jim whispered, 'and I know you love me, and I know I don't deserve it.'

They lay together.

'The *Royal William* arrives in the next few days,' Jim said. 'We have a private journey to make. Pack your bags.'

'When will we be coming back?'

'This is our place,' was all he said.

The *Royal William*, stinking of livestock, carried them to Emu Bay. Its next stop was Kangaroo Island for a cargo of salt and skins, so as there was no railway they transferred to another vessel for the voyage along the north coast of Van Diemen's Land to the Tamar, being towed the forty-five miles upriver by the steam-tug *Henrietta Thompson*, whose smoke left the decks and sails streaked with greasy black soot to the fury of the captain. The Launceston shipyards were busy, wooden skeletons ranking the shore in various stages of completion, completed hulls ready to be launched down the iron ramps imported from England, or bobbing high in the water being fitted out and stepped with masts. Launceston was rich from supplying the new settlements expanding so rapidly around the estuaries of mainland Australia, Melbourne, Adelaide, Geelong. Plumes of steam hung over the shipyards and a steam whistle blew with an unearthly shriek that made Annie jump.

'I feel like a country cousin,' she said as they threaded the bustle of Queen's Wharf.

Jim booked them in at the Tamar Hotel, in William Street close to the river. The room was on the second floor, which felt strange to them. Annie disliked such sumptuousness, and the bed was much too soft. Jim took something from his valise and put it inside his jacket.

'What's that?' she asked sharply.

He looked awkward. 'My last will and testament,' he said, then kissed her cheek. 'I've got some things to arrange.'

'Jim,' she said with a frisson, 'you realise that technically I'm still a criminal? I might not be here by the time you get back.'

'I know what you feel, and I'm going to do something about it,' he said. She watched out of the window as a minute later he appeared below and crossed the street to the Union Bank of Launceston. She saw him take the thick envelope from his pocket and stare at it, then look up at the legend above the door. *Subterranean Vaults. Safe Deposits Taken.* Again a steam whistle shrieked somewhere, an alien sound of whose purpose she had no idea. Jim shoved the envelope back into his pocket, then went into a notary's office for a few minutes – *Oaths taken* in gilt on the bow windows – but when he came out, he had the envelope with him. He turned on his heel and she watched him walk rapidly away. When he returned to the hotel room several hours had passed, his boots were dusty, but he still had the envelope in his pocket. Annie said nothing.

They ate supper in the restaurant downstairs, the coal gas lights hissing.

Later she held him in the too-soft bed. They lay listening to the unfamiliar sounds out of the dark, horses clopping down the street, drunken cries, laughter, doors opening and slamming closed.

'It didn't feel right to leave it there,' he said.

She waited.

'It just wasn't right. The lawyers reminded me of — ' he shrugged. 'Another place. Long ago. Not my place.'

'Why's that envelope so important to you, really, Jim?'

'It's everything,' he said at last. 'The truth. My whole life. I never saw it until it was written down. I wasn't guilty.' He reached out and weighed the pale rectangle in his hand. 'My life in an envelope.'

She was chilled. He was talking as though it was all over.

'We'll be married at the Registry Office tomorrow,' he said and she closed her eyes, understanding. *He* had achieved innocence.

Annie lay beside him, happy and envious, because *she*, guilty and bound for hell when she died, unpunished in this world, had been blessed with all she desired: and if he wondered when he heard her weeping, he didn't ask.

About a hundred and thirty miles south of Mr and Mrs Jim Pride's chartered yacht returning them down the Tamar estuary to King Island, Ezzie was teaching their grandson Jack to swim in the Derwent. 'The water's icy!' he called through chattering teeth as she plunged in from the new bathing sheds at Beachside. Jack had passed his eighth birthday last May, and Ezzie was sure he was going to be a terrific athlete. One day he would swim as fast as she but for the moment she took long strokes with her right arm while he thrashed enthusiastically beside her, then let him pull ahead. They hung together from the gunwhale of the anchored jollyboat that had been their objective, recovering their breath.

'You won,' Ezzie said.

'You slowed.'

'No, I didn't,' Ezzie said, brushing the sandy locks out of his eyes. 'It's just my weak arm. Think you can beat me back to the shore?'

'If we can run along the beach to get warm.'

'You can run faster than me,' Ezzie said. 'You'll beat me for sure.'

Jack hugged her. 'I know,' he grinned. 'Come on!'

The yacht anchored in Franklin Roads and Jim and Annie were rowed ashore to Yellow Rock in the shallow-draught skiff. No party was there to greet them or bring their horses to the jetty. The crew swung up their baggage onto the sunsplit boards and departed with a tug of their forelocks before the wind changed. Annie said to the emptiness: 'I thought Johnny was supposed to meet us.' They waited with the sand hissing about their legs: Annie sighed and changed out of the fine dress Jim had bought her in Launceston, and they started walking. Johnny's hut appeared in its niche between the rustling, sand-blown grass and the great sombre stands of blue gums, the canvas blades of the windmill used to pump water whirling and clattering. Selina was ladling hefty portions of meat and potatoes from the pot for the twins's supper. She turned with a smile and wiped her hands on her hips.

Annie didn't say anything she'd planned. The words burst out of her. 'We're married!'

Selina whooped and lifted Annie clear from the ground. 'Where was it?'

'William Street at Launceston – it was beautiful – you'll never believe–'

'I can see the difference in you already!'

'I made an honest woman of her,' Jim said, ruffling Peter's hair. 'Where's Johnny?'

'Didn't he meet you?' Selina shrugged. 'Where that man gets to is a mystery to me. He was going to do

285

some firing while the wind's easterly. I sent Billy out to fetch him from Sean's this morning.'

'We saw no smoke,' Jim said. 'It doesn't matter. Lend us a couple of nags, would you?'

'You've got to stay for supper.' She threw down a tattered journal brought by the *Royal William*. 'There's something Peter wants to show you. Some new invention.'

'It's called a calotype,' Peter said eagerly. 'Can I have one, Grandad?'

'Eat your potatoes,' Jim told him. 'What does it do?'

'It draws pictures,' said Peter with shining eyes, 'with light.'

Busy with the ladle, Selina scoffed: 'Sounds like a toy.'

'Then I can have one?' the boy came back instantly, quick as a terrier.

Jim laughed. 'Maybe when you're older,' he said. 'Ask your father.'

Johnny didn't make an appearance so Jim and Annie rode home alone. Dead calm reigned, and the motionless Huon dominated the moonlit valley. 'Do you notice?' Annie said casually from the door. 'It's grown since we've been here. Just a little, but it has.' A tree that old still flourishing in its way, bone-slow, giving their little lives a sense of connection to eternity; it made a warm and pleasant thought for Annie to hold in her mind as she went to sleep beside her husband.

She woke. Iron rang faintly on stone, the sound thrown back by the outcrop.

At first, incredibly, she thought they'd had a thief. In a cold shaft of moon her jewellery, mostly cheap nostalgic dross salvaged from the *Paragon* but precious to her, lay scattered on the table. Her padded brass box that had once held the ship's monies behind its lock and key was gone too.

Jim's side of her bed was cold under her hand. She

crossed the moonlight and looked through the scratched, gleaming window at the silvery darkness beyond. Jim was digging beneath the tree, almost lost in the shadow, but she saw the echoing flash of the pickaxe blade, then heard the steady chinking of a spade into the soil. A pile of it, black as velvet, speckled with quartzite stones, already rose high as Jim's waist.

She watched for a while, then went back to bed. She did not own his life.

The sunlight was brilliant – they had overslept. The hammering on the door drove any thought of the previous night from her mind as Annie scrambled over Jim's sleeping body. She pulled the door open and shielded her eyes.

'Billy,' she mumbled. 'What brings you here?'

The young man looked at her with the piercing gaze of his right eye. His left, watering and concussed, peered over her shoulder. 'I've found my father,' he muttered.

Annie tried to collect her wits. 'Where is he?'

'My father is dead in a gully.' Billy's face crumpled. 'His horse threw him. Maybe yesterday or the day before. It can't have happened. No one was a better horseman than my dad.'

Annie thought she would collapse. 'My son can't be dead.'

'I didn't know what to do, I had to lift him across the saddle and – the birds.' Billy stared at his hands. 'His eyes.'

'Our son is dead,' Annie said to Jim who came out, yawning.

'Bob?' he cried, instinctively clutching his chest. 'I should never have let him go – '

'Johnny,' Annie said.

Jim drew a deep sigh when they told him Johnny had fallen from his horse. 'He must have been drunk,' he said.

287

'No.' Billy cocked his head. 'I'll never forgive you. He was loyal as a dog and the more you kicked him the more he loved you until you broke him.'

'You're very young,' Jim said.

Billy's face distorted, with fury or tears they could not tell.

'Be quiet, Billy,' Annie said frantically. 'I can't take any more.'

'There's lots more,' Billy said, but he backed down when Jim pushed past. Then Jim turned and put his arm round Billy's shoulder. 'Come on,' Jim said gently, 'there's work to do.'

Annie watched them dig, the new pile of velvet earth spreading across the brilliant grass of the graveside. Jim seemed invulnerably at peace, but she knew part of herself had died.

'There's no question of my returning to run the farm,' Bob wrote in his letter that arrived with the *Royal William* during the blazing hot Christmas of 1845. *'My life is here in Hobart Town. Ezzie and Jack are happy here. This is our home now, dearest Mama.'* The letter went on, *'We have bought some land out of town at Dunkley Point and are thinking of building a little summerhouse there with a boat for Ezzie and our dear boy. . . .'* Annie put the town-talk letter down impatiently. All she cared about was Jim. Through the cloudless new year, with the river the lowest they had ever seen, it was obvious that no man of his age could take up the burden of running the spread alone, but he wouldn't admit it. Billy wasn't much help. The dams dried out to puddles of mud and through the night the stock lowed piteously. Daylight flattened the cleared paddocks with shadowless glare, the grass so dry that it seemed white, the paddocks looking like white, desiccated pits among the sombre green climax forest where the only shade was to be found. The animals huddled there in the shadows, devoured by flies,

trailing out in search of water at night. Jim wouldn't give up. But Annie was terrified of his collapses. His heart was weak and he didn't seem to care.

At last the rains fell.

'He's really ill,' Selina said. 'I saw him with blue lips the other day, and Rebecca said "poor Grandad." '

'You tell him,' Annie said bitterly. 'He doesn't care what I say.'

'He's the most selfless man I've ever met,' Selina said.

Annie said: 'I wish he'd think of me.' She watched Peter sitting on a log, his household chores completed, staring across the vista of dune grassland towards the sunset, and something in the way he sat reminded her so much of how Bob had loved to watch the mutton-birds flying out of the great red ball of the sun. Bob had called them *yollas* and young Peter did too. He was great mates with Josh, Isaac's boy.

'Jim's wealthy enough by now, isn't he?' Selina said.

'It's only money.'

'And respected.'

The two women sat close. 'It doesn't mean a bloody thing to him,' Annie tried to explain. 'I just want him to live.'

When Jim came back they were still sitting there. 'You're exhausted,' Annie said.

'I don't want to eat,' he muttered. 'Stop fussing!' There was silence.

Peter piped up: 'We just want you to be with us for ever.' He ran from the log and hugged his grandad.

Next morning Jim went to Sean's pub, early, and talked to Billy. 'One day this land will be in your hands. You've got to learn responsibility.'

'That's what you told my father,' Billy said, staring. 'You won't fool me. I'll get it anyway.'

Jim sighed and heaved himself back on his horse. A band tightened around his chest: his heart, some sort of genetic deterioration ticking in his blood. The ache easing with the gentle movement, he let his horse take him along Corduroy road to the Simmonds place. Powwidde, greeting him with pleasure, now asked to be called Peggy because of the embarrassment her real name caused Josh with other boys his age. Twelve was a sensitive age; Josh was an outsider amongst outsiders, and he wasn't sure why.

Peggy held the horse's bridle and Jim swung down. 'Isaac's out back,' she said. She had no shoes; and her clothes were in rags. But Joshua wore leather shoes and neatly darned trews. Brown feathers clung to his chest where he had been plucking the supper chicken. Across the yard Isaac was repairing the head of a hoe that had been wired up a dozen times before. They shook hands. 'Since I lost Johnny my land's been a disgrace,' Jim said without further preamble. 'I'm not up to it any more and I need help.'

'Always ready to help.'

'I mean help I pay for. Formal. Couple of days a week maybe.'

Isaac chewed it over, his tousled hair showing the first streaks of grey.

'What's Billy think about this, mate?'

'Maybe it'll put some ginger in him,' Jim predicted mildly.

But he was wrong. Billy just smiled. 'Sure,' he said, and bided his time. But it took much longer than he had thought, because Jim Pride just wouldn't die.

It was the height of summer, the start of 1850. Jim lay alone in bed in the broad day. Through the half-open ship's door of Paragon House he glimpsed the green vista of paddocks and treetops, a brilliant vision of the world he had carved from the wilderness. Annie was preparing the midday meal and the clatter of pots and pans seemed very loud at first. Then that sound faded and all he heard was his own laboured breathing, the frantic running of his own heart.

'Won't be long,' Annie called cheerfully.

Jim's fingers gripped the counterpane.

'Potato soup. Are you all right? All right?' Now Annie's voice faded away.

Silence. Jim's fingers moved. Eve's voice said: 'He cannot die.'

His fingers scribbled across the counterpane as though he held a pen.

My dearest Eve, tomorrow I shall die, if tomorrow comes without you. The new world is the prisoner of the old, and I cannot live without my freedom, without hope, without the woman I love.

Eve, I love you. That day had come.

He looked up, hearing creaking wood, seeing a shadow cross the room. Eve opened her arms to the struggling figure. He smiled because she looked so beautiful in her fine English fashion clothes, cream wool, a long cape. William Prideau stood beside her, smug and cold, terrified of her even in his dominance, holding her back.

James, Eve whispered, *don't accept your fate.*

'I love you,' James Prideau said with all his strength.

Annie unbent his fingers from the counterpane, kissed his lips, and closed the blue eyes she had loved all these years.

27

1850

John Prideau's legacy (2)

It was the start of 1850, the very depth of the English winter, and it seemed dawn might never come. Then growing light eroded the darkness from the features of William Prideau and his wasted form was revealed to the sun's cruel illumination.

Eve Prideau sat out her vigil at her husband's bedside listening to him heave breaths into his bony chest. His closed eyelids were almost transparent, revealing the dreaming orbs twitching beneath. This was the man who had possessed her almost all her adult life, taken over her life. There was almost nothing of him left now; these gasping breaths, the stink of him.

She was numb with the hours of sitting and her cold hands were folded inertly in her lap. The fire had gone out long ago but she didn't bother the maid. Eve's hair, such a pale white it looked almost blonde knotted by the royal blue ribbon, was untouched since the dinner party last night when William, having endured years of illness, collapsed and entered his final decline.

Their son John stayed with him for a while, then he and his wife Adelie returned to their home further down Chesterfield Street. It was a Monday morning, and John must arrive before morning prayers at Prideau & Prideau, as strict as his father about setting a good example to the staff.

Eve wept without moving. It was silly; she felt beyond summoning any emotion at all, yet the tears slid down her cheeks. She crossed to the window and opened it on the breeze from Hyde Park, acid with the tang of coalsmoke and horse manure, so familiar that it passed for fresh.

Straw had been laid in the street so that the clopping of hooves, the rumblings of wheels, would not distract an important man from his death. The silence in the room was eerie; only William's wrestling breaths behind her.

A knock came on the door. She composed herself. The little maid knocked again and entered shyly. 'Shall I make up the fire, ma'am?' she asked.

Eve could not bring herself to speak. She turned away with a wave of her hand. The poker clinked in the fireplace, then the door was closed.

In the street a tinker, dressed in neat castoffs, pedalling a whirring grindstone, was sharpening knives. From Adelie Prideau's doorway further down the street appeared the formidable figure of the nanny, Mrs Turton, pushing a perambulator with Eve's grandson Winston sitting upright holding onto the sides, at nearly four looking rather large for the vehicle – by his mischievous expression he might without warning vault out of it. Hunching her shoulders, Mrs Turton turned him towards the Park for his morning constitutional. The monopoly that had eased London's traffic jams by excluding omnibuses from the central parishes had been revoked, and now as Mrs Turton came to Curzon Street an old Shillibus pulled by three horses stopped by her, the cad swinging down to stuff as many passengers aboard as possible. That never would have been the case in the old days when the conductors were gentlemen, usually proudly retired from the sea – nowadays the cads always seemed to have accents from east of Aldgate Pump. The wind gusted strongly from the south, suddenly whirling the straw along the road. Eve smelt the grey-green, rotting-vegetable odour of the river driving down the wind, and faintly heard the distant, steamy roar of a train pulling into the Waterloo terminus from Nine Elms. The trains created enormous numbers of travellers; doubtless underwriting the railway companies was one of the ways William had made money, before this more important termination claimed his attention.

And now he looked back on his life, what did he see?

Behind her, William groaned.

She crossed to his bedside. The smell of William: his mouth had opened in a circle, his head thrown back into his thin white hair. His gums were ridiculously pink, his porcelain teeth in a glass on the bedside table by the papers left there by John for his attention, as though he were not dying.

During the night Eve had felt a most curious sensation flood through her, filling her heart with grief, then passing on like the wind, and she knew she had felt a death. She looked at William sadly, sure her premonition was the grief for her husband that she should be feeling, sadness at the disease eroding his heart finally claiming him – *I must love him a little after all*, she thought sadly, then shook her head.

William stared up into her face. 'I have sinned,' he said harshly, and when he began to speak she could not believe what her ears were hearing.

He confessed to her all the evil he had done: his crime against James Prideau, his identical twin brother, whom she loved.

And, Eve realised, loved still.

William, all smoothness gone from his features, gazed at her with ghastly eyes. 'Forgive me.'

Eve ran to the window. She put her hand over her mouth. All was clear to her – all her guilty feelings that she hated her husband and blamed herself for, when she had been right all along. He had lied to her. She could hardly encompass the enormity of what William had destroyed. He had lied his way into her life, her love, her *self*, and left her with this. Nothing. Once she had been young and in love.

'Now you understand,' William whispered, 'do you forgive me?'

He watched her.

'He didn't deserve you.' William crooked his finger, and she found herself going to him. Her throat was so tight she could not weep.

'I shall make amends,' William whispered. His hand knocked against the bedside cabinet, papers whirled down. 'That one,' William said, grasping. She passed a document into his fluttering hands without looking at him. 'I shall earn your love.'

Again she shook her head.

'And salve my conscience,' acknowledged William. 'Money and property. The only way I know.'

'I can't bear to be in this room!'

'One half to my son John. One half to my brother James Prideau in Australia and his descendants, if any.'

'But he's dead,' Eve shouted. The servants would hear.

William dragged a breath. 'It's written down. It's enough.'

'It's not anything,' she shouted.

'Is it enough?' William groaned. 'I'm dying. Let me touch you. I'll sign.' His hand slid up her dress. He held out his other hand for the pen, then took it himself when she didn't move, writing down his name with the painful concentration of a child. 'I love you, Eve, I did it all for you.' He closed his eyes. 'Tell me you love me now.'

'I do not and I never have.' Her features wrinkled with the pain of her admission. It was herself she was throwing away. He had nothing to lose.

'Just let me touch you.' His hand shivered on her thigh, then slid to the softness of her sex. 'I'll go out of this world the same place I came in,' William muttered victoriously, and the breath went out of him.

Eve closed the window. She covered his awful face with the counterpane, snatched up the documents and almost ran out into the hall.

'Ma'am!' said the little maid, Jenny, waiting patiently on a three-legged stool.

Eve calmed herself. 'The master is –' Eve nearly said *dead*. 'He is passed on.' Jenny burst into tears; people who had not known William would mourn him. 'Call the doctor to make the arrangements,' Eve directed.

William's manservant bowed to her in the entrance hall, and she waved him upstairs. 'This is a sad day for us all, ma'am,' he whispered.

'Yes,' Eve said too loudly.

William's butler bowed to her and opened the front door since she seemed so eager to be out of it. 'Madam. . . .' he said in an anxious voice, 'Madam should not. . . . Madam is not wearing black.'

Eve walked into the street and drew a deep breath. The butler came down and draped round her shoulders a black cape he must have been holding ready. The wind whipped around her, sending motes of straw whirling in the cold sunlight. 'I don't want it to get in my eyes,' she said, and he bowed again. The straw would be swept up immediately.

Eve wandered to Adelie's door and knocked. Adelie Prideau, her son John's wife, opened it herself. 'Eve! Mama! My poor darling! Is it really over?'

Eve allowed herself to be drawn inside, comforted by the effusive lamentations. Adelie always called her Mama, her rich chocolatey enunciation making Eve feel warm and enriched. If anyone knew her, it was Adelie.

Adelie, wearing a pink satin gown, was a big effusive

woman with the plump double chins of an opera diva, and a throat girded with chains of jewellery even at nine in the morning. She had never lost her theatrical ways; Adelie's double-jointed fingers made her florid gestures extraordinarily expressive. Her voice, once stormy and magnificent, had become booming since she relinquished the stage, but her eyes had lost the shallowness and suspicion Eve first knew and their friendship was genuine.

They went into the parlour and Adelie threw herself on the chaise-longue, saying nothing while Eve prowled: Chinese wallpaper, Thackeray serials in yellow paper covers and the three novels by the Bell brothers, Dickens in green covers, piles of sheet music and, extravagantly, two pianos; and, most extraordinary of all, Adelie's wedding portrait taken by a photographist.

'Poor Mama! Of course you're utterly devastated.' Adelie's naturalness and vivacity sounded aristocratic. She had learned well. Nine years older than John, she had spent almost thirty years of her life on the stage, mostly in the chorus, as Mrs Lawson – because *Mrs* was respectable, not because she was married. With no powerful patron behind her, only approaching middle age, as her voice matured, was her hard work and talent rewarded with leading rôles. Eve wished she had Adelie's powers of application: she would have liked to have lived such a life, devoted to a voice, a vision, an achievement: to sing. Her voice was *almost* as good as she thought. In the shock of her disappointment Adelie gave it all up for a man of thirty-seven, nine years her junior. John knew how lucky he was. Her florid magnificence was the warmth in his life, his sole indulgence, and he had defied his father to marry her.

There had been more to William's point of view, of course. There always was. His inquiries had established that Mrs Lawson was a stagename: her real name was Miss Gumboge, and she lived in uneasy harmony with her eldest sister, also a spinster, in the old Sotheby rooms west of Somerset House. Eve had never visited Prideau and Prideau, as William's place of work in the Middle Temple was his castle, but it seemed that a Lawson Gumboge had been his partner until the late 1820s, and the name did seem vaguely familiar to her. 'What does it matter?' Eve asked when William brought up his new barrier of Adelie's lower class origins. Apparently this Mr Gumboge had spoken with a south London accent.

'I do not wish my son to marry the daughter of an employee,' William had huffed.

'Oh,' Eve smiled.

But John, who overheard this intensely restrained disagreement and recognised it for a furious argument, was a match for his father in the matter of cold rationality: he too had a mind like an analytical machine. He silenced his mother with a kiss. 'Father, I recall Mr Gumboge's youngest daughter married Mr Wray at the age of sixteen, and *he* is now Head Clerk,' John said quietly to William. 'Wray's loyalty and the quality of his work is exemplary. Adelie is my sole indulgence!' he exclaimed. 'Only in her have I ever disobeyed you. What is the real reason for your opposition?'

William wriggled uncomfortably on the hook, but would not admit the truth.

The truth, of course, was that a wife of forty-six would not produce an heir.

So John had married Adelie five years ago, at St Paul's church on the west side of Covent Garden market, two months after she gave up her career. Almost at once the last thing she could have expected happened: she fell pregnant with Winston. It was the baby that won over William to the match.

With Winston's arrival, William's attitude was transformed. Dying, he doted on the baby.

But now William was dead.

*

In Eve's lifetime London had changed beyond belief; and London had not changed at all. After the funeral she drove down to the Middle Temple, staring through the sidewindow at the heavy traffic, omnibuses, dog-carts and heavy waggons, a fool weaving between them on a Dalzell bicycle in the bitter cold. Two guardians of the imperial metropolis, tall moustachioed Metropolitan Policemen wearing the hated white gloves – *they* didn't get their hands dirty – marched along the pavement. Many ancient street markets had been closed down by the Crushers as hotbeds of crime, rookeries invaded, practices regulated. Detectives infiltrated themselves in communities in plain-clothes, in the Continental manner. Eve was grateful because William had been. As rookeries were broken up to make way for new roads and railways, crime diminished, though specialist crimes like garotting – violent robbery, the victim grabbed by the throat from behind – were increasing. The poor were being driven out of the town centre in the hope that they would find somewhere else to go, the Common Lodgings Act allowing the police much closer surveillance powers off the street, but the outbreaks of cholera from drinking water supplies draining from cesspools and burial grounds, as in Clerkenwell, now seemed to Eve less the fault of the immoral poor than of the indifference of the travelling public. She knew William would have considered these thoughts of her own, slowly emerging now he was dead, a heresy. Her gaze swept past Buckingham House where the young Queen played with her children – the grand East Front was finished, and the Marble Arch now rebuilt at the top of Park Lane, over the old Tyburn gallows.

The carriage took her into Trafalgar Square, the openness and light of that sudden space still startling her. St Martin-in-the-Fields was now a view, unencumbered by slums; William had never got used to this windy emptiness where once the stinking mass of the

Bermudas and the Caribbees spread over to Charing Cross, and preferred to walk through the warren of Covent Garden.

Eve leaned forward, staring out: the Nelson Column still awaited its bronze lions, and the sky looked like snow.

Even the Strand had been cobbled and widened. The penny post was being delivered, the letters enclosed in envelopes, though she still found herself folding her letters the old way and reaching for sealing-wax instead of a penny black or tuppenny blue. Here was Newgate, that dark monster of her memory with its modern public gallows where twenty villains could be strung up together, although beheadings were no longer performed. They seemed a much less humane policy than transportation, which nowadays continued only to west Australia and Van Diemen's Land, at the New South Wales colonists' own request, despite their shortage of labour. Many had once been such men, and now they wanted to forget.

The jammed traffic stopped her reaching Temple Bar so she got down and walked. She had to ask a clerk the way to 2 Brick Court, and finally entered her husband's secret heart, where he had hidden so much from her.

It was crowded! Clerks scurried everywhere, descending from above, hurrying up from below, clutching tomes and sheafs, legal documents, account books. Eve stood confused. The Head Clerk, Wray, whom she had met for the first time at the funeral, looked startled when her name was whispered in his ear, then bowed. He looked lively and efficient, but painfully thin, and if his wife was as generously proportioned as the rest of the Gumboge line seemed to be, he must have been almost swamped.

Eve said breathlessly, 'Is it always as busy here as this?'

'As you know, we shall shortly be opening additional offices in the City.'

'No, I didn't know.' He bowed politely for the second time. Of course she hadn't known; it was none of her business.

'It will give us more room,' he said, making conversation, preceding her up the narrow stairs. His footsteps were slow and she realised he was unwell. The door of the inner sanctum opened as they arrived, a warning having been passed somehow, and John strode out.

'Mother!' he said in his deep voice, taking her hands. 'You should have told me you were going to come. I would have prepared – ' he gestured with a shrug of his shoulders. Anything. 'A welcome.'

'I decided on the spur of the moment.'

John, except that one time in his life, with Adelie, did nothing on the spur of the moment. 'Yes, of course,' he said solidly, and she realised how little he understood her. A son's mother was a different animal; more symbol than real woman. Eve accepted her fate. Only once had she asked him about his feelings: why had he chosen Adelie? William had been away, she was desperate to know. Unspoken behind her question was that John, handsome and with a strong personality, and every prospect of becoming wealthy, could have picked any woman of his class he wished. John, standing by the mantelpiece, looking her in the eyes with his straightforward blue gaze, twirling a forgotten sherry in his large muscular hand, simply replied: 'Because I never met a woman I loved more.' That had been the closest they ever were. They did not speak of feelings now.

'May I go in?' she said, looking into his office.

'Bring us tea,' John told someone as he closed the door behind her.

It had been William's; now it was John's. The office was spartan and dark, with a single bright window holding the edge of a view down to Blackfriars Bridge and the cold grey river. The furniture was very heavy.

John sat behind the desk and clasped his hands in his lap; her own mannerism. They stared at one another, then both started speaking at once and both stopped. John began again.

'We weathered the 1847 economic crisis. We're the largest Regimental Agents in the country since taking over Cox's. Some of that will be handled in the City by The Prideau Merchant Bank, probably by summer. As you see we have no room here. Prideau & Prideau will remain, dealing mostly with corporate law, it's the most rapidly expanding field there is, and an excellent way of introducing ourselves to customers who later use our more profitable services.'

Eve wore an interested smile. 'What about all this gold that's being discovered in California? Are you investing there?'

'Who would we finance? A bunch of down-and-outs digging dirt.' He admitted: 'We are investing in South America with Baring Brothers.'

'I see. What in?'

'Reputable silver-mining companies, Argentinian beef, and so forth.'

That was all she was going to get. He poured the tea with total concentration: William had taught him well. 'I brought this.' She laid an envelope on the desk. 'It is your father's. He signed it before he died.'

John flicked up the unsealed flap and scanned the single page with professional speed and indifference. 'Yes, that's definitely his signature.' He put it down in front of him.

Eve quoted: ' "One half to my son John. One half my estate and interests to my brother James Prideau in Australia and his descendants, if any." '

'You've left out the heretofores and whereofs,' he

302

objected, and Eve was delighted to have scratched his lawyer's skin.

'You have the sense of it,' she said, picking it up. ' "My Trustees may employ in the business of the Companies such part of my residuary estate as they in their uncontrolled discretion think fit, which they may advance to the Companies on the security of debentures or debenture stock, or by the issue of additional shares, and the income shall fall into and be applied as income of my residuary estate. . . ." '

'Yes, quite,' John said smoothly. *Oh, Father, what have you done?*

Eve read on: ' "It is my wish that my Trustees shall retain the shares for as long as they consider it beneficial to do so, and that they may if they think fit carry on, or cause to be carried on, the business of the Companies. . . ." '

He looked at her with wounded eyes, provoked to cutting to the heart of the matter. 'I did not know my father had a brother,' he accused her.

'More than that, a twin brother. James was his twin. He was transported to Australia for a crime. . . . not his crime. That was how your father made this firm his. James's ship foundered in the Southern Ocean.'

'My father never mentioned this to me,' John said, and she had to admire his self control. 'He cannot have considered it important. This piece of paper makes no difference to anything, you understand.'

'Your father considered that piece of paper very important,' Eve said softly.

'Very well. I will have the matter looked into most carefully.' When he saw that she was waiting for him to continue he explained, 'We'll apply to the Court for probate with the presumption of James Prideau's death by shipwreck while we look for him. There are established procedures for everything. My father wholly owned all his business concerns.' For the first time she

303

heard a bragging note in his voice. 'We even own Versucchi outright. Apart from that it's entirely run by the Versucchi family of course, keeps the Italians happy. One doesn't buy a dog and bark oneself.' He returned to the matter of the will. 'You and I are Executors and Trustees of these monies, which are mostly in the form of shares. When the time comes to distribute my father's estate we'll apply to the Court for, in the legal phrase, "half his growing fortune" to be paid into Court because the beneficiary, James, is believed dead.' A ghost of a grin showed. 'Convicts are legally dead anyway.'

'I'm sure you know what you're doing,' Eve said. 'It's just that, if there is the slightest chance – '

'I understand,' John said, looking at her thoughtfully. But for her insistence, it would be the easiest thing in the world for this will to be lost. Did she so deeply desire James Prideau to live on, even if only in her memory? 'It was forty-five years ago,' he said. 'Why should you care?'

'Oh – you know what women are like! Is this very bad news for the firm?'

'No.' He went to the window and stared out. 'You cannot really think James Prideau alive.' She did not answer. 'Well, Mother, the truth of the matter is that I could not possibly afford to purchase one-half share of my father's enterprises, and I certainly wish to prevent any other firm purchasing them! So the longer the matter remains locked up with the Court, frankly, the safer I feel.'

'Thank you, John.' She got up gratefully. *Don't you feel you had a twin sister, John, my little baby daughter Eve, even though she lived for only an hour? Don't you feel her spirit at all?*

'I shall begin inquiries as to James Prideau immediately,' John said. 'You may rest assured, the matter is safe in my hands.'

He escorted his mother to the door, and outside through the falling snow to her carriage which had now arrived, exchanging pleasantries all the way. Then as Eve got inside she looked back at him through the white, whirling flakes. 'Did I fail you, John – as a mother?'

He kissed her as though she had not spoken and closed the carriage door, stood waving goodbye until the vehicle had disappeared behind the falling white veils.

Eve Prideau was an innocent in Babylon.

John, however, was not.

Having promised his mother to make a search for James Prideau, he let it linger. The search was entrusted to an inexperienced junior clerk, Nicholas Murphy. No James Prideau had been embarked on a hulk or prison transport. No trace of a James Prideau could be found during a lengthy, very lengthy examination of the Colony's records. Such omission or losses from the records were not uncommon after almost half a century. The trial record survived: James Prideau pleaded *po se*, no contest.

John became interested in James Prideau. What was he really like? From the old account books and papers in the Depository downstairs he formed a picture of a man full of life. John stayed in the office late at night, considering. What was Eve's part in all this? When it came down to it, how much did he really know about his mother? She was a doctor's daughter, he thought mistakenly, from Lynmouth in Devon – at a party he had heard her talk knowledgeably of the place when Coutts the banker, whose family had made the place famous, mentioned it. Eve had come to London having known the two Prideau brothers. But William, John slowly realised, was not the one she had really loved.

John was beginning to learn more than he wanted to know.

The more he looked, the more he discerned his father's hand in James Prideau's fate. A smile crossed his features. John admired a man who got what he wanted. It made life simple.

Nevertheless, the matter would have to be handled carefully.

It seemed that the *Paragon*, the ship James Prideau must have been assigned to, went down off King Island. Young Murphy, as fascinated in following the story as he, found it on the map. In dangerous waters, without any obvious harbour, the place was ignored until 1830. Twenty years ago two interesting things happened: King Island became administratively part of Van Diemen's Land, and the lieutenant-governor granted a series of conditional pardons. These, of course, were gazetted in papers held by the Colonial Office in London. There was no mention of Prideau, but then Murphy, who was becoming too zealous, started going through the almost endless lists looking up similar names. And there it was. *Jim Pride, also known as James Prideau.*

John thanked the clerk, paid him a raise, and had him transferred to much more important work.

He despised colonials: the only one who had come out of this honourably was the man John was most proud of, his father. The man who got what he wanted.

John loyally concealed anything that might appear to slur William's name and thus reflect on his own. He sidetracked his mother, and as his own legal representative, once the Court had finished with it let the will find its way into the Depository downstairs, where it was left to moulder.

The two women stuck together. Eve and Adelie sat, concealed from the eyes of the crowd, in their sixth-

'You've got dust on your knees, Daddy,' Lily piped, and he straightened her lavender pinny.

Una, Vanessa's sister, stood a couple of paces behind them, and Fergus sensed her dry eyes fixed on the back of his head, her mouth pinched down. Una disapproved of displays of feeling. She wore a black dress and a black hat with a few bits of black ribbon, much as at her father's funeral those twelve years ago. That day Fergus had been wearing black, too – broad black arrows on his yellow slops. . . .

The two girls had ignored the ever-present men in black and yellow, busy comforting their mother. The convict gravediggers, pushed back by the overseer, lay sprawled in the pale shade of a gum while the cheap service ran its brief course. Only Fergus the Scot remained standing, six foot four inches tall and wide in every dimension, with a brutal face when he chose, full of blunt features. He had spent most of his life in pubs, the scar from a broken bottle now almost hidden by his beard, but in repose his eyes were gentle and kind. The men were chewing stalks, laying odds which girl would give the best time. Fergus stood a few paces apart, saying nothing, watching quietly as ever. The thin girl in black, the one the mother kept calling Una, looked round at him.

She threw him a look of such raw passion that he blinked.

'Fergus, lie down, you bastard,' the overseer yawned.

Fergus stared at the other girl. The mother called her Vanessa, a name he'd never heard. Vanessa's complexion was dark and interesting, her hair subtle shades of brown – a harmonious face, with deep blue eyes. Her warmth and gentleness with the old woman attracted him. Fergus liked a woman who cared: Vanessa filled his eyes. Una was the one the men chose.

Through the gap in the hedge he watched the girls

walk away down the dusty road. *Walk* – so they lived close.

Fergus Matheson didn't forget them. Sometimes, when he was sent on the road-gang out in the Blue Mountains, his great arms swinging in the punishing heat and dust, it seemed he thought of little else but the two sisters he had seen that day.

Fergus Matheson, once of Glasgow but later of all places south, had been transported for seven years for forgery – those hands, later so calloused and toughened, were capable of the most delicate caresses of paper or metal. He had a fine intelligence too, and a fatal weakness for drink. Drunk and humiliated, he was caught over a very amateurish piece of work passed across the pub counter, and learned his lesson well. He never touched a dram again, or ever wanted to.

His philosophy these days was simple. He wanted to be rich and happy.

A man sent down for seven years usually received his ticket-of-leave, which began his rehabilitation in society, after four. Fergus went round the district sharpening knives. It took him a year to find the sisters, but they had their own house and he recognised Una immediately. As the door was opened, he swept off his hat and bowed.

'Good morning, Miss Una,' he said.

He was skilful at gaining their trust, chatting while he sharpened the cutlery, repairing a broken handle. There was no charge. He began doing little jobs around the place, the garden needed work and the paling fence was broken; embarrassing them because they could not pay. 'There's no charge,' he said politely. Their mother was ill and he easily carried up the iron bedstead they could not manage on the stairs. As their confidence in him grew Vanessa and Una began waiting on him with cups of tea or bread and cheese for lunch, talking while he ate. They were very lonely. Una's face lost its pinched look, her thin mouth smiled, but her conversation was quick and direct. Vanessa, the shy one with the top of her head hardly reaching the height of his chest, fetched the hot water when he cut his hand, and Una wound the bandage round, looking into his eyes. He had never seen such a naked need to be taken. But Vanessa dropped the bowl with an enormous clatter and the moment was broken. When she glanced at him with her deep blue eyes he could not tell whether her amusement was mocking or innocent. Una ran from the room.

He liked them both.

He decided to marry one or other of them. Una asked him to move the skillion table, and they both knew what was really running through their minds. A faint blush bloomed on Una's flat cheeks and such was her need she already lifted herself on tiptoe to be kissed. 'Una, do you believe I'll be rich one day?' he said.

'You?' she said. 'You'll have to shave that beard off first!'

He bowed politely, and moved the table for her. Una followed him round the house all morning, but at last he found Vanessa alone beside the apple tree in the tiny garden. She was hanging out the washing and handed him the pegs. 'Vanessa,' he said, 'do you believe I'll be rich one day?'

She looked at him seriously. 'I believe,' she said.

They were married at the Registry Office exactly three weeks later, the old woman whining tearfully and demanding in a sudden loud voice who would look after her now. Una was sitting beside her, pinched and pale, and the answer to that question was obvious.

Vanessa had faith in Fergus, and she never lost her admiration for the delicate intelligence that guided his iron will. He could balance a china teacup in its saucer politely on his knee, or guffaw with the drinking crowd at the Rocks and never touch a drop. Like most emanci-

311

pists he loved gambling, but he quit when he was ahead. The winnings staked them for the store he built out of town on the Blue Mountain Road, a hut with blue-gum walls that split in the sun, and a living that barely supported them. Nevertheless, he persevered, and learned his trade. Vanessa fell pregnant, worked until her lying-in, and had her baby in the appalling heat of the tiny back room. Fergus shut up shop that day.

They named their little girl Lily, after Vanessa's mother, by now bedridden in the house Sam had left her, with Una's life devoted to looking after her. She took no pleasure in Vanessa's visits but only complained about Una. 'Be quiet,' Una whispered, 'be quiet, you wicked old woman.'

Fergus worked himself in the store until he was almost beaten. The work was hard and the hours were endless. It was time to try something new. This was what had brought them back to Sydney that day: they were saying goodbye. Fergus watched Vanessa lay flowers against the burning stone, and Lily cried because her mother did. Fergus knelt between them, and put his arms round them both.

'The ship's waiting to take us to Melbourne,' he said at last, and Vanessa kissed Una goodbye. Lily curtseyed prettily.

'Are you sure you won't come and see us off?' Vanessa asked.

'I've got to get back!' Una said. Fergus bent to kiss her and Una pressed her fingernails into his arms. 'Goodbye, Fergus,' she said, 'look after her.' Then she turned away.

A year later, in the supposedly booming state of Victoria, running a ramshackle pioneer store seventy miles west of Melbourne on the road from Geelong to Buninyong, Fergus would know he had made the biggest mistake of his life. Gold had been discovered in the Wellington district of New South Wales and his old store on the Blue Mountains Road, which he had sold out for a few pounds, was now besieged by the constant stream of prospectors fighting for the privilege of buying anything they could lay their hands on, pans, shovels, sugar, boots, paying any price demanded of them, such was their greed to reach the goldfield.

And so Fergus had lost.

Buninyong, the knee-shaped hill, was the end of nowhere – Mother Jamieson's pub and a few huts built by sawyers and splitters. George Innes was 'King of the Splitters' and Dr Power, who saved Lily's infected finger when her tame kangaroo bit her, was the only doctor nearer than Geelong. All men carried firearms as the aborigines had murdered some settlers, and everyone kept clear of their mia-mias on the Yarrowee. The days when Captain Ross, dressed in kilt and full Highland regalia, had walked peacefully from Ross Creek to Geelong were long gone.

The country had been opened up by Scots, which was partly what attracted Fergus to it: twelve years ago everywhere to the northwest of the Bay of Corio was unknown, an ocean of forest and native hop out of which stuck hills like islands. Cattle had been grazed here for a decade and in the last few years a Presbyterian minister arrived, and three years ago Mr Bedwell opened his school, but at ten pounds a year the fees were too high for Fergus to afford.

So Fergus Matheson would sit his daughter on the empty counter and play knuckles with her, or talk about anything that came to mind, together listening out hopefully for the tread of a customer, or the Cobb & Company coach creaking from Bacchus Marsh on its leather springs. Vanessa sat in the back room, waiting. Her face was worn and her eyes had lost their lustre. She'd inherited her father's luck and she knew the end of the road when she saw it. She went out and hugged Fergus and Lily without saying a word.

But it wasn't the end for them: it was only the end of the beginning.

Part III

Lily

29

January 1850 – 1858 January
Blood and gold

Bob and Ezzie brought young Jack with them from
Hobart Town, of course, to pay their respects to Jim
Pride's memory, and doubtless they hoped for a reconciliation with Annie. She was too proud to be won
over so easily. Jim Pride's funeral on King Island had
been quick, Billy roaming nowhere to be found. Annie
began digging the grave with no one to help her. The
velvety soil was cruel with stones, her bones cracked,
the high summer sun beat down on her back. She was
determined to lay him to rest beside Johnny, his son,
the two of them so far apart in life lying together at
the foot of the rock outcrop. Below her was the lagoon
and the tree. This was tearing the heart out of Annie –
not the work, she was used to that. She was emotionally
devastated. Jim's death brought back the ache of Johnny's loss, the unfairness of it, she could think of nothing
else.

Another shovel was helping her. Selina had arrived
without a word and they worked together. Peter and
Rebecca kept the soil, now increasingly sandy, from
sliding back. Isaac came on horseback to talk over the
day's work, saw what was happening, slid down and
took Selina's shovel. His boy Josh took over with Peter,
and Rebecca went into the house to make a pot of
'Giraffe' tea. Annie wouldn't rest. Then the shovels
sank into the black band of rich loam, decayed vege-

table matter from the ancient forest, and they knew they were six feet down.

'We haven't got a minister to put it right,' Selina said when they were ready.

'We don't need anyone like that.' Annie wore her face of stone. 'Isaac, say it.'

Isaac took off his soft hat. They stood around the graveside.

'Jim Pride was a good mate,' Isaac said, 'he did everything for the best.'

Annie shrugged away Selina's hand. 'And we're going to miss him,' she said. She missed them both. Johnny still seemed so alive to her, manly and inarticulate, but whatever heaven Jim had gone to wouldn't include her.

'Isaac,' she called, when the job was finished, 'there's work to do!'

When she had given him his orders – a bullock had strangled itself in the wire beyond the small creek – Isaac rode off, Josh galloping his pony beside him. Selina put her arm round Annie's shoulders.

'Don't look so sad,' she said. Annie shrugged.

So it was Selina who had written to Bob.

The letter took a month to reach Hobart Town, then within the week Bob arrived with his family. Annie stood at the Yellow Rock jetty, watching the steam launch he had chartered drop a jollyboat, the sailors wearing neat blue-striped jerseys, and understood for the first time that they were wealthy. She snorted. Bob would re-learn soon enough that money meant nothing here.

'I didn't ask you to some,' Annie said. She was wearing belted trousers of Botany Bay tweed, a red shirt and a leathery broad-brimmed hat against the sun. Bob, office-pale, came towards her with his hand outstretched, both smiling and tentative. He wore a slim black suit with a stiff white shirt. His hat was very tall and fashionable. Annie kept her hands on her hips.

'Nevertheless, here we are,' Bob said. 'You're always in our hearts, Mother, and our prayers.'

Ezzie scrambled out of the boat, lithe as the day Annie first saw her, though her pinned-up hair was paler, and her skin darker. 'I see you don't spend all your life beneath that parasol,' Annie said briefly, and Ezzie smiled at her with eyes frank and innocent. Everything about her frightened Annie with its echoes of Annie who had been. The punishment was bitter.

'You haven't met Jack,' Ezzie smiled, ignoring the awkward silence.

Annie's grandson was two months from his thirteenth birthday. Jack's shy eyes were the blue of Annie and Bob's, but his long delicate nose, high cheekbones, and dark complexion were Ezzie's. His hair was paler, almost blond. Annie thought he looked quick rather than strong – he reminded her of Peter – and uncomfortable in his black suit; he had eased one foot out of his too-tight shoes. Annie's heart softened. 'You'll find Peter and Rebecca in the dunes where they're supposed to be working. They're probably looking at insects or fishing in the Yellow Rock river. Peter will show you the yolla flying in this evening, if you ask him pretty nicely.'

'I used to do that,' Bob said.

'You were a dreamer in those days,' Annie said. 'This isn't your home now.' Jack ran off like the wind, looking forward to getting out of those shoes, Annie thought, and dabbling his toes in the cool river. She almost said so, but saw Ezzie thought it too. Annie turned away quickly. 'You'll pay your respects,' she told Bob gruffly, 'and then we'll eat a simple supper.'

But it wasn't simple; one thing led to another. Annie had become so obsessed with keeping it unspecial that it turned into a feast, looking like a welcome home, the last thing she had intended. She had early decided they would have to use the *Paragon* cutlery to which she was sentimentally attached, but the ivory handles had spotted and yellowed and it took her hours to whiten them with emery. Then she saw how stained the brass kettle looked – the first thing another woman would notice – and restored its shine with salt and vinegar. She scoured the table, hesitating before removing with milk the inkstains Jim had left, then touched where they had been with her fingertips. She had Isaac bring in an echidna, which would taste like suckling pig, removed the porcupine quills and soaked the pale skinned carcass in salted water. It looked too plain; she made a stuffing of breadcrumbs and chopped bacon, then added rosemary, thyme and fennel from the herb garden. Tasting it, she put in grated lemon and a pinch of nutmeg. After sewing it up she decorated it with fat bacon, then went out to pick the vegetables. After all that she didn't have time to change. They would just have to take her as they found her.

The table was set outside. Bob swept off his ridiculous hat – his hair didn't move in the evening breeze, stiff with macassar oil, not supple Jamaican rum, so Annie knew he'd signed the pledge – and he said a long grace, he'd caught religion properly. Peter and Jack scoffed their food; Rebecca observed Annie. Annie hardly ate. She missed Jim terribly. She drank brandy, defying Bob to say a word. Bob and Ezzie complimented her how good the food was, their Hobarton manners irritating her further. It was all unreal. City people! Ezzie found the pudding and brought it out, a feathery jam roly-poly so light it tickled their throats. Annie watched them eat. 'I'm letting you down, aren't I?' she demanded.

'You're very upset,' Bob said tenderly.

She frowned when they sent Jack off to play instead of making him help with the washing up. 'I'll do it,'

Ezzie smiled. Annie looked at the smooth, servant-fed hand that took her plate and wondered if she knew the difference between washing soda and caustic soda. They were left alone.

'You're taking it pretty hard,' Bob said, dropping his Englishy Hobarton accent.

'What do you know about it. What do you know what you've put me through.'

'Come on, Ma. Don't be sad. Don't exclude us.' He made to hug her, which was what she wanted, but she lifted her glass.

'You look smug in that jacket,' she said.

He took it off. Then he took off his stiff white collar and undid the top button of his shirt.

'Is Jack included in your vendetta?' he said. 'It wasn't my fault, Ma. I didn't want to leave the Island.'

'Ezzie's my daughter.'

Bob laughed.

'*Stop*,' Annie said.

He stopped.

'Everything about her. You can see it now, Bob.'

Finally he said: 'You couldn't possibly know.'

Annie touched her heart. She threw away her glass. 'Believe me,' she said, 'I'm truly sorry. I had to tell you. It's God's truth.'

Bob said: 'You shouldn't have told me.'

Ezzie came out with a laugh. 'What shouldn't you have told him?' she smiled, leaning down from behind where Bob sat and sliding her arms around his shoulders. Her horn sidecomb pulled out, her unpinned hair streamed down his shirt-front and she kissed his jaw. Bob sat rigid.

That night Annie quickly persuaded herself she'd done no harm. On the contrary, she felt better now the weight was off her shoulders – a worry shared was a worry halved. And it wasn't as if Bob and Ezzie had

321

deliberately done anything wrong – they had been wronged, but Bob hadn't blamed her. He was a good son. It seemed that her crushing burden hadn't been so important after all. Everyone in the world was related and intermarried or they wouldn't be human. The royal families of Europe had intermarried for thousands of years. Annie turned over and pushed her fist into the bolster, settled her face comfortably, and slept. . . .

In the next bedroom, Ezzie touched Bob with her wicked fingers.

In the usual way of girls Rebecca was far more mature than the two boys of her age. Peter was ignoring her, infatuated with his new friend Jack – they'd brought each other right out of themselves with their playing about. The house was full so the boys slept in the woodshed, and Rebecca was supposed to bed down with her mother on the parlour floor. There was a secret that neither of the twins ever referred to outside the family – and with a secret this big, even Annie was an outsider: Selina *snored*.

Rebecca sat sleepless by the window. She had pulled on her dress because the night was clear and chill, and Annie's thin ships' blankets were bald with age. She knew Peter and Jack had sworn they would whisper ghost stories to one another to see who was toughest, and they wouldn't let her join in. It was the first time in her life Peter had excluded her.

She thought she heard the door of the woodshed creak, but then her mother exhaled noisily and she couldn't be sure. Perhaps it was ghosts! Then in the starlight Rebecca saw the two boys sneaking down to the lagoon, silhouetted against the speckled waters. She pulled a blanket round her like a shawl, and slipped outside after them.

The dew was icy on her bare feet.

'Oh no,' came Peter's low voice out of the dark, 'it's her.'

'Stop it,' Rebecca hissed, 'let me join in.'

'Let's send her back,' Peter said. Jack didn't say anything, and Rebecca realised he was still shy with her.

'It was nothing very interesting,' he said, making space for her on the fallen treetrunk where they were sitting.

Peter flicked a pebble in the water. The star-speckled ripples expanded across the lagoon.

'I'm sorry I was nasty to you, Rebecca,' Peter said. 'It's more fun with you, really. Doesn't the Milky Way look huge?'

'I wonder if it would be possible to count all those stars,' Rebecca said.

'Oh yes.' Jack broke a twig. 'Just a matter of time, and method.'

'Let's tell ghost stories,' Peter said.

'We're sitting here just being friends,' Rebecca said. 'What were you really going to do?'

Jack said shyly: 'We were going to run races in the dark.'

'But suppose you ran into something?'

He laughed, coming out of himself. 'It's a possibility.'

'It's fun, isn't it,' Rebecca said softly. They watched the stars. 'The three of us.'

'You're the only friends I've got,' Jack said.

'Aaah,' Peter said, clasping his hands over his heart.

'Stop it!' Rebecca said.

'Honest,' Jack grinned.

'But you must have lots of friends in Hobart Town,' Rebecca said.

Jack shook his head. He shrugged. 'Some do, some don't.'

Peter was looking at Jack intensely and she wondered what he saw. She wished Peter would go away. Suddenly Peter said: 'Let's swear an oath to be friends for ever!'

'To be celibate for ever,' Rebecca said. She was intensely aware of the two boys sitting beside her on the log. 'We'll swear we'll never marry.'

'That's silly girl-talk,' Peter said.

'Except each other,' Jack said. 'I swear it.'

'No!' squealed Rebecca.

'Sssh!' hissed both the boys.

'What's the matter?' Ezzie demanded tearfully. It was a week later; they were back home.

'Nothing's the matter.'

'Is it me?' she asked at last. 'Don't I attract you?'

'There's no need for that talk.'

'Isn't there? Is it *you*?' she asked.

'Don't accuse me!' he shouted, and she jerked.

'I'm not accusing you! I just. . . .' she stopped. 'I just have to know.'

'What?' he said.

'Who is she?'

Ezzie sat by their parlour window, the dark green gum trees behind her, and the vivid blue Derwent. The morning light shone round her sunbleached hair, making it shine so pale and bright she was almost blonde. His heart ached to look at her.

'That's a wicked thing to say, Ezzie.'

'You don't touch me. You don't love me. What have I done?'

'There's more to love than bed.'

'Is there?' she said tearfully.

'You know there is.'

She had been sitting up all night. He was preparing for work, pinning his necktie while out of hearing Graves brushed his coat in the anteroom off the tall, tiled, Italianate hallway. The parlour was furnished to Ezzie's taste, with soft rugs and supple furniture. The coloured ribbon she wore in her hair was hardly in keeping with Wesleyan simplicity either; plain French ribbon would have been more proper.

'You are my wife,' he tried to explain, 'you must simply be my wife.'

'Then treat me like you know how to do.' He knew what she meant.

He turned away with pursed lips.

'You look just like your mother,' she condemned him. She was so desperate for his touch, a kiss, the embrace that would end this estrangement between them, that she followed him into the hall. Lazarus Graves appeared on cue with the brushed black coat. 'I'll do that,' Ezzie said. Bob turned his back to her and shrugged his arms into the arms. She held the shoulders for an extra moment, her cheek against the expensive material.

'Is it trouble at work?' she murmured, knowing how hard times were for so many. Annie, the initial awkwardness of her welcome passed over by the second day, had fulminated cheerfully against the Anti-Transportation League who would end convict labour without giving the farmers anything to replace it with. Free settlers wouldn't work for only ten pounds a year plus food, slops, beer and tobacco, as the convicts did, and many farmers Bob lent money to faced ruin. Free grants of land had been stopped nearly twenty years ago to prevent labourers becoming landowners, but even so in a few years farmers wouldn't have enough men to bring in the harvest, and wages were already soaring. The depression in England had pushed prices at local wool sales as low as tuppence a pound, and even the London markets paid only a shilling, which was nothing after costs. To cap it all Lieutenant-Governor Denison's Legislative Council had passed an Act that sheep were no longer permitted to graze Crown lands. The farmers led isolated lives, seeing few people and developing a conservative outlook to preserve what they believed to be civilised standards, but since the crisis they lost their influence. Two in three new free arrivals settled in the towns, radicals demanding self-government. But who would pay for it? The economy of Van Diemen's Land hung on a knife-edge.

Bob held out his hand for his hat.

'Please, speak to me,' Ezzie begged.

'It's nothing for you to bother your head over,' he said protectively.

She rested her forehead on his chest. 'Just say you love me.'

'I love you!' That was the odd thing: it was so obviously true. Ezzie began to search for guilt in herself, but she could not find how she had offended him. Then gradually the reasons became clear. Jack was running a little wild, and it was the fault of her casual ways. Her openness had always invited censure from the Hobarton set, so Ezzie concluded they must be right. Jack attended James Bonwick's school at three guineas a quarter, and they were not strict enough. Ezzie decided that Jack would have the best opportunity money could buy: a place at the Hutchins School, run by the nephew of the famous Dr Arnold of Rugby School in England. Staffed by Cambridge graduates and designed as a feeder grammar school for Christ's College – Hobartons had always felt closer to England than to Sydney – two ex-pupils, the Crisp boys, had already been put through the Inns of Court in London and Samuel Crisp, called to the Bar, had returned to practise law in Hobart Town. This was the sort of grounding Ezzie dreamed of for Jack, though Bob wanted him to join the Bank. But at the end of the first term Jack came home to find Ezzie sitting in the parlour.

'May we talk, Mother?' He sat opposite her, crossing his long legs defensively. 'You know I'm not happy at school,' he accused her. 'Whatever I do I can't please both you and my father. You seem so far apart.'

'You'll settle down, dear.' She wanted to reach out and touch him.

He said: 'Is it my fault?'

'Why, no! Nothing is wrong.'

Jack whispered: 'Are you ashamed because Grandpapa and Grandmama were transported? Is that why my father is so ashamed?'

Every solid citizen denied the convict stain; whispers destroyed reputations. Even a distant relation stigmatised by the broad arrow, a convicted grandparent or cousin, marked an innocent man down. No man wore a yellow waistcoat, a woman never chose a yellow dress, because of the colour's convict associations. 'Why should we be ashamed?' Ezzie laughed.

Jack had been attending classes. 'Original Sin,' he said. 'Four out of five of us are tainted by the Stain whether we admit it or not.' He put his head on one side, eyeing her with his quick bright eyes, but showing no expression. 'What do I have to do?' he asked.

'Everything we do for you is for your own good,' Ezzie said. 'Really, I won't be badgered like this. The subject is closed.'

'I'll show you,' he said, 'I'll show you you're wrong about me.' He sprang lithely to his feet. 'You've changed,' he said.

The more Ezzie denied it, the more it was true.

'We love you,' she called after him.

Jack went into himself. His 'disappearance' coincided with the arrival of spots, just like any adolescent boy, Ezzie told herself. Jack's bright and incisive mind would be perfect for the law, and when she broached this to Bob one evening he simply glanced up and said, 'Then let Jack study the law.'

'But what about the Bank?'

'What does it matter?' he shrugged.

'Bob, please don't.' She knelt by the arm of his chair. 'I know you wanted him to follow in your footsteps – '

He hid his elbows in his lap and said casually, 'I could sell the Bank. Business isn't so good any more.'

'Don't withdraw from me.'

'Jack isn't interested in banking, he looks down on it. And me. Let him have the law if that's what he wants.'

'It isn't like you not to care.'

'Peter Pride has a good head on his shoulders,' he said.

'But Peter isn't your son.' She glanced at the door, hearing a floorboard squeak. 'Dear, you're so tired. Come with me to bed.'

He rustled the papers propped against his thighs.

Ezzie whispered, 'Don't push Jack out of your heart too.' He rustled them again, and she crossed to the door, paused before opening it, then went to bed alone.

She met Jack in the Royal Society of Tasmania's botanical gardens. Set up in the days of Sir John Franklin – his wife Lady Jane had started a fashion for the name Tasmania in honour of the island's discoverer Abel Tasman – the gardens were in the grounds of the new Government House, still being built. The stone monsters and gargoyles that would adorn its three massive Tudor-Gothic towers lay scattered like vast chess pieces across the grass. The 42nd Regiment's band piped cheerfully down to the water's edge and back again between the flowering plants, shrubs and fruit trees, many of them discovered in the wild and donated by Ezzie's friend Ronald Gunn, once Sir John Franklin's private secretary. Honeyeaters fluttered round the gravillea shrub. A mighty Tasmanian blue gum rose straight as a plummet for a hundred and fifty feet before spreading its perfumed branches, the scent of their oil so familiar from expensive soaps. Ronald had seen eucalypts twice that size growing in the wilderness – one he had measured at head-height around the base with a piece of string was fifty feet in circumference alone. Ezzie and Jack walked by the heated chimney-walls growing espalier vines and came to the stream. It amused her that he was already taller than her. She sat, but he stayed on his feet examining a pomegranate tree nervously.

He said: 'I'm going to fail my exams.'

She was startled. 'But you were doing so well.'

He went to the cutting of Huon pine struggling to grow on a patch of moss by the waterfall. It was no higher than his knee.

When he turned she saw something of his agony. His age felt things so deeply, and she wouldn't patronise him by saying *It will pass*. 'I know I've failed my father. Is he really serious about training up Peter Pride for the Bank?'

Ezzie backed down. 'I'm sure he isn't,' she said reassuringly.

'Then I'm sure he is,' Jack said, and brought home to Ezzie the gulf that had opened up in her marriage. She was deceiving herself trying to paper over the cracks.

'Calm down,' she advised for Jack's sake, feeling for a moment very close to panic.

He held out his hands like a drunk demonstrating he did not have *delirium tremens*. 'I am perfectly calm.' He smiled his smile, and she was astounded by his self-control. 'I have decided,' he said. 'It's simple when you've decided. I'm going into the Bank.'

'But your exams – the Inns of Court! You can't deliberately fail.'

'Then my father won't have any choice,' he said over his shoulder, and left Ezzie disturbed. Jack was too clever, and she hated his new coldness. He had the overconfidence of one who has discovered a too-simple truth. Ezzie closed her eyes for a moment. She was no part of his plans; he knew his mother would always love him. It was his father's respect he must earn. Jack's first step was not to do as he was told, and he didn't do it by drinking or gaining a reputation with women.

Jack failed his annual exam, though not by much.

Ezzie's opinion of Jack became tinged with respect. He fought Bob in every way he knew, forcing him to pay attention. Bob had to go and see the headmaster to arrange extra tuition. When Bob lectured Jack for laziness Jack stood there taking it, close enough to touch. But Bob didn't reach out.

But never once did Jack risk losing Bob's respect.

Only once did Ezzie see genuine hurt in Jack's eyes. It was a foot-race one summer day at school, the boys haring along the streets with their jackets flapping. Jack slipped on the last corner and came in second.

Bob said: 'Second isn't good enough.'

Ezzie realised that Jack wasn't the problem; Bob was.

Gold is usually found near pubs.

There were many sly-grog pubs in the Buninyong area, near Fergus Matheson's store, and even a proper licensed inn at Ballan. Men staggered out of the pubs and relieved themselves not noticing at first the glitter their streams revealed in the soil. The first real gold was discovered at Buninyong with a pan lent by Mother Jamieson to an old digger, Tom Hiscock, who hardly dared believe the gleams his eyes were seeing.

All gold belonged to the Government, so at first everyone pretended this was California gold. But then gold was discovered everywhere, and the secret could not possibly be kept.

The first sensational gold-rush along the road to Golden Point, Ballarat, followed the find there in August 1851. Tom Dunn's ten-foot hole on the little quartz hill looked like a gingerbread basket sunk into the earth, the soil was so yellow with gold. The result was what the Scots feared most: society lost its ordinary conditions, those at the bottom rose to the top, those at the top fell to the bottom, and within a month four and a half thousand diggers, mostly Irish, had arrived and taken the place over. Then followed the Chartists, radicals, continental revolutionaries, and Americans who believed in colonial independence. The Chinese, everyone's enemy, arrived in clucking coolie-hatted droves. Six thousand Aussies disappointed by the downturn in California joyously took ship for their homeland, bringing back with them skills and devices. With his own eyes Fergus saw a hundred and thirty pounds of gold taken from a single crevice. Fourteen thousand men, some with wives and families, were said to be arriving from Van Diemen's Land; God knew who was keeping the farms going there, who would bring in the harvest.

Around Ballarat the forests were chopped down for firewood, and the diggers slathered in mud. Democracy was on the march and loaded pistols protected the day's winnings. The Government clambered on the bandwaggon with digging licenses at thirty shillings a month, doubled to three pounds in December, for a claim eight foot square. Government regulation had failed in California, but here the highly developed bureaucracy of the state could enforce its will. Licences were checked at musket-point, and men had to carry a document proving they were free.

But of course it was not the shicers who dug their hearts out for gold, who were grubstaked by the store-keepers with eggs at six shillings a dozen and tobacco at ten shillings a pound, who stayed in hotel dormitories at up to a pound a night, who made the money; or even the quick-rich diggers buying brooches as big as warming pans for their potato-faced women reeking of eau-de-cologne, brandy and onions. The real money was made, as always, by the storekeepers.

'I always had faith in you,' Vanessa said, nestling. 'I knew we'd be rich one day.'

'You're right.' Fergus kissed the top of her head. Downstairs it sounded, as always, as though a riot was going on: he could count fifty-nine bullock-drays and thirty-seven horse drays parked outside the hotel. The store was almost empty of stock, though a gigantic order was being carted in convoy from Geelong, and the new hotel had taken four thousand pounds in the last ten days. 'I just never expected it to happen this way,' he said. Fergus wore a lavender-coloured jacket and trousers, a red necktie and waistcoat, and his fingers were heavy with gold rings. No licensed pubs were allowed near the diggings, so sly-grog profits were immense. He had cultivated a personality as gigantic as his frame to impose his authority on his customers and kept a double-barrelled shotgun handy beneath the bar: he was strong enough to drag back both hammers with a single sweep of his thumb, and the loud double click ended most trouble before it began. 'Want to make a mess?'

This was no place to bring up a child – and no sort of life for a lady like Vanessa. Both of them wanted to stay with him, and nothing bad had happened to them yet, but Fergus had a simple motto: *Quit while you're ahead.* He took a hard decision to send them to his house 'Yallambee' in Melbourne, where he didn't have to worry about them, and where Lily could go to a proper school. But it was hard to say goodbye.

Back at Ballarat, the Golden City, the gold ran out.

Fergus' gigantic shipment for the store arrived from Geelong, at a transport cost alone of £100 a ton, all pulled on bullock-drays and thoroughly pilfered on the way. He had already spent £14,000 on his new hotel, complete with clocktower, in the centre of Ballarat, and added a further hundred rooms to another of his properties; suddenly all were empty. He had the over-flow tents at the back pulled down before they fell down. Fergus sat on the empty counter, his gold rings rattling the rough-cut wood as he tapped his fingers in worry.

In May, the Eureka Lead was discovered, and the earlier rush paled into insignificance. Bendigo was opened up, Castlemaine, Yackandandah, The Wool-shed, Beechworth with its gold like fine rich dust, worked by pumps. Fergus built his hotels in corrugated iron, brilliantly painted for a very pretty effect. Tough-looking men ate at the hotel tables with their ferocious mongrel-dogs guarding the gold-heavy saddle bags at their feet. Outside, a woman tightrope-walker swayed above the street, her hands as red as raw beef, inching amateurishly from the clocktower to the flagstaff flying above one of the billiard-gaming rooms. Below, the Germans had arrived, dressed in lederhosen and green feathered caps, blowing through trumpets while their vast pendulous women kept time on accordions. Packs of wild dogs howled dolorously. Fergus watched leaning against the verandah-post, a cigar clamped between his teeth.

Quit while you're ahead.

The gold streams of Ballarat were leading deeper as the easy alluvial gold was exhausted. To work the wet gold-bearing substrata needed pumps, machinery, organisation, capital. The next wave of expansion would be financed by mining co-ops, not grubstaked diggers. The co-ops would grow into mining companies as heavier machinery was needed, and the mining com-panies would need loans. Fergus quietly bought stock in the Royal Bank of Ballarat from the top-hatted men in Lydiard Street. Pit-props and steam-driven pumps required vast quantities of wood: Fergus bought land in the Bullarook Forest. The mining company employees would need housing and feeding: he bought land and built flour mills. And very quietly, he sold his hotels, and retired to Melbourne.

Vast and filthy, the town had changed out of all recognition. The miners were the new aristocracy. Fergus went down to the harbour and bought a schooner from among the hundreds whose crews had jumped ship to dig for the yellow metal. He had her re-rigged, with her hull painted white and the decorations chased with gold leaf, the cabins sumptuously outfitted. At the re-launching ceremony champagne was broken over her bow and Vanessa renamed her the *Golden Girl*. Fergus walked proudly on the holystoned decks. The crew wore white ducks and white shirts with the ship's name embroidered in gold thread on the back. Fergus puffed his cigar contentedly and turned to Vanessa.

'We're quitting,' he explained, 'while we're ahead.'

Lily was fourteen, a young lady now. For a moment Fergus felt his eyes burn, she looked so like her mother the first time he saw her: those deep blue eyes, shy glancing smile. 'Daddy says we're going to sail around the world.'

'Oh, Fergus!' Vanessa said. Then she laughed. He was irrepressible. Fergus cuddled her shoulder possessively.

The day before they were due to leave, when Vanessa was out riding one last time, her horse threw her, she struck her head on a stone, and was killed instantly.

Twice a year Bob Pride took the Royal Mail coach to Launceston, then rode by horseback along the north-west coast path to report progress on the vast, infertile properties of the Van Diemen's Land Company back to the Directors in London. Losing money, like every business in Tasmania that was not supplying goods to the gold rush in Victoria, the Company was building townships to attract free tenants as the convict system withered on the vine. Rumours that gold had been discovered on the Calder River, just outside Company property, seemed to have no foundation. Bob enjoyed these jaunts, but Ezzie stayed back at Launceston at Newstead House with old Ronald Gunn.

Called by the *London Journal of Botany* Tasmania's 'most active and intelligent botanist', Gunn had nearly been drowned investigating the Calder River gold theory. The *Flora Tasmaniae* that would make his name, with its foreword by Charles Darwin, was under preparation at Kew in London. It was the height of summer but Newstead House, with its green-painted shutters over the long windows, remained cool downstairs. Ronald's family by his first wife was grown up, but his second family ran breathlessly after one another around the large Spanish oak. Sitting in the garden beneath a scented tree Ezzie put back her head, listening to the children's laughing games among the *ranunculi*, letting the sun caress her throat.

'I have a theory,' Ronald Gunn said, a cool drink at his elbow, watching wattle-birds stalk across the rough-scythed grass, 'that the climate was not always as it is now, and that species are not immutable but adapt to changes. I know, it is shocking! The Carboniferous Era was warmer than the present. The sea level rises and falls. Europe was once covered with glaciers; so, I believe, was Tasmania.'

She let his pleasant voice, polite, tentative, enthusiastic, wash over her. 'I travelled overland to Macquarie Harbour,' he said, 'did you know?

She opened her eyes. 'Macquarie Harbour?'

'You look surprised. It is, of course, no longer a prison. That hell was closed down long ago. The place has reverted to nature.'

'I wasn't aware an overland journey had been attempted – not since Sir John Franklin's expedition fifteen years ago.'

'It is not likely to be soon attempted again; fortress mountains, forest mazes. It is impossible to maintain a sense of direction without a compass; the wilderness has been so distorted, ripped up and re-deposited by glaciers and volcanoes that it is very difficult to say where the real Tasmania *is*. We are, dearest Ezzie, the inhabitants of a mystery.'

Imposing side-whiskers gave authority to his slightly effeminate features; he was about the same age as she. His wife Margaret came by and straightened his necktie. 'Don't let him bore you,' she warned.

'Oh!' Ronald said, looking alarmed, 'am I?'

'On the contrary, I am most interested.'

'For example,' he continued, flattered, 'the shorelines of Macquarie Harbour run almost parallel – but why! A most odd but unremarked feature – a rectangle fifteen miles long, its mouth blocked by sand said to be hundreds of feet deep. . . .' His voice droned on. She was thinking of Bob, hearing something Annie once said to Jack, '*Peter will show you the yollas flying in this evening, if you ask him pretty nicely. . . .*'

And she remembered Bob butting in, with an odd note of enthusiasm and wistfulness in his voice: '*I used to watch them. . . .*' then stopping as if there was so much more he wanted to say.

'*You were a dreamer in those days,*' Ezzie remembered Annie saying. Poor Annie; always afraid of being soft with her men. '*This isn't your home now.*'

Ezzie realised that Bob was trying to get back home, and always had been.

'Everything is covered with lichen and moss. The trees drip constantly into impassable undergrowth and the gullies glow at night with phosphorescent fungus.' Gunn spieled Latin names. 'The Gordon River cuts its way through magnificent landscape, below hillsides clothed in Huons, *Dacrydium franklinii*, a thousand, two thousand years old and more – you saw my cutting in the new Government House gardens? Not much to look at now, but just wait ten centuries! And then at the end of the journey Macquarie Harbour opens up in front of you like heaven. Convict labour and piners long ago cleared the forest around Farm Cove.'

He went on to talk of the flowers he had found and discoveries he had made, but Ezzie's mind was far away. When Bob returned, dusty and tired, she said nothing at first. To her surprise he broached the subject as they walked in the orchard. 'The Van Diemen's Land Company is winding up its farming operations. In future they will all be leased to private individuals – who will make a pretty penny. Hundreds of thousands of acres up for grabs at Woolnorth and Emu Bay – which I am tempted to lease myself – Macquarie Harbour, Circular Head – the Prince brothers made nine thousand pounds there out of us!'

'Don't do it all for me, don't put it all on me. Don't you see? Only *you* matter to me.'

'You'd soon change your mind if we couldn't pay the bills.' Paragon-Pride had taken over a bank in Launceston to participate in the supply boom; parts of Hobart were like a ghost town.

'Bills and worry!' Ezzie said. 'Let's have a holiday. For our sake.'

Bob sighed, but then he nodded.

The Launceston they now returned to was a solid, prosperous town with solid, prosperous houses illuminated by coal gas. At Morton House Ronald's friend Dr Pugh performed operations using anaesthetic ether. Ronald also introduced them to the merchant John Thompson, and while his wife Henrietta took Ezzie to Thomas Bock's studio to have her photograph 'taken' on glass by the Daguerre process, Bob negotiated to hire one of Thompson's little steamships. The deck thumped beneath them, the paddles churning as they left, and the start-cannon for the Tamar Regatta boomed, sending gigs and whaleboats tacking across the bright water in a fluttering mass of coloured flags.

Still largely unexplored, the green right bank of the Tamar slipped by, the lifeless forest throwing back the gasps of the boiler. Ezzie held out a slim parcel wrapped in paper to Bob.

'My gift to you,' she said.

'Jack is your gift to me.'

'Take this one,' she said. He opened it. It was the photograph of herself.

'It's beautiful,' he said sadly, 'it doesn't do you justice.' But when she kissed him, again he turned away.

They found no motion on the glassy sea. A serpent of smoke and sparks trailed them across the humid surface as they wound through the tortuous sand-channels between the islands off Cape Grim. They spied sheep dotted across the bleached pastures of Woolnorth, then as they turned southward past Flat Topped Bluff the mountains above the west coast raised their pale teeth in tiers. It was a wondrous sight reflected in the sea's mirror mile after mile, like an endless toothy smile.

'Faith must have seen this before she died,' Bob said, and Ezzie was startled, realising how differently from her he saw this – and how bleakly. To him the mountainous wilderness was deeply threatening.

She was up early and stood at the railing in the soft dawn. The deep ocean swell lifted them, half a mile between each breath, and let them drop in a slow exhalation. By midday a pale glare reflected upward into the sky ahead: this was the vast white swathe of Ocean Beach shining in the sun, not the surf over Hell's Gates as the captain feared, today calm and blue as a millpond for them. The semaphore which Faith had written of was gone; everything was deserted, as empty as the days before man. As they crossed the bar the leadsman in the chains called out the depth beneath the keel at less than four feet, then they were through the channel and entered the waters of Macquarie Harbour, brighter than the sky.

'It's so beautiful, yet it's a place where such ugly things were done,' Bob murmured. Clouds drifted across the mirror beneath them as though they were flying; the pointed fingers of headlands slipped towards them showing infinity above and below. In the evening, with the engine slowed to a heartbeat and the paddles chuckling lazily in the water, the little vessel slipped between the points of Farm Cove and anchored within the friendly enclosure of the bay, close to Soldiers Island.

In the night it rained like they had never heard rain before.

Next day, in bright sunlight, they explored the steaming grassland. Ezzie ran on the greensward like a child – the smooth curve of land behind the beach had been sown with European grasses by the convicts to bind the soil. Once the officers' garden – Sarah Island was just visible as a low stain across the harbour – Ezzie was delighted to find strawberries growing wild, raspberries flourishing among enormous stands of bramble, blackcurrants and blackberries, a profusion of potatoes, turnips, carrots and other root vegetables planted for the proud, hungry and homesick officers of the 48th. Improving the soil took many years and they had never fared well; now all the work the convicts had done was paying off.

Ezzie ran on the sand to Pine Point, ribbons flying and bare ankles flashing. From a grassy knoll, across the tops of fruit trees growing in its wind-shadow, she surveyed the fertile green and gold bowl of the Cove below her. The shimmering golden water reflected the sand; Soldiers Island stood in its golden reflection. To the north Coal Head, where the convict mines had been, jutted dark against the shining harbour waters.

Inland the encroaching rainforest – gums, Huons, King Billys and a paler haze of blackwoods amongst the dark ever-present myrtle – rose rapidly towards Mount Sorell and the other bare peaks. There was no treeline, the forest simply dwindled away as though the slopes had risen too quickly to catch. Beyond that jagged horizon she glimpsed Frenchman's Cap, seeming no larger than a thimble, but almost a mile high and sheer down one side for thousands of feet.

In the afternoon they rowed to Sarah Island. She could not read Bob's expression: but it was he who insisted they come to the terrible island.

The jetties had been thrown down so they landed on a low tongue of reclaimed land, the stones held together with Huon pine logs as fresh as the day they were cut. Cleared of all vegetation by the convicts, the island was again thick with poor scrub clinging to the clay-quartzite soil, but vegetables survived in the old house-gardens leavened with topsoil shipped from Farm Cove – that was the only way they could tell where the houses had been. Bob searched for the walls Faith would have known. The gaol, massively constructed, was in pristine condition, though Bob had to hack with a cutlass through the laurel shrubbery blocking the entrance. Ezzie picked an apple and followed him inside the penitentiary. Piners had camped here from time to time; flash-fires had burned out the doors and window-frames, also the wooden floors over the dungeons where the aborigines had been kept, pissed on by the convicts from above: lower even than they. Intricate shafts of light crisscrossed the shadows of the pit.

Bob lifted a handmade brick and held it.

Outside, they found the cemetery. The thick slabs of Huon pine were fire-blackened but still readable, though they didn't recognise the names until they got to the slab marked: *Sacred to the Memory of Samuel Fisher*.

'Without him,' Bob said, 'I wouldn't be here. The Bank wouldn't exist. Did you love him, Ezzie?'

'His intentions were good and I respected him.'

Bob couldn't leave it alone.

'I love *you*,' she interrupted.

They returned to the mainland. Bob still hung on to the brick and she knew he was fascinated. Evening was drawing in and the sailors had built a great bonfire on the beach.

'It's a thought,' Bob said. 'Building something from the wilderness. Something real.'

She held his arm, smiling innocently.

'Why are you smiling?'

'Because,' she said, 'I've got you back again.' She held her finger to her lips, silencing him. Bob held his secret, that had almost gushed out of him, back in his mouth: *I know who your real mother is*: and in that moment, looking down into her smiling face, he decided that she must never ever know. Ezzie was so happy, he loved her so much.

Across the harbour the sky was brilliant with sunset, tufts and streaks of carmine and ochre above and below the darkened hills, and a spreading cloud of wings. The yollas were returning.

30

1860

Blood and fire

King Island never changed. The wind blew, the trees
grew. The little paddocks won from the forest fed the
cattle for a year or two, the sheep for a year or two
more, then the scrub proliferated and the victorious
forest encroached. Most of the land fenced by Jim Pride
had disappeared, first beneath razor-sharp blades of
cutting-grass, then tall thin stands of tea-tree, finally
eucalypts growing as though they fed on fire; and new
fires had to be lit, new land opened up, constantly
moving on. The valley remained fertile, a small oasis
fixed in the sullen green, but everything else won by
human hands was in continuous flux. That also never
changed.

Annie Pride's indomitable figure – she must be
within spitting distance of seventy, her skin browned
and wrinkled, tanned like leather by the sun – sat
astride her horse as stiffly as though her whole body
was made of leather. Without her commanding presence there would be no order, no one to guide the
rotation of the fields now that Billy was sulking at
Surprise Bay. Her family – by now Isaac and Joshua
too were almost part of the family – could not imagine
life without her, and difficult though Annie was they
did not want to. Only Billy in the south of the island
was not subservient.

Annie wanted everything just as Jim would have
wanted it. Everything she did was for him, the life she

lived was in Jim's memory. She didn't let on about this sentimental secret, fearful of losing her family's respect. Selina, round-faced and jolly, was her only real friend, and even to her Annie could sometimes be cruel. There was something savage and despairing buried deep inside Annie and Selina feared such emptiness. Selina, who had grown very plump despite her energy and enthusiasms, had taken up religion after Bishop Nixon's visit to King Island. The south arm of Quarantine Bay was briefly renamed Nixon Point in honour of the Anglican Bishop of Tasmania, until the ship *Whistler* was more memorably wrecked there a year later. But Annie denied life after death, her angry atheism a challenge to Selina and finally almost an obsession to her. Selina blamed Annie for driving Billy away.

'That's long ago, it's all water under the bridge,' Annie said briskly. Such metaphors suddenly revealed her foreignness: there was little free water on King Island, and no bridges.

'Why don't you ease off on him,' Selina said. Since Billy had moved down to Surprise Bay she rarely saw him – Annie's fault – and by rights, as Selina's eldest son, all this should be Billy's. Selina closed her eyes: if only Johnny hadn't died. She still longed for him.

'You don't understand,' Annie said, with that warning look in her eyes, and Selina was afraid to go on because she didn't want to hear anything bad about Billy. The incident was well known – Billy dismissed Isaac Simmonds after Jim Pride's death, Annie reinstated the half-caste Blackfellow, and Billy had drawn a knife, almost berserk with grief. Annie never forgave him. Isaac remained Head Stockman, and Billy had to back down humiliated. But he still wouldn't accept it, wouldn't return to the fold.

Selina couldn't make Annie understand forgiveness, or explain how deeply Billy had suffered. It wasn't that

343

Annie was wrong – Selina was determined to be fair – but Billy wouldn't apologise or even show remorse. As Selina lost her grip on her unhappy boy, he roamed further from her. At first she always knew she would find him at Sean's, drinking himself into a stupor: and even that was a kind of comfort, knowing where he was. She loved Billy with a desperate sadness, seeing in his slumped figure the shadow of the little boy wearing his father's jacket. She would put her arm round him sometimes and just close her eyes, holding him.

Billy wanted to come back to her. She knew he did.

But when Sean's hut burned down – the blaze in which Sean was burned alive, his dark figure stumbling back and forth between the jars of rum and brandy spouting fire – Billy still wouldn't come home. He sobered up, and worked hard improving his Surprise Bay land. He was proving something, but Annie wouldn't relent.

'It's not good for the twins,' Selina told her.

'They have to learn.'

'Learn?'

'You don't get something for nothing in this life,' Annie said. She threw down her hat and plumped into the rocker on the verandah at Paragon House, where Selina and the twins lived since the second storey was added. 'Well, have you considered any more about a husband for Rebecca?'

'That's her own business,' Selina said. 'Don't push her.'

'Young people don't know what's good for them,' Annie yawned. 'It's time she was married. And Peter, too. It's unhealthy for the twins to spend so much time together.'

Obviously Annie hadn't heard the latest news, or it had slipped her mind. 'Peter's had a letter from Jack Pride in Hobart Town,' Selina said. 'They've been firm friends for ages and Jack calls him "country cousin".

You know Jack more or less runs the Bank in Bob's name – '

That set Annie off again. 'Bob should have come back here,' she said stiffly. 'He'll never make anything of the outstation at Macquarie Harbour. He's bitten off more than he can chew. He should have come back to King Island!' Selina started speaking, but Annie interrupted her: 'Jack's brain is over-active. He was supposed merely to learn the business. Instead he feeds his father's appetite for loans for that west coast obsession. Jack has never even been there! It's not good practice.'

'Jack is almost twenty-three,' Selina pointed out, 'and a married man.'

'Twenty-three is still a child. What can one know at that age?'

Selina exploded. 'Yet you insist Rebecca should be married and she is exactly the same age!'

'She's pretty,' Annie said darkly.

'Jack has invited Peter to stay with him in Hobart Town.'

'What about Rebecca?' demanded Annie. 'There is no one suitable for her on the Island, you know.'

Selina hid a smile. Annie had always liked Rebecca, who was vivacious and intelligent, but much too content – the old woman thought – to drift on life's stream in the shadow of Peter's enthusiasms. It was almost impossible to imagine the twins apart, they were almost like husband and wife, with a wise toleration of each other's foibles beyond their years, perfectly matched. Rebecca's mind was precise, her emotions cool; she had received three proposals of marriage and dismissed them lightly. Selina knew that the only boy – man, now – to really be lovesick for her was Joshua, Isaac's son, a liaison so obviously out of the question in Annie's view that it was never raised. Selina was sure Rebecca had not understood his depth of feeling, and if she had, would have been angry with him for spoiling their friendship. 'She really ought to take a hold on herself, she's completely out of it socially,' Annie said. 'You should have sent her to the boarding school in Hobart Town.'

'Jack's experience was not good,' Selina pointed out, 'and Rebecca is rather too similar to Jack – though that's probably why Peter and he get on so well together, even if it is only by letter.'

'And what is Peter's latest obsession?'

'It still comes back to photography.'

'I'm ashamed of him. When's he going to get down to some real work, d'you reckon?'

'When you stop nagging him and trying to force him to do something he doesn't want!' Selina snapped.

'He needs discipline,' Annie said in a self-satisfied voice. 'You've been too soft on the boy. God help us if he turns into another – ' She didn't say *Billy*, but that was what she was thinking, and for a moment Selina hated her. Annie put back her head, drinking in the evening sun. 'It's lovely here,' she said.

Selina said: 'Peter wrote to Jack and said he wants to visit Hobart Town. Thus the invitation. Jack invited Rebecca too, but she refused.'

'What's Peter up to? He loves the Island.' Peter's watercolour landscapes hung in the room behind the open door. The colours deceptively simple, the views of King Island confused Annie with their intensity of feeling – so unlike, Annie thought, the boy himself, at least in the carefree side he showed her. Peter was so likeable she felt she couldn't really know him. 'What he needs is hard work!' she repeated.

'He's artistic,' Selina said. It was her ultimate defence.

'He's like my Bob,' Annie decided, finishing the conversation off as Selina got up to start supper.

Annie sat in the sun. She wondered how much longer she could go on. She wanted to live for ever.

'I climbed the tree,' Peter said.

It was written in some book Peter had forgotten that no love was more pure than the love between brother and sister. He remembered the feel of that sentence: the letters on the page a clear picture glowing in his mind's eye, and perhaps Rebecca's too. Around them the land beneath the stars was seamlessly dark.

Tomorrow Peter would catch the steam packet from David Howie's Boat Harbour to Launceston.

'I can see Aldebaran,' Rebecca's voice came. She knew all the stars; nine of the ten brightest stars in Earth's sky could be seen from King Island.

'I climbed it right to the top,' Peter said, 'and the wood was smooth, as though somebody had been there before.'

'This is a female tree,' said Rebecca authoritatively. 'The male cones producing pollen and the female cones producing seed are on separate trees. Because this female Huon stands alone she can never reproduce.'

'Wipe my eyes.'

'It's not sad,' Rebecca said, 'it's just the way it is. Why are you going?'

'You could come with me.'

'You've decided to find a wife,' Rebecca said.

Peter corrected her: 'To fall in love.'

'Do you remember our oath?' she said wistfully. 'The three of us. It seemed so serious. I took it seriously.'

'Well, Jack got married.'

'Not for love.'

Peter sounded surprised. 'But they had a wonderful wedding!'

'He married Dora Briggs because she's the daughter of a director of the Van Diemen's Land Bank, and the

347

VDL's the largest bank in Tasmania, and Paragon Pride was one of the smallest. Was.'

'Good on Jack.'

'Yes, I admire him. But I'm not going to be treated as any man's breeding stock. I'll never marry.'

'What about love?' he said.

She said: 'I don't believe in love.'

Alone, Billy had achieved a fulfilment working his own land in self-imposed exile at Surprise Bay that he had never known following orders at Yellow Rock. Surprise Bay was good land but for one man the work was crushingly hard: better than that, it was a challenge. Making a success of it was a kind of revenge. He could afford to bide his time – the old woman couldn't go on for ever and when Annie died, as Johnny's eldest son he would inherit all that had been taken from him. The Blackfellows who she had brought in his place would be sorry when Billy got his property back. Meanwhile Billy held his peace. He would inherit the benefits of Isaac and Joshua's labour; in a sense they were already working for him.

Since he had made the break Billy never drank. The sun had leached the colour of his hair almost to white as he was in the saddle from dawn to dusk – he kept four good horses. His father had taught him all he needed to know: how to ring-bark, fell a tall tree from a springboard inserted above head height in the trunk, and always to carry matches when the land was dry. Johnny was depending on Billy to carry on: Peter was a dead loss, still clinging to his ma's apron strings, and Rebecca didn't count. Everything Billy did, he did for his father.

Billy loved burning-off better than anything, the cool flames sweeping across grassland, the black ash tasting bitter as pain. Setting off the dried swathes of tea-tree was best, hot fires rippling into the night, clumps of ground glowing for a week. Billy would sleep all the next day, then ride through the black landscape scattering seed. After the rains the land bloomed green in memory of Johnny.

Peter arrived in Launceston and went straight to Thomas Bock's studio to collect the new camera he had ordered. Standing tall as a man, it was a work of art in dark polished mahogany, with a milled brass focus-ring and shiny lens-cap hanging on a fine chain. Peter examined it with delight. The focal length was the longest he had seen.

'It's not bad,' old Bock remarked, 'not bad at all. If you can get enough light, and the glass photographic plates don't crack, and you can persuade your subject to sit still, you'll get a good picture.' He smiled modestly and pulled his sidewhiskers, and that was the picture Peter took.

Because of the precious camera he decided not to risk the bumping of the Royal Mail coach to Hobart Town but went by steamer. He leaned on the rail watching the desiccated white hills roll by, each tree standing in its yellow shadow where the stock lay exhausted by the heat. The drought of 1857 had broken all records and decimated the farmlands of Victoria, to the great profit of Launceston merchants, but now it looked as though the same would happen to them.

The Clyde-built steamer pulled slowly between the sailing boats plying the Derwent even so early in the morning, Hobart Town dwarfed beneath the roseate bulk of the mountain. The white warehouses of Hunter's Wharf glowed a delicious pale amber. The scene on the dockside was one no camera could catch: the busy cocksureness of an Independent Colony and an independent people who knew the future was theirs. The Legislative Council had approved the eradication of thistles and the introduction of salmon.

Peter waved from the deck.

Jack stood motionless among the motley crowds of young men strutting with gold rings and pins, colourful waistcoats that showed off silk linings, and the women in dresses as brilliant as birds with the new dyes, wearing extravagant plumes in their hats. Dogs ran in yapping hundreds – the Colony considered the dog licences imposed on them by London to be taxes by the back door, and by now the issue had thrown the colonial statute-book into chaos. Jack Pride disliked chaos; tall and immaculate in banker's black, he stood out by his very immobility. Peter ran down the gangplank and embraced him. 'You look good!'

Jack shook hands. 'My carriage is over here,' he said. Peter grabbed his scuffed valise and a porter followed with the camera. The driver of the coach cracked his gutta-percha horsewhip.

In the privacy of the carriage Jack's manner changed completely. His features relaxed as though unpinned and he threw his silk hat on the seat opposite, put up his feet there, and brushed back the locks of his sandy hair that his hat had restrained. 'Well, cousin! What can I do for you?'

'I want to see the sights. I want to see everything there is, Jack! I want to meet your wife.'

'Dora's fine,' Jack said automatically.

'And your daughter. I'll take a photograph for the folks back home.'

'How's Rebecca?'

'She's fine too.'

'What can I really do for you?'

Peter looked from the window. If only Rebecca had not been so determined not to come. Hobart Town had a quaint, neglected look she would have loved.

Jack was talking. He'd begun working at the Paragon-Pride Bank in 1855, when he was eighteen, as a clerk on the bottom rung getting all the worst jobs from

350

his tyrannical father. But after the lean years, gold prosperity followed, and banks were so flooded with money they turned away depositors. When Jack learned the business a banker could hardly go wrong, surfeited with an embarrassment of riches, but that changed soon enough. After his father's mental breakdown – and Jack obviously considered Bob's decision to retire to Macquarie Harbour at the age of forty-seven to be such a symptom – Jack was left, as he put it, 'in control of a rapidly deteriorating business situation. I moved rapidly to consolidate my position. Obviously the interests of the Paragon-Pride Bank are my own interests. An alliance was in order.' He really talked like this.

In Hobart Town bust followed boom as unerringly as a rise in the number of marriages followed rising birthrates – though not amongst the Hobartons, insulated both from economics and moral stain. Jack married Dora Briggs having no more than kissed her hand.

Now the British subsidy was being slowly withdrawn. Jack pointed out to Peter the impressive barracks standing with blinded windows as the garrison was run down, and the convict-built roads, stone buildings and stalwart bridges falling into disrepair. Yet their new, shabby mellowness lent them an air of provincial charm. While Peter remained silent Jack made smalltalk: workmen were lazy and depraved, wages too high, yet the island's trade with the mainland had dwindled to a trickle; exports were under a million pounds for the first time in a decade, Jack grumbled. The whale fleets couldn't find whale except in the far south, grain exports were halved and timber found no buyers at all. Bank deposits in coin were only one-sixth of a year ago, and yet the shop windows were full of imported Stoke pottery, shingled roofs re-covered with imported Welsh slate, and kitchen appliances were all stamped *Birmingham, England*. Eight hundred houses stood empty yet no one was starving, thanks to the earnest street-scouring of hungry or shoeless children by social reformers. An air of disillusionment stained the self-confident atmosphere of this comfortable, conceited backwater. Many of those who had clawed their money from the rough-and-tumble of the mainland had retired to enjoy respectability in the tranquillity of Tasmania.

'I want a wife,' Peter said. He hadn't heard a word, Jack realised.

'That's easy. I know the perfect girl. Seventeen and. . . . perfect.'

He sounded so serious Peter thought he must be joking. 'She's got to be beautiful too,' Peter said, but Jack did not return his smile.

'She's the most beautiful girl I've ever seen,' Jack said wistfully.

'Are you stringing me along?'

'She came to Hobart Town two or three years ago with her father, a widower. Paragon-Pride are his Agents here, and Dora and I met them socially, once. He bought a mansion on Davey Street for just the two of them. They're almost never seen out; he's a bit of a recluse and something about him doesn't quite add up, if you ask me.'

'She sounds irresistible. What's her name?'

The carriage turned into Elboden Place. 'Lily Matheson,' Jack said.

It was the first time Peter had been to Bob and Ezzie's old house but though it seemed that they had removed their personalities with them to Macquarie Harbour, there was almost no stamp of Jack's personality here either. His wife Dora, pretty and pale with her wide-spaced eyes, sat in the parlour, a sample of embroidery folded across her blue-satin knee, a plump white ankle showing beneath. Her breasts were full,

352

their daughter being weaned. 'Jack!' she sulked, 'I woke all alone.'

'May I introduce my friend and cousin, Peter.'

'Jack,' she commanded, lifting her cheek, and he kissed it. She turned to Peter with a petulant chuckle. 'He likes to think he surprises me. I didn't know Jack had any friends – outside the office, of course.'

Peter told the driver to put the camera in the corner, then dropped into a chair. 'Trouble you for some toast.'

Jack turned to call but Dora rang for the maid. 'Please may we have some toast. We say please may we have here, Peter,' Dora smiled, cocking her eyebrows.

'It's all right, dear,' Jack said.

This was the unhappiest marriage Peter had experienced. The interplay fascinated him. The new art of photography had taught him to look at people's souls through a lens. Jack was highly intelligent, perhaps even talented, and ruthless with himself, sacrificing his private life to marry into the Bank of Van Diemen's Land. Peter looked around him. The furniture was expensive and tasteless, the watercolours poorly executed provincial scenes – *English* provincial scenes – and he could see Dora expected him to make conversation. They sat in silence waiting for the toast to come.

'You must tell me all about yourself!' Dora exclaimed.

'There's not much to tell,' Peter said because he disliked her. Jack sat in the background.

'Everyone has something about them that's interesting,' she said blankly.

Peter said: 'May I take your photograph?'

Lily Matheson hadn't stepped off the *Golden Girl* in Hobart Town 'two or three' years ago: it was exactly two years and three months, as Jack well knew. Peter was watching Jack's face as their party guests arrived.

Jack had been married two and a half years and his baby daughter Emma lay asleep upstairs.

Peter met the eyes of a girl looking at him. The crowded room seemed empty.

'This is my cousin, Peter Pride,' Jack introduced them. 'Miss Matheson.'

Peter kissed Lily Matheson's hand then shook it. He didn't look away from her eyes.

'Pleased to meet you, Peter,' she said quizzically. Her eyes were a deep and wonderful blue, looking up at his height because they were standing too close. He moved his head for the pleasure of seeing her respond.

'Jack tells me you're a photographer.'

'That was one of my interests,' Peter replied.

'Was?' Jack said, and both of them looked at him in irritation.

It was strange and lovely to see eyes so dark so warm. Peter didn't know how to cope with her. The orchestra struck up.

Jack said brightly, 'Excuse me! I must – my wife. . . .'

They were alone. Dancing couples jostled them.

Lily Matheson frowned. 'You do look a little like your cousin,' she said. Her unusual accent: a mainland nasal twang, Sydney or Melbourne, overlaid with mock-English finishing school. But there was Scotch in there too.

'He's all right,' Jack said, gliding past with Dora in his arms, unable to leave them alone.

'Does he talk?' Lily said, and Peter smiled, loosening. She wasn't the type to say *please may I have*, he decided.

'Get you a drink,' he said, snagging the sherry waiter.

'Champagne.'

'You know your mind!'

She looked at him peculiarly – almost a look of relief. 'I like a man who knows *his* mind,' and he knew she had been attracted to Jack. Peter steered her casually between the crowd, their voices drowned in the constant movement.

'I know what I'm thinking.'

'He walks, he talks, he thinks.'

'I'm thinking – '

She waited curiously.

He said: 'There's only one girl in this room.'

'Yes, and her father is looking for her,' she said.

'Tell me about yourself.'

'My mother died and my father lost heart.'

'You're all he has.'

She swirled her champagne. Between dances Hobarton conversation flowed around them.

'I can't believe we're talking like this,' he whispered.

She laughed, her head thrown back, showing white teeth, the white upper slopes of her breasts. He touched her elbow where it emerged from her evening glove.

'Dance with me,' he said.

He sat next to her at supper. Every muscle in her body was loose: she could feel the way her petticoats lay over her knees as she listened to him, and the warmth of her cotton undershift. Peter had little of Jack's chilly maturity, he was hot and malleable, unformed. She tried to concentrate on what he was saying. His manner was completely unforced – he was obviously close to his sister, unfrightened of treating a girl as a real friend: that made him very different. But all this missed the point. He was the one.

There was only one man in the room who could come between them: her widowed father, Fergus Matheson. He dominated the room in a way only the young lovers could not have noticed. Dora's anger with Jack showed in her social smile. 'How could you do such a dreadful thing to me,' she whispered between her teeth, with polite nods from side to side at guests.

'Business reasons,' Jack lied. 'Fergus Matheson – '

'Look at him,' she said disdainfully, 'here in our house – a man blackballed by the Tasmanian Club!'

Fergus Matheson didn't care who knew about his convict past. His outsize figure was impossible to ignore and with his blunt features, scar and beard, brilliant yellow paisley waistcoat and hairy fingers clotted with gold rings, his grey hair in ringlets, he even let himself look like a convict as though he was proud. That was unforgivable: he didn't care about the Hobartons.

'How could you have invited him? He treats us with contempt,' Dora said.

'The man can afford to do what he likes!' Jack said.

'He should know better. It's like inviting a dog – heaven knows what he might do.'

'He didn't want to come. He wants to protect his daughter from – ' he left it tactfully unsaid.

'From whom?' Dora said icily.

Jack said: 'From such people as we, perhaps. He is simply devoted to his daughter. Look at his eyes. They follow her everywhere.'

'She's a poor guest, she has permitted your cousin to monopolise her.'

Jack said: 'But doesn't she look happy?'

Fergus Matheson, standing alone with a glass dwarfed in his fist, watched Lily. It was the first time he had seen her laugh since coming to Hobart. He watched her with his gentle eyes, then took a mouthful of champagne.

His grief for his dead wife was intolerable. Vanessa, her laugh, her radiance that he had treasured, was now reborn in her daughter.

On the way home in the carriage he said: 'I forbid you to see him again.'

'Will you hide me away for ever?'

'I care only for you. My interests are your interests.'

'And my happiness?'

'Is mine too,' he said fondly.

'No,' she smiled with her mother's steel, 'is *mine*.'

She thought about Peter.

Of course she saw him again; it was impossible not to. She saw him while the maid drew her bath, while the maid undressed her; she lay in the bath and touched her fingertips to her lips like his kiss.

Peter Pride and Lily Matheson both wanted to fall in love; the moment they saw each other, they had no choice. It was their secret. It was easy for her to walk into a shop and straight through, crossing the empty green centre of the block behind where the children played, into the street on the far side where Peter was waiting in Jack's carriage, the blinds up, and they kissed hungrily. 'Look at me, I'm shameless,' she said, filling his hands with her breasts, her knees apart, touching the doors, 'quick. Quick!'

'What have we done?' they smiled secretly to one another, listening to the horse's hooves slowly clopping, the driver's sleepy commands. Sometimes it was raining, sounding gorgeously loud on the wooden roof, sometimes they lolled in the dimness while the sun beat down outside, their bodies intimate with perspiration. But most often they took the ferry and went walking on Kangaroo Bluff, just to be in love, among the orchards and the houses being put up, every place seeming like a new adventure between them.

Nobody had ever been in love before, never like this.

'I never thought I'd let anyone do this,' Lily said. 'I love to watch your face. I feel you everywhere.'

Later she murmured: 'Tell me about King Island.'

'There's nothing to tell.'

'Tell me everything.'

'It's home.'

She cuddled him silently.

'I swore an oath never to be married,' he said.

'I reckon,' she said, pressing the end of his nose,

'that I know you better,' twisting it, 'than you think I do.' She kissed him with the tip of her tongue.

'You'd never made love before,' she said suddenly. 'You're not like other men. There's two people inside you.'

'No.'

'Suppose I have a baby?' Lily said.

'I hope you do,' he said, looking in her eyes. 'Then we can get married.'

Sydney, New South Wales

Sam Summers was long dead; Una's mother only recently so, a year, or two, or three ago, her loud sudden voice from upstairs ceased for ever, yet it seemed to beat on and on in her daughter's head, for tea, or pillows, or this, or that. The old woman had died weeping in Una's arms. Una, her spare form tightly dressed all in black except for her smart flowery hatband – dressing like this even indoors, alone! – now sat at the kitchen table, like a servant. Alone – of course. Her tea was untasted in its cup, and beside it was a long bread-knife with a sharp, serrated blade. She sat looking at the unfolded letter as though, with her straight back, she could read it from here. Her ladylike hands were neatly clasped in her lap. Una was not what she seemed to be.

Una was always the one the men chose. There was something in her face, the way she held herself, that proclaimed to the man who was looking, and men were always looking, that here was no virgin. She didn't need love, only possession, the shuddering moment of erasure. In the death of desire was her release; there was nothing worse than the soft men who fawned, still in her bed when she woke in the morning, and she screamed inside, kicking them out with her bare feet.

She was not ashamed of the dragon inside her. It

358

was her *father's* blood, *his* lust, *his* weakness: how Una had despised him.

The letter on the table was from the third sister, Emily, the eldest, who had remained in London. A year older than Una, at the edge of twenty she had married Edward Smith, her girlhood sweetheart; as the children followed they were one of those happy, reckless, itinerant families moving around the country one step ahead of their creditors. Smith, though feckless, was a man of great charm, and his brother had done well and could be relied on to save them from disaster from time to time, and it seemed, as the number of Smith daughters grew, that his shabby-genteel ensemble lived charmed lives. Sam, the only son, was born after three years of marriage and the family followed father through a dozen homes in Sam's first dozen years: the boy was called Samson because of his great strength, though he was not, from what Una could gather from Emily's carefree writing style, particularly tall or long of hair. Samson had gone to sea, perhaps attracted by the rootless, intimate, unpredictable life before the mast – he must know it so well from home. Emily wrote to Una with infuriating irregularity – only when she was flush, no doubt, but her letters were always jolly, and irritated Una unbearably.

There was no doubt about it: Emily had done everything wrong, and yet had been rewarded. Her daughters had, 'like her,' Emily gushed, 'all found good husbands before they were twenty,' and now the doting woman was positively hemmed in by lively, mewling grandchildren, from what Una in her envy could gather. Emily's latest letter from London was on good quality paper – Edward's brother had left them a small legacy – but Emily's real news was about Samson. God, she was proud of her children! Captain Samson Smith, master of the emigrant frigate-ship *Clara* from London to the Swan River colony in Western Australia, had fallen in love with one of the ladies on the passage, Bess Smail, and married her in the Fremantle Wesleyan chapel. Their daughter Ernestina had been born last year, and now Samson was master and part-owner of a clipper on the wool run, and dreaming merrily of settling down with his own family.

Alone at the kitchen table Una put back her head, and laughed until she wept.

On a rainy day in Hobart Town in February Peter walked to the echoing mansion on Davey Street. The butler took his coat, hat, and umbrella. Lily was upstairs: it was all arranged.

But the interview with Fergus Matheson did not go as he thought it would – only the start of it, with Fergus predictably lighting a cigar, his back turned, broad and indomitable.

But then Fergus turned from the window and Peter saw his face was dragged into unhappy lines of sadness and doubt. There were no pleasantries. 'You love my daughter, Mr Pride.'

'That's not the point,' Peter said.

The views were stunning: Davey Street ran along the ridgeline above the smells and crowds of the town. Around the sawdust oval grooms walked racehorses in sweat-rugs. Gardeners were watering the steep lawns despite the rain and the flowers and flowering shrubs looked vivid against the grey squall-streaked Derwent far below. Fergus was on the board of the Racing Association and Jack had advised Peter to make small talk about horses. But this was too serious a business.

'What is the point,' Fergus said.

'*She* loves *me*.'

'Damn you, laddie!' Fergus waved his hand, a circle of smoke in the air. 'There's no need to call me Mr Matheson.'

'Sir, you can order her not to see me again.'

Fergus admitted, 'And break her heart.'

'I'm sorry, sir.'

'I love my wife. If I let Lily go, I lose my wife too.' Fergus walked from the window to the cold fireplace, his shoes clicking on the marble. 'She came back to life. I saw her in Lily's eyes.'

'She must have loved you very much, sir.'

'More than that.' Fergus tossed away his cigar and it missed the bin. 'Vanessa had faith in me. She was prepared to back a loser.'

'I'm no loser, sir.'

'Aren't you, Mr Pride? I was.' The emancipist bent and picked up his cigar, began smoking it again. The grey rainy light glowed across his gold rings, the tip of his cigar made an amber point in his eyes. 'I *am*. All this is illusion, money. None of it is Vanessa. You ask me to give up my daughter.'

'I demand it, sir.'

The clock ticked. They stared at one another through the rising coils of cigar-smoke. Then Fergus chuckled. 'You're tougher than you look.'

'So's Lily, sir.'

'Isn't she?' said Fergus, delighted. 'I'm not really so selfish, am I? This is almost the unhappiest day of my life.' He put his arm round Peter's shoulder, then threw his cigar into the fireplace with a sigh. 'My answer is yes. Go and tell her.'

But Lily was waiting in the doorway. She ran across the marble and threw herself into her father's arms. 'I'm sorry!' She was weeping.

'Ssh, hush,' he said tenderly. 'You'll want the day to be as soon as possible, I know, I know. But leave it a week or two longer. It will take that long for the west wing to be redecorated for you. The builders – '

'No, daddy,' said Lily, taking Peter's hand, 'you're very kind. You're too kind. But you see, when Peter is my husband, we won't be staying here.'

'This is your home.'

She said gently: 'This is *your* home. Our home is King Island.'

On King Island no rain fell.

Billy waited until dusk. The wind on his left cheek, he rode out of the last light of the huge orange sun, throwing down matches where the wind would blow the flames south. A trail of sun-coloured bonfires springing up behind him hid the curve of Surprise Bay and the final, southern headland of the island where night rushed across the darkening sea. As night deepened the bonfires joined into a line like a thread following him from the bay. Billy grinned, feeling his power.

The brightening glare dimmed the light of the stars, then they were obscured by churning smoke. It streamed round Billy as the wind changed. He pressed on blindly beneath the roof of smoke. Shortly he must come either to the sea or the paddocks of Denby's squat. He was not at all afraid.

He found the track and followed it north through the trees, orange smoke flowing above the treetops faster than he rode. But he had to stop for a minute, it was such a beautiful sight, a red river rushing down the sky.

He topped a rise. Down on his left the Denby place was well alight. He hoped Chas Denby got his children out, but Chas had been slow since his wife died. There was nothing Billy could do for them now, or would if he could. That would be very good land soon.

Smoke washed round him, very fragrant, and he knew the big blue gums had started burning somewhere. That was worst about being ahead of a fire: you couldn't tell where it was, only it was coming, the smoke spoiled the view. He hoped people would appreciate the fine smell, it would perfume the air of the whole island by dawn.

He trotted his horse down to Pioneer Lagoon, the broad strip of marsh that would stop the flames, opened the gate and passed through. At the forest border beyond, he stopped to enjoy the entertainment. Flames billowed down the far side as fast as smoke billowed up; the shallow patches of water glared upward like orange eyes, each holding a reflection of fire and smoke.

The flames jumped across dry patches and followed paths like hands and fingers, wrapping the bushes in fire. Billy felt the first, gentle caress of heat on his face. His horse whickered softly.

His spare horses and all his fenced-in cattle would be charcoal by now. They could be replaced. So could his hut, though he'd have to cut down a new handle for his tomahawk to split the shingles and hack out the frames. But where would he get the wood from? There could be very little left on the headland. He began to laugh: it was a ridiculous situation.

The heat exploded, scalding the sweat on his face. He turned his horse and spurred into the cool darkness beneath the trees, losing his hat, riding northward towards Seal River. Other animals ran determinedly beside him, Tasmanian devils and white wombats, jumping wallabies and pademelons and the biggest kangaroo he had ever seen, bounding beside him with its extraordinary blunt face turned towards him, and birds fluttered crazily white and black amongst the trees. The path forked, they went one way and he went the other. Light gathered itself behind Billy, flinging his shadow ahead of him. He spurred for his life. The path curved and fire burst through ahead of him.

'Jesus!' Billy said, reining in. 'Give me a break!'

There was no break. The flames leapt the path in streams from tree top to tree top. Billy held his hands over his head, but the pain was too bad. He fell from the saddle and crouched close to the earth, his hair burning. He ran after his horse but she retreated, then was gone.

He knew he was finished. At least he knew what he'd done.

'Burn it.' Billy tottered proudly, and drew his last breath of flames.

Selina, undressing at Paragon House, did not sense the death of her eldest son. She ballooned her voluminous calico nightdress over her head, put up her arms and let it slip down, then knelt by the bed and prayed like a child, elbows propped, hands pressed together under her nose. Rolling between the sheets, she ate a doorstep of bread and jam, then put out the lamp.

Rebecca sat reading in the front room. Annie was in the rocker on the verandah watching the last glow of sunset fade from the western sky. She put her hands on her cracking knees and got up with a groan. 'I'm turning in,' she said, then saw Selina had already gone.

Annie yawned and drew the parlour curtains, less to keep the night out than to stop the early morning sun fading the carpets. 'G'night,' she said to Rebecca, then stopped awkwardly. She never felt quite at ease with Rebecca, whose coldness matched her own – a coldness Annie had learned, but seemed part of her granddaughter. 'One of your clever books, girl?'

Rebecca smiled up. 'It's *The Origin of Species*, by Mr Darwin.'

'And what does your Mr Darwin have to say for himself?'

'That we come from a common ancestor, and evolve by mutation.'

'Evolve?'

'Get fitter to survive.'

'Rubbish. He's the one who says our grandfathers were monkeys. Your friend Joshua Simmonds is a bit of a monkey, isn't he?'

'That's a rotten thing to say,' Rebecca said coldly.

'Now, I saw Edward Preston the other day. . . .'
Annie hesitated. 'I wish you weren't so clever,' she
said, 'I don't know where you get it from. It can't be
me.'

'Oh, Gran,' said Rebecca, holding Annie's hand.

'It doesn't do you no good,' Annie grumbled, 'it isn't
what matters.'

Finally Rebecca had to ask. 'Well, what does
matter?'

'If you don't know, girl, I can't tell you.'

'Then I'll never know!'

Annie regarded her with a half smile, then shrugged.
The word, of course, was *marriage*.

Rebecca watched the infuriating old woman shuffle
off to bed. Rebecca sat up for a while but couldn't
concentrate on the book. Peter had stayed much longer
than planned in Hobart Town and she was terrified
he'd found some girl; he had no sense and she was
worried for him. No letters; he'd found a girl and was
afraid to write, not even a telegram – the undersea
cable from Victoria now ran across King Island on its
way to Tasmania. The one-and-sixpenny fee would
have been a small price for a pledge of loyalty. Rebecca
swore she would hate her, then examined her feelings
with surprise.

She splashed cold water over her face from the pitcher, took off all her clothes in one sweep over her
head, dress, cotton chemise, jaconet muslin petticoat,
flannel petticoat, dropped them in a pile and fell
exhausted into bed. Soon she was asleep.

Fifteen miles to the south, beyond the valley's rim,
the sky grew orange with smokeclouds, and below
them, the land glowed like lava.

At the Electric Telegraph Office in Launceston's
George Street, which was closed, the engineers testing
the Melbourne circuit through Cape Otway cursed as
the line went dead. 'Not a bloody peep,' said the top-

hatted chief engineer. 'It's King Island again, it's that bloody reef cut the cable, pound to a penny. Close the bloody thing down. I'll tell the directors in the morning, God knows if they'll reopen it this time.'

The crew of a ship anchored in David Howie's Boat Harbour were woken by a sound like a furious thunderstorm. Melting pitch dripped through the deck-seams. Crossing themselves, they rushed on deck: the ship floated on a mirror of fire and the thunder was flames. Out of the inferno struggled silhouetted figures from the little township, across the blazing humps of the dunes down to the beach, where the sand shone like red glass. Drowned by sound, O'Henry's store blew up in a silent expanding circle of white vapour as the gunpowder and fuel supplies caught, black figures tumbling as the blast knocked past them. The *Angelica*'s hull rang like a gong. 'Up anchor!' The Italian captain, brought up in the shadow of Vesuvius, bellowed orders for buckets to douse the deck and masts, putting out the pitch hanging in burning strings from the rigging, drenching the volatile tuns of whale-oil in the hold. Steam drifted from the ship against the wind, sucked into the furnace along the shoreline. Under a single stormsail Captain Carboni got the ship's bow turned out to sea, and closed his eyes to the shapes struggling in the water. He was far from home, and his business was whales.

Driven by the wind, the fire rolled northward up the island like a wave. The eucalyptuses, standing two hundred feet high from beds of shucked dry bark, burst into flame in one flash as though waiting for this moment. The flames raced ahead across grassland, cleared blocks, paddocks, a hand grasping with long burning fingers. Many smallholders woke to find themselves already surrounded. Mothers threw their children in the dams and jumped after them, standing up to their necks in warm water, watching their lives

366

burn, counting the heads of their children over and over in hope and terror.

Josh Simmonds wasn't asleep. He dreamed of touching Rebecca Pride's legs.

He had never felt any different from other men of his age, but he knew he *was* different. His father Isaac was half Aborigine and so was his mother. That was a whole world of difference. Everyone *knew* Josh was a Blackfellow even though his skin was nearly as pale as a European's. He dreamed of moving away from King Island, of becoming anonymous, of being accepted. He could have moved away any time, and would have.

But that would have meant leaving Rebecca.

It was a fact of life that a man wanted most what he could least have. Josh desired Rebecca's respect. He didn't need her love, or to put her on a pedestal, or think she was perfect. Rebecca lacked something. That single flaw made her deeply attractive to him. She never noticed him, never cared about him, but not because he was part-Aborigine. She was indifferent to everyone. Josh crawled with jealousy when Edward Preston called on her to pay court, but she'd looked on him as if he was an insect – and yet Edward was a Quaker. He had backed down in humiliation from her cold demeanour. Josh told her he loved her and she showed no reaction at all, but Josh had grinned with admiration before turning away.

'She looked at me,' he had told his father as they worked. 'What a woman.'

'You stick clear of that one,' Isaac warned. 'Don't forget she's been brought up to pay your wages one day.'

'I don't have to like her. She still looked at me.'

'Don't you forget who you are,' Isaac said crushingly. But still Josh lay awake and dreaming, his hands clasped behind his head, staring at the glow on the ceiling. He sat up slowly, still staring up.

He took two quick steps to the window. The sky was alight.

'Oh my God,' Josh whispered. He got one leg into his trousers. 'Oh my God!' He hopped to his parents' room, hammered on the open door. 'The Pride place is burning!'

Isaac sat up calmly. 'Boy, either get those trousers on or take them off.'

'The whole bloody Pride spread is on fire!'

Isaac drew the curtains and let in the light, then covered his eyes. 'The whole island is on fire.' He pulled his hands down his face. 'I knew this must happen.' He strode to the skillion and tossed the long wooden box of sulphur matches to Josh. 'Ride like the wind. Open the gates, let the stock out. Then light a fire downwind, clear the ground. It's their only chance.'

'What about our house?' Powwidde cried.

'It's lost. It's only a house, save what you can.' Isaac turned back to Josh. 'Meet us at the Yellow Rock River.'

'What about the Pride house?'

'Everything's finished!' Isaac roared. 'Don't you understand? We'll be lucky to get out with our skins.'

Josh rode bareback, hanging on to the bridle. The horses he released from the stable flew like the wind after their shadows. The fire made the night air scented and lovely as he reined in at every gate, knocking it open. Dropping matches as he went, he topped a grassy dune, struck his last match, and watched the cool flames race away from him. Then he turned.

Tears streamed down his face.

He rode south, towards the fire. The Pride fields were outlined in flames, the valley a dark groove. He got to the north gate but as he knocked the bar open with his heel the stud bull came out in such a fury of fear that the horse tossed Josh into the dust, and he heard hoofbeats fading into the distance. Josh scrambled over the splintering fence rail as the bull charged him, then fell into the trampled grass amongst the milling herd of cows. Weaving between their legs, his mouth full of dust and animal stink, he crawled to the far side of the herd, and ran, cutting his bare feet on the sharp grass.

Fire enclosed the valley like the pincers of a giant red crab.

Josh ran in the river. It was quiet and dark in the valley. He splashed alongside the lagoon then onto the knoll of dry mossy land, jarring his foot on a root of the Huon. He hopped, agonised, then trudged uphill towards the lightless house. It was the deepest hour of the night.

Flames curled over the valley rim and rushed down, split around the rocky outcrop, swept towards him. The heat was explosive. The blackwood shingles on the roof of Paragon House caught fire from above; fire curled like snakes up the wooden supports of the verandah. Josh hit the burning double doors with his shoulder and fell inside.

'Is it fire?' Rebecca said, crossing the parlour. 'Have you released the stock?'

'Yes, miss.'

'Have I time to get dressed?'

'Roof's on fire,' he croaked, 'get out. Lagoon.' He limped towards the stairs, but everything was burning up there. The house creaked and shook under the weight of fire like a ship in a gale.

'Joshua,' she said, 'I'm frightened.'

Dawn rose. Rebecca screamed when a blackened human torso fell from the flame-guttering shell of Paragon House and rolled down towards them, splashing into the shallows. She thought it was Annie.

It wasn't. It was the ship's figurehead, the paragon of virtue.

They never found Annie's body, or Selina's.

The lagoon was blue and still. The marsh was a vivid ring of moss encircling the shore, everything of the valley above was ash or smoke. The Huon stood alone from its mossy bed, a shaggy green sentinel touching the blue sky.

Josh held out his hand.

Rebecca climbed the tree, and looked at what was revealed.

31

The light of the world

'My father started a new life in Tasmania because the scenery reminded him a little of his native Scotland – at least as Sir Walter Scott writes of it – and because he can live there like a king.' Lily smiled under the steady, swaying glow of the night-lamp hanging from the *Golden Girl*'s deckhead. 'Once Fergus wished to sail round the world. But the world has no roots.'

'Now he has lost you.'

'I remember Aunt Una,' Lily said gently.

'Who was she?'

'Nobody, finally. I never want to be like that!'

The ship's bunk was very narrow and two of them were a crowd. They lay as though still making love, pretending they were saving space, Lily on top with her knees bent and ankles twined, her arms folded across his chest, her hair draped over his face.

'I'm glad I married a light woman,' Peter said. 'I could lie like this all day. But your hair tickles.'

She trailed it mischievously from side to side, creasing his face.

'I'll sneeze,' he said.

'You'll blow me off.'

He hugged her. She put back her hair and kissed him. A knock came on the door, and the steward's voice: 'Sorry to .... er .... wake you, sir. The cap'n wants you on deck, something he reckons you ought to see.'

'Thank you.' Peter rolled over and pulled aside the drape across the porthole. Lily stroked his back, her fingertips tracing the nobbles of his spine. He put his hands behind him with jutting shoulderblades, holding her without looking at her, staring from the porthole.

'Lily,' he said. 'My God, Lily.' The drape fell back. They knelt facing one another on the bunk and she could feel him shaking.

He jumped down and pulled on his trousers and shirt, then the door slammed and she heard his feet on deck. She flicked the porthole drape and pressed her nose to the glass.

'Saw the glow most of the night,' the captain told Peter on deck.

'You should have woken me,' Peter said.

'Didn't like to,' said the captain, and Peter gave him a guilty glance.

'I can smell it from here,' Peter said. 'Can't you go faster?'

'Talk to the wind,' advised the captain. The wind had faded to a breeze; now it was failing altogether.

When Lily came on deck she was dressed as carefully as ever, in her full green dress, a proper lady, her face calm and strong. For a long time she said nothing, standing quietly behind Peter. The sun was hot and the jagged shadows of the sails swung over them and back again with the rolling of the ship. The coast moved slowly past them.

They stared at the waste land.

The schooner negotiated the channel into the Yellow Rock River, barely a foot beneath her keel, on the last of the wind, and tied up in the pool at the old jetty. No one spoke. The blackened humps of the dunes stretched round them, the sand-blows making brilliant yellow tiger-stripes. Tussocks still trailed smoke. Nearer the river tallow-wood glowed like coals. No birds flew.

'Peter,' Lily whispered.

He turned. 'Yes?'

'You have to do something.'

He jumped down into the shallows and pulled up a bundle floating there. 'I've got Isaac Simmonds here,' he said, and let it flop back. He went into the dunes and they heard him vomiting. He returned and ploughed into the wavelets, lifted a ballooned face in his hands. 'His wife, Powwidde,' he said. 'Thought they'd be close.'

The captain turned to Lily. 'You'd better go below, Mrs Pride.'

'No,' Lily said, determined to live up to her responsibilities. She had the gangway let down and walked to Peter across the beach. 'Look at me,' she said. 'Don't turn your back on me.'

'I'm all right now. I love you.'

'Were they burned to death?'

'No, look at their faces. Asphyxiation. Smoke.' He shook his head. 'You're going to need trousers and heavy boots. We've got a long walk ahead of us.'

Rebecca and Josh watched the party of sailors approaching in the distance, two figures in trousers leading, plumes of ash trailing their footsteps across the featureless plain. 'That's where the forest was,' Rebecca murmured. 'Peter caught butterflies there. I first read Berkeley's *Principles* there.'

'Stop it,' Josh said.

'Look what we've done.'

Josh eyed her frankly. She'd be any man's handful, crazy and wonderful, and he desired her hot or cold. But she talked too much.

'We're savages,' she said. 'No, not you. Me. *Us.*'

Her hair hung in mats and her face was striped with charcoal where her nervous fingers had rubbed it, her whole body filthy with greasy ash.

'I just want to cry,' she said. 'I wish I could.'

He gazed at her superb profile against the backdrop

of the tree, the brilliant lagoon, and took her into his arms.

'It's finished,' Peter said coldly. Annie was dead, and Selina. And King Island.

'Look at him,' Rebecca whispered to Josh, '*that*'s Peter.'

Peter's youthful exuberance was gone. The survivors were gathered on the beach, a few dozen, one or two still arriving, the rain trickling greasy beads down their blackened faces. Half a century of work and dreams had been annihilated, whole families gone. Many men had battled the fire; their widows and children, saved by the dam pools, stood around in a weary state of shock. Some of them had saved their cattle, sheep, on beaches or cleared ground, but there was almost nothing for them to eat. The stink of smoke was so strong that everyone was sick. They stared at the surf breaking in black waves on the black beach, the Yellow Rock River and smaller streams sluggishly washing the black cargo off the land. They turned their black faces up to the rain. The rain that had come too late.

'It's the first of March,' Peter said, and their faces turned towards him. 'It's too late in the year for anything to grow.'

'Tell them what to do,' Frank O'Henry called.

'Eddie Preston,' Peter said, 'you know about seeds. How long before the island grows again?'

Eddie shook his head.

'No, we ain't beaten,' Ricky Yates said. He looked around him.

'You got your kids,' Chas Denby said in a low voice, standing alone.

'We're beaten,' Peter told them. 'We are beaten here.'

'Tell them, Peter,' Rebecca shouted, 'tell them they asked for it!' There was an angry chorus from the other settlers and Eddie Preston, beetroot-red, bunched his fists.

'Listen.' Peter raised his voice. 'We can rebuild our homes, our herds and flocks, but not here. There'll be no pasture this year or next year; it'll probably take decades for the island to re-seed properly from the patches that survived the fire. King Island's finished and we've got to face up to that.' They fell silent and Rebecca went and stood beside him, then held out her hand to Josh. Peter pointed at the *Golden Girl* and the *Angelica*, which had brought the survivors round from Preston and David Howie's Boat Harbour, anchored in Franklin Roads.

'I know we can get all the good stock aboard those ships. I know where there's all the grass they can eat. I know where we can start a new life.'

'This is just a ploy to increase the importance of the Pride family,' Edward Preston told the others.

'That's not true,' Rebecca said.

'You cold bloody bitch.'

Rebecca turned and kissed Josh Simmonds in front of them all.

'Anyone who wants to come, comes,' Peter said. 'There's nothing for us here. We make new lives at Macquarie Harbour.'

'What do you think of my brother?' Rebecca whispered to Lily by the ship's rail.

'I love him, I don't think of him,' Lily said. 'He's there, that's all.' The rising sun lit her lovely blue eyes as she glanced at Rebecca.

'That's the way I feel about Josh,' said the older girl sadly. 'That's all it is, and it's somehow everything. I wish I was seventeen again, I wasted so much time.'

They watched Josh help Peter set up the camera by the sternrail.

'We've come of age, haven't we,' Rebecca whispered

as water began to slide past the hull. 'I know Peter has. I think I have.' They looked round as ropes squealed in the blocks, the sails unfurled in the morning sun. 'We've all lost our homes.'

'I lost mine when I left Hobart Town,' Lily said.

'Now we're making a new home together,' said Rebecca.

They watched Peter remove the bright brass lens cap. King Island was a cindered and terrible desolation behind them, pluming steam and smoke downwind. The green line, the fertile plateau was gone.

'Goodbye,' Lily said, and turned to face forward.

'I'll never forget,' Rebecca said, looking back until there was only the sea.

A man landed on the northern tip of King Island. He wore a black coat and dusty grey trousers, and from his head rose a stovepipe hat almost as tall as Isambard Kingdom Brunel's: this man too was a engineer, sent by Messrs Turner & Swan under the auspices of the Tasmanian Clerk of Works.

He had come to build a lighthouse.

The closure of the hazardous – but quick – Bass Strait short-cut by punitive Lloyds' rates and London Board of Trade restrictions meant vessels travelling from London to Sydney sailed all the way round the south tip of Tasmania, making Hobart Town their first landfall, to the great profit of the town. Even trade between Sydney and Melbourne went that way. This was intolerable; so the lighthouse would be generously funded by the federation-minded governments of Victoria and New South Wales. Tasmania had been a greedy parasite on the body of Australia for too long: now that would gradually change.

The Legislative Council in Hobart Town could hardly disapprove of an improvement in maritime safety. Cape Wickham would be the site of the highest lighthouse in the southern hemisphere, a light visible to mariners for more than twenty miles. The walls at the base of this massive tower would be more than eleven feet thick.

The contract was priced on the assumption that all this stone would be quarried on the mainland and landed somehow on the beach.

'I saw it further south, sir,' said the Irish convict-navvy, nearing the end of his term, his hairy arms grizzled with grey hairs. 'Further south it was, a granite outcrop of good smooth stone, a matter of six or seven mile mayhap, but with the beach as level as a road for carting.' He had done time here as a track-cutter near the start of his sentence, and now it was nearly finished he was anxious to ingratiate himself with a possible employer.

'What a godforsaken place this is,' the engineer commented dourly to the foreman as they walked south along a vast, empty beach. The convict working-party followed a respectful distance behind them. The island seemed almost treeless, shimmering under the heat, wasted, timeless, disconnected.

Trefoil grass crunched sparsely under their feet as they turned inland and reached the valley. The party drank from the lagoon then sprawled in the shade of the single tree while the engineer examined the outcrop. He kept looking over his shoulder. The silence was enormous.

'We'll import wooden sleepers and build a light railway,' he decided. 'I'll have a surveyor on the route right away. We'll cut through the valley wall *there*,' he pointed, 'and run by gravity to the beach. . . .'

Messrs Turner & Swan would make their fortunes saving the cost of transporting the stone from the mainland. For many years the staff of the lighthouse would be the only permanent inhabitants of King Island, tending the massive ticking, whirring mechanism that set the great lenses revolving.

In November 1861 the clean, white light of the world first shone out from the empty island.

32

The safe harbour

The two ships crossed Hell's Gates where the swell lifted high and broke in brassy bursts of spray, and entered the calm waters of the safe harbour.

They looked around them at this new land that was their home.

Rebecca, of course, knew all about Macquarie Harbour: a rectangle of brackish water, a hundred feet deep, almost closed off from the sea by the vast sandy tongue of Ocean Beach that all but blocked its mouth. Fifteen miles long by five wide, it pointed like a shining brick into the heart of the unexplored southwest wilderness of Tasmania.

'You'll love Ezzie,' Rebecca assured Lily. 'Everybody does. She's fun.'

'How long have you been friends?' Lily worried about her welcome.

'I've never met her,' admitted Rebecca, 'some silly family quarrel. But her letters are fun. And she's Jack's mother, so she can't be far wrong.' Rebecca still admired a man who decided what he wanted, and got it.

'What a strange place this is,' said Lily, gazing at the tiers of pale, dolerite peaks rising into the far distance. She pointed at an inlet in the trees close by as the ships tacked among the flocks of black swans. 'What's that, Rebecca? An uncharted river?'

'The King. Ezzie goes sailing and catches eels, native trout there. Its course was only mapped last year. The largest, fastest rivers in Tasmania flow into Macquarie

Harbour, but almost everything about them is a mystery.' North of the grey spine of Mount Sorell, she nodded at a flattened-looking bulk of a mountain showing above the horizon, beyond about a dozen misty miles of sombre tree tops. The peak's grey-green colours almost matched with the forest, but a landslide showed up red and yellow streaks. 'The Queen River joins the King there at Mount Lyell. Mr Gould only discovered it last year; he named the Chamonix Valley – after Donizetti's *Linda de Chamonix*, he being rather operatic – because it is so full of *wind*! Listen,' she explained, trying to cheer Lily up, 'Ezzie's an active person, she loves entertaining, and having guests and – parties!'

'Here?' Lily said, seeing not a single habitation, nor any welcoming curl of smoke breaking the enormous parallel shorelines.

'Mr Gould,' continued Rebecca, 'is a British geologist. The forest is impenetrable, except by river, and so only the rivers and mountains have names. Mr Gould,' she said with a frown of disapproval, 'opposes *The Origin of Species*, so he named the three biggest mountains Jukes, Owen and Sedgwick after the three most famous opponents of the theory, and the three smallest after its supporters, Mounts Darwin, Huxley – and Lyell.'

'Has anyone ever climbed Lyell?'

'Doesn't look much of a challenge,' sniffed Rebecca, 'looks like it's been worn down – you can't really tell because of all the trees.' They retreated under the tarpaulins sheltering the animals as a rain-squall rattled across the smooth water. The mountains here picked up the moist sea winds on their cold rocky shoulders, wringing out huge quantities of rain, and Macquarie Harbour's rainfall was twice that of Hobart Town; a few miles inland it was twice as much again, creating the great rivers that somehow broke through the mighty shield of mountains. As the rain eased they saw the Gordon River, clothed in Huon pines, flowing into the harbour's southern end beyond Sarah Island.

'Don't these cattle smell,' Lily said suddenly.

'You'll get used to that.'

'I'm so excited!' Lily laughed, and Rebecca, who had been so ready to dislike any wife of Peter's, couldn't resist hugging her. Peter, watering the animals in their pens, looked up from his buckets and watched them with approval.

Rebecca, her arm round Lily's shoulder, pointed enthusiastically as the ships tacked close to shore again. 'That must be Coal Head.' Bands of brown coal about six feet thick, separated by layers of sedimentary rock, ancient sandy beaches, angled down to the water's edge. The waves had washed them away to give a striped effect. 'One more tack,' Rebecca predicted, 'and we'll be at Farm Cove.'

Rebecca was right, as always.

The ships rounded Gould Point and entered the enclosed bay, then turned into the wind and anchored by Soldiers Island. Lily looked around her in awe at the beauty of the scene: round the ships stretched a bowl of hollowed grassy slopes made fertile by the volcanic rock beneath, as if there had once been a volcano here, still showing jagged outcrops where the grazing animals sheltered, or wended their way towards the stalls and rustic byres built of rough-hewn beams as evening approached.

Above, just below the green ridgeline, a large house had been built. The figure of a woman, the wind blowing her hair, stood on the balcony. She went inside, then reappeared a few minutes later running from the door, through a bright garden, then following an invisible path down to the beach. Discarding her clothes without affectation, leaving only a flannel shift, she plunged into the water and swam out to the *Golden Girl*.

'That's Ezzie,' Rebecca decided. 'She has a crippled arm but she swims like a mermaid. Isn't she lovely?' The woman swam out through the dark waters painted with reflections of mountains and farmland, then hung onto the Jacob's ladder dropped over the ship's side. Everyone aboard was silent, reluctant to be the first to speak.

'Annie?' called up the woman from the water.

Peter said: 'Something terrible has happened.'

'You can't stay,' Bob said. 'This is a terrible place.'

'Don't pay any attention to him,' Ezzie said briskly. 'He doesn't like to admit he's happy as a sandboy.'

'I was happy on King Island,' Bob said. 'Was – was her end truly dreadful?'

'Annie never knew what was happening,' Peter said. He shivered; this southern night air struck cold, and he put his coat round Lily.

'She didn't even wake up,' added Josh.

'Burned alive!' Bob exclaimed, and they fell quiet round the long table. His hair was receding, his eyes gaunt hollows. Half a dozen years younger than Ezzie, Bob looked much older, the outdoor life suited her so well.

'You're all welcome here,' Ezzie said. Bob put down his knife and went into the house. She looked after him sadly. 'I'm so glad you've all come,' she said softly, the bonfire shining in her eyes, 'now we'll really make something of this place.'

It didn't take them long to find out who, for all her gentleness, was boss. 'Listen up, folks,' Ezzie called, holding out her hand for Lily to help her on a chair, 'this is pretty sudden. But we're lucky. Charlie Gould and his party are away on an expedition up the Gordon, that means we can use his men's tents in Kelly Basin, just on the other side of the ridge there. It's a good place for houses, you'll find plenty of timber begging.

There's some old convict huts too. I recommend you get to it because when it rains here, it rains.'

'We'll decide what to do and when to do it,' Edward Preston said. 'We aren't second class citizens, and we won't take second class territory.'

'Get working or get wet,' said Ezzie indifferently. 'It's up to you. You've brought some pretty good stock, springers, yearlings, heifers, and I saw a couple of fine bulls.' Peter looked at Bob's shadow standing in the balcony window; quietly, he drifted away from the crowd.

'Porkers go into the piggery on Soldiers Island,' Ezzie went on. 'We grow wheat and barley on Philips Island, vegetables and fruits on shore. The sheep runs are on higher ground.'

Preston called: 'How about branding?'

'We sink or swim together here,' Ezzie said. 'Anyone who doesn't like the way I run things can sail on with the *Angelica* to Hobart Town and I reckon my son Jack will do what he can for you. Some of you girls with families, who lost your men, will want to go. That's the way it is. Who stays, works.'

Lily looked round for Peter.

'Reckon we'll make it?' shouted Ezzie in her clear, ringing voice. It was quite extraordinary, Lily thought: one slender woman in her mid-fifties standing on a chair and still hardly taller than half the men shuffling around her, holding them in the palm of her hand like a congregation.

'I've never worked with my hands,' Lily said, finding her voice, 'but I'll work them to the bone.'

'Enjoy it,' Ezzie said with her hurt, fierce grin.

'We don't need you to tell us one damned thing,' Edward Preston said, speaking for the men behind him.

'Then go to hell,' Ezzie said. 'There's your damned ship.'

Josh whispered to Rebecca: 'What are you smiling at?'

'I've found a woman with a dream,' Rebecca said. 'Put your hand up in the air, Josh.'

'Oh,' he said, 'I already found her.'

In the house, Peter stopped in the hall. He had brought two gifts on the ship with him: one was too heavy to carry and remained on the ship, the other weighed almost nothing and he held it now in his hands, a small, fragile square of photographic glass.

'Uncle Bob?' There was no reply from upstairs.

Banking money had built this house: tall sash windows in every room, fine furniture and Persian rugs, Irish crystal, Dutch pottery, absolutely undefeated by the trackless wilderness that lay beyond those thin glass panes, this small green oasis between the harbour and the rainforest.

Peter climbed the stairs, noting the expensive brass carpet rails between each riser, and came to the big open rooms of the top floor. Bob was standing at the balcony windows staring into the dark. Peter could see his own reflection hesitating in the doorway, and the reflection of Bob's face looking at him. Then Bob spoke.

'Doesn't she have a beautiful voice? I have everything a man desires.'

'Yes.'

'Welcome to our green and pleasant land,' Bob said, 'welcome to hell.'

'I'm sorry if I've disturbed your thoughts.'

'You're the same age as that son of mine Jack, to the day, maybe to the hour.' Bob turned abruptly. 'D'you reckon the hand of God in it?'

'No, sir,' Peter said.

Bob sighed. 'He used to smile like that, when he was a child.' He turned back to the window. 'You've come a long way to be here, chum.'

'Yes, sir.'

384

'A penitentiary.'

'I'll take it as I find it, sir.'

'A hell made by men. You don't have to face it. We could find you a better life in Hobart Town, letters of introduction, a place in the Bank.'

'I want to be here,' Peter said.

'No future here, mate.'

Peter showed him the cruel photograph of King Island, the cinder on the sea. Bob stared at it for a long time, holding the sharp edges of glass between the palms of his hands.

'I am going to hang that on the wall where I can see it,' he said. 'Good night, Peter.'

Peter met Ezzie in the hall. 'How's he taking it?' she asked him.

'Badly.'

'Was he talking about hell again and all that rubbish?'

'Is it true?'

'We make our own.'

'I'm sorry for him,' Peter said.

'Don't be,' she said, and pushed past him. 'Just be half the man he is. Work starts six in the morning, sharp.'

'I've got a present for you,' Peter called after her.

'What is it?' She turned as quickly as a young girl.

'See you at quarter to six, sharp,' Peter said. 'Outside.'

She laughed.

Yawning, Peter waited by the dinghy in the grey pre-dawn glow; the sun wouldn't rise from behind the Cracroft Hills until much later. He blew on his hands, the pocked sand crunching underneath his boots as he paced. Streamers of white mist hung over the glassy black water, the two ships pointing in different directions, motionless over their vertical anchor chains. He knew Ezzie wouldn't let him down, and such was the stillness he could hear the parlour clock striking the quarter-hour up in the house. She appeared wearing a filmy muslin ankle-length gown, and she had bound up her hair. 'I was going to row you out to the ship,' he said, offering her his cape, but she made him hold it up and took off her outer clothes, then slipped into the water wearing only a costume.

'We'll swim out,' she called. 'Come on, man, it won't be the first time I've seen a man in woollen long johns.'

He grinned then hopped out of his boots and followed her into the dark water, grimacing and sucking through his teeth. Their heads towed black ripples to the white hull of the *Golden Girl*.

'Well?' Ezzie said on deck when he had recovered his breath.

He went onto the foredeck and unwrapped the shape beneath a tarpaulin.

'This is what you saved?' He nodded, put off balance by her amusement.

'The Paragon of Virtue,' Ezzie murmured. 'My, she's got blackened!' She touched the wooden figurehead tenderly. 'I was married very close to her. Peter Pride, you couldn't have chosen a finer gift, almost.'

'Anything.'

'My son Jack.' Her voice was naked.

'Ah, well, Jack is a paragon of virtue in his own right.'

They spoke lightly now. 'Yes, bankers always are, Peter, it must go with the job. I'm glad you're friends. All we ever seem to do is ask him for loans.'

Peter said: 'He's happy where he is.'

'I know.'

'Jack was born to be a banker.'

'No,' she said, 'he was not.'

Ezzie pushed the figurehead over the side and they swam back to shore pushing the bobbing wooden carving in front of them. One of the Yates boys saw them and called his mother. The children splashed out and gathered round them in the shallow water, rolling the figure onto the beach. The adults arrived, the men naked to the waist and smelling of carbolic soap, and helped carry the figurehead in turns, finally a party of them carrying it like a totem over their heads to the house.

'Paragon House,' Ezzie said.

It was the most exciting time of their lives.

The *Angelica* had sailed for Hobart Town within a few days, crammed with families who could not or would not stay. 'You're fools to try to stick it here,' Edward Preston shouted back over the ship's rail. 'You'll end up playing second fiddle to the Prides. Why else d'you reckon they want you?' The sails snapped and fluttered as the ship turned, drowning his words.

Peter looked at Josh, whose face wore a wide grin, no doubt relieved to be free of his rival: Edward had repeated his proposal of marriage to Rebecca. She turned him down flat.

'Let's get to work,' Peter told Josh, and they spat on their hands.

For the moment Fergus Matheson's *Golden Girl* remained at anchor off Soldiers Island, their only tenuous link with civilisation.

'I almost wish she wasn't there,' Peter told Lily with a kiss. 'This is a wonderful land. I wish it was just *us*.'

'That's enough of that. I thought your hands hurt.'

Peter's torn hands glistened red and black from wielding the four-foot smoke-hardened handle of the felling axe, and she dabbed salt on the blisters to harden them. The wind rattled the bark roof of their slab-hut, they could hear it flapping Gould's tents below them by the Kelly Basin beach, and the shallow waves washing across the sandbars around the mouth of the Clark River.

'You look strong now,' she said, relenting.

'Got to keep up with Bob. Finished?'

'Rebecca told me a secret.' She held her tongue between her lips in her concentration, took another dab of salt.

'Told *you*?' Peter was drifting apart from his twin.

'Josh asked her to marry him.'

'Ouch.'

'She told him no,' Lily said. 'She'll change her mind.'

'You don't know Rebecca – ouch!'

'She will change her mind,' Lily said.

Among those who remained at the settlement there was a feeling of youth and vitality, of everything being fresh, and of togetherness. It was Ezzie who brought them together, her door always open, her table always set, even dragging Bob in with her enthusiasm, no longer the outsider.

Some of the men, unused to the company of women, or of considering them at all, didn't like it. Women cramped them and they longed for the lonely mateship of campfires, where tobacco smoke and male talk could rise as high and free as the stars. These men drifted over to Captain Lloyd's place on Sarah Island, ferried by Ezzie herself, and gradually made their way up the Gordon to the captain's pining camp on Butler's Island.

The *Golden Girl* was sent back with Frank O'Henry to Hobart Town with Bob's draft on the Bank for winter supplies – flour, sugar, tea, yeast, matches, canvas, glass and ironwork for the houses they would build, and blueys for them to wear, thick cloth leggings and hobnailed boots, and red flannel shirts they hung in the chimneys for a week to smoke them and make them waterproof.

They were all aware they were in at the birth of a

388

new community, something fresh and exciting against the wilderness, carving out lives where there had been nothing. Together their energy seemed boundless, and winter was coming.

By May the mountain peaks were white with snow.

Beneath the trees there was almost no wildlife, only the gloomy green density of overclimax rainforest. It took a man a day to hack his path for a mile through the horizontal scrub growing higher than his head, the bauera that filled every gully twenty or thirty feet deep. Bob, his muscles standing out in cords and his set face streaming sweat, almost mindless with exertion, led the logging party up to a fine stand of trees for their houses – no one wanted to pass the winter in a slab-hut. When they reached the Huons they worked up to their knees in swamp. Celery-top pines and myrtle, growing so thickly their branches could not be seen, preferred drier ground, and the men built muddy sassafras skidways to slide the felled trees down. The air whined with the rip of cross-saws, the creak of falling timber, and the groans of the piners manhandling the trunks with hand-spikes, crowbars, blocks and tackle. When night fell the men packed it in, exhausted, and returned to their wives.

Gradually they discovered that the forest was not so lifeless after all. They knew of the snakes of course, and mosquitoes. Now they discovered any clearing attracted wombats and wallabies, fluttering cockatoos and brilliant whizzing parrots, vivid streaks of colour in the half-light; other parrots, drab green, ran like quails on the ground. In the mud they found scattered prints of the Tasmanian tiger. In the forest sound was more important than sight, and many times they heard the lapping of these large half-striped creatures from forest pools.

Bob told them that the acid brown waters of the harbour were too poisonous to support life. Ezzie wasn't having that. 'What about the mussels on Nigger Head Rock? There's cod, ling and flounder, you've just never looked – and freshwater crays in the rivers – '

'All right,' Bob said.

'Eels too,' said Ezzie. 'Big ones.'

Next morning there was frost on the ribbon-tree roof of Frank's store by the river. The *Golden Girl*, newly returned, floated in her gilded white reflection. The yacht was their talisman: if anything went badly wrong for them, they could use her to escape.

They smoked bacon and eels for the winter, salted pork and beef. Bob didn't make them unwelcome, but his silence became domineering, his lack of expression cheerless and finally oppressive. Ezzie told Peter: 'Give him time.' Bob accompanied the parties that went out to catch crays, leaping from the punt with forked sticks and splashing across the sandbars by the mouth of the Gordon. This was how Josh caught the black swan, or rather the swan caught Josh, Josh chasing the swan then the swan chasing Josh, beak open and wings outspread. The two of them fell in a tangle and spray flew up, Josh getting a grip on the swan and the swan's wings clouting him off his feet again. Bob's face cracked a smile. Josh and the swan dashed back and forth until Josh fell into deep water, then the swan cruised slowly past him, stretching her neck and wiggling her tail feathers victoriously. Bob laughed so hard he hung from Peter's shoulders.

'That's the funniest thing I ever saw,' he said. 'Let's get Josh ready for the table.'

The Government geologist, Charles Gould, and his men returned to Kelly Basin with the first wet snow, exhausted and dispirited by their exploration of the Gordon. Ezzie threw a party, an opportunity for the ladies to change out of their rough skillion dresses, brush the mould off their finery, and feel for an evening their lives were not an endless drudge. Ezzie's hot rum punch and roaring fire soon loosened tongues.

Gould, little older than Peter, told of the wonders he had seen in a cool and stoic tone.

This year he turned his attention to the lower Gordon and the wild river that ran into it, the Franklin: he had pushed as far upstream as Devil's Hole, struggling up to his chest in freezing waters on the rapids.

'No part of this land is flat. Waterfalls plunge from the sky and gorges open at one's feet as though the earth has split. Exploration of such an extraordinary and confusing landscape cannot be carried out as hasty forays by individuals. The Government must find money for thorough geological surveys.'

'I don't think that's likely,' Bob said.

'Gold,' the geologist replied.

'I knew it!' exclaimed Rebecca. 'You have no interest in science at all, you are purely in search of gold!'

'There's none here,' Bob said firmly.

'How do you know that, sir?'

Bob dismissed him. 'We came here to escape the worship of the yellow metal, Mr Gould.'

'You are a man of the world, sir, and you know that just the rumour of a gold find at Otago in New Zealand has once more decimated the Tasmanian labour market. The Government is desperate for a Tasmanian mineral find. What other chance do we have?'

Lily asked, 'Have you found colours?'

Gould looked at her keenly, then gave a small bow. 'I see you know a little of prospecting.'

'My father was a Ballarat merchant.'

'Then you are aware that the Reverend William Clarke is Australia's foremost geologist.' Gould spoke quietly and calmly in the rapt silence. 'He has advised the Government that the Victorian gold-reefs are, if you will pardon a mixed metaphor, merely the tip of the iceberg. He believes the ore-bearing strata run south from Victoria below Cape Otway, pass beneath King Island, and that the mother lode is to be found somewhere down the 146th parallel.'

'But that's here,' Lily said.

Gould drained his glass and it was refilled.

'Yes,' he said. 'The Eldon Range, to be exact. Last year I found gold in the King River, and now the Franklin too, but not in payable quantities. None in the Eldons – but to be honest the country is so difficult, and the geology so confusing, that no man knows what he will find round the next mapless bend.'

'You're on a wild goose chase,' Bob said.

Gould smiled politely, 'The Government is paying me £600 a year to do work which fascinates me anyway.'

They sat at the table and Lazarus Graves served rich eel soup. 'You really believe there is gold, Charles?' Rebecca murmured.

'I am certain it exists.' Gould sipped from his spoon.

'And you believe in sea monsters.'

'Yes, I am certain they exist. . . .' Gould glanced at Bob, aware that he had lost face, then tried to brazen it out. 'And phoenixes, too.'

'But you do not believe in evolution.'

'I do not.'

'Even the land evolves, does it not?' Rebecca said, popping a piece of bread into her mouth with her fingertips.

'I see that I am talking to a disciple of Mr Darwin, a man who married his cousin, an unnatural selection which doubtless explains his experience in interbreeding.' Gould grinned wittily.

'Mr Darwin has also been Secretary of the Geological Society, I believe?'

'Before my time,' Gould said uncomfortably, changing the subject back. 'The land evolves?'

'The sea level was once higher than it is now; you

392

can see the ancient sea cliffs and beaches high up Mount Sorell,' Rebecca said, 'and Tasmania was once connected to Australia. Huon pines thrived on King Island, part of the huge forest. Mountains rise and fall. Glaciers –'

'I know all about glaciers,' Gould said gloomily, 'it is their movement which has made the geology of western Tasmania incomprehensible. I believe the King River is a glacial moraine – debris! – and that debris contains minerals, but where do they come from? The glaciers have destroyed the evidence. If there *were* ore deposits, I suspect they have been removed by erosion and deformation – after all, where else in the world do rivers deliberately flow *through* major mountain ranges instead of *along* them. . . . but this is beside the point, young lady. What you are describing is simply chaos, not evolution to a higher order.'

'A hidden order,' Rebecca said, hoping Uncle Bob would keep quiet.

Gould said quickly: 'Mysticism!'

'The hand of God,' Bob said.

'No more mystical than sea monsters,' Rebecca said to Gould.

Gould, defeated, resorted to an amused laugh.

'I wasn't *trying* to annoy Uncle Bob,' Rebecca told Ezzie defiantly, 'it was the truth.'

'Introducing your atheism at the dinner table didn't improve his digestion.'

'You're one,' Rebecca said.

Lily looked at Ezzie in surprise.

The three women were in the skillion, working with short razor-sharp knives, gutting cod caught off the rocks, Rebecca laying them in the barrel of brine for the winter. They shivered despite the pelts across their shoulders.

'At least it's too cold to smell the fish,' Lily sniffed

393

through her reddened nose. It was the first time she had taken off her wedding ring and her fingers had swollen; she hoped she could get it back on. Josh put his head in, ostensibly to get a bandage for his cut knee but really to look at Rebecca. They slept together and his eyes were full of her.

'You'll live,' Rebecca said, and packed him off.

Lily was singleminded and she found her older friend difficult to understand. Most people disliked Rebecca, but she fascinated Lily. Rebecca obviously loved Josh but she wouldn't admit it; her head and her heart pulled different ways, but Lily was determined that they would marry.

Charlie Gould had turned into a good friend. He and Rebecca fought like cat and dog as soon as they saw one another: the Government-chartered schooner *Anne* that was to fetch his party was overdue.

'Perhaps the tides are keeping her out,' Rebecca had called, catching him alone on the beach.

'Macquarie Harbour has no regular tides,' Gould responded argumentatively. 'The level rises and falls in response to changing barometric pressure.'

'It's going to be fine,' Rebecca laughed, 'look, the tide's out!'

Josh watched them from the fence rail he was working on, his face stiff with jealousy.

'You don't understand,' Ezzie was telling Rebecca, throwing a fish towards the barrel, 'Bob would love *not* to believe.'

'After the fire on King Island we discovered more bodies than we could account for,' Rebecca said.

'How could that be?'

'Some were skeletons in caves; they may have been aboriginal, perhaps very old.'

'How ghastly!' Lily said.

But Ezzie found it easy to accept. 'Life's more

interesting, more hidden than we can guess,' she said mildly, 'like people, really.'

Rebecca said: 'There's something I've never told anyone. On King Island, in the dunes where Peter and I were digging down to the layer of shells, the level of the old beach – we burned them to make lime, to sweeten the grass. . . .' She stopped.

'Yes, we used to do that here,' Ezzie said, 'but now we use the old convict lime-kilns up near Butler's Island.'

'I found a knight's helmet,' Rebecca said in a rush.

'We'll never know,' Ezzie said.

'Maybe it was a miner's helmet or an old saucepan,' Lily said practically, blowing on her numb fingers.

'It was a old Portuguese helmet,' Rebecca murmured, 'just an outline of rust really. A conquistador's helmet lost on the beach three or four hundred years ago.'

'Tea time!' Ezzie decided.

'Charlie Gould doesn't really know what he's looking for,' said Rebecca, and Lily was suddenly quite sure that Rebecca felt nothing beyond friendship for the personable young geologist. 'He'll try and persuade the Government to mount a bigger expedition next year just so he can lead it.'

'I hope he doesn't find anything!' said Lily with her quick impetuosity.

'I hope *it* doesn't find *him*,' Rebecca said. 'That's what I meant, that's what a wilderness is all about, isn't it?'

Lily wondered if Rebecca was quite right in the head. But then they heard the gun going off, signalling the sighting of the *Anne*, and next day Charlie Gould departed from the safe harbour through the spray of Hell's Gates, having found neither gold nor sea monsters.

33

1862

The river-spirit

Charlie Gould's third expedition to Macquarie Harbour was by far his biggest, and his last chance. The Government staggered from economic crisis to economic crisis, and there would be no fourth expedition if he failed them again. The politicians couldn't care less about intellectually rigorous geological surveys, they wanted gold, and it was Charlie's job to find it.

Thirty-one men came with Gould to Macquarie Harbour in December 1862. This time they would scatter in small parties to make sketch maps of the widest possible territory: Burgess the surveyor would head up towards Deception Gorge, Ibsen would attempt to find the Gordon River tunnels beneath the mountains, while Gould himself planned to locate the headwaters of the Franklin and explore its tributary, the Jane.

As before they set up their base camp at Kelly Basin, and were greeted like old friends by the stockmen at the jetty. By chance Lily, still childless, and Rebecca had taken Ricky Yates's youngest children and the others for a picnic on the grassy sward of Picnic Point, the curving promontory which provided a spectacular view of the mouth of the Gordon and the ranges of mountains behind. Lying back with their heads in the wild flowers, the excited calls of the playing children all around them, they didn't hear the signal gun and the first they knew of Gould's arrival was the appearance of the *Anne* tacking across the blue waters below them.

The children ran down at once, scampering along the beach waving, keeping up with the ship.

'I'd better keep an eye on them,' Jennie Pillinger said tolerantly, brushing stalks of phalaris from her dress and running down.

Rebecca held back Lily's arm. 'There's something I want to tell you.'

'It's not because Mr Gould is coming back, is it?'

Rebecca shook her head impatiently. 'I'm pregnant,' she said. 'It's Josh's of course, but I don't want to marry him.'

Lily looked shocked. 'But you must.'

'I want to live my own life.'

'But you have to set an example. Does Josh know this?'

'I'm swearing you to secrecy.'

'You mustn't do this,' Lily whispered. Her eyes filled with tears.

'I thought you'd understand. You're talking like one of the new moralists, Duty, Family, Country. I'm confident of my own identity.'

'But what about the baby?' Lily said, glancing at Rebecca's still-slim waist.

'Oh, it's months away yet!' Rebecca stood up angrily shaking her hair. 'I really thought you'd understand!'

'I'm sorry you're disappointed in me,' Lily said, but Rebecca just flicked her fingers and walked down to the jetty by herself.

Gould's weary battles with the Treasury and the Committee of the House of Assembly had visibly aged him, but Rebecca noticed his face light up when he saw Ezzie, and on the quayside he presented her with an astonishing gift: the two volumes of Ronald Gunn's *Flora Tasmaniæ*, with two hundred plates in colour interleaved with tissue paper, and many more exquisite illustrations in pen-and-ink. 'I shall treasure it for ever,' Ezzie said.

'No sea monsters for me?' Rebecca demanded challengingly.

She must have sounded strident. Gould stepped back. 'Perhaps one day.' He greeted Peter. 'I knew of your skill in the science of photography,' Gould said, 'so I hope you will find my small token not without interest.' It was a slim book of silk-screen photography, not the usual panoramas of London or portraits of the Royal Family, but something quite new.

'They are photographs of the Crimean War,' Gould said. 'Not the Charge of the Light Brigade but the war as it really was. Look at those figures in the mud. Do you see those rows of wounded men, their faces? And this little figure – she is Florence Nightingale.'

Peter stared at the book.

That night Bob and Ezzie invited Gould and his team to supper at Paragon House. Peter and Lily came with Rebecca, but not Josh. Rebecca liked to think herself not dependent on him.

Bob held court in the drawing room. 'I expect you've noticed some changes, Mr Gould, since you were last here.'

'No one can doubt that you are beating back the wilderness,' Gould said. 'You have made the most encouraging progress.'

'I thought I'd be alone,' Bob said, 'now I find the world has come to me.'

Peter and Lily had built their long, low single-storey house out of bricks stolen from Sarah Island, and King Billy pine. Fergus Matheson in Hobart Town, still not quite able to let Lily go, had selected imported furniture and fittings to his own florid, exuberant taste from Lewis's store, and sent it with his compliments on the *Golden Girl*. Lily had been really quite annoyed, and relegated the gilt chairs to a back room.

The wranglers and stockmen lived in shingled wooden huts near the barns. During the summer Bob employed half a dozen piners who lived in tents clearing land ready for burning and lime-spreading. Twice a year vessels brought them supplies, newspapers, *Walch's Catalogue of Books* and the latest episodes of Dickens's novels to while away the long winter evenings, and loaded up with Huon pine logs and livestock to sell. 'Our bloodstock is the finest in the southern hemisphere,' Bob bragged in high spirits. 'Next year we'll import prime Herefords from the old country. We're succeeding where the Van Diemen's Land Company failed.'

'The spread will turn a profit one day,' Peter said.

'Ah, if only my son Jack were here, we'd show him the place! We'll bring him here one day, Ezzie old girl.' *One day* was a game he and Peter played.

'Jack's got his own life,' Ezzie said. 'He'll never come here.'

Bob turned to Gould, who was examining the frameless photographs hung baldly along the wall as Bob liked them: the burnt island, and a single tree growing tall without another in sight, a deserted curve of beach, a view from a high point along a discordant rocky coastline of an empty sea, an empty land.

'Listen, Gould,' Bob said. 'I'm coming with you and Peter up the Franklin.'

'More hands are always welcome.' Ezzie had discussed this with Gould earlier.

But then Rebecca dropped her bombshell. 'I'm going too,' she said, tilting back her head, her mind made up.

'But you *can't*!' Lily whispered.

'Why not? Jane Franklin did.'

'Not on foot. In a blackwood sedan-chair carried by relays of convicts! And she – ' *She wasn't pregnant.* Lily turned to Ezzie for help.

'I couldn't possibly dissuade her,' Ezzie said mildly, 'you see, I'm coming too.'

*

'One. Two. Three.' Rebecca counted off the seconds.

'Don't you feel it?' Ezzie whispered. 'The rivers are the heart of this country.'

Rebecca, throwing twigs into the sliding water to estimate the rate of flow, gave her a scoffing look. 'You made me lose count,' she said.

'Don't be stupid,' Ezzie said. 'Listen. Feel.'

Away from the flat rock where they stood the water bent downwards in a black curve, then broke into a glittering tangerine foam down the ramp of the Devil's Hole. A small tree rotated in the whirlpool below, sucked down and spat up almost regularly enough for Rebecca to count by.

Away from the water's roar, the forest was intensely peaceful.

From hills that seemed almost vertical, trees cascaded silently into their pictures in the river's curve. All round them pandanus dangled ropes of white blooms, flowering bauera twisted its beautiful, impassable chains across every gap, and the dark limestone cliffs, riddled with caves, echoed to the thwack of tomahawks bouncing off the tough vine; there was nowhere to put it when it was cut, and there was always the fear of snakes beneath the rotting maze of fallen trees the rainforest fed on. Fungus, sometimes luminous as glowing orange eyes, sprouted from every piece of decayed wood, and the two women, wearing long moleskin skirts and waistcoats over cotton blouses, groaned privately to one another as they shouldered the forty-pound knapsacks they had insisted on carrying.

They had made their first camp near the limestone cliffs of Butler's Island, then followed the track Burgess was cutting and clearing to the Franklin River, far too wild-running for the heavy, unstable boats Gould had used on the Gordon. It would be all on foot from now on.

'I love the river,' Ezzie said. The party had climbed

up into the windy Elliot Range and were staring across the brown button-grass heathland of the Western Plains to the dark stain of the Black Forest, where the Jane River joined the Franklin. Far below them, the Franklin came winding beneath its green walls.

'Once all this was Ice Age rainforest,' Gould said, pointing against the wind towards the distant coast, 'but the aborigines burned it off. They're long gone, thanks to Robinson, but button-grass burns easily from lightning-strikes, and the rainforest never grows back – there's no Huons north of the King River for fifty miles. Heemskirk is just an open coastal plateau blasted by the wind. Probably an aboriginal fire got out of control in prehistoric times – it takes thousands of years for rainforest Huons to regenerate.'

'It's a temporary landscape,' murmured Ezzie.

'Robinson said that aborigines never came here into the river country,' Rebecca called to Gould, 'they never left the coast.'

'I wish this wind would stop,' Bob said.

'Robinson only followed the coast!' Gould laughed. 'Even in the late 1840s, Jamie Calder was sure at least one tribe was still hiding out in the river valleys.'

'And now?' Rebecca said.

Gould pointed. A figure moved among the eucalypt shrubs downhill, but then they saw it was the tireless surveyor, Gordon Burgess. He waved and Gould ran down to meet him.

He returned with a flushed face, cradling a few smooth, glittering flecks in the palm of his hand. 'Gold has been found in the middle gorge of the Jane River,' he said. 'Come on!'

They camped overnight in the Franklin valley, then pushed on early into the Black Forest and crossed the river on a pine raft at Calder Ferry, following Calder's old path through stands of Huon to a forest-tunnel of dark myrtle, sassafras, pepper, laurel, manferns with their tops like huge pineapples, and the most gigantic tea-trees they had ever seen. The waters of Humbaba Gorge echoed unseen on their right, then after three hours' hard walking they broke through to the pale pebbly quartz of White Hill Plains. It took them almost until dark to descend the few hundred yards to Gilgamesh Gorge, cutting steps and making handrails so steep was the fall. Scrambling over the boulders of the river bed, foam and mist all round them and the solid water thundering below, they found Burgess's men working a pool. It had collected a small shaly beach where the men were swilling sandy gravel around their wooden prospecting dishes.

Dark, dolomite cliffs towered above them.

Gould shouted: 'Have you found it?' They shook their heads, showing him a few shining flecks, not payable quantity. Gould felt them. 'They've been washed smooth,' he shouted over the river's roar. 'It doesn't come from here, look upstream.' But the gorge was already filling with gloom, and they had to hurry to set up blanket-tents and find driftwood for their campfire.

'You see, the rougher the gold, the closer it is to the reef,' Gould told them by firelight.

'I don't think there's anything here,' Bob said. All of them were weary of the thunder of the river, its fine mist soaking them.

'Why is this called Gilgamesh Gorge?' asked Ezzie, but the men shrugged and turned in a few minutes later.

'Gilgamesh wanted to live for ever,' Rebecca told Ezzie in their tent. They lay shivering, too cold to sleep.

'Did he live for ever?'

Rebecca shook her head.

Ezzie said: 'Are you crying?'

'I'm not crying. It's so freezing cold.'

Ezzie curled her good arm around Rebecca and they cuddled.

'I'm going to have a baby,' Rebecca said.

'I know.'

'Lily told you.'

'You told me. Your walk, your eyes, hands, everything.'

'You're the only friend I have in the world. You understand, Ezzie. Tell me you do.'

'Yes.'

'Lily has given away her life to Peter. The obedient little woman.'

Ezzie said: 'Lily risked everything to marry Peter.'

'Why?'

'She loved him!'

'I don't know if I love Josh. I'm so angry with myself. I just don't know.'

'Rebecca,' Ezzie murmured, 'Rebecca, Rebecca. . . .'

Rebecca lay awake, thinking: *I don't love Josh.*

She woke alone. In the early morning light, Ezzie was crouched by the river's flood, the white blouse she wore looking like a flower over her rumpled moleskin dress. She splashed silver drops on her face, then stared across the water. Gould had already departed with his party of prospectors to explore the valley of the Acheron River, and they seemed to be alone. Rebecca walked down shyly. By daylight she was ashamed of her night secrets. 'It's so powerful,' Ezzie said. 'The river. Look at the driftwood caught in the forks of those trees. Must be thirty, forty feet above the present level.'

She pointed, and now Rebecca saw Bob climbing carefully among the shrubs clinging to the cliff face above. 'He saw a gravel bed up there. Might be gold.' They watched Bob crawl along a ledge, tiny stones sliding from his hands and feet, then he pulled aside a shrub – and disappeared.

'Must be a cave,' Ezzie said. 'Could be we'll sleep dry tonight. Do you feel up to a climb?'

Bob's scream echoed in the valley and his figure

teetered on the ledge. For a moment they thought he would fall fifty feet onto the rocks. Then he sat down. Rebecca followed Ezzie climbing up to Bob who was sitting on his hands, his face very pale.

Ezzie said: 'Is it a skeleton?'

'No,' Bob said. He showed no inclination to move.

Rebecca slipped through the tall entrance-slit into the cave. At first she saw nothing; the walls were black, and when she pulled the palms of her questing hands away she could hardly see them for soot. Her long laced-up boots crunched on animal bones, fragments of meteoric glass, a wooden haft stained with ochre: aboriginal. 'Is there anyone here?' There was no answer, only her whispering echo, and she realised the cave was deep.

Suddenly her feet were silent, touching on some sort of woven material, and she almost screamed. She caught its flash of blue by the glow of the entrance, then Ezzie's silhouette blocked the light. Bob pushed past. He knelt by the dress.

The pale glow shone on his face.

'Faith had a blue dress,' he said.

'She was drowned when the *Prince Leopold* went down thirty years ago,' Ezzie said. 'You can't possibly know.'

'This is her blue dress,' Bob said. 'Oh my God.'

34

1870

Beginning and end

London.

'My boy,' John told Winston, 'it will be a shock. You must betray nothing of what you feel.'

'Why not, Father?'

'Don't be more stupid than you have to be. She is dying; she is hideous!'

Winston paused. Improbably for the season he was carrying a glorious display of varicoloured, hothouse flowers.

John Prideau, morning-suited, stiff-collared, black-hatted, walked on like a lanky steam engine with his arms and legs pumping, an impression reinforced by the puffs of white breath that squirted from his nostrils. Across kerbs, jerking up his stick to warn the traffic, there was something mechanical about him – not amusing, or ridiculous, but *efficient*. No wasted movement, and an implacable indifference to whether the heavy drays pulled up or not. He lived a charmed life; Winston had always thought so. John Prideau, in life as in business, seemed to his son to possess the magic touch.

Winston, almost twenty-four years old and very long-legged, was dressed in a grey suit at the very limit of respectability for his profession and a paisley waistcoat several steps beyond it. Nor was he redeemed by his mirror-black patent shoes – he looked more like a somewhat foppish gentleman of leisure than a banker – how he irritated his father!

Winston tilted his broad-brimmed hat and loped a few long-leggedy paces to catch up. 'I will betray nothing, Papa,' he said with an earnestness he hoped would impress.

His father surveyed him frostily. 'See that you do not, Winston.'

They turned into Chesterfield Street. John Prideau, in so far as his cold heart hated anything, hated this street: once he had lived here. Winston could just remember those good times, though he could not pick out the door he must have known as a child: his mother, Adelie, had been killed by a dray as she came out of the Royal Italian Opera House in January 1850. It had been snowing, and the roads must have been slippery. He had been almost four years old and his grand-mother, Eve, returned home to the silent house and simply took him in her arms. He'd understood every-thing from her face, and cried.

'*Will I see her in heaven?*'

'Yes.' He remembered her saying the word, no doubt in it at all. He had loved Eve ever since.

Now Eve was dying, and he didn't want her to go.

In little over two years the Royal Opera House had been rebuilt, much changed, and turned through ninety degrees to face Bow Street. The great Corinthian port-ico provided a covered carriageway, ridding the dangerous steps of ham-sandwich sellers, touts and pickpockets, permitting playgoers to ascend to their carriages with their dignity intact, and in safety. Win-ston never attended the Opera without his throat tight-ening with what might-have-been. He had a fine clear voice, his birthright from his mother no doubt, and the bohemian life of the stage attracted him; he might have been a singer.

Alone, he could not resist his father.

John Prideau rebuilt his life with almost frightening speed – especially to his sensitive son. John Prideau married Alexandra Pelham the moment respect for the dead permitted, as though he had never loved Winston's mother at all, and Winston never forgot that hurt.

His new mother was pale and shy, frightened that Winston was closer to her new husband than she. It was not necessary for love to exist for another son to be born: Winston was brought home from school to be shown the swaddled child. 'What's his name?' he asked.

'Ernest,' replied both parents at once.

'How soon can he come out and play?'

'Don't touch!' they said.

Mrs Turton, Winston's nanny, packed her bags. This dreadful loss was almost greater than the first: the familiar black figure and friendly red face never to be seen again, many small kindnesses never to be repeated. Winston sat in the window watching her dwindle and shrink.

Winston was sorry for Ernest. Ernest had never known Mrs Turton, the small secret cartons of Italian ice-cream in Hyde Park, or the Christmas stockings freshly ironed, empty at the foot of the bed, but rich with promise; Father Christmas always came treading in slippers whose leather soles squeaked like Mrs Turton's. So Winston pitied Ernest for the love he had not known, but there was no need. Ernest was a good boy. He was a marvellous boy, the apple of his mother's eye. He was no fun.

Winston, who liked almost everyone, found his half-brother difficult to like; and Ernest thought Winston, with his flash mannerisms, unsound. One day Ernest would join the Prideau & Sons Merchant Bank of Threadneedle Street, nestled between the Threadneedle Street Branch Post Office and the Bank of England in a sea of stock jobbers and brokers, insurance offices and Peruvian railway companies; but for the moment he was safe behind the high walls of Trinity College, Cambridge. Winston was brilliant at the human side of banking, dealing with staff and winning new customers, and his financial touch was quick and sure; it was he who took ship to Rio and somehow extricated the Bank from the financial débâcle that almost dragged down Baring Brothers. Sometimes he was spectacularly wrong. John Prideau liked to sum his two talented sons up like this: Winston was gifted, but Ernest would be sound.

Sound was respectable.

John Prideau was at the age, with such a fine Head Clerk as Oliver Wray to oversee the day-to-day running of the business, when a man starts thinking of retirement, of handing over his life's work to his sons. Certainly he would not do that until Ernest had settled in.

First, John Prideau must visit his dying mother. He dreaded it; he had not even objected to Winston, who by being so much closer to her would exclude him, accompanying him.

Along Chesterfield Street the snow fell in slow veils, cartwheels rattled through the slush; straw had not been laid on her explicit command, she was an eccentric old lady. John Prideau rapped twice on the door knocker with the head of his stick and it was opened. The butler shook his head to John Prideau's raised eyebrows – there was no hope – and led them upstairs.

'D'you see this wallpaper,' John Prideau gloomily confided to Winston as they went down the passageway, 'William Morris. Arty-crafty. Her mind's failing, you know.' Eve Prideau had owned this house for the twenty years since her husband's death and filled it with colourful fripperies and continental knick-knacks. This was a woman's house, all ornamentation and dusting, where a sneeze could cause disaster. Women were no longer classed with children and lunatics, incapable of taking care of themselves or others – the Married Woman's Property Act allowed them to own houses, which drove men out to the clubs; which was no bad thing, having saved many a marriage, thought John with the nearest his thin lips approached to a smile. Time would show! He supposed Eve would leave him the house and he would sell it, his property in Red Lion Square being so satisfactory; and with Chesterfield Street gone the last link of his memorably happy life with Adelie, which never ceased to cut at him, would at last be severed.

The butler opened the door. Dressed in white bedclothes, Eve was sitting in a tall red armchair by the window. John Prideau crossed to her. 'Mother,' he said in his deep voice. He kissed her hand.

She looked straight past him.

'Oh Winston,' she said, 'those clothes.'

'How are you, Gran-Mama?' Winston kissed her on the lips and slouched on the arm of the chair, presented her with the flowers as though he had only just thought of them. 'Hothouse blooms straight from the Wellington Street flower market – and a pineapple from the Floral Hall.'

'How d'you expect her to eat a pineapple in her condition?' John Prideau demanded.

'I didn't think. Sorry, Gran-Mama.'

'He never thinks,' John said with the pride that masquerades as contempt.

'It was the most wonderful lack of thought, Winston,' Eve murmured patiently, as though she had all the time in the world. 'You remind me – '

Winston knelt beside her.

She was still beautiful, not hideous at all; her eyes sad, like dark blue flames, her sultry skin etched and meshed by the years of experience. Even – or especially – at the age of almost eighty-two, it was a kind of perfection, and he wished he could touch her.

He prompted: 'Who do I remind you of, Gran-Mama?'

'No one,' Eve murmured. 'Oh, I'm so full of pain.'

'I'll send for my doctor,' said John Prideau at once.

'John, my dear, take the pineapple downstairs to the cook and bring me the juice, would you?'

'If that's what you wish!'

'And a vase to put the flowers in,' she said.

Alone with her, Winston looked out of the window. It was dark and the gas lamps had been lit. A hansom cab rattled past.

'No straw,' Eve murmured, her head on one side as though she watched the street, but really watching Winston. 'I shall die in this chair.'

'You won't die.'

'I was in love and I died. It was long ago.' Her gaze was not so much looking *at* as looking *through*, the gentle clear gaze of a dying person marking everything for the last time. He knew she was failing. She glanced around the fine room. 'I've made such a mess of my life.'

'I love you, Gran-Mama,' Winston said in a voice as vulnerable as a little boy's, and he really looked as though he would cry.

She stroked his face. 'Don't let your father do it to you,' she said. It was her last wish. 'Be yourself, Winston. Be yourself.'

Part IV

Emma

35

1878

A sound man

'Again!' came Peter Pride's muffled voice from beneath the velvet cloak, and they stiffened into the demeanour they wanted posterity to remember them by.

The photograph of them hung on the wall of Dunkley Point House for many years. There in the garden, the monochrome vista of the Derwent to one side, for a frozen moment stands Jack Pride, slim as a dancing-master – a touch too slim to look properly prosperous – still with an athlete's build in his forty-second year but with his grim little jowls stiffening into sagacity, and his eyes remorseless: no longer the face of a young man but of the upstanding paterfamilias.

His family was only his daughter Emma, but she was the world to him.

The photographer's skill reveals Jack's glinting self-satisfaction rather than confidence, and the hands folded in front of his buttoned-up frock coat look suddenly self-doubting, protective under the burden of his many responsibilities. But then the shutter clicks, and there stands the Victorian paterfamilias proudly with his wife beside him, and on his other side the yard-long brass telescope that signifies his cultured interest in astronomy. Behind him, his residence with its windows shining in reflection of the bay – and not too close to his neighbour's house, St Helena, just visible through the trees.

In front of him sits Emma, precious and delicate, the

sunlight gleaming on her long blonde hair, her rosebud lips turned up prettily in the conventional pose for a young lady. There is a wonderful artless innocence about the peep of her ankle beneath her long dress.

'Once more,' came Peter's voice, 'cheese!' – and caught the moment. He pulled his head out for a breath of fresh air, the wind blew, a bee buzzed, and suddenly his niece Emma was solid and real, the right way up.

'Emma,' Jack said, 'how about more lemonade for our guests.' Dora rang for the maid. 'Make conversation,' she murmured in her daughter's ear, embarrassed by the girl's painful shyness.

'How long have you been taking photographs, Uncle Peter?' Emma asked in her stilted way – a flood of words followed by a sudden silence.

'Long enough,' Peter said, wondering what he could say to this gorgeous creature that would not make her jump. 'Long enough, Emma.' Despite the length of her arms and legs she moved with the fluid bodily grace of one who has been taught deportment.

Dora said: 'How long is long exactly?'

'Fair part of a tidy bit,' Peter said looking past her. Dora's rouged lips flicked a smile like a tiny whip.

'Come, Emma,' she said.

But there was nowhere to go; the lemonade was being passed round. The West Coast Prides – as Jack called them – sprawled on the grass between the rather unkempt shrubs. Peter looked awkward in his formal clothes but Lily had grabbed the chance to dress up – or maybe the crimson skirt with its lime-green waistcoat, and hat full of flowers, was her father's gift. She seemed to be thoroughly enjoying herself, making Fergus Matheson, who sat observing them from the patio, happy.

Dora appropriated Lily. 'I trust you are enjoying your annual teaspoonful of civilisation . . . ?'

Lily was finding their visit to Hobart very stuffy.

They came to the shops once a year, and she used to start looking forward to the next visit the moment they returned home, but now she couldn't wait to get back to the vast windy spaces of the wilderness, the rough, good-natured hard work of the Macquarie Harbour spread. Even the tea tasted better at home.

Emma, embarrassed, circulated back to Peter who was always kind. He was talking to Ezzie, who was dressed in bright youthful clothes not the sombre shades old ladies usually wore. Her vivacity fascinated Emma, who listened anxiously, wishing she could think of something wise to contribute. Before she could, Peter's eight-year-old boy Morgan tugged his coattails. '*She* was showing her leg,' he said, and Emma felt herself flush. She was sure everyone was staring at her. Ezzie was smiling.

'Only her ankle, Morgan,' Peter explained.

'I don't know how you can endure the primitiveness out there,' Dora went on. 'How can that terrible desolation be fair on the children?'

'Come and try it sometime!' Lily flared, and Dora looked disappointed but unsurprised at such poor manners. Lily was a convict's daughter and always would be. Nevertheless, Dora decided to use the disrespectable Fergus Matheson, unredeemed by his enormous wealth and charitable good works from the Stain, to her advantage.

'Your father still hopes you will come back,' Dora said.

'My home is Farm Cove now,' said Lily. 'You must come and visit us.'

'One thing I can promise you,' Dora said, 'is that Jack is Hobart Town through and through and he would certainly never dream of making such a journey.' Having said her piece she helped herself to something from the cakestand with a silver fork. 'Is it true – ' she

415

smiled sweetly, 'that you still find convict bones in the forest?'

A new voice interrupted. 'Yes, Dora, and other bones too.'

Age and experience had seamed and stitched Ezzie's sun-darkened skin like leather, but her eyes were still bright, and though her hair was now white it looked almost blonde in the brilliant sunlight. Rheumatism had bent her spine, but the old woman's authority quelled Dora. Ezzie was the only person in the world close to Jack.

But Jack was deep in conversation with Fergus Matheson on the patio.

'Oh, you mean the bones you found somewhere on the river,' Dora sailed on bravely. Emma listened, entranced, half a pace behind her.

'Not at all,' Ezzie shook her head. 'We found no bones.'

'What, then?'

'A ghost,' Ezzie said.

'I don't think you should listen to this,' Dora told Emma.

'It was only a dress,' Ezzie said. 'That was what made it so awful. It was the blue dress Faith wore the day I was married to Bob.'

'How could it have got there!' Emma exclaimed, then looked down.

Ezzie grinned and gripped the girl's long, pale hand in her own short brown fist. 'That's the thought that occupied. . . . or I should say, *consumed*, Bob for the last years of his life, dear Emma,' she said mildly. 'He searched for her almost to the day he was – '

'Lost,' Dora said quickly, bowing her head.

'He'd been lost years before,' Ezzie said. 'He died.'

'How did he die?' asked Emma timorously, not looking up from the hand clenched on her own.

'Bob was travelling to Hobart Town to sell up his

holdings in the Paragon-Pride Bank to Jack. The Macquarie Harbour spread has never turned a profit and never will.'

'It will,' Peter said, 'it'll pay its way.'

'It's our place,' Ezzie said urgently, 'our home. Poor Emma, don't look so sad! Bob never reached Hobart Town. The *Golden Girl* was lost at Hell's Gates and Bob. . . . Bob. . . .'

'Couldn't swim,' Lily said.

'Didn't swim,' said Ezzie. 'Well, Emma, now you know.'

'It was a happy ending,' Emma said.

Ezzie looked at the beautiful young girl with surprise, then nodded. 'You must tell me some of your secrets, Emma.'

'Oh, I don't have any!' Emma flushed, dreadfully embarrassed.

Ezzie smiled infectiously, and Emma found herself smiling back. Ezzie spirited her away from Dora, who was plainly anxious to defuse Jack and Fergus's too-earnest conversation. Ezzie and Lily, with Emma gangling between them, impulsively stopping to pick daisies as though she was alone, walked down the garden to the reclaimed land of the Point. Beyond the blue wavelets bright-sailed sabots weathered the yellow buoy and raced along the downwind leg towards Battery Point. Emma wove a daisy chain.

'Emma, tell me about yourself,' Ezzie said.

'There's nothing to tell!'

'Yes, I suppose it was a happy ending,' Ezzie sighed. 'We'll never know what really happened to Faith. I suspect that she was taken in by aborigines, but it's almost impossible for a small group to survive in true wilderness, and nowhere else was left for them. God knows what she suffered, willingly or not, friendless or among friends. They made their last stand at the cave. That's what I think. Her fate – her *unknown* fate, the

417

anonymity of it, the tiny scale of her life – was a dreadful shock for Rebecca too.'

'My husband's sister was a terrific romantic in those days and to be honest she was big-headed,' Lily confided. 'She was a know-all. She thought the world turned around her and she could do whatever she liked.'

'The aborigines believed in river-spirits,' Ezzie said. 'The rivers were their souls.'

'After it all Rebecca married Josh Simmonds, the head stockman,' Lily said, 'and had her baby in wedlock. We're great friends now. Gideon is old enough to help round the place, and now they have two lovely daughters – the youngest, Rachel, is Morgan's age.'

'It's all over now,' Ezzie murmured. 'Does Jack still swim?'

'No,' Emma said.

'I used to swim to that yellow buoy out there.'

'I do!' Emma confessed, delighted.

'Do you still see whales off Battery Point?'

Emma said: 'I wonder if Faith had any children.'

Lily clapped her hands to her face. 'I never thought of that!'

'That was the first thing I thought of,' Ezzie said. 'Your parents don't appreciate what they've got in you, Emma.' She sighed. 'Oh, we'll never know.' She took Emma's daisy chain and threw it over the waters. 'We don't know almost anything, I think.'

On the patio Fergus was leaning back in the cane chair, his stick between his knees, squinting beneath his tufted white eyebrows at the figures of the three women down by the water. 'God knows what women talk about, eh, Fergus?' Jack prompted.

'They're talking about Bob,' Fergus said.

'I wish they'd use the croquet lawn. I had it laid especially.' Jack had long ago decided that everyone

418

but himself was slightly peculiar. 'Towards the end my father wasn't quite sound, you know,' he sighed.

'Bleak prospect for you,' Fergus said in his economical way.

'Like father, like son? I hardly think I shall go down that road!'

'Aye, you've always been a sensible one,' Fergus grunted. 'I don't reckon you've ever made a wrong decision, have you?'

'A man in my position can't afford mistakes.'

'I see you're still not an executive director of the Van Diemen's Land Bank.'

'The shareholding is in my wife's name,' Jack admitted. 'I have complete confidence in my father-in-law, Councillor Briggs. In any event, there is no finer or more substantial bank than the VDL.' He wished he were talking with Lily, but had avoided her for fear Dora would see the expression in his eyes. Jack's feeling for Lily was one of the many secrets – although Jack thought of her with a banker's word, *confidences* – that he had perforce to live by in his trusted position. Gradually they had become confidences even from himself; he no longer thought of the word *love* but saw her still as the pure young girl of fifteen or so on her arrival from Melbourne, stepping from the *Golden Girl* onto the quayside, the prettiest thing he had ever seen. Dora, pregnant with Emma and temperamental with morning-sickness, had pointed at Fergus Matheson on the gangway and exclaimed: 'That is the ugliest man I have ever seen!'

Jack had not been intimate with Dora since Emma was born. After twenty-one years his marriage had achieved its majority and he and his wife were strangers. Dora seemed so angry all the time but when he asked her why, she could not explain. Obviously there was no problem, then. But her shareholding dominated his life.

And increasingly, Dora spent her real life at her father's house, St Helena, through the trees. Dora's younger sister, Helen, had died in infancy. Only recently had Dora moved out from her shadow and become reconciled to the old man, though he had always doted on her and expected Jack to. But now Councillor Briggs, wealthy through the Bank of Van Diemen's Land and powerful through his non-elective seat in the Legislative Council, was being slowly eaten by a cancer, and he needed Dora more than Jack did.

The Bank of Van Diemen's Land was huge, the single great pillar of the Tasmanian economy. As the Paragon-Pride Bank lived in the shadow of that great rococo building – literally so, on winter afternoons, being close to the corner of Elizabeth and Collins – so did Jack Pride's relationship with his wife live in the shadow of her father. Jack put up with this because it was all part of his strategy. One day the Bank of Van Diemen's Land, known all over the island as the VDL, would be his.

And Emma was his. The dear girl went with her mother when commanded to do so, but otherwise was daddy's girl. Jack, staring at the figures, felt his eyes moisten. 'One day this will be her house,' he told Fergus.

'You'll have to let her go,' Fergus said. 'They fly, Jack. What wonderful wings she has, if only she knew.'

Jack shook his head. 'I have always disliked the name Dunkley Point. This land has been wrest from the sea, Fergus. Wrest Point it shall be – and this house shall be hers.'

'Don't be a fool.'

'I have no son and I never shall.'

'You can't own her.'

'I won't let anyone take advantage of her,' Jack said doggedly. 'Look what happened to Lily. Look at her hands, that awful place. I don't know how you could let her.'

The same old stuff; Fergus wondered how much he could say to poor Jack, who had only one happiness in the world. Jack Pride was that rarity in Hobarton business circles, a truly honest man, and his friend. Fergus trusted no one, except Jack. 'You aren't really close to her.' Fergus ignored Jack's protests and pointed with his stick at the figures of the women on the shore. '*She's* close. Your mother, Ezzie. Look at the way they're standing: she and Emma.'

'My mother is shortly returning to Macquarie Harbour. The refit of her yacht is nearly completed,' Jack said stiffly. 'John Ross took her out of the water on his slipway.' The *Ezzie* had been specially designed and built eleven years ago, with a hull of Huon pine and a shallow draught, but a very heavy lead-ballasted keel to get her across Hell's Gates in safety. John Ross said the white-painted hull, with its graceful yacht lines, would last for ever. Her decks were laid in celery-top pine, and her two tall masts, densely rigged against the west coast gales, were of Douglas fir. The steeply raked counter sported large gilded sternwindows but at the last moment Ezzie had left the ship's figurehead, the Paragon of Virtue, above the doorway of her house in Bob's memory. 'And Emma,' Jack said, 'remains with me.'

'I'm going to end my days at Macquarie Harbour,' Fergus said.

'You can't leave Hobart Town!'

'I want to be near Lily, in the end that's all that matters. They've been badgering me to go for years. They're my family, Jack. I've been a fool to stick it out here as long as I have. I won't see seventy again.'

'But what about the Racing Club?' Jack was aghast. 'And who will run the Hobart Regatta without you?'

'D'you reckon the middle classes will ever let the

lower classes race against them? Or the nobs allow themselves to be beaten across the finish by the little shopkeeper who sells them tea? I've had a lifetime of it and I'm weary of it, Jack. The littleness of it. I'm beaten. Farm Cove is a good place for me.'

'But your business interests.' Fergus had invested early on in the hugely profitable tin mines at Mount Bischoff, inland of Emu Bay on the north coast. The richest tin mine in the world, it was situated behind country belonging to the Van Diemen's Land Company, so rugged that no railway had been built to it. This year four thousand tons of ore, worth a third of a million pounds, was carried to the coast by pack-horse. Jack badly wanted to be the man to fund that railway, but the expense would break him. On the other hand Bob Pride's almost worthless shares in the Van Diemen's Land Company, which had been willed equally to Ezzie, Peter and Jack himself, had been transformed into bonds of great value: no one could build a railway without their say-so. It would be a huge and fearfully dangerous investment. The northwest was a ferment of speculation, with new bubble companies launched and failing every day, and most men lost their shirts. Very few cashed dividend cheques twice a year, like Fergus.

'The west coast is the coming place – you know they've found tin at North Heemskirk.' Jack nodded glumly: all the reports indicated it was in country so harsh it made Bischoff look a treat, with no possible harbour. Prospectors stocked up at Frank O'Henry's store at Smith's Cove, just inside Macquarie Harbour, and ignored his good advice. 'Take a fool's advice, and let other fools face these forests.' But he grubstaked the poorest of them, and watched them go: rugged, ragged loners hunched under eighty-pound swags, following the enormous sweep of Ocean Beach northward, the old aboriginal route.

'Those fools can't tell black stream tin from black

titanic iron,' Jack told Fergus. 'It's worthless shicer. I saw them quietly dumping bags of the stuff off the Kangaroo jetty.'

'The Ballarat School of Mines analysed another claim and it was good.' Fergus spoke the prospectors' language. 'I heard there's plenty of cassiterite around and you know what that means.'

'It's not a sure sign,' Jack said.

'I might speculate a penny or two,' Fergus murmured. His paisley waistcoat gleamed peacock colours beneath his white tropical suit.

'You know how highly I rate your advice,' Jack admitted. Nearly twenty years ago Fergus had advised Paragon-Pride to buy into the Bank of Ballarat. It had been Jack's first really big decision, but the holding had multiplied many times in value. Marvellous Melbourne boomed on and on while Tasmania languished. Still, the Hobart Town banking community jealously maintained its financial independence from the predatory Australian banks.

Dora called up the steps, 'Why are you two hiding away?'

'We're talking,' Fergus said.

'You must be boring each other to death.'

'Money,' Jack said.

'How gauche,' she said, then turned away angrily. 'Come on, don't leave your relatives all to me!'

'It's business,' said Jack. He sat beside Fergus in a cane chair and put his elbows on his knees, clasped his hands in front of his lips.

'Watch her,' Fergus said, following Jack's wife with his eyes. 'She's no friend of yours.'

'Does it show?' Jack sounded amazed. 'Dora's all right. Everyone can see we get on all right.'

'You're in love with Lily,' Fergus said. He held up his hand. 'Don't worry. Dora wouldn't credit it if I told her. Ezzie knows, I'm sure, and Peter, but not Lily.'

423

'I'm ashamed,' Jack said.

'I wish *you'd* married her,' Fergus said wistfully, 'that would have been the ideal situation. None of this Macquarie Harbour business.'

'But would I have made her happy?'

Fergus sighed impenetrably.

Jack said: 'Do you think Emma guesses?'

'Great God, man,' Fergus said angrily, 'look at her, look at her eyes and the way she moves, listen to the way she speaks. She knows everything.'

'She's the one person who loves me. I'd die for her, Fergus.'

Fergus could be brutal. 'You died the day you married Dora for her shares and her family's political clout.'

'It's turned out better than I thought,' Jack said sadly. 'I never thought I would have such a lovely daughter.'

'I can't help admiring you,' Fergus said. 'I've met some ruthless types in my time, but you take the biscuit.'

'Dora's a marvellous woman,' Jack said earnestly, 'you should see the work she does for the Temperance Alliance and the Girls' Home Industrial School.'

'I'm sure she has her reasons.'

Jack closed his eyes.

Fergus changed the subject. 'I hear you're entertaining a visitor from Home next week. You're playing your cards very close to your chest, Jack, as always. I had to find out from George Salier.'

'I shall be entertaining Mr Winston Prideau formally at the Tasmanian Club on Friday. Why don't you join us?'

'You know very well the Tasmanian Club permits no one with a past through its august portals.'

'Mr Prideau represents the Prideau Merchant Bank of Cornhill, London,' Jack said. Below them the three women were skipping stones across the water now; he could hear their happy laughter on the evening air.

'A banker,' Fergus said thoughtfully. 'Your father-in-law and the Bank of Van Diemen's Land aren't going to be too pleased about this pre-emptive move of yours, are they?'

'My position is perfectly proper.'

'Of course.'

'Mr Prideau will be staying privately as my house-guest.'

'Sound move.'

'I am managing director of the Paragon-Pride Bank and my responsibilities are to – ' Jack nodded at his cousins – 'my voting shareholders.'

'What are you up to, Jack?'

'Sound business management,' Jack said. 'You see, Fergus, I have always known what I wanted. That's why people trust me.'

'And what have you always wanted?'

'To serve my shareholders and the people of Tasmania.'

'Money and power,' Fergus acknowledged. 'Very sound.'

36

Profit and loss

'Do it just for me,' Jack said. He didn't want to leave
Emma alone in the house, except for the servants, who
didn't count. Dora might return from her father's bedside or whatever charitable work occupied her. There
was a bright side to her absences: Dora's grip on Emma
had been shaken by the visit, now ended, of the easy-
going West Coast Prides. Jack made the most of his
opportunity. But now Emma said she didn't want to
come with *him*.

Emma's cheeks were flushed. Jack indulged her with
a smile he did not feel – not yet twenty-one years old,
and arguing with him! It was his mother's fault; Ezzie
had treated the shy young girl, *only* a girl, like a grown
woman.

'Have you forgotten your manners?'

'I don't want good manners,' Emma stuttered, 'I
want – I want – '

Jack sighed.

Jack's marriage wasn't an unhappy mess, they were
very, very happy, as happy as a man and a woman
could possibly be, but his home must take second place
to his occupation. In confidence, he had a mistress, a
widow of good breeding who lived near Elboden Place,
and they sat down and drank tea, and he talked. . . .
well, about himself. This gentle woman knew more of
his business affairs than his wife or any of his directors.
Jack was Paragon-Pride. His occupation was Jack.

'We'll go and meet the big ship together,' he told
Emma. 'Wouldn't you like to see her?'

426

Emma could have wept at his obtuseness. 'I just don't want to come!'

He didn't listen. 'Do it for me,' Jack said tenderly. 'Please?'

She gave in. The house was empty except for the servants and the time she had looked forward to alone, perhaps dancing alone in *her* bedroom, or walking alone with *her* thoughts on the seashore, would have to be sacrificed on her father's whim. He patted the long brass telescope through which he had studied the steamship *Flinders* coming up the Derwent, a thousand tons of iron and speed with smoke pouring from her tall black funnel and the Tasmanian Steam Navigation Company pennant fluttering proudly from the masthead.

'Our money built her,' he told her in the open carriage. It was breezy and he held his impressive black hat on with one hand; her hat was secured with a plain silk sash under her chin and she looked so pretty his heart beat twice. 'You're my girl,' he said, sounding so in awe of what he had created that she almost laughed or cried, helpless in the face of his ignorance.

'You never talk to me,' she said.

'There are nearly a thousand empty houses in Hobart Town because of the recession.' Jack talked of what he knew. 'A recession despite tin and gold exports of over three hundred and fifty thousand pounds sterling, my dear, almost more than the wool cheque, and look at all the trouble they took to rid us of sheep-fluke. The most ghastly crisis is coming, but we're decadent and lethargic – see the dull faces of that class of people waiting for the horse-bus! Doctors believe it is because phosphates have not been spread on the land: we lack essential minerals. Our race is not fit. Rabbits are ruining the grasslands and the apple crop has been decimated by moth. . . .'

Emma said: 'What do you feel?'

'What an extraordinary question,' he said after a moment. 'What did they teach you at that school?'

Labouring, the horse climbed the Davey Street ridge-line and then the smart gig turned right, downslope towards the harbour. Now they had entered the square mile of Hobart Town and Jack resisted the urge to hold his nose. Stinging, cindery smoke blew from the Derwent Iron Works on the Salamanca wharf. The Rivulet, once an open stream but now contained between deep walls of rendered brick, discharged its cargo of brown human slurry, soapsuds and fomenting scum from the Cascades Brewery into the dock where the *Flinders* was tying up. Beyond the masts of the ship and the jam factories rose the abattoirs.

'I feel this is a time of opportunity,' Jack told his daughter. 'We have government by faction, and crooked politics. The premier, Crowther, who hasn't paid his civil servants for months because the Treasury is empty, won't last long. The autumn typhoid, diphtheria and cholera epidemics appear to be something to do with poor drainage and we must have sewers. Public works must be paid for; the Government must raise revenue. If elected, Giblin will slap a duty on beer and spirits, taxes on property and unearned income. Even so, enormous Government borrowings will be required. How are they to be financed? Giblin is a senior director of the Bank of Van Diemen's Land, and they can use their overdraft permission of more than £30,000 from the London and Westminster Bank to increase their loans by a huge amount. . . .'

To his amazement, she seemed to understand. 'You mean the banks will fight to loan money to the Government?'

'The lucky ones will. The ones who can afford it.'

'And this London bank – '

'Loans to governments are very profitable,' Jack explained, 'and they grow and grow.'

428

'Can we go home now?'

He patted her hand. 'I'm sorry I've been boring you.'

Emma watched the seagulls soaring around the masts of the ship. Only a few days ago the *Ezzie*, shining with fresh white paint and rigged with new yellow cordage, had swung at anchor here in Sullivan's Cove and Emma had gone aboard to say goodbye. On the gleaming holystoned deck she had clung onto Ezzie's hand with a sensation almost of terror at what she was missing. 'Can I come with you, one day, when I'm old enough?'

Ezzie had laughed and kissed her. 'If you have to ask,' the old woman whispered, with sudden seriousness, 'you are not old enough.' But when it was time to go Ezzie deliberately sought her out and gripped Emma tight with that strange little hand of hers. 'Don't pull away,' Ezzie whispered. 'My dear, you're twenty years old. The age of female consent is twelve. You're not as young as you've been told, do you understand?'

As the sails were raised Emma, standing between Dora and Jack, waved goodbye with her lace handkerchief from the dockside. She didn't know what she felt. Ezzie had opened Pandora's Box to her – and Emma found it empty.

The carriage moved slowly through the crowds along the dockside towards the iron wall of the *Flinders*. Emma heard her father say: 'Are you quite well? You're very quiet.'

They went up the gangway onto the deck. A tall man wearing a waistcoat as bright as Fergus Matheson's pushed through the passengers and tapped Jack's shoulder. 'Carry these, would you.' He hefted his suitcases into Jack's arms. 'Don't let anyone touch them and there's sixpence in it for you.'

Emma hid her smile behind her hand.

'Who does that bloke think he is?' Jack was outraged.

'I'm no bloody porter!' He threw the cases at the man's departing back and they clattered on the deck by the gangway. Emma laughed outright. The man turned back and glanced at her with irritation, but seemed to take no offence at his now-scuffed leather bags. 'Some mistake, is there?'

'You've bloody well mistaken your man if you think we behave like that here, mate,' Jack said, from his highest horse.

'My apologies.' A hand was languidly held out. 'Winston Prideau, at your service.'

'Oh!' Jack said.

Emma thought she would burst. 'I'm Emma Pride,' she introduced herself, 'and this is my father.'

Winston bowed to her. 'Pleased to meet you, Emma.' She had thought all Englishmen, like their officious officials, called one another by their last names – and the *Mr* dropped only between lifelong friends, too. 'How d'ye do, Jack,' Winston Prideau said. 'Got a better climate here than Sydney. I like that mountain, lovely little pocket city.'

'We like it,' Jack said stiffly. 'We're very proud of our Mount Wellington.'

'Pleased to hear it, Jack.' No one spoke to Jack Pride like this; it was the way he spoke to his doorman or the night janitor.

'Don't this wind never stop blowing?' Winston grinned, pushing his long brown hair out of his eyes.

'No, it don't never stop,' Emma said.

Winston had very dark eyelashes and pleasant lines curved around his mouth. 'Let's find a man to carry my bags,' he said, 'and we can get going.'

'I'll carry them,' Jack growled. 'My pleasure.'

'Suit yourself.' Winston held out his elbow. 'Lead on, Emma. Show me the sights.'

They sat facing one another in the carriage, the sun between the buildings flicking shadows across their smiling faces. Jack, obliged to recover his temper, was determined to do his duty as host. He ordered the carriage to a tour of the museum and imposing town hall and other buildings he thought his visitor must find impressive. Then he tapped the driver's shoulder with his stick: 'Turn right!' They avoided the site of the derelict Murray Street gaol – Jack was ashamed – and the old men, invalids, paupers, idiots and lunatics, sitting by force of habit in Franklin Square they had known so well when they were convicts. Nevertheless, Winston had keen eyes and commented on the numbers he saw sitting hopelessly in doorways. 'These leftovers of Mother England are your fault,' Jack said. 'The imperial subsidy was withdrawn long ago but these poor needy remnants remain, their time expired, unable to look after themselves.'

'No one likes to talk about them,' Emma said, 'or even sees them.'

'That's the Paragon-Pride building,' Jack pointed. 'You'll want to see inside! We imported marble from Carrera.'

'Not now,' Winston yawned. 'Seen one bank, seen them all.'

Emma studied him.

Away from the windy shore the banker – and it was becoming very difficult to think of Winston as a banker like her father – had relinquished his waistcoat for a striped brown and yellow summer-jacket, which Emma decided was a cricket blazer in public school team colours, but she didn't even know what school. His white shirt was open at his neck, which was sunburned despite his straw hat, and his long legs were crossed in flannel trousers. His foot almost touched her knee with the jogging of the carriage and she looked away. He was infernally casual.

'You must be tired after your journey,' Jack said, and ordered the driver to turn for home. Never had he felt so demeaned. Winston Prideau's superiority was unbearably irksome. At least Emma seemed able to tolerate him, and Jack relied on her. 'He's a pakapoo ticket,' he confessed to her in the hall while Winston was being shown his room upstairs. 'That man thinks he's Christmas and the Angel Gabriel rolled into one. I just want to make money out of him!' He went into his study and slammed the door behind him.

Emma met Winston on the stairs. 'You've upset my father.'

'That's a start.'

'Surely you don't have to pretend all the time?'

He betrayed surprise. Then he said: 'It's a serious business.' He moved a step below her so that their eyes were on the same level. She supposed he was almost old enough to be her father, well into his thirties.

'Will you not change for dinner?' she asked.

'If you ask me to.' He watched her, then leaned forward and kissed her on the lips. She kept her eyes open. 'I think you're the one to watch,' he said, running lightly up the stairs, then turned with his jacket over his shoulder. 'I'm thirty-two. I live in Chesterfield Street.'

She stared at the place where he had been. Then she ran downstairs, her face burning.

Her father's ignorance astounded her. He noticed nothing.

The three of them sat at the long table. Through a gap in the velvet curtains the moon was rising over Bellerive. On the sideboard the butler served soup from a silver tureen into thick cold dishes. 'We send out all statements of accounts written with goose-quill, and always will, people expect it,' Winston said, talking to Jack but glancing at Emma. 'But for office work my father introduced typewriters. Faster than a pen. Efficient.'

'I understand your father died last year. Please accept my condolences.'

'Heart. Ernest, my half-brother, has taken over responsibility for home affairs while I look for new opportunities to expand.'

'The loss of confidence in the markets after the South American crash hit the colonies very hard – especially independent colonies like Tasmania here.'

'That's why I'm here.'

'We're underfunded, undercapitalised. This is the land of opportunity.'

'I'm afraid we're boring Emma.' Winston forced her to smile at him, and returned her smile. 'Listen, Jack, you're going to want to build a railway from Emu Bay to the mining town of Waratah to bring out all that tin from Mount Bischoff.'

So he knew about Jack's holdings in the Van Diemen's Land Company. 'We're talking of hundreds of thousands of pounds,' Jack said. 'You cannot imagine the mountains. The narrow-gauge pastoral line just from Launceston to Deloraine cost four hundred thousand.'

'And was secured by a system of re-guarantees. Not acceptable.' Winston hadn't blinked at the enormous figures. The lines around his eyes had come from more than smiling: he had burned the midnight oil. Emma understood pretence, and hid her smile behind her hand. His gaze lingered on her white knuckles. 'Jack, everyone I've talked to says you're the best. You can be Hobart Town's biggest banker. I'm prepared to make available an overdraft guarantee for half a million.'

'My God,' Jack said.

'If Giblin is elected the Government will need to borrow at least that much this year, more next. The railway will be operated by holding companies with you up front and in control.'

'But?'

'We speak the same language. A sprinkling of English directors will give you political leverage.'

'How so?'

'If any disagreements arise between the railway companies and the government, for example over land rights, or freight charges, in fact anything, then the English directors can threaten to obstruct loans sought by Tasmania in London.'

'It's brilliant,' Jack said.

'It will make Launceston for ever the second town of Tasmania, and Hobart Town firmly the financial capital. That can't be bad for your standing in the community, Jack.'

'There will be many details to consider.'

'We'll work something out,' Winston said casually, and Jack had to let the business talk lapse. Winston ate his steak while Jack only toyed with his, obsessed by the vision that had been revealed to him: the great London banks pouring their money out into Tasmania. Winston said: 'Perhaps you will allow me to appropriate Emma and your driver to show me the sights tomorrow?'

'No,' Emma said.

'Certainly,' said Jack.

'That's settled,' Winston said.

She taught him a lesson.

The only lesson Emma understood was *absence*. When Winston came down yawning to breakfast in the morning, her carriage was already turning out of the driveway.

She smiled to herself as the horse clopped along the Sandy Bay Road.

Her name was shouted, and she turned and looked back over the folded canopy: Winston had appeared at the gate. He stood looking after the carriage with his blazer hanging from his hand, then shrugged it on and ran after her.

Emma called impulsively to the driver: 'Faster!'

The carriage weaved between the horse-buses. Winston's long legs carried him like the wind. Emma stared over her shoulder, excited. His jacket fluttered and his head was thrown back. The hill to Davey Street slowed the carriage and he pulled closer, then the slope told against him and he slipped back. The carriage slowed behind a plodding horse-bus, and Emma watched with her fists clenched as Winston put in a superhuman effort, grabbed the canopy-rail and threw himself over. For a moment she thought he would slip back and grabbed his sweating hand.

'Thank you,' he said.

'For goodness sake pray sit down. People are watching.'

'*This* is me,' Winston said, holding his arms wide. 'I'm no banker, Emma. He's not me.'

'You're drawing attention to us,' she murmured. 'Please sit down.'

But he liked attracting attention to himself. The carriage turned left along the Huon Road, Winston standing up.

'You're mad,' Emma murmured.

'You wouldn't want me any different.' He threw himself into the seat beside her. 'How does a stiff, sour old fish like your papa have such a radiant daughter as you? Let's run away.'

'You merely show how little you know him. He's very kind.'

'I didn't say he was unkind, I said he was all tight and bound up inside himself.' Winston wrapped himself in his long arms. They were in open country, Mount Wellington looming overhead. The road twisted and turned.

'You're twelve years older than me,' Emma said, 'and you come from the other side of the world.'

'His love for his daughter is the only brightness in the dull accountancy of his life.'

'That's cruel.'

'I promise not to be truthful again. It's my day off.'

'But aren't you meeting – '

'Don't be boring. Let's climb the mountain.'

'That's quite impossible in one day. And I have only these shoes.'

'You were ordered to entertain me. Surely there is a hut where we could drink lemonade.' He was suddenly quiet, slumped beside her. He said no word until the driver stopped about four miles out of town, then lifted her gaily down. They followed the wide path through the sun-speckled forest, he carrying her cape and performing the occasional pleasant duty of lifting her over some mossy fallen log, the only times they touched. She talked of nothing: clematis and waratah, grass trees and honeysuckle, her voice echoing in the curved green spaces.

As the slope steepened and the day grew warmer, he held her hand. They were quite alone.

'Doubtless your father has much better men lined up.'

'I do not think he has considered such a fate for me!'

'It was an electric shock when I first saw you and it was only yesterday. It seems like a lifetime.' He said no more and neither did she. He lifted her up a staircase of logs and they stopped to rest at the top. Through the tree tops they could see the first sheoakers coming up the Derwent loaded with sheoak firewood for the coming winter. 'We're like gods up here.'

'You angered my father,' she said.

'Frightened him. He married without love; he cannot understand his daughter's love. Now I've made you angry too. It is anger, isn't it?'

'Stop pushing me.'

'You're pushing you.'

'Stop it.'

'You're as I am,' he said.

'You are foolish.'

'In love head over heels, as I am with you.' He took her hand lightly before she could reply. She followed him uphill silently. Anything she said seemed to change her life.

'I am not.'

'I have seized you in both hands.' Then he took her in his arms, their faces close. 'Let's run away.'

'My father would never permit you to hold me like this.'

'Or touch you like this, or this.' He touched her lips in a kiss so brief it was already past. She snatched at the memory. He would depart on the Union steamer and she would never see him again.

'Don't!' she shuddered, holding him with all her strength.

'I love you. Don't answer. Don't spoil it with your denials.'

She followed him through tree-ferns whose fronds arched so thickly around them as to almost cut out the sun. 'Winston!' she called.

He had come to a low turf-roofed cottage, the Spring. Hobart drew part of its fresh water supply from here and an area of grass had been cleared beneath a tall gum-tree. 'Lemonade,' Winston told the innkeeper, who brought them a stone jug kept ice-cold in the stream.

They sat with it between them, sipping from the dew-beaded glasses. The magnificent birds' eye view encompassed the tiny rooftops of Hobart Town, the azure Derwent and the Bellerive settlement on the far shore, an interval of burning scrub, and the distant hills around Port Arthur.

'You're right,' Winston said, 'we're mad.' She held him tight.

She knew everything about him. Winston in black was transformed. His man Toynbee, delayed by fever in Sydney – Winston allowed nothing to interrupt his schedule – had arrived in Hobart Town with a portmanteau of clothes complete to the ironing board. Winston's black tails, a high white collar pushing out his chin, made him a man to be reckoned with by the grimmest colonial Quaker.

'You look so serious,' she whispered at the top of the stairs. Tonight he was making his speech at the Tasmanian Club dinner. Women, of course, were not invited.

'Tonight is money,' he said, 'money is serious.' She straightened his collar. 'Tonight is Ernest's part of the plan.'

'And tomorrow?'

'Tomorrow is my plan.'

'And what,' she chided him, 'is that?'

'You.'

He bowed to kiss her hand. His hair was parted in the centre and his thoughts were on tonight; his eyes were cold. Then he gave his smile and went downstairs to join Jack, similarly dressed and only about ten years older, but looking a lifetime older, waiting in the carriage beneath a lofty hedge crimson with autumn berries. As they drove, overripe fruit was falling from the plum-trees that lined the road, the burst plums looking like splotches of blood.

'We'll do the signing first,' Winston said.

'I have a pretty fine sherry.'

'I am in love with Emma.'

'They're lighting the gas lamps. I beg your pardon?'

'I am in love with Emma.'

'No,' Jack said.

'Emma is in love with me.'

'She cannot possibly know her mind at her age. I've forgotten my speech.' Jack patted his pockets. 'We must keep our minds on the business in hand. Everyone will be there. William and Tom Giblin, the Dobsons – '

'I'm informally asking for your daughter's hand in marriage.'

'You're coming in on the grouter, damn you, you can't do this to me.'

'I know what I want,' Winston said, and Jack gave him a frightened look.

'You'll have to give me time to think. I'll give you my considered answer after the signing.'

The raised voices of the Hobart Glee Club, singing English village songs in welcome of the Tasmanian Club's English guest of honour, prevented any further discussion on the steps.

The documents were to be signed in an upstairs room. Jack wondered how he had ever thought this self-possessed foreigner casual or relaxed: Winston was stiff as starch, icily formal. He wrote his signature slowly, ending with a flourish, then looked up expressionlessly. All Jack could think about was Emma. He bent down and signed.

'Well?'

'Believe me, I speak wholly with Emma's interests at heart,' Jack said smoothly. 'I've got to tell you my answer is and always will be no.'

'You Australians never use one word where ten will do,' Winston grunted. He held out his hand and Jack shook it, thinking that was the end of the matter. They exchanged papers, Jack handing his to his clerk, Winston to the cadaverous Toynbee. 'Let's eat.'

'I trust this won't affect our business relationship,' Jack said. Winston smiled at him.

'I mean to have her,' he said.

Three long silver-laden tables led away from the

gleaming head table where the Committee and Winston, as guest of honour, sat. Around the walls group portraits of former committees gazed gloomily down on the diners, all identical in white tie and tails. The seven courses were in French, *potage* Windsor, *filet de barracouta, agneau de Tasmane*, sorbets, local cheeses. 'Not bad,' Jack said, patting his pockets, then read a grandiose welcoming speech introducing their special guest.

'Thank you.' Winston spoke without notes. 'I've been impressed by my visit to your island.' Jack let the words wash over him, nodding wisely from time to time, then pricked up his ears at what Winston was really saying. 'You are all rightly proud of your status as an independent colony. However, the Tasmanian Navy has only one launch and the Royal Naval Squadron, paid for by the British taxpayer, protects your coasts. Tasmania is too small to be independent, gentlemen. With no very great wealth, you must for ever remain a colony of Britain or Australia.'

Jack leaned back in his seat, horrified. His guest's words would be interpreted to have his stamp of approval.

'I have this evening,' said Winston, 'signed papers with Jack Pride. . . .'

Jack closed his eyes. *I am a traitor to my own country,* he thought, but forced his face not to betray his feelings. Beyond doubt Winston had made him Tasmania's foremost banker – second only to the Bank of Van Diemen's Land; but what a price he had paid.

Winston was ending his speech.

'Sir, I formally ask for your daughter Emma's hand in marriage,' Winston said.

'You're a man after my own heart,' Fergus Matheson said. 'In public! He'll never let you get away with it. I don't blame him.'

'It's what Emma wants.'

440

'Emma is in her minority. Her opinion is worth nothing. If you touch her it could be rape. Jack is the Chief Justice's personal banker. That's the way it is here, sonny. There's a Union steamer in the Cove; better be on it.'

'I'm not due to leave for another week. I must speak to Emma.'

'Jack won't let you.'

'He can't keep her for ever,' Winston said.

'Unless she stands up to him, her life is his,' Fergus said. 'He'll choose her husband. And he'll do it soon. You and your lust have made a mockery of his good standing in this stuffy community.'

Winston stopped pacing. 'You're on my side,' he said.

After the speech he had given at the Tasmanian Club, with its explosive climax that set every Hobarton tongue wagging, he could no longer remain as Jack's houseguest with Emma at Wrest Point. 'You are no gentleman,' Jack had said in the carriage, stopping outside Heathorn's Hotel, and that was that. 'We have a business relationship, and no more.'

'You broke your word,' Winston accused hotly.

'I said I'd give you my reply after the signing, old choom,' Jack swore, 'not that my reply would be yes. Good night!'

Winston took the verandah suite and Toynbee was sent for the portmanteaux.

Next day in the lobby a white-bearded gentleman, dressed in a white tropical suit and flamboyant waistcoat, but with measuring eyes, handed his card to Winston who was hurrying through the lobby. 'Come up to my house and see me when you have the time, but don't be long, or I shall be gone.'

Winston had read the card later. 'Fergus Matheson.'

Workmen were busy in the great mansion, Southland, on Davey Street, as the house and contents were prepared for auction.

'I'm old,' Fergus Matheson said, turning from the broad window with its stunning view, a cigar clamped between the stumps of his teeth. 'I'm going home. I've been a fool not to see it all these years. Home is where my family is. I'm moving to Macquarie Harbour.' Grunting, he sat in the sole Louis chair remaining by the fireplace, then braced his hands over the top of his stick as he looked around the empty room. 'So few memories. This house once had my wife's name. I had to let her die.'

'I'm sorry, sir.'

Fergus Matheson got down to business: 'You're the first man who ever stood up to Jack – and won.'

'But I'm afraid I haven't won, sir.'

'I like Emma and I know her. And I know love,' said Fergus sadly, 'and I know she loves you. And you love her. From your behaviour you're plainly not in your right mind.'

'I know what I feel, sir.'

'Then,' Fergus Matheson said, 'it's simple. You know what you must do.'

Winston sat in the trees on the edge of Wrest Point, his polished shoes scuffed by the rocks of the reclaimed land he had scrambled around to get here. In the nearby house the clinking of breakfast cutlery had ceased. Jack's carriage departed for the Bank at eight-thirty sharp, Fergus Matheson's arrived a few minutes later. Winston took out his watch, then looked up hopefully when the house garden door slammed and a woman appeared, but it was only Dora, and his spirits sank again. He watched her walk across the corner of the lawn towards St Helena, her invalid father's mansion. She carried a wicker basket over her arm.

At last Fergus Matheson and Emma came out of the

garden door. Winston licked his dry lips. They strolled towards Winston between the flocks of plovers strutting on the grass, Emma holding up the hem of her skirt from the dew, showing her ankles. He stood up, and she began to run, then held out her arms.

Winston clenched her tight.

'Together,' he whispered in her hair, 'together, or not at all.'

Jack stood on the empty quayside with tears streaming down the papery planes of his face.

Fergus sat in the open carriage watching seagulls swirl above the vacant swathe of water. The Union steamer had sailed in the mid-morning, would have dropped the pilot by now and be in international waters.

'I've lost my little girl,' Jack said.

Fergus did not move a muscle. Jack, who married without love, didn't know what he'd missed, but knew that in Emma he'd lost all he had.

'You got everything else you ever wanted,' sighed Fergus Matheson.

Jack's face distorted like a child's.

'I just don't want her to be unhappy, as unhappy as I have always been.'

'You're wrong to feel sorry for yourself, Jack.' But still Fergus didn't move from the carriage, or try to comfort the friend he pitied. Poor buttoned-up Jack; no man was his own master, human will was a puny force, and love paid for all. The tyranny of that was both beautiful and terrible. Fergus was very tired and he longed for Macquarie Harbour.

'Let's go home,' he said.

'Together,' Winston murmured, 'or not at all.'

'You're all I have,' Emma whispered against his chest. It was chilling to hear the terror in her voice.

He touched her, stroked her, kissed her. The first class had been called to supper so they were alone on the pounding deck. Smoke boiled from the tall funnel above their heads, trailing a horizontal cloud of black grime and smuts towards the green coast of Tasmania, the inexhaustible forests dwindling northwards towards the Bass Strait and the thin red line of Australia. The light was failing and the forests lost their colour, the stars came out over her homeland. 'I can come back,' Emma said.

'No.'

'One day.'

'We never can.'

She was silent in her happiness and grief. Her childhood days were done, and she looked up eagerly. 'We'll be together for ever. I thought it was just a story.'

'What?'

'That the captain of a ship in international waters can marry people.'

'They can under certain circumstances.'

She teased him: 'What are those?'

'Money,' Winston said.

37

March 1878–1892 Christmas
The antipodean

'So you are Winston's little crime of passion! Who would have guessed he would return from the Antipodes with his own little Antipodean!' Not even *Australian*, but like a koala bear, or a kangaroo. Many possible wives had looked forward to Winston's return, and greeted the joyous Mrs Prideau with English jealousy, patronisingly masking their disappointment. Plenty of other fish in the sea!

The pretence mattered to Emma. *That* was what their tittle-tattle did to her marriage. In Winston's arms, she had lived happily ever after on the ship. She stepped onto the Southampton dockside an outsider.

On the boat she had not known what to expect as he unbuttoned his shirt, seeing the pale skin beneath the red ring of his sunburned neck, then his hairy chest revealed, and everything else, covered in hair and not at all like a Greek statue as she had imagined. *All for love* – she knew what she must do, nothing, but the shock of her submission was very great. The anguish of what he did to her, and his murmured endearments, confused her, and she cried.

'My love, my darling,' he whispered, and they lay cemented by her pain. She vowed to herself she would do anything for him.

She could not bear to be separated from him for a moment. Their stateroom was one of only two on the boat with a private bathroom, and she went to the toilet with him, holding his thing while he urinated, helping him lather his face with shaving soap, holding the shaving-brush which he told her was made with black-and-white bristles of British badger hair. It was all very luxurious between them, as if all married life was purely sensuous, and it lasted for ever.

Until the ship docked.

Winston strode casually down the gangway with her in tow. Emma wore a slim bottle-green dress bought at Cape Town, gathered at the knees then flounced like petals round her ankles. Her hair, uncut during the voyage, allowed long blonde strands to escape from beneath her bottle-green hat.

From Winston's descriptions of his half-brother, she recognised Ernest Prideau at once. In his late twenties, wearing black tails, black top hat, black shoes, a stiff white collar and grey-striped trousers, he stood by the carriage that would take them to the railway. 'His first words will be,' Winston whispered, *it's all arranged.* Then he'll say we can just catch the train if we hurry.'

'Winston,' Ernest said nastily, 'what have you done?'

'Hallo chum,' Winston said, examining his fob-watch. 'This is Emma, my wife.'

'Pleased to meet you!' Ernest said rudely.

At last Winston asked: 'Aren't we late?'

They sat silently in the compartment.

Ernest said discreetly to Winston, 'May I have a word.' He bowed to Emma, who nodded inarticulately in the face of such hostility. Before the door was closed she heard Ernest saying in the corridor: 'What were you playing at, Winston? How could you be so irresponsible? How *could* you do this to us?'

Winston's reply was lost in the roar of a bridge.

Emma sat rocking miserably with the train, then pressed her ear to the wooden partition, and after a moment heard Ernest's voice moving, as though he were pacing up and down in front of Winston. 'Did you not consider the Bank at all? What of Lucinda? Why this inarticulate Australian nonentity who talks through her nose as soon as she opens her mouth? She has no *class*, Winston. What sort of dinner parties are you going to hold? You'll be a laughing-stock! That's your right – but what about the Bank, the employees? What about *me*?'

She heard Winston's voice. 'I love her,' Winston said.

Emma sat without moving when he returned. He took her in his arms.

'It's us against them,' she whispered.

'Oh,' he chuckled, 'they'll come round.'

The London of Nelson was gone, the slums pushed from the city centre into the east end out of sight and out of mind, and the gutters no longer ran with stinking human filth, which instead was carried smoothly along sewers hidden deep beneath an expanding network of underground railways; smoke from these fountained abruptly from chimneys disguised as walls or trellises of climbing flowers. Policemen in blue patrolled the impressive public boulevards. Solid and dark, interspaced with fine houses and marvellous squares with trees in leaf, the London Emma Prideau gaped at was a vast imperial metropolis whose Queen ruled the widest Empire the world had seen. The day had turned rainy and the streets were canals of shiny black umbrellas.

'This is my home now,' Emma said.

She fell in love with Winston's house in Chesterfield Street, soothing her homesickness away. She marvelled at its lovely wallpapers of rural scenes, hundreds of pictures, and pretty ornaments. Except for his sombre upstairs study with its deep armchair and view of the street, and the plain bedroom he had left behind with a single bed, it was not a man's house. The furniture was delicate and feminine; a music-stand holding a page of music signed by Chopin next to an old-fashioned piano, a Georgian chaise-longue in the reflection of a bright window.

'Yes, this is your house,' Winston said. 'It belonged to Gran-Mama Prideau long ago. I have always felt its strange attraction. My father was furious it was willed to me, which accounted for the coolness between us during his final years. He tried to exclude me from my share of the Bank, you know, its trading interests. He trusted Ernest.'

'But now you have proved yourself.'

'Yes, I believe our Australian investments will prosper.' But that was not what she had meant: she meant he had married her, and asserted himself as his own man. But she wisely held her tongue. 'Don't mind Ernest,' Winston said suddenly, 'he does not know what passion is.'

'Hold me tight!'

Winston buried his face in her neck.

Two weeks passed arranging the welcome-home party, and no debutante ever prepared herself for her coming-out more anxiously than Emma. She agonised over her choice of dress, settling for a plum-coloured one that showed off her waist. Even Winston looked shocked. 'Is it too frightful?'

'It is wonderfully daring!' he laughed.

'You don't care what they think,' she said impetuously, 'neither do I!'

When they were introduced in the hall the men bowed, very cool and proper, but afterwards in the salon their wives were very friendly and admired the dress, especially Lucinda Fleur-Boyes who wore a beautiful maroon satin dress and lustrous pearl earrings, almost ten years older than Emma but still unmarried. She had teeth of finest West African ivory. 'So you are Winston's little crime of passion! He has returned from the Antipodes with his own little Antipodean!' And there it was: the irresistible phrase coined, the damage done. Lucinda's ancestors had probably come over with William the Conqueror, her lineage, like her teeth, impeccable.

'Don't you patronise me,' Emma said.

Lucinda laughed like a sailor. 'Say *Australia* for me.'

'Australia.'

'There you are – *Oztralia*!' hee-hawed Lucinda for the benefit of the circle of women. 'Divine!'

Emma cried later. 'I hate your friends,' she told Winston. 'They classify me, like . . . like a Neanderthal!'

'They mean no harm. They're just having fun. You'll learn to deal with them.'

She did, of course, but now she was always the outsider looking in. Words never came easily to her, but she learned to speak English like an Englishwoman. 'Be yourself,' Winston begged her, shaking his head. But no one but he would accept her as herself. All she had was Winston; she wrote letters to her father, but Jack never answered. His business relationship with Ernest was immensely profitable, work on the mining railway from Emu Bay to Waratah (the homeliness of those names!) was proceeding apace. Jack blamed her, not Winston, for her elopement – the man in such an affair might be a scoundrel, but at least his point of view, knowing the power and rightness of male desire, was understandable; Emma was beautiful; *her* action was inexcusable. 'You turned your back on me,' was the way Jack's mind worked, 'therefore my back is turned to you.' But still Emma wrote the long letters, until gradually her spirit faltered and she wondered if he ever even read them.

She fell into a sullen mood.

One winter's day whirling with sooty snowflakes, she discerned a grey caped figure cross the street, then heard the jangling of the bell. She waited in suspense while the butler, Cayman, responded to the summons, and the parlour door was opened.

It was Ernest. He looked lean and tense as always. She turned up the gas in the firelit room with its view of the swirling street. Cayman had taken his cloak and hat and she wondered whether she should call for tea and cakes; he looked like he needed feeding up. 'Sit down, Ernest, why don't you.'

'I shan't stay. Your mother has communicated to me that her father, Councillor Briggs, has died of cancer.'

'I see. I shall write my condolences.'

'Is that all? You will not be returning to the Antipodes?'

'Can't you bloody well bring yourself to call it Australia? Why do you hate me?'

'I don't hate you,' Ernest smiled. 'You are an ambitious woman, you seduced Winston for your own purposes.'

'That's quite untrue!'

'I'm glad we're talking. He deserved better than you, Emma. Lucinda is worth two million and is the same circle with the Burdett-Coutts clan. She is in love with Winston. I arranged it all,' he accused her.

'I'm glad I spoilt your scheme. Winston isn't like that.'

'Oh, I know that,' he admitted breathtakingly. He sat primly in the armchair opposite her, hitched up the trouser of his crossed leg. 'You have brought Winston no benefit, you know. You're destroying his work. He's lost his edge, his brilliance. You could save him, you see.'

'By going back to Australia.'

'If you really loved him you would go. It could be arranged.'

'I'm sure it could!' Emma's lips quivered, she could not help them; her dark eyebrows drew together into a single line, which her mother had always said was her worst feature.

He stood. 'You will consider what I have said. You are without friends here, Emma. At this time your mother would welcome you back, and if *she* did, then your father would.'

She called to him at the door: 'Why didn't Winston tell me about Briggs's death?'

'Because he was frightened you would go.' There was an implacable truthfulness about Ernest. 'I should add that in a way. . . . actually I haven't yet told him. My message awaits him on his desk.' Ernest allowed Cayman to put the cape over his shoulders, then touched his stick politely to the brim of his hat, and left.

Emma waited by the fire for Winston to come home.

'My darling,' he said, 'I have some very bad news for you.'

'Thank God!' she said, and threw her arms round him.

She had won her small victory over Ernest, but gradually she realised he was determined to win the war. She could think of no reason for his hostility and did everything she could to allay it, but he just smiled at her weakness. He was impeccably polite, classically educated, conservative and rapacious. She knew nothing of his business life and could not talk to him on his own terms. Before Winston's visit to the Far East and China – Ernest said, smiling, 'Get some of that brilliance back, Winston, eh?' – Emma became convinced that they must conceive a child before he left, but it was not to be. When he had gone she told herself the child would have given her legitimacy as his wife; she told herself she had missed her opportunity. But why did she have to prove herself?

If only she had some real chums – she'd thought

London would be like Hobart Town but bigger, brighter, closer to heaven, and in a way it was. She could buy anything in the shops, and the theatres and shows were magnificent. But though she was often surrounded by brilliant people and witty conversation, it never seemed to include her; or she never included herself, unsettled by Ernest's opinion of her. Perhaps she really was just the colonial adventuress his eyes said she was.

She was not quite so sure of Winston's love when he returned, greeting her almost absent-mindedly on the Southampton dockside exhausted by his year's travels, kissing her forehead then falling at once into deep conversation with Ernest about far-eastern financial matters. Winston had put on too much weight before he left, but now she was sure he had lost too much, and she was determined to feed him up. Cook was ordered to prepare duffs and roly-polys. By a multitude of such small signs did Emma show her love for the husband she had given up everything for.

'You have never left my heart,' he whispered in bed.

But she couldn't be sure. He was always away at work; the Bank required him to meet large numbers of people, but she met almost none, so she wanted to talk when he most needed silence; her days were empty so she was full of life when he returned home exhausted, too tired to notice all the little things she did for him. Tired of taking decisions about everything under the sun, he could not really care about her chatter over the colour of new curtains or carpet, or enjoy her pleasurable indecision. It irritated him. And as he grew older, and heavier, he lost his quick grace and languid charm, acquiring the forceful indomitability of middle age. He travelled as far as Canton and San Francisco, but she never got further than Deauville.

Sometimes she felt he was dealing with her like a customer. If she had a problem, he settled it. Perhaps an elopement had been fine and fierce in the flood of it, but after a decade. . . . a man of forty wished it had been done differently.

They lived the lives they were expected to lead, formed by the expectations of others. Winston's solidity was expected of a man in his position, just as her too fashionable clothes were demanded of her, and must be discarded the moment they were *passée*.

But what about *them* – Emma and Winston?

A child would bind them. Emma desired that noisy bundle to the point of obsession as a panacea to all her ills. But the years passed, and despite one or two false promises nothing happened.

She was not totally alone; she had one real friend, a world away, Ezzie.

Although they had never imagined it at the time – but Ezzie had sensed it – a true bond had been forged between the three women, Emma, Ezzie and Lily, that day on the reclaimed shore of Wrest Point. Emma had been too young, but Ezzie had seen into her as though her flesh were transparent. Without Ezzie there would have been no Winston, no London, no love or grief.

The old woman's letters from Farm Cove, densely scrawled in her strangely cramped handwriting, were postmarked *Strahan Post Office, Macquarie Harbour*, on hardy yellow paper watermarked *Frank O'Henry's Pioneer Stores*. The letters took at least three months to arrive, but one arrived every month and Emma could visualise the chain of them crossing the ocean, small litanies of daily life. Sometimes the lives of the families there seemed closer to her than her own London acquaintances. The names of those distant places clinging to the edge of the wilderness acquired a kind of magic to Emma: Trial Harbour, less a harbour than a pool behind the reefs; the King and Queen rivers, the Gordon River deep as the Thames, plunging through endless forest, and ravines that cut out the light of the sky. This was life at a place Emma had never been to but could visualise perfectly. After the glaciers retreated Britain, even London, had been like this for nearly all its history: rivers and forest. The word was home.

She unfolded the latest letter. *'Dearest Emma –'*

She folded it again and ran upstairs, threw herself down on the bed in a shaft of mellow autumn sunlight, then luxuriously began again. Ezzie's writing was old-fashioned with funny capital letters.

22 June 1886

> *Farm Cove*
> *Macquarie Harbour*

Dearest Emma

Midwinter has come again and rain lashes the windows, every Time I look up the cloudscape has changed, and the harbour is full of breaking waves the colour of Mud. . . .

Emma closed her eyes, seeing the scene.

My news, of course, if Lily has not already written to You, is that she has, surprise surprise, already given birth to her New Baby!

Emma's eyes filled with tears.

We are calling him Lawrence, so everyone calls him Larry. I think we should call him the Throwback – the child has Brown Eyes! We have no idea where he gets them from – something cropping up from the distant past I suppose. . . .

Emma skipped ahead until she came to news of Lily.

Lily thought she had completed her Family – her first was Morgan, who is now sixteen and very practical-minded about the place, I am sure he will be Ordering us about soon enough – and then she had the two girls, and thought her childbearing days were over – and then, there appeared another! But a very wonderful surprise He is, gurgling away with His curly Brown hair and bright Brown eyes. . . .

Emma wondered how old Lily was. At Wrest Point Lily had worn colourful clothes and tight stays to disguise her dumpiness, but Emma guessed Lily would have been rather older than her own age now, twenty-seven: if Lily had been thirty-five – Emma's mind worked busily – the Surprise would have happened when she was over forty! Emma breathed a sigh of relief. There was time for her yet.

But when *she* was forty, Winston would be well over fifty.

Life was so short.

Gradually, as nothing happened, her fretting turned to worry, and she could hardly bring herself to eat.

'You're prettier than ever,' Winston grunted as the flunkey opened their carriage door and they stepped down into the porte-cochère of the Royal Opera House. 'You've lost weight, Emma.'

'Thank you.'

'It's not fashionable. Don't want you to get skinny,' Winston said.

He loved the opera, and loved to boom snatches from his favourite arias on their way home. Although she was tone-deaf and preferred the theatre, she pressed his hand with the light of tenderness in her eyes at the pleasure the evening had given him. 'You could have been a great opera singer,' she told him, and he looked at her strangely.

'Nonsense!' he said. The carriage turned along the darkened streets. 'You didn't enjoy the evening,' he said at last. 'You don't care anything for singing.'

'It pleased you, so it pleased me.'

'That's one way of looking at it, I suppose!'

After they had undressed and got into bed, she knew how to touch him, and he rolled over and took her although he was half-asleep. Afterwards she quietly put back the covers and lifted her legs in the air.

'What are you doing?' he grumbled.

'I want to be sure to have a baby.'

'You look ridiculous,' he grunted, turning over, 'you are ridiculous!'

I don't mind, if I have my baby, she thought but did not say.

Nearly all her social acquaintances had children, often six or eight of whom survived, now that drinking water was fresh and sewers discharged downriver. The bored women Emma knew all complained about nannies and schools, but it seemed to her that they didn't see nearly enough of their children, and she bit her lips at their ingratitude.

She decided to privately consult a gynaecologist. The man recommended to her was very good, a great deal better than she wanted to hear. Doctor Henry Summers, clever to the point of sharpness, pronounced her in marvellous health. 'No fault lies with you, I assure you.'

'But it must!'

'Conception is a matter of chance; you must be patient.'

'I have almost lost hope.'

'Perhaps you do not have a propensity to conceive – just one of those things – heredity – have you not heard of the work of Gregor Mendel? Characteristics can be passed on in humans, it seems, just as they can in plants.' Fifteen years ago he had married Jemima Fox of Holywell in Kent, where generations of that family had lived in the same house reputedly for centuries. 'What do you know of *your* family, Mrs Prideau? We stand on the shoulders of our ancestors, you see.' He watched her face. 'You are Australian, are you not?'

'That's no sin,' she said, angry and defensive.

'Then I should examine your husband, not you.'

She shook her head. Winston would never permit such an astounding interference in his affairs, being treated like bloodstock. She stood impetuously.

'Mrs Prideau, perhaps you should examine your marriage.'

456

'There's nothing wrong with our marriage,' she said miserably.

Ernest was waiting for her one day in Hyde Park; it could not have been an accident. He walked along the yellow gravel beside her, uncharacteristically silent in the fresh spring sun. Like Winston he was a man of property, proud with the confidence of third-generation wealth and social standing, condescending in the home with the tyranny of good manners, and capable of ruthlessness to the point of rapacity in business. Though younger, he was subtly the senior partner, never not at work. He cleared his throat nervously. 'Emma, we have never been friends.'

'I wouldn't put it even so high, chum.'

'I believed you were bad for Winston, and thus for the Prideau Bank, and I have remained loyal to both.'

'You're stuffy, Ernest.'

'Well, then – you are the first to know. I am to be married.'

'Why honour me?'

He shrugged. 'I wanted to tell you first.'

'You've fallen in love!' she taunted him. 'Is she well-connected or just rich?'

'Since you ask, she is the second daughter of an hereditary peer. The Lockhart family have vast estates in Yorkshire. However her father, Edward, the ninth Lord Cleremont, prefers London. He has been a Gentleman-in-Waiting to Her Majesty. We handle his accounts. I merely wish you to understand.'

'I certainly do understand you. What's the name of your prize?'

'Diana – Lady Diana Lockhart. Emma, I want you to be friends with her.'

Emma stopped. 'Why?'

'Because it's important to me.' He dug the ferrule of

457

his stick among the tiny pebbles. 'I wish a quiet, decorous home life, no waves.'

Emma said: 'Leave Winston alone.'

Ernest looked genuinely surprised. 'Hasn't he told you? Winston is off to the far east. Singapore, Hong Kong, Manila, he will be away at least a year.'

Emma greeted her new sister-in-law like ice, but the miracle was that she and the shy Yorkshire girl rapidly became firm friends. Diana and Ernest were married very early in 1889 at St Andrew Undershaft, the afternoon sun streaming through the faces of the Monarchs of England in the west window – William the Third looking rather new, and the wainscotting still smelling of turpentine after the recent renovations. Her aristocratic father was yawning at his fob watch as Diana, her mousy hair and dry skin hidden beneath her virgin white veil, beautiful for a day, said 'I do' and became The Honourable Mrs Ernest Prideau. Her pallid hands shook visibly and Emma's heart went out to her. After a wedding breakfast at the Londonderry Hotel paid for by the parsimonious peer, of warm gravy poured over cold roast beef, the happy pair honeymooned in Yorkshire. To Ernest's relief the Boulanger crisis on the Continent depressed the money markets and he had to rush back to London.

Diana and Emma had both everything and nothing in common. Diana had been brought up, with her other sisters, in a draughty pile of a castle on the Yorkshire moors. Pampered, repressed and deserted – only the eldest boy, the heir, mattered – they were tolerated as liabilities in the lottery of chance required to achieve the birth of the male. Shadows, they rarely saw their father, who lived in London.

'You're so lucky,' Diana murmured, 'you had a father who loved you!'

'I'm not lucky,' Emma said.

Diana touched Emma's hair, which had gone darker

458

in the soft English sun, but retained its curl and lustre. 'You are,' she said.

'My father tolerated my elopement with Winston, I see that now. He put his bloody prosperity ahead of everything.' Emma's mouth twisted into an ugly line in her bitterness, and her eyebrows drew together.

The two women knelt by the fire, their arms round one another in their loneliness.

They were not lonely for long. Diana's pregnancy – the pregnancy Emma could not have – might have destroyed their friendship with envy, but instead it drew them even closer together. Diana told Emma everything, excited and afraid, and as Diana's waistline swelled it became a shared enterprise, going out to the Oxford Street shops together to choose cradles and christening-robes, the gowns Diana would wear for her lying-in, arranging a room at home and a wet-nurse and all the myriad details. Emma almost felt she was having the baby herself, and was the second – Dr Summers was the first – to hold Diana's pink, mewling bundle.

'John Ernest,' Ernest proclaimed, handing him to the minister as the child was baptised, inevitably, in Leadenhall only a few minutes walk for the men from the Bank, and the business world from which they excluded their wives.

Playing with baby, watching him begin to smile, watching for the first time he turned over by himself, waiting for him to slide forward into a crawl, then watching anxiously for him to take his first tottering steps, Diana and Emma entered the home-world from which they excluded their men. But by the time Ernest came home, Emma would be gone. She was still the outsider.

She had put on her hat and gloves and was going down the steps for her morning visit to Diana's house in Red Lion Square just before Christmas when the second post arrived. She recognised the cramped, old-styled writing immediately. It was postmarked Hobart Town; but it was from Ezzie.

Dear Emma,

I am not Aware if you knew I was here in Hobart Town when your mother Died, but I assure you she suffered no Pain near the End. . . .

Emma stared at the letter with stony eyes. Her mother was dead after some sort of long illness, obviously, and her father had not told her. Neither had Ezzie. No pain *near the end* must mean she had suffered it before. How much did Emma not know?

38

Christmas 1892–1896 January
The throwback

Sails close-hauled and tight as boards in the gale, the yacht *Ezzie* clawed around in a turn beneath the bleak spray-fountained cliffs of Cape Sorell and flew towards Hell's Gates. The rising waves kicked up by the shoaling water roared into foam as high as the masts, and ahead of them in the narrowing channel Nigger Head Rock surged up black and streaming, and still the wild wind blew.

Old age must make its pleasures where it would, recapture youth where it could. Ezzie Pride defied her frailty, standing stiff and crutched at the rail near the two seamen on the helm, a third seaman behind her with his hand clenched in the rigging, almost touching her shoulder with his arm, ready in an instant to catch her should she tremble; her bones were brittle as chalk, but her dignity was indomitable.

Ahead of them in the white breakers they glimpsed the yellow sea bed, the deck inclining forward as though to bury the bowsprit in the racing sand, flip them end over end as the wave gathered under them; but instead it carried them through into the calm waters of Macquarie Harbour.

One of the seamen began to laugh, looking superstitiously back at the woman. No one knew how old she was, not even she; Ezzie's face was riven and cracked, her bound hair thin and pale, blue eyes boiled and ancient.

'Thank you, gentlemen,' she said in her strong voice, including them all in her gaze, and they realised how tough she was.

She stood alone now, staring over the railing at the distant mountains. Once all had been forested, but now the green shoulder of Mount Lyell was streaked with sulphurous orange-yellow smears of bare rock above a haze of sulphur fumes and woodsmoke.

She alone knew how frail she was, feeling the unremitting ache of her life – of her withered arm, which had always been part of her, but now of almost everything else, muscle, bone, heart – the ache almost totally possessed her, her personality and memory leaking back to the earth which conjured them. But her spirit was still her own: these small bright moments of pleasure, of not being defeated, standing out like islands from the rising tide of darkness.

Old age conferred dignity and wisdom but in return endured the greatest indignities. Her brain achieved scope and simplicity but her body was unable to put it into action. At her great age, what lay before her was not death but childhood.

Where do I come from? Here I come home.

Here at last were the calm waters. Far to the north across the dunes of Ocean Beach and the terrible bauera country she saw the line of the Heemskirk highland, its worthless tin mines drowned in forest, and with them the money Jack Pride had speculated. Inland she saw the sharp peak and wooded ridges of Mount Zeehan, source of silver and lead and a squalid, squelching boomtown of tents that seemed to double in number each year. She chuckled: poor dear Jack, blowing on his burnt fingers no doubt, had missed out on that opportunity – though Fergus Matheson, playing roulette with the confidence of dotage and immense wealth, had not. Jack, on the other hand, all those leagues away in Hobart Town and egged on by the enthusiasm of Thureau, the government geologist, had dropped £20,000 into the King River Syndicate, which found enough alluvial gold to justify such enormous expenditure on mining machinery, and then no more; the money was gone literally into a hole in the ground.

But only the small men went bankrupt. Until last year.

The crash of the Van Diemen's Land Bank ended the days of the Hobartons: many of Tasmania's finest families lost their wealth. Desperate investors and depositors gathered unavailingly outside the Bank's slammed doors. It turned out many of the loans had been unsecured; gold bullion bolstering accounts that did not exist. Thomas Giblin and Burgess, the managing director, begged personally for Jack Pride to intervene, but he set his face against them like stone. Within days his late wife's shares, which he had hungered for as a young man and which had hung over him all his business life, were worthless. The assets of the great institution were raffled, houses, businesses, hotels, even the Bank's gracious premises, changing hands by the drawing of a number, no doubt to Jack's advantage. By now cunning and success were second nature to him. As the terrible worldwide depression of the 1890s deepened, Jack was by far the colony's pre-eminent banker.

Ezzie sighed, staring over the railing as Long Bay opened up to port, revealing the red tin roofs of Strahan. From the smart fore-and-aft schooner *May Newton* moored at the jetty on west Strahan beach, the wharfies had already unloaded a string of ore-cars ready for when the railroad opened. But still she thought sadly of her son. Once Jack in his cleverness had pretended to have a cold heart; now it had come true.

The Depression shut most of the fledgling West Coast mines – the capital investment was too great for Tasmanian banks to risk. The Australian banks, who stood by while the Bank of Van Diemen's land collapsed, had moved in, and through them the British tightened their grip. Talk of federation with Australia was now open in Tasmanian political circles; there seemed no alternative. Jack had had London backers for years, but only collaborated with them on the railway projects and the large Hydro hotel now planned in Hobart Town. The railways were fine investments and the original Emu Bay project to Waratah had now been extended south to booming Dundas and Zeehan. The railway the syndicate was building from the Strahan docks had now fought its way across dunes and through bauera swamps to within half a dozen miles of Zeehan.

Ezzie ordered the captain to bring her yacht into Risby Cove. Strahan, built along one shore of the inlet – the old settlement at Smith's Cove turned out not to have enough fresh water – was the coming place. Where ten years ago there had been only marsh, Ezzie gazed at proud wooden buildings along the Esplanade, the Grinings' boatyard, Frank O'Henry's pioneer store, Herr Zeplin's King River Hotel in the middle of the road where the Christmas celebrations, from the sound of his expert piano playing, were in full swing. The yacht turned and cruised by new wharves where two years ago there had been only ramshackle jetties. Piner topsail-schooners laden with sawn Huon were tied up among the two-man fishing skiffs, waiting for Hell's Gates to fall calm, and for the end of the festivities. Men spilled out of Zeplin's place, rough but good-natured in their best clothes and dusty slouch hats, millionaires and stony brokes dancing man-to-man in the street. Ezzie watched: it seemed this shimmering moment in the early afternoon must live for ever. A Huon had been set up as a Christmas tree hard by the Risby brothers' sawmill.

'Send ashore a couple of cases of Cascade beer,' Ezzie

said suddenly, 'with my compliments.' A whoop went up. They would drink to her health; she needed that. The yacht turned towards the open water, heeling past Regatta Point, and gradually the cheerful sounds on the Esplanade faded astern.

Almost immediately the remoteness of the wilderness enclosed Ezzie, a limitless expansion of spirit. The wind died away during the afternoon and it was not until the light airs of evening that the *Ezzie* rode slowly into Farm Cove.

The candlelight flickered golden slits inside Larry's brown eyes, like a cat. The impression was so strong that it gave even dull Morgan pause. What was the kid up to now? Morgan, pale and tall – in his early twenties he was a full foot taller than his mother, and Lily had once joked, in the days when she joked, that as a baby he had come out like a long piece of string – Morgan slipped back into the shadows, watching Larry cup the candleflame in his hands against the breaths of air. Larry was six-and-a-half-years-old, and keeping that candle alight was everything to him as he followed the trail to the seashore.

Morgan followed him at a distance, stumbling. The twilight had almost failed and the Cove was a pale sheen silhouetting the graceful blackwood tree, the Christmas tree. No one was here yet, Morgan saw: only the candleflame and the little figure of Larry, staring out into the gleaming silence.

'Hey, Throwback,' Morgan said, and blew out the candle. 'What are you carrying that for? Are you mitching off from your chores? The party doesn't start until it's proper dark, you know. It's no good you thinking you'll be allowed to light the fires!'

'Look,' Larry whispered.

Her sails rigged goose-winged to catch the last breaths of air, the white yacht drifted soundlessly in

465

her reflection by Soldiers Island. Larry ran to the jetty and swarmed over the rail as the yacht slid alongside. 'We're having a bonfire!' he informed Ezzie breathlessly. The old woman hugged him while Morgan watched.

'Come on!' she said. 'Let's get ashore!'

Peter came down leading the party from the ranch house. Larry was allowed to light the bonfire and as the flames rose, making the tree's tinsel glitter and the long red and yellow ribbons shimmer like colourful tails, the children ran down, the boys drawn to the bonfire, the girls around the tree holding candles. Then the parents came down carrying babies in swaddling, hurricane lamps, and food baskets that the babies would be put in later when the mutton chops and steaks were eaten; the smell of frying food began to rise. Ezzie, bolt-upright in an armchair set on the grass, watched the scene with all her attention, as if fixing it for ever in her memory. Peter put his hand on her shoulder, then he winked at her and said nothing. She squeezed his hand gratefully.

You're all my family, she thought, and remembered when she was young, when she was alone and had nothing of this to be part of. For all its faults and failures, what a marvellous life she had lived. A feeling of sadness suffused her rambling, unstitching mind, not for Bob who had long gone on, but for Jack her son who was not here, her one great regret.

There were others who were not here – the Prestons had loaded all their possessions on Captain Reid's coaster *Yambacoona* and steamed back to King Island for another try. The Island had been surveyed by John Brown in 1887 and reported green again; even the trees had come back, mostly fast-growing gums, and Brown reckoned that with modern agricultural techniques, superphosphate fertiliser to enrich the soil and hedges of African box-thorn to break the wind, settlers were in with a chance.

Ezzie reached out to Peter. 'If only Rebecca were with us,' she murmured.

'If only,' he said. Rebecca and her children, with Gideon her precious only boy, were no longer living here with Josh Simmonds. It was impossible to imagine Peter's chief stockman moving from Farm Cove; his lean, striding form, sinewy muscle and open-neck red flannel shirt were as much part of the landscape as the trees. Standing by the fire guarding other men's children from the flames, Josh saw them looking down at him, and touched his hat. They sensed the hurt within him, the wound that would never heal. He loved Rebecca still, and she loved him.

'If only,' Ezzie said, then grunted. It was Rebecca's stock phrase, *if only* this were different, *if only* that. It had been Rebecca's sure conviction that Gideon deserved better than outback life, he had such a fine discerning brain, and the thought of her only son stopping school – such as school was, in the backroom of Paragon House – at the age of fourteen like the other children, wasting their lives to help their fathers in manual work, was almost unbearable to her. If only things could be arranged differently. *She* must arrange them – the men of Macquarie Harbour kept their women in their place, and called anyone with ideas a hungry bastard – but everyone agreed Gideon was bright, which meant he stood no chance, Rebecca thought bitterly. So she arranged, by herself, without telling Josh, for Gideon to be placed in supervised lodgings in Hobart Town with a lady who provided that service to out-farmers. But soon Rebecca had fretted at her lack of control. She was frightened that Gideon would slip away – just *slip away* out of her fingers into the chaos that lay beneath them, everywhere, but if she went to him that meant leaving her

467

little girls, so they would have to go to Hobart Town too. She convinced herself that Rachel, her youngest daughter, was backward. If *only* she could have the push she needed! 'Josh, I'm going to move to Hobart Town where there are specialist doctors who can help Rachel, and Ruth can go to a proper school.'

'But you're my wife and I love you,' Josh protested. 'You can't be odd like this. What will people say?'

'Don't take this from me, my darling!' Rebecca said earnestly, 'our love is so strong, we don't need to cling to one another like children, do we?'

'But I *love* you,' Josh said.

She kissed her fingers and pressed them to his lips. 'We don't need to be together,' she told him, 'if you really love me.'

She never came back. She visited from time to time, but she never really came back, and they lay together embarrassed like strangers. It was better she stayed away; that way they were still in love, still had each other.

Rebecca's life was in Hobart Town now. Gideon had passed effortlessly – of course – through the High School and the University, and was now working in a law office in Sydney. Rebecca was glad because, though he was far from her, he was sure to meet a better class of girl. In her opinion the young ladies of Hobart Town were simple, gigglish creatures with no social graces; she made sure that Ruth was put through the Proprietary Ladies College, and Rachel plodded on with private tutors until finally Rebecca took her over herself.

They were both happily married now with children of their own, far from Rebecca who remained in Hobart Town.

'Do you think she'll ever come back?' Ezzie whispered.

'*If only*,' Peter said. Lily called him peevishly to start

cooking the chops. Ezzie thought what a fine couple they looked in the flaring flamelight, Peter tall and muscular with his long swept-back hair. Lily, ever the practical one, her well-rounded shape seeming shorter than ever despite the chunky heels on her shoes, her greying hair scraped back and a certain piercing hardness in her eyes from the hardness of her life, suddenly softened and put her arms round Peter, standing on tiptoe and kissing him in public. Morgan pretended not to notice – Rebecca would have had that young man in university long ago – but Larry was young enough to stare curiously, the firelight dancing in his brown eyes. Ezzie crooked her finger.

He ran over to her. Ezzie's arthritis was too bad to take him on her lap, but he curled himself along the padded arm then cuddled warmly in beside her.

'What have you done today?' she asked, intensely attracted to him.

'I went swimming,' he said, and she shivered. 'I swam to Soldiers Island to feed my pig there, Grandma.'

'You be careful,' she said, 'the water's deep.'

'I've given her a name and she's mine.'

'What name have you given her?'

'Esmerelda.'

'I was a fine swimmer when I was young,' Ezzie said fondly, 'I thought I would never grow old.'

'Morgan says you've always been old.' Larry was awed.

She said sadly: 'It must seem like that to a child.'

'Larry, don't be a nuisance!' Lily came over, her mouth strict, but then she didn't pull him away. Fergus Matheson, buried at Strahan, had left Lily a very large fortune, enough for her to do anything she wanted, but she stayed for Peter's sake, and she didn't act like a rich woman. With Larry her touch was a little hesitant – perhaps it was because he was born so late, in her forty-fourth year, perhaps because he was a dreamer, like Peter. But those brown eyes! Morgan called him 'Throwback' out of half-affectionate sibling rivalry, Ezzie from half-proud amusement, and of course Lily hardly noticed them most of the time, but there they were, always, suddenly excluding her, a mystery. She was at pains to love him carefully because of this, which Morgan knew well. She could relax with neither of her sons.

'Run away and play,' Ezzie told Larry, patting his hip.

'Shall I bring you a chop, Gran?' he asked eagerly. 'And a baked potato?'

'I reckon I can handle that,' Ezzie said tolerantly. She was almost beyond food. The conviction was growing on her that this was her last Christmas. She was wrong.

The flow of letters between Ezzie Prideau at Macquarie Harbour, and Emma Pride in London, continued. Ezzie became housebound after a fall towards the end of the year, the arthritis in her hips by now so bad that it seemed she would never walk again. Her bed was turned by the French windows during the day, and in the summer the doors were left open on the green vista below her to the shining bowl of Farm Cove, a caldera, the eroded mouth of an ancient volcano filled by the waters of the harbour. When the weather was set fine and windless for the day, her bed was wheeled out on the upstairs verandah and a large, square, white-tasselled parasol put up to protect her head from the sun. Sometimes Larry brought her small surprises, honey if he'd found a bee-tree on his childish explorations, and once a small bright parrot. Lily looked at it doubtfully and searched out a cage, but Ezzie trained the little bird to return for crumbs from her lips. These small pleasures were the limits of her life. She was vaguely pleased Lily and Peter had moved into the house to look after her; Ezzie called him Bob by mistake. The captains of the steamers who passed the entrance to Farm Cove with increasing frequency tooted their sirens, and Lily said they were saluting her, but Ezzie murmured that it was for the Paragon of Virtue, sunfaded and splitting, bolted to the verandah railing.

Yet none of this seemed quite real to her.

Her memories of London grew more vivid than the world around her and Emma's letters seemed invested with echoes, shadows glimpsed, an emotion of loss. The friends her granddaughter wrote of seemed more real than the family around Ezzie. She wasn't unhappy; she had never been happier. Unfolding Emma's gracefully written lilac-coloured letters, or writing painfully with her own clawed hand, the sensation grew on Ezzie that she was going home.

Emma had come to marvel at the city where she'd made her life, and finally to love smokey, sooty, infernal, aristocratic London. She had everything to make her happy, except contact with her widowed father, Jack, who obstinately refused to forgive her desertion; and except a child of her own.

From her own hard experiences Ezzie felt what her granddaughter was going through. Emma had come to feel her lack was her own fault, a failure of her wifely duty, and so blamed herself that Winston no longer seemed so close to her – he had become absorbed in his City work to the point of obsession, she wrote, just like his brother Ernest. Winston was invulnerably self-confident in his success, clubbing with men rather than his wife, their only holidays the male company of grouse shoots; leaving her with the women playing cards. This was hellish for Emma, because she loved him.

She had learned to play the piano, with her grace and dexterity Emma picked up any manual skill quickly, and she even learned to sing. She must have been born with a fine voice, although her ears could not discern it, but for Winston's sake she learned to sing parlour-songs tolerably well. For his sake she forced herself to like the opera. For his sake she learned these things, but still her brain fed her tongue Australianisms that made her stand out.

Then a letter arrived for Ezzie and Lily opened it for her. Ezzie grunted and held it in her claw. The wind from the sea fluttered the paper: it was dated, of course, two months ago, November 1895.

Emma was going to have a baby.

Ezzie knew what she must do. She said: 'I'm going back to Hobart Town to see Jack.'

'She can't!' Lily said. 'She can't, she's too old, she's dying.'

'She knows it,' Peter said sadly. 'She's nearly as old as the century; there can't be much she doesn't know.'

'She's *dying*, Peter. She won't survive the voyage to Hobart Town. We can't take the responsibility.'

'You try stopping her,' Peter said.

Ezzie walked step by painful step along the path leading down the curved green slope of Farm Cove to her yacht waiting at the jetty, Peter propping her up on one side, Josh on the other almost carrying her. Lily had dressed her in black bombazine and Larry was given her valise to carry. He scampered ahead, joyful in his youth and strength. Morgan, who would accompany Ezzie to look after her, was already on deck. He had never been away from Macquarie Harbour before.

'I'll be back for your tenth birthday, Throwback, so you be good,' he threatened. 'You look after your mother, now.' Morgan's cool temperament was very dutiful, or maybe he was just trying to cling on. He put out his hand for Larry to shake, but the little boy hugged his elder brother without affectation.

'I'm going to miss you, Morgan.'

'I'll be back soon!' Morgan said desperately, very tall and trembling. 'For God's sake go away, Larry,' he said roughly, and snatched the valise, 'or my mates will see me like this.'

Ezzie looked back at the house and said goodbye. Lily and Peter embraced her, Josh shook her hand, Larry gravely presented her with a seashell. The sails caught the breeze and the yacht turned away on the dark water. Larry swam alongside as far as Soldiers Island. He was a strange boy.

39

1896

A death, a life

It was an awful voyage, the south-westerlies from the Antarctic unrelenting, but the old woman bore her misfortune with equanimity. She could have had the vessel put in at Launceston and taken the railway, but by now, she said, the yacht was part of her. In truth she was too weak to leave her cabin.

'You look old,' she told off Jack spiritedly, as he followed the nurse helping her upstairs at Wrest Point House. It was a single man's house now. The staff kept it dusted and immaculate, but inside was gloomy, the curtains kept half-drawn against the hot blue light of the Derwent.

'Me – old!' Jack said in his dry, calm voice.

Ezzie looked around the nurse's shoulder. '*You* know, Jack, why I have come back.'

Jack braced his hands on his lapels. 'You won't leave again,' he said. Then he called earnestly: 'Why here?' and she saw his baffled look.

'Where my son is, my home is.'

'Mother, you just want to interfere in my life,' Jack said.

'The privilege of a dying woman.'

'Don't talk in that manner.'

'Emma is having a baby.'

Jack turned, hearing a rustle behind him. 'It's true,' Morgan said. 'It's in a letter.' He held it out.

'I won't read it,' Jack said. He ordered the nurse: 'Put her in the bedroom.'

With Nurse Lyons living in, the old woman was no trouble at all, yet her presence behind the closed door dominated the house. Morgan settled in, eating with Jack at the long table every night; Lyons fed Ezzie upstairs.

'She wants to die here,' Morgan said at last. 'Won't you at least hear why, sir?' He could not bear to keep his mouth shut any longer; his own father was too emotional to be fully trustworthy, but the dry-as-ice coldness of his uncle surveying him from the far end of the table was something he had never encountered before, both frightening and admirable in its self-control.

'She's a cunning woman,' Jack explained, 'you can't trust them.'

'No, sir.'

'I'll give you good advice here, Morgan,' Jack said, 'never marry. I swore once I'd never marry. Swore it.'

Morgan said, surprisingly, 'Who was she, sir?'

Jack looked at him with respect. 'You're a sharp boy. Lily's boy. You're clever, aren't you.'

Morgan instinctively hid the feeling of excitement which ran through him. 'I've had no proper schooling, sir.'

'That's good. I'll give you all the schooling you need.' Jack sighed and drained his glass. 'Come with me to the Bank tomorrow. Eight-thirty sharp.' He got up with a last glance at the ceiling. 'We can't escape women, you know. Especially our mothers.'

But Morgan's life was transformed.

There was nothing dry or cold about Jack Pride at work in Hobart's Square Mile: he came to life, yet such was his confidence in himself that he appeared almost casual in his rapidity. He took decisions with extraordinary efficiency, his brow unmarked by any of the furrows of worry that concerned him at home. Astonished and fascinated, Morgan watched, and waited, and learned.

'You can do this too, can't you,' Jack said one weary evening, glancing over the fur collar of his greatcoat. 'You've got the feel for it.'

'Not like you, sir.'

'No,' Jack said, 'no one will ever be as good as me.' They were sitting in the open carriage even though it was winter – Jack abhorred the fast new hydroelectric trams running to Sandy Bay, shooting sparks from the overhead lines, frightening the horses and populating suburbs previously the province of the rich with the middle classes. The carriage was returning them to Wrest Point. Jack grunted: 'Fergus Matheson left Lily a good nest-egg, I guess?'

'He did, yes.'

'I'll give you a pretty good tip. Heard of Bowes Kelly? One of the richest men in Australia, a great gambler, an Irish-Australian sheep grazier who risked a couple of hundred pounds on a fourteenth-share of Broken Hill, and inside five years it was worth a million. Broken Hill wins out fifty pounds' worth of silver for every miserable pound sterling we scratch out of Zeehan, shows how small we really are.'

'I hadn't realised.' Everything had seemed so new and vast to Morgan and to learn differently was a deep shock.

'Now, what d'you reckon happens when two Irishmen get together?' Jack asked rhetorically. 'Heard of Mount Lyell?'

'Sure, I've seen the smoke. There's a smelter there, yes?'

'But no money to pay for it. There's silver and gold at Lyell, but the *real* gold is copper – the ore body is seven per cent copper! If only Kelly can raise the money to get it out.'

476

'How much?'

'A hundred and fifty thousand pounds.' About one-fifth of the entire annual income of the Tasmanian government.

'Have they tried London?'

'Rothschild's and the copper corner wouldn't touch it last August, and all the rest of the City was on holiday shooting grouse.' Jack smiled with vindictive pleasure. 'Since the bank crashes in Marvellous Melbourne no one believes in "Australia for the Australians" more than the English do.'

'So,' Morgan asked, 'what deal are Mount Lyell having to offer?'

'Their one hundred pounds debenture pays six per cent, plus the right to exchange each one for thirty-three Mount Lyell shares any time in the next two years. It's dead bird, Morgan! If the shares soar your mother makes her money back three or four times over, and if they don't, she still collects the interest.'

'I don't think my father and mother really care about money,' Morgan said sadly. 'Since Fergus died Farm Cove doesn't even have to make a profit.'

'Everyone cares about money,' Jack said as the carriage turned into the drive.

He had almost succeeded in forgetting his own mother. Jack's evening visits to Ezzie's room were dutiful and brief, and it itched at him like a kind of guilt to see her wasting away. Partly he feared it happening to himself. There were things they must say and time was running out, but he put it off like a visit to the headmaster's study.

Nurse Lyons was waiting for him in the hall. 'Something broke in her today, Mr Pride. I really think you should see her. She's been so lonely.'

'You should have telephoned me!' he snapped.

She called after him: 'She's in terrible pain.' Morgan

took the nurse's elbow and guided her smoothly into the front room to wait. Jack went on up.

'Well!' he said heartily, 'what's this I hear!'

She didn't answer. He had never realised how deformed she was. The length of her good arm lay down the coverlet, her short arm crabbed over her chest distorting her. Her face was crumpled but her eyes were bright.

'It hurts,' she said, 'it isn't easy.'

'What? You just rest.'

'Dying,' she said. 'Midwinter. How it hurts.'

'I'll call the doctor to give you something.'

'The sun's gone down.' Her fingers closed round his like butterfly wings. 'Emma,' she said.

'Don't talk now.' A steam crane raised its rusty head, hissing and clattering beyond the trees where St Helena used to be. Jack took the chance to glance peevishly at his fob. Ezzie's fingers fluttered round his own.

'Emma,' she insisted.

To be literally full of life was a sensation not at all as unpleasant as Emma had expected. After the first few wobbly months of her pregnancy the weight inside her seemed to hold her down and give her confidence, to content her with pleasurable anticipation. She felt no worries despite her age – she was thirty-seven, which Dr Summers assured her seriously was old for a first baby, but she knew he would be there, with a lying-in nurse, and a wet-nurse, and that she would receive the finest attention. Her complexion had never been clearer, she had never felt better, she was carried forward on a swelling onrush of exultation. She made Diana laugh.

'You were born to be a mother!' Diana said walking in Hyde Park.

'Winston was completely bored by me,' Emma said carelessly, wearing a broad-brimmed hat against the midsummer sun. 'I had to do something!' It was as though the natural chemicals coursing in her blood had intoxicated her.

'You're going to be so proud,' Diana said admiringly. She looked at how Emma waddled beside her. Working men considered it indelicate for a woman to be seen out in her condition. 'You *are* making a bit of an exhibition of yourself. Shall we take a taxi home?'

'You mustn't fuss! Winston and I are going to the Haymarket Theatre this evening, will you come? It's *Trilby*.'

'You really are making no concessions! You're just as impulsive as Winston used to be!'

'It runs in the family.'

Ezzie screamed, jolting him awake, and for a moment in the dark Jack did not know where he was.

'This is my last wish,' Ezzie said clearly. 'You have made a disaster of your life, Jack, because you would never admit you've ever done anything wrong. Make it up with Emma; you aren't getting any younger.'

At arm's-length he found the switch for the electric light.

'I will,' he said, blinking.

'It's no fun being old,' Ezzie said. 'Swear to me, dear Jack.'

'Mother, treat me like a grown up.'

'Swear it!'

'Save your strength.' He sighed. 'I swear, if it makes you happy.'

'It is not a reconciliation for me, it's for you.'

He squeezed her hand tenderly, nodding.

'*This* is for me,' she whispered. 'I want to be buried at sea, in the ocean, in my yacht. Do you hear me, Jack.' Her eyes had slipped closed.

'I do hear you, yes.'

'A Viking burial,' she murmured, while Jack listened

in horror, 'the *Ezzie* burning at sea. Set sail for the great south land.'

Jack tactfully said nothing; he could foresee all sorts of insurance difficulties, and certainly the medical authorities would never permit it.

'Swear,' she said.

'I swear it.'

Ezzie raised her stunted arm. 'Now we are free,' she said, lowering her arm, and such had been her power over him that he waited for her to move again.

Emma had read George du Maurier's book *Trilby* of course; everyone had. Dying, his eyesight failing, the elegant *Punch* cartoonist had turned novelist to support his family when he could no longer see to draw, and had written a romantic masterpiece. The stage-play of the book had been the London sensation of the last two years: profits at the Haymarket were paying for the building of a brand new theatre, Her Majesty's.

Emma had seen it before, of course, like most of the audience, but it was a wonderful story. The hauntingly beautiful heroine, Trilby, was mesmerised by Svengali into becoming a brilliant singer. No wonder Winston loved the story, but tonight Emma could not quite concentrate on it: iron bands seemed to have wrapped themselves around her body, pulling tighter with ever-increasing frequency. 'Oh!' Emma said.

'Oh no,' Winston said.

The play had reached the climax where Svengali throws his hands up out of his cloak, eyes glittering and long fingers extended.

'Quick,' Emma was muttering. They had to help her up from her seat and empty the whole row to get her out, people milling in the dark gangway as the performance continued, Winston murmuring apologies, Diana holding Emma's hands to lead her. Emma was sure if she stumbled on these steps she would have

her baby there and then, but they reached the top
without incident. Half-carried, the electric-lit corridor
seemed endless to her, red and gold, doors opening and
closing.

'I can't,' Emma said.

Winston opened the door to some sort of office, then
they rushed her in, and Emma leaned back against the
desk.

'I'm sitting on my baby's head!' she said. 'Oh! Oh!'

BOOK TWO

TRILBY

Thou didst create night and I made the lamp,
Thou didst create clay and I made the cup,
Thou didst create the deserts, mountains and forests,
I produced the orchards, gardens and groves;
It is I who turn stone into a mirror,
And it is I who turn poison into an antidote.

Mohammed Iqbal

Part V

Esme

40

June 1896–1897 December

One nation

Jack did not keep his word. There could be no reconciliation. He made sure too that his mother was buried properly in a stone sarcophagus in a small mausoleum plot kept decently plain, by a minister in a cassock, with a respectful cortège of mourners wearing black hatbands as long as their faces. As for the yacht, *Ezzie*, he arranged for it to be taken back to Macquarie Harbour. Morgan didn't want to go; and Jack wanted to keep him on at the Bank. When Jack died, there would be no one to mourn him. It was winter, and Morgan stayed.

Jack felt guilty; no doubt about it. He didn't admit it to himself, but his behaviour became guilty. He took to putting on his overcoat and walking down his garden to the sea. Drops of seawater spattered his shiny black brogues, and his stiff collar hurt his throat.

Nowadays Jack often walked slowly down the Sandy Bay road and drank a glass of milk at Lipscombe's place, then sometimes he stood on the soft wet sand of Nutgrove Beach – the convict stockade long gone, the bathing huts he remembered from his childhood already rotting and ridiculous, and wondered, was it really so long ago? He watched the sleet draining from the clouds turning to rain before it hit the water, and the modern steam ferries plying busily the chilly gap between Sullivan's Cove and Bellerive. He could not quite feel part of what he saw.

487

And there was his anger, which he did not recognise – his staff were incompetent, cab drivers were rude and greedy. Federation was inevitable though no patriot wanted it; the Mineral Isle could not afford to stand alone, was sure to be gulped into the Australian maw. In his despair Jack decided to sell up Wrest Point House. There was no reason why the Hydro Hotel project, the 'Sanatorium of the South' so long in gestation and backed by a £20,000 guarantee from Ernest Prideau, should not now go ahead. Part spa-hotel, part convention centre with croquet lawns, golf, archery and tennis for the ladies, the Hydro would be a genteel place for Jack to grow old in and be treated with respect. An annexe of rooms by the roof garden would suit him well enough. He was the last of his line; everyone he respected either was dead or had rejected him. In his private life he was free! He might as well enjoy his freedom.

Seriously, there wasn't very much to enjoy nowadays. His pleasure in his cousin Rebecca's company – his first love, and still a deeply attractive woman – had decidedly cooled. Her long grey hair set into the appearance of girlish curls, she bumped into him in Collins Street and hauled him into the new Coffee Palace – she was extremely active in the Temperance Alliance and, he told himself grumpily, any other fad. He watched her across the table, finding her mannish certainty repellent. 'One Hobart Town house in every sixteen is a Public, or was.'

'Was?'

'We're doing something about it!' She gulped her steaming brew.

'*We?*'

'You've never liked me, Jack. I don't mind. I just want you to admit it,' she said brightly.

He disliked her intensely. When she first arrived in Hobart twenty years ago – but she had never fitted in here, and was still a stranger – with her baffled children in tow, Jack had almost asked her to stay in his house. Now he was glad she had gone into lodgings. She was a cuckoo, he would never have got her out.

'We must meet again,' she said, and for a moment he saw how frightened of being alone she was.

'I don't think so,' he said. Her simplicity repelled him, her worn black gloves, scuffed shoes, her righteousness. Because she was Peter's sister he had assumed she was rich, but really she was just Mrs Simmonds, the stockman's wife. Jack saw through her, and stood to go.

'You can help us,' Rebecca called. 'Each night there are children who sleep on the street. And there are children who must be taken from their parents.'

He paid the bill and left. An itinerant magician, Cadwaller the Great, had set up his cart and was working a crowd on the corner of Murray Street: a little bouncy man with Welsh patter, sticking-out front teeth and receding hair – but the sharpness of his eyes attracted Jack. A monkey was advertised but did not appear, so Mrs Cadwaller, introduced by her husband with a showman's flourish but looking appallingly nervous, made do. She had been skimpily dressed and her plump legs were goosepimpled by the freezing August wind. When, obviously in her late thirties, she clambered unsteadily into the box to be cut in half, wags in the crowd shouted it was cruel. The careworn face sticking out of the end of the box began to cry. The Great Cadwaller worked his saw with a will. 'Where's the monkey?' someone yelled. The crowd took up the chant. 'We want the monkey. We want the monkey!' It was pure entertainment, wonderful and very cruel. Afterwards a little girl of ten or so, probably the Great Cadwaller's daughter, was sent into the crowd with a hat and suddenly, of course, the street was empty. She

489

held up the hat to Jack and he thought how pretty she was, but her eyes asked for no pity.

He dropped a penny into the hat and her expression did not change.

'Good day!' Jack said, touching his stick to his hat, and turned away.

Going back to his place for lunch, a letter had arrived, placed neatly by the butler on the silver tray. Jack recognised the writing; she couldn't deceive him. The letter was from Emma in London and he knew what news it contained: the news that she had had her baby.

For the first time he hesitated, but too many years separated them, too long a distance and too much time. He threw it unopened on the fire like all the others.

The Bank was old Jack Pride's life. And Morgan knew what news would interest him. 'Look at this!' Tall, black-suited and suave, Morgan strode into Jack's office without knocking and banged the subscription telegram from the Melbourne stock exchange on the desk.

'What is it?' Jack wasn't wearing his half-glasses.

'Winston Prideau of London has purchased £70,000 of shares in Crotty's North Mount Lyell Company.'

Jack grinned: 'But that's worthless ground!'

'Yeah,' Morgan said. 'I reckon that about sums it up.'

James Crotty was a wealthy Melbourne business-man, but his North Lyell lease was just barytic hemat-ite, good as barren rock.

'Crotty did a fine job raising money in London,' Morgan said, reflecting Jack's cheerfulness, 'bought newspapers and journalists, claimed the Mount Lyell ore-body extended under his North Lyell lease, claimed *his* land contained the massive 146th-parallel lode pre-dicted by Clarke.' He shrugged. 'Fraud, pure and simple. Crotty's a genius – he even got the Tasmanian government to pay half the cost of a road to his barren mine, like an official stamp of approval.'

'Winston Prideau's luck has run out,' Jack said savagely. 'This will break him. We've got him! He won't get out of it this time.'

Morgan looked at the quiet old banker with interest. Every man had his passion.

On 20th October 1897 a road-building gang, half their six shillings a day wages paid by the Government, blasted a quartzite outcrop on James Crotty's worthless shicer North Mount Lyell lease. The white quartz was stained a rainbow purple-blue with the richest copper ore they had ever seen. The rush was on. By Christmas, Winston's £70,000 investment had boomed to a million pounds.

Morgan, coming quietly into the office, wondered what Jack wanted to hear.

'The man must be in league with the devil,' he said.

Jack's face was perfectly calm. A lifetime's pretence had made his expression automatic: it always lied when anyone was looking.

Jack cleared his throat. 'Luck of the draw,' he said.

When he returned to his place, already gutted and soon to be knocked down for the Hydro development, the cruellest deception awaited him: an envelope on the silver tray. He examined it without expression. A letter postmarked London. He instinctively checked the handwriting but did not recognise it.

He opened the letter.

The slip of paper that fell out, an unspoken invitation written by Emma's best friend Diana, so distant from her own father, contained only two words: a name.

Trilby Prideau.

He knelt to pick it up and held it at arm's length, squinting without his glasses, then tore it up.

41

1904

The secret society

The girls – that was how Emma thought of herself, Diana, and Trilby – had a fine time. For years their circle had existed below the sightline of their husbands; the secret society of women. When evening arrived, Diana and Emma must do the other half of their duty, look after the head of the house, all proper and correct, meals ordered and prepared, everything coped with: they changed for dinner, and the whisper of their shifts and petticoats around their legs, the skill of their maids' fingers with the fashionable Edwardian bows, each husband's kiss on their left cheek, was repeated in a hundred thousand homes across comfortable, imperial London.

Winston put his feet up in front of the fire, laid back his head and sighed, then read the paper. Ernest had pulled him deeper into the Bank. A whisky in a beautiful, very heavy leaded crystal cut-glass, with a small water jug on the silver tray beside it, was convenient to his left hand. He didn't hear the door opening. Emma, waiting in the doorway, bent down and whispered to Trilby. Dressed in a frilly nightdress, with white satin house-shoes with blue bows, the little girl slipped across and stood by the overstuffed leather arm of her father's chair, waiting to be noticed.

'Ah!' Winston said, putting down his paper. 'Trilby! Has my little girl been good today?'

'Yes, Papa.'

'Ah. Good night!' She hugged him and he kissed her. Emma held out her hand and Winston did not pick up the paper until the door was closing again. He was a good father.

But their days were free. The three girls walked in Hyde Park – rather, Emma and Diana walked, Trilby swinging from her hands between them – or picnicked by the Serpentine, or watched the Changing of the Guard and any of the innumerable free shows of the capital. Sometimes they had lunch in one of the great stores, sitting among the gloved women who had come up by train from the country, like a vast social club united by a single purpose: purchase. The weary dirt and violence all around them did not touch them; they had worked hard to be so lucky.

At Ernest's insistence his son John had been sent to boarding school at the age of eight, and now he was attending Eton – he would doubtless follow his father's footsteps to Trinity, then the Bank. So Trilby had almost as good as two mothers.

No reply to Emma's letters had ever come from Australia.

At noon on the first day of the twentieth century the people of Tasmania, without enthusiasm but with the hope that the price of meat would fall and new markets be opened for their apples and potatoes, had federated their island to the Australian Commonwealth. Their proud independent colony was now merely a state, an adjunct to a vast yet tiny land of four million people, fourteen parliaments and thousands of constitutional lawyers. There were no ringing declarations of independence. The Tasmanians had gained a Commonwealth and lost a country.

After Trilby's birth Emma had desperately wanted Jack Pride to know of her – Trilby, his own blood, a family he could be part of if only he would reach out. But as the stony, wounded silence from the Antipodes

493

prevailed she lost hope. Perhaps there was guilt on both sides. Emma's attempts at a reconciliation dwindled.

Diana was so sad. Her own father was long dead, and Jack Pride's playing dead hurt *her* more than it did Emma. Diana tossed her best friend's silent unhappiness over and over in her mind at night, magnifying it. Finally she went through to Ernest's bedroom, knocked on the door, and lay in his arms. Could they not force Jack to accept the news by inserting it in a routine business telegram through the Prideau Bank? Ernest was offended because she raised such a matter while they lay together, which was a time for action not talking; he was doubly offended because her personal interests must not be allowed to interfere with official Prideau business practice.

'Where would it stop?' he demanded.

'I'm sorry, dear,' she said, closing her robe. 'It was my fault.'

'Women, damn them,' muttered Ernest to the pillow when he was alone.

So she had sent only the name in her own handwriting, *Trilby Prideau*, but she might as well have done nothing for all the response there was. Diana couldn't know that Jack Pride cared more that Winston's infuriating speculation in Crotty's worthless mine had paid off; couldn't know that to Jack's way of thinking the sneering Englishman had put him in the dirt twice, *and* got a daughter.

It really was the three of them now. The men, Winston, Ernest, young John away at boarding-school, didn't count. For the secret society it was always summer, always fun, even running to catch the omnibus was fun. It was even fun standing on Blackfriars Bridge when a steam-tug shot underneath, and Trilby screamed as a fountain of smoke shot up over the stonework, showering them with cinders and smuts, smudging their faces like raccoons as soon as they wiped their eyes. They spat on their handkerchiefs and dabbed off the worst, trying to hold Trilby still from laughing at their antics. 'You look like hot-chestnut sellers!' the little girl laughed.

Nothing seemed to stick to Trilby.

'They've got a wonderful marble washroom in the Hotel Cecil,' Emma said. 'Come on, Screamer.'

'I *didn't* scream.'

'You *did*!' A South Eastern and Chatham Railway locomotive chuffed and clanked between the rooftops on their right, and rather than follow the new Embankment crowded with strollers and itinerants, they cut past the Guildhall School of Music then across the Middle Temple gardens, Trilby in her once-white pinafore skipping over the signs saying *Keep Off The Grass*. 'Look. . . .' Emma said suddenly, stopping at a brass nameplate by an old door in a shabby-looking courtyard.

Trilby read aloud, following her sooty fingertip: 'Prideau & Prideau.' Her eyes enormous in her smudgy face, she turned excitedly. 'Is that us?'

'It must be,' Diana said. Time and generation was familiar to her: the Lockharts could trace their aristocratic ancestors back through the male line to Elizabethan times. 'Maybe the Prideaus were lawyers once. Maybe that's why Ernest wants John to have a legal grounding when the time comes.'

They walked on to the Cecil and cleaned themselves up for tea, but it was only a few days later – she always mixed the two incidents up in her mind – that Trilby's life was changed for ever. Emma was playing the piano and Trilby, by the window, was singing along concentrating more on the scene outside than the song. She saw Diana arriving in the street and waved, then sang to show off until the music-room door was opened.

Diana just stood there.

Emma stopped playing. Trilby looked frightened.

Diana said: 'Can't you hear, Emma?'

'Hear what?' Emma looked thoroughly alarmed.

'My God, she's got a voice,' Diana said. 'The girl has a *voice*.'

42

November 1906–1907 August
No man's island

His seventieth year approached and Jack was weary,
his body as trim as ever and almost irritatingly healthy,
giving him no excuse to slow down, but sometimes
there seemed to be no reason for him to get up in the
mornings. The windy roof garden of the Hydro had
been planted with shrubs for commercial reasons,
labour being the extortionate price it was, all the good
flower gardeners worked along Davey Street, or for
the municipal parks department, or in the Botanical
Gardens. Jack stared at the merciless sun withering the
foliage between the white parapets. He was fed up
with the enterprise; the Hydro had never made much
money, his countrymen were not tourists much in their
own country. At his age one of his few, increasing,
pleasures was spying on the giggling girls playing
tennis.

Jack gazed across the roof.

Sometimes it seemed he had no more identity than
a guest in an hotel.

Years ago Fergus Matheson had told Jack: 'I'm going
home.'

And that was where, at Macquarie Harbour, he had
ended his life.

Morgan Pride, now general manager of the Bank,
would look after things for the few days the boss was
away. 'Enjoy your holiday,' Morgan said indifferently,

holding open one of the doors to the 8.10 morning express train to Launceston. 'Give my regards to everyone at home.'

One foot on the carriage step, it crossed Jack's mind he had taught Morgan all too well, if that was possible. The shy boy he had nurtured had disappeared. As a man Morgan had even learned to smile, lean and dangerous, elegant rather than trim, beautifully turned out, with a clean, instinctive ruthlessness, like a shark. Morgan had the confidence, the heartless lack of sympathy, of a man who knew exactly what and where he was, and how to make things happen. Morgan had never suffered, Jack told himself: Morgan was unstained. He would be rich one day through his parents Peter and Lily, and Jack had let drop the hint his own controlling interest in Paragon-Pride would pass to him, the fittest successor. The son Jack should have had; the man he should have been.

Jack feared his creation.

Then Morgan smiled. 'Don't forget me to the Throwback – I mean to Larry,' he said, and Jack realised: *Morgan's jealous!* Larry had *home*, and youth – he must be about twenty whereas Morgan was thirty-five or so – Larry had everything Morgan thought he had been denied. Jack grinned through his old-fashioned sidewhiskers, finding Morgan humanised by the small weakness.

The carriage door slammed, the guard whistled, steam roared. What within living memory had been a dangerous coach journey across rolling hinterland – once exhausted but now greened with superphosphate – the Tasmanian Government Railways' express traversed in five hours to the minute: at ten minutes past one Jack stepped down at Evandale Junction in time to eat a good solid lunch at the inn. Launceston was less than half an hour further on, but Tasmania's second port did not interest him; instead Jack stepped

498

smartly aboard the Western Line's 1.50 train to Emu Bay. He had to change at Deloraine and arrived at the Burnie Hotel to find a late repast laid out in his room. Rather than eat, he fell exhausted into bed. He was not used to travelling, and tomorrow he would set out into the rough and tumble of the wilderness.

Mr Stirling, the Emu Bay Railway's Burnie manager, introduced himself to his largest shareholder after breakfast and escorted Jack personally to the station. 'The bloody Crampton loco broke its bloody Walschaert valve, log on the line. We rushed about like blue-arsed blowflies to find you a Belpaire loco but the bloody rolling-stock's up a gumtree – you'll have to go second.'

'Second class!' Jack said. He had watched his stock in the railway fall to a quarter of its value after the Government's decision to fund Napier Bell's plan for Hell's Gates: a huge breakwater had been built to funnel the tides. Now the channel could take K class colliers and thousand-ton freighters, and at a stroke wiped out all hope of dividends to the shareholders of the Emu Bay Railway.

'Travelling second's not so bad,' Stirling reassured him. 'You get there just as fast. Wooden slat benches. Get you a cushion if you need it.'

'Don't bother,' Jack said.

At the ticket office a man with sticking-out teeth was arguing angrily with the clerk, trying to get the twenty per cent discount allowed for parties of six or more applied to his family of three, himself, his wife and daughter. Jack was relieved because they sat opposite him in the draughty carriage, which was otherwise full of navvies in blueys with shovels tied on their swags, or slouch-hatted fossickers smelling of sweat and sour bacon. Americans travelled too, which was why the Railway provided spittoons, and clusters of Frenchmen sounding excitable, but gradually their chatter subsided into boredom. The carriage rocked appallingly on the narrow-gauge rails and Jack gazed glumly through the grimy window at the endless forest, endless button-grass plains, the occasional cutting through a hill or shuddering trestle-bridge over a foaming torrent. The daughter stared at him as though she remembered him. He nodded politely but she just stared. Perhaps it was just hostility to the world in general.

His eyes moved around the carriage, then came back to her. He smiled, but she didn't move. He looked down at his fingers in his lap. Her mother stared silently out of the window.

The man with the sticking-out teeth said: 'I see you're travelling on business, my good sir.' A fawning Welsh lilt, but hard black eyes beneath the tightly-rolled brim of his bowler. He wore a suit of moderate quality, and shoes down at the heels, but carefully polished.

'Do you indeed!' Jack said.

'There's copper in these hills,' said the Welshman idly. He took out his handkerchief from his top pocket with a flourish. 'I happen to know – '

Still the girl stared at Jack.

Jack snapped his fingers. 'I know you,' he told her father, 'you're The Great Cadwaller!'

The woman said: 'Oh, Ewan,' in despair.

'Cadwaller is my name indeed.' The Welshman flourished a card from between his fingers. 'Ewan Cadwaller, at your service. Perhaps you are thinking of my brother.'

Jack remembered the girl. 'I'm bloody sure I'm not.' She would have been about ten – he remembered her pitiless blue gaze. It had been many years ago, but that remained the same. Jack said to the young lady in an avuncular voice: 'I gave you a copper penny.'

She said not a word. The woman stared from the

window at the slow march of telephone poles that swung their shadows across her weary face.

'This is a hateful, empty land,' Jack said.

'But rich,' said Cadwaller. His card was embossed in gold, *Share Promoter*. 'I have friends in the very best Melbourne syndicates and – '

'Not interested.'

'My wife is accompanying me. And this is my daughter, Esmerelda.'

'Esme!' she said, colouring, stung out of her silence.

'You know what girls are like,' Mrs Cadwaller apologised. Cadwaller just grinned smoothly but succeeded in looking both toothy and smug.

The delay in starting meant they missed their connection with the Tasmanian Government Railways train to Strahan and must stay overnight in Zeehan. Jack phoned ahead to the Shelverton Hotel from Dundas, the easily remembered telephone number 8, and the proprietor, Mr Quinn, personally assured him of a corner suite with a verandah. 'Where are you staying?' Jack asked Cadwaller as he reclaimed his seat.

'I have already taken a suite at the Grand,' Cadwaller promised airily. 'Perhaps we shall have the pleasure of your company on the continuation of our journey to Strahan tomorrow?'

He repeated that hope on their arrival in Zeehan, though Esme jerked her head impatiently. Jack noticed how slim her waist was as she stood to pull down their heavy case from the rack. The wooden Shelverton Hotel was less than a minute from the railway station and the house porter carried Jack's suitcase; the Great Cadwaller, his trailing women carrying the cases, strode into the gloom along the slimy street in the direction of the Grand.

Jack wondered at the sensation of pleasure he felt on seeing them on the station platform next morning, and told himself it was not the girl. Of course it was – the little things, the way she moved her fingers, that slim waist, the auburn curls escaping onto her shoulders from beneath her silly little hat. Even at his age – *especially* at his age! She was wearing the same dress as yesterday and it was crinkled, a piece of straw caught in the hem. Yet he could not turn his attention away from her. Esme reminded him a little of Lily Pride as he remembered her long ago, with a harsh edge of determination in her eyes, and the bronzed planes of her face, that the rich girl had never needed to acquire.

'I trust you spent a comfortable night,' Jack said.

'Not as comfortable as yours,' said Esme without looking down. Her accent had a lower-class snuffle that disappointed him.

'Most comfortable,' asserted Mrs Cadwaller bravely. There were little red marks on that good gentlewoman's neck and Jack was sure they were flea-bites. If they'd slept in the Grand, it was in the stable. But Cadwaller, when he appeared, was sleek as you please, his thumbs buttonholed in his lapels with the air of a man who has enjoyed a good breakfast. His wife greeted him nervously. 'I met up with some boys from the Royal Welsh Male Choir,' he told her cheerily. 'Don't fuss, I sang for my supper, that was all.' Jack telegraphed ahead for Larry Pride to meet him at Strahan, then paid his four-and-tenpence at the ticket office and climbed into the first-class carriage. 'Is it two classes?' Cadwaller exclaimed angrily, and for a moment Jack was tempted to lend them the difference in order that he might ride opposite Esme again. But the guard blew his whistle and the opportunity was gone.

The sudden tin-roofed shanty towns rising bravely out of the bush, a couple of brick hotels the stamp of supreme confidence, the wooden post offices and Waxman Halls, stores with hundreds of little huts surrounding them, were already rotting in the rain and split by the fierce sun, battered by the violent gales from the Southern Ocean. Many bore the marks of bushfires; Penghana had been completely wiped out. The trees had been cut down for buildings and firewood, and to feed the furnaces in the early days, and now fires raced eagerly across the cleared ground. An old miner told Jack some men had their shacks burned two, three times. 'All bloody forest here once,' the old man shook his head, 'none of these places was here ten, fifteen years ago. Mount Lyell made a profit of half a million last year. Good news for us shareholders.' He laughed at Jack's surprise. 'Why, I invested fifty pounds in Mount Bischoff thirty years ago, and never done a day's work since. And I always travels first class!'

Jack glimpsed Ewan Cadwaller's profile beside his daughter in the trailing carriage. 'I see what brings people to this part of the world.' He meant *money*.

'Hope.' The old man slapped Jack's knee. 'Hope.'

The train rattled over a turntable and came to the end of the line in West Strahan. There was a fault on the telegraph and no one was waiting by the workshops to meet the passengers, no porters, and no Larry Pride – Jack imagined he must look like Morgan, and there was certainly no one like that here. Jack hefted his case and followed the others along the gravel track beneath the cliff dividing West Strahan from East, the port.

'I'll carry that, chum, allow me.' Ewan Cadwaller looked Jack in the eyes and took the case smoothly. His women tottered behind with his own cases.

'No problem, mate,' Jack said, hanging on. 'You look after your own.'

They walked along with him, except Esme, who went ahead. Jack kept flicking his eyes at her when he thought he wasn't noticed.

'We're catching the ferry to Teepookana, on the King

503

River,' Cadwaller said, offensively knowledgeable, 'and taking the rack-and-pinion train to Queenstown.'

'Goodbye,' Jack said firmly. Cadwaller, eyeing the women, drew him aside with his finger to his lips.

'This is no place for a woman,' Cadwaller confessed sadly. 'You know what my situation really is, sir, and what I am. . . . but my wife was gently brought up, and knew better.'

'I wish you luck,' Jack said.

'I have pursued luck all my life,' Cadwaller murmured, 'and it has brought me down to this.'

'This?'

'Sir, I have lost everything. I do not have even the ferry fare.'

Jack dug his hand in his pocket and tossed the man a couple of sovereigns without looking at him. Cadwaller followed him past the grand new Commonwealth Buildings, whistling cheerfully. Suddenly Jack was plunged into the crowd milling along the Esplanade.

It seemed incredible that such a small place should be Tasmania's third largest port – first, sometimes, by wealth – but Strahan was brim-full of bustle. Wharfies swung drums down from half-loaded decks to be lost in the swarm and scurry below, steam cranes whistled and nodded, donkey-engines clattered. The shouts of men were everywhere, throngs of men smoking and spitting outside the hotels and stores, men reading comics on the steps of Harvey's but with restless eyes, hungry for opportunity. The air hung thick with the smell of Boag's ale, fresh-sawn wood, smoke, johnny-cake, carthorses, and men's unchanged clothes. Above the ringing of the blacksmith's anvil hawkers shouted the titles of steam launches for hire, the *Nellie* for Marble Cliffs, the *Lottah* already pouring smoke across the bay setting out for a drinking trip up the scenic Gordon River.

He met Mrs Cadwaller looking anxious, and Esme

sitting on an upturned case, making the men push round her to get past. Her expression was as hostile as ever, not just for Jack. 'I. . . . we seem to have lost Mr Cadwaller!' bleated Mrs Cadwaller apologetically.

'He'll be probably in the pub,' Esme said, uncrossing her arms. She looked accusingly at Jack. 'He's drinking it away. He'll make a dozen new friends and God knows what'll happen to us.'

'I tried to help.'

'Didn't you read the railway timetable?' she exploded. 'There *is* no ferry to Teepookana. The railway's been extended and all we have to do is walk to Regatta Point.' She pointed angrily across the narrow bay at the terminus.

'Nothing to do with me,' Jack said.

She pushed herself up with her hands on her knees. 'I'll go get him in the pub!' she said.

Jack touched his hat to Mrs Cadwaller and pushed his way through the crowd to the curving shorelines ending the bay. He had seen a familiar shape tied up at the jetty: the yacht *Ezzie*, her hull needing a coat of paint, her vanished topsides blistered, brass fittings tarnished, and one of her masts with an iron band round it where the wood had split. A dark young Hercules was loading crates of supplies from Frank O'Henry's Mammoth Store aboard.

'Larry?' Jack said, and knew at once he was right, just from the way the young man turned, his energy – the blood didn't lie. But the brown eyes were unfamiliar, their *thinking* gaze. This shirtsleeved boy had a brain and it worked. Jack shuffled uneasily, pierced.

'So you are Uncle Jack.'

'Sure. Yes. Pretty busy place here, not what I expected.'

Larry shook Jack's hand. Everyone seemed to know Larry – men were knocking past them all the time, saying hallo, clapping Larry on his red flannel shoulder.

None of Larry's attention wandered from Jack. 'Business opportunities?'

'Just to see you.' That simian gaze didn't waver. 'Looks like a place with opportunities,' Jack said finally.

'You see what you want to see.' Larry's stillness broke. 'Let's get you aboard! Lily's going to want to see you.' He called his parents by their Christian names, apparently. Jack felt very far from Hobart Town. Larry went back to the store for another load, calling the Pillinger boys to take Jack's swag and get him aboard the boat: they made them big here on the west coast, and Jack followed them meekly. There was a disturbance on the quay.

'Looks like trouble,' asserted the elder of the Pillinger boys.

'Looks like a woman,' drawled the other.

Jack recognised the girl being shoved through the crowd. He watched the scene from the deck of the yacht. Esme's hair had been knocked over her face; strange how easily a woman looked disreputable, deserving of her punishment. At first only the young men of Larry's age, but suddenly everyone in the crowd, black moustaches moving in unison, was shouting. Esme was shouting back now, giving as good as she got. The mood changed. Someone knocked her and she dropped into the water, her dress flying up around her like an umbrella. The crowd laughed – good-natured again – as she reappeared, drenched, her hair drowned like a cat. She spat dirty water. The larrikins roared with laughter. Esme looked up.

'You bloody bastards,' she said clearly.

There was silence as the girl in the water swam for the ladder. 'You bloody bastards!' Esme screamed up at them. They let her get to the top, then someone put their hand over her face and pushed her down. She floundered in the mud, weeping now.

Larry returned to the quay.

'Bloody violent women in this town,' the Pillinger boys explained reasonably to Jack, 'got to keep them down.' She hung on the bottom of the ladder and now an older man scrambled down, losing his hat in his haste, and knocked her off.

'Hey, she's cost me my bloody hat!' shouted the man furiously.

They saw Larry coming.

'Going to be a donnybrook,' said the youngest Pillinger eagerly.

But Larry went down the ladder and said politely, 'Shift over, mate,' to the man already on it.

'I won't,' the man said, 'she's lost me my hat, and I'm going to teach her for it.' Larry pushed him in the water and reached out to the girl. She stared up at him.

'Come on,' Larry said, outstretched. He gripped her cold hand. 'Don't look anyone in the eye. Walk with me.' They walked slowly and the crowd parted.

'Better cast off,' said Jack nervously as Larry and Esme scrambled aboard. She stood dripping on the deck. One of the Pillinger boys tossed her a towel but she screwed it in a bundle and threw it on the deck at her feet.

'She's going to Queenstown with her parents,' Jack confided to Larry as the water rippled past.

'I'm not!' she said.

'Look at the way she's looking at you,' Jack murmured.

Larry pushed the towel into Esme's hands. 'I'll put you ashore on Regatta Point, you can meet your parents there.'

'I'm not going with them!' she cried impetuously.

'It's a free world,' shrugged Larry.

But she just shook her head.

Nevertheless, they put her ashore on the point near the Railway Hotel where she could clean up, but she stood motionless on the wharf looking after the departing yacht, and Larry looked back.

'Be careful of that young lady,' Jack said. 'She just wants your money.'

But he was a very unworldly young man; never thought about money or cared about it. Never needed to here in this godforsaken land, so long as he could sail up to Strahan and lay in stores once a week. Jack couldn't find anything very much that this romantic young Hercules *did* care about. Larry was Peter's side of the family all right. With Lily's money in addition to his Paragon-Pride stock and immense land rights Peter must be the wealthiest man on the West Coast, but you'd never know it to look at him. He dressed like a stockhand. Jack was disappointed that Paragon House, though it had a new wing in the Federation style, wasn't bigger and had no billiard room. The view was spectacularly broad; but who wanted to see Macquarie Harbour's brown waters, sere backdrop of mountains and empty tree-covered hills, and to cap it all the distant ruins of Sarah Island – a convict settlement! Surely they wanted to put all that behind them? But Peter was artistic and had chosen to paint his life, not in oils, but on this broad canvas. Jack, spreading leatherwood honey on his toast next morning, tried to get through to him. 'Peter, you're as arrogant, in your way,' he said, 'as Rebecca.'

'But he has *me*,' Lily said across the breakfast table. Jack still could not look at her without aching; her eyes had lost none of their life that he longed to possess.

'That's true,' he admitted spinelessly.

'Last year the spread turned a profit,' Peter said.

'Five thousand pounds from the sale of blackwood and Huon. The bloodstock is the finest – '

'But look at the amount of capital you have invested!' Jack said earnestly.

'We can afford it,' Lily said.

Larry threw his leg casually over the arm of the chair. 'Did pretty well leasing out the ground for Pillinger, too.'

'I'd like to see that,' Jack said tartly. 'Never seen a ghost-port.'

Larry took him at his word. 'I'll ride you over,' he said, and next morning, early, Jack found himself out on the mare. The valleys beneath the dim hill-lines were full of shadows and Macquarie Harbour oily black, crowded with stars under the breathless air. They topped the ridge and stopped.

'In ten years' time,' Larry said, sounding very young, 'you'll never know it was here.' Jack saw the outlines of streets, a crooked jetty with a barge half-sunk beside it, still secured by rotting mooring ropes. Some huge, slumped pieces of ironwork cluttered the beach like sculptures.

'You're wasted here,' Jack said angrily. 'With your brain you could go a long way.'

Larry laughed and they followed a smooth, grassy gradient, all that remained of the ghost-port's railway threading inland between the hills, the lemony essence of Boronia wafting in their nostrils as the sun rose. This high the trees were the size of shrubs. The horses skirted cushions of alpine flowers by the watercourses. Larry pointed across the broad, level plain that opened up ahead. 'See it?'

'What?' puffed Jack, raising himself uncomfortably in the saddle.

'The town of Crotty.'

Jack peered at the vista of scrub with narrowed eyes. 'I don't see it.'

'That's right,' Larry said.

'My God.'

'Ceased to exist within three weeks when they shut the smelters. A thousand people packed their bags and left overnight. The Parer brothers dismantled the hotel and shipped it off to King Island.' Larry turned suddenly to Jack. 'My father opposed all these developments. He hated them.'

'Peter's done well enough out of them, through Fergus Matheson.'

'I don't remember Matheson,' Larry said absently. 'Morgan does.'

'You two brilliant brothers,' Jack said idly. 'Morgan envies you.'

For the first time Larry looked surprised. 'What?'

'Your happiness. The life you live. The person you are.'

'That's nonsense.' Larry sounded unsettled. They were riding north along the plain, following the easy country. The pink conglomerate peak of Darwin rose on their left, scrub already hiding the scars of tailings tipped from the mine mouth.

'She really just wanted me for my money?'

'Oh, her,' Jack shrugged. 'Esme? Her father's a hungry bastard.'

'So she's one too. I haven't got cash, I don't care about *money*. I thought she looked damned good.'

'For someone so intelligent,' Jack sighed, 'you're pretty bloody stupid.'

'Here's Linda,' Larry called back later. Jack turned up his collar against the wind rising along the bare sweep of the valley, denuded hills white and yellow beneath grey crags. 'Not a woman,' Larry said, 'a town.' Only two concrete hotels were left, the railyards were derelict, silent. 'A year ago, before the price of copper rose, you could buy houses for a pound, a church for a few guineas. Bargain, don't you reckon?'

'Someone had to bear the loss.'

Larry put his head on one side, then nodded. After that he kept looking over his shoulder at Jack as they rode. He had decided Jack wasn't so bad.

As they followed the track uphill to a windy saddle-back ridge, Jack called ahead: 'What's that pong!'

'Queenstown.' Larry reined in on the brink of a great bare valley surrounded by yellow hills. 'Sulphur from the smelters. Kills everything, trees, scrub, that's why Queenstown doesn't have a fire danger. More than a hundred thousand tons of sulphuric acid went up the chimneys every year until they started exporting it for fertiliser. Sometimes the fogs are so thick the miners can't find their way to work. Looks like the moon, I reckon.'

'It has a kind of beauty.'

'The richest copper mine in the world. Gold and silver too.' Larry nodded. 'I guess it does. And the deeper they go the more they find. They're at a thousand feet and the ore-body is still opening up like a ship in the earth.'

'And it's only found at this one place? It seems incredible.'

'Like a woman,' Larry grunted, 'keeps her treasure in one place.'

Jack's visit extended to a fortnight, a month, then even longer; an eerie, slightly horrified fascination had enveloped him at the sight of this strange locality, its scale dwarfing the people who struggled to make their small lives here. It was reverting to nature, to chaos. The railway mounted on piers across Hell's Gates to carry stone for the huge breakwaters had been dismantled, and for all the puffing of the Marine Board Jack was sure Phase Two, the East Breakwater and training walls, would never be built and the work already done would be wasted, reclaimed by the sea. The bleakness of the prospect depressed him and he felt unwell. He longed to return to Hobart Town but could not face the journey. He wouldn't admit his exhaustion, and each week when Larry sailed up to Strahan in the *Ezzie*, Jack said: 'I'll go next week.' Lily looked at him, but didn't suggest sending for the doctor.

Larry didn't go to Strahan just for stores.

In the late afternoon he walked below the cliff into West Strahan, and followed the wavelets lapping the shallow sandy beach, where he waited. Esme had not followed The Great Cadwaller to Queenstown. She had made her own life.

During the day she worked behind the counter of Harvey's circulating library, hair bound back and face stiff – Larry had glanced at her through the window, but she did not look at him. She worked fast, and towards five her work was done; she was just opening and closing books.

Esme lived in West Strahan, just by the road's sharp turn towards the railway yards, close to the constable's house. Larry glimpsed her fine figure striding on the road, her steps striking her steel-grey skirt ahead of her, her hands clasped primly. She turned down to the beach, the dense tea-tree bush at her back, and pretended to stare over the water until they were sure they were alone.

They had little time; she worked again from eight till midnight in the cottage hospital on Regatta Point.

He laid his hand on her shoulder and she turned into his arms, their mouths wet, her eyelashes fluttering, and he stroked the lobes of her ears with his fingertips then slipped his hand between her buttons and moulded, inside the pressure of her bodice, her breast in his palm. For the first time their eyes opened and now he pressed his fingers into the obscuring folds of her skirt.

'I love it when you touch me down there!' she said,

512

and he had her amongst the thin trunks of the trees, which latticed the coppery sunset with darkness. Afterwards, both of them lying in her skirts, he exhausted and she in command of him, she hugged him to her. 'Oh my darling,' he sighed.

'I'd do anything for you,' she said fiercely.

'Why?' he murmured.

She looked around her as though her eyes pierced the tea-tree that surrounded them, the gathering gloom, to reveal the township straggling along the shore and the shapes of all the men asleep or in pubs. 'Because you're the only man worth having,' she said. 'Will I see you next week?'

'Maybe,' he taunted her, pleasing himself.

'It's so easy for you,' she whispered.

And still, when Larry asked Jack if he wanted to come to Strahan, Jack said: 'I reckon I'll stay another week, if that's good enough by you, Lily, what do you say?' He was always very shy with Lily.

Lily told him gently: 'That's good enough, Jack.'

So Larry kept going to Strahan alone, but he didn't stay there alone. He wouldn't go in Esme's house, using the old landlady as an excuse, but really keeping his girl at a distance. He didn't want to see her room, her things, to come too close to her, he only wanted what she possessed.

She gave him everything and asked nothing in return.

As winter came he didn't meet her for a month, then two, because of the storms, and almost forgot her. One morning they learned that a five-hundred-ton ship, overwhelmed by enormous seas, had struck on the breakwater at Hell's Gates. Two women and four children were drowned – the children could be heard screaming but could not be saved – and a couple of days later another two men drowned trying to save the ship's papers from the wreck.

Larry called through the door of Jack's room: 'Are you coming with me to Strahan tomorrow?'

Jack opened the door. 'Yes,' he admitted finally. 'I'm going. My father was right. This is a dreadful place. I don't think I can bear it any longer.' He packed his bags and carried them downstairs, but had a second thought and turned back for something. His suitcase dragged him down and as his dizziness increased he saw the stair riser, the brass carpet-rod, close in front of his eye, receding. He reached out for it, but the steps slipped away under his fingers like the minutes and hours and years of his life, and he flew backwards down the steep perspective, reaching out, but he couldn't quite touch whatever it was. He died ten minutes later, his head cradled in Lily's lap, her arms around him.

43

September 1910–1930 Christmas Day

Two nations

It was a time for death.

The suddenly shallow waters at the mouth of the King River almost caught Larry out, and he tacked the yacht just in time. The milky green burden of the river's flow rippled across the slimy new tongues of mine tailings it carried from Mount Lyell, and he barely avoided grounding.

'I thought you knew this shore like the back of your hand,' Morgan said icily, and Larry coloured, the younger brother.

Rounding Dead Horse Point and the bright-painted misery of ramshackle cottages built among the trees for holidaying miners, the *Ezzie* moored between the ships at Regatta Point. They walked slowly up to the cemetery. Jack lay beside Fergus Matheson, the two clematis-twined headstones left with an empty space between them as though waiting for a third. She had now come.

Lily had died after a short illness, a chill that came from riding out on horseback to Braddon Creek in the rain, taking Peter and the men their lunch. They were draining the marsh to make use of the rich loam beneath the rank network of mosquito pools. Peter looked exhausted; he was too old for such serious work, but he wouldn't ease up. Yet it was she, returning home, who grew feverish and light-headed, and retired gratefully to her bed for a few days well-earned rest.

But the chill was pneumonia, and she died without regaining awareness.

Morgan arrived within thirty hours by private train from Hobart Town: that touch of drama, of earnest flamboyance, was very Morgan. Larry observed him with a journalist's eye. *Morgan envies you.* Yet Morgan had everything.

Larry was tired, almost burnt out by a questing sense of disappointment. He wrote the 'Fossicker' articles for the Strahan *Banner*, now taken up by the Hobart Town *Mercury*. They were written on the American model of country wisdom Will Rogers had made so popular. Fossicker drolly asserted that Tasmania was so inbred, indigent and irrational that it shouldn't be a state at all, but a folk museum under federal control. This so epitomised the mainland view of their new island that the Melbourne *Age* reprinted them in full. At the windy cemetery on Regatta Point, standing beside Morgan who was so slim and self-confident, so *organised*, Larry felt more in common with Peter his father, who still wore his red-check working shirt under the black frock coat, decades old, that hung from his shrunken frame. The lines in Peter's face contained fine white hairs the razor had missed. Larry was a fine swimmer who used to challenge himself by diving from the high volcanic cliffs at Gould Point; who at slack tide had swum across Hell's Gates, and climbed Cape Sorell to watch the yollas swirling around Bird Islets, blackening the sky above the whole mighty white crescent of Ocean Beach. Now his childhood's impulsive exuberance, his joy, had leaked from him and he looked older and less innocent than sleek Morgan beside him.

A figure moved. Larry looked up at the weatherboard fascia of the cottage hospital. Esme in her white apron, having come to a decision, crossed the verandah, and approached the cemetery gate.

Morgan glanced between her and Larry and understood everything from the girl's face. He kept his eyes on her. 'So this is your secret,' he murmured in Larry's ear.

'My secret?' Larry frowned.

'Well, it isn't *hers*,' Morgan said.

'I haven't seen her for years.'

'You expect me to believe that,' Morgan slyly winked.

Esme watched them. Larry seemed to be in thrall of his elder brother, and her hands tightened on the white fence-palings that separated her from him; he was so impressionable, so unaware of his qualities that she longed to protect him. Even his imperfections filled her with tenderness. She had used his lust to seduce him, trying to teach him her love, and so in her arrogance had failed him. She had merely taught him distrust.

Morgan jogged Larry's elbow, and Larry came over to the gate.

Esme knew she had this one opportunity. 'I want us to erase everything that happened between us. I'm ashamed.'

That got him. She saw the hurt in his eyes. So she had meant something to him. 'Forget the past, the happy times we had,' she said. 'I love you, Larry, but I know you can't love me.'

He looked frightened. 'What are you talking about?'

'You're too happy as you are,' she said, 'just you, by yourself.' She walked back to the hospital.

'Larry?' Morgan called.

'Esme,' Larry had followed her quietly. 'I treated you very badly.'

'Don't you *see*?' she told him from the top step, 'the fault was mine.'

'I don't know how to express myself.'

'But you write.'

'I write for the paper Morgan owns.' He spread his hands. 'I am bright but there's nothing to me.'

'Stop it!' she said.

'You know how much you mean to me.'

'No,' she said finally, 'I don't think I do. I don't think *you* know.'

He reached out, then realised Morgan, with his pleasant smile, was observing their every move.

Esme said gently: 'You aren't ready for me, Larry.' Still she couldn't get that light to come out of his eyes. She couldn't break through Larry's rich-boy disconnection to the real him, if he existed, and she was sure he did. Larry would not force himself to acknowledge her, really care about her, and she feared he never would. Yet her faith in him was real and desperate.

'Larry,' she called after him, and he stopped at once, uneasy that Morgan was listening. 'I'll wait for you,' she said publicly, showing her naked feelings in front of them both, then added in a whisper for Larry alone: 'Larry, even if you come back to me.... I'll never sleep with you unless we are married.'

Morgan watched with interest the now-silent movement of their lips: Larry had done it again, got a girl who would humiliate herself for her emotions, mere emotions. But then Larry left her standing alone, and Morgan frowned.

London

'My God,' Emma Prideau whispered ecstatically, in awe of her daughter, living through Trilby's success in her ambitions, 'she *can* sing.'

'I warned you years ago,' Diana said.

On the stage at the front of the hall, the tall, slim figure of Trilby, flat-chested and sexless in a baggy cardigan, wearing no makeup, waited under the klieg lights whose glaring rays had tanned her face to the now-fashionable shade of healthy brown. The pianist started rehearsals again, and the two women were able to spy indulgently from the shadows at the back of the hall.

'She's too tall,' Diana said critically, 'her gestures are too extravagant.' Diana's youth had dreamed of marrying princes in small central European principalities, and nowadays to be a ballerina in Diaghilev's Ballet Russe was all the rage, with ballet schools springing up everywhere crammed with leggy hopefuls bound for disillusionment; but Trilby's dream was coming true. She had a voice.

'She's doing perfectly!' Emma asserted.

But as yet it was only a voice; it was not *the* voice. The prosaic Herr Stompel was no Svengali.

Trilby, irrepressibly vital and vibrant within that unprepossessing frame, too full of life to impress the mannered high society of Emma's set, was her mother's joy and despair. The girl was an ugly duckling with a voice as beautiful as a swan. Teased, and pampered, and endlessly trained, the shrillness had gone, a wonderful melodious power taking its place, though still too variable, and Trilby would *not*, complained Herr Meistersinger Stompel – as Diana called him – concentrate on the proper breathing: too much out, not enough in, the sin of overconfidence. The trouble was, most often she got away with it.

'She is good,' Emma had insisted, hard-eyed.

'She is no good without the discipline,' asserted the Prussian.

'Then give her the discipline.'

Trilby was fifteen at this time, when they had started taking her talent very seriously.

'But her mind wanders, she knocks props over. She reads the books too quickly. She thinks her voice is easy for her.' The German sounded bitter.

'She *is* a natural!' exclaimed Emma.

Herr Stompel's profile, with its Kaiser moustache, acknowledged her with the smallest click of the neck. 'Yes, she is almost a natural. Is she content to be an amateur, a drawing-room singer?' He paused. 'Or is she serious.'

'Oh, she's serious enough,' Emma said, 'aren't you, darling.'

'Yes,' Trilby said.

'*Serious*,' said Herr Stompel.

'Yes,' Trilby said.

'Then!' said Stompel, laying down the law, 'there are certain natural disadvantages she must overcome.'

'Tell us,' Emma said devoutly.

'Dear lady, you are banned from my music lessons.'

'But that is outrageous!'

'She is too tall also,' said Herr Stompel, 'not enough bosom.' Whatever the opinions of the young, the paying customers favoured plumpness; operas were not written for slim divas, and theatrical costumiers did not stock dresses for them. 'You will drink milk.'

Trilby laughed: 'But I hate milk, it gives me catarrh.'

'If you are serious, you will drink milk.'

Trilby drank milk. She was too tall; she wore flat shoes. She even wore the saucy new French invention, a brassière, to lift her bosom. She was forced to forego her traditional British reserve and sing with *attack*, roaring with her open mouth into a mirror, locking eyes with herself.

'Louder! Deeper! More brilliant!' thundered Stompel.

'Better,' he whispered afterwards, 'a little better.'

Shortly after Trilby's successful audition with the Guildhall School of Music and Drama in John Carpenter Street, Herr Stompel disappeared, afraid of being interned. After the outbreak of war he was said to have been a spy.

'They say *everyone* with a foreign accent is,' Trilby

told David Earle, walking with him to John Carpenter Street. David was a childhood playfriend and she knew him well enough to be jocular with him, though she was tongue-tied by shyness with every other boy. The Embankment was shrouded in fog, the public buildings around them protected from Zeppelins by ghostly roof-nets and sandbags. Trilby and David worried about the sooty, stinging river-fog at their throats and wore identical woollen scarves. The college was too close to the river and sometimes David had to tap with a stick between the fog-flares blazing on the bridges and at important junctions. They were almost alone in liking the fog: it gave them an excuse to hold hands.

'Your mother has an accent.' David was a year older than Trilby, like her exceptionally young to be accepted for the Guildhall. His father was a barrister who tolerated the singing only because David was his second son.

'My mother was an Australian,' Trilby said uncomfortably.

'Australians are fighting in France,' David said. 'We can hardly call them foreigners any more.' Smuts the South African was a member of the War Cabinet, the war had tightened links between the Dominions and the Mother Country, and Canadian, South African and Australian troops were cheered in the streets.

The lights of the college gathered like balls of cotton wool in the murk ahead of them. David stopped. With an effort he said: 'You know I have to go.'

She knew. She held his hand miserably. 'You don't have to,' she said.

'Everyone else is.'

'That doesn't mean *you* have to.'

'Yes,' he said, 'it does.'

'Don't let's talk about it!'

He kissed her cheek, and she looked at him shyly. She could not concentrate for the rest of the day. She dreamed of young David doing something terribly heroic in the army, leading a cavalry charge, swords drawn, guns booming, and coming home with an officer's moustache and a medal.

But she didn't want him to go.

Emma laughed to reassure her daughter. 'You just worry about your exam results. I rely on you to do better when David's gone.'

'I don't care about singing or anything.'

'That's enough of that talk,' her father said. 'I expect you to come first in the exams, you're a Prideau, even if you are a girl.'

Walking alone through the fog, Trilby confided to her scarf: 'If he was killed, I could not survive.'

When David returned to Chesterfield Street to say goodbye, his private soldier's uniform looked shabby to her eyes, mass-produced, unadorned, as though he were unimportant to everyone but her. She had never felt such a strong sensation of loss. They shook hands and she promised to write every day. Neither of them had any idea where he was to be sent; France, probably. He waved as he went away, and her mother said, 'You'll get over that young man.'

'I never will.'

Emma said: 'Nineteen is too young to be in love.'

Trilby stared at the empty street, still waving. She loved David Earle more even than she loved singing, but nobody understood.

Naturally Larry followed in his father's footsteps, willy-nilly whether he wanted to or not. He had grown up knowing Peter Pride's photographs in the various rooms of Paragon House better than anyone, family pictures in the dining room and parlour, Josh Simmonds and a black swan, old Jack proudly holding up a salmon trout he had caught in the Gordon; and in Peter's study, where the old Bock camera still stood on its tripod, were the landscapes of Macquarie Harbour shimmering like steel, ringed with mountains as solid as eternity, the distant sun illuminating a sea of tree tops with sudden fingers of light. Larry had grown up with these.

And there was the book of war photographs from the Crimea.

But the pictures that formed him most were those up the stairwell, the faded daguerreotypes of King Island black under a white sky, meaningless and powerful.

Larry knew he, himself, alone, had made a mess of his life. He had been a luckier bloke than anyone had a right to expect, good parents and a fine house, wealth, a girl who loved him, but still he wanted more. He loved Esme. All he had to do was say *marry me* and everything would be dinkum, his own family, no problems. Wasn't there anything more?

Esme waited for him, but there must be more.

On Larry's last day he threw a towel over his shoulder and went down to the beach, swam out towards the island. Treading water, he looked back at the curve of the shore, the bowl of green hills dotted with cattle, Paragon House near the ridge and over to one side the ranch house where Morgan summered, kept in touch with his business empire by coded telegraph. Morgan could get up in the middle of the night and with a few taps of his finger order shares bought or sold on the London Stock Exchange, and the telegraph would beep acknowledgement of the transaction before he got back to the bedroom. Such a life had filled Larry with dread.

Larry's gaiety, his loneliness, had become frantic. He was a prisoner of himself; he could not go to Strahan because Esme was there. He was cruel to her because he was ashamed of himself. Still he could not bring himself to go to her.

Morgan was his salvation. 'You've got insight, Larry. These newspapers of mine could use a bit of that sort of stuff. Tell us what the war really feels like – not dry reports, I want *correspondence*. No blood and guts, something for the women.'

'And photographs?' Larry said.

'Right, pull the old heartstrings,' Morgan said. 'No more backs going over the top, no more shellbursts and landscapes, I want faces. Well?'

'I'll go,' Larry said simply.

'What makes you tick?' Then Morgan had called after him: 'It's that girl, that's what I reckon.' He pretended to forget her name.

'Esme,' Larry said, looking round slowly with his brown eyes. 'I haven't seen her for years.'

'Forgotten her?' Morgan said.

'I don't need her,' said Larry Pride.

25 April 1915
Aboard the River Clyde, *V Beach, Cape Helles*

Nearly three thousand men were crammed into the ship's gritty iron hold, which still stank of damp coal, like a cold furnace. The *River Clyde* had also been used for transporting mules, the old animal smell now drowned by the new animal smell of frightened men. 'What the bloody hell are you doing here?' A pair of knuckles tapped Larry's hand and a cigarette was passed to him. A match sparked then died, but he had glimpsed the face of the young soldier beside him in the dark.

'Mix-up on Tenedos,' Larry whispered. 'The *Times* man's gone with the Tommy Kangaroos.' He stuck out his hand and it was taken. 'Larry Pride.'

'David Earle.' The voice cursed the damp matches fluently. 'I saw you earlier on the foc'sle-head. A lot of these chaps are Royal Munsters and Dubliners but I

524

thought you didn't look Irish, and you aren't a Hampshire. Looking forward to it, Aussie?'

'What?'

'The stroll in the park!'

Larry hesitated, unsure how to react. He hated English humour, didn't know how to take it. 'Just as long as it's not a Turkish bath, choom,' he said. That went down well with the group of woodbines, encouraging him, sweeping him, a tinkle-tinkle correspondent, into the sense of togetherness with them, the camaraderie that united fighting men the world over. 'Listen, what are you blokes up to?'

'Well,' David Earle said, 'when the ship stops, we're going to get off.' Someone lit the cigarette for him. 'We're going to win the war.'

'Nah, it's a sideshow,' came the voice of one of the leavening of regular soldiers. He sounded happy to be here. The regulars revelled in the opportunities a sideshow provided as a stepping stone in their careers. Anywhere was better than France. 'Churchill's baby.'

None of these boys was frightened, Larry thought for his notebook, *they were all looking forward to the sport.*

'What did you do before, ah, your present occupation?' Larry asked.

'I was going to be a great singer.' The others laughed.

'Were you? I mean, *were* you?'

'No,' David's voice came. 'No, I wasn't nearly good enough.'

'Yeah, well I can't write that frogshit down,' Larry said.

'Then I'm going to be a great singer.'

'Jesus, I guess that's dinkum brave.'

'Can you use it?'

'Goodoh, mate.'

David held forward the glowing tip of his cigarette for Larry to light his own, and for a moment they

525

stared into each others' eyes from a distance of a couple of inches. '*Are you frightened?*' Larry whispered.

'No,' David Earle said quickly, mellifluously.

Larry clapped his shoulder and climbed the gangway, winced at the brightness of the misty dawn air hanging over the flat blue Aegean. He found a place out of the way below the bridge superstructure. On his right, beyond the shabby flotilla of worn-out merchant ships accompanying them stretched the plains of Troy, ahead of them the ancient Hellespont of the Greeks with its treacherous currents. Men were a crowded mass in the well-deck forrard of Larry's position; steel plates had been rigged to deflect small-arms fire. The *River Clyde* dragged a bevy of barges and lifeboats alongside her, full of men in tropical gear with white sun helmets. Gangways and wooden staging had been constructed below the tall iron bows of the old collier where the men in the well-deck and hold would jump ashore when she grounded on the beach.

Battleships shelled the shore, obliterating the gorse-covered hills with drifting smoke. Yet it looked so peaceful, apart from the sound like railway trains crossing the sky, the shells going over – then suddenly there were ships everywhere, a traffic-jam of them, and the yellow beach ahead.

Horribly, the *River Clyde* grounded eighty yards off-shore. The broad river of sea foamed with hostile fire from the hilltops and cliffs. Men jumped from the bow gangways into the sea up to their necks, white hats, upraised arms keeping their rifles dry, all that was visible of them. Little rowing boats struggled to pull heavily-laden lifeboats ashore, tiny spiders dragging enormous prey. Larry scribbled in his notebook. The ship rang and belled and shuddered around him with gigantic sounds. Men poured up from below, their heavy boots tinkling on the steel.

It was bitterly cold, and quiet, and Larry was alone.

He was soaked with freezing water; shells must have been bursting in the sea near the ship, which was full of debris, uniforms, shattered wood planking. Men lay as motionless as if they were asleep like sunbathers on the beach, but fully-clothed. Larry put his hands over his ringing ears, and tasted blood in his mouth. He was very frightened.

He slithered loudly below, so silent was it, his soft footfalls clanging on the iron. Number Four hold was full of wounded, quiet as death. The bulkheads were streaked and peppered with shrapnel. He backed out.

Night was falling but the light of a burning village illuminated the holes through the hull like stars. The large hatches, where the men had been unloaded earlier, had been cleared but now each carried a shambles of curious dead. Larry stepped over them onto the staging bolted to the hull, the water slapping below, and felt something soft below his feet. David Earle had been shot through the throat and his eyes stared. He must have been lying out in the sun all day, one side of his face baked red as fire in the light of the burning buildings.

His hand closed on Larry's heel.

Larry took David's head against his loins, his hands under the wounded man's armpits, and dragged him into the darkness inside the ship. In a glowing patch beneath a porthole they lay down.

Larry put his ear to David's lips. 'Go on, Dave.'

A bubble burst in David's throat and he began to rattle. His hands clenched something into Larry's grip, a letter soaked and the writing run everywhere, all tears and dark blood. The name at the end of the last page was clear: TRILBY.

David grunted.

'I'll make sure she knows.' Larry said. 'You did it right.'

*

Because of the confusion it was Larry's letter to Trilby, not a War Office telegram, which brought the news of David's death to her. She was devastated, and told herself she would never recover.

'You'll get over him,' Emma said. She lay in bed dying of stomach cancer, believing it to be an ulcer, full of hope.

'You'll feel better soon,' Trilby said, patting her mother's hand.

But Trilby did not recover. She had discovered a driving force, a seriousness. She held David's loss within her. Her Svengali was an emotion, not a man.

Trilby began to sing, to *really* sing. She seemed to mourn David not at all and people said she hadn't really cared for him, she was cold.

At the end of her ninth full-time term, in 1917 at the age of only twenty-one, she was Guildhall silver medallist to Dora Labette's gold. Her father was in the audience. Afterwards they rode home in the back of Winston's blue Rover landaulette, the same model and colour as the one driven for the Governor of the Bank of England, so spacious that Winston did not need to remove his top hat.

'I had anticipated gold,' he said. 'I rather promised it to Beecham in fact.'

'I'm afraid I don't quite – '

'You're a fanatic, Trilby. I don't understand that sort of thing, don't care to. But I know a voice when I hear it, better than ever your mother did,' he asserted, then waited for her to respond.

It was a compliment. 'Thank you, father.'

'As you know the Royal Opera House is being used as a government stores, but the war won't last for ever, life will go on. I'm not without influence. That unpalatable little man Beecham will be the next musical director and you will be in the chorus.'

'I want to achieve success by my own efforts.'

528

'Oh, naturally.' Winston touched his nose with his gloved finger. 'It's the golden rule, everyone *says* that.' Winston grunted and smiled as they got out. 'First rung on the ladder. Done my bit. After this it's all up to you. You'll have to find some young man to look after you,' he said with the ponderous and chilling wit he had affected since Emma's death.

'I'll never marry,' Trilby said.

Winston gave her an old-fashioned look, but Trilby set her lips in her determination. *I shall succeed by my own efforts*, she promised herself.

But when after an empty year the Armistice was declared, and the Royal Opera House announced a crowded season of operas in English under Beecham's direction, and no other work was offered her, Trilby allowed herself to be persuaded to join the back row of the chorus. She had put her foot on the first rung of the ladder.

Larry had left a Dominion, a place far from Home, unsure of its own identity. He returned home to find an Australian nation. Britain's casualty rate had been little more than half her fighting men; Australia's more than two-thirds. The Great War was a birth, a dividing line of pride.

The past was past.

Larry knew he was an anachronism as he sailed the ketch *Ezzie* into Strahan. This nation of battlers had its eyes set firmly on the future. A petrol-engined speed-boat swept past him on the smooth waters of Risby cove, a party of fishermen returning from a trip on the Gordon, and bagged the last empty mooring on the Esplanade. Larry double-moored and walked slowly along the crowded quay. Brash young men elbowed him aside, motor cars hooted, there had been a bad fight in one of the pubs and a man sat on the steps with blood streaming down his face. The constable was there with a gun on his hip, ignoring the illegal games of two-up played by discharged bronzed Anzacs inside. Too many diggers had learned to fight in the war, and too many got a taste of sex: Strahan was going to take time to settle back to being a man's town. Larry sat on the dockside with the doorway to Harvey's circulating library behind him, drinking a bottle of Cascade beer, swinging his legs and screwing his nerve up. At five o'clock precisely, the door slammed and her shadow fell across him. He scrambled to his feet.

'You know why I have come, Esme.'

'Go to hell!' she said.

He chased after her. 'I have been there. Without you.'

She stopped.

'Don't pay any attention to me,' she said, almost tenderly. 'I just promised me I'd say that when you asked me at last to marry you.'

'I can't ask you to do that. You must be married, there must be someone else.'

She peeled off her glove and held out her bare hand. 'Don't waste any more of my life, Larry.'

He held both her hands.

'Don't fight me any longer,' she whispered. 'I can't bear it if you do.'

Still he said nothing.

People were looking at them; they couldn't hold hands in public, a man and a woman, their faces naked with feeling. Larry stuck his hand in his pocket and lit a cigarette in the corner of his mouth, and they walked over the dusty track to Regatta Point. Jack Pride, last of his line; Peter Pride, dead of a heart attack just into his eighty-second year.

'Morgan won't marry,' Esme said, 'he's not that sort of bloke. He's here all the time now, you know. Overland telegraph, radio, even a telephone. The world at his fingertips. A man like that doesn't need a woman.'

'I do,' Larry said, 'you're all I need.'

'Say it.'

'Marry me.'

She put her arms around him and hugged him tight. 'Shout it.'

He shouted the words at the top of his voice.

'I won't work at the hospital tonight,' she said.

They honeymooned at Parer's Hotel on King Island. They delighted in exploring the island, which held no memories for them, even identifying the single Huon from Peter's photographs, still miraculously growing in a small valley sheltered from wind and fire. They could recognise hardly any other features beneath the tangle of tea-tree and gums; of the funny rickety little batch-house the photographs showed here, they could find no trace whatsoever. Only a few wild raspberries and silver beets indicated where possibly a vegetable garden had once been sited.

'You see,' Esme whispered, 'it does grow again, it all works out. Have faith, Larry.'

'Oh, I guess we still own the ground,' Larry said. They could hear the axes of the Soldier Settlement Scheme work-teams clearing the forest on adjacent blocks to make farms for the returning heroes to till, a couple of hundred acres and desperately hard labour with no living to be made at the end of it. Larry cranked the hired Ford motorcar to return to the hotel, and only glanced back over his shoulder one more time. 'Let's leave it alone,' he said, the plume of blue exhaust smoke drifting away behind them as they departed.

And so the past was forgotten.

'It's a girl – no, it's a boy,' the midwife said. 'Sorry about that, chum,' she told Larry, 'sometimes it's difficult to tell when they lie like that.' Esme had had her baby almost sitting up so that she could see, but Larry had been so fascinated by the process that he kept forgetting to flannel her forehead and the sweat rolled into her eyes. 'Pay attention to the other end!' the midwife from Burnie kept telling Larry, but it was more interesting below. 'Men,' the ginger-haired midwife snorted. Morgan's influence with the railway had arranged for her to arrive by special train. 'The Prides are never ordinary,' Morgan said, 'and neither are their women.' Morgan, ruthless and introverted, claimed never to have travelled by a scheduled service in his life.

Larry called his son Ian, and let him run as wild and free as he had been. Ian inherited Esme's blue eyes. His hair was very dark, and he was frightened of the water. This upset Larry. 'Don't be frightened!' he told the youngster.

But Ian shook his head.

'Don't force him to if he doesn't want to,' called Morgan from the long verandah of the ranch house, where he was breakfasting alone. He never had company there, female or otherwise. Ewan Cadwaller was his eyes and ears on the Melbourne Stock Exchange. It seemed sure that Morgan, dressed always in white cotton shirt and fawn slacks, a fanatic man of action in business but totally inert with women, really would never marry. Larry couldn't imagine a woman who'd want to marry such a cold man. 'How little you know,' Esme had said mischievously, in bed.

'Would *you*?'

'He's very masculine. Not a thought in his head, greed, desire, possession, but not a real thought. Typical man.'

'Your sort.'

'I'd kick him in the balls,' Esme had said.

'My family is *my* business,' Larry told Morgan tersely. 'You worry about your own business.'

Now that Morgan sent the stepped-hull speedboat to Strahan four times a week for stores and the post,

Larry ended up leaving the old yacht *Ezzie* tied up at the Farm Cove jetty. The ketch acquired a list to starboard when Larry forgot to pump her out.

'Ought to sell that old thing,' Morgan said, roughing Ian's hair. Morgan kept himself very fit, doing expanding exercises on the gym equipment he'd had installed among the climbing plants in the sunroom, and now in his fifties his shoulders had broadened. He liked the working-man's look and often took the speedboat up to the pubs, clubs and hotels of Strahan on Saturday night for a weekend with the boys, now check-shirted and a true-blue cobber.

The letters from Trilby Prideau had been fading away; Larry was reminded of this, and of his own guilt in not writing more often, when one arrived out of the blue. 'She's obsessed, like Morgan,' Larry mused as he read aloud fragments to Esme. 'About singing, though.'

'They'd get on great,' said Esme, looking over her sewing.

'She isn't interested in men any more than he's interested in women.'

'Poor girl. Suppose – ' she stopped. 'Nothing.'

'Suppose what?'

'You hadn't come back from the war, my love.'

'Go right ahead, cheer me up.'

'And David Earle had.'

'She'd have married him and you'd be doing the cockeye bob on Morgan.'

Esme sewed. 'No, I'd be like Trilby, an embittered spinster, in my case sinking all my energies into the library.' She glanced up with a shudder; Larry didn't notice.

'She isn't embittered,' Larry said, 'you've missed the point. She's successful at what she does. She sings solo at Covent Garden and does provincial tours and everything. She's well-regarded.'

'I think she has something more important,' Esme said.

'What's that?'

'The gift of friendship.' They stared at the letter. 'Here we are, eleven thousand miles away, talking about her. You must write back.'

'I'll do that,' Larry said. But somehow he never got round to it. They had never met, and of course Trilby had heard nothing of Larry from her mother Emma – he had not been born until years after Emma's elopement with Winston, and that once-saucy story, a tasty tidbit of dinner-table gossip for the 1880s, a skeleton in the family cupboard by the turn of the century, was ancient history and forgotten after Winston's death in 1926. Names and dust; the living got on with living, swept on day after day, meaning to write letters.

Trilby's career in opera was successful, and after the early years were past – especially after that first, disastrous Beecham season – her reputation grew, and her lonely life was solid and satisfying. She sang many times at Covent Garden, was a hit at New York's Met, and most memorably at La Scala. She recorded on Deutsche Grammophon and the technical mastery of her pieces would stand equalled but never excelled for half a century; greater voices would outrange her, more exuberant prima donnas make more headlines, but the sheer disciplined suppression of her own identity into a role put her in her own way beyond comparison. Independently wealthy and the last of her line, she had no real reason to undertake the grind of touring, nor did she after the end of the decade. Among her peers in the ingrown, inbred, inward-looking world of opera, she was famous. With the public at large she remained peripheral, impeccable in character parts, wholly lacking the bankable vanity and greed of a star. Buffs were awed by her chill professionalism, critics liked her, but audiences wouldn't pay to hear her: there were no fights in the box-office queues where Trilby was singing.

'You're cold, young Trilby,' Ernest wheezed at her with a flicker of self-recognition. 'You're an unignited fire.'

Trilby whispered: 'Who are you to talk, Uncle Ernest.' He was dying; overwork and the Depression had exhausted his heart, his wife Diana was dead, his home empty, and his fond memory was of the knight-hood he had almost succeeded in purchasing from Lloyd George in 1921. Now Ernest supported charities grandly and dreamed of the plain white envelope from Downing Street. . . . an old man's dream. His son John, five years older than Trilby and her closest childhood friend, did the work at the Bank now. He had returned from his war in the Guards Regiment a captain and a DSO, a different man, with a strange gloss to his skin and a barking laugh that bit at his lips: he had haunted eyes. Yet just when he was recovering his old exuber-ance, he returned to the Bank too soon, his father's palace, then quickly and unexpectedly married Lady Patricia Fleur-Boyes in St Andrews Undershaft, with hardly time to book the Savoy for the wedding break-fast. Patricia was a willowy neurotic who screamed with laughter or tears, but she was a girl of extreme beauty in the right mood, almost eleven years younger than John; she brought with her a deal of money but more importantly connection to a rock-solid respectable family name, so Ernest (almost Sir Ernest that year) sanctioned the union joyously. Also in the church was Patricia's great-aunt, Lucinda Fleur-Boyes, who had re-entered Winston's orbit after Emma's death. John bought his new wife an Elizabethan farmhouse in Surrey with a fine garden, but during the week he stayed at his pied-à-terre in the city.

Trilby had watched them wed without a tear in her eye.

She had almost everything a great singer needed, but she took herself too seriously. Trilby searched for the fire. It must be within her; it must be within everyone, or else the world was unutterably cruel. Sometimes late at Covent Garden, when the auditorium was empty and only a few yellow bulbs remained glowing amid the plush and gilt, she climbed up to the box on the highest tier and looked down into the pit far below. When the performance had gone well she almost sensed *it* floating in the dusty abyss – the *it*, the something missing: as if she could reach out and touch *it*, brush it with her fingertips. One time, when she had sung herself nearly out of her skin, one of those magical, unrepeatable performances when she had done it but didn't know how she had done it, she went up and knew *it* was there. The passion. She could reach out, touch *it*, and fly.

Trilby drew back. The moment passed her by.

Morgan came up behind the boy on the windy cliff at Gould Point. 'What's on your mind, Ian?'

'Nothing.'

'Nothing's nothing,' Morgan laid down the law, 'not one single detail. Now, what's on your bloody mind?'

'I'm frightened,' Ian said without looking round.

'Don't you ever be frightened,' Morgan ordered. 'That's your father talking. I know you. You're frightened of too much, don't you reckon, boy?' There was no answer from the ten-year-old; Ian's misty blue eyes reflected the horizon. 'If a man is frightened of one thing, just one thing, he ends up frightened of everything. I know, and I'm telling *you*.'

'Yes, Uncle.'

'What's this bloody business about then?' Morgan pulled the boy round and stared angrily into the tearfilled eyes. 'You're frightened of falling, right?'

'I'm frightened of swimming,' Ian confessed.

536

'That father of yours doesn't understand you,' Morgan said.

'He can do anything,' Ian said proudly. 'He dives down from here and you can see him go down underwater for such a long time. He looks changed down there – like a golden man.'

'Yiss,' Morgan said shortly, the Hobart accent he'd learned off Jack. 'Swimming isn't everything. It's almost nothing a-bloody-tall. Your pa and ma have got pretty odd ideas. You got to stand up for yourself, Ian,' Morgan said, standing. 'I did, found a proper man to teach me, and look at me.'

The wind ruffled the hair over their eyes.

'Don't let them spoil you,' Morgan said gently. 'They're manic depressives.'

'Daddy makes me laugh!' Ian looked up eagerly, there was so much he wanted to express, a whole world inside himself, but Morgan had turned away to watch a speedboat streaking along the harbour below them. It passed the mouth of Farm Cove and curved out of sight beyond Picnic Point, and the drone of the engine faded towards the ghost-port of Pillinger. 'Nothing to do with us,' Morgan grunted. He looked for Ian, but the boy was running back down the slope as fast as he could, hair and coat flying. 'Hey,' Morgan called, 'you aren't frightened of me too, are you? Jesus Christ!'

The man who climbed out of the speedboat onto the deserted jetty of Pillinger was in his thirties, smartly but conservatively dressed in a suit, not flannel, and tie, silk. The gold wedding band on his little finger still looked new, and the boatman looked appreciatively up the titless, bumless little skirt of the woman climbing the ladder. 'Come on, Dee!' called the man impatiently from above, glancing at his watch. 'I want to get all the way to Butler's Island before lunch.' A hamper was propped on the sternseat, and a bottle of champagne would be hung into the icy waters of the Gordon on a string. The boatman scratched his stubble: not poms, but something almost as bad. Hobarties.

'Wait for us,' ordered the man, then strove for the common touch, 'mate.'

'Where'd you think I'd go?' spat the boatman, putting back his greasy peaked cap with his thumb, and the woman giggled. She opened a small crystal bottle from her handbag, pressed her fingertip to it and dabbed the fingertip under each ear.

The man looked across the crumbling tarmac to a weedy block that had once been the centre of the town. 'You're sure he's still alive?' The boatman, who had busied himself coiling a rope, pointed with a nod of his head. The pair picked their way through the rubbish and decayed industrial ironware, Dee wobbling on her heels, then crossed the smooth grass and climbed to the white house halfway up the hill. Dee took off her shoes but the man did not even loosen his tie.

The old brown man, wizened and bald, rocking on the verandah with all the time in the world, watched their approach equably.

'Heard you coming, stranger,' he said, and they realised he was blind. Over the door hung a huge curved pair of Hereford bull horns, like a primitive emblem.

'Am I speaking to Josh Simmonds?' demanded the young man authoritatively.

Dee hung on to her husband's elbow.

'Who's asking, eh?' The old boy was well into his nineties, obviously.

'My name is Joseph Simmonds.'

'Who's your woman!'

'I'm sorry,' Dee said, 'I was sure you couldn't see me.'

'Smelled you.' The old brown hand reached out and she took it. 'Simmonds, eh? Now there's a coincidence.'

Joseph said: 'We've been a long way away, Grandfather.'

'Don't speak to me like I'm a child, I'm old but not stupid,' the old man said irritably. 'Gideon's boy?'

'Gideon moved up to Sydney – '

'Knew that! Broke Rebecca's heart.'

'And established a very prosperous constitutional law practice there, married Pamela, my mother. He founded the Mendonça Society and I share his historical interests. We believe Australia was discovered by the Portuguese in 1522. You see, our history is longer than we – '

'Rachel and Ruth,' rambled old Josh, 'they were your father's sisters, one of them moved up to Oatlands. God knows how many children they had. . . .'

'We don't talk to that side of the family. I am in charge of my father's Hobart office, and I want to delve – '

'Women didn't smell like this when I was young. Honest sweat and horseshit. What's her name?'

'I want – there's something I want to know,' Joseph said stiffly. 'I want, I need to know. . . . where did I come from?'

'Between your mother's legs of course!' cackled the old man, and Joseph flushed brick red.

'Dee is my name,' the girl said gently.

'I like the sound of your voice. Not so sure about his.'

'I want to know something of my ancestry, *who*, the person I am,' Joseph said. 'I can face the truth – if there. . . . you know. The Stain.'

'You can really face it, can you, boy?'

'I think so, sir.'

'Well, your grandma Rebecca was a Pride, and all the Prides was convicts through and through. So was my grandad, I believe, but he'd gone back to Pommieland before I arrived.'

'I was hoping – but thank you for telling me, sir. It's better to know.'

'He was hoping for someone famous,' whispered Dee.

'Can do better than that,' old Josh drawled. 'My own father was a half-aborigine.'

Joseph's face froze. '*Abo*? A *boong*! But that can't be right. We – '

'*He* was half-abo, and he married Powwidde, and *she* was half-abo.'

Dee tugged Joseph's arm mischievously. 'Darling, you never told me.'

Old Josh went on remorselessly: 'My grandmother, now what was her name, Wayanna, she was a prime full-blooded Tasmanian abo. . . .'

'Forget it,' Joseph said.

'It's the truth. I'm part wonk, part boong, and so are you. You're the same man, aren't you?'

'Just forget it,' Joseph said, pulling away. 'Come on, Dee.'

She called back to the old man: 'Goodbye!'

Josh sat rocking, his blind eyes turned up to the sun, recalling.

'Looks like he's spoilt your bottle of champagne,' Dee told Joseph gleefully. 'You look like you need a *real* drink.'

'Shut up!' he said. He pushed her suddenly, and she fell over, her shoes flying from her hand.

Every year, the muttonbirds – few now remembered them as yollas – returned to the great rookeries on Cape Sorell, Bird Islets, and the vast sweep of dunes behind Ocean Beach. Each summer evening the sunset was dark with their wings and beaks and bodies.

Each dawn, clouds of them rose into the sky, swirling and gathering and sweeping out to sea, following the pointers of their shadow in front of them.

Larry stood on the rough igneous clifftop of Gould

Point, his bare feet curled on the sharp rock, the water a black mirror below him. And he dived.

Ian watched.

He was quite clear now what the test of manhood was. It was this.

Far below, Larry swam ashore with powerful strokes. Esme, bathing her toes fastidiously, her hair pinned up like a goddess, handed him his towel.

Above him, on the clifftop, Ian unbuttoned his shirt.

Below him, Larry towelled his hair.

Ian pulled down his trousers and stood looking into his shadow streaming ahead of him in the air. He dived.

He lost control, falling, twisting, and the water hit him like a brick. Ian went flailing down and down into the darkness, the pressure crushing the breath from his lungs, pressing into his eyes like fingers. Then a hand grabbed him and he overtook the bubbles streaming from his mouth. He surfaced gushing phlegm and spit, Larry shaking his neck like a dog, and shouting.

Larry shouted: 'Where is she?'

Ian could not comprehend.

He struggled back to the rocks. Out in the channel, beyond the jostling bombora of waves over the reefs, the water made a smooth swathe where his mother had been swimming to him. Larry appeared, duck-dived, reappeared, swept along, coming up further along, further out each time with the ebbing tide, and Ian followed him along the rocks. Now the surface remained empty.

Ian went into the water up to his thighs and screamed.

Esme's body, her face cloaked in hair, was taken out before midday over at Sarah Island, by a man fishing for the cod and ling feeding off the rocks.

Three days passed before they found Larry, rolling on the sand at Hell's Gates, his arms outstretched above his head and a woman's hairpin through the palm of his hand. The lighthouse keeper brought him back.

Morgan and Ian went in the speedboat to the Dead House on Regatta Point.

'Look at the expression on his face,' Ian whispered.

'Cramp,' Morgan said, 'fish. Don't look.'

Larry stared upwards with enormous pink eye-sockets. They had nibbled out his brown eyes.

'He saw something amazing down there,' Ian said. 'Look at his face! My daddy saw something before he died, something amazing, and he *understood* it.'

'You got to stop talking that nonsense,' Morgan said, irritated. 'Look at me, Ian. Stop dreaming. He never lived up to his promise.'

Ian shuddered in the refrigerated air, so much that Morgan held his arms. Ian cried: 'He saw it! But I went down there too, and there's nothing there. Nothing. Blackness.'

'You've got to learn not to talk like this,' Morgan said. 'You come home with me. It isn't going to be so easy for you from now on. But I'll make it worth it for you. I'll make you happy, son. You'll see.'

It was Christmas Day.

44

1931–1975

One world

When Ian died they said he had loved money more
than his own son.

Ian lived a life as cold and opportunist as his Uncle
Morgan's; it had been bought at the finest schools,
given every opportunity, nothing withheld, no secret,
no trick: old Morgan let the boy, who so soon became
a man, into his heart.

'I'll teach you all I know,' Morgan said.

The aristocracy of money.

Ian learned what he must learn. He lived in doubt
and fear of everyone but Morgan. Ian's bright, smiling
silk-screened face was double-spread across the society
pages, a man constructed of ten thousand dots: a man
of a thousand Features from the gossip columns of
New York and London to the tittle-tattle of the Hobart
backwoods. His eighteen-metre yacht in Sydney Harbour, his Tiger Moth seaplane trailing foam across
Farm Cove, the teddy-bear women on his arm, or preceding him through the racecourse crowd: behind the
bright smile, a private man.

'I've virtually adopted you as my own son,' Morgan
once said.

'I'm not your son,' Ian replied.

A frightened man.

Morgan smiled and watched him go.

Ian loved to look at what people wrote about him,
the pictures of *him*: the man hidden behind boat and

plane and the plumage of single, beautiful women: the man he wanted to be.

Ian was frightened of what he hadn't seen down there. Only blackness.

He hated his father; hated the most important person in his life for not being with him now, deserting him. He never went up on the clifftop again.

He hardly noticed when Morgan died, suddenly, of a heart attack. The plans for the transfer of power had long been complete. By now he almost was Morgan, except for one enormous difference. In 1939, Ian was married.

But she made almost no difference at all. Jilly Fitzroy of Davey Street was a quiet and reliable young woman who would neither let him down nor bother him. She, of course, dreamed of more; but he did not.

He wanted an heir for his Australian dynasty, the group of corporations that were his inherited family, not many of which bore the name of Pride but were controlled or influenced by him: Paragon-Pride, its satellites the loans houses, real estate, a brewery and his share of the fashionable new thirties-style Wrest Point Hotel, shares in Mount Lyell and railways, radio stations and even, he discovered, yellowing scrip in the Bank of Ballarat, which he sold.

'Am I important to you?' Jilly asked one night in bed, in the almost-dark.

'Yes.'

'Say you love me,' she murmured comfortably in his arms. He stared at the nightlight, its dim orange glow, then let her go. Swinging his feet out of bed, he crossed to the window.

'Yes, I love you.'

'Oh darling,' she said, irritating him with her sentimentality.

He parted the curtain and stared at the moonlight beating its path down the black surface of Macquarie

Harbour. It was terribly silent. Her image appeared behind him, wearing a kimono of lovely Japanese silks. 'I know what you want,' she said tenderly, sliding her wrists around his neck.

Johnny was born swiftly and painlessly in the middle of 1942, with gas, in the bed where he had been conceived with indifference, and was the son his father wanted, which was not easy. But Johnny grew up knowing his duty.

'Never relax,' Ian told Johnny, getting his lesson in before the boy went to the University of Tasmania, 'never trust anyone.'

'Sure, Dad.'

'Never tell the truth. And don't get caught.'

'Yes, Dad,' Johnny said, and grinned as his father's hand gripped his head, tousling his hair.

'You're my boy,' Ian said, and coughed. He put his hand on his chest, there it was again: his mortality. His heredity, the small strange weakness of the heart that had been passed down the generations, the ever-present reminder. 'My father was drowned young,' Ian said, gripping his son's hand: Johnny had sandy hair, sunstruck blue eyes, an open tanned face, Australian manhood shone through every youthful pore. 'Oh,' Ian groaned, 'you're *my* boy. Morgan, now, he died over his heart. But *his* father didn't, old Peter lived to a ripe age. . . . Jack Pride died of a heart attack long before I was born. Don't know about any of the others.'

Johnny glanced at his watch. 'I got to go.' Hobart Town in 1960 was little more than an hour away by Cessna seaplane, and there was a girl he wanted to see. In fact there were several.

'Remember,' Ian said, 'we aren't big, we're small. By American standards, European standards, even to those yellow Japs, our business operations are small. The British are going down the pan but they're still too big for us.'

'For now,' Johnny said.

A flicker of a smile crossed Ian's face. 'You know, in my father's time British shareholders even owned Mount Lyell. They sold it in the twenties, as the War had taken their wealth. The second War broke them completely, Johnny, they're burned out. Our one-time masters have more strikes than we do.'

Johnny looked at his watch impatiently.

His father mused: 'When I was a boy the globe was British Empire red. Fading away, Johnny. . . . they've lost the will to fight. The Huns and the Japs and the Yanks are moving in. And us. . . .'

'Then London sounds a good hunting ground,' Johnny said from the door. He didn't like his father, but he admired him, respected him. 'Thanks for the words of wisdom, Dad. Anything more I can do for you?'

'No,' Ian said, 'there's nothing more.'

'Thank you, Dad,' Johnny said, and left the door open.

He too married the right woman, in 1967, Mary Deems, daughter of one of the oldest pastoralist families on the island, who had been on the same course at the Tassie Uni. Ian was not there at St David's Cathedral, too ill to attend, but he was sent a wedge of the wedding cake, and the photograph: their hands clasped together on the knife. They would honeymoon between the Far East and London; the world was shrinking every day.

Pale as death in his wheelchair at Macquarie Harbour, Ian held the photograph, but he was staring from the window. When the portico was added to the front of the house there had been the silly sunsplit wooden statue of a woman to dispose of; he almost had it burned but a visitor, an American lady professor, said it had something, it was so charming, so he had it painted white and mounted on the lawn, near the fine marble swimming pool and the tennis court he'd had built for Johnny. Soon this house would be Johnny's. He could do with it what he liked; Johnny would do right. A large white H within a circle on the grass identified the helipad where his Jetranger would land. A Riviera speedboat, its immaculate ebony hull and decks varnished like a black mirror, floated at the jetty; the old wreck of a ketch left by Morgan to decay there had long been towed round the point to what remained of the hardwood wharves of Pillinger, and left there to hang from its mooring ropes.

Around them stretched the wilderness. The enemy.

Ian closed his eyes, then grasped his chest. What had his father seen? Ian struggled to his feet, collapsed across the windowsill. The parallel shorelines of Macquarie Harbour stretching into infinity. Ian struggled, but saw only blackness.

In Strahan, declining with the decline of Mount Lyell, the railway to West Strahan closed, Hell's Gates silting up and the wharves of the Esplanade and Regatta Point almost empty, the few battlers left put their threadbare elbows on the pub counter and drank to Pride's epitaph: the hungry bastard who loved money more than his son.

In London, staying at the Ritz, Johnny and his new wife walked out with a camera into Piccadilly and there, amongst the smelly long-hairs and hippies gathered around the steps of Eros in the centre of the Circus – no one now knew it as the Hub of the Empire – they saw a fine old lady, probably in her sixties, but straight and tall, her eyes piercing. "Scuse me there,' Johnny touched her elbow as she hailed the taxi he had his eye on. He stared after the departing vehicle angrily, hating to be bested by anyone in anything, and that was the photograph Mary took.

'She did that because she knew I was an Ocker,' Johnny said. 'Believe it, Mary.' The taxi was lost to view between the double-decker buses browsing about Eros like big red dinosaurs.

Trilby Prideau had not sung on stage since the great years of Sir Thomas Beecham at Covent Garden, in the thirties. In the end her great talent was not for singing. During Hitler's War, when the Royal Opera House was used as a dance hall, she had discovered that she could teach and loved teaching: her talent was for spotting talent. Only gifted young people got close to her, and to them, the ones who were best and most difficult, her criticism was unflinching. She did not believe in encouragement. No voice was a natural, each one had to be trained, its owner distorted to fit the shape of the glorious sound. Trilby's reputation was at the very least formidable, and some believed her to be cruel. Many left her master classes in tears, and many young hopes, and parental dreams, were dashed.

'If it's clay I can only make pots with it,' Trilby snapped. 'Give me gold and I'll make it shine.'

'You have no children,' the distraught parents said, 'you can't possibly understand.'

'I do understand what you mean,' Trilby said gently.

Yes, she had no child of her own; but she had brought up a child and, like them, always felt she had failed him, though she could not tell how. She did her best and it wasn't sufficient. William Prideau was the only human she could not do enough for, though she would have died for the boy.

It had been no secret that his father's first marriage, to Pamela Fleur-Boyes, was unhappy. Sir John, sole heir to The Prideau Merchant Bank and its conglomerated interests after Ernest Prideau's unnobled death in 1932, received his knighthood from the lips of the stuttering King in 1938 and saw no reason not to divorce his demented wife. Having achieved the knighthood his father dreamed of, Sir John did not care if he was never invited to the Palace again. Pamela went on

548

to marry a professor, and lived for many years on the banks of the Isis, showing no sign of any characteristic more alarming than happiness. Before the outbreak of war Sir John, whose sexual peccadilloes were in danger of becoming public, married Maud Woolstone for appearances' sake. The daughter of an impecunious duke, she was bluff and practical and knew how to turn a blind eye, so long as she was seated at the head of the table. In 1942 she gave Sir John, now in his fiftieth year, his son.

'You'll be his godmother of course,' Sir John told Trilby.

'How sweet of you to ask.'

'Good, that's settled. You're too old to have a pipsqueak now, Trilby, you're the last of your side of the family.'

'Yes, I know,' Trilby said quietly.

'Someone had to do it,' Sir John said genially. 'Got me a son, dammit. Not bad.' But the glint in his eye was pure ruthlessness.

'And what name,' asked Trilby in her quiet, penetrating voice, 'have you given my godson?'

'William. Don't know anyone called William, do you?'

'No.'

'William it is, then. Don't worry, Trilby, you won't even have to hold the brat.'

But she did. She had to hold him at the font in St Andrew Undershaft's because Maud was ill; the child had been a difficult birth and Maud, her apparent indifference to her husband's affairs worn down, relapsed into deep depression. 'Maud's illness,' Trilby told Sir John pointedly, 'is tears.' But he just laughed; she'd get over it! He never saw how he hurt people.

At the end of the War, while Sir John was working at his desk in the City, a V2 rocket reduced his Belgravia home to rubble. One moment everything was normal, women in overcoats, soldiers on leave, prams, sandbags, the next moment the earth exploded. Trilby, who had been coming to see Maud for tea, arrived almost immediately at the smoking pit. Her mind went blank with terror, but then a woman shouted that William had been sent to play next door with a neighbour's boy. Trilby helped the firemen pull the boy, shocked and terrified, out of the wreckage, and held him to her with all her strength.

His mother was dead.

'For the moment you'll just have to look after the child, Trilby,' Sir John said. 'You haven't got one of your own; you'll enjoy it.'

'I don't want one of my own.'

'You're his godmother, Trilby.'

So Trilby found herself playing the role of a mother, and she did her best. She ended up providing a home for William well into the 1950s. Sir John cared little for his son, but William, his attention focussed by the distance between them, tried to imitate his father in everything. Trilby found herself both irritated and fascinated. She tried to teach William to sing, but his voice was not very good, and she had the sense to give up rather than force the boy.

One day when he was fourteen, now in long trousers, he came home to Chesterfield Street from school and held out his hand to Trilby. 'Daddy's taking me back,' he said.

'Do you want to go?'

'Of course I do.'

'There will always be a room for you here, William. If you need me.'

William shook his head. 'Isn't it exciting!' he said.

So his father took William back.

Trilby continued with her committee work, fundraising activities for the National Opera, her weekly master classes at the Guildhall and meetings of the Board of

Trustees. She kept up her friendship with William and watched him model himself on his father. Busy, she knew that life was a mystery. Sometimes, still, with the gift of age, she felt quite close to understanding something very important. Sometimes she almost reached out, but then shook her head, and it was gone.

Four years after Johnny Pride married Mary Deems she gave him a son, and four years after that, in 1975, she was divorced from Johnny. She received a large settlement, which was what she really wanted, for she had another man in her eye; and so Johnny got what he, too, wanted. His son.

The boy had been christened James; but that, of course, was not what his many friends called him.

551

Part VI

Eve

'It's wonderful to live dangerously again!' her brown-eyed mother gushed. 'Just when I thought I'd lost my touch.'

Eve Summers put down her mug. 'I really must – '

'That isn't really your terrific car.'

'I had to pick it up for my employer.'

'Things have changed since *I* was in the typing pool, obviously.' The car parked by the railings below Carrie's first floor rented flat was a Bentley Turbo R, in Lichfield black, with coupé coachwork by Hooper. 'Tell me all about this marvellous boss of yours! Is he dishy? Or he's probably a *she* nowadays. Is it one of those Arab banks?'

Eve glanced at her ladies' Piaget. 'I was supposed just to pick the car up from its valeting at Jack Barclay's. I wish I could stay, Mum.' The temptation to show off the car had been irresistible.

'Have a big wedge of cake, Buzz-wuzz!' Carrie held it out in her fingers, as natural as ever; or perhaps that was her secret of dominating her daughter. Or by her sheer unflagging energy, her sheer unflagging flapping tongue.

Eve returned the slice to the dish.

Her earliest memories were of her mother's silliness, and Eve still hated being called Buzz-wuzz. Her mother had even trilled the name in front of the whole first hockey team at the comprehensive school, the neat row of girls in white shirts and black shorts with kneepads about to be photographed, hockey sticks held like weapons, and everyone broke up in giggles, except Eve. 'Chin up, Buzz-wuzz! *Chin up, Buzz-wuzz!*' Lara and Sharon had taken up the chant in the showers, towels over their shoulders and wet hair in rats'-tails, then Leeane and Keri Scott, as always, her spotty face gleaming with vindictive envy at the chance to take the piss out of Eve. *Chin up, Buzz-wuzz!*

'Shut up, Keri, you're such a shithead.' Eve had flicked out the corner of her towel, then backed away. She always remembered the white tiles. *Chin up, Buzz-wuzz!*

Eve had changed schools before the next term; not her decision, another of her mother's moves, another man. Mummy had never grown up. She was in search of true love, but what she really wanted was true fun. She looked unmollified about the cake, as though Eve's rejection was for the whole maternal lifestyle. Strong-featured, doe-eyed with curly brown hair, Carrie Summers, née Carmen Paz, had been a heartbreaker in her day; and she'd broken Daddy's heart when she left him.

'I can't,' Eve said, patting her slim stomach.

'Oh you're such a bore darling.' Carrie looked down at her own, now ample frame filling her cheerful printed kaftan, with plenty of vertical pleats let in like gills over her bosom. Eve supposed she was still attractive, in a plump, blowsy, uncoordinated way. 'I wish you wouldn't be so disapproving,' Carrie grumbled. She was talking of her latest boyfriend, a cultural attaché at the Spanish Embassy, who gave her little brassy gifts of prancing horses for the mantelpiece and was wonderful for free théatre tickets. She was dying to tell Eve all about him. 'It's an old-fashioned romance,' Carrie warned her, 'we have to be very discreet.' They didn't really. Who cared? Fun!

Eve closed her eyes for a moment. Her mother had no idea of how discreet discretion had to be for some people; discretion as complete as though there was nothing really there, even when they were together, if anyone else might look at them; so discreet it was almost like living a lie.

'Does he come here?' Eve flicked her eyes at the bedroom door.

'Don't be like that. Why can't I have my bit of nooky? It's all safe sex nowadays. You're so cold. I won't have you look down your nose at me just because we all know the only person you ever loved is yourself. Your silly qualifications hide *you*. You'll discover romance one day then you'll be sorry for all you've missed and you won't be so proud. There's more to life than work.'

Eve didn't say *I know*.

'One day you'll discover true love,' chanted her mother.

I have.

'And *then* you won't laugh at your embarrassing old mum.'

'You're not embarrassing,' Eve kissed her cheek, 'and you're not old.'

Eve's skirt and jacket were the shade of white coffee, and her shoes and handbag matched the darkest Kenyan roast, the burnt glow of her hair: the glossy curls that swept over her shoulders, finally pulled almost straight in the small of her back by their own soft weight. Her complexion was dark – the sultry blood of Eduardo Paz, her grandfather, had come through her mother – Eve was tanned-looking, with a touch almost of carmine across her high cheekbones and lips. It seemed that only her eyes were inherited from Sam Summers, her estranged father: like dark blue flames. She had learned to smile with care.

'I always feel you're keeping secrets,' Carrie

557

grumbled as they went downstairs, past the bicycles parked in the hall, the smell of drying anoraks from last Monday's rain. Someone's mother had unlocked the park and children were playing in Cornwall Gardens. The spring foliage was vivid below the sun dropping behind the rooftops and the voices of the children echoed on the evening air. Chin up, Buzz-wuzz. 'Aren't they sweet?' Carrie sighed the happy sigh of one whose child has left home.

'I hate the little buggers,' Eve said. She shushed her mother's fingertips from the gleaming paintwork and sank into the pale leather and boxwood interior of the car, thumbed the toggle that lowered the window.

'A woman isn't really like a man,' said her mother through the gap.

'Mummy, you're such a hippy.'

'I had my moments. That's the trouble with life, suddenly it's such a long time ago. You're only twenty-one.'

'Two.'

'Suddenly it's all over.' Nothing kept Carrie down for long: she was irrepressible. 'Look!' she pointed, 'that's Lord Snowdon's house. It's a quite nice area, honestly.'

Eve tapped the gear selector with her fingernail, and blew her mother a kiss. She drove very carefully. A respray on this car would probably cost half her year's salary, before bonus. Bonus was the way things were done at The Prideau Merchant Bank, everything rated on performance, promotion fast-streamed. Despite her degree from Exeter University she'd started off literally making the tea. She could have had a much better job almost everywhere else.

The traffic lights changed to red. She waited, then at green turned right along Kensington High Street. People swarmed for the Underground, several girls running trying to look chic, long legs with knees together, in slim calf-length business skirts. A young man with nice glossy short hair crossed in front of her, very full of himself in his smoothie Next jacket, looking through the windscreen.

Eve glanced at herself in the rear-view mirror. Her eyes were a little too slanted, she always thought. It embarrassed her that men looked at her and didn't see *her*, just what she looked like. Yet at the same time she was grateful for the shield, and put her chin up. With her chin up her determination showed.

The expensive car wafted her forward, but only for a few hundred yards: the traffic was locked solid along Hyde Park and the Bentley inched along beside a mini, the driver picking his nose as though she couldn't see him. After he turned off towards Sloane Heaven she rested her elbow on the door capping, steering with one finger on the thin rim of the power-assisted wheel, and wondered how to operate the radio. Some kids got up in punk gear for the tourists were fighting on the pavement. They milled between the herded cars and horns sounded menacingly: the violent city. As the traffic moved on near Apsley House some guys in jeans and different-coloured bright sweatshirts with identical logos, *Guildhall School of Music and Drama*, were swinging their legs amiably on the wall near the bus stop. One young man, with the others and yet *not* with them, looked straight through the open window at her.

The road ramped down here, entering the tunnel beneath Hyde Park Corner, and as she looked away she realised he could see her profile against the pale concrete cladding the entrance. She looked directly at him, unmoving in the traffic, then lifted the toggles and the windows swept up into place. He smiled broadly. She sat in the silence, glancing at him.

He was laughing.

The traffic moved, leaking down into the tunnel, and she let herself be carried forward. Over her shoulder she saw his silhouette against the rectangle of daylight, hands on hips. Then he was gone. In the dark she relaxed. It was ridiculous, her heart was hammering, she felt like she had been in an advertisement for expensive chocolates – girl in posh car, athletic stranger, very blue eyes, Grade One blond hair darker near the roots. But not smooth enough for chocolates. And too intense. Much too powerful all round for chocs, she decided. Aftershave maybe. Very cleanshaven, simple, strong features. Too lively. She had summed him up.

The traffic inched forward, gleaming artificially.

There was something much too *light* about him, too unharmed.

Too young.

Suddenly, alone in the orange dark of the tunnel, tears pricked her eyes: that her lover should be old enough to be her father – was in fact *older* than her father, wherever Sam was. This was the first time she had felt shame, even a moment. Shame to find there must be something lacking inside her, to be in love with a man more than twice her age.

Baby, you can drive my car. Beep beep! Yeah!

The traffic oozed forward into daylight.

There, he was waiting, leaning calmly on the railing trying to pretend he wasn't puffed. A grin split his face. She pressed the central locking.

He vaulted over and came winding through the cars towards her, and Eve realised how defenceless a girl in a car was, her fear accentuated by the locked doors. He was altogether too confident, and too young. He held up his hand in greeting, still grinning. The other side of the road was clear.

She pushed down her foot, twirling the wheel, and the car shot forward down the wrong side of the road. She was too terrified to look back. The lights ahead changed and an avalanche of traffic came towards her down Piccadilly. She tried to get back in the left lane but the cars she had overtaken wouldn't let her in. A bus with its headlights on put its radiator almost against the Bentley's door. Eve twisted and looked over the seat-back – jeans, white sweatshirt, running. She took her toe off the brake, praying not to scratch the car, forcing a Sierra to give way, then the bloody lights went red. She was head of the queue. She flicked her eyes between the mirrors, rear and door mirrors, but saw only the Sierra driver glaring at her.

There he was, running.

The lights wouldn't change. She leaned forward over the wheel, he was coming up beside her, belt-buckle almost touching the glass. He put his arm on the roof, leaning down, and she looked away. The lights flashed green and she kicked the accelerator to the floor, leaving him standing. She caught up the next pulse of traffic clearing the lights ahead and clung determinedly to its tail through the amber warning.

He was running along the pavement. A man could run as fast as London traffic. The lace of one of his Nikes had come undone and flapped at his jeans but still he came on. Then the traffic eased and she pulled ahead. In the distance he stopped, legs akimbo, then turned up a sidestreet.

Eve's hands were trembling. She had heard such terrible things, read of them every day. Men did not chase after girls for innocent purposes.

She turned downhill. Her mother would have chatted to him, they would have turned into firm friends in two minutes. Probably he'd just fancied her.

Still, she had been frightened.

Now she found the confidence to try one of the buttons on the radio and melodious sound filled the car: Mozart. Outside the Haymarket Theatre, she saw a single headlight weaving through the traffic behind her.

It followed her across the side of the big square.

Some sort of big motorbike, and he wasn't wearing

561

a helmet. Cars hooted him officiously. The last of the sun flickered between the buildings.

Eve felt completely frantic and actually put her hand on the door-pull to get out. There was a church in front of her, St Martin-in-the-Fields. The road to Charing Cross Station cleared and she jabbed at the throttle, got well ahead, the Bentley screamed round the corner into the Strand, the fastest she'd ever driven.

The bike came out of a sidestreet, she slammed on the brakes, opened the door furiously.

The faint sound of tinkling glass. He stood up, brushing his jeans, then stepped across the sprawled carcass of the bike and held out his hand.

'I'm sorry! I'm sorry!' he laughed in a broad, cheerful accent.

He wasn't English. Relief washed over her. There had been a misunderstanding.

'Jim Pride,' he said, still holding out his hand.

'Eve Summers,' she told him absently, staring at the broken glass.

'I've always been impetuous,' he said cheerfully, 'it's my best fault. I always meet girls like this.'

'You bloody liar. Don't you talk to me.'

'Pity about the old headlight there.'

'You're right,' she said. He picked up the pieces. There was blood from the graze on his arm. 'Does it hurt?'

'Yes.'

'Good!' she said.

'Mozart,' he grinned, popping the glass neatly into one of the green sponsored bins. '*Così fan tutti*. Not Solti's best recording.' She went back and turned the radio off. 'I like living dangerously,' he said, picking up the bike, watching her. He propped it on its stand.

They must get down to the routine. 'We'd better swap names and addresses.'

'That's the idea,' he said. 'I see you're unmarried.'

She looked at him furiously. 'You shouldn't steer with one hand,' he pointed out her naked finger, 'it's a lazy habit.' Traffic was curving around them, faces looking down delightedly from the bus windows to see the dented Bentley.

'So that's how you knew,' she said. 'No luck, Mr Pride. I'm spoken for.'

'I'm always lucky,' he told her seriously, then glanced at the piece of paper she handed him. 'Cornwall Gardens.'

'My mother's house.'

'I'd love to meet her.'

'Can't you control yourself? You're welcome to her, you deserve one another. I don't live there.'

'Do you live anywhere? You're too glamorous to be true,' he said, and she looked at him very sharply indeed.

'Oh? You're so experienced. What let me down?'

'Nothing,' he told her, 'not one single thing.'

He fired up his bike, waved, and was gone.

She stared at the piece of paper in her hand, crushed it up, then put it in her handbag. Her stomach was full of butterflies. She hated young nerds who pretended they were personal friends of Mozart and Sir George Solti.

Getting back in the car, she made the ten minutes' drive along the Strand and the sad deserted newspaper offices of Fleet Street to the City. She parked in the underground car park and turned on the vanity lights, checked her face in the mirror. She'd be forgiven for the broken headlight, but she looked like she had been crying. She dabbed her cheeks, but it was a strange fact that eyes looked brighter and better after tears: she shut the car door quietly, patted the dusty roof of her Fiat Panda in the next bay, and took the lift to the penthouse feeling like a call-girl.

*

563

'I love the heat between your thighs,' William whispered, stroking her sheer tights inside her skirt with the palms of his hands. 'I love the smell of you.'

She clung onto him, faintly embarrassed. If he stroked her much more through the nylon the poor man would probably get an electric shock.

He promised her: 'I shall penetrate your heart.'

He was on his knees in the deep carpet in front of her, pretending to be her slave, secure in his dominion over her: 'I *covet* you.' She held his head tenderly, murmuring, telling herself she was in love with this older man with his sandy hair flashed with grey at the temples, his silk paisley dressing-gown. William Prideau was forty-nine years old, mature, complex, powerful, and he needed her.

'And I covet you,' she said, trying to play it by his rules.

He looked up.

She confessed: 'There's something I have to tell you.'

'You're upset,' William said suspiciously.

'The car.'

'Wasn't it ready?'

'The silly headlight.' He clasped his hands behind her legs, pulling her against him, laughing.

'You worried me.'

She said foolishly: 'I thought nothing worried you.'

He stopped. 'Only you.' He stood up, much taller than she, blue eyes twinkling. 'Do you love me, Eve?'

'My love.'

'I don't know how to show you more than I do.' He was too good-looking, rich and far into middle age to have remained celibate – he must have reached his physical maturity in the 1960s, the great age of sex according to Eve's hippy mother, when no one over sixteen wasn't on girls and pills and drugs. Carrie, of course, had ended up marrying an older man in besotted love with her as an ideal woman, determined to make a housewife and mother out of her, and that had not been Carrie's scene at all.

Eve had few illusions.

'Take me to bed,' she said.

'Does my body really mean as much to you as yours. . . .' he slipped his fingers over, with a gulp, the swell of her breasts, unbuttoning her out of her blouse, almost shy, '. . . . as yours does to me?'

She murmured and sighed.

He held her in his hands: 'As *you* do to me?'

He talked too much. Yet, he did love her, she was sure. She felt it too. He spoke this artificially believing it meant as much to her as to him. Only words. Yet they did add a sophisticated dimension to the prosaic act of doing it. If she hadn't loved him she wouldn't be like this, going into the bedroom with him, all clothes gone, lying over his body on the bed.

That look in his eyes.

'I wanted so much to give you pleasure,' he whispered. 'I wanted to touch you.'

'You did touch me.'

'Not just with that.' He wasn't so proud now he was limp.

She kissed him.

At his level love was the rarest commodity, anything genuine was precious. She'd been honest. Were they in love? She didn't know. That took two.

By the lights of the NatWest Tower, a glowing column beyond the drapes, she looked at William Prideau's sleeping head on her breast, her nipple in the circle of his snoring mouth, and stroked his sleek hair.

William looked up at her through slitted eyes. The world was full of ambitious women, and he encouraged ambition ruthlessly; when all the cute boss-talk about teamwork to losers was over no corporation prospered without dog eat dog, or bitch eat bitch. Yet Eve baffled him. He was in love with her, and that love made her supremely dangerous to him. It was a well-known business maxim that when successful older men discovered their sexual vitality they were finished.

He sucked her nipple, pretending he was asleep.

Her career profile said Eve Summers was ambitious, but was she *this* ambitious? Of course she loved him, otherwise she wouldn't have let him exploit her this far – unless she was hugely ambitious. He couldn't penetrate her motivation, understand her, only love her body. Her mind defeated him. The real she remained untouchable, an *absence*, essential femininity, when he possessed her there was nothing there. What was her price? Unless it was really all very simple.

Just love.

He sucked, and caressed.

He didn't believe he could be so lucky as he was in her. No one could be that naive, he told himself in the pride of his possession.

He wondered if he could successfully enter her again, without her waking, and come without her knowing.

When his moment came he cried out and gripped her in her sleep with his elbows and knees, possessing all, losing all.

Do I love her? he asked himself afterwards, *or do I hate her?*

Jim sat on his Kawasaki motorcycle, one leg across the fuel tank, holding his ankle comfortably, looking up at the harlequin of lighted and dark windows soaring into the night sky. He didn't know the building, any of these buildings, had never been into the City before. The piece of paper she had given him was still crumpled in his pocket. He had simply followed her.

He noticed the lace of his sneaker was undone and did it up in a thoughtful way. Then he fired up the bike and swept back the way he had come.

*

566

Eve glanced back. As head of the privately owned Prideau Merchant Bank, William Prideau was one of the wealthiest men in Mr Major's Britain. Immaculate, tall, dark-eyed with silver temples, he looked what he was: successful. Eve crossed the raised car-way – the chauffeur dealt with the car door – and waited for the three men in the car to finish talking.

William got out and instructed the chauffeur: 'Six o'clock sharp.' As he crossed the pavement towards her, Eve looked away from his face. He passed her without a word, everything between them secret, unacknowledged, totally real.

'Come on, Ray,' he called back coldly, then disappeared inside.

Eve pondered him. Mrs Laidlaw, his devoted secretary for twenty years, her face powdered below beautifully permed hair – a woman with the confidence to wear lovely hand-knitted pullovers and comfortable shoes in this man's world where the girls dressed like men, and behaved like they thought men did – had confided to Eve: 'Mr William's just like his father, lass, Sir John. There was a difficult man!' *Difficult* was a compliment from this practical Scotswoman. Her gaze had softened. 'Not that William realises it, of course. William wanted to be so *faithful* but Sir John wouldn't let him close. That put William in a tricky pickle when Sir John died in 1972. William hadn't done his homework, almost lost the company to Ray Higgins.'

Having met the immaculate Mrs Laidlaw, now retired, Eve was sure *she* had never bedded William – but she had been Sir John's secretary for eleven years. Eve had joined the company as an analyst, a nobody, thinking she was important. Alone in her leaky Clapton flat after work she listened to the boom-bass ghetto blasters of the blacks breaking cars in the street, or through the walls, like an all-night party, then the revving of car engines, and she cried herself to sleep at night. She was so lonely it was like a kind of paralysis.

William supported the Royal Opera House because that is what a successful man does. For the same reasons he collected art, because that's what is done, not because he cared. For the same reason, like his father, he collected women. Until he was collected. The most beautiful girl he had ever set eyes upon, more than pretty, more than desirable: wanting her hurt him. She was getting on the bus when he was leaving work, he saw her from the back of his car, couldn't get her out of his mind. Looked out for her. Then he discovered she was working for Prideau Bank, *his* bank.

So he owned her.

Ray and Kelvin hurried past Eve. Kelvin puffed, 'Thanks, love.'

The group crossed from the brassbound plate glass doors. The award-winning atrium was seven storeys high inside, originally Mayan in ethos, with concrete circles to represent the sun that the Mayans worshipped, but lately all that had been softened and empathised with fashionable Gaia motifs, real boulders imported from northern Italy and lots of hanging greenery, trees, plants, all genuine. Eve's raised heels made a lighter, more rapid click than the steady footsteps of the men; it was impossible to forget she was a woman. She clicked ahead to summon the lift, all three men eyeing her bottom.

There was a moment to wait; Eve held the briefing folders against the swell of her breasts, the hem of her woollen dress tickling her lightly behind her knees, her face as businesslike and averted as William's own.

Kelvin Barridge was nervous. He had folded his pudgy arms, looking too relaxed. Ray Higgins, slim and aristocratic-looking with his silver hair and aquiline nose, wore a Trotter suit he would never have purchased, his wife had been power shopping. It was the first time Eve had seen Ray nervous; it showed in his easy-going manner, his quick smile for employees who probably only recognised him from the company magazine. The securities trading room, full of computer consoles, served day or night as the time zones marched on the big screen around the world, occupied three floors behind the glass wall.

The lift door opened, *ting*, upper C, and she followed her seniors inside, turned the key, pressed the top button on the steel keyboard. A year ago such status would have seemed so glamorous, a dream come true, but already she took it as prosaic. Behind her the two men stood casually, like conspirators, paying court to William by the curved glass wall of the external lift, the horizon expanding as they rose: the pale windowless stone of the Bank of England close by, then a sudden vista of roof-slates gleaming after last night's rain.

'Give me the numbers,' William said.

Kelvin Barridge murmured: 'Thirteen billion.'

Ray's face froze. Those weren't his Prideau Trust figures. He didn't like New Guard banking men like Kelvin reworking his numbers. Obviously William knew what Kelvin would estimate; even guided the estimate. Twenty years ago, when he lost the battle, Ray Higgins had been put in Outer Siberia at Prideau Trust, the wholly-owned conglomerate – screw factories, car parts, all the old rubbish left for dead. He'd transformed it. Ray couldn't win against the man who had his name on the building, who carried the Board in his pocket, but Ray had a genius for marketing assets. He was valued, pampered with limousines, the corporate jet, William even waiving for the family's Riviera junkets the double first-class fare rule for personal use. But lately the success of Hanson Trust, especially in the United States, had eclipsed Ray's achievements. People were beginning to say Ray only picked on the leftovers from Hanson's table.

'Thirteen billion Australian or American?' asked Ray heavily.

'Same difference,' William said.

'Pounds sterling,' Kelvin said, and cleared his throat.

Ray saw that William had it all planned. 'It's going to cost more than the Channel Tunnel,' William smiled. 'But this time, no sharing. No common cause. No consortia. *We* shall control the costs.'

'Jesus,' Kelvin shuddered, the financial expert.

'It's copper-bottomed,' William said, 'gold-plated.'

He forced himself to look away from Eve, turning to the sharp glass blades of the City that pierced the skyline around them. Far below dwindled the dwarfed spires of churches, winding streets, and so many people they hardly seemed human now: strings and ribbons of little yuppies like ants. William said in a low voice: 'One small item of information there's no need to bother people with today. We are not alone.'

The lift gonged and Eve stepped out first, the most junior.

'There are other players,' murmured William to the two men as they walked along the corridor. Ray tried to pretend he wasn't getting left behind.

'Dammit!' he said, 'if there's a leak, it doesn't come from my boys!'

'I never suggested it did,' William said icily. Ray glared at Kelvin and other members of the New Guard dressed in dark pinstripes waiting in the rotunda – some wags called the circular, galleried space the Panopticon, the centre of a prison from which every convict could be seen.

These waiting men were not commercial bankers, the 'spaniels', men with nice mortgages and nice wives who helped out at the kids' playgroup: these investment bankers were the Master Race, lean and hungry Essex men of vision, career sharks who bilked their clients and kept dogs that bit. The Masters of the Universe

570

were a Roaring Eighties breed who had been believed to have no place in the Nice Nineties. But they had always been insiders.

'Gentlemen, I'm ready.' William led the way.

They followed him past the curving walls hung with aboriginal art, a $150,000 Albert Namatjira water-colour of gum trees under an alien sky, a Lin Onus in acrylics, Janet Forrester and Michael Simmonds Lowreene working in traditional dots. William's public relations consultant, Elmer Kryne, accompanied them smiling as though he knew what it was all about. 'You'll see,' he kept saying, 'and you'll be *wowed* when you see.'

Eve opened the door.

This was the main boardroom, where fire procedures and pension arrangements were discussed: a long refectory table familiar from Eton or Trinity, even to the beeswax smell disciplined into the dark wood. From dull gilt frames round the panelled walls stared the faces of past chief executives, dark and severe as head-masters. Eve opened the door on the far side and the men filed past her into the Inner Circle.

Nothing changed in the uses of power. Prideau was a global corporation, one of many, by no means the largest or oldest, built on the American corporate model of wheels within wheels, clubs within clubs, secrets within secrets. Here, with a dash of European subtlety, was the nexus: the centre of the centre, where everything fitted together.

William smiled. More influential than directors, boards or cabinets: a committee. And he controlled it.

'Gentlemen,' he said. The table was constructed from one single sheet of black ebony, flawless. Into the wall was set a large Hitachi video screen. The presentation manager, Vernon Wachinski, nodded almost impercep-tibly from the rostrum and the lights went down. Wil-

571

liam nodded for Eve to stay, and she sat unobtrusively in a chair by the locked door.

'Today I'm wearing two hats, gentlemen,' William said. 'I am speaking to you as chairman of Prideau Trust as well as chairman of our Bank. An opportunity has arisen. Vernon.'

The video wall became a brilliant planet Earth viewed from space.

Someone said, 'Whoo-hoo!' The effect was stunning.

Then somebody said: 'That's not Earth, where the hell's that?' One vast red archipelago, each island green around the edges, shimmered over most of the northern hemisphere; the rest was a mighty, world-covering ocean.

'Shit, it's Venus,' said one of the dealmakers.

The voice of the narrator, a well-known actor, spoke over the soundtrack.

'Our world, four hundred million years ago. The Devonian – Devon – period. The islands drawing together to form a supercontinent, a vast red desert ringed with life, volcanoes, shallow seas, where south-west England now is. Mighty rainstorms deposited minerals in huge river-deltas. This sediment becomes rock.'

The continent split slowly in two. The visual effects were by Industrial Light and Magic, as totally convincing as *Star Wars*.

'Our world, two hundred million years ago. Pangaea shears into two supercontinents, Laurasia the north, Gondwana the south, from which all our modern continents derive. Australia, torn away, drifts through a Persian Gulf climate together with Antarctica, touches the South Pole, separates and is swept slowly northward.'

The continents suddenly stopped. The globe was now the modern world.

Most of these men would have left school without an

O-level in geography. The world obligingly rotated, the tiny triangle of Britain disappearing, the vast red continent of Australia turning into view, its green heart hung beneath it like a pendant.

'Tasmania, Australia,' the narrator said helpfully.

Slowly the island grew until it seemed it would overflow the screen.

'Tasmania,' purred the narrator. 'The Apple Isle. Tasmania's geology goes back a billion years – in the Devonian period, a thin line of volcanoes fringing the shore of the great desert, the Devon environment of shallow seas and sediment. The very edge of the splitting supercontinent.' The narrator paused, having anticipated the ripple of more than interest, *fascination*, his remark caused. 'The lava carried minerals from deep in the earth's crust.'

The southwest wilderness of Tasmania seemed to rush forward out of the screen. Several watchers tilted their seats back involuntarily.

'This land is fractured by volcanic activity, uplifted mountains, and, very recently, glaciation. Population almost zero. It's wilderness. Good for nothing.'

The voice stopped, the screen went dark.

As the lights came up William said: 'It's incredible how much we know.'

The presentation continued. A tame professor of geology had already braced his hands on the lectern, surveying them with eagle eyes. Then he looked down. 'There is a mystery,' he confessed.

The southwest coastline of Tasmania brightened behind him, silhouetting the professor's profile between forest and ocean. He tapped a rectangular blue shape, almost cut off from the sea, with a white baton like a conductor's.

'Macquarie Harbour, gentlemen.' The scale expanded slowly. 'Nearly twenty miles long, cut off from the sea by Hell's Gates. You may have seen it on

573

the news ten or fifteen years ago during the Gordon River dams controversy, the No Dams movement. The greenies won the battle, lost the war. Other hydro-electric damming projects went ahead and much of the area mined-out in the early part of this century has been flooded in the King River and other schemes, submerging chunks of the island, forming enormous bodies of water.'

William interrupted: 'They're used for big projects.'

'Thirty million years ago Tasmania was part of a huge forest attached to Australia, now submerged beneath the sea. The Vale of Macquarie was covered with flowers, fruit, beech, pine.'

'Coal,' said one analyst, 'oil.'

'We believe the land sank down between two parallel faults. Macquarie is a *graben*, gentlemen – first a lake, collecting sediments washed from the mountains by the prehistoric Gordon and other rivers, becoming a harbour as the sea rose. The barrier of Hell's Gates is a natural creation of the sea's currents depositing sand. This sand is a hundred and twenty-five feet deep – as deep as the harbour – the drowned fault continues far out to sea along the coastline. Two days before he discovered Tasmania, Abel Tasman's compasses became useless from the amount of Macquarie Harbour magnetite on the sea bed beneath his ships. Lost, he navigated by the mountains Zeehan and Heemskirk which appeared over the horizon, naming them in his gratitude after his ships which they had saved.'

The map changed to odd colours: the geology, each rock-type labelled with its own hue.

A trader said in disgust: 'Christ, a riot in a disco.'

Terry Olsen said, 'No, a broken vase no one has been able to glue together.'

'The geology of Queenstown today, gentlemen, sheet SK–55 issued by the Department of Mines, the latest available.' The professor tapped his baton. 'Twenty-five thousand years ago glaciers smashed the whole geology of the area. Once the picture was simple, almost all significant primary mineralisation in this area is middle Devonian – copper, zinc, tin, gold, silver. Mount Lyell is part of the Mount Read volcanic sequence which runs north-south near the 146th parallel and reaches Macquarie Harbour at Farm Cove. Now, after glaciation, it's unbelievably complex. We believe the mother lode of mother lodes is there somewhere, but we have no idea where.'

'Who owns Mount Lyell?' Kelvin Barridge asked. 'Not us.'

'Consolidated Gold Fields,' Ray Higgins said, 'purchased by Hanson Trust for £3.5 billion in August 1989. Often about to close down, always reprieved. That old copper field's never going to die, just goes deeper. They've dug down through the mountain to a level equal to below the floor of Macquarie Harbour, and it's *still* going on down.'

Eve saw that William permitted himself a small smile. *Do I love him?* she wondered, *do I really touch him?* She hadn't seen him look at her once. He hid everything inside himself. That reassured her.

'Mount Lyell was lifted by a freak chance with its original Devonian mineral beds at a thirty-degree angle, and we know much has been eroded away – in the last century prospectors fell over the strata lying on the surface, gold, copper being washed away in front of their eyes by the rain.' He paused. 'In Mount Lyell, gentlemen, we have merely glimpsed the tip of the iceberg. We have to ask ourselves a question. Where is the original deep, level strata preserved from the time before the upthrust of the mountains? And where has all the exposed, eroded rock gone to?'

There was a silence. Someone said: 'Oh my God. Macquarie Harbour?'

The professor stepped down.

Still Eve watched William's face. He had planned all this, the fumbling audience led gently towards the extraordinary truth. William looked at her and a flicker of excitement glittered for a moment in his eyes, for her alone. How much more remained hidden? She smoothed her dress over her knees. He kept looking at her as though he could hardly concentrate on the presentation for which he had worked so hard and so long.

Now a young, lanky man with long brown hair, looking very awkward in a beige sports jacket and loosely-knotted blue tie, took the stand. The resident genius, Mark Hattowyer, the mathematician. He scratched his ear then put back his hair with the palm of his hand.

'Right,' he said, 'right on. Macquarie Harbour, on both counts. When the Macquarie Harbour *graben* sank, it took down the virgin strata beneath it out of harm's way. Then the mountains eroded billions of tons of richly mineralised sediment into the basin. Then the evidence was covered with a hundred and twenty feet of water, and at Hell's Gates with sand.' He swept back his hair again. 'That was our hunch. The problem was how to prove it.'

'Secrecy,' William said.

Hattowyer continued: 'In March 1983 the Tasmanian State Government dropped its moratorium on mining in the Southwest Conservation Area and invited mining companies to apply for exploration licences. Six years ago the Australian Government began the largest-ever geological survey of the area. Many companies subscribed or did their own surface work: base minerals in Mount Sorell, gold a couple of miles from Strahan. An oil rig test-drilled a couple of miles off Cape Sorell. Four hundred million tons of iron ore were found at Birthday Bay, brown coal at Coal Head, asbestos at Asbestos Point – Jesus, the old fossickers who named

576

these places knew it was there, but they couldn't get the stuff out. Soon it's gonna be worthwhile.'

William stepped in for a moment to explain. 'Gold and copper are dirt cheap right now so everybody's happy, we can all afford to follow the fashion, get cute about the environment. But when the Antarctica anti-mining treaty is signed and ratified, gold and copper prices are going to rise, and *rise*. The only other main sources are Africa, where the tribes are swinging in the trees again as the old colonial order goes, and the Soviet Union with the same scenario. Our investment is simply a matter of common sense. New resources will be desperately required, because without them we are talking the economic end of the world, mass unemployment, and the time comes when people don't vote for the trees but for their jobs.'

The illuminated map changed smoothly between its various formats, the same picture viewed in different ways: a plain simple school-map with the sea painted blue and the land painted green, then deeper perceptions revealing what lay beneath, gravity vortices showing up denser lenses of rock, electromagnetic lines of force spiralling deep into the earth, seismic graphs with their jagged whispers echoing from the hidden world below.

'We had to be dead careful,' Hattowyer said, 'couldn't let off seismic charges in case we gave our game away. Then we discovered that storm-waves breaking on the cliffs at Cape Sorrell – those southern ocean seas can be eighty, a hundred feet high – went off like bombs, and the shock was boomed for miles through the stratiform lenses of deep rock below the harbour. There it was: the real entrance to Macquarie Harbour. Of course all this microseismic activity, and the overlay of glaciated rock, gave us figures like rubbish. Noise. Others have had that problem.' He palmed his hair proudly. 'We crunched *our* numbers through a

577

Cray supercomputer. Bingo. We found the ore horizon, deep and smooth.'

Terry Olsen, the bright young analyst now totally bald from chemotherapy in his battle with cancer, leaned back with a sigh. 'So El Dorado is underneath Macquarie Harbour.'

William said: 'We're talking the biggest copper mine in the world. One of the biggest gold mines. Zinc – '

'Doesn't that have to be extracted using electricity?'

'Hydro-electricity. No pollution. The Gordon dam will be built, the Tasmanian government always wanted it. The Federal government won't dare overrule them again. This time there's too much at stake.'

Kelvin Barridge said: 'We have majority control of leases covering the harbour. An oil company has a couple of blocks – oil and gas have been known for years to bubble up in the harbour. Others are in private hands going back more than a hundred years – they were allocated in eighty-acre parcels and if some of it was over water, tough.'

Terry Olsen held up his hand. 'You'll mine from shore, through a complex of slanting drives under the harbour?'

'The mining subsidiary of the Prideau Trust will. Standard practice, forget about Victorian winding-shafts and black-faced miners. Whole new towns, hospitals, town halls, tunnels big enough to take sixty-ton Komatsu trucks a thousand feet below the harbour.'

'What about tailings, all the useless rock from these enormous drives? Where does it go?'

'Jesus, Terry,' Mark exploded, 'it's Australia! There are regulations.'

'They'll want the jobs,' William smiled, 'they'll want them badly enough. Besides, Lyell fought tailings dams for years, discharged four million tons of pyrite silt and base metals down the King River, there's a delta of the stuff fifty or a hundred feet deep at the mouth of the

578

river, and the silt covers three-quarters of the harbour bed. It's drowned most of the rocks so the fish have nowhere to feed – those that weren't killed off years ago by the cyanide and arsenic by-products. The University of Tasmania couldn't even find any shellfish to test.' He waved his hand in dismissal. 'The place is already a desert.'

The maps were replaced by a still photograph of Macquarie Harbour, the mountains held perfectly in their own reflections.

Eve stared.

'But it's kind of pretty,' Terry Olsen said.

The room was emptying, everyone claiming they knew about Project Zain right from the start: William had played them off against one another.

'Oh yes, it's pretty,' said William to Eve, suddenly dropping his wary, confident business face, for her, 'it's a place without people.' His wistfulness touched her, and as soon as they were alone, she squeezed his hand. 'I can't sleep with you tonight,' William said. 'I am at the Opera.'

'Your dear aunt.'

'One of her charities. And entertain afterwards. I'm sorry.'

Someone appeared and they walked apart.

'It's all right,' Eve said. 'Really. I'll go to Clapton, wash my hair.'

'We can't go on like this,' William said. He didn't look at her, spoke almost without moving his lips, like a ventriloquist. 'I love you, Eve. I really, really do.'

The Variety Concert in Aid of Ethiopia was presented by the Corporation of London at the Royal Opera House. In the audience jewellery flashed. Jim Pride, dressed in white tie and scissor tails, his collar though oversize as always seeming too tight as he breathed deeply to relax, waited in the wings before his performance. The smell of sweat was very strong here. In front of him stretched blinding light and dark, the announcer's silhouette at the microphone introducing him: '*And now –* '

Jim walked into the glare onstage, into the wave of heat. The microphone had been removed: in front of him there was nothing, only air. Below him in the pit the score-lights glinted off the instruments of the Young Musicians Symphony Orchestra, waiting. Silence. Now he saw the conductor's baton, the glow of James Blair's blond hair, his pale hands slowly rising.

O du mein Holder Abendstern, Wolfram's aria from Wagner's *Tannhäuser*, would demonstrate Jim's virtuosity. He would sing or die. There would be almost no introduction, only the single chord, the rest must be from his throat.

Jim was calm, concentrated, using his nerves properly. In only a few minutes, Wolfram's princess would cut her throat and leave him alone for ever. He stared into the darkness and filled his lungs.

The chord filled the theatre, and Jim launched himself, the column of sound summoned from within his heart and throat, his spirit.

In a private box high in the darkness, William Prideau noted his aunt's concentration. The back-glare illuminated her withered features in hooks and seams of light. She was so motionless that he really thought she was dead.

'William,' she said, turning to him.

Jim Pride did not need to be told it was a triumph. Backstage, he wandered almost blindly, glad it was over, yet filled with sadness too. The echoes had died, the sound was gone, and he wanted to be alone. But girls in tutus knocked past him, then he was in the flaking, cream-painted brick corridor leading to the dressing rooms. There were always people waiting after a performance to say how good it was as if they knew something about music. They pressed their business cards into his hand or slipped them into his top pocket, and slapped him on the back just to touch him.

'Young man.'

Jim turned.

William Prideau said: 'Come to my party.'

'I've got my own party on, thanks.'

'You aren't my choice. My aunt asked to see you.' He called after Jim: 'Do you know who I am, young man?'

'No,' Jim called back, 'but I'm busy, OK?'

One of the other singers whispered, 'Pamper the punters. Think of your career.'

'All I care about is singing.' Jim drove his bike through the backstreets of London to his Southwark flat, the slipstream tugging his coattails, humming as he went.

'James, my boy, this is Dad here!' came the voice down the phone, and Jim, lying on the sofa with a tin of Ruddles on his chest, told himself his father had somehow heard of his solo earlier in the evening and rung up to congratulate him. He hated being called James and was sure his father knew it. He put his hand over his other ear: Babs and Mac made a racket washing glasses in the kitchen, the drama girls were in fine form, and some lizard Jim didn't know was trying to sell Tark insurance.

Johnny Pride, in his room at the Savoy, a very expensive blue pinstripe jacket hanging unbuttoned from his barrel chest, his tie off and shirt collar pulled open around his bull neck, was fifty years old today. He looked no more than forty-five. No card, no present, no surprise party. His son had forgotten.

'Hi, Pops!' Jim's youthful exuberance, everything was water off a duck's back to him. If only the boy would get serious.

Alone in his London room Johnny said: 'I reckon you're enjoying yourself, as usual, from what I can hear in the background.'

Jim clicked the muting switch on his red cordless phone for a moment. 'Hey, guys, I got my old pops calling from the other side of the world. . . .'

'How you doing, chum?' came his father's voice heartily down the line, strangely lacking, Jim thought, the usual satellite delay.

'Good,' said Jim automatically, wondering why his father was really calling, what he was trying to bully him into now. Johnny Pride always sounded as though he spoke through clenched teeth: as though everything was a battle. Jim once admired his father unreservedly, partly because his divorced mother tried so hard to turn Jim away from him – it was she who had first encouraged Jim's singing, because Johnny Pride hated it, wanted Jim to study maths at the Uni in his image, and Jim did go there. But then he left before he got a degree and played off his parents, ran away to England, and they still fought one another over him. Jim was important to them because he showed they had once been in love. But he was like neither of them.

Jim had a voice.

Jim, out of his formal penguin suit and into jeans but still wearing the white shirt, now crumpled, with the winged collar unstudded, lay on the sofa in his Southwark flat with its wonderful view of the twinkling lights receding down the Thames past London Bridge. The flat his absent father owned, the view his absent father paid for. 'Good!' he repeated heartily. One of the drama girls reading the Godot soliloquy giggled. The ugly, generous one blew a squeak on her recorder. Jim pulled a Phil Cool face, pointing at the phone: keep the noise down.

'Partying *again*,' Johnny Pride said. 'Don't you ever get down to some work?'

'Celebrating a gig, Pops. Tonight I sang solo at Covent Garden – ' Jim told his father, but Johnny Pride cut him off like a knife.

'Gig? You still doing that Barbershop nonsense?'

'Yeah, but hold on, Pops, it's not – ' He wanted to tell his father *Tonight I sang a solo on the stage at the Royal Opera House*. But he couldn't find the words to explain it. Not words his father would understand.

'When are you going to grow up? Pennies in a hat. Jesus.'

'That's called busking, Pops.' He held the phone at arm's length and crossed his eyes at it. The giggly girl giggled and the serious one said: 'But Becket is all soliloquy, after all, Lena.' Tarquin had folded his legs like a stick insect and was poring over his ingrowing toenail, and Jim attempted again to make some kind of contact with his father. 'The guys and I do a little busking, we enjoy it. But tonight, I – '

His father said: 'That's not what I pay the Guildhall School five thousand pounds a year to hear, James. I know you're just pissing me off doing something I don't like.' He drew a deep breath. 'I want you to behave responsibly, James, that's all. None of our family have ever been interested in singing. Look, if you want to be rebellious, do it in a way I can respect, not this. . . . arty stuff. The police come down on you for busking, being a public nuisance, don't they? If you drag our name into the papers – ' He let the threat hang.

'Why do you care?' Jim had rolled forward and put one hand on top of his head. When the giggly girl spilt her bolognese on the carpet nobody laughed, someone quietly got the cloth to wipe it up.

Johnny Pride hadn't even paused. 'Because I'm in London, James, and I'm here on business, and I'm not going to have you let me down, is that clear?'

Silence.

'Why didn't your secretary tell me you were here?'

Jim's voice trembled. 'Have I ever let you down? *Have I?*'

'Don't tell me you wouldn't do it,' Johnny Pride raged down the line, 'you haven't a thought in your head!' His heart was thumping and he calmed his temper the boy aroused so easily. 'Look, let's get together for a meal. You come here, wear a tie. Sorry if it isn't fun, but do it for me.'

'You didn't tell me you were in London.'

'Shit, James, it's lucky I didn't bump into you singing for your supper in the Underground! You listen to me. I'm in the *Financial Times* tomorrow, I'm doing photocalls in the City. An Australian raider in London.'

'What is it, buying another brewery? Why didn't you come and see me?'

Johnny Pride said the nastiest thing he could think of. 'I don't know what goes on in that flat of yours.'

He was so out of court that Jim laughed. 'Come off it, Pops, orgies went out of style with the Rolling Stones.'

'Don't rock the boat,' warned his father. 'You just keep your head down quietly with all your warbling pals and don't make trouble. I'm here on the biggest deal of my life – whether you care or not!'

'I'm not working for you – ' Jim looked at the phone, startled. 'He hung up on me. My old man hung up on me.'

'I spilt the bolognese,' Lena said nervously. She was a drama student and didn't usually mix with the singers, only knowing Jim Pride by his reputation for easy-going friendship. Of course, she told herself bitterly, he could afford it: a white carpet, Adirondack furniture. 'What was the fuss?' she asked cockily, but he didn't look at her.

'He wants me to be someone I'm not,' Jim said with a shrug, as if it didn't matter. 'Shit! I forgot his birthday!'

'He's welcome to this toenail,' lamented Tarquin in his deep bass voice, looking very black against the carpet.

'I want you at the rehearsal tomorrow, Tarka,' Jim said, finishing his beer and opening another. '*On time* this time, and we'll do a session on *The Deitch Company*.' Then he sat sipping his beer moodily by the speaker, his friends trickling away.

At the Savoy Hotel, a knock came on the door. Johnny Pride opened it.

The bald-headed young man said: 'I wasn't followed.'

'Did the meeting happen? Is Project Zain what we thought?'

'It's just as you predicted. More.'

Both men looked down the empty corridor. 'Come in, chum.'

Terry Olsen, looking ill, shook the drops off his raincoat while Johnny Pride picked up the phone and ordered sandwiches. 'Right, talk to me.'

Terry Olsen talked, and Johnny Pride, twice the other man's size, listened to him. When the sandwiches came Terry shook his head: his therapy.

'Are you going to make it?' Johnny Pride asked.

Terry closed his eyes for one moment.

Johnny Pride sat splayed over a gilt chair, resting his forearms on the back, occasionally feeding a salmon sandwich, or tuna and lettuce, into his mouth. Everything the bald man said added up: his own father had always felt there was something wrong about the harbour but that had been because of his parents drowning there in the nineteen-thirties. What was Terry's motivation in giving him this priceless information? 'So you're telling me this because you're dying or is there some other reason?' He had met Prideau just once and instinctively disliked him; both were invulnerable men and didn't trust their reflections. Later Prideau won back a Triple-A deal that Paragon-Pride had almost sewn up. That was business, but it had been done with a superior arrogance that said: *Just an Ocker.*

'It's true my life insurance is on the company scheme. So is the pension payable to my wife and two boys in the event of my death.'

'You can't afford to rock the boat!' grinned Johnny Pride. It was difficult not to mock a man so soon bound for the next world for fretting about the future of this one. 'Secretly, Terry, you're Greenpeace, right?'

'I am,' Terry said earnestly, more relieved than he could express by the sincerity and strength he saw in the other man's face, 'and I know you are.'

It was true. The English *Independent* newspaper had reported the poacher turning gamekeeper, Australian banker John Pride's conversion to environmentalism, his acceptance of a post-industrial world. The leopard had changed his spots, very publicly disposing of his controlling interest in America's fifth or sixth largest lumber company because of its 'cut and git' policy. 'The sequoia groves,' he had declared, 'must be given World Heritage status.' The interviews were managed from the verandah of his mansion in western Tasmania, his business headquarters and also his home: there was Johnny Pride, sitting on the step in a red flannel fossicker shirt and slouch hat, a straw in his mouth, saying so. 'The pursuit of greed is yesterday's creed. We have too much money.'

There were no fools like clever fools; the traitor Terry Olsen's eyes were hollowed by tears of relief.

'I've been there, Mr Pride, like you. I've seen the Wilderness. I've stood under a Huon pine older than Jesus Christ. I've stood on the float of a seaplane on the Gordon River, drifting with the current and listening to the silence. The cathedral of river and trees. Prideau must be stopped.'

'Yes, he must. You Poms have exploited Australia for long enough.' Johnny made himself chuckle to rob his words of offence. *Without my son, the real emptiness is inside myself*.

Terry grasped his hand gratefully. 'What shall I do? No one will believe me, I cannot reveal my name – it's not for my own sake, you understand, but for the twins. But *you* can go public and arouse the opposition. It's your home, Mr Pride, the home of one of the last great wildernesses of the world.'

Johnny Pride said compassionately: 'You must tell me all you know. Then we can stop him.'

He listened, smiling inside himself.

He had glimpsed Prideau's plan and his own mind went leaping ahead. He saw history in the making, and his own place in it. Immortality.

Jim Pride's motorcycle swooped across London Bridge, the ebbing tide swirling below, and swept uphill to the Monument then along King William Street, past the Bank and into sight of the vast brutalist blocks of the Barbican. The bike swayed in the sudden gusts of wind they pulled down. He was late as always, ignoring the gaping mouths of the underground car parks, instead swung across the main entrance to the Guildhall School, leaving the machine in the care of the old keeper of the car park serving the private flats. The complex was a 1960s celebration of culture modelled on Costa del Sol hotels, and a few chilly people sat round the rectangular lake, wearing overcoats against the wind.

Jim ran inside, blowing on his hands and half frozen from his brief ride, wearing only jeans and white shirt, kicking open the heavy green doors that got in his way as he ran. With no time to check his pigeonhole for post, he ran down the Music Hall foyer beneath the Gold Medal boards that once hung in the old John Carpenter Street school, and plunged into the warren of singing and teaching rooms with their pale green walls and fluorescent lights. Students were singing in the endless corridors.

In practice room 234 Tarquin heard the doors banging, signalling Jim's approach. 'I hear the man,' he said.

Jim bounced in. 'Sorry, mates.' He combed his hair in the broad mirror.

'Late!' mocked Tark, tapping his watch, 'the man's late, late, late!'

Barbershop singing was slicker and quicker than traditional village glee songs. Charlie Nestor did most of the organising and Jim Pride had most of the fun. The audiences always liked Tarquin Williamson the West Indian, six foot four in spats, who usually played the fall guy but never missed a beat. The tenor was new, and Paul was escorted today by singers' common complaint, a nose cold. Using their voices like musical instruments for rhythm and backing vocals, the five-member group slicked back their hair and dressed thirties-style, calling themselves the Charleston Hestons and doing gigs mainly at birthday parties, weddings, Guild and City dinners. By now they'd built up a repertoire of thirty or forty songs and a smooth act that required endless practice. Today they all wore jeans, even Thomas, and Paul favoured his cold with a long Lenin overcoat.

Nestor the Wise was lying on one of the yellow bentwood chairs ranked along the wall eating a lettuce sandwich. 'Rabbit food,' he said. Their overdrafts were a virility symbol. Some worried about it more than others and Wise Man was a worrier. He gave the lettuce a sick look.

'Smoke it,' Jim suggested.

'What are we doing today?' Thomas touched his toes once, twice, thrice. Paul was practising his golf swing.

Wise Man wiped his lips. '*Deitch.*'

'Let's get to it,' Jim said. 'Let's hustle, guys.'

'You vill line up!' Tark commanded in a German parade-ground voice. The others goose-stepped. 'Hey, man, mind my toenail.'

'Inspect the line, keep the time,' Jim said. 'One two three stop talking gentlemen.'

'Fore!' Paul said.

'You vill do as you are told. Jim, give us a G, at vunce.'

Jim gave them the note. He had perfect pitch, an eerie ability. '*Oh ven you hear ze roll of ze big bass drum. . . .*' Tark inspected the line, stepping immaculately between the rhythm of kicking feet.

None of them noticed the door had opened.

'Give yourself more time!' Jim said. 'Three, four – hey, that note sequence sounds almost medieval, we need more third, it's too open.'

A voice murmured: 'It's not too open, it's just flat.'

They looked round in the silence.

The old woman leaned on her stick by the piano. Her movements were tortoise-slow, her face a mask of age, but her eyes were clear and steady. 'You will permit me to listen?'

'No worries,' Jim said.

Paul whispered: 'A fossil?'

'Achtung,' Tark said.

A woman companion helped the old lady, who wore smooth pale pearls round her wattled neck, onto the piano stool. Her archaic style of clothes, the pearls, carried a distinct whiff of the twenties as though she had ceased there. Wise Man had recognised her. 'For God's sake,' he fussed behind his hand, 'it's one of the Governors. . . .'

'The Charlestons never sing flat,' Jim said, and she

589

was sure he had hardly noticed her years, saw through her.

She hummed the key. Perfect pitch.

'That was better,' Jim admitted when they had finished.

The old lady watched him without moving.

'You are better than this,' she said. She held up her hand and her companion gave her a card.

'Do you reckon?' Jim grinned. Even his sentence structure, the way he put words together, was as familiar to her as though the years had dropped away. She still kept Larry Pride's letters, echoes from the life unlived.

'Don't be so young.' She held out the card so he must come towards her to take it. 'I heard you sing last night. You need to talk to me, Jim Pride.'

The address on the card was Chesterfield Street. Her name was printed archaically: Miss Trilby Prideau.

'Tea time,' she instructed. 'Four o'clock sharp. You will not wear those clothes.'

The others looked at Jim. They all thought *they* were the best.

Trilby settled gratefully into her wheelchair waiting in the corridor and clasped her stick in her bony knuckles as she was pushed. She said nothing. Finally Edwina, her companion, leaned forward over Trilby's shoulder.

'*Is he the one?*'

Jim ran up to the library to return his overdue copy of Tovey's *Musical Analysis*, ducked his professor, decided he didn't have time for the toasted cheese and bacon sandwich he'd ordered and found a note waiting for him at the main entrance. It was from his father. *We rubbed each other up the wrong way last night. Peace. Let's get together for a meal tonight and sort things out.* Jim thought *oh-oh*. But he had no time to think, the rehearsal had overrun, he pulled on his helmet and drove the Kawasaki through the City back to the Shakespeare's Globe development at Southwark. Across the river the dome of St Paul's looked misty and beautiful against the afternoon sky. He hopped into a quick bath, the Duruflé *Requiem* on the CD, then dressed in a dark suit with a red and gold tie, and left. As he came out of the Underground at Hyde Park Corner he slipped on his sunglasses as he hurried past the Hilton Hotel into Mayfair. It was already four-thirty. He had to consult his *Visitors' London* to find Chesterfield Street.

The butler let him in and as he was ushered into the large elegant room upstairs Jim realised this was not really a tea party. It was a *salon* like the eighteenth century. Miss Prideau, withered and ancient, sat in a tall crimson armchair with the light from the window behind her. Her long hands were massively knobbled with arthritis; her face was rather shadowed by the light. He wondered if he should kiss her but there was an impatience about her that dissuaded him. Some of the smartly dressed young people gathered round her glanced at him and he realised he was an outsider.

But Trilby said: 'Jim Pride.'

He came forward. 'Hi. You asked me, so I came.'

One of the girls said: 'Are you singing for us?'

'No, I'm not.'

'Oh, it's rather a tradition.'

'If only I'd known,' Jim said, 'I would have brought my voice.'

Trilby looked amused, and one of the other girls laughed.

Jim did a double-take. The picture of her standing in front of the Bentley with the smashed headlight flashed across his mind. She held her fingertip to her lips: accompanied on the piano, a baritone in a dinner jacket filled the room with sonorous chords. His face was very well known. Silver-haired men listened seri-

591

ously to him, their fingers curled on their chins in knowledgeable concentration. Jim kept meeting Eve's eyes. A maid handed him a cup of tea and he realised the singing had stopped. He helped himself to a cucumber sandwich. Someone else was deep in conversation with Eve, one of the learned men, so he ate a couple more. The man glanced at him, hands in his pockets, then strolled over, and Jim realised it was the man who had buttonholed him last night. 'William Prideau.'

'Jim Pride.' Jim stuck out his hand. It was left hanging there.

'My aunt told me you would be here.' Jim looked at his hand then shook it by his ear as if it was a watch. William dismissed the playacting as not worth his attention.

'No,' Jim said, 'can't find anything wrong with it.' He held his hand out again.

'I believe I did business with your father once!' William shrugged the proffered hand quickly between his fingers.

'My father does a lot of business.'

'Give Johnny my regards,' William said disdainfully. 'I hope I see him around.' He put his hands back in his pockets. 'Sniffing around London for wounded and carrion, I suppose?'

'How did you know he was in London?'

'It's my business to know. And I read the *Financial Times* this morning. I don't think he'll find anything for him here, you know.'

'You're out of my depth. I'm just a singer.'

'Just!' said Trilby. 'No, no. William, you will observe this boy. To be a singer is the greatest thing in the world.'

William took his hands out of his pockets. 'I absolutely must be going, Aunt. I've enjoyed myself so much. Eve, ask the maid for my coat please.' He glanced at Jim. 'It's been so nice meeting you. I should

592

stick to singing. Tell your father to stay at home with his sheep.'

'Cattle. I've really, really enjoyed making your acquaintance.'

Trilby said: 'He has a voice, William. You heard my star baritone. Jim is better.' William coloured as though she was accusing him of his own lack of application as a child.

'I chose business,' he told his aunt, 'one cannot do both.'

'I know,' she said. 'Kiss my cheek, dear, then you may go.' Alone, she looked up at Jim from her wheel-chair. 'He's such a little boy really.'

'He's totally charming.'

'William is under intense pressure.' She sat watching Jim. Out of the window William Prideau's figure appeared in a navy-blue wool overcoat, crossing the road below. Ankles flashing, Eve hurried after him to the car. They got in and the black Bentley sped away.

'You've got it, Jim Pride,' Trilby said.

He looked impatiently at the empty street, then turned back to the room.

'Some are born, some are made,' Trilby said simply. 'There's no need for you to be second best. I have never been moved so powerfully as I was last night. You were born. What was created by God can be shaped by woman.'

What was she offering him?

'Not *it* yet but the foetus of it, Jim. You're too young. You're too confident, too untouched, too immature.' She searched for breath. 'But you lack. . . . all the empty things, swagger, arrogance. You have the passion, the reserve to succeed – don't you?'

'Don't tire her,' Edwina whispered in Jim's ear.

'You have the voice I would have given my limbs to have,' Trilby said wistfully, '*the* voice. I know you never needed to work for it until now.'

'I want to succeed,' Jim said. He had never admitted this to anyone.

'Don't abuse your gift. It's more precious than you know.'

He shot back: 'How do *you* know?'

She held her finger to his lips. 'I have been there. And I failed. Don't *you* fail.'

When he had gone, Trilby closed her eyes. There was always the fear that she was just a gaga old fool, her words of wisdom senile drivellings.

'Did he understand?' she murmured. 'He's so full of life.'

'He knew,' Edwina said, pulling the bedroom curtains closed against the streetlights. 'He listened.'

'He won't reach full flower for twenty years,' Trilby murmured, 'and I'll never hear him. I detest being old. Not having lived.'

Jim ran along Piccadilly, jacket flapping, snatching a glance at his watch, late as always. He almost fell over the taxi turning out of a sidestreet. 'Old Compton Street,' he told the driver. His father, who preferred the 'Ecu de France' with its rows of wooden heraldry shields and sense of history, wanted to meet Jim in Wheeler's, which he thought of as a younger person's restaurant. Johnny Pride was making a concession.

Jim would have chosen Pollo's, the Italian restaurant Italians went to.

Among the mahogany and brass of Wheeler's, Johnny Pride was sitting at the counter. He came through the gloom and shook hands, smiled, clapped Jim on the back. They took the corner table, almost enclosed, very private. Only one or two businessmen entertaining their secretaries remained, the theatre crowd had arrived and was eating busily, mostly Americans with their forks in their right hands. Jim wished he hadn't eaten so many cucumber sandwiches

'Hungry?' Johnny Pride said.

'Sure.'

'You haven't changed!' He ordered an enormous prawn salad to start. He hardly touched his but Jim felt obliged to plough through his own plateful.

'Here, have some of mine, I'm not hungry,' Johnny Pride said. What did he want? Jim wished he was somewhere else. 'Jim, we've pulled apart, kind of. Sure, it's my fault, I know, I know. We won't be so far apart in the future. It's time you faced up to your responsibilities.' He pulled the head off a Mediterranean prawn but didn't eat it, placed the meat neatly on his plate. 'You're my son. I know you've had an unhappy time. I know your mother turned you against me.'

'That's not true.'

'It wasn't all my fault. She's getting divorced a second time.' He shrugged. 'Jim, you can't remain a child for ever.'

They leaned back as their plates were taken. 'Smoked salmon,' Johnny Pride ordered, looking up with eyes like blue marbles. Jim ordered Dover sole. 'Give him plenty of chips.' Almost as if it was part of the order he continued, looking straight at his son, 'I want you to join the business.'

'We've had this discussion before, Pops. You don't own my life.'

'No, I don't want to. I own your Kawasaki, your flat, I pay your Guildhall fees, and thereafter I get out of your life? I'm not going to have you walk all over me like that, mate.'

'What do you mean?'

'I want you to learn to value yourself, earn your living, pay your way.'

'Why won't you accept I don't want to be like you?'

'I want you to learn to be a man,' Johnny Pride said bluntly. 'It's a jungle out there.'

'You just want me to do as I'm told.'

'I damn well do. The most important lesson a man learns, doing what he's told. You learn what you're told, you learn to do the telling.'

'Tell me about home,' Jim said.

Johnny Pride tried to reach across the table.

'You're the only battle I ever lost.'

They ate. Johnny Pride pushed his salmon onto Jim's plate. 'I don't want to fight you. I'm up to my neck. . . . oh, everything's fine at home. You really love that place, don't you. You didn't like going away with your mother to Hobart.'

'I hated going there!' Jim's outburst surprised them both.

'It was the one thing I gave you. Macquarie Harbour.' Johnny Pride looked at his empty plate, shaking his head. 'That's why I'm here. . . . oh hell, Jim. I just wish I understood you. I do respect your desire to sing. But believe me, it is so irrelevant. . . .'

His father's voice seemed to fade away. Jim ate mechanically, remembering the 1983 America's Cup and the winged-keel yacht so vividly in his child's imagination that suddenly he was there, eleven years old, living in the great house at Macquarie Harbour, a child alert to every vibration, his mother's impending departure. And he must go with her. The fighting over him was intense, their voices raised behind shut doors. . . . a child running between the boundaries of the shaved lawns, numb with a sense of loss he was too young to comprehend, imagining their eyes watching him from the closed windows. In the cove floated his father's sleek high-tech racing yacht *Pride of Australia* with alloy masts like shining spears, the crew working out in orange survival suits, and if they brought the Cup home the next competition would be held amid the foamy billows of the Southern Ocean, a channel blasted through Hell's Gates to take the deep keels, an Observation City built on Cape Sorell . . . But there had been technical problems with the hull and, now renamed *Pride of Tasmania*, the faded dream floated on a weedy waterline in the Wrest Point Marina. But then all that was in the future.

Jim had wandered away from the lawns, seeing things as if for the last time. He had not discovered his voice and did not know what he wanted from life. In an overgrown area of bush, once a rubbish-tip, was a place he hid to smoke cigarettes or just lie with his hands behind his head. He had found a totem, a wooden figure. Larger than life-size, the woman's bust was cracked and the paint had flaked from her eyes. It seemed she had lain here for ever.

To a child everything was magical. Jim crossed between the grazing cattle on Picnic Point and came down to the water's edge: once there had been a town here, the port of Pillinger. Nothing remained but the hardwood jetties, split, bleached white by the sun and terribly dangerous, but that made it all the more fun. A hulk lay beached half in the water, full of sand. But when he banged the hull with the flat of his hand, the wood was sound as though it had been cut yesterday. He scraped away layers of faded white paint with his penknife, layer after layer, each brighter than the one before, until he came to golden wood. There was no name on the bow. The stern was awash; he reached down into the tea-coloured water and there his child's hands found a raised outline: it was the letter E.

He never forgot it: the intoxicating romance of that moment as the name was revealed by his fumbling fingers. *Ezzie.*

Jim looked up from his plate. 'You gave me the *Ezzie*,' he said.

'You're my son, I'd do anything for you. She's a great piece of restoration. But she was no good for racing.'

'She'd sail across Hell's Gates without being dismantled. I put the figurehead of the woman on her.'

'The Paragon of Virtue,' Johnny Pride said, drinking his iced wine, 'our Company symbol.' How differently they looked at everything.

'Once there must have been a boat called *Paragon* –'

'Jim, let's keep our feet on the ground, shall we? I'm chasing the biggest business opportunity of my life. It's Macquarie Harbour, and it's *mine*. You never knew my father, Ian. He was convinced there was something beneath the harbour, but he didn't know what it was. Blackness. Oil. We own several leases where we've been test-drilling. It's there, and coal, from the drowned primeval forest. But the Poms have found something more, deeper. Gold. Copper. Zinc. Lead. Opals. Very deep down, maybe diamonds. We aren't going to let them have it.'

Jim imagined a seafloor map of drowned forests beyond the shore, riverbeds still winding their prehistoric courses beneath the ocean.

'But it's all part of the Southwest Conservation Area!' he exploded. 'It has World Heritage status.'

'This,' said Johnny Pride, 'is quite a bit bigger than that.'

It's time you grew up. I want you with me, I mean it. Be a part of the real world, Jim. You're my son. Singing's a good joke, but let's get serious.

Jim lay on the sofa with his hands behind his head. London was never really dark. It was 3 a.m. He stared at the reflections of the river moving on the ceiling, his father's voice whispering in his brain.

They had gone back to the Savoy. A council of war was held in Johnny Pride's suite. He introduced Jim casually to his lieutenants, 'This is my son. He's not doing anything,' he added quickly, seeing the objection rise on Jim's face, 'just listening in. OK, Jim?'

Jim sat in the corner.

'That's all,' Johnny Pride said. 'Meet Dan Arby my Chief Financial Officer, Ken Dickson my lawyer you've met before, Jonesy, Vince. . . .' An Australian club, all top men, experts in their fields. Johnny Pride ordered eighty pounds' worth of sandwiches from room service and talked with one flapping in his hand. 'Our own figures bear out my source's information. Prideau isn't the only one who can buy time on a Cray.'

'William Prideau?' murmured Jim, and for the first time the other men paid attention to him.

'Mean anything to you?'

'Not a thing,' Jim said gently.

They turned away, impatient to get on. It had been a long day. The decision to go ahead had been taken. Paragon-Pride must now demonstrate that it could obtain the lines of credit for its mining subsidiary. Such a load was far more than the Australian banking system could bear: it must come from the great financial centres of London, or Tokyo, or New York.

'There are only three American banks with the clout,' Dan said, 'Citibank, Chemical Banking Corporation and Nationsbank. I tried them all, but the dollar's no good with that deficit, and the Yanks don't like our long time horizon. We're talking fifteen, twenty years before we make a cent profit. And they wanted a slice of the management action. That's almost as bad as having shareholders.'

'This project is *ours*.' Johnny Pride ate another sandwich, putting the parsley on the side of his plate. 'The Japs?'

'They have a saying,' Vince said: 'invest in the south and watch your honourable share price also head south.' Vince hated anyone he needed, even if they did build wonderful golf courses. 'The Japs don't *need* to invest in us when they're just buying us – the reason we had a high standard of living was because we sold our country for Toyotas.'

Jim looked at his watch. He was very sleepy.

'There is a further real problem with Japan,' Dan said. 'They're nice quiet people who don't like to make waves. This is going to be very high profile politically and environmentally, mass protests, TV crews, heat in the State parliament, the raising of constitutional issues – '

'Not a problem,' Johnny Pride said, 'an opportunity.'

'We're going to trash the Salamanca Agreement,' warned Dan. 'That sort of radical outcry worries the Corporate Jap. Added to that their share prices are down through the floor – Japanese banks get a lot of their capital through equities – they're up to their necks in loans to their sky-high domestic property market, and the London credit rating agencies keep re-rating them downwards. . . . They're being forced to borrow at a half per cent above Libor, the benchmark interest rate, and that's a hell of an expense.'

'I thought the Japanese were tigers,' Jim yawned.

'Paper tigers,' Dan said. 'They're in the same boat as the Americans.'

'That's why we've come to London,' Johnny Pride said. 'Prideau has raised the money,' he pointed out.

Vince dropped his bombshell. 'Prideau has signed exclusive loan agreements – he's even tied up banks he's not going to borrow from. Expensive, but it works. He's done his best to cut us off from the New Eliza-bethans.'

'Who are they?' Jim asked.

'A hundred years ago the Brits owned the world,' Vince said sourly. 'They lost the lot in the two world wars. Ten, twenty years ago net British portfolio invest ment abroad was almost nil. Now Britain has investe eighty, ninety *billion* pounds abroad. The Empire go them used to thinking in global terms. London own twice as much of America as Japan. It's a revolution and it's happened in the last ten years: the New Elizabethans. Don't forget, the Japs only take the ore from Mount Lyell, the Brits own the whole bloody mountain.'

Johnny Pride said: 'Britain joined Europe for about the same reasons Tasmania joined Australia, I guess.' He spoke so casually that Jim, half-asleep, woke up. He realised he knew his father better than the others: they had missed something. What was his father hiding? 'Same symptoms,' grinned Johnny Pride. 'You know, I've been doing a little research. Before Tasmania became an independent colony from Imperial Britain in the 1840s, there was a furore about dog registration, no joke, it almost brought down the government: the principle that licences are taxes. The Brits are splitting on the same issue. Social stress. Europe united and Great Britain isolated. National sovereignty. Now there's a powerful issue if ever there was one.'

Dan scratched his head. 'Why the sudden interest in history, mate?' He thought Australia had no history beyond the First Fleet and the biographies of the great explorers he'd been taught in school.

Jim stared at his father, thoroughly alert now. But Johnny Pride smiled and shrugged off the question. *He's on to something*. Jim closed his eyes in case his father thought he was interested in business.

Johnny Pride said: 'Just think of it as national, well, pride. Patriotism. Australia. I'm a fighter. How I hate these arrogant sods whether they're in London or Canberra. This is our chance to prove we Tasmanians can stand on our own two feet, *and we will*.'

After the meeting broke up Johnny Pride stood looking down at his sleeping son. *We Tasmanians*. He took off his coat and covered him, then went quietly to the bedroom.

When the bedroom door was shut Jim's eyes opened. He sat up, then folded the coat over the arm of the chair, and stole quietly away.

There were no taxis around at this time of night but it was only a short walk across Blackfriars Bridge, the moon silver on the water, to Southwark. When he entered his flat he put up his feet on the sofa, his hands behind his head.

His father appalled him; the energy of the man, the waste of it on these futile schemes. But now, for the first time, Jim Pride found something to admire in his spirit.

But I have my voice, Jim thought.

This, his father had said, *is quite a bit bigger than that. Let's get down to business. I want you with me. And I mean to have you.*

William Prideau lay in bed with Eve Summers, her long slim legs tangled over his, her sleeping face framed by the curls of her hair. She was so lovely he ached. This divine creature belonged to him, and he was terrified.

What could be possessed, could be lost.

Did he possess her? She cried out when they orgasmed. But was that enough? He loved her. But how could he be sure about her? They must marry.

He was now fifty years old. Age was the battle no man could win – but he felt so young with her; in her love he recaptured what he never had.

He gently slipped out from between her legs, smiling as she murmured in her sleep.

He left the door open and crossed the soft carpet to the area he used as his office, clicked on the desk lamp, winced at its brightness on the top secret report he laid out. *The Mount Lyell deposit has always been considered unusual because most of its metal reserve was probably formed beneath the sea floor.* . . . *Mount Read volcanic belt intense*

mineralised. . . . Western Sequence believed to recur in Macqua-
rie Harbour area. . . . stratigraphic and structural complexities
such that many facets of evolution remain unsolved.

Not now. Supercomputers had revealed everything.

Below the sand, gravel and lignite floor of Macquarie Har-
bour, first to be encountered is a deep layer of eroded polymetallics
washed down from the ore-rich mountains. Below this level lie
the sunken, virgin strata of the Devonian period: the stratiform
barite lenses are copper-rich at the base, zinc-lead higher, with
gold found between the bands of ore. . . . silver. . . .
osmiridium. . . .

William snatched a look over his shoulder: his bed
in the backwash of light, the covers deliciously rumpled. Eve's pale knees raised as though he were still
there, one hand lying open across his pillow. He turned
his attention back to his desk. The assay results in front
of him were sufficient to give any man an erection.

Copper 13% by weight. Silver 260 grams per tonne. Gold
37 grams per tonne. Osmiridium, tungsten, part of the band
that stretched clear to King Island. *Tin, lead. . . .* the
list was long. The most conservative estimate put the
copper reserve at twenty million tonnes, twenty times
the size of the Mount Lyell deposit. This was a prize
worth paying any price for.

Eve watched him from beneath her eyelashes: his
naked figure bent over the white papers, his scrawny
backside and the lines around his armpits. Did William
Prideau love her? Yes, he was over his head in love
with her. He came back to bed and she closed her eyes
as his shadow fell across her. Then he got in beside her
and soon he was snoring.

She loved him. His maturity. His power. The fact
he wanted her.

The light irritated her and she got up to turn it off.

The top sheet of paper lay directly under the lamp.

The ancient rivers of Gondwana – the Gordon, King and
Pieman rivers – have followed their courses for more than a

quarter of a billion years, while Tasmania was swept around the world. As the mountains slowly rose around it, the Gordon cut through them spectacular gorges so deep they were once believed to be tunnels. . . .

Fascinated, Eve closed the door. He was still asleep. She returned to the desk and a land she had hardly heard of came to life in front of her eyes.

Thirty thousand years ago, carrying their firesticks with them, Aborigines walked through the forest to Tasmania. The mountaintops were occupied by glaciers less than nine thousand years ago. The Aborigines, never more than a few hundred in the Wilderness, are believed to have burned the forest to make grassland for game – wallaby, echidna, possum, shrubs for fruit and berries. But the grassland was swept by fire and lost its fertility, and when the first white explorers arrived they found the Aborigines wandering, starving in the land they had destroyed.

Jim was at Trilby's house. Gradually it turned into a lesson – an *education*. Her energy was prodigious, singleminded. She wanted to be his Svengali.

He could not listen to her and believe she was ninety-five years old. 'Visualise the sound you want to make. Breathe. Exhale that sound.'

The effort of bringing forward the energy from him exhausted her and Trilby sat in the wheelchair with her eyes closed. The doorbell had rung downstairs and Edwina had gone down. Trilby's eyes flickered as her mind wandered. . . . perhaps she was young.

'Miss Trilby, you should rest,' Jim murmured.

Her clear blue eyes opened in her ancient face. 'Again,' the strict disciplinarian said. 'Pull all the air in the room into your chest, all of it this time.' The door opened. 'Brighter, James, fuller. . . . extend. . . . extend. . . .'

Jim's voice warbled and he coughed. The girl by the door continued to watch him. She wrapped her arms around the sheaf of papers and folders she held, protectively he thought. She was businesslike and yet defensive.

'I'm so sorry,' she said, embarrassed, 'don't let me stop you.'

'Eve Summers, James Pride.' Trilby looked between their faces. 'Ah!' she said. 'I see you know Eve.'

'Hallo,' Jim and Eve said together, then both struggled not to laugh. 'No, we haven't – ' they said. Both stopped.

'Met,' Jim said. 'We haven't met. Except once or twice.'

'Miss Summers is my nephew's personal assistant,' Trilby said.

'I've brought the routine papers,' Eve said, colouring. She was determined not to look at him.

'Ah. Well, James, you sang much better – right at the end. Edwina,' she called her companion, 'I am weary. I think I shall take my rest now.' She allowed herself to be wheeled out without a further word.

In the silence Eve busied herself arranging some of the papers she held in a folder on the piano. She was as aware of him as if she wore a sign on her back. She glanced round.

'I hope I didn't get you into trouble,' he grinned.

'What?'

'The Bentley.'

'Oh, that.' But she didn't reply. Checked the page numbers.

'You wanted to see me,' he said, touching the door lightly so that it closed.

'Why should I? Why do you have to be so juvenile all the time?'

Jim leaned against the piano beside her. 'Eve.' He nodded at the closed door. 'That old woman knows so much it's amazing.' Eve's fingers slowed. 'Not just technique and motivation, how to express a voice, all that stuff. Everything. She knew my great-grandfather,

Larry Pride, they exchanged letters for years. You know, once Prideau and Paragon-Pride were friends, business partners. Now we're deadly competitors.'

'There is always competition, it's a fact of life.'

'That's a hard view.'

'It's a hard world,' she said, clamping the papers that remained to her breasts. That characteristic pose of hers looked so familiar to him.

'You couldn't resist me after all.'

'You're so big-headed! Trilby is a shareholder through her father's estate, Winston Prideau. These are just routine papers for her to sign. We try not to burden her. . . .'

They stared at one another. He saw himself deep in her eyes.

'We'd better go,' he said.

Outside he stood by her taxi in the street. As she got in he took her arm seriously. 'Say what you came to say.'

They walked in Hyde Park. He stopped at the kiosk and bought ice-creams. Despite the warm sun the wind was cold and they both shivered as they ate.

'Jim. Your home is at Macquarie Harbour, isn't it?'

'Yes, it is.'

Eve said: 'You wouldn't really destroy it, would you?'

'*Me*?' He shrugged irresponsibly, nothing to do with him.

'Prideau will destroy it,' she said.

'It'll never happen.'

'You don't know William Prideau.'

'Not nearly as well as you do,' he said.

They looked at one another angrily. She coloured.

'I'll have you know,' she said, 'I'm damn good at my job.'

'You make your own choices.'

'That's right!'

'It's a man's world.'

606

They glared at one another with rigid faces.

'Oh, Eve,' he said. 'You're lovely.'

'You sound so soppy when you talk like that.' She unclamped her arms, showed him the papers.

'You've got ice-cream on it.'

'They're only photocopies.' Still he hardly glanced at them.

'Eve, are you a leaker?'

'The whole thing will go public in a couple of days anyway. It's not just Macquarie Harbour, don't you see the scale of the thing? It's everything, they're going to dynamite Hell's Gates to get modern ore-carriers in, the full Gordon hydro-electric dam scheme from ten years back will be resurrected.' She waved a sheet of paper. 'Back then, the Tasmanian State Department of the Environment estimated that with the full scheme nearly two-thirds of the wilderness would be logged out, flooded, destroyed.'

'Don't get emotional about this,' he advised. 'Don't get emotional and forget the facts, the bottom line.'

'I don't care about facts, only the truth.'

'Within half a second, I knew I loved you.'

'Lowland forests dominated by myrtle,' she murmured. 'King Billy pine, Huon. All gone.'

'You heard.'

'For God's sake stop smiling. This is William Prideau's position paper.' She held it against her, not letting him see it. 'The State Government will support Project Zain. Ten thousand jobs. Billions of dollars, the whole Tasmanian economy transformed. No more non-jobs subsidised by the Federal Government. Tasmania will be like Hong Kong.'

'The Wilderness Society would never permit it.'

'You don't understand what William Prideau is. This is *big*, Jim, it's so big it's – ' She looked at him appealingly. 'I didn't realise until last night. Suddenly it isn't a game.'

'Is it a game between us?'

She looked down. 'The Government will say the aboriginal fires produced less fertile soil, it's no good, so it doesn't matter if it gets submerged.'

He said: 'Eve.'

'Your father is trying to stop it, isn't he? Johnny Pride's trying to raise the money so he can buy the leases, save the harbour – isn't he?'

'I'm on your side.'

'This is the first project of William's I could see all the advantages to be gained and I still think it's wrong.'

'I guess there are plenty of advantages in being William Prideau's girl. To him you're more than just his Personal Assistant.'

'Don't make it sound so dirty, it's just a fact of life.'

He found a bench to sit on. She sat on the other end.

Jim called: 'Are you going to marry him?'

'He hasn't asked – ' But she couldn't help sounding excited. 'Do you really think he will?'

'Surely.'

'Why are you so sure?' She looked at him uncertainly.

'Because I would.'

He slid down the bench.

Jim said: 'You won't marry him.'

'Oh?'

He kissed her: just a touch of their own lips together

Suddenly they both laughed, the park around them spring, sun, and the wind murmuring in the trees, the green unfolding leaves.

Eve lay in the dark.

'I love you,' William Prideau sighed.

His shoulders slid under her hands. The woolly fee of his chest against her naked breasts, the lines unde his armpits snagging her fingertips. Tears trickled fron the corners of her eyes.

She had told Jim Pride she was going back home to Clapton. That was the destination she gave the taxi driver. She was so afraid of losing Jim. As soon as the vehicle was out of sight she tapped on the glass.

'The City,' she had said.

William groaned as though he was in pain.

'Was it good for you?' he asked her tenderly.

'Yes.'

'I'd do anything for you.'

She closed her eyes. It was no darker. 'I know,' she said.

He ran the palms of his hands down her body. 'Your swoops and curves,' he murmured more lyrically than anywhere but bed. He was constantly trying to please her, like someone anxiously popping their supper back into the oven to keep it hot.

Earlier Jim Pride had left her on his flat's balcony staring at the flowing river while he changed into a white shirt, starched white collar, dinner suit with black satin lapels, trouser-stripes, patent shoes. He was singing at St John's, Smith Square. With his golden hair, gleaming eyes and beaming smile he looked so young, so *alive*, that she had ached.

They had made smalltalk in the taxi to Smith Square. But nothing between them was really smalltalk. If he had said '*It's a cool evening,* ' she might have jumped with excitement.

They hardly spoke.

She sat in the hall near the back. His figure looked so small. St John's was kind to lower voices, resonating, but even so the power and depth of Jim's voice was extraordinary. She listened to his sound, keenly aware of her own body, the simple physicalness of it, the wooden seat beneath her buttocks and her shoes on her feet. She didn't have the courage to get rid of William. Any change now required such courage. She felt demeaned.

She felt she demeaned herself.

Yet, she knew, William did love her.

After the singing Jim wound down with a beer in the pub. She sat unhappily beside him, desperately wanting to say all the things she hid inside herself to him. She felt so dull. 'Only tonic water?' he said.

'Yes,' she said. He found a taxi to take them back to Southwark. As they pulled up she wondered what he would do. Would he invite her in?

He kissed her lightly on the lips. 'Tomorrow.'

'Always,' she said.

The taxi driver asked, 'Where to?'

She told him: 'Clapton,' and Jim slammed the door. She watched through the back window until he was gone before tapping on the glass.

'The City.'

It wasn't hard.

William Prideau was hungry as a starving man. She lay beneath his caresses. It was easy.

I am not corrupted, she told herself.

She knew she had to run away.

It was past midnight. Today Project Zain was made public.

'We want a rush!' the Hobart *Mercury* had proclaimed more than a hundred years before, and human nature had not changed. 'So far, nothing to equal it in extent,' wrote the mining experts, 'has yet been discovered in Australia.'

The scheme had been sold to Sydney businessmen and Canberra politicians as The Macquarie Harbour Initiative, an *Australian* initiative. The front companies were Australian owned and everyone who knew what side their bread was buttered on would benefit from the bonanza. Australia would not become a wholly-owned economic colony of Japan. The price was Mac-

quarie, the Empty Harbour – who'd even heard of it?
Who cared?

The clever chorus of public relations firms hired in
Hobart by apparently Australian companies told Tasmanians that their island, less than one per cent the
size of Australia, would become the new Jewel of the
East, the new island financial centre to rival Singapore
or Hong Kong. Macquarie, the poisoned harbour
beneath the bare sulphurated hills of Mount Lyell –
how many Tasmanians had even been there?

The Chambers of Commerce embraced the development with open arms. At last the brave new highways,
built as part of the political package to compensate the
region for its disappointment after cancellation of the
Gordon Dam, would be used. The Hydro-Electric
Commission had never let the Gordon project die and
now it was resurrected, all the planning infrastructure
ready in place. The silent majority had no need to
speak.

Vociferous minorities, young people out of work and
students who did not need to work, grouped outside the
offices of the Wilderness Society at 189 Davey Street, or
crowded into the Wilderness Bookshop on Salamanca
Place. During the Saturday Market earnest-looking
girls harangued fringe meetings. Schoolchildren were
organised. Greenies dressed up as trees for the television cameras, and held a procession outside the State
Parliament.

Middle-class lower-middle-managers with safe, ster-
ile, non-jobs in air-conditioned offices contacted the
Department of Parks, Wildlife and Heritage. They were
assured that due process would be observed: the Salamanca Agreement was a promise to consult. There would
be Economic Impact Statements. Nothing would
happen quickly.

After a few weeks the news went away. There were
scares invented to keep the issue alive: bulldozers and

611

mining machinery would carry cinnamon fungus into the area, and a rare phosphorescent mushroom found only at Macquarie Harbour was under threat. Quietly the HEC beat the drum for hydro-electric power. There would be no Greenhouse Effect, and any excess Tasmanian electricity could be sold to mainland Australia through undersea cables.

The Director of Mines was empowered to approve environmental disturbance within the Southwest Conservation Area, including bulldozers and excavators, having only to consult with the National Parks and Wildlife Service and the Forestry Commission. The Mining Wardens Court was not obliged to take into account environmental matters in the granting of exploration licences. The fighting fringe was urged to ease up while environmentalists in suits went through the proper channel of consultation, the Salamanca Agreement.

Mikey Simmonds Lowreene was outraged. This was conservatism, not conservation. The entire process, all this chatting over coffee round a table, had got too comfortable. He sat crosslegged on the floor of his bright, airy studio overlooking Victoria Dock, near the art gallery on Hunter Street, listening to the rain patter on the sloping glass roof. He breathed in and out through his flared nostrils. His nose was not as broad, nor his lips as full, as he would have wished, yet he was a Tasmanian Aboriginal.

Someone had only to *feel* that they had Aboriginal blood in order to register at the Tasmanian Aboriginal Centre. Mikey called his mates 'coes' and added the southwestern tribal name 'Lowreene' to his own. What his father and grandfather had been most ashamed of, Mikey was most proud. The Lowreene had been burning Cape Sorell when the first white men entered Macquarie Harbour in the 1820s under the cover of the smoke. Mikey's ancestors, he was convinced, had been locked up on Sarah Island – treated worse than the convicts because they were *black*, and the convicts made their lives unbearable. Mikey claimed to be a descendant of the great chieftain Towterer, kept at Sarah Island then exiled on 5 June 1833 to Flinders Island, far from the forests and rivers he loved.

Mikey proclaimed his status, wearing jeans to see the British Queen when she visited Australia, and stitched the yellow sun, black people, red earth Aboriginal Flag on the pocket of his blue denim shirt. From the Lands Department Library he learned what tribes claimed dispossession from which lands, although the last true Tasmanian Aborigine died out more than a hundred years past, and he supported the Aboriginal Land Claim for return of ownership, or compensation.

He learned to speak like a Tasmanian Aboriginal, discovering his lost past, rolling his *r*'s rough and deep, putting a gutteral throatiness on *ch* and *gh* like a Scot saying *loch*, extending *u* like a Frenchman.

The few hundred members of the Lowreene tribe had moved in nomadic bands of less than fifty, the land was so poor. They burned tracks through the forest and swam across Hell's Gates, but Mikey was sure they must have had boats to keep their fires alight. And if they had invented boats, what else might his people not have invented? White men had no ears for the song of the trees and streams that the Aborigines believed in. Whiteys had made respectful treaties with the warlike Maoris of New Zealand, who had pride in their land, treaties enforceable in law even today. But because Aborigines had no sense of property, their property had been stolen.

Mikey did not believe in the Law. It had never worked for the Tasmanian Aborigines. His great-grandfather Gideon had tried to deny what he was by founding the Mendonça Society, trying to prove white men had some long-ago historical claim on the land;

his grandfather Joseph, a Hobart lawyer, successfully passed himself off as white until his nomination to the Supreme Court of Tasmania in the 1950s, when hints of a 'creamy' background surfaced. Some said that their source was his own wife, Dee; their marriage had been deeply unhappy for years. Mikey's own father, a respected lawyer, had never shaken off the nickname Skip from school because he was so long-leggedy, with the distinctive black eyebrows.

But by the eighties, as many white people reckoned there was no shame in having a crim for an ancestor – it added spice – a lot of skeletons came rattling out of family cupboards to evaporate guiltlessly in the light of day. But Mikey's new-found pride in his aboriginal ancestry demanded guilt: the Australians, Mikey decided, had stolen Australia. In Tasmania they had got away with genocide. These people *should* be made to feel guilty.

'I'm not an Australian,' he told journalists. 'I'm a Tasmanian Aboriginal.'

Mikey created his world in his paintings. Now it was to be stolen again.

Traffic fumes hung over London on the hot summer days. Eve Summers made love with William Prideau, helpless to stop what she had started even though it now had a very different meaning for her; once doing it had not mattered, now it did. Johnny Pride plodded around every bank and investment house he could think of, trying to assemble a consortium that could stand against the formidable muscle of The Prideau Merchant Bank, but the City was politely, firmly, sewn up tight. One bank asked for a deposit of five million Australian dollars just to look at the financial papers. For Johnny the summer was turning into a lonely excruciating humiliation, but he couldn't let go. He had to win. Macquarie Harbour had always belonged to the Prides.

His son didn't give a damn. Jim Pride rode his motorbike to Chesterfield Street and sang his heart out for Trilby. Johnny went to see the Opera and it bored him sick. He dragged the boy up to Newmarket in the Toyota Lexus to lay a few bets on the gee-gees, but most of the time the boy sat in the car playing with the stations on the radio.

Then Johnny saw his opportunity. For Jim's birthday, he bought him a Porsche 911 Carrera 4 with leather seats. 'Time you settled down,' Johnny said.

'Why's that so important to you?'

'I can't do it all,' Johnny Pride said. 'Time you joined the family firm, chum. You see, I know what William Prideau's plan is, and I think it'll work. Start the engine.'

Both men listened to it rev. 'I still think the federal government will turn the project down,' Jim said.

'You don't know shit.' Johnny Pride reached over and turned the ignition off. In the silence he said: 'The federal government won't be there.'

'What do you mean?'

'Tasmania is going to secede from Australia.' Johnny Pride dangled the keys then dropped them in Jim's lap. 'Tasmania will be a sovereign nation, a world financial centre.'

'Jesus Christ.'

'Not the pauper of Australia subsidised by Victoria and New South Wales. Tasmania will be for the Tasmanians, with the muscle to insist on their rights. It'll happen,' Johnny Pride promised, 'and by a landslide.'

'But the voters – would they? The politicians would never – '

'You really need it spelt out? Tasmanians have never forgiven Australian federal lawyers for finding the constitutional loophole that killed off the Gordon Dam last time. *We* Tasmanians. Well, revenge is a dish best eaten cold. Secession from Australia.' He nodded. 'That's what William Prideau wants.'

'And what do *you* want?'

'Us.' Johnny opened the car door. 'I want you in it with me.'

'Not my scene, Pops.'

'It will be,' Johnny said, getting out and giving the car's roof a proprietorial slap.

Jim drove to Chesterfield Street for his singing lesson and had a hell of a job parking the car; he wished he had the bike.

'Pops sees himself as being part of history,' he confessed to Eve, meeting her in the hall as he left. 'He wants his name in the history books. The man who unbundled Australia.'

She followed him along the pavements searching for the Porsche. 'What colour is it?'

'Red. There it is.'

She held the monthly papers with Trilby's signature on them against her, the hot wind blowing her hair and her light green summer dress, watching him unlock the door, then brushed the red Porsche with her red-painted fingernail. 'Daddy's boy,' she teased.

'You know very well that's not true,' Jim said. She got in and sat, waiting. Jim started the car and drove down past Buckingham Palace. 'All right, what's the matter?'

'He asked me to marry him.'

'You can't let it go on and on like this, Eve!' He gunned the motor across Westminster Bridge, turned left. 'You don't love him.'

'You don't care what I feel. At least he knows what he wants.'

He glanced at her, braking. She stared straight ahead. She had shaken him.

'Ah, come on.'

'No,' she said, 'think about it, Jim. Don't you care about anything except yourself? And having – ' she almost spat the word, '*fun.*'

She couldn't penetrate him; couldn't break through that jaunty self-possession. If he laughed at her now she'd kill him.

He stopped the car in the underground car park. 'You and William,' he said, then cleared his throat. 'I didn't think it was so serious.'

'*He* is serious,' she repeated, '*you* keep on opting out. You can't opt out of life. When the press hassles you about joining forces with your father you say it's not your fight. Your father needs you. I need you. Jim, you're even trying to opt out of my life.' He slammed the doors. They both knew what they felt for each other but they hadn't made love. If she was accusing him of cowardice maybe she was right.

Jim tried to explain to her. 'It wouldn't be easy, not *easy*, with you. Do you understand?'

They rode up in the lift in silence.

When they reached the top Eve was crying. 'When they cry,' Johnny Pride had warned him long ago, about Mum, 'that's how they manipulate you.' It was a lesson Jim didn't know how to forget.

He tried to touch Eve's shoulder but she twisted away.

He drew the curtains, busying himself with make-work. The lights, a brandy for her. He held out the glass.

'Touch me,' she said.

He put down the glass slowly. 'Eve, have you ever made love with William Prideau?'

She said: 'No.'

It was terribly hot in bed. Eve said: 'Oh my love, you're hurting me!' so he knew she had told him the truth. The evening sunlight outside still glowed across the drawn curtains, the sweaty sheet lay across their bodies. She lay with her cheek cuddled into the soft underside of his upper arm. Jim lay staring up.

'I *love* you,' he said, 'this is just. . . . cement.'

'Was I good?'

'Don't be old-fashioned. I don't want you to be good, just to be.'

'I've never been naked with a man before,' she told him shyly, 'never *really* naked.' She sat up, showing him her breasts, her tummy-button, one knee raised. He threw off the sheet. 'Everything open between us,' she said.

'Oh, Eve. What are we going to do now?'

'William has asked me once. He'll ask twice.'

'Leave him!'

'And leave my job. I need more, Jim.'

'I love you, but I love singing too.'

'Let's run away. Anywhere!' she said.

'I can't leave my course at the Guildhall.'

She leaned down and wiggled her tongue in his ear. 'Compromise,' she whispered. But he hadn't for his father, and he wouldn't for her. She liked that a lot.

'I can't compromise over my singing,' he told her. 'You know I can't, even for you. Especially for you.'

He watched her silently dressing and said: 'What will you tell William?'

'Oh, that I was washing my hair.'

'Eve,' he said, watching the green dress slide down over her body, and she tossed back her hair, 'we haven't had sex. It was making love.'

She kissed him, and left. She already knew that.

William Prideau tried to face his obsession.

With Eve Summers he felt more alive than he had ever been; he had given himself heart and soul for her, and lived in her youth, her immature funniness, impetuosity, her quickness that entranced him. He

618

intoxicating scent, the lightning caress of her lips and fingertips, then her resistance, her submission, gave him courage. Without the strength he derived from her, he might never have dared commit himself to the Macquarie Harbour Initiative.

When he asked her to marry him she turned him down. That made him hotter for her. The coolness of judgement he prided himself on was lost. He was well aware he was infatuated and loved the feeling. In the wild race he now found himself, he was gambling all, risking all, in a sense all for her. It seemed glorious.

But some said he had lost his business touch.

He was *not* a young man. He must make her secure. He must organise his feelings. He must domesticate her so that his desire no longer threatened him. She must marry him.

But she would not marry.

What did she feel? He did not know what a woman felt.

William Prideau threw himself into his work with ferocity. But the more he put her out of his mind, the more her unattainable image consumed his passions.

There must be another man.

William stood beside his desk as Kelvin Barridge, the chief financial officer, came into his office accompanied by Eve, who sat in the corner. William could not take his eyes off her. Kelvin was speaking: William's only competitor in the Macquarie Harbour Initiative was Johnny Pride, by now hanging on only by his fingernails, but unable to let go. . . .

William dragged his attention away from Eve. Johnny Pride,' he said. More than money was at stake or that man. William had got him wrong. Macquarie Harbour was the man's home, his feelings were involved, William understood that now. He knew his misjudgement had made some of his lieutenants uneasy. Only now was William learning the power of emotion to turn everything on its head, the world upside-down. He *must* marry Eve Summers. He dragged his mind back to the business at hand.

'It's affecting your credibility,' Kelvin said. 'You told the banks there would be no contest. Johnny Pride is your enemy.'

'Yes!' William said eagerly.

'You can destroy him,' Kelvin said. 'Paragon-Pride is wholly owned and invulnerable, but all these Australians are vulnerable on loans and credit now since the crashes, and he is divorced. There have been various women and lots of gossip. We can smear him.'

William Prideau listened to Kelvin, but he watched Eve.

Johnny Pride's bid to be taken seriously by the London banks was a lost game and he knew it. The British Establishment had closed ranks against the Australian: once number two, always number two. How he hated the bastards.

'Take it easy,' Dan Arby advised, 'you don't help our cause by losing your cool.'

'Polite bastards,' gritted Johnny Pride as they strode out of the meeting and along the marble corridor, his heart beating like a hammer, 'they belong to the same Club. Sharks in Eton ties. Grinning bastards.' The two men reached the top step outside First Boston and Crédit Suisse and Johnny put his foot out. His heart cranked over faster, then suddenly a vice clamped on his chest so tight he could not move his arms or even cry out. He tumbled slowly from the top to the bottom dead.

Dan Arby knelt beside the body. 'Johnny?' he said. Secretaries walked around them.

'What do I do?' Dan wondered. He got out his handkerchief but he didn't have a clean one to cover the staring, indomitable face. At last Dan heard sirens wailing. He fussed around the ambulancemen, then suddenly the pavement was empty. He blew his nose on the handkerchief.

Dan went back to the Savoy and started phoning. He couldn't contact Jim at the Guildhall but he got through to his flat. 'Jim, it's – '

'Hi, Pops.'

Dan was embarrassed. 'No, it's not him. Jim, your father's, your father's gone.'

'When did he go?'

'No, I mean not back to Australia,' Dan said, aghast at the impression he had given. 'I mean he's dead.'

'Oh my God.'

'I'm sorry to have to be the one to tell you. . . .'

The boy sounded pathetic. 'What will Mum say? I'll have to tell Mum. I'll fly back to Hobart right away.'

'Jim, I'm sorry. It was his heart.'

'What hospital – '

'It was a heart attack,' Dan said. 'He never knew what hit. . . .'

'He's dead,' Jim said. 'Mum and he liked one another really. It wasn't a love match. She'll blame herself you know.'

Dan Arby let him ramble on.

'You can't go back to Hobart,' he said firmly. 'Johnny Pride is dead, Jim. It's all yours now.'

Nothing on the line.

'The Bank, Jim.'

'I can't handle this,' Jim said. 'I never thought this would happen.'

'No one did. It's happened.' Dan waited. Suddenly the line was broken and he heard only the blank purr of the dialling tone. He tried to get through again and again through the afternoon, but there was no answer. Damn the boy. His father would never have fallen to pieces like that.

He began phoning round for Ken and Vince, and other members of the team. It was going to be a long night.

No one had the stomach to order sandwiches. The men sat in shirtsleeves around the table in Johnny Pride's Savoy Hotel room. 'The boy's a dead loss,' Dan said. 'We won't get anything out of him for weeks, if ever.'

'Now Johnny's gone,' said Ken soberly, 'we have a real, real problem. The press release has got to go out before ten.'

'William Prideau has won,' Vince said.

'Let's just keep our jobs, I reckon,' Ken said. 'This could go very, very bad. Shit, I wish I'd made that jump to Bank of Australia last year.'

'The ship isn't sinking yet,' Dan said, but he sounded unconvinced. 'I reckon the first thing we should do is get back to Tassie, save what we can. You know the boy *is* Paragon-Pride now? Johnny was going to bring the boy in.'

'Johnny is absent,' Vince reminded them. 'We can't even hold a board meeting without the chairman present. Johnny had too much faith in himself.'

'We going to say that in this press release?'

They struggled to deal with the problem.

The door opened quietly. Jim Pride came in. He had been crying, it showed in his face.

'Jim!' Vince got up, holding out his hand. 'Great to see you! Look, no worries, but oh boy he chose a hell of a time. We just want to say how sorry we are.'

'You look sorry,' Jim said. He splayed his legs across a chair and sat with his arms across the back, his chin on his wrists, surveying them.

'I never knew him, I never really knew my father. I guess you've got a thing or two to tell me.'

Jim circled Clapton several times in the dark before h

found the block of brick flats. He parked by the Fiat Panda and went up to the fourth floor. The door opened even as he raised his hand to knock.

'Jim, I heard about your father on the news, I'm so sorry.' Eve took his hand. 'William's in Geneva. Come in.' She led him into a lounge, surprisingly large with the battered sofa and chairs pushed back to make a large bare space where open newspapers, magazines, old books lay scattered, enough almost to hide the cheap carpet. 'I expected you to call.'

'I had your mother's address in Cornwall Gardens that you gave me, and she told me where you lived.' Jim trod cautiously between the papers. Eve was wearing a white towelling wrap over her nightdress. He said: 'I didn't really believe you'd be here. I thought you'd be in William Prideau's penthouse, watching the television or whatever it is you do together.'

'I didn't deserve that.'

He sat on the arm of the sofa. 'I am going to fight William.'

She held his head between her hands. 'I'm so glad.'

'I've been pushed to the point. I can't be a bystander any longer.' Jim closed his eyes. 'He'll destroy everything I love.'

She was touched. 'Do you really love me so much?'

'Without my father Paragon-Pride would have ceased to exist. He didn't care about it when he was young any more than I did, but he learned to care. Our heritage was built up by our family for God knows how many generations, from *nothing*.'

'I love you when you speak this way.'

'William will transform the Tasmanian wilderness into a lake surrounded by foreign-dominated heavy industry. He destroyed my father. He may yet win you.'

She denied it.

'And he has destroyed my singing.'

623

'Oh, no,' she said. 'You feel like this because it's been a terrible day.' She knelt on the sofa. 'Jim, you mustn't give up singing. You can't let William do this to you. Hatred isn't the answer.'

'Hatred? I *envy* William, his age, experience, his self-confidence. His superiority. He has you. I've found my enemy.'

'Then I promise I will never see him again.'

'Yes,' Jim said, 'that would hurt him.'

She shivered.

'I think you should keep working for him,' Jim said. 'Whatever you want.' He was exhausted and overexcited and had changed into a person he would have despised this morning. 'Jim, you'll feel differently tomorrow. I'll make up the couch. Sleep here, darling.'

'Has William slept with you here?'

'Jim, I can't bear it when you're like this to me!' He stared at her wondering if she would cry. 'You can't let William do this to you,' she said. Suddenly she picked up the phone. 'If you won't listen to me – ' she punched the numbers – 'I know who you *will* listen to.'

'You're lucky I don't sleep nowadays,' Trilby's voice said, when the situation had been explained. 'You'd better come round.'

Eve put down the phone and went into the bedroom leaving the door open, and got dressed. Jim didn' look at her, lost in thought. When she came out, ver businesslike in a soft tweed jacket and skirt, he gaze at her steadily. 'Now I'm doing what everybody wante me to do,' he said, 'but it seems that's wrong too.'

He drove the Porsche along the glittering streets, th windscreen wipers swinging shadows across her fac along the brilliant perspectives of shop windows. Th pubs were closing and the police were out in forc Chesterfield Street was quiet, each streetlamp a pa sphere of drifting rain, and the railings gleamed li black prison bars. As they hurried across the paveme

624

they saw the old woman's shape waiting without movement in the illuminated window above them. 'She's watching for us,' Eve said.

Edwina opened the door reproachfully. Jim strode upstairs; it was left to Eve to apologise for the lateness of the hour.

Trilby Prideau sat in the tall red armchair like a throne by the opened curtains of the window. The lamp standard behind her glinted on the raindrops streaming silently down the glass, and made a silvery halo of her thin, uncombed hair.

'I don't know how I can still bear to like you,' she told Jim, 'but I do.'

'Miss Trilby,' Eve said, coming in, 'it's been a terrible business. I've tried to persuade him but he won't listen to me. He's like a child who's found a new toy.'

'I know what I'm giving up,' Jim said, 'but I must. What else can I do?'

'I know a man cannot have two mistresses.' Trilby raised her shadowed face. 'Oh, Jim, all this goes back such a long, long way. You have the talent I do not. Now you throw it away.'

Jim Pride said nothing.

'You see, all my life,' Trilby said, 'I have been a witness.'

The light fell across her eyes, her young blue eyes. Her grief was fierce but silent.

'Who knows the truth about anything,' she whispered. The web of blood between them was greater than they could possibly know. 'Pride and Prideau. . . . all this goes back a long way, between nations, between families, between men and women. It would be amazing were our families not connected.'

She told them of her mother, Emma Pride of Hobart, Jack's daughter, who eloped with Winston Prideau and made a new life in London. She talked of Larry Pride, and of the man she had loved, David Earle, the love of her life, who died in Larry's arms at Gallipolli. 'Larry was artistic, Jim. A photographer like his father.' She searched for the name. 'Peter, Peter Pride.'

Eve sat in the chair by the other window. She was very tired.

Jim was saying, 'I remember his old photographs, ancient faded daguerreotypes on glass. . . . my father gave them to the Hobart Museum. The originals used to hang up the stairs in the house at Macquarie Harbour. King Island, I think. . . . there was always supposed to be a family connection with King Island.'

Trilby said: 'Winston my father told me of a rumour that my grandfather, John Prideau, knew of a dreadful family secret – which he kept – a skeleton in our family cupboard.'

'A skeleton?' Eve said, alerted.

'It seems we Prideaus have a Devon ancestor who was transported for a crime. His name was James Prideau. He was sent to Botany Bay early in the nineteenth century, but his ship was lost and the wreckage was never found; all were believed killed. The names are close, aren't they. Prideau, Pride. . . .'

Eve looked eagerly at Jim.

But he only shrugged. 'So what? Prideau is a common name in Devon.'

'James Prideau had a twin brother, William,' Trilby said. 'William, the worker, founded Prideau & Prideau and the family's fortune, while James committed a crime and paid the price. And the name of his convict ship was the *Paragon*.'

Eve clapped her hands with excitement.

'There must have been lots of ships called *Paragon*,' Jim said. 'Paragon-Pride is just a coincidence. All this is just women's talk!'

Trilby took hold of Eve's hand in her own. In the

excitement the old lady and the young girl barely glanced at him. They had eyes only for each other.

'Women's talk,' Jim stormed. 'My battle with the Prideau Bank is being fought *now*, today, don't you understand?'

Outside on the pavement the rain had cleared and stars poked wanly through the streetlamp-coloured sky. The night wind, suddenly chilly with the changing of the seasons, gusted and slapped wet autumn leaves at them. Eve held her hair as Jim took out the keys to the Porsche, but he didn't put them in the lock. Instead he turned to her.

'Eve. There's something I want you to do for me.'

'Let's do it in the road.'

He said irritably, 'I want you to continue in your job.'

'Working for William? You can't be serious.'

He tapped his fingers on the car roof, gazing at her.

'I wouldn't ask you to be a spy,' he said.

'You *are* serious,' she said.

He kissed her.

'No, don't ask me that way,' she said.

'Please,' Jim said. 'We need the time, if we're to save Macquarie Harbour.'

She searched his face.

'For the sake of our unborn children, Eve.' He clicked the key and the central locking whined. 'And the last haunt of the Tasmanian Tiger.' Later he kissed her again.

'All right,' Eve said.

'I heard the Tiger,' said Mikey Simmonds Lowreene. 'I heard the Tasmanian Tiger.'

'What it sound like, man?' called Nick, a long-haired white chum who followed Mikey.

'Beautiful,' Mikey said, 'sort of friendly, but wild, you know?'

They had set off from the People's Park at Strahan wearing waterproof anoraks and backpacks, walking southeast along the shore of Macquarie Harbour. They crossed the King River on the Teepookana Bridge, once derelict but now repaired as a tourist attraction, and camped off the track near Lignite Creek.

Their bible was the Tasmania Lands, Parks and Wildlife booklet: their boots were lightweight with rounded heels and smooth soles so as not to damage the bush, they faithfully ploughed through any bog or morass in their way, rather than widen it by avoiding it, hauled water to wash their billies and cooking gear several hundred feet from the stream so as not to pollute it – using sand not soap which was alien to the wilderness environment – and dug their toilet at least three hundred and thirty feet from their camp and from the creek. Behind them the bush slanted upwards to the bare shoulders of Mount Sorell, and Mikey looked for footprints of the tiger he had heard in the night.

'This is my land,' he called over his shoulder as they walked.

'Ours,' Nick said.

'You're only a white. You wouldn't understand.'

They came to the crest beyond the Coal Head track and there below them, on the shore opposite Philips Island, was the peace camp they had come to join where they were welcomed as old friends by people they hardly knew, young upwardly-mobile couples taking a day or two's break to get back to the soil, older middle class ex-hippies sentimental for comradeship, all united by genuine concern for the environment. Some preferred to walk in like Mikey, others arrived on the fast planing-hull motor cruisers that took half-day trippers up the Gordon. The beach was dotted with CNN an

Australian Broadcasting Corporation satellite dishes and everyone was talking.

For political reasons the tent camp on the Braddon River was just beyond the Strahan municipal boundary. The livelihood of Strahan's two hundred and eighty permanent residents came from some thirty-five thousand tourists in an average year. Few stayed overnight since the start of high powered half-day cruises roaring down Macquarie Harbour to the Gordon, where radar speed traps operated; the coach-lagged visitors glimpsed a few tame wallabies skulking by a raised tourist boardwalk in the rainforest, then the boats jetted back for a glimpse of Hell's Gates, returning to Strahan in time for the coaches to depart. But this year, more than a hundred thousand visitors would come, attracted by the furore, and they would stay and spend money. The news networks rented entire hotels and Strahanians loved them.

But Queenstowners hated the greenies. Queenstown was a mining town. Australia was a mining country. Quarter-acre plots in Strahan brought postal votes and all the owner had to do – from anywhere in Australia, without even being naturalised – was write to the council clerk for a voting application form. The municipal elections put the pro-mining lobby in the office of the Warden of Strahan with a majority greater than the actual population of the town, and the greenies were thrown out of the People's Park.

So they put up their tents here, beyond the municipal boundary, on the Braddon River.

Police speedboats circled offshore, outboard motors buzzing.

The celebrities had started arriving, Greenpeace boats, Friends of the Earth, representatives from hundreds of voluntary organisations and clubs.

This was the land the Lowreene tribe had known. Mikey closed his eyes and put out his arms, imagining their energy, their *memory*, flowing up through the soles of his feet. Someone took his photograph.

Mikey listened to the song of the river dreaming its name.

Generators mumbled among the trees. In a glade he found yellow bulldozers parked in a circle and a long scar of raw earth. Chainsaws whined in the distance. As the light faded into evening the rain began.

It rained all night.

Mikey thought about the bulldozers.

It rained and rained. The TV crews splashed through the mire in bright dayglo oilskins, their cameras wrapped in black plastic dustbin bags, but all the dispirited faces they filmed made a bad impression and they went back to Strahan.

Rumours swept through the camp; there were going to be mass arrests. The Prideau Trust had applied for an injunction against anyone intending trespass. The application had been granted; rejected. Jim Pride was coming from London specially to get himself arrested, get headlines. The rumours were believed, then denied.

'It's a battle, man,' Mikey told one interviewer, 'this here's the Battle of Australia.' He corrected himself. 'Tasmania.' The interviewer gave up her battle against the sheeting rain and sloshed back to the speedboat waiting for her on the dirty rain-pocked water.

Mikey thought about those yellow bulldozers a lot.

That evening he turned on the charm and organised Nick and a few girls. 'I'm going to chain myself to a bulldozer,' Mikey said. 'You make sure there's some people there. Dress up. I guess a Tasmanian Aboriginal chained to a dozer will make people view things in different light.'

He already affected the long Lowreene pointed beard and tribal moustache. Now he took off his hiking boots and fried some bacon for fat, which he mixed with charcoal from the fire and yellow ochre he had brought

630

with him, and smeared it over his legs and torso. He hung shells around his neck. 'The spirit Moinee cut the ground and made the rivers,' he told the people watching him, 'cut the land and made the islands.'

The girls called their friends.

In the morning, they all stole out through the forest. Many in the camp had left it to get to a big rally to be held in Hobart; more than six thousand people were expected. Rain dripped through the branches and Mikey's little group slithered behind him in the mud, filling him with a sense of elation as he realised that his own bare feet gripped the mud better than their expensive footwear. The rain slid off his naked, greasy skin and he slipped easily through the tangles of bauera that snagged the clumsy clothes of his companions. His right hand clenched itself, like a race memory, as though he held a spear. He began to move faster, leaving them behind, the heavy chain swinging from his neck.

When the others arrived at the sleepy depot in the clearing, Mikey's silhouette against the massive yellow stern of the lead bulldozer was already kneeling, chaining himself to the iron towbar. The workmen were coming out of the Portakabin wiping the breakfast off their chins, and they ran to their machines when they saw Nick and the protesters hurrying from the trees. The engines started with a roar. One of the bulldozers lurched forward in a spray of red mud. Nick and the girls joined hands in front of Mikey's bulldozer. The driver raised the blade on the hydraulics.

Nick looked round. 'Where are the police?'

'We don't need them,' said one of the girls' blokes. The driver jiggled the dozer blade menacingly. One of the girls had wrapped herself in greenery and was singing. The stink of diesel was very strong, and blue smoke swirled in the gloomy first light striking across the forest glade.

'Hey, look,' Nick said urgently, 'we need the police, we need those guys to arrest us if these cases cut up rough.'

'So what if they do?'

'I didn't come here for this,' Nick said.

One of the girls cried out: 'Think of the ground parrot, think of the azure kingfisher, think of the pigmy possum and all the lives that are threatened, think of the world.'

The driver, whose name was Gus Honeyman, a kindly fellow with three kids, ended the confrontation. He backed down, throwing the bulldozer into reverse, massive treads churning, and the chain from the towbar sang taut beneath. The big yellow vehicle bumped as it clanked and slithered backwards.

'Listen, you bloody idjits,' Gus shouted out of the cab door as he killed the engine. 'Sooner or later there's going to be a bloody accident.'

'Prideau will win,' Jim said. With Eve he was honest dropped his smiling face. 'The William Prideaus of the world always win.'

Eve said nothing. An icy rain fell beyond the fluor escent-lit plate glass window, and battered cars, Dat suns and Cortinas with thudding megabass stereos splashed through the puddles, and went prowlin around the London street corners. A few dirty kid were trying to let off fireworks from the shelter of cramped doorway. Jim, resting his elbows on the fibre glass table of the Clapton Burger King, wore his nav blue woollen overcoat unbuttoned, the collar up, an it still seemed slightly odd to see him wearing th business suit beneath it, a very nice tie neatly knotte at his throat. Which she had chosen.

'You still root for him a bit, don't you,' Jim told he 'You don't even admit it to yourself. But William do

632

exert a kind of hold over you.' He sucked his Coke, watching her over the plastic lid.

'I had my career to consider. What he felt wasn't important to me. Jim, it was simply a matter of survival.' She touched Jim's hand. William Prideau always talked of marriage, but Jim never did.

'Dan Arby says my father was right,' Jim said. 'If William wins, Tasmania will secede from the Australian union. Pops knew the political situation all along, and so did William. And William will win because the Tasmanians see something they desire, the conservationists only see something they fear.'

'The mining lobby have been getting pretty bad headlines.'

'Of course they do, but people make up their own minds. That greenie guy that got run over was played up as a hero, but most real guys just thought he was a twit. These issues aren't fought out by headlines. At bottom it's always people who matter.'

'You really believe that?' Eve said.

'Yes, I do.'

He sounded so innocent that she kissed him impulsively. 'Then so do I,' she said.

Consequently, when she returned to work on Monday, curiosity rather than treachery prompted her that evening to access computer records on the VDU behind her desk. The green cursor blinked: ENTER.

She hesitated, uncertain. What had Trilby said? '*John Prideau knew of a dreadful family secret – which he kept – a skeleton in our family cupboard. . . .*'

Eve's fingers, usually so swift and sure, hesitated over the keys.

The green cursor flashed patiently: ENTER.

Eve typed: JOHN PRIDEAU.

The VDU monitor should have responded with the box numbers relating to any papers of John Prideau's held in the vaults of The Prideau Merchant Bank.

A question mark appeared. ? (*II*) *JOHN PRIDEAU 1891–1972?* Only then did a string of green box numbers scroll down like magic; keys to a lifetime preserved on paper in a concrete and steel, antiseptic, fireproof Chubb vault.

Early in the nineteenth century. . . . 1891 was far too late. The computer had accessed (*II*) because it would be the more recent, more obvious choice. The real John Prideau was further back.

She keyed: (I) JOHN PRIDEAU.

Nothing happened. Then a code appeared: *BCR*.

Eve frowned. She tried again.

(*I*) *JOHN PRIDEAU 1808–1877 BCR*.

That was all. She was stonewalled.

Eve rolled her chair back from the screen and flipped through her telephone index. She found the number. 'Mrs Laidlaw?' she chatted to her predecessor. 'It's Eve Summers here. . . .'

Mrs Laidlaw had retired to Inverness to live with her sister. Her smart voice, after the initial startlement, and perhaps pleasure, had lost none of its precise notation. 'Now, lass, what may I do for you?'

'It's nothing really. An obscure reference. BCR.'

Grace Laidlaw sounded disappointed. 'That's only the Brick Court Repository.'

'What's that?'

'Brick Court, the Middle Temple. The foundation o the core Company, Prideau & Prideau. A law firm Only the regimental agency work is carried out ther now, and that only on the top floor. Originally it wa a Wills Repository before Somerset House was buil It's still our Registered Office for the serving of docu ments on the Company even though we – ' she sti said *we* – 'we have had our offices in the City since th 1830s or so, but we didn't store legal documents at th Bank until the 1870s, when the new vaults were buil Enough for you?'

634

Eve permitted herself a small smile. 'Wonderful. Sorry to interrupt your afternoon.'

'It really was a pleasure,' said Grace Laidlaw pathetically.

Eve put down the phone.

She twirled her chair and looked at herself in the big black window behind her desk, seeing herself suspended speckled with lights, the street-map of London. A million people were going home. How could she access the Brick Court Repository? Was it stored on disk? No one would have bothered – just old papers. The door opened and William's image appeared behind her own. She hit the EXIT key with the tip of her little finger and the screen went blank as he leaned over her shoulder.

'I'm going home, Miss Summers.' William put his hand against her neck, inhaling the scent of her hair, then turned her chair to face him. 'Eve?'

He put his hands over the arms of her chair, enclosing her, his chin almost touching her forehead. She stiffened slightly.

'Eve, will I see you later?'

'I've got some work to finish up.'

She said nothing. They had not made love since he asked her to marry him.

'Eve,' he begged her, and she could see the bulge in his trousers. 'We won't go out. I'll cook and we'll watch the television.'

'I've got some work to do.'

'Soon you won't have to work. You know what I will ask you, and next time I won't take no for an answer.'

Eve promised she would come to his penthouse later. In the ladies' loo she leaned her hands on the counter between the basins, still trembling. Then she combed her hair, smiled for the lipstick, made smalltalk with the other girls off home. The lift seemed to take forever going down.

From the payphone by the bus stop she phoned the Savoy Hotel. Jim was at a meeting. 'I really, really want to talk to him,' she said, then put the receiver down. A bus for the Monument growled away from the stop and she jumped onto the rear platform, then took the Circle line Underground to the Temple.

The pubs, blazing with electric light, were already deserted.

Beyond them, everything was quiet. She stepped back a hundred years: a silent maze of narrow cobbled alleyways and wandering courtyards overhung with eaves, no cars, glimmering dusty windows peering from age-bent walls. Here was the Law. Above the occasional quaint iron streetlamp rose a jigsaw of black rooflines, the orange sky. Her footsteps clicked, echoing.

Numbers 2&3 Brick Court was ridiculous, a Dickensian confection that made her shake her head in wonderment even while her body was crying out with nerves. Newer buildings were all around it, rebuilt after bomb damage in the War probably, but this odd little place survived, somehow more real in its oddity: not a wall was straight, but the brass plaque by the low doorway was brightly polished: Prideau & Prideau.

There was no bell, not even a knocker, but the door opened under her hand and she ducked inside, then almost turned her ankle on the scoop worn into the stone.

'Careful,' came a man's voice, 'that's tradition.'

She peered into the gloom. By the yellowish glow of a forty-watt bulb she saw a man dressed in old dark clothes, a battered blue cap like a captain's on his head sitting upright at a desk. As she came closer across the creaking boards, limping slightly and wafting her hand in the dusty air in front of her, he neither took his eye from her, nor moved. His hands, with very long double jointed fingers, lay on a magnificent old desk of some

636

beautifully inlaid wood, broad as a bed. A half-eaten apple, the bitten white flesh already brown, lay in a brass ashtray on the blotter between the man's hands.

Eve wondered if there was anyone else here. The building was totally silent. Now that she had come further in the room seemed to have many corners, and in one of them an open fire burned, smokelessly, with little licking flames sending shadows across the ceiling.

'Don't worry about me,' the janitor said, 'I've got it pretty good here. What can I do for you?' His eyes twinkled roguishly.

Eve smiled. 'I think you can help me,' she said.

He didn't let her make friends with him that easily. 'I don't know about you headquarters people,' he said.

'How did you know –' She stopped when he lifted one finger, pointing at the security tag on her lapel. 'Oh.'

He looked proud of himself.

'My name is Eve Summers, personal assistant to Mr Prideau. You really can help me –' She stopped as he stood up, extended his hand across the desk.

'Mr Murphy,' he said. Not to be hurried, he took her hand and shook it. He moved sadly round his desk and knelt by the fire, prodded it with a poker into a gush of cheerful flame that illuminated the room for a few seconds. 'Mr Norman Murphy. You saw at once what I was, silly old fool you thought, I can see you don't miss much. My father was clerk here for forty-five years, never made Head Clerk. My grandfather now, he was Head Clerk.'

'I've got to move you on, I'm in a rush,' Eve said in her business-like way.

'It's not been what you would call an interesting life, though it's had its moments. The burial of Sir Winston Churchill was something. That window there, you could just see him pass on the river.' He pointed, encouraging her to be interested. 'This is a terrible place. In the night you can feel it, that's why I like the night. The night's the time. The tales these boards could tell. I'd talk all night, but you wouldn't listen.'

'Try me.'

He looked at her with his head on one side, very far from stupid.

'I haven't made the best,' he said, 'of my opportunities.'

'Mr Murphy, do you keep papers here, I mean *old* papers?'

He went to the desk, opened a drawer and came up with a pipe. He coiled his fingers round the stem, then plucked up a tuft of tobacco from the drawer and tamped it into the bowl.

'You mean the old documents repository.'

'Yes!'

'They're going to give it to a museum.' Norman Murphy lit a match, let the flare subside, wafted it over the aromatic tobacco. 'There's papers there going back to the Restoration, one or two from the days of Henry VIII. Can't hardly read the writing but those old boys sure knew how to flourish a signature.' He chuckled 'Cup o' tea?'

'Afterwards. I need to look up anything that ha been preserved of John Prideau's papers.'

'Anything of Sir John's is kept in the main vault at the Bank. You'd need security clearance, all tha nonsense.'

'I'm interested in an earlier John Prideau wh doesn't matter any more. He died over a hundred year ago.'

Murphy inhaled from his gurgling pipe, watchin Eve thoughtfully. Then he rattled the keys on his bel 'Let's have a look.'

Narrow stairs wound upwards, but he opened a do beneath them. They went down into a room like schoolroom, with ancient tiers of desks and barred tu nel-windows, now used as a storeroom, crowded with split cardboard boxes marked *Fresh Laid Eggs* and *The little lion means Quality*, piles of old office papers, memos, expense slips, spilling from them. 'From the 1950s,' Murphy commented sourly. 'Don't suppose they'll last much longer now recycling's all the rage.' He unlocked another door and they went down lower.

The repository was real chaos; beneath the curved vaulting old trunks were bundled every which way, bundles done up with string, sacks with mouths gaping open, teetering piles of brown envelopes waiting for a breath to fall. 'It's like the end of *Raiders of the Lost Ark*,' Eve said helplessly.

He watched her search.

'I can help,' he said suddenly. 'I liked the way the firm was run like this, not the way it's done nowadays. Computers. A man could understand this way, it was sort of human, flawed.' Flicking on the yellowish lights as he went, he led her to a winding corridor between stacked trunks. 'They filled up going away from the doors. That's common sense. Eighteen thirties. Eighteen fifties.' The smell of his pipe-smoke flooding over his shoulder mingled chokingly with the dust and damp as Eve followed him. 'Here we are.' He pulled at this and that, then kicked a portmanteau, smeared at the grime covering it with the sole of his boot. 'John Prideau, ma'am. I'll get that tea now.'

Eve found a piece of sacking to kneel on and began to sort through the household accounts and personal correspondence. The dates were all 1877; it seemed his death had been very sudden, in the midst of apparent health. She lifted a bundle and found a letter underneath dated 1863. Of course, the latest papers had been dropped in last; the oldest would be at the bottom. Eve had no idea of the exact year she was searching for, or exactly what she was searching for. A secret. A secret that was kept.

Her back grew stiff. She broke a nail. When she really thought her knees would crack, she crouched amidst the pile of papers she had turfed out and rubbed them, then knelt again. And there it was, right in front of her eyes.

'I nearly died,' Eve told Jim Pride. 'This is it.'

The meeting in his suite at the Savoy was still going on, cans of Foster's on the table, advisers sprawled in shirtsleeves.

'Jim, you clever devil,' Dan Arby said, not knowing of the dying traitor, Terry Olsen, 'so this is your source. She's quite a piece.'

'We have to talk,' Eve told Jim.

'These guys were just on their way.' The men got up and pulled on their jackets, put out their smokes. Eve stood awkwardly next to Jim in the silence, the only woman there, dying to tell him how she had forced herself to sit drinking tea with the crazy janitor while the documents she was holding so casually almost burned her. 'I nearly died,' she told Jim as he closed the door, 'This – '

He turned on her angrily. 'You shouldn't have come here. Now everyone knows about us – '

She burst into tears.

'I'm sorry, I'm sorry,' he admitted reluctantly, dabbing her cheeks with his handkerchief.

'Say you're sorry properly,' she said.

He kissed her.

She smiled radiantly. 'You see, Jim, it's all a lie.' She held out the papers. 'Prideau & Prideau is founded on a lie.'

He glanced at the top sheet without comprehending its old-fashioned handwriting at first. Then he said, 'My God.'

'The first thing I did was get the janitor down t

witness what I was discovering. I had to drink tea with him for hours afterwards.'

'You did the right thing.'

He pulled absently at his lower lip. 'My God,' he repeated. 'The last will and testament of the founder of the firm, William Prideau, dated the second of January, 1850.'

One half to my son John. One half my estate and interests to my brother James Prideau in Australia and his descendants, if any. . . . Jim skipped on: *the income shall fall into and be applied as income of my residuary estate. . . . my Trustees shall retain the shares and carry on the businesses of the Companies. . . .* He looked up, utterly pale. 'My God, after more than a hundred and forty years – it's haunting.' He leafed through other pages. 'The Prideaus never diluted their shareholding, they kept reinvesting in the company. They bought a concern called Versucchi with their own money and that was the start of the Prideau Trust. They always *owned* whatever they bought lock, stock and barrel. . . . application to the Court for probate. . . . half "his growing fortune" to be paid into Court – it's never been wound up! – because the beneficiary, James, was believed dead. . . .'

He picked up the phone and asked for a room number. 'Ken? Get back here.' He sat on the edge of the table, his hand on Eve's waist. 'See what a lawyer says.'

Ken Dickson seemed to leaf through the pages for hours. He was wearing half-glasses and a bottle-green dressing gown over his striped pyjamas, but in his haste he had forgotten his slippers.

'Well?' Jim said when Eve thought she was about to die from the suspense. The lawyer's bare feet irritated her unbearably.

Ken glanced over the top of his glasses. 'The will is valid, the Court accepted it. It obviously suited John

Prideau that the matter remained there. The key phrase is *and descendants.'*

Jim said: 'Is that me?'

Eve gripped his hand.

'You must prove that Prideau became Pride.' Ken tapped the papers with his fingernail. 'Some clerk must have researched deeper than that bastard John Prideau wanted. The *Paragon* was believed to have gone down off King Island, then there's a gap of twenty-five years until 1830, when a conditional pardon was granted to *Jim Pride*, also known as *James Prideau*.' He shrugged, destroying their hopes. 'It's a persuasive coincidence, but it's not proof.'

'Half of Prideau & Prideau and all its companies are mine,' Jim whispered. 'It's my birthright.'

'If you can prove that, Jim,' Ken said, 'you can break William Prideau's balls.'

When the lawyer had gone Jim and Eve stared at one another across the table. 'I promised William I'd go to the penthouse tonight!' she said.

Jim Pride held out his hand to Eve Summers.

She hardly remembered if they made love; it didn't seem necessary to be accomplished. They lay in one another's arms, neither sleeping nor waking, slipping between the two states, and Eve wished the sun would never rise.

After their first elation they realised that everything they hoped for against William was valueless unless they proved beyond all doubt that James Prideau survived the wreck of the *Paragon* and founded the Pride dynasty, and that Jim was his descendant. Jim phoned his mother in Hobart but got no reply; he tried Paragon House at Macquarie Harbour and she answered once. Mary had driven over to sort through Johnny old papers. 'The love letters I wrote him,' she said gaily, 'I'm burning them.'

642

'Don't burn anything important,' Jim said tersely. 'This is really urgent. I want you to look through the old family papers, I mean the really old ones. Last century. Peter Pride's photographs, any connection with King Island. Diaries, letters. . . .'

'It's so sad here,' came her voice. 'The place is very empty without you.'

'Just do what I said.' He put the phone down. 'It felt so odd,' he admitted to Eve. 'I'm the head of the family now.'

They were eating breakfast in the restaurant, the waiters gliding among the white linen-covered tables. The silver-domed trolleys rolled noiselessly on the deep carpet, towing a mouthwatering scent of crispy bacon, and the scrambled egg was a luscious deep yellow, made with fresh cream. In the murmur of low conversation, the swing door opened and William Prideau came in.

Jim didn't move. William stood behind Eve.

'Welcome, partner,' Jim grinned. 'I believe you've met my fiancée.'

William looked even more shaken, if that was possible. He was holding a newspaper in his hand. 'Is this true?'

'I haven't asked Jim yet,' Eve said. 'You know how impulsive he is.'

'Shut up, you vicious bitch,' William said hoarsely. He brandished Ken Dickson's letter. '*Is this true?*'

'Better shake my hand properly this time,' Jim said. 'Partner.'

'I'll see you in hell first.'

Jim stood up. 'Don't reckon I like you much, mate.'

William spoke in a low voice so as not to disturb the other diners. 'You're just speaking like that to annoy me. You are very, very young. You cannot compete.' He crumpled the letter slowly. 'You will drop this charade.'

Jim laughed at him.

William hissed: '*Miss Summers?*'

'You've lost out, Bill,' Jim said. 'She's come over to the other side.'

William recovered himself. 'Eve.' He laid his hand politely on the back of her chair.

She shook her head.

William threatened: 'You will find that I am a formidable enemy.' Then he turned on his heel and walked away.

'Britannia no longer rules the waves,' Jim said, and sat. But when he leaned down and looked up into Eve's face, he saw that she was crying.

'I never understood Johnny,' came Mary's voice. 'I see that now, you always meant more to him than I did. The gifts he spent on you, never on me.' Jim sat in his father's Savoy Hotel room, still rented by Paragon Pride, listening to his mother's faraway voice come down the phone. 'And now he's dead, it's too late. looked back through the old rubbish for you. I kep seeing Johnny there, bits of him, gleams.' The lin sighed.

'Mum, what did you find?'

'Peter Pride was born on King Island in 1837.'

'That's close,' Eve said.

Jim held up his hand: he hung from his distar mother's every word.

'The family still own the property there, Jim. It been a wildlife reserve since the 1920s.'

'Yeah, but what about Peter?'

'King Island obviously meant a great deal to hi even as an old man Peter remembered his childho there. You never recover from your childhood, do yo He'd just been married. His mother was burn alive. . . . Oh, Jim, it must have seemed like the end the world. I don't know. The guilt he must have fe

His happiness with his new young wife,' she said rapidly, and he knew she was remembering her own young hopes.

Jim said gently: 'Did Peter Pride keep a diary? Write a memoir?'

'In later life he was just a farmer, he worked with his hands. But as a child, before the fire, he was *talented*.' His mother's voice was wistful. 'When he was very young he wrote ghost stories. . . . you can't tell where fact ends and the story begins. . . . recollections, young friends swearing never to marry, horsemen falling into gullies. . . . Peter's grandfather was shipwrecked on King Island. It seems it was he who started everything off, the valley, the herd. . . . a bull that got so angry that it swam across the sea. An old man with flowing white hair who sat in the top of a tree staring over the ocean. I mean. . . .' She laughed. She was a practical woman. 'I'll fax this stuff to you, but. . . .'

Jim asked: 'What was the name of the ship?'

'The *Paragon*.'

Eve said, 'Are there trees on King Island?'

Jim shrugged. He'd never been there.

'Don't you *see*? I think your mother's right,' Eve said, 'your families are close. William and James Prideau. William never forgave James for being a criminal.'

'James pleaded *po se*, no contest.'

'He accepted guilt. He allowed his condemnation!'

'He *didn't*!' Jim said, and the telephone receiver creaked under his hand. He threw Eve a hot glance. He didn't. . . . or if he did he had a reason.'

Eve kissed his lips. 'James never forgot the home, the identity he had lost. Jim, you identify with him, don't you?'

Jim Pride frowned.

He asked his mother the most important question. 'What name did James Prideau call himself on King Island?'

645

She said: 'I thought you knew! Jim Pride.'

'You're right, Eve. I do identify with him. Jim Pride's world is gone, I suppose, but people, and cities, and feelings don't change.'

Jim and Eve lay on the carpet with the faxed documents spread out in front of them, disappointingly few: there must be more family papers in attic trunks, or hidden away in the records of the Paragon-Pride Bank of Hobart, dry accounts waiting for light to bring them to life.

They had so little time. Every day that passed gave William Prideau time to unbundle his business empire in some way to keep it out of their grasp; but for such fundamental change he required Trilby Prideau's approval.

And Trilby, after a minor stroke, sitting in her old chair with her eyes closed, her withered face wooden in her determination, sleeping when she slept and waking when she woke, was living an instinctive life. Her knuckled hands clung onto the arms of the chair, and she withheld her approval.

'William's next step will be to obtain power of attorney over her,' Ken Dickson had warned them.

Eve asked Jim, 'Why is Trilby hanging on?'

'She knows what love is. She thinks you'll bring me back to singing.' He touched his throat. 'This won't be lost.'

'Will you?'

'When this is over. Yes. Of course I'll come back.'

'And the wilderness is saved,' Eve murmured as the faxed documents arrived. They propped themselves on their elbows and examined them for hours.

Johnny Pride had been laid to rest at the huge Golders Green crematorium far from the land he knew.

Jim sat up on crossed legs looking at the grainy

reproduction of an old photograph, a single tree growing from a cindered desolation.

'You're right,' he told Eve, 'we're close. His loss. . . . I can feel Jim Pride. He wouldn't have let his story die, his *fury* would not have let him fade away.'

'What would you have done?'

'I don't know. Written something down, registered my outrage, my innocence, somehow. That I was not what I appeared. At the end of his life William Prideau, the founder of the firm, was driven to confess his guilt in his last will and testament. But there's no will for Jim Pride at the Hobart Records Office. *Was* there one?'

'He would have used it to say he was innocent.'

'That's all we need, a statement that would prove he was James Prideau. Ken says there was something called the Statutory Declarations Act passed in 1835. An oath sworn under that would be unimpeachable.'

'You'd put it in a bank,' Eve said, 'a solicitor's office. . . .'

'The hell I would. No, Eve, he didn't trust those places, they were the cause of his downfall. He stayed on King Island all his life.'

They pored over the papers. 'I'll go blind if I look at these any more,' Jim said at last, rubbing his eyes.

'Wait! Trust Australian bureaucracy,' Eve exclaimed, picking up a paper by its corner. '1845: Jim Pride made an honest woman of Annie Day, the mother of his children, at the Registry Office by the Union Bank, William Street. In *Launceston*.'

'It's time I went home,' Jim said. 'We can't see it from here.'

was a strange and, she found, intensely endearing ature of young Jim Pride that he was utterly unaffec- d by the power and, now, wealth that had come to m so young. Although at business meetings he

dressed like a businessman, as soon as they were finished he was her Jim Pride. While they waited for their
flight she watched him stroll in Heathrow's Terminal
3 wearing jeans, a bright shirt and old sneakers; if
there were spare seats, she thought, he wouldn't get
upgraded. When he asked her what was so funny she
said she didn't care; everything was wonderful.

Even the flight seemed wonderful, a constant bright
adventure to her that would have no end, their lives
moving forward together across the blue, brilliant sky.
Between meals they sat with their fingers entwined, and
while he slept she stared from the window at Moscow
passing beyond the wingtip, then the desert of the Aral
Sea with its ships sunk like toys in the sand with the
changing climate, the cities of India like endless swathes of burning straw stirring in the wind through the
night. She slept over the ocean, the plane weaving
between moonlit thunderheads billowing up from the
storm below, and woke to see the great red continent
of Australia sailing beneath the wings. In Sydney a
giant koala bear dressed up as Santa Claus solemnly
wished them Merry Christmas, and the thunderous
summer heat struck them like a blow.

The cyclones that used to track well out into the
Pacific now clawed their way down the eastern sea-
board of Australia. Jim and Eve swung their travel
bags over their shoulders and followed the file of tan,
numbered, law-abiding Australians winding across the
concourse between handlers and security guards to
catch their connection to Hobart. Foreign car adverts
admired their frontier spirit, and newspaper headlines
were laying odds on whether it would be the air contro-
lers, baggage handlers or pilots who jinxed Christmas
travel this year. The flight was full.

'No smoking,' the stewardess warned passengers over
the intercom, 'and don't try it on in the toilets, guys,
because smoke detectors have been fitted.'

'Home,' Jim said, relaxing. 'I reckon we can't feel comfortable unless we're treated like crims, or children.' He slept, but Eve pressed her face to the porthole as the sea ended and a magical land was revealed below, pointy purple mountains towing grey feathers, the wriggling coastline drawn in fits and starts with a child's yellow crayon.

The plane banked steeply onto the short runway near Hobart and suddenly they were in the real world, a limousine to meet them for the short ride into town. Crossing the Narrows Bridge the highway descended to the harbour and Jim told the chauffeur to take them straight to the manager's house on Battery Point.

'Tony, Eve Summers.' Tony Briggs had brown receding hair and a face as long as a potato. As it was a Saturday he wore a white open-neck shirt and slacks. Tony, we'll be going on to Launceston first thing.'

'Not worth it, you'd be better off trying the house at Macquarie.' Tony took them onto the patio, opened a tubby of Toohey's beer for Jim, a glass of orange juice or Eve, and introduced them to his wife Sara, who smiled decoratively. Tony's house straddled the curve of the hill, rooftops on the left tumbling to Salamanca Place and the busy market, the sailing boats of the harbour, and on the right an open view down the Derwent to the concrete cylinder of the Wrest Point Casino.

'Tony, give me the good news and the bad news,' Jim said.

'Sure, Jim. The good news is that the Union Bank at Launceston moved to the corner of St John and Paterson Streets in 1865. The bad news is that your ancestor bloke would have deposited any Statutory Declaration at the old William Street address, where the archives remained after the move, and it certainly isn't there now.'

'How can you be so positive?' Eve asked.

649

'The 1929 Launceston floods. When they opened the old vaults next day all that came out was dirty water and wood-pulp. Total loss.'

Eve looked at Jim. 'So William Prideau has won.'

'No,' Jim said, 'we lost.'

'It was only an outside chance anyway,' Tony said, 'no bother.'

Eve flushed red. 'You don't know what sort of a man he is. I do.'

Tony said, 'Yeah, well, we reckon it's in the national interest of Tasmania if the project goes ahead. And of Paragon-Pride, Jim.'

'I know.'

'We can get a slice of the action, no problem.'

'I *know*,' Jim said.

'You're not interested in a slice of the action!' Eve said.

'Sara,' Tony said, pulling his earlobe, 'you haven't shown Eve your kitchen.'

Eve watched through the glass patio door the mouths moving silently. Jim had to go along with these men who carried thousands of jobs dangling from their hands. Tony would be telling Jim his *duty*, his *responsibilities*, how he must fight for that *slice of the action*. 'Your father would have had it, Jim.'

'We're totally electric here, Eve,' Sara gushed, 'hydro-electricity is so wonderful and so cheap, and there's no greenhouse effect. We like to say it just falls from the skies!'

When they left Eve, getting into the limousine, knew Jim was angry. 'I don't need Tony Briggs to tell me my business.' He ordered the chauffeur to take them to the Victoria Street multi-floor car park, where his father's car was stored. 'We're going to drive to Macquarie Harbour. You'll find it pretty breezy.'

'I'd better buy some proper clothes.'

In one of the boutiques in the Centre Point mall

used her card for a Laura Ashley dress, a warm cashmere scarf and a long, caped ulster in pure Tasmanian knotted wool. The shops were already shutting though it was hardly midday. She waited for Jim in Liverpool Street, already feeling lost among the identical broad highways that cut between the islands of city blocks. Jim came into view driving the red sports car he had described, a Chrysler Viper with the hood down, and she swung into the passenger seat.

Almost at once, despite the high hot sun, she was grateful for the ulster as they rocketed through Glenorchy and climbed between the hills, the wind now blowing cold in her hair. The Derwent narrowed and raced beside them. There was very little traffic; it felt odd how good the roads leading west were. They stopped for a couta sandwich at Ouse and there in the dark store with its single table, Eve had never felt so happy, so alive. The woman at the fryer watched them like a wooden Indian. 'She knows we're in love,' Eve whispered.

The country was more beautiful than she imagined. As they rose out of the shimmering plains along the blacktop looping into the mountains, suddenly it rained torrentially, drops flying back over the top of the windscreen, then they were amongst brilliant peaks, blazing sun, shadowed valleys. It hailed near Lake Sinclair and snowed as they crossed the shoulders of Mount Arrowsmith. Eve put up the collar of her ulster, excited. Jim braked and there from the roadside she caught her first glimpse of Frenchman's Cap jutting between the clouds, its broken dolerite dome making a sheer, glinting drop of thousands of feet where young men proved their virility with parachutes.

'Is that the Wilderness?'

'It can't be touched,' Jim said, 'without being destroyed.'

They skirted the vast new lakes and entered the

moonscape of bare hillsides around Queenstown. Smelting had stopped twenty years before and trees were returning to the ochre, sulphurated slopes, much to the disgust of Queenstowners: 'It's the fire risk,' said the driveway attendant at the petrol station on roster, 'I like our hills the way they are, I grew up with them, and I don't like these greenies in Volkswagens telling me what's the right way to live. That's their religion not mine, right?' He patted the bonnet. 'This is a car,' he said.

The old miners' road to Strahan was part of the landscape, winding like a serpent the easy way along the ridgeline instead of driving straight through it. Strahan, with its empty quays, was quiet, the short remaining row of shops along the Esplanade shut up for Christmas. The historic F. O'Henry Mammoth Store was a bare skeleton of beams awaiting reconstruction, and Jim left the car in a lock-up garage round the back. Eve saw not one single person as they walked past the offices of Wilderness Air and Jim pulled the Riva speedboat in from the buoy on a long weedy rope. Macquarie Harbour was a mirror of the evening sky and at fifty knots Farm Cove opened up in front of them in a quarter of an hour.

From its green swards the house overlooked the shining crater of smooth water. Jim killed the engine and the boat glided in total silence alongside the jetty. The remnants of their wash lapped with sudden loudness against the white hull of the ketch moored there: the *Ezzie*.

They lay in bed. 'It isn't here,' Jim said.

Eve held him sensuously. 'I thought this was everything.'

'You know that's not true.'

'I'm in love and everything's true.'

He sat up. They had emptied the attic until the du

made them sneeze. Age-stiffened letters and papers, Victoriana – Eve kept being distracted by bits of furniture, frames, or personal effects discarded as almost worthless by following generations: old photographs of faces who had become anonymous, a locket of a woman with eyes as brown as her hair, cheap bracelets and rings now unloved and meaningless, the wearers who had treasured them long dead.

Jim drew the curtain and stepped on the verandah into the hot Christmas sun. 'I always thought this was home. But it isn't here. James Prideau didn't become Jim Pride here. Where did we come from? There was a time before this. The proof isn't here.'

Eve followed him. Her nightdress moved with filmy swirls in the faint morning breeze. She could smell flowers and a lemony scent she could not identify. He touched her, growing ardent.

'If not here, where?' She whispered in his ear: 'King Island.'

'We still employ a few men at the old scheelite mine there. I've had the banks in Currie checked. No files for Pride.'

'I know Jim Pride,' she whispered.

He groaned passionately, stroking her thighs.

A single tree growing from a cindered desolation.

She wrapped her arms round him with a cry as he entered her.

'He buried it,' she whispered. 'In the earth. Beneath the tree.'

'I love you,' he cried out in his ecstasy, and the golden water below them filled her eyes, ruffled with catspaws, the white yacht in its shimmering image, the gathering wind and a deep sense of peace.

'I thought this was my home,' Jim said sadly.

She held him in her.

The white yacht stole across the still waters, only the

ripple of foam, the occasional hum of an electrically-assisted winch, the luffs of the sails fluttering in the veer of the wind, to break the silence. Jim tried the radio again but the commercial helicopter service was closed down for Christmas, and the Hobart Flying Club, his last hope, was closed by rising winds from the east. 'We could do with more wind here,' Jim said. 'Got the hang of steering now?'

'No worries, cobber,' Eve said. The helm was taller than she was, but she had braced herself elegantly on the tilted deck, her hair over one shoulder, holding the wheel slightly to port against the tension of wind and water. The wind hardened and she lifted one foot. Tea-coloured bubbles streamed out behind the ketch, showing their course from Farm Cove.

Jim pointed beyond the bowsprit. 'Hell's Gates,' he said as the channel narrowed. 'I'll take over.'

'I can handle it,' Eve said.

Only the broken rocky spine remained of a break-water along the glassy surface. Now ships themselves no longer kept the harbour entrance stirred and moving, no one knew how deep the channel was silted. A plume of spray rose above Hell's Gates, the ocean swell rolling from a distant storm into the calm waters. The spray drifted like smoke, turning in on itself as the wind gusted. Eve spun the spokes. The yacht swayed dragged forward by the surge, then broke through into the mighty ocean. Jim kissed her.

He flicked the switches for the Satellite Navigation and the autopilot, but Eve stood there still holding the helm.

'If we win – ' she said.

'We?'

'Macquarie Harbour development stops in its track is that right?'

'Yes.'

'You won't go ahead with it.'

654

'No. You're a bossy sheila, are you?'

'I know what I want.'

'Trust me,' he said, then went back to raising King Island on the radio.

Her eyes filled with tears. 'I'm so happy,' she said, but thought of her life with William Prideau. *Did you sleep with him? No.*

Jim and Eve sailed northwest with the wind still gathering behind them, sending little grey breaking waves hurrying past them, though the swell still rolled deep and blue from the west. Jim signed off the radio. 'Success. They'll meet us at Yellow Rock. We'll anchor in the lee of the New Year Islands.'

Jim took a couple of tucks in the sails, then at sunset, with the sun throwing red shafts of glare between clouds the colour of bruises, he reefed down for the night, but still the wind rose. For supper they ate sandwiches on deck, but they tasted of salt. The yacht heeled on the endless slopes of the swell, foam roared across the crests, and they glimpsed ragged stars.

'It's fun!' Eve shouted.

He looked anxious. Something else in his face frightened her. It was a kind of anger, the wind pushing at them like enormous hands, flapping his wet-weather gear – the lights failed, and she could only hear its flapping, and the rattle of spray across the decks, not see him. His anger at his helplessness. Did he know she had lied to him, because she loved him? The yacht dropped and rose like a cockleshell, the darkness flying round them.

Suppose he was washed away? She was frightened of losing him. She clutched on to his arm but he wasn't there.

'Jim!' she shrieked.

He was behind her. She hung on. 'I thought I'd lost you.'

'No danger of that,' he said grimly. But there was

danger of it. In such a small vessel the storm seemed gigantic. Yet it almost comforted her, the way the walls of wind enclosed them.

A part of her was disappointed when he said: 'It's dying away.'

The wind was dropping. At first the seas seemed higher, but then they began to fall.

He said: 'Dawn in an hour.'

She could already see a grey line.

'We've beaten it,' he said exultantly.

But the grey line widened and now they could hear its roar, see the bursts of spray rising like explosions the rolling slopes of surf breaking grey along the horizon. On both sides of them the darkness was solid. The *Ezzie* was being swept down the channel between two islands. Before Jim could react a black face of rock seemed to thunder from the sea beneath them, breaking the railing as though it would come aboard.

The sun rose behind the bare dunes, the treeless agricultural vista of King Island, its level rays illuminating the white wreck thrown up on a vast curve of smooth yellow sand.

The surf broke black, full of kelp.

The sky was blue, cloudless, windless. Only the soggy thudding of the surf, its endless push and drag.

Along the beach, flotsam. Broken white planks. Cordage. A glinting chromium-plated winch still attached to its ropes like arteries, but they led nowhere. A girl in a dress, sitting in the scoops her buttocks had made in the sand, her head between her parted knees, her face buried in her hair.

Her hair was full of sand and salt.

The sun was warm on her back.

She was alone.

After the storm the seagulls were returning; s

heard the mewling cries. Then: 'Eve.' His voice. She looked round.

'Eve, are you coming?'

Jim Pride was standing in the dunes.

'Eve!' he shouted when she didn't come at once.

Half sunk in the sand beside her, her fingers found a length of wood broken at each end. She touched an E. Then a Z. A truck was coming bouncing through the dunes, the gearbox whining and big tyres spraying sand.

She heard Jim tell the men: 'You took long enough.'

She got up and walked on her bare feet beneath the flocks of gulls towards Jim. She could manage him. One of the men who had been standing with his back to her looked at her suspiciously then put a blanket around her shoulders. She pushed through the group to Jim.

'We were lucky,' she told him.

He just grinned. He had a wonderful grin. He almost looked as if he was laughing at her.

'We'll be lucky again,' he said, 'and again.'

He swung her into the cab beside the driver, the rest of the men sitting behind them in the open back as the truck churned along the track by the Yellow Rock River. Out of the dunes, a flat, treeless landscape stretched ahead of them dotted with cattle. A perspective of dirt tracks dwindled between box-thorn hedges to break the wind, a few clumps of tea-tree. The truck turned along the dune margin. Eve thought she saw a golden eagle but the men just shook their heads.

The truck climbed a rise, sand blowing behind it, and Jim pointed through the windscreen. The valley below them was so much smaller than they had pictured. A yellow generator trailer stuttered blue smoke. Vehicles were scattered about, a circle of men in jeans and check shirts playing cards, drinking beer. They were getting their money.

Eve was bitterly disappointed by the reality. She had so badly wanted to find something of value. The 'lagoon' was no more than a small lake, its surface rank with dense green weed. The Yellow Rock River was not a river but a slimy path, churned by the hooves of grazing cattle, glinting in places with rainbow hues. Jim pointed through the windscreen. The tree remained, but it was smaller than she had imagined.

'It's a Huon pine,' one of the men said. Only a pine; Eve had never heard of it, she had imagined something vast and noble, not this gnarled thing trailing its foliage like tattered clothes.

They stood on the bare slope looking at the tree.

'It's the last remnant of the Bass Forest,' said an earnest young man in glasses. 'The valley was formed by prehistoric dune systems during the high sea level, thirty thousand years ago.'

Jim walked down. Eve hesitated, then followed him. She had seen the men with chainsaws.

'You were right, Eve.' Jim was standing with his hands on his hips. 'It is here. This is where he buried it.'

'I wish I'd never come,' she said miserably.

He turned on her with his boyish grin, kissed her jovially.

'I reckon it'd take you a lifetime to dig down through them growing roots,' judged one of the men. 'We need heavy machinery. No good cutting down the tree, go to pull it out like a tooth.'

'Burn it,' Jim said.

The smell of gasoline filled the air as the trunk was doused. It happened so quickly. Eve ran after him.

'Jim, look at me.'

'What do you want of me?' he said angrily. 'I can't back down, Eve. I thought you wanted to save the harbour.'

He turned away. 'Burn it!' he shouted.

One of the men tossed his cigarette.

'Jim, I'm sorry,' Eve said. 'You're right.'

The Huon was not a fire tree; the ancient wood made a terrible noise as it burned. Clear streamers of flame stood out from the grooves in the bark, the oils that made the golden wood expanding in the heat, the vapours igniting. Eve had thought the business would be over in ten minutes, but each time she looked back at the tree, it burned more.

The tree burned all day.

They sat around drinking coffee. The perfumed smoke hung in the sky. Some of the men went home to finish Christmas with their families. Later most of the others followed them. The generator ran out of fuel and stopped.

When darkness fell Eve sat in the shadow of the fiery illumination, her arms wrapped around her knees. The foliage and branches were a black skeleton. They turned to sparks and ash as the wind blew. The trunk still stood, wreathed in flame pulled downwind like streaky bacon.

Fall, she whispered.

'Eve, there was no other way.'

'Yes, I know.' She squeezed his hand. 'Nothing seemed important before.'

'Eve,' he said, 'there's something I want to ask you – '

'No,' she said.

'At least ask you.'

'That's not the way we're going to do it.'

The tree creaked, leaning. The men who remained began to cheer.

'*Eve*,' whispered Jim Pride. The tree burned in his eyes and she was sure of her victory.

At dawn the tree fell, still burning, streaming transparent flame and bitter smoke. The roots clung in the soil, pulling up, creaking and snapping, stretching out stiff as bars as the trunk keeled over, then crackling upward in showers of steaming earth.

The head of the bare trunk splashed into the lagoon and the weed flowed over it.

Eve and Jim searched amongst the clods and clumps of the churned soil, the net of overturned roots that still defied them. They dug down through the charred, brittle layers into the past, Jim working like a madman. Surely they must be below the soil of 1845 by now, into the virgin earth, the forest floor before men walked the earth: only the taproots of the fallen tree to delay their frantic quest.

Almost part of the soil: filthy and black, a tarbox. They pulled at the clinging dirt, revealing its shape like a black egg, a box wrapped in solidified, age-stiffened layers of canvas and pitch.

Jim cut the first layer, then, grunting, prised open the layers beneath with his fingertips. He unwrapped them with increasing speed: and there it was.

A small brass box, a woman's jewellery box.

Eve laid her hand lightly over his. 'There's something I want to ask you first.'

The lid broke from its corroded hinges as Jim pulled it open. It could never be put back.

He stared, then reached inside.

He said: 'Now we can do what we want!'

Eve said: 'Jim Pride, marry me.'

Thanks

Big books like this are not written without the help of many friends. In Tasmania, my thanks to Ian Pearce, Chief Archivist, State Library of Tasmania, and to Sue Ridd and Barbara Valentine of Tasmaniana for unlocking their bookcases to me; to Geoff Lennox at the Lands Department Library, Roger Brammidge and his friends who went to so much trouble at the Wesley Centre, Hobart, and to Russ Smith at the Launceston Maritime Museum and Local History Centre. Howard Clayton took me a thousand memorable feet down the Mount Lyell Mine – in a Toyota Landcruiser. Thanks to Mark and Pam McDermott of Sharonlee for their introduction to the Wilderness and to geology, and to Harry McDermott, Warden of Strahan, for his time.

On King Island, my gratitude to Robyn Eades for a picnic at Quarantine Bay, her local knowledge, and the journey of discovery which led to Pride's Valley; to Alf Button for his long memory and for what a forest fire really feels like; to Whato Whately of the Boomerang; and to all, my apologies for the liberties I have taken with the history of their island.

In Hobart, thanks to Ronald and Jean Porter for putting up with us for so long, and to David and Miriam Grieve.

In Perth, my gratitude to John Thorpe for the stars, and to Susanna for making possible the idea of King Island.

In England, thanks to Mark Bowen for the light, as always, he sheds on legal matters.

My most special thanks are to Simon Thorpe, for the singing.